Angela B

Volume 2
Novels 5 To 8

Bosom Friends: A Seaside Story
The Manor House School
A Fourth Form Friendship
The New Girl at St. Chad's

®2018 Neo Books (Neoeditorialbooks@gmail.com). This book is a product of its time, and it does not necessarily reflect the same views on race, gender, sexuality, ethnicity, and interpersonal relations as it would if it was written today.

CONTENTS

BOOK FIVE. BOSOM FRIENDS: A SEASIDE STORY 1
  CHAPTER I. FELLOW-TRAVELLERS. 1
  CHAPTER II. MRS. STEWART'S LETTER. 8
  CHAPTER III. A MEETING ON THE SANDS. 14
  CHAPTER IV. THE SEA URCHINS' CLUB. 21
  CHAPTER V. A HOT FRIENDSHIP. 27
  CHAPTER VI. ON THE CLIFFS. 34
  CHAPTER VII. THE "STORMY PETREL." 40
  CHAPTER VIII. CROSS-PURPOSES. 50
  CHAPTER IX. SILVERSANDS TOWER. 56
  CHAPTER X. WILD MAIDENHAIR. 62
  CHAPTER XI. THE ISLAND. 68
  CHAPTER XII. A FIRST QUARREL. 74
  CHAPTER XIII. READING THE RUNES. 81
  CHAPTER XIV. A WET DAY. 88
  CHAPTER XV. TEA WITH MR. BINKS. 95
  CHAPTER XVI. BELLE'S NEW FRIEND. 102
  CHAPTER XVII. THE CHASE. 109
  CHAPTER XVIII. GOOD-BYE. 115

BOOK SIX. THE MANOR HOUSE SCHOOL 120
  CHAPTER I. Nora's News 120
  CHAPTER II. An Interesting Stranger 127
  CHAPTER III. A Strong Suspicion 134
  CHAPTER IV. Haversleigh 141
  CHAPTER V. An Unexpected Development 150
  CHAPTER VI. Monica 157
  CHAPTER VII. Lindsay's Luck 165
  CHAPTER VIII. Pendle Tor 173

CHAPTER IX. The Plot Thickens 181

CHAPTER X. Under the Hawthorn Tree 190

CHAPTER XI. Sir Mervyn's Tower 199

CHAPTER XII. An Enigma 207

CHAPTER XIII. Lindsay Makes a Resolve 213

CHAPTER XIV. The Lantern Room 220

CHAPTER XV. Hide-and-Seek 227

CHAPTER XVI. A Surprise 234

CHAPTER XVII. Good-bye to the Manor 241

BOOK SEVEN. A FOURTH FORM FRIENDSHIP **249**

A School Story 249

CHAPTER I. Aldred's Sketch 249

CHAPTER II. Mabel Farrington 260

CHAPTER III. The Model Cottage 270

CHAPTER IV. Domestic Economy 281

CHAPTER V. Out of Bounds 291

CHAPTER VI. An Awkward Predicament 299

CHAPTER VII. False Colours 307

CHAPTER VIII. Amateur Theatricals 316

CHAPTER IX. Chinese Lanterns 323

CHAPTER X. A Frosty January 331

CHAPTER XI. Venus in the Snow 339

CHAPTER XII. The New Teacher 347

CHAPTER XIII. Aldred pays a Visit 360

CHAPTER XIV. An Alarm 368

CHAPTER XV. On the River 377

CHAPTER XVI. An Opportunity 386

CHAPTER XVII. Loss and Gain 397

BOOK EIGHT. THE NEW GIRL AT ST. CHAD'S **405**

A Story of School Life 405

CHAPTER I. Honor Introduces Herself..405
CHAPTER II. Honor's Home 415
CHAPTER III. The Wearing of the Green.................................423
CHAPTER IV. Janie's Charge 434
CHAPTER V. A Riding Lesson 445
CHAPTER VI. The Lower Third...456
CHAPTER VII. St. Chad's Celebrates an Occasion 464
CHAPTER VIII. A Mysterious Happening.................................476
CHAPTER IX. Diamond cut Diamond..483
CHAPTER X. Honor Finds Favour 490
CHAPTER XI. A Relapse...500
CHAPTER XII. St. Kolgan's Abbey 509
CHAPTER XIII. Miss Maitland's Window.................................520
CHAPTER XIV. A Stolen Meeting 528
CHAPTER XV. Sent to Coventry...538
CHAPTER XVI. A Rash Step...546
CHAPTER XVII. Janie turns Detective.......................................555
CHAPTER XVIII. The End of the Term 562

BOOK FIVE.
BOSOM FRIENDS:
A SEASIDE STORY

CHAPTER I. FELLOW-TRAVELLERS.

"Say, is it fate that has flung us together,
We who from life's varied pathways thus meet?"

IT was a broiling day at the end of July, and the railway station at Tiverton Junction was crowded with passengers. Porters wheeling great truckfuls of luggage strove to force a way along the thronged platform, anxious mothers held restless children firmly by the hand, harassed fathers sought to pack their families into already overflowing compartments, excited cyclists were endeavouring to disentangle their machines from among the piles of boxes and portmanteaus, a circus and a theatrical company were loud in their lamentations for certain reserved corridor carriages which had not arrived, while a patient band of Sunday-school teachers was struggling to keep together a large party of slum children bound for a sea-side camp.

The noise was almost unbearable. The ceaseless whistling of the engines, the shouts of the porters, the banging of carriage doors, the eager inquiries of countless perplexed passengers, made a combination calculated to give a headache to the owner of the stoutest nerves, and to drive timid travellers to distraction. All the world seemed off for its holiday, and the bustle and confusion of its departure was nearly enough to make some sober-minded parents wish they had stayed at home.

Leaning up against the bookstall in a corner out of reach of the stream of traffic, clutching a basket in one hand and a hold-all full of wraps and umbrellas in the other, stood a small girl of about ten or eleven years of age, her gaze fixed anxiously upon the great clock on the platform opposite. She was a pretty child, with a sweet, thoughtful little face, clear gray eyes, and straight fair hair, which fell over her shoulders without the least attempt at wave or curl. She was very simply and plainly dressed—her sailor suit had been many times to the laundry, the straw hat was decidedly sunburnt, and her boots had evidently seen good service; but there was about her an indescribable air of refinement and good breeding—that intangible something which stamps those trained from their babyhood in gentle ways—which set her apart at once from the crowds of cheap trippers that thronged the station. From the eager glances she cast up and down the platform she appeared to be waiting for somebody, and she tried to beguile the time by watching the surging mass of tourists who hurried past her in a ceaseless stream. She had listened while the circus manager button-holed the superintendent and excitedly proclaimed his woes; she had held her breath with interest when the slum babies, with their buns and brown-paper parcels, were successfully bundled into the compartments reserved for them, and had craned her neck to catch a last glimpse as they steamed slowly out of the station, their small faces filling the windows like groups of cherubs, and their shrill little voices over-topping all the other noise and din as they joined lustily in the chorus of a hymn. She had witnessed the struggles of several family parties to secure seats, the altercation between the young man with the St. Bernard dog and the guard who refused to allow it in the carriage, the wrath of the gentleman whose fishing-rod was broken, the grief of the lady whose golf-clubs were missing, and the despair of the young couple whose baby had gone on in the train; then, growing rather weary of the ever-moving throng, she turned her eyes to the bookstall, and tried to amuse herself with admiring the large coloured supplements which adorned the back, or reading the names of the rows of attractive books and periodicals which were spread forth in tempting array. She was fumbling in her pocket, and wondering whether she would spend a certain cherished penny on an illustrated paper, or keep it for a more urgent occasion, when her attention was aroused by a pair of fellow-travellers who strolled in a leisurely fashion up to the bookstall, and, standing close beside her, began to turn over some of the various magazines and journals.

They were a tall, fashionably-dressed lady, carrying a tiny white lap-dog under her arm, and a little girl of about her own age, a child who appeared so charmingly pretty to Isobel's eyes that she could not help gazing at her in scarcely-concealed admiration. An older and more practised observer would have noticed that the newcomer's face lacked character, and that her claims to beauty lay mostly in her dainty pink-and-white colouring and her curling flaxen hair, and would have decided, moreover, that the elaborately-made white Japanese silk dress, the pale-blue drawn chiffon hat with its garland of flowers, the tall white French kid boots, the tiny gold bangles and the jewelled locket seemed more suitable for a garden party or a walk on the promenade than for the dust and dirt of a crowded railway journey. To Isobel, however, she appeared like an enchanted princess in a fairy story, and she looked on with thrilling interest while the attractive stranger made her choice among the supply of literature provided for the wants of the travelling public. She seemed somewhat difficult to satisfy, for she threw down one magazine after another in a rather disdainful fashion, declaring that none of them looked worth reading, and, calling to the assistant, bade him show her some story-books. A goodly pile of these was handed down for her inspection, and Isobel, who stood almost at her elbow, could see over her shoulder as she turned the pages. So endless was the variety of delightful tales and illustrations, from legends of King Arthur or the Red Cross Knight to Middle Age mysteries or modern adventures and school scrapes, that it should not have been hard to find something to suit any taste, and the little girl in the sailor hat looked on so fascinated with the snatches she was able to read that she did not notice when a sweet-faced lady in black came hurrying up, until the latter touched her on the arm.

"Why, mother dear—at last!"

"Did you think I was lost, darling? I had such terrible difficulty to get a porter, and the brown box had been put in the wrong van, and has gone on to Whitecastle. I was obliged to telegraph about it, but I hope we may get it this evening. Come along! That's our train over there. We've only just nice time, for it will start in a few minutes now. Give me the wraps."

She took the hold-all from the child's hand, and the two hurried across the bridge on to the opposite platform.

"Here's our porter!" cried Mrs. Stewart.—"Have you put all in the van? Yes, these things in the carriage, please. Third class. It seems almost impossible to find a seat. Is there room here? How fortunate!—Come, Isobel; get in quickly."

"Plenty o' room here, marm," shouted a stout, gray-haired, farmer-like old man, as he reached out a strong hand to help her into the carriage, and found a place for her wraps upon the already crowded rack.

The compartment was more than half full. A party of cheap trippers with a wailing baby, and a "pierrot" with a banjo, which he occupied himself with tuning incessantly, did not offer much prospect of a peaceful journey; but Mrs. Stewart knew it was impossible to choose one's company at a holiday season, and wisely made the best of things, while travelling was still such a novelty to Isobel that she would have enjoyed any experience.

"It's no easy job catchin' trains to-day, marm," said the old farmer, with the air of one who enjoys hearing himself talk. "How them porters gets all the folks sorted out fairly beats me. It's main hot, too. I've come all the way fra' Birmingham. Bin travellin' since eight o'clock this mornin', and I shall be reet glad to find myself back at Silversands again. Little missy 'ud like to sit by the window here, I take it?" good-naturedly making room for her.—"Nay, no need o' thanks! You're welcome, honey. I've a grandchild over at Skegness way as might be your livin' image. Bless you! I've reared seven, and I know what bairns like. Sit you here against me, and when the train gets out of the station you'll see the sea and all the ships sailin' on it."

Isobel settled herself in the corner with much content. She had never expected such luck as to secure a window-seat, and she surveyed the ruddy cheeks and bushy eyebrows of her kindly fellow-traveller with a broad smile of gratitude.

"Goin' to Silversands, missy?" he inquired. "Ay, it's a grand place, and I should ought to know, for I've lived there, man and boy, for a matter of sixty year. Where might you be a-stayin', if I may make so bold? Mrs. Jackson! Why, she's an old friend o' mine, and will make you comfortable, if any one can. You ask her if she knows Mr. Binks of the White Coppice. I reckon she won't deny the acquaintance."

"Tickets ready!" cried the inspector, breaking in upon the conversation. "Take your seats, please! All stations to Groby, Heatherton, Silversands, and Ferndale."

There was a last stampede for places among excited passengers, a last rush of porters with rugs and hat boxes; the guard had already unfurled his green flag, and was in the act of putting the whistle to his lips, when two late-comers appeared, racing in frantic haste down the platform.

"O mother!" cried Isobel, "that lady and the little girl are going to be left behind! It's the little girl in the blue hat, too! They were buying papers at the bookstall. Just look how they're running! Oh, the guard's stopping the train for them! I think they'll catch it, after all. Why, they're coming in here!"

"Put us in anywhere—anywhere!" cried the lady in desperate tones, as the inspector flung open the carriage door.

"Here you are, m'm!" cried the porter, seizing the little girl with scant ceremony, and jumping her into the compartment.—"Luggage in the front van, and the light hampers in No. 43. Thank you, m'm.—Stand back there!"

He pocketed his tip, banged the door violently, nearly catching Isobel's fingers thereby, the whistle sounded, and the train started off with a jerk that almost threw the newcomers on to the lap of old Mr. Binks, who had watched their sudden arrival with open-mouthed interest. The lady apologized prettily, and finding room between the pierrot and a market-woman with several large baskets, she sank down on the seat with a sigh of relief, and taking a smelling-bottle and a large black fan from her dressing-bag, leaned back with an air of utter exhaustion.

"Mother! mother!" cried the little girl. "Do you see they've put us into a third-class carriage?"

"Never mind, dear," replied the lady. "I was only too thankful to catch the train at all. We can change at the next station if we wish, but it seems scarcely worth while for so short a journey. The carriages are so crowded that the firsts are as bad as the thirds."

"That porter's dirty hands have made black marks on my dress," said the little girl disconsolately. "Why couldn't the train wait for us? They needn't have been in such a hurry when they saw we were coming."

"Trains don't wait for any one, dear. It was your own fault, for you wouldn't come away from the bookstall. I told you to be quick about choosing."

"I didn't see anything I wanted. Books are all just the same. I don't think I shall like this one, now I have it. Give me Micky, please," taking the pet dog on to her knee. "Shall we have to stay very long in this carriage? I'm so terribly hot."

"Get the scent out of my bag, dearest, and the vinaigrette. You'll soon feel better, now this nice breeze is coming in through the window. If the train's fairly punctual, we shall be there in half an hour."

"It's past three o'clock already!" consulting a pretty enamelled watch which was pinned on to her dress. "Oh dear! I'm so tired! I hate travelling. Why can't we have a carriage to ourselves? This basket's knocking my hat off. *Do* let us change at the next station. How the baby cries! It's making my head ache."

"Young lady don't fancy her company," said the market-woman, moving her basket as she spoke. "I've paid for my ticket same as other folks 'as, and my money's as good as any one else's, so far as I can see."

"Some people had better order a train to themselves if they're too fine to travel with the likes of us," observed one of the trippers with sarcasm.

"I'm sure I'm sorry as he cries so," apologized the weary mother of the wailing baby. "The heat's turned the milk sour, and I durstn't give him his bottle. He won't go to sleep without it, neither, so I can't do nothing with him. Husht! husht! lovey, wilt 'a?"

"Bairns will be bairns," remarked old Mr. Binks sententiously. "I ought to know, for I've reared seven. Live and let live's my motto, and a good un to get along the world with. I'll wager as young missy there meant no offence."

"Indeed she did not wish to hurt anybody's feelings," said the lady hastily, adding in a low tone to the little girl, "Be quiet, dear. Take off your hat, and perhaps you'll be cooler."

Wedged between fat old Mr. Binks and the window, Isobel had sat watching the whole scene. She was terribly hot, but the crowded carriage and its miscellaneous occupants only amused her, and she divided her attention between the quickly passing landscape and her various travelling companions, stealing frequent glances at the pretty stranger opposite, who had closed her eyes in languid resignation, having drawn her white silk skirts as far as possible away from the market-woman, and placed her pale-blue hat in safety upon her mother's knee. The baby was asleep at last, worn out with crying, and the trippers were handing round refreshments—large wedges of pork pie, sticky buns, and cold tea, which they drank in turns out of a bottle. They pressed these dainties cordially upon everybody in the carriage, but the only one who consented to share their hospitality was the market-woman, who remarked audibly that "*she* was not proud, however much some folks might stick theirselves up." In return she produced a couple of apples from her basket, which she presented to the two little tripper boys, who promptly quarrelled which should have the bigger, and kicked each other lustily on the shins, till their father boxed their ears and threatened to send them home by the next returning train. The pierrot created a diversion at this point by playing a few selections upon the banjo and singing a comic song, handing round his tall white hat afterwards for pennies, and informing the company that they could have the pleasure of hearing him again any day upon the pier at Ferndale at 11.30 and 3 o'clock prompt.

"I'm glad we're not staying at Ferndale," thought Isobel, "if all these people are going there! I'm sure Silversands will be ever so much nicer." And she turned with relief to look out through the open window.

After running for a long distance between high embankments, the train had at last reached the coast, and Isobel watched with rapture the sparkling blue sea, the long line of yellow heather-topped cliffs, and the red sails of the fishing-boats which could be seen on the distant horizon.

On the shore she could catch glimpses of delightful little pools among the rocks left by the retreating tide, and Mr. Binks, who seemed to enjoy acting as guide, drew her notice continually to rows of bathing-vans, children riding donkeys or digging sand-castles on the beach, or fishwives gathering cockles at the water's edge, pointing out the various objects of interest with a fat brown finger. The few stations which they passed were crowded with tourists, one or two of whom opened the door of the compartment in the hope of finding room, but slammed it again quickly when they saw the number of its occupants.

"They did ought to put on more carriages, so nigh to August Bank Holiday," said Mr. Binks. "We're close on Silversands now—you can see it there, over at t'other side of the bay—so you won't be long waitin' of your tea. You'll be rare and glad to get some, I take it, if you feel like me."

Isobel thought it was the longest and hottest journey she ever remembered; but, like most things, it at length came to a close, and after several halts and tiresome waitings on the line the heavy train crawled into Silversands. It was a little wayside station, with a gay garden running alongside the platform, and the name "Silversands" elaborately done out in white stones upon a green bank. A group of Scotch firs gave a pleasant shade and a suggestion of country woods; the sea and the sands were just visible over a tall hedge of flowering tamarisk, the meadows were full of buttercups, while cornfields, beginning already to yellow with ripening crops, and gay with scarlet poppies, made a refreshing sight to dusty travellers.

"Here we are, mother!" cried Isobel, with delight. "This is really Silversands at last! Oh, look at the poppies among the corn! Aren't they lovely!"

"Ay, it's Silversands, sure enough," said Mr. Binks, opening the carriage door and descending with the caution his bulk demanded. "Main glad I am to see it again, too. Take care, honey! Let me help you down, and your ma too. You're welcome, marm, I'm sure, to anything as I may have done for you; and if you and missy here is takin' a walk some day towards 'the balk,' just ask for Binks of the White Coppice, and my missus 'ull make you a cup of tea any time as you likes to call. Good-day to you!" And he moved away down the platform with the satisfied air of one who again finds his foot on his native heath.

Silversands seemed also to be the destination of the two travellers in whom Isobel had taken such an interest, as they got out of the train with

but also critical of snobbery

much apparent relief, and were greeted by quite a number of enthusiastic and smartly-dressed friends who had come to the station to meet them.

"We've had the most *terrible* journey!" Isobel overheard the little girl saying. "We were obliged to go in a third-class carriage with the rudest and dirtiest people! I'm sure I'm black all over. Oh, I'm *so* glad to have got here at last!"

She retailed her experiences to a sympathetic audience, while her mother, who, it appeared, had lost a handbag, insisted upon calling the station-master and giving a full description of both its labels and contents; and until their numerous boxes and portmanteaus had been collected and disposed on a carriage, and they and their friends had finally passed through the gate at the bottom of the platform, it was quite impossible for Mrs. Stewart to secure the services of the solitary porter. She managed at last, however, to gather together her modest luggage, and leaving it to follow upon a hand-cart, set out with Isobel to walk to the lodgings which she had engaged.

CHAPTER II.
MRS. STEWART'S LETTER.

"'Tis half against my judgment. Kindly fortune,
Send fair prosperity upon this venture!"

IT will be quite easy to find our rooms, mother," said Isobel. "We know they're close to the beach, and there only seems to be one row of lodging-houses down on the shore. I suppose that must be Marine Terrace, for there isn't any other. What jolly sands! Can't you taste the salt on your lips? I feel as if I shall just want to be by the sea all the time."

"I hope it will do you good, dear," said her mother. "I declare you look better already. I shall expect you to grow quite rosy before we go home again, and to have ever such a big appetite."

"I'm hungry now," replied Isobel. "I hope Mrs. Jackson will bring in tea directly we arrive. I mean to ask her first thing if she knows Mr. Binks. Wasn't it nice of him to let me sit by the window? Do you think we shall be taking a walk to the 'balk'? I don't know in the least what a 'balk' is, but I suppose we shall find out. I should like immensely to go to his farm."

"I dare say we might call there some afternoon. He seemed a kind old man, and I believe he really meant what he said, and would be pleased to see you."

"Weren't the people in the carriage funny, mother? How tiresome that pierrot was with his banjo, and the poor baby that wouldn't stop crying! I was so glad the little girl in the blue hat didn't miss the train. Isn't she lovely?"

"She's rather pretty," said Mrs. Stewart; "but I couldn't see her very well—she was sitting on my side, you remember."

"I think she's perfectly beautiful!" declared Isobel, with enthusiasm—"just like one of those expensive French dolls at the stores. Did you see them drive away in the landau? I wonder where they're staying, and if we shall ever meet them again?"

"Perhaps you may see her walking on the beach, or in church," suggested Mrs. Stewart.

"I hope I shall. I wonder what her name is. Do you think she'd mind if I were to ask her?"

"Perhaps her mother might not like it," replied Mrs. Stewart. "I'm afraid it would hardly be polite."

"But I do so want to get to know her. I haven't any friends here, you see, and I think she looks so nice."

"I'm sorry, dear, but I shouldn't care for you to try to scrape an acquaintance with these people. We shall manage to have a very happy time together, hunting for shells and sea-weeds. You must take me for a friend instead."

"You're better than any friend!" said Isobel, squeezing her mother's hand. "Of course I like being with you best, sweetest; only sometimes, when you're reading or lying down, it *is* nice to have somebody to talk to. I won't ask her her name if you say I'd better not; but I hope I shall see her again, if it's only just to look at her. Why, this is the house—there's No. 4 over the doorway; and that must be Mrs. Jackson standing in the front garden looking out for us. I think she ought to be Mr. Binks's cousin; she's as fat and red in the face as he is."

"The place is very full, mum," said Mrs. Jackson, showing them to the little back sitting-room, which, at August prices, was all Mrs. Stewart had been able to afford. "I had three parties in yesterday askin' for rooms, and could have let this small parlour twice over for double the money but what I'd promised it to you. Not as I wanted to take 'em, though, for they was all noisy lots as would have needed a deal of waitin' on. I'd rather have quiet visitors like you and the young lady here, as isn't always a-ringin' their bells and playin' on the pianer till midnight, though I may be the loser by it. I'm short-handed now my daughter Emma Jane's married, and not so quick at gettin' up and down stairs as I used to be."

"I don't think you'll find we shall give more trouble than we can help," said Mrs. Stewart gently. "We seldom require much waiting on, and we hope to be out most of the day."

"I'm only too glad to do all I can, mum, to make folks feel home-like," declared Mrs. Jackson, showing the capacities of the cupboard, and calling attention to the superior comfort of the armchairs. "And if there's anything else you'd like, I hope as you'll mention it. I'm a little short in my breath, and a bit lame in my right leg, bein' troubled with rheumatics in the winter, but I do my best to please, and so does Polly (she's my niece), though she's a girl with no head, and can't remember a thing for two minutes on end."

"I'm sure you'll make us comfortable," said Mrs. Stewart, "and we hope to have a very happy time indeed at Silversands. We should be glad if you could bring in tea now; we're both very hot and thirsty after our long journey."

"That you will be, I'm sure, mum," returned Mrs. Jackson. "We've not had a hotter day this summer. Little missy looks fair tired out. But there's nought like a cup of tea to refresh one, and I'll have it up in a few minutes; the kettle's ready and boilin'."

"The room feels rather stuffy," said Mrs. Stewart, throwing open the window when her landlady had departed to the kitchen regions. "I'm sorry we have no view of the sea; but we can't help that, and we must be out of doors the whole day long. Luckily the weather is gloriously fine, and seems likely to keep so."

"What queer ornaments, mother!" said Isobel, going slowly round the room and examining with much curiosity two stuffed cocks, a glass bottle containing a model of a ship with full sail and rigging, a case of somewhat moth-eaten and dilapidated butterflies, a representation of Windsor Castle cut out in cork, some sickly portraits of the Royal Family in cheap German gilt frames, and a large Berlin wool-work sampler, which, in addition to the alphabet and a verse of a hymn, depicted birds of paradise at the top and weeping willows at the bottom, and set forth that it was the work of Eliza Jane Horrocks, aged ten years.

"I think we shan't need quite so many crochet antimacassars," laughed Mrs. Stewart. "There seems to be one on every chair, and there are actually five on the sofa. We must ask Mrs. Jackson to take some of them away. We would rather be without all these shell baskets and photo frames on the little table, too. If we moved it into the window it would be very nice for painting or writing if it should happen to be a wet day."

"I hope it won't be wet," said Isobel. "At any rate, there are some books to read if it is," turning over a row of volumes which reposed on the top of the chiffonnier. "I've never seen such peculiar pictures. The little girls have white trousers right down to their ankles, and the boys have deep frilled collars and quite long hair."

"They are very old-fashioned books," said Mrs. Stewart, examining with a smile "The Youth's Moral Miscellany," "The Maiden's Garland," "A Looking-Glass for the Mind," and "Instructive Stories for Young People," which, with a well-thumbed edition of "Sandford and Merton," a battered copy of "The History of the Fairchild Family," and a few bound volumes of *Chambers's Journal*, made up the extent of the library. "I should think they must have belonged to Mrs. Jackson's mother or grandmother for this one has the date 1820 written inside it."

"Of course they don't look so nice as my books at home," said Isobel; "but they'd be something new."

"You're such a greedy reader that no doubt you will get through them, however dry they may prove," laughed her mother. "Here comes our tea. We shall enjoy new-laid eggs and fresh country butter, shan't we?"

"I wonder if they're from Mr. Binks's farm," said Isobel, seating herself at the table.—"Do you know Mr. Binks, Mrs. Jackson? He said I was to ask you, and he was sure you wouldn't deny the acquaintance."

"Know Peter Binks, miss!" exclaimed Mrs. Jackson. "Why, there isn't a soul in Silversands as doesn't know him. Binks has lived at the White Coppice ever since I was a girl, and afore then, and him church-warden too, and owner of the *Britannia*, as good a schooner as any about. His wife's second cousin is married to my daughter, and livin' at Ferndale. Know him! I should just say I do!"

"I thought you would!" said Isobel delightedly. "We met him in the train as we were coming. He gave me his seat by the window, and asked us to go to his farm some day. You'll be able to tell us the way, won't you?"

"Another time, dear child," said Mrs. Stewart "Mrs. Jackson's busy now, and our tea is waiting.—Thank you; yes, I think we have everything we need at present. Polly might bring a little boiling water in a few minutes, and we will ring the bell if we require anything more.—Come, Isobel, you said you were hungry!"

"A nice-spoken lady," said Mrs. Jackson afterwards to her husband in the privacy of the kitchen. "Any one could see with half an eye as they was gentlefolk, though they've only taken the back room. I wonder, now, if they can be any relation to old Mr. Stewart at the Chase. They did say as the son—him as was killed in the war—had married somewhere in furrin parts, and his father was terrible set against it, havin' a wife of his own choosin' ready for him at home. A regular family quarrel it was, and both too proud to make it up; but they said the old man was nigh heartbroken when his son was taken, and he'd never sent him a kind word. I had it all from Peter Binks's nephew, who was under-gardener there at the time."

"It might be," said Mr. Jackson oracularly, taking a pinch of snuff as he spoke, "and, on the other hand, it might not be. Stewart's by no means an uncommon kind of a name. There was a Stewart second mate on the *Arizona* when we took kippers over to Belfast, and there was a chap called Stewart as used to keep a snug little public down by the quay in Whitecastle, but I never heard tell as either of 'em was any connection of old Mr. Stewart up at the Chase."

"It weren't likely they should be," replied Mrs. Jackson, with scorn. "But that don't make it any less likely in this case. I remember Mr. Godfrey quite well when we lived at Linkhead, and I'd used to walk over with Emma Jane to Heatherton Church of a Sunday afternoon. A fine handsome young fellow he was, too, sittin' with his father in the family pew, takin' a yawn behind his hand durin' the sermon, and small blame to him too—old Canon Martindale used to preach that long! I can see him now, if I close my eyes, with his light hair shinin' against the red curtain of the big square pew. Little missy has quite a look of him, to my mind."

"You're always imaginin' romances, Eliza," said Mr. Jackson. "It comes of too much readin'. You and Polly sit over them stories in *The Family Herald* till you make up goodness knows what tales about every new party as comes to the house. There was the young man with the long hair as played the fiddle, whom you was sure was a furrin count, and who only turned out to be one of the band at Ferndale, and went off without payin' his bill; and there was a couple in the drawing-room as talked that grand about their motor car and their shootin' box and important business till you thought it was a member of Parliament and his lady, takin' a rest and travellin' incog., till you found out they was only wine merchants from Whitecastle after all. Don't you go a-meddlin'. Let them manage their own affairs, and we'll manage ours."

"How you talk!" declared Mrs. Jackson indignantly. "Who wants to meddle? As if one couldn't take a bit of interest in one's own visitors! There's the drawin'-room a-ringin', and the dinin'-room will be wantin' its tea. Stir the fire, Joe, and hold the toast whilst I answer the bell. Where's that Polly a-gone to, I wonder?"

In spite of her husband's disdainful comments, Mrs. Jackson's surmises were not altogether groundless; and if she had peeped into her back sitting-room that evening, when Isobel was in bed, she might have seen her visitor slowly and with much care and thought composing a letter. Sheet after sheet of notepaper was covered, and then torn up, for the writer's efforts did not seem to satisfy her, and she leaned her head on her hand every now and then with a weary air, as if she had undertaken a distasteful task.

"I do not ask anything for myself," wrote Mrs. Stewart at last. "That you should care to meet me, or ever become reconciled to me, is, I know, beyond all question. My one request is that you will see your grandchild. She is now nearly eleven years of age, a thorough Stewart, tall and fair, and with so strong a resemblance to her father that you cannot fail to see the likeness. I have done my utmost for her, but I am not able to give her the advantages I should wish her to have, and which, as her father's child, I feel it is hard for her to lack. She is named Isobel, after your only daughter, the little sister whose loss my husband always spoke of with so much regret, and whom he hoped she might resemble. You would find her truthful, straightforward, obedient, and well-behaved, and in every respect worthy of the name of Stewart. It is with the greatest difficulty that I bring myself to ask of you any favour, but for the sake of the one, dear to us both, who is gone, I beg that you will at least see my Isobel, and judge her for yourself."

She addressed the letter to Colonel Stewart, the Chase, sealed it, stamped it, and took it herself to the post. For a moment she stood and hesitated—a moment in which she seemed almost inclined to draw back after all; she turned the letter over doubtfully in her hand, went a step away, then suddenly straightening herself with an air of firm determination, she dropped it into the pillar-box and returned to her lodgings. Going upstairs to the bedroom, she tenderly lifted the soft golden hair, and looked at the quiet, sleeping face of her little girl.

"He cannot fail to like her," she said to herself. "It was the only right thing to do, and what *he* would have wished. I'm glad I have had the courage to make the attempt. He will surely acknowledge her now, and my one prayer is that he will not take her away from me."

CHAPTER III. A MEETING ON THE SANDS.

"What's in a name? That which we call a rose,
By any other name would smell as sweet."

THE little town of Silversands was built on the cliffs by the sea, so close over the greeny-blue water that the dash of the waves was always in your ears and the taste of the salt spray on your lips. The picturesque thatched fishermen's cottages lay scattered one above another down the steep hillside at such strange and irregular angles that the narrow streets which led from the quay wound in and out like a maze, and you found your way to the shore down flights of wide steps under low archways, or by a pathway cut through your neighbour's cabbage patch. It was not difficult to guess the occupation of most of the inhabitants, for fishing-nets of all descriptions might be seen hanging out to dry over every available railing; great flat skates and conger eels were nailed to the doorways to be cured in the sun; rosy-faced women appeared to be eternally washing blue jerseys, which fluttered like flags from the various little gardens; and the bare-headed, brown-legged children who gathered cockles on the sands, or angled for crabs from the jetty, seemed as much at home in the water as on dry land. The harbour was decidedly fishy; bronzed burly seamen were perpetually unloading cargoes of herrings which they stowed away into barrels, or lobsters that were carefully packed in baskets to be dispatched to the neighbouring towns. There was a kind of open-air market, fitted up with rickety stalls where you might buy fresh cod and mackerel still alive and shining with all the lovely fleeting colours which fade so quickly when they are taken from the water. You could afford to be extravagant in the way of shell-fish, if you liked such delicacies, since a large red cotton pocket-handkerchief full of cockles and mussels only cost a penny, and whelks and periwinkles sold at a halfpenny the pint.

At high water the quay was always agog with excitement, the coming in of the boats being accompanied with that hauling of ropes, creaking of windlasses, shouting of hoarse voices and general confusion both among toiling workers and idle loungers that seem inseparable from the business of a port, while the occasional advent of an excursion steamer was an event which attracted every looker-on in the harbour. All the talk at Silversands was of tides and storms, of good or bad catches, the luck of one vessel or the ill-fortune of another, and to the fisher-folk the affairs of the empire were of small importance compared with the arrival and departure of the herring-fleet. The schools gave a thin veneer of education, but it seemed to vanish away directly with the contact of the waves, so that the customs and modes of thought of most of the people differed little from those of their forefathers who slept, some in the churchyard on the edge of the cliff, with quaint epitaphs to record their virtues, and some in those deeper graves over which no stones could be reared.

Standing apart from the old town was a modern portion which was just beginning to dignify itself with the name of a seaside resort. To be sure, it was yet guiltless of pier, promenade, band, or niggers; but, as the owner of the new grocery stores remarked, "you never knew what might follow, and many a fashionable watering-place had risen from quite as modest a commencement." There was already a row of shops with plate-glass windows and a handsome display of spades, buckets, shell-purses, baskets, china ornaments, photographic views, and other articles calculated to tempt the shillings from the pockets of summer visitors; there were several streets of lodging-houses near the railway station, as well as the long terrace facing the sea, dignified rather prematurely by the name of "The Parade," and an enterprising tradesman from Ferndale had opened a tea-room and a circulating library. The proprietor of the bathing machines was doing a good business, and had set up a stand with six donkeys; a photographer had ventured to erect a wooden studio upon the beach, where he would take your likeness for eighteenpence; and the common was occasionally the camp of some travelling circus, which, though *en route* for a larger sphere of action, did not disdain to give a performance in passing.

Like a link between the old and the new, the ancient gray stone church stood on the verge of the cliff above the harbour, looking out to sea as if it were always watching over those of its children who had their business in great waters, and sending up silent prayers on their behalf. In the square tower the bells had rung for seven hundred years, and the flat roof with its turreted battlements told tales of wild times of Border forays, when the people had fled with their goods to the one spot of safety, and watched the smoke of their burning farms, as the victorious Scots drove away their cattle over the blue line of hills towards the north.

But I think the great attraction of Silversands was its delightful beach. The sands were hard and firm, and covered in places with patches of sea holly or horned poppies and the beautiful pink bindweed growing here and there with its roots deep down among the clumps of stones. Above rose the cliffs in bold craggy outlines, their tops crowned by a heather-clad common which stretched far inland, while the low tide disclosed attractive rocky pools where anemones, hermit crabs, sea urchins, jelly fish, mermaids' purses, starfishes, and all kinds of fascinating objects might be captured by those who cared to look for them.

The afternoon of the day following her arrival found Isobel wandering along this shore alone. Mrs. Stewart had been unfortunate enough to meet with an accident that morning: slipping on the rocks she had twisted her ankle severely, and it was only with the greatest difficulty that she had managed to limp back to the lodgings.

"It's a bad sprain, too," said Mrs. Jackson, shaking her head as she helped to soak cold water bandages. "You won't be able to put that foot to the ground for a matter of ten days or more. It's a good thing now as I didn't sell the sofa, which I nearly let it go in the spring, as it do fill up the room so; but you can rest there nicely, and keep puttin' on fresh cloths all the time, though it do seem a pity, with your holiday only just begun."

"I must try to be patient, and get it well as fast as possible," replied Mrs. Stewart.—"I'm afraid it will be very dull for you, Isobel, my poor child, while I'm lying here. You will have to amuse yourself on the beach as best you can. I certainly can't have you staying indoors on my account."

"It will be much duller for you, mother dear," said Isobel. "I shall be all right—I like being on the shore—but you won't have anything to do except read. What a good thing we brought plenty of books with us! I'm so sorry our sitting-room hasn't any view. I shall try to find all the shells and sea-weeds and things that I can, and keep bringing them in to show you."

It was on a quest, therefore, for any treasures which she thought might interest her mother that Isobel strolled slowly along, looking with delight at the gleaming sea, the red sails of the herring-fleet, and the little white yacht which came slowly round the point of the cliff, waiting for a puff of wind to take her to the harbour. The tide was coming in fast, and the churning of the waves, as they ground the small pebbles along the beach, had the most inspiriting and refreshing sound. She stooped every now and then to pick up a shell, or to clutch at a great piece of ribbon sea-weed which was dashed to her feet by an advancing wave; she had an exciting chase after a scuttling crab, and missed him in the end, and nearly got drenched with spray trying to rescue a walking-stick which she could see floating at the edge of the water. She had filled her pockets with a moist collection of specimens, and was half thinking of turning back to retrace her footsteps to Marine Terrace, when from behind a crag of rock which jutted out sharply on to the sands she heard a sound of children's voices and laughter. Moved with curiosity she peeped round the corner, and found herself at the edge of a small patch of green common that ran along the shore between the cliffs and the sea. It was covered with soft fine grass and little low-growing flowers; the broken masts washed up from a wreck made capital seats; and, altogether, it appeared as pleasant a playground as could well be imagined.

So, at any rate, seemed to think the group of boys and girls who were assembled there, since they had set up some wickets, and were enthusiastically engaged in a game of cricket, for which the short fine grass made an excellent pitch. It looked so interesting that Isobel strolled rather nearer to the players, and finding an upturned boat upon the beach, she curled herself under its shadow, and settled down, apparently unnoticed, to watch the progress of the game. She could hear as well as see, and her ears were keenly alert to the scraps of lively conversation which floated towards her.

"Have you found the ball?"

"Yes; under a heap of nettles, and stung my fingers horribly. Just look at the blisters."

"Don't be a baby. Go on; it's your play."

"I can't hold the bat while my hands hurt so."

"Then miss your turn.—Come along, Bertie, and have your innings; Ruth doesn't want hers."

"Yes, I do! I'm older than Bertie, so I must go in first. If you'd only wait a minute, till I can find a dock leaf."

"We can't wait. How tiresome you are! Here, Bertie, take the bat."

"It's not fair! We were to go in ages, and I'm six months older than he is."

"You can have your turn after Joyce."

"Joyce! She's only nine, and I'm eleven."

"Then miss it altogether, and don't make yourself a nuisance!—Now then, Bertie, look out for a screw."

"It's a shame! I always seem to get left out of things!" grumbled the little girl, with a very aggrieved countenance, sitting down upon a rusty anchor, and nursing her nettled hand tenderly.

"It's your own fault this time, at any rate," said a companion, with scant sympathy. "There are plenty of dock leaves growing under the cliff if you want them."

"Bravo, Bertie! Well hit!"

"Quick with that ball, Arthur!"

"Play up, Bertie!"

"Well run! Well run!"

"Oh, he's out! Hard luck!"

"Whose turn is it now?"

"Belle's."

"Where is she?"

"Here I am, ready and waiting. Now give me a good ball. It's Hugh's turn to bowl, and if he sends me one of his nasty screws or sneaks I shan't be friends with him any more."

Isobel gazed at the last speaker, entranced. There was no mistaking the apple-blossom cheeks and the silky flaxen curls of her fellow-traveller in the crowded carriage, though to-day the white silk dress and the blue hat were replaced by a delicate pale pink muslin and a broad-brimmed straw trimmed with a gauze scarf. She looked even more charming than ever, like some fairy in a story-book or one of the very prettiest pictures you get upon chocolate boxes; she seemed to put all other children round her in the shade, and as she stood there, a graceful little figure at the wicket, Isobel's eyes followed her every movement with an absolute fascination.

The first ball was a slow one, and she hit it fairly well, but did not make a run; the next she merely slogged; the third was high, and as she wisely let it alone, it cleared the wicket; the fourth was a full pitch: she tried to play it down, but unfortunately it hit the top of her bat, and went right into the long-stop's hands.

"Caught!"

"She's out!"

"What an easy catch!"

"Come along, Aggie, your innings."

The vanquished player put down her bat somewhat reluctantly, and walked slowly away in the direction of the old boat. She sat down on the sand close by Isobel, and taking off her hat, began to fan her hot face with it After stealing several glances at her companion, she at length volunteered a remark.

"It was too bad, wasn't it," she said, "to be caught out first thing like that?"

"Much too bad!" replied Isobel. "But I think they were horrid balls."

"So they were. Hugh always sends the most mean ones. Weren't you in the train with us yesterday?"

"Yes. I saw you first at the bookstall at Tiverton."

"Didn't you think the people in the carriage detestable? I nearly died with the heat and stuffiness."

"It was dreadfully hot and noisy."

"Noisy! I don't know which was worse—the baby or the banjo! You were better off sitting by the window, though that fat old man would keep talking to you."

"He was rather kind," said Isobel; "I didn't mind him."

"I suppose you're staying at Silversands, aren't you?"

"Yes, at 4 Marine Terrace."

"We're in Marine Terrace too, at No. 12. We have the upstairs suite. They're not bad rooms for a little place like this, but they don't know how to wait. Mother says she wishes they'd build a hotel here. What's it like at No. 4?"

"It's quite comfortable," replied Isobel. "We have a nice landlady."

"Are there only just you and your mother?"

"That's all."

"Have you no father?"

"He's dead. He was killed in the Boer War."

"Was he a soldier, then?"

"Yes; he was a captain in the Fifth Dragoon Guards."

"My father is dead too. Have you any brothers and sisters?"

"No. I never had any."

"Neither have I. I only wish I had. It's so lonely without, isn't it?"

"It is, rather; but I'm a great deal with mother."

19

"So am I; still, when she's at home she's out so much, and then I never know what to do."

"Don't you read?" said Isobel.

"I'm not fond of reading. I only like books when there's really nothing else to amuse myself with."

"You were buying a book at Tiverton. Which one did you get? Is it nice?"

"It's just a school story. I forget its name now. I haven't looked at it again."

"Then you didn't choose 'The Red Cross Knight' after all?"

"Oh, that's too like lessons! I've had all that with my governess, and about King Arthur too. I'm quite tired of them. Have you a governess?"

"No," replied Isobel; "I do lessons with mother."

"How jolly for you! I wish I did. I'm to be sent to school in another year, and I don't think I shall like that at all. When are you going?"

"Not till I'm thirteen, I expect."

"How old are you now?"

"Almost eleven."

"Why, so am I! When's your birthday?"

"On the thirteenth of September."

"And mine is on the tenth of October, so you're nearly a month older than I am. You haven't told me your name yet?"

"My name's Isobel Stewart."

"What!" cried the other, opening her blue eyes wide in the greatest astonishment. "That's *my* name!"

"*Your* name!" exclaimed Isobel, in equal amazement.

"Of course it is. *My* name's Isabelle Stuart."

"How do you spell it?"

"I-S-A-B-E-L-L-E S-T-U-A-R-T."

"And mine's spelt I-S-O-B-E-L S-T-E-W-A-R-T, so that makes a little difference."

"So it does. I'm called 'Belle,' too, for short. Are you?"

"No; never anything but Isobel."

"It's funny. We're the same name and the same age, and we're staying in the same terrace. I think it is what you'd call a 'coincidence.' We came to Silversands on the same day, too, and in the same railway carriage. We ought to be twin sisters. You're really rather like me, you know, only you're pale, and your hair doesn't curl."

Isobel shook her head. She had a very modest opinion of her own attractions, and would not have dreamt of comparing her appearance with that of her pretty companion, so very far did she think she ranked below the other's style of beauty.

"I should like to be friends, at any rate," she said shyly. "Perhaps I shall see you again upon the shore. I'm afraid that's your mother calling you. I think I ought to go home now too; I didn't mean to be out so long."

Isabelle Stuart sprang to her feet.

"Yes, it's mother calling," she said. "She's walked up with Mrs. Rokeby. I must fly. But I hope we shall meet again. I shall look out for you on the sands. Good-bye!"

"Good-bye!"

Isobel stood watching her as she ran lightly away; then turning, she hurried home as fast as possible along the beach, for she was very excited at this strange meeting, and was anxious to give her mother a full and detailed account of it.

"I didn't ask her *her* name, mother," she explained. "It was she who asked me mine. You told me I'd better not speak to her; but she spoke to me first, and asked me ever so many questions. Isn't it queer that our names should be just the same, and our ages too? You'll let us be friends now, won't you? I think she's the nicest girl I've ever met in my life, and I can't tell you how much I want to know her."

CHAPTER IV. THE SEA URCHINS' CLUB.

"'Twas here where the urchins would gather to play,
In the shadows of twilight or sunny midday."

ISOBEL found her namesake waiting for her on the beach next morning.

"I thought you'd be coming out soon," announced Belle, "so I just stopped about till I saw you. We're all starting off to play cricket again on the common down under the cliffs, and I want you to go with us. I've taken *such* a fancy to you! I told mother I had, and she laughed and said it wouldn't last long; but I *know* it will. I feel as if you were going to be my bosom friend. You'll come, won't you?"

"Of course I will," replied Isobel, accepting the offered friendship with rapture. "Mother told me to do what I liked this morning."

"Let us be quick, then. The others have run on in front, but we'll soon catch them up."

"Are you going to the same place where you were playing yesterday?" asked Isobel.

"Yes; we call it our club ground. We mean to have matches there almost every day. It'll be ever such fun. You see there are several families of us staying at Silversands that all know one another, so we've joined ourselves together in a club. We call it 'The United Sea Urchins' Recreation Society,' and it's not to be only for cricket, because we mean to play rounders and hockey as well, and to go out boating, and have shrimping parties on the sands. We arranged it last night after tea. There are just twenty of us, if you count the Wrights' baby, so that makes quite enough to get up all sorts of games. Hugh Rokeby's the president, and Charlie Chester's secretary, and Charlotte Wright's treasurer. We each pay twopence a week subscription, and at the end of the holiday we're going to have what the boys call a 'regular blow-out' with the funds—ginger beer, you know, and cakes, and ices if we can afford it. I wanted to make the subscription sixpence, but Letty Rokeby said the little ones couldn't give so much. I'll ask them to elect you a member. You'd like to join, wouldn't you?"

"Immensely. But I haven't any money with me now."

"Oh, never mind! You can give it to Charlotte afterwards. Here we are. I expect they're all waiting. I see they've put the stumps up. You don't know anybody except me, do you? I'll soon tell you their names."

The party of children who were assembled upon the green patch of common certainly appeared to be a very jolly one. First there were the Rokebys, a large and tempestuous family of seven, who were staying at a farm on the cliffs by the wood.

"A thoroughly healthy place," as Mrs. Rokeby often remarked, "with a good water supply, and no danger of catching anything infectious. We've really been so unfortunate. Hugh and Letty took scarlet fever at the lodgings in Llandudno last year, and I had the most dreadful time nursing them; Winnie and Arnold had mumps at Scarborough the year before; and the three youngest were laid up with German measles at Easter in the Isle of Man; so it has made me quite nervous."

Just at present the Rokebys did not seem in danger of contracting anything more serious than colds or sprained ankles, for a more reckless crew in the way of falling into wet pools, climbing slippery rocks, or generally endangering their lives and limbs could not be imagined. It was in vain that poor Mrs. Rokeby dried their boots and brushed their clothes, and implored them to keep away from perilous spots; they were full of repentance, and would vow amendment with the most warm-hearted of hugs, but in half an hour they had forgotten all their promises, and would be racing over the rocks again as wet and jolly as ever.

"I really do my best to keep them tidy," sighed Mrs. Rokeby pathetically to Mrs. Barrington. "Their father grumbles horribly at the bills, but they seem to wear their clothes out as fast as I buy them. Bertie's new Norfolk suit is shabby already, and Winnie's Sunday frock isn't fit to be seen. As to their boots, I sometimes think I shall have to let them go bare-foot. Other people's children don't seem to give half the trouble that mine do. Look at them now—dragging Lulu down the sands, when I told them she mustn't get overheated on any account! The doctor said we were to be so careful of her, and keep her quiet; but it seems no use—she *will* run after the others. Oh dear! I can't allow them to turn her head over heels like that!"

And Mrs. Rokeby flew to the rescue of her delicate youngest, administering a vigorous scolding to the elder ones, which apparently made as little impression upon them as water on a duck's back. The untidy appearance and unruly behaviour of her undisciplined flock were really a trial to Mrs. Rokeby, since they generally managed to compare unfavourably with the Wrights, a stolid and matter-of-fact family who were staying in rooms near the station.

"You never see Charlotte Wright with her dress torn to ribbons, or her hair in her eyes," she would remonstrate with Letty and Winnie. "Both she and Aggie can wear their sailor blouses for three days, while yours aren't fit to be seen at the end of a morning."

"The Wrights are so stupid," replied Winnie, "you can hardly get them to have any fun at all. They spend nearly the whole time with that mademoiselle they've brought with them. They're so proud of her, they do nothing but let off French remarks just to try to impress us. She's only a holiday governess too—they don't have her when they're at home—so there's no need for them to give themselves such airs about it. I believe their French isn't anything much either, they put in so many English words."

"Arthur Wright actually brings his books down on to the shore," said Letty, "and does Greek and Euclid half the morning. He says he's working for a scholarship. You wouldn't catch Hugh or Cecil at that."

"I'm afraid I shouldn't," sighed Mrs. Rokeby. "To judge from their bad reports at school, it seems difficult enough to get them to learn anything in term time. As for mademoiselle, you might take the opportunity to talk to her a little, and improve your own French."

"No, thank you!" said Winnie, pulling a wry face. "No holiday lessons for me. I loathe French, and I never can understand a single word that mademoiselle says, so it's no use. If the Wrights like to sit on the sand and 'parlez-vous,' they may. They're so fat, they can't rush about like we do. That's why they keep so tidy. Charlotte's waist is exactly twice as big as mine—we measured them yesterday with a piece of string—and Aggie's cheeks are as round as puddings. You should see how they all pant when they play cricket. They scarcely get any runs."

"And they really eat far more even than we do, mother," said Letty. "Aggie had five buns on the shore yesterday, and Eric took sixteen biscuits. I know he did, for we counted them, and he nearly emptied the box."

"The Chesters are five times as jolly," declared Winnie. "Both Charlie and Hilda went out shrimping with us this morning, and got sopping wet, but they didn't mind in the least, and Mrs. Chester only laughed when they went back. She said sea water didn't hurt. She's far nicer than Mrs. Barrington. I wouldn't be Ruth Barrington for all the world. She and Edna never have any breakfast, and they're made to do the queerest things."

The unlucky little Barringtons were possessed of parents who clung to theories which they themselves described as "wholesome ideas," and their friends denounced as "absurd cranks." Many and various were the experiments which they tried upon their children's health and education, sometimes with rather disastrous results. Being at present enthusiastic members of a "No Breakfast League," which held that two meals a day were amply sufficient for the requirements of any rational human being, they had limited their family repasts to luncheon and supper, at which only vegetarian dishes were permitted to appear; and the poor children, hungry with sea air and with running about on the sands, who would have enjoyed an unstinted supply of butcher's meat and bread and butter, were carefully dieted on plasmon, prepared nuts, and many patent foods, which their mother measured out in exact portions, keeping a careful record in her diary of the amount they were allowed to consume, and taking the pair to be weighed every week upon the automatic machine at the railway station. Their costumes consisted of plain blue over-all pinafores and sandals, and they wore neither hats nor stockings.

"It's all right for the seaside," grumbled Ruth to her intimate friends, "because we can go into the water without minding getting into a mess; but we have to wear exactly the same in town, and it's horrible. You can't think how every one stares at as, just as if we were a show. Sometimes ladies stop us, and ask our governess if we've lost our hats, and hadn't she better tie our handkerchiefs over our heads? We shouldn't dare to go out alone even if we were allowed, we look so queer. We went once to the post by ourselves, and some rude boys chased us all the way, calling out 'Bare-legs!' It's dreadfully cold in winter, too, without stockings, and when it rains our heads get wet through, and we have to be dried with towels when we come in again. I wonder why we can't be dressed like other people. I wish I had Belle Stuart's clothes; they're perfectly lovely!"

Ruth's rather pathetic little face always bore the injured expression of one who cherishes a grievance. She was a thin, pale child, who did not look as though she flourished upon her peculiar system of bringing up, which seemed to have the unfortunate effect of completely spoiling her temper, and making her see life through an extremely blue pair of spectacles. This summer she certainly thought she had a just cause of complaint, since her two schoolboy brothers, instead of spending their holidays as usual at the seaside, had been dispatched on a walking-tour to Switzerland with a certain German professor, who, in accordance with the latest educational fad, was conducting a select little party of boys on an open-air pilgrimage, the main features of which seemed to be to walk bare-foot by day and to sleep in a kind of wigwam at night, which they erected out of alpenstocks and mackintoshes.

"It's too disgusting!" said Ruth dolefully. "Just when Edna and I had been looking forward all the term to the boys coming home, and making so many plans of what we would do and the fun we would have, some wretched person sent father a copy of *The Educational Times*, with a long account of this horrid walking-tour, and he said it was the exact thing for Clifford and Keith, and insisted upon arranging it at once. I think mother was really dreadfully disappointed. I believe she wanted to have them home as much as we did, because she said they ought to go to the dentist's, and she must look over their clothes, and she should like to give them some phosphates tonic; but father said they could have their teeth attended to at Geneva, and she could send the tonic to the professor, and ask him to see that they took it. I know the boys will be furious; they hate taking medicine: they generally keep it in their mouths, and spit it out afterwards. They'll have to talk German all day long too, and they can't bear that. You've no idea how they detest languages. I had a picture post-card from Clifford yesterday, and he said his feet were horribly sore with walking bare-foot, and his tent blew away one night, and he was obliged to sleep in the open air."

No greater contrast could be found to the Barringtons than the Chester children. Charlie, the elder, a lively young pickle of twelve, was on terms of great intimacy with all the fishermen and sailor boys whose acquaintance he could cultivate, talking in a learned manner of main-sheets, fore-stays, jibs, gaffs, booms and bowsprits, and using every nautical term he could manage to pick up. He had a very good idea of rowing, and would often persuade the men to let him go out with them in their boats, taking his turn at an oar, much to their amusement, and setting log lines with the serious air of a practised hand. His jolly, friendly ways won him general favour, and he was allowed to make himself at home on many of the little fishing smacks, learning to hoist sails, to steer, and to cast nets, though sometimes a too inquiring mind led him to interfere on his own account in the navigation, with the result that he would be unceremoniously bundled back to shore again, with a warning to "keep out of this" in the future.

He was the envy of his eight-year-old sister Hilda, who would have liked to follow him through thick and thin, but the sailors drew the line at little girls, and would politely request "missy" to "return home to her ma," as there was no place for her "on this 'ere craft," much to her indignation. She consoled herself, however, by organizing the games of the younger Wrights and Rokebys, making wonderful sand harbours with their aid, and sailing a fleet of toy boats with as keen an enthusiasm as if they were real ones.

At the end of a morning on the common Isobel found herself on quite an intimate footing with the Wrights, the Rokebys, the Barringtons, and the Chesters, besides being a duly elected member of "The United Sea Urchins' Recreation Society."

"I've never had such fun in my life," she confided to her mother at dinner-time. "We played cricket, and then we went along the shore, because the tide was so low. I picked up the most beautiful screw shells, and razor shells, and fan shells you ever saw. I had to put them in my pocket handkerchief because I hadn't a basket with me. Bertie Rokeby got into a quicksand up to his knees, and Lulu sat down in the water in her clothes. You must come and see our club ground, mother, when you can walk so far. We have it quite to ourselves, for it's right behind the cliff, and none of the other visitors seem to have found it out yet; and if anybody else tries to take it, the boys say they mean to turn them off, because we got it first. They're all going to carry their tea there this afternoon, and light a fire of drift-wood to boil the kettle. So may I go too, and then we shall play cricket again in the evening?"

CHAPTER V. A HOT FRIENDSHIP.

"I was a child, and she was a child,
In this kingdom by the sea."

BY the time Isobel had been a week at Silversands she had begun to feel as much at home there as the oldest inhabitant. She had won golden opinions from Mrs. Jackson at the lodgings, and had been invited by that worthy woman into the upper drawing-room during the temporary absence of its occupiers, and shown a most fascinating cabinet full of foreign shells, stuffed birds, corals, ivory bangles, sandal-wood boxes, and other curiosities brought home by a sailor son who made many voyages to the East.

"Don't you wish you could have gone with him and got all these things for yourself?" said Isobel ecstatically, when she had examined and admired every article separately, and heard its history.

"Nay," replied Mrs. Jackson, "I've never had no mind for shipboard, though my second cousin was stewardess on a Channel steamer for a matter of fifteen year, and made a tidy sum out of it too. She could have got me taken on by the Anchor Line as runs to America if I'd have signed for two years. That was when my first husband died, and afore I married Jackson; but I felt I'd rather starve on dry land than take it, though it was good wages they offered, to say nothing of tips."

"Why, it would be glorious to go to America," said Isobel, sighing to think what her companion had missed. "You might have seen Red Indians, and wigwams, and medicine men, and 'robes of fur and belts of wampum,' like it talks of in 'Hiawatha.' Do you know 'Hiawatha'?"

"There were an old steamer of that name used to trade from Liverpool in hides and tallow when I were a girl, if that's the one you mean. I wonder she hasn't foundered afore now."

"Oh no!" cried Isobel hastily. "It isn't a steamer; it's a piece of poetry. I've just been reading it with mother, and it's most delightful. I could lend it to you if you like. We brought the book with us."

Mrs. Jackson's acquaintance with the muse, however, seemed to be limited to the hymns in church, and a hazy remembrance of certain pieces in her spelling book when a child, and being apparently unwilling to further cultivate her mind in that direction, she declined the offer on the score of lack of time.

"Not but what Jackson's fond of a bit of poetry now and again," she admitted. "He sings a good song or two when he's in the mood, and he do like readin' over the verses on the funeral cards. He pins them all up on the kitchen wall where he can get at them handy. What suits me more is something in the way of a romance—'Lady Gwendolen's Lovers,' or 'The Black Duke's Secret'—when I've time to take up a book, which isn't often, with three sets of lodgers in the house, and a girl as can't even remember how to make a bed properly, to say nothing of laying a table, and 'ull take the dining-room dinner up to the drawing-room."

The much-enduring Polly, though certainly not an accomplished waitress, was the most good-tempered of girls, and an invaluable ally in saving the treasured specimens of flowers or sea-weeds which Mrs. Jackson, in her praiseworthy efforts at tidiness, was continually clearing out, under the plea that she "hadn't imagined they could be wanted."

"She even threw away my mermaids' purses and the whelks' eggs that we found on the sand-bank," said Isobel to her mother. "But Polly climbed into the ashpit and grubbed them up again. She washed them in a bucket of water, and they're quite nice now; so I shall put them in a box, to make sure they'll be safe. Polly's father is part owner of a schooner, and sometimes they fish up the most enormous fan shells. She says she'll ask him to give me a few when she's time to go home, but she hasn't had a night out for nearly three weeks, the season's been so busy."

"Perhaps old Biddy could get you some large fan shells," suggested Mrs. Stewart. "I believe they find them sometimes very far out on the beach when they're shrimping."

Biddy was a well-known character in Silversands. She was a lively old Irishwoman, with the strongest of brogues and the most beguiling of tongues. In a blue check apron, and with a red shawl tied over her head, she might be seen every morning wheeling her barrow down the parade, where her amusing powers of blarney, added to the freshness of her fish, secured her a large circle of customers among what she called "the quality." She had a wonderful memory for faces, and always recognized families who paid a second visit to the town.

"Why, it's niver Masther Charlie, sure?" she exclaimed with delight, on meeting the Chesters one day. "It's meself that knew the bright face of yez the moment I saw ut, though ye're growed such a foine young gintleman an' all. Ye was staying at No. 7 two years back with yer mamma—an illigant lady she was, too—and your sister, Miss Hilda, the swate little colleen. Holy saints! this must be herself and none other, for it's not twice ye'd see such a pair of eyes and forgit them."

What became of Biddy during the winter, when there were no visitors to buy her fish, was an unsolved mystery. "Sure, I makes what I can by the koindness of sthrangers during the summer toime!" she had replied when Isobel once sounded her on the subject. "There's many a one as gives me an extra penny or two, or says, 'Kape the change, Biddy Mulligan!' The Blessed Virgin reward them! Thank you kindly, marm," as Mrs. Stewart took the hint. "May your bed in heaven be aisy, and may ye niver lack a copper to give to them as needs it."

Besides Biddy, Isobel had a number of other acquaintances in Silversands. There was the coastguard at the cottage on the top of the cliffs, who sometimes allowed her to look through his telescope, and who had an interesting barometer in the shape of a shell-covered cottage with two doors, from one of which a little soldier appeared when it was going to be fine, while a nautical-looking gentleman in a blue jacket came out to give warning of wet weather. Then there was the owner of the pleasure boats, who had promised to take her for a row entirely free of charge on the day before she was going home; and the bathing woman, who always tried to keep for her the van with the blue stripes and the brass hooks inside because she knew she liked it. The donkey boy had christened the special favourite with the new harness "*her* donkey," and made it go with unwonted speed even on the outward journey (as a rule it galloped of its own accord when its nose was turned towards home); and the blind harpist by the railway station had waxed quite confidential on the subject of Scottish ballads, and had allowed her to try his instrument.

As for the members of the Sea Urchins' Club, she felt as if she had known them all her life, and the sayings and doings of the Chesters, the Rokebys, the Wrights, and the Barringtons occupied a large part of her conversation. Jolly as they were, none of them in Isobel's estimation could compare with Belle Stuart, who from the first had claimed her as her particular chum. The two managed to spend nearly the whole of every day together, sometimes in company with the other children, or sometimes alone on the beach, hunting for shells and sea anemones, picking flowers, or just sitting talking in delicious idleness under the shade of a rock, listening to the dash of the waves and the screams of the sea gulls which were following the tide.

"I'm not generally allowed to make friends with any one whom we don't know at home," Belle had confided frankly. "But mother said you looked such a very nice lady-like little girl, she thought it wouldn't matter just for this once. I told her your father had been an officer, and she said of course that made a difference, but I really was to be careful, and not pick up odd acquaintances upon the beach, for she doesn't want me to talk to all sorts of people who aren't in our set of society, and might be very awkward to get rid of afterwards."

Isobel did not reply. She would never have dreamt of explaining that it was only due to her most urgent entreaties that she, on her part, had been allowed to pursue the friendship. Mrs. Stewart, from somewhat different motives, was quite as particular as Belle's mother about chance acquaintances, and had been a little doubtful as to whether she was acting wisely in allowing Isobel to spend so much of her time with companions of whom she knew nothing, and whether this new influence was such as she would altogether wish for her.

"But I can't keep her wrapped up in cotton wool," she thought. "She has been such a lonely child that it's only right and natural she should like to make friends of her own age, especially when I'm not able to go about with her. She'll have to face life some time, and the sooner she begins to be able to distinguish the wheat from the chaff so much the better. Thus far I've perhaps guarded her too carefully, and this is an excellent opportunity of throwing her on her own resources. I think I can trust her to stick to what she knows is right, and not be led astray by any silly notions. She'll soon discover that money and fine clothes don't represent the highest in life, and I believe it's best to let her find it out gradually for herself. She's like a little bird learning to fly; I've kept her long enough in the nest, and now I must stand aside and leave her to try her wings."

For the present, at any rate, Isobel could see no fault in her new friend. Belle had completely won her heart. Her charming looks; her fair, fluffy curls; her little, spoilt, coaxing ways; the clinging manner in which she seemed to depend upon others; her very helplessness and heedlessness; even the artless openness with which she sought for admiration—all appealed with an irresistible force to Isobel's stronger nature. If it ever struck her that her companion was lacking in some of those qualities which she had been taught to consider necessary, she thrust the thought away as a kind of disloyalty; and if it were she who generally carried the heavy basket, searched for the lost ball, fetched forgotten articles, or did any of the countless small services which Belle exacted almost as a matter of course from those around her, it certainly was without any idea of complaint. There are in this world always those who love and those who are loved, and Isobel was ready with spendthrift generosity to offer her utmost in the way of friendship, finding Belle's pretty thanks and kisses a sufficient reward for any trouble she might take on her account, and perhaps unconsciously realizing that even in our affections it is the givers more than the receivers who are the truly blessed. Belle, who usually found a brief and fleeting attraction in any new friend, was pleased with Isobel's devotion, and ready to be admired, petted, and waited on to any extent. I think, too, that, to do her justice, she was really an affectionate child, and at the time she was as fond of her friend as it was possible for her light little character to be. She would not have troubled to put herself out of the way for Isobel, and it would not have broken her heart to part with her, but she enjoyed her company, and easily gave her the first place among the dozen bosom friends each of whom she had taken up in turn and thrown aside.

One particular afternoon found the namesakes strolling arm in arm along the narrow sandy lane which led inland from the beach towards the woods and the hills behind. It was the most delightful lane, with high grassy banks covered with pink bindweed and tiny blue sheep's scabious, and bright masses of yellow bedstraw, and great clumps of mallows, with seed-vessels on them just like little cheeses, which you could gather and thread on pieces of cotton to make necklaces. There was a hedge at the top of the bank, too, where grew the beautiful twining briony, with its dark leaves and glossy berries; and long trails of bramble, where a few early blackberries could be discovered if you cared to reach for them; and down among the sand at the bottom of the ditch you might find an occasional horned poppy, or the curious flowers and glaucous prickly leaves of the sea holly. Isobel, on the strength of a new bright-green tin vasculum, purchased only that very morning at the toy-shop near the station, and slung over her shoulder in the style of a student in a German picture-book, felt herself to be a full-fledged botanist, and rushed about in a very enthusiastic manner, scrambling up the banks after pink centaury, diving into the hedge bottom for campions, or getting her hair caught, like Absalom, in a prickly rose-bush in a valiant endeavour to secure a particularly fine clump of harebells which were nodding in the breeze on the stones of the old wall.

"They're perfectly lovely, aren't they?" she cried. "I've got fourteen different sorts of flowers already, and I'm sure some of them must be rare—anyway, I've never seen them before. I'm going to press them directly I get home. Do you think this stump will bear me if I climb up for that piece of briony?"

"I'm afraid it won't," said Belle, fastening some of the harebells in her dress (they matched her blue sash and hat ribbons). "It looks fearfully rotten. There! I told you it wouldn't hold," as Isobel descended with a crash. "And you're covered with sand and prickly burrs—such a mess!"

"Never mind," said Isobel, the state of whose clothing rarely distressed her. "They'll brush off. But I must have the briony. I'll climb up by the wall if you'll hold these hips for a moment."

"Oh, do come along—that's a darling!" entreated Belle. "I don't want to wait. They're only wild things, after all. I wish you could see our garden at home, full of lovely geraniums and fuchsias and lobelias, and the orchids and gloxinias in the conservatory. They're really worth looking at. Carter, our gardener, takes tremendous pains with them, and he gets heaps of prizes at shows."

"But I like wild flowers best," said Isobel. "You can find them yourself in the hedges, and there are so many kinds. It's most exciting to hunt out their names in the botany book."

"Do you care for botany?" said Belle. "I have it with Miss Fairfax, and I think it's hateful—all about corollas, and stigmas, and panicles, and umbels, and stupid long words I can't either remember or understand."

"I haven't learnt any proper botany yet," said Isobel, "only just some of the easy part; but when we come into the country mother and I always hunt for wild flowers, and then we press them and paste them into a book, and write the names underneath. We have eighty-seven different sorts at home, and I've found sixteen new ones since I came here, so I think that's rather good, considering we've only been at Silversands a week. How hot it is in this lane! Suppose we go round by the station and up the cliffs."

The little lane with its high banks was certainly the most baking spot they could have chosen for a walk on a blazing August afternoon. The sun poured down with a steady glare, till the air seemed to quiver with the heat, and the only things which really enjoyed themselves were the grasshoppers, whose cheery chirpings kept up a perpetual concert. In the fields on either side the reapers had been busy, and tired-looking harvesters were hard at work binding the yellow corn and the scarlet poppies into sheaves. Little groups of mothers and children and babies had come to help or look on, as the case might be, and brought with them cans of tea and checked handkerchiefs full of bread and butter.

"Don't they look jolly?" said Isobel, peeping over the hedge to watch a family who were picnicking among the stooks, the father in a broad-brimmed rush hat, his corduroy trousers tied up with wisps of straw, wiping his hot forehead on his shirt sleeves; the mother putting the baby to roll on the corn, while she poured the tea into blue mugs; and the children, as brown as gypsies, sitting round in a circle eating slices of bread, and evidently enjoying the fun of the thing.

"Ye-e-s," said Belle, somewhat doubtfully, "I suppose they do. Are you fond of poor people?"

"I like going with mother when she's district-visiting, because the women often let me nurse the babies. Some of them are so sweet they'll come to me and not be shy at all."

"Aren't they rather dirty?"

"No, not most of them. A few are beautifully clean. Mother says she expects they know which day we're coming, and wash them on purpose."

"Babies are all very well when they're nicely dressed in white frocks and lace and corals," remarked Belle, "so long as they don't pull your hair and scratch your face."

"One day," continued Isobel, "we went to the *crèche*—that's a place where poor people's children are taken care of during the day while their mothers are out working. There were forty little babies in cots round a large room—*such* pets; and so happy, not one of them was crying. The nurse said they generally howl for a day or two after they're first brought in, and then they get used to it and don't bother any more. You see it wouldn't do to take up every single baby each time it began to cry."

"I wish you'd tell that to the Wrights; they give that 'Popsie' of theirs whatever she shrieks for. She's a nasty, spoilt little thing. Yesterday she caught hold of my pearl locket, and tugged it so hard she nearly strangled me, and broke the chain; and the locket fell into a pool, and I couldn't find it, though I hunted for half an hour. The nurse only babbled on, 'Poor pet! didn't she get the pretty locket, then?' I felt so cross I wanted to smack both her and the baby."

"And haven't you found the locket yet?"

"No, and I never shall now; it's been high tide since then."

"What a shame! I should have felt dreadfully angry. I don't like the Wrights' nurse either. She borrowed my new white basket, and then let the children have it; and they picked blackberries into it, and stained it horribly. Why, there's Aggie Wright now, with the Rokebys. What *are* they doing? They're hanging over that gate in the most peculiar manner. Let us go and see."

CHAPTER VI. ON THE CLIFFS.

"We saw the great ocean ablaze in the sun,
And heard the deep roar of the waves."

THE gate in question proved to be the level crossing, which had just been closed by the man from the signal-box to allow a train to pass through. Charlotte and Aggie Wright and five of the Rokebys were all standing upon the bars, hanging over the top rail and gazing at the metals with such deep and intense interest that you would have thought they expected a railway accident at the very least, and were looking out for the smash.

"What *is* the matter?" cried Belle and Isobel, racing up to share in whatever excitement might be on hand. "Do you see anything? Is it a cow on the line?"

"No," said Bertie Rokeby, balancing himself rather insecurely upon the gate post; "we're only waiting for the train to pass. We've put pennies on the rail, and the wheels going over them will flatten them out till they're nearly twice as big. You'd hardly believe what a difference it makes. Would you like to try one? I'd just have time to climb down and put it on before the train comes up. I will in a minute, if you say the word."

"I haven't a penny with me, I'm afraid," answered Isobel, rummaging in her pockets, and turning out several interesting pebbles, a few shells, a mermaid's purse, and the remains of a spider crab. "Stop a moment! No, it's only a button after all, and a horn one, too, that would be smashed to smithereens. If it had been a metal one I'd have tried it."

"I've nothing but a halfpenny," said Belle. "It's all I possess in the world till to-morrow, when I get my pocket-money. But do put it on, Bertie; it would be fun to see how large it makes it."

Bertie climbed over the gate and popped the coin with the others on the rail, much to the agitation of the pointsman, who ran in great anger from the signal-box, shouting to him to get off the line, for the train was coming. He was barely in time, for in another moment the express came whirling by with such a roar and a rattle, and making such a blast of wind as it went, that the children had to shut their eyes and cling on tightly.

"You'll get into trouble here if you get over them bars when I've shut 'em," grunted the pointsman surlily, opening the gates to admit a waiting cart from the other side. "I'll take your name next time as you tries it on, and report you to the inspector, and you'll get charged with trespassing on the company's property."

"Oh, bother!" cried Bertie; "I wasn't doing any harm. I can take jolly good care of myself, so don't you worry about me." And he rushed impatiently after the others, who were already picking up their pennies from the rail.

"It's crushed them ever so flat!" exclaimed Aggie Wright, triumphantly holding up a dinted copper which seemed to be several sizes too large.

"You can scarcely see which is heads and which is tails," said Arnold Rokeby.

"Just look at my halfpenny," said Belle; "it's twice as big as it was before."

"Why, so it is! Any one would take it for a penny if they didn't look at it closely. Come along. They want to shut the gates again for a luggage train, and we shall have to clear out. We're all going to the Pixies' Steps. Are you two coming with us?"

"No, I think not," replied Belle. "It's too hot to walk so far. Isobel and I just want to stroll about."

"Then good-bye. We're off.—Come along, Cecil. For goodness' sake don't go grubbing in the hedge now after caterpillars. Even if it *is* a woolly bear, you'll find plenty more another day.—Here, Arnold, you young monkey, give me my cap." And the Rokebys tore away up the road with a characteristic energy that even the blazing August heat could not quench.

"If we go behind Hunt's farm," said Isobel, "we can turn up the path to the churchyard, and get on to the cliffs just over the quay. It's a short cut, and much nicer than the road."

So they crossed the line again by the footbridge, passing the station, where the porter, overcome with the heat, was having a comfortable snooze on his hand-barrow; then, facing towards the sea, they climbed the steep track which zigzagged up the face of the cliff to the old church. The door was open, and the children stole inside for a minute and stood quietly gazing round the nave. It was cool and shady there, with the rich glow from the stained-glass windows falling in checkered rays of blue and crimson and orange upon the twisted pillars and the carved oak pews. The choir was practising in the chancel, and as they sang, the sun, slanting through the diamond panes of the south transept, made a very halo of glory round the head of the ancient, time-worn monument of St. Alcuin, the Saxon abbot, below. Crosier and mitre had long ago been chipped away by the ruthless hands of Cromwell's soldiers, but they had spared the face, and the light shone full on the closed eyes and the calm, sleeping mouth. Isobel moved a little nearer, trying to spell out the half-effaced letters of the inscription. She knew the story of how the pagan Norsemen had sacked the abbey, and had murdered the abbot on the steps of the altar, where he had remained alone to pray when his monks had fled to safety; but the words were in Latin, and she could not read them.

"For all the saints who from their labours rest," chanted the choir softly, the music of their voices mingling strangely with the shouts of the children at play which rose up from the beach below.

"He looks as though he were resting," thought Isobel; "not dead—only just sleeping until he was wanted again. I suppose he's one of the 'saints in light' now. What a long, long time it is since he lived here! I wonder if he knows they built a church and called it St. Alcuin's after him."

"Here's the verger coming," whispered Belle, pulling at her hand. "I think we'd better go."

"Let us sit down; shall we?" said Isobel, when they were out in the glare of the sunshine once more on the broad flagged path which led from the church door to the steps looking down on to the sea.

"Not here, though," replied Belle; "I don't like gravestones—they make me feel horrid and creepy."

"Under the lich-gate, then," suggested Isobel. "It'll be cooler, for it's in the shade, and there's a seat, too."

"What a simply broiling day!" said Belle, settling herself as luxuriously as possible in the corner, and pulling off her hat to fan her hot face. "I don't like such heat as this; it takes my hair out of curl," tenderly twisting one of her flaxen ringlets into its proper orthodox droop.

"It's jolly here. We get a little wind, and we can watch everything all round," said Isobel, sitting with her chin in her hands, and gazing over the water to where the herring fleet was tacking back to the harbour.

The children could scarcely have chosen a sweeter spot to rest. Below them lay the sea, a broad flat expanse of blue, getting a little hazy gray on the horizon, and with a greenish ripple where it neared the rocks, upon which its waves were always dashing with a dull, booming sound.

The old town, with its red roofs and poppy-filled gardens, made such a spot of brightness against the blue sea that it suggested the brilliant colouring of a foreign port, all the more so in contrast to the gray tower of the church behind and the wind-swept yew trees which had somehow managed to survive the winter storms. The grass had been mown in the churchyard, and filled the air with a fragrant scent of hay; a big bumble-bee buzzed noisily over a bed of wild thyme under the wall, and a swallow was feeding a row of young ones upon the ridged roof of the sexton's cottage. In the great stretch of blue above, the little fleecy clouds formed themselves into snowy mountains with valleys and lakes between, a kind of dream country in purest white, and Isobel wondered whether, if one could sail straight on to the very verge of the distance where sea and sky seemed to meet, one could slip altogether over the invisible line that bounds the horizon, and find oneself floating in that cloudland region.

"It's like the edge of heaven," she thought. "I think the saints must live there, and the cherubim and seraphim much farther and higher up—right in the blue part. One could never see *them*; but perhaps sometimes on a day like this the saints might come back a little way out of the light and nearer to the earth where they used to live, and if one looked very hard one might manage to catch a glimpse of them just where the sun's shining on that white piece."

"O blest communion! fellowship divine! We feebly struggle; they in glory shine!"

came wafted through the open church door, the sound of the singing, rather far off and subdued, seeming to join in harmony with the lap of the waves, the hum of the bees, the cries of the sea-gulls, the twittering of the swallows, and all the other glad voices of nature. It looked such a beautiful, joyful, delightful, glorious world that Isobel sat very quietly for a time just drinking in the sweet air and the sunshine, and feeling, without exactly knowing why, that it was good to be there.

"Are you asleep?" said Belle at last, in an injured tone; "you haven't spoken to me for at least five minutes. I'm sure it must be getting near tea-time. Let us go now."

"All right," said Isobel, recalling herself with a start—she had almost forgotten Belle's existence for the moment. "It's so nice on these steps, one feels as if one were up above everything. It's like being on the roof of the world. Perhaps that was why St. Alcuin and the monks built the abbey here; it seems so very near to the sky."

"What a queer girl you are sometimes!" said Belle, looking at her curiously; "I believe you're fond of old churches and musty-fusty monuments. Come along. We'll buy some sweets or some pears as we go home."

It was a change indeed from the cliff top to the bustle and noise of the little town below. Most of the fish-stalls were empty in the market, for the stock of herrings and mackerel had been sold off earlier in the day; but a travelling bazaar was in full swing, and exhibited a bewildering display of toys, tea-cups, mugs, tin cans, looking-glasses, corkscrews, and many other wonderful and miscellaneous articles, any of which might be bought for the sum of one penny. The main street, narrow and twisting, ran steeply uphill, the high gabled houses crowding each other as if they were trying to peep over one another's shoulders; from the side alleys came the mingled odours of sea-weed and frying fish, and a persistent peddler hawking brooms shouted himself hoarse in his efforts to sell his wares. Under the wide archway at the corner by the market stood a tiny fruit-shop, where piles of plums and early apples, bunches of sweet peas and dahlias, baskets of tomatoes, lettuces, broad beans, cauliflowers, and cabbages, were set forth to tempt customers.

"There are the most delicious-looking pears," said Belle, peeping through the small square panes of the window, "and so cheap. I shall go in and get some."

"Yes, love, six for a penny," said the woman, a motherly-looking soul, as Belle entered the shop and inquired the price. "They're fine and ripe now, and won't do you no harm. A pen'orth, did you say?" And picking out six of the best pears, she put them into a paper bag and handed them to Belle, who, turning to leave the shop, laid down on the counter the coin which she had placed that afternoon on the railway line.

The woman did not look at it particularly, but naturally supposing from the size that it was a penny, she swept it carelessly into the till.

"Belle! Belle!" whispered Isobel, catching her friend hastily by the arm as she went out through the door, "do you know what you've done? You paid her your big halfpenny instead of a penny."

"Oh, did I?" said Belle, flushing. "I didn't notice. I never looked at it."

"What a good thing I saw the mistake! Give her a proper penny, and get the halfpenny back."

Belle fumbled in her pocket in vain.

"I don't believe I have another penny, after all," she said at last. "I thought I had several. I must have lost them while we were up on the cliffs, I suppose."

"What *are* we to do?" exclaimed Isobel anxiously. "We can't take the pears when we haven't paid for them properly; it would be stealing."

"I'll bring her another halfpenny to-morrow," suggested Belle.

"But suppose before that she looks at the money and finds out; she'll think we have been trying to cheat her."

"Perhaps she won't remember who gave it to her."

"Oh! but that wouldn't make it any better," said Isobel. "Look here; let us take back the bag, and tell her we paid the wrong money, and ask her to give us only half the pears."

"Very well," answered Belle. "You go in, will you? I don't like to."

Isobel seized the parcel, and quickly re-entered the shop.

"I'm ever so sorry," she said breathlessly, "but we find we've made such a dreadful mistake. We meant to give you a penny, and it wasn't a penny at all—only a halfpenny squashed out flat on the railway line; so, please, will you take back half the pears, because we neither of us have a proper penny in our pockets."

The woman laughed.

"I didn't think to notice what you give me," she said. "But you're an honest little girl to come and tell me. No, I won't take back none of the pears. You're welcome to them, I'm sure."

"It was very nice of her," said Belle sweetly, peeling the juicy fruit slowly with her penknife as they turned away down the street. "So stupid of me to make such a mistake! Have another, darling; they're quite delicious, though they are so small."

Isobel walked along rather silent and preoccupied. Though she would not allow it to herself, down at the bottom of her heart there was the uncomfortable suspicion that Belle had known all the time, and had meant to give the wrong coin.

"She *couldn't!*" thought Isobel. "She *must* have made a mistake, and thought she really had a penny in her pocket. Yet at the level crossing she certainly said the halfpenny was all she had until she got her weekly money to-morrow. Perhaps she forgot. Oh dear! I know she didn't mean to cheat or tell stories—I'm sure she wouldn't for the world—but somehow I *wish* it hadn't happened."

CHAPTER VII. THE "STORMY PETREL."

"A boat, a boat is the toy for me,
To rollick about in on river and sea,
To be a child of the breeze and the gale,
And like a wild bird on the deep to sail—
This is the life for me."

THE United Sea Urchins' Recreation Society usually met every morning upon the strip of green common underneath the cliffs which they had appropriated to their own use, and were prepared to hold against all comers. The Rokebys, who were enthusiastic bathers, had a tent upon the shore, and spent nearly half the morning in the sea, where they could float, swim on their backs, tread water, and even turn head over heels, much to the envy of the Wrights, who made valiant efforts to emulate these wonderful feats, and nearly drowned themselves in the attempt. The two little Barringtons were solemnly bathed each day by their mother in a specially-constructed roofless tent, which was fixed upon four poles over a hole previously dug in the sand, and filled by the advancing tide. Here they were obliged to sit for ten minutes in the water, with the sun pouring down upon them till the small tent resembled a vapour bath, after which they were massaged according to the treatment recommended by a certain Heidelberg doctor in whom Mrs. Barrington had great faith, and whose methods she insisted upon carrying out to the letter, in spite of Ruth's indignant remonstrances and Edna's wails.

"Ruth says bathing's no fun at all," confided Isobel to her mother; "and I shouldn't think it is, if you can't splash about in the sea and enjoy yourself. Mrs. Barrington won't let them try to swim, and they just have to sit in a puddle inside the tent, while she flings cans of sea-water down their backs. Edna says the hot sun makes the skin peel off her, and she can't bear the rubbing afterwards. Her clothes fridge her, too; they always wear thick woollen under-things even in this blazing weather, their mother's so afraid of them taking a chill."

"Poor children!" said Mrs. Stewart; "I certainly think they have rather a bad time. It must be very hard to be brought up by rule, and to have so many experiments tried upon you."

"Ruth says she has one comfort, though," continued Isobel: "they're allowed to speak English all the time during the holidays. At home they have a German governess, and they talk French one day, and German the next, and English only on Sundays. Ruth hates languages. She won't speak a word to mademoiselle, but she says the Wrights simply talk cat-French—it's half of it English words—although they're so conceited about it, and generally say something out very loud if they think anybody is passing, even if it's only *Il fait beau aujourd'hui*, or *Comment vous portez-vous?* The Rokebys poke terrible fun at them; they've made up a gibberish language of their own, and they talk it hard whenever the Wrights let off French. It makes Charlotte and Aggie quite savage, because they know they're talking about them, only they can't understand a word."

"What's the club going to do to-day?" asked Bertie Rokeby one morning, looking somewhat damp and moist after his swim. ("He never *will* dry himself properly," said Mrs. Rokeby; "he just gets into his clothes as he is, and he's sitting down on the old boat just where the sun has melted the pitch, and it will be sure to stick to his trousers.")

"Don't know," said Harold Wright, lolling comfortably in the shade of a rock, with his head on his rolled-up jacket; "too hot to race round with the thermometer over 70°. I shall stay where I am, with a book."

"Get up, you fat porpoise! You'll grow too lazy to walk. Unless you mean to stop and swat at Greek like old Arthur."

"No, thanks," laughed Harold. "I'm not in for a scholarship yet, thank goodness! I'm just going to kick my heels here. The *dolce far niente*, you know."

"Let us go down to the quay," suggested Charlie Chester, "and watch the boats come in. It's stunning to see them packing all the herrings into barrels, and flinging the mackerel about. Some of the men are ever so decent: they let you help to haul in the ropes, and take you on board sometimes."

"Shall we go too?" said Belle, who, with her arm as usual round Isobel's waist, stood among the group of children; "it's rather fun down by the quay, if you don't get *too* near the fish.—Are you coming, Aggie?"

"Yes, if Charlotte and mademoiselle will go too.—Mam'zelle, voulez-vous aller avec nous à voir le fish-market?"

Mademoiselle shivered slightly, as if Aggie's French set her teeth on edge.

"Qu'est-ce que c'est, chère enfant, cette 'feesh markeet'?" she replied.

"I don't know whether I can quite explain it in French," replied Aggie; but seeing the Rokebys come up, she made a desperate effort to sustain her character as a linguist. "C'est l'endroit où on vend le poisson, vous savez."

Unfortunately she pronounced *poisson* like the English "poison," and mademoiselle held up her dainty little hands with a shriek of horror.

"Vere zey sell ze poison! Non, mon enfant! You sall nevaire take me zere! Madame Wright, see not permit zat you go! C'est impossible!"

"It's all right, mademoiselle," said Arthur, taking his nose for a moment out of his dictionary. "Aggie only meant *poisson*. The mater'll let the kids go, if you want to take 'em."

"Come along, mademoiselle, do!" said Charlie Chester cordially. "Venez avec moi! That's about all the French I can talk, because at school we only learn to write exercises about pens and ink and paper, and the gardener's son, and lending your knife to the uncle of the baker; a jolly silly you'd be if you did, too! You'd never get it back. Suivez-moi! And come and see the *poisson*. You'll enjoy it if you do."

"I'm sure she wouldn't," said Charlotte Wright, who liked to keep her governess to herself. "We haven't time, either—we must do our translation before dinner; and Joyce and Eric can't go unless we're there to look after them."

"All right; don't, then! We shan't grieve," retorted Charlie. "We'll go with the Rokebys."

But the Rokebys, though ready, as a rule, to go anywhere and everywhere, on this particular occasion were due at the railway station to meet a cousin who was arriving that morning; so it ended in only Belle and Isobel, with Charlie and Hilda Chester, setting off for the old town. The quay was a busy, bustling scene. The herring-fleet had just come in, and it was quite a wonderful sight to watch the fish, with their shining iridescent colours, leaping by hundreds inside the holds. They were flung out upon the jetty, and packed at once into barrels, an operation which seemed to demand much noise and shouting on the part of the fishermen in the boats, and to call for a good deal of forcible language from their partners on shore. The small fry and cuttle-fish were thrown overboard for the sea-gulls, that hovered round with loud cries, waiting to pounce upon the tempting morsels, while the great flat skate and dog-fish were put aside separately.

"They're second-rate stuff, you see," explained Charlie Chester, who, with his hands in his pockets and his most seaman-like gait, went strolling jauntily up and down the harbour, inspecting the cargoes, trying the strength of the cables, peeping into the barrels with the knowing air of a connoisseur of fish, and generally putting himself where he was decidedly not wanted.

"They only pack the herrings, and they salt and dry the others in the sun. You can see them dangling outside their cottage doors all over the town, and smell them too, I should say. When they're quite hard they hammer them out flat, and send them to Whitechapel for the Jews to buy—at least that's what the mate of the *Penelope* told me the other day."

"They eat them themselves too," said Hilda. "I went inside a cottage one day, and they were frying some for dinner. The woman gave me a taste, but it was perfectly horrid, and I couldn't swallow it. I had to rush outside round the corner and spit it out."

"You disgusting girl!" said Belle, picking her way daintily between the barrels; "I wonder you could touch it, to begin with! Why, here are the women coming with the cockles. What a haul they've had! There's old Biddy at the head of them."

"So she is!" cried Charlie; "her basket looks almost bursting!—Hullo, Biddy!—

'In Dublin's fair city,

Where girls are so pretty,

There once lived a maiden named Molly Malon

She wheeled a wheelbarrow

Through streets wide and narrow,

Singing, "Cockles and mussels alive, alive-O!"'

Change it into Biddy, and there you are! I've an eye for an 'illigant colleen' when I see her!"

"Sure, ye're at yer jokes agin, Masther Charlie," laughed Biddy; "colleen, indade, and me turned sixty only the other day! If it weren't for the kreel on me back, I'd be afther yez."

"I'd like to see you catch me," cried Charlie, as he jumped on a heap of barrels, bringing the whole pile with a crash to the ground, greatly to the wrath of the owner, who expressed his views with so much vigour that the children judged it discreet to adjourn farther on along the quay.

They strolled past the storehouse, and round the corner to where a flight of green slimy steps led down to the water. There was an iron ring here in the sea wall, and tied to it by a short cable was the jolliest pleasure boat imaginable, newly painted in white and blue, with her name, the Stormy *Petrel*, in gilt letters on the prow, her sail furled, and a pair of sculls lying ready along her seats.

"She's a smart craft," said Charlie, reaching down to the painter, and pulling the boat up to the steps. "I vote we get inside her, and try what she feels like."

"Will they let us?" asked Isobel.

"We won't ask them," laughed Charlie. "It's all right; we shan't do any harm. They can turn us out if they want her. Come along." And he held out his hand.

It was such a tempting proposal that it simply was not in human nature to resist, and the three little girls hopped briskly into the boat, Belle and Isobel settling themselves in the bows, and Hilda taking a seat in the stern.

"It almost feels as if we were really sailing," said Isobel, as the boat danced upon the green water, pulling at its painter as though it were anxious to break away and follow the ebbing tide.

"She'd cut through anything, she's so sharp in the bows," said Charlie, handling the sculls lovingly, and looking out towards the mouth of the harbour, where long white-capped waves flecked the horizon.

"Can't you take us for a row, Charlie?" cried Belle; "it's so jolly on the water."

"Yes, do, Charlie," echoed Hilda; "it would be such fun."

"Do you mean, go for a real sail?" asked Isobel, rather aghast at such a daring proposal.

"Oh, we'd only take her for a turn round the harbour, and be back before any one missed her. It would be an awful lark," said Charlie.

"But not without a boatman!" remonstrated Isobel.

"Why not? I know all about sailing," replied Charlie confidently, for, having been occasionally taken yachting by his father, and having picked up a number of nautical terms, which he generally used wrongly, he imagined himself to be a thorough Jack Tar. "Wouldn't you like it? I thought you were fond of the sea."

"So I am," said Isobel; "but I don't think we ought to go without asking. It's not our boat, and the man she belongs to mightn't like us to take her out by ourselves."

"I suppose you're afraid," sneered Charlie; "most girls are dreadful land-lubbers. Hilda's keen enough; and as for Belle, she's half wild to go, I can see."

"I should think I am; and what's more, I mean to!" declared Belle; and settling the dispute as Alexander of old untied the Gordian knot, she took her penknife from her pocket, and leaning over, cut the painter off sharp.

"*Now* you've done it!" cried Charlie. "Well, we're off, at any rate, so we may as well enjoy ourselves.—Hilda, you must steer while I row. If you watch me feather my oars, you'll see I can manage the thing in ripping style."

There was such a strong ebb tide that Charlie had really no need to row. The boat went skimming over the waves as if she had been a veritable stormy petrel, sending the water churning round her bows. Although all four children felt a trifle guilty, they could not help enjoying the delightful sensation of that swift-rushing motion over the sea. Nearly all Anglo-Saxons have a love for the water: perhaps some spirit of the old vikings still lingers in our blood, and thrills afresh at the splash of the waves, the dash of the salt spray, and the fleck of the foam on our faces. There is a feeling of freedom, a sense of air, and space, and dancing light, and soft, subdued sound that blend into one exhilarating joy, when, with only a plank between us and the racing water, it is as if nature took us in her arms and were about to carry us away from every trammel of civilization, somewhere into that far-off land that lies always just over the horizon— that lost Atlantis which the old navigators sought so carefully, but never found.

Isobel sat in the bows, her hand locked in Belle's. She felt as if they were birds flying through space together, or mermaids who had risen up from the sea-king's palace to take a look at the sun-world above, and were floating along as much a part of the waves as the great trails of bladder-wrack, or the lumps of soft spongy foam that whirled by them. Charlie rested on his sculls and let the boat take her course for a while; she was heading towards the bar, straight out from the cliffs and the harbour to where the heavy breakers, which dashed against the lighthouse, merged into the rollers of the open sea.

"Aren't we going out rather a long way?" said Belle at last. "We've passed the old schooner and the dredger, and we're very nearly at the buoy. We don't want to sail quite to America, though it's jolly when we skim along like this. If we don't mind we shall be over the bar in a few minutes."

"By jove! so we shall!" cried Charlie. "I didn't notice we'd come so far. We must bring her round.—Get her athwart, Hilda, quick!"

"I suppose if you pull one line it goes one way, and if you pull the other line it goes the other way," said Hilda, whose first experience it was with the tiller, giving such a mighty jerk as an experiment that she swung the boat half round.

"Easy abaft!" shouted Charlie. "Do you want to capsize us? Turn her to starboard; she's on the port tack. Put up the helm, and make her luff!"

"What *do* you mean?" cried Hilda, utterly bewildered by these nautical directions.

"You little idiot, don't tug so hard! You'll be running us into the buoy. Look here! you can't steer. Just drop these lines. I'd better ship the oars and hoist the sail, and then I can take the tiller myself. There's a stiffish breeze; I can tack her round, you'll see, if I've no one interfering. Now let me get my bearings."

"Are you sure you know how?" asked Belle uneasily.

"Haven't I watched old Jordan do it a hundred times?" declared Charlie. "I'll soon have the canvas up. I say, look out there! The blooming thing's heavier than I thought."

"Oh, do be careful!" entreated Belle, as the sail went up in a very peculiar fashion, and beginning to fill with the breeze sent the boat heeling sharply over.

"She'll be perfectly right if I slack out. The wind's on our beam," replied Charlie; "I must get her a-lee."

"You're going to upset us!" exclaimed Belle, for the sail was flapping about in such a wild and unsteady manner as seemed to threaten to overturn the little vessel.

"Not if I make this taut," cried Charlie, hauling away with all his strength.—"Hilda, that was a near shave!" as the unmanageable canvas, swelling out suddenly, caught her a blow on the side of her head and nearly swept her from the boat.

Hilda gave a shriek of terror and clung wildly to the gunwale.

"O Charlie!" she cried, "take us back. I don't like sailing. I want to go home."

"Oh! why did we ever come?" shrieked Belle, jumping up in her seat and wringing her hands. "You'll send us to the bottom."

"Sit still, dear," cried Isobel. "You'll upset the boat if you move so quickly.—Charlie, I think you'd better take down that sail and try the sculls again. If you'll let me steer perhaps I could manage better than Hilda, and we could turn out of the current; it's taking us straight to sea. If we can head round towards the quay we might get back."

"All serene," said Charlie, furling his canvas with secret relief. "There ought to be several, really, for this job; it takes more than one to sail a craft properly, and none of you girls know how to help."

He gave Isobel a hand as she moved cautiously into the stern, and settling her with the ropes, he once more took up the oars.

"I shall come too," wailed Belle. "I can't stay alone at this end of the boat. Isobel, it's horrid of you to leave me."

"Sit still," commanded Charlie. "It's you who'll have us over if you jump about like that. We can't all be at one end, I tell you. You must stop where you are."

He made a desperate effort to turn the boat, but his boyish arms were powerless against the strength of the ebbing tide, and they were swept rapidly towards the bar.

"It's no use," said Charlie at last, shipping his sculls; "I can't get her out of this current. We shall just have to drift on till some one sees us and picks us up."

"O Charlie!" cried Hilda, her round chubby face aghast with horror, "shall we float on for days and days without anything to eat, or be shipwrecked on a desert island like Robinson Crusoe, and have to cling to broken masts and spars?"

"We're all right; don't make such a fuss!" said Charlie, glancing uneasily, however, at the long waves ahead. They were crossing the bar, and the water was rough outside the harbour.

"I *know* we're going to be drowned!" moaned Belle. "It's your fault, Charlie. You ought never to have brought us."

"Well, I like that!" retorted Charlie, with some heat, "when it was you who first thought of it, and asked me to take you. I suppose you'll be saying I cut the painter next."

"You want to throw the blame on me!" declared Belle.

"No, I don't; but there's such a thing as fair play."

"O Charlie, it doesn't matter whose fault it was now," said Isobel. "I suppose in a way it's all our faults for getting in, to begin with. Couldn't we somehow raise a signal of distress? Suppose you tie my handkerchief to the scull, and hoist it up like a flag. Some ship might notice it."

"Not a bad idea," said Charlie, who by this time wished himself well out of the scrape. "You've a head on your shoulders, though I did call you a land-lubber."

Between them they managed to tie on the handkerchief and hoist the oar, and as their improvised flag fluttered in the wind they hoped desperately that it might bring some friendly vessel to their aid.

They had quite cleared the harbour by now; the sea was rough, and the current still carried them on fast. Isobel sat with her arm round poor little Hilda, who clung to her very closely, watching the water with a white, frightened face, though she was too plucky to cry. Belle, who had completely lost self-control, was huddled down in the bows, shaking with hysterical sobs, and uttering shrieks every time the boat struck a bigger wave than usual.

"I wonder no one in the harbour noticed us set off," said Isobel after a time, when the land seemed to be growing more and more distant behind them.

"They were busy packing the herrings," replied Charlie, "and you see we started from round the corner. Our only chance now is meeting some boat coming from Ferndale. I say! do you think that's a sail over there?"

"It is!" cried Isobel. "Let us hold the flag up higher, and we'll call 'Help!' as loud as we can. Sound carries so far over water, perhaps they might hear us."

"Ahoy there!" yelled Charlie, with the full strength of his lungs. "Boat ahoy!" And Hilda and Isobel joining in, they contrived amongst them to raise a considerably lusty shout.

To their intense relief it seemed to be heard, as the ship tacked round, and bearing down upon them, very soon came up alongside.

"Well, of all sights as ever I clapped eyes on! Four bairns adrift in an open craft! I thought summat was up when I see'd your flag, and then you hollered.—Easy there, Jim. Take the little 'un on first. Mind that lad! He'll be overboard!—Whisht, honey! don't take on so. You'll soon be safe back with your ma.—Now, missy, give me your hand. Ay, you've been up to some fine games here, I'll wager, as you never did ought. But there! Bairns will be bairns, and I should know, for I've reared seven."

"Mr. Binks!" cried Isobel, to whom the ruddy cheeks, the bushy eyebrows, and the good-natured conversational voice of her friend of the railway train were quite unmistakable.

"Why, it's little missy as were comin' to Silversands!" responded the old man. "To think as I should 'a met you again like this! I felt as if somethin' sent me out this mornin' over and above callin' at Ferndale for a load of coals, which would 'a done to-morrow just as well. It's the workin's of Providence as we come on this tack, or you might 'a been right out to sea, and, ten to one, upset in that narrer bit of a boat."

It certainly felt far safer in Mr. Binks's broad-bottomed fishing-smack, though they had to sit amongst the coals and submit to be rather searchingly and embarrassingly catechised as to how they came to be in such a perilous situation. Their plight had been noticed at last from the harbour, where the owner of the boat, missing his craft, had raised a hue-and-cry, and there was quite a little crowd gathered to meet them on the jetty when they landed, a crowd which expressed its satisfaction at their timely rescue, or its disapproval of their escapade, according to individual temperament.

"Praise the saints ye're not drownded entoirely!" cried Biddy, giving Charlie a smacking kiss, much to his disgust. "And it's ould Biddy Mulligan as saw the peril ye was in, and asked St. Pathrick and the Blessed Virgin to keep an eye on yez. Holy St. Bridget! but ye're a broth of a boy, afther all."

"I'm main set to give you a jolly good hidin'," growled the owner of the boat, greeting Charlie with a somewhat different reception, and fingering a piece of rope-end as if he were much tempted to put his threat into execution. "Don't you never let me catch you on this quay again, meddlin' with other folk's property, if you want to keep your skin on you."

"He really was most dreadfully angry," Isobel told her mother in the graphic account which she gave afterwards of the adventure. "But Charlie said how very sorry we were. He took the whole blame to himself, though it wasn't all his fault by any means, and he offered to pay for having borrowed the boat. Then the man said he spoke up like a gentleman, and he wouldn't take his money from him; and Mr. Binks said bairns would be bairns, and it was a mercy we hadn't gone to the bottom; and the man shook hands with Charlie, and said he was a plucky little chap, with a good notion of handling a sail, and he'd take him out some time and show him how to do it properly. And Mr. Binks said I'd never been to see him yet, and I told him you'd sprained your ankle and couldn't walk, but it was getting better nicely, and you'd soon be able to; and he said, would we write and give him warning when we'd made up our minds, and his missis should bake a cranberry cake on purpose, and if we came early, he'd row us over to see the balk. I said we should be very pleased, because you'd promised before that you'd go. So you will, won't you, mother?"

"I shall be only too glad to have an opportunity of thanking him," said Mrs. Stewart. "I feel I owe him a big debt of gratitude to-day. Perhaps in the meantime we can think of some pretty little present to take with us that would please him and his wife, as a slight return for his kindness. You would have time to embroider a tea-cosy if I were to help you."

"That would be lovely," said Isobel. "And then they could use it every day at tea-time. We could work a teapot on one side and a big 'B' on the other for Binks. I'm sure they'd like that. May I go and buy the materials this afternoon? I brought my thimble with me and my new scissors in the green silk bag. I feel as if I should like to begin and make it at once."

CHAPTER VIII. CROSS-PURPOSES.

"Though a truth to outward seeming,
Yet a truth it may not prove."

ALTHOUGH Mrs. Stewart had now been more than ten days at Silversands she had not yet received any reply to the letter which she had dispatched with so many heart-burnings on the evening of her arrival.

"Does he mean to ignore it altogether?" she asked herself. "Will he never forgive? Can he allow his grandchild, the only kith and kin that is left to him, to be within a few miles and not wish at least to see her? Does he still think me the scheming adventuress that he called me in the first heat of his anger, and imagine I am plotting to get hold of his money? I would not touch one penny of it for myself, but I think it is only right and fair that Isobel should be sent to a really good school. It would be such a small expense to him out of his large income, and it is simply impossible for me to manage it. I have done my best for her so far, but she is so quick and bright that she will very soon be growing beyond my teaching. He will surely realize that for the credit of his own name something ought to be done. Perhaps he may be ill or away, and has not been able to attend to my letter. I must have patience for a little longer, and wait and see whether he will not send me an answer."

The waiting seemed very long and tedious to poor Mrs. Stewart as she lay through those hot summer days on the hard horsehair sofa of the small back sitting-room at No. 4 Marine Terrace. As the lonely hours passed away, the lines of trouble deepened in her forehead, and she stitched so many cares into the winter night-dresses she was beguiling the time by making that every gusset and hem seemed a reminder of some anxious thought for the future.

In the meantime Isobel remained sublimely unconscious of her mother's hopes and fears. To her the visit to Silversands was nothing but the most glorious holiday she had spent in her life, and her jolly times with the Sea Urchins, and especially the delight of her friendship with Belle, made the days fly only too fast. The latter was still as clinging and affectionate as ever, and would scarcely allow Isobel out of her sight.

"I'd rather be with you, darling, than with any one else," she declared enthusiastically. "I used to think I liked Winnie Rokeby, but she was very unkind once or twice, and told such nasty tales about me, actually trying to make out I was selfish, just because I wanted her to do one or two little things for me that *you* don't mind doing in the least. She splashed sea-water all over my best white silk dress too, and I'm sure it was on purpose, and she said my hair looked exactly like sticks of barley-sugar." And Belle tossed back her curls as if indignant yet at the remembrance.

"She really *is* fond of me," said Isobel to her mother. "And it's so nice of her, because, you see, although she doesn't care for Winnie Rokeby, she might have had Aggie Wright or Ruth Barrington for her special friend; she knows them both at home, and goes to all their parties. Charlotte Wright says it's too hot to last, but that's just because Aggie was jealous that Belle didn't ask her to go to tea the day I went; and Letty Rokeby says we're bound to have a quarrel sooner or later, but I'm sure we shan't, for there never seems anything to quarrel about, and I couldn't imagine being out of friends with Belle."

On the afternoon following Isobel's adventure in the *Stormy Petrel*, any one seated in the front windows of Marine Terrace might have been interested in the movements of an elderly gentleman, who for the last ten minutes had been slowly pacing up and down the broad gravel path in front. He was a very stately old gentleman, with iron-gray hair and a long, drooping moustache; he held himself erect, too, as if he were at parade, and he had that air of quiet dignity and command which is habitual to those who are accustomed to seeing their orders promptly obeyed. Whether he was merely enjoying the fresh air and scenery, or whether he was waiting for somebody, it was difficult to tell, since he now lighted a cigar in a leisurely fashion, and cast an anxious, quick look towards the houses, and, frowning slightly, would walk away, then come back again as if he were drawn by some magnet towards the spot, and must return there even against his will.

He was just passing the garden of No. 4 when the front door opened, and Belle, who had been spending an hour with Isobel, sauntered down the path, and closing the gate behind her, seated herself upon one of the benches which the Town Council had put up that summer on the gravel walk in front of Marine Terrace, as a kind of earnest of the promenade which they hoped might follow in course of time. She spread out her pretty pink muslin dress carefully upon the seat, rearranged her hat to her satisfaction, and slowly fastened the buttons of her long kid gloves. It was too early to go home yet, she thought, for her mother was out with friends, and their tea-time was not until five o'clock, so she sat watching the sea and the fishing-boats, and drawing elaborate circles with her parasol in the gravel at her feet. She was quite unaware that she was being very keenly observed by the old gentleman, who, having followed her, walked past once or twice with an undecided air, and finally settled himself upon the opposite end of the bench where she was sitting.

"That's certainly the address she gave me," he muttered to himself, "and it might possibly be the child. She tallies a little with the description; she's fair, and not bad-looking, though I don't see a trace of the Stewarts in her face. As for resembling my Isobel—well, of course, that was only a scheme on the mother's part to try and arouse my interest in her. What the letter said is true enough, all the same: if she's my grandchild it isn't right that she should be brought up in penury, and I suppose I must send her to school, or provide in some way for her. I can't say I'm much taken with her looks. She's too dressed-up for my taste. Where did her mother find the money to buy those fal-lals? It doesn't accord with the lack of means she complained of. I wonder if I could manage to ask her name without giving myself away."

He took a newspaper from his pocket, and spreading it out, pretended to read, stealing occasional glances in Belle's direction, and racking his brains for a suitable method of opening a conversation. Belle, who was beginning to be rather tired of her occupation, and was half thinking of moving farther on or going home, became suddenly conscious that she seemed to be arousing an unusual degree of interest in her companion at the other end of the bench. Constantly petted and admired by her mother's friends, she was accustomed to receive a good deal of attention, and it struck her that a short chat with this distinguished-looking stranger might beguile her monotony until tea-time. She therefore let her fluffy curls fall round her face in the way that an artist had once painted them, and began to cast coy looks from under her long lashes in his direction, hoping that he might speak to her; both of which methods she usually found very engaging with elderly gentlemen, who generally asked her whose little girl she was, and ended by saying she was a charming child, and they wished they owned her, or some other remark equally flattering and gratifying.

In this case however, her pretty ways did not seem to have their due effect; either the old gentleman was really shy himself, or he found a difficulty in starting, for though he cleared his throat several times, as if he were on the very point of speaking, he seemed to change his mind, and kept silence. Somewhat disappointed, Belle nevertheless was not easily baffled, and after having sighed, coughed, opened and shut her parasol, taken off her gloves and put them on again, thereby exhibiting the small turquoise ring that was her greatest delight, and finally even got up a sneeze, all without any result, she at last pulled off her bracelet, and in refastening it managed with considerable skill to let it drop on the ground and roll almost to her companion's feet. It was but natural that he should pick it up and hand it to her.

"Oh, thank you so much!" exclaimed Belle, in what some one had once called her "Parisian" manner. "It was so careless of me to drop it, and I wouldn't have lost it for the world. Things so easily roll away on the shore, don't they?"

"I suppose they do," replied the colonel. "It certainly isn't wise to send your trinkets spinning about the sands."

"I value that one, too," said Belle, shaking her curls, "because, you see, it was a present. A friend of mother's gave it to me on my last birthday.

He was going to choose a book at first—he always sent me books before, the most terrible ones: Shakespeare, and Lamb's 'Essays,' and Ruskin, and stupid things like that, which I shan't ever care to read, even when I'm grown up—so this birthday I asked him if he would give me something really nice; and he laughed, and brought me this dear little bangle, and said he expected it would suit Miss Curly-locks better than solid reading."

"Ugh!" grunted her new acquaintance, with so ambiguous an expression that Belle could not make out whether he sympathized or not; but as he put down his paper, and seemed quite ready to listen to her, she went on.

"It's very nice at Silversands. Mother and I have been here nearly a fortnight. We think the air's bracing, and the lodgings are really not bad for a little place like this. One doesn't expect a hotel."

"Are you staying in Marine Terrace?"

"Yes; it's the nicest part, because you get the view of the sea. I don't like the rooms near the station at all. Mother looked at some of them first, but there were such dreadfully vulgar children stopping there. 'This won't do, Belle,' she said. 'I couldn't have you in the same house with people of that sort.'"

"Is your name Belle?"

"Yes, Isabelle Stuart; but it's generally shortened to Belle. Mother says a pet name somehow seems to suit me better. Last winter I went to a party dressed all in blue, and everybody called me 'Little Bluebell,' and asked if I came from fairyland."

She paused here, thinking the old gentleman might take the opportunity to put in a compliment; but he did not rise to the occasion, so she continued,—

"Other people asked if I were one of the bluebells of Scotland; but we're not Scotch, although our name's Stuart. My father was English. I can't remember him properly, I was so little when he died, but mother always says I'm his very image."

"Rubbish!" growled the colonel suddenly.

"Why!" exclaimed Belle, in astonishment, "how can you tell? You didn't know him? He was very tall and fair, mother says, and *so* handsome. She cries when I talk about him, so I don't like to speak of him very often."

"What is she doing for you in the way of lessons? Is it all parties and trinkets, or do you ever do anything useful?" asked her companion.

"Of course I have lessons," replied Belle with dignity, feeling rather hurt at his tone. "I learn French, and drawing, and music, and dancing, and a great many other things."

"And which do you like best?"

"I don't know. I'm not very fond of history or geography, but mother hopes I'll get on with music. It's so useful to be able to play well, you see, when one comes out. I think I like the dancing lessons most; we learn such delightful fancy steps. Some of us did a skirt dance at the cavalry bazaar last winter, and I was the Queen of the Butterflies. I had a white dress lined with yellow and turquoise, and I shook it out like this when I danced, to show the colours. People clapped ever so much, and it was such a success we had to do it over again, in aid of the hospital. Our mistress wants to get up a flower dance for the exhibition *fête* next winter, and she promised I should be the Rose Queen, but mother says perhaps I may go to school before then."

"Time you did, too—high time—and to a school where they put something in the girls' heads," remarked the colonel, almost as if he were thinking aloud. "It ought to be history and geography, instead of Bluebells and Rose Queens. I don't approve of capering about on a stage in fancy dress."

Belle was much offended. The conversation had not turned out nearly so interesting as she expected. Instead of being appreciated, she had an uneasy sensation that the old gentleman was making fun of her; and as this was not at all to her taste, she thought it time to beat a retreat; so, noticing the Wrights approaching in the distance, she rose and put up her parasol.

"I see some of my friends," she said, in what she hoped was rather a chilling manner, "and I must go and speak to them."

And to show her displeasure, she marched off without deigning even to say good-bye. Colonel Stewart sat watching her as she walked away, with a somewhat peculiar expression on his face.

"Worse than I could ever have imagined!" he groaned. "Vain, shallow, and empty-headed, caring for nothing but pleasure and showing herself off in public places decked out like a ballet dancer! She's pretty enough in a superficial kind of way—the sort of beauty you get in a doll, with neither mind nor soul behind it. *She* worthy of the name, indeed! Oh, my poor boy! Is this the child on whom you had set such high hopes? And is this little French fashion-plate really and truly the last of the Stewarts?"

CHAPTER IX. SILVERSANDS TOWER.

"Say, what deeds of ancient valour
Do thy ruined walls recall?"

FOUR o'clock on the next afternoon found Belle tapping at the door of the little back sitting-room in No. 4 with a very important face.

"Why, what's the matter?" she exclaimed, as she entered in response to Mrs. Stewart's "Come in," for Isobel was sitting in the big armchair propped up with cushions, looking as limp as a rag and as white as a small ghost.

"It's only one of her bad headaches," replied Mrs. Stewart; "I think it must be the heat. She ought not to have played cricket this morning in the blazing sun.—No, Isobel, you mustn't try to get up. Belle may sit here and talk to you for a few minutes, but I'm afraid I can't ask her to stay long."

"I'm *so* sorry!" said Belle, sitting down on the arm of the big chair and squeezing her friend's hand. "I've brought an invitation. It's mother's birthday on Saturday, and she's going to give a picnic at Silversands Tower, and ask all the Sea Urchins. Won't it be splendid fun? You simply *must* be better by then. It will be quite a large party: Mr. Chester and a good many other grown-up people are coming.—Mother wonders if your foot will be well enough, Mrs. Stewart? She would be so pleased to see you, if you don't mind so many children."

"Thank you, dear; but I can scarcely manage to hobble on to the beach at present," replied Mrs. Stewart, "so I fear it is out of the question for me, much as I should have enjoyed it. Isobel, of course, will be only too delighted to accept. I believe the very thought of it is chasing away her headache."

"We're to drive there on two coaches," said Belle, "and have tea in the ruins, and afterwards we can play games or ramble about in the woods. There'll be twelve grown-up people and twenty children. We didn't invite the Wrights' baby, because mother said it was too young, and she really couldn't stand it. She's asked all the Rokebys, even Cecil, though he *is* rather a handful sometimes; but Mr. Rokeby's coming, I expect, and he'll keep him in order. The Wrights are bringing an aunt who's just arrived back from a visit to Paris. I'm afraid we shall scarcely get them to talk English. And Mrs. Barrington hasn't decided yet whether she'll let Ruth and Edna go—she says it depends upon how they do their health exercises; but they're going to try and get their father to persuade her. Well, I mustn't stay now if your head aches, but I'm very glad you can come; I think we shall have a glorious time, and I *do* hope Saturday will be fine."

Not one of the numerous members of the Sea Urchins' Club could have been more anxious for a brilliant day than Isobel. She tapped the glass in the hall with much solicitude, and even paid a visit to her friend the coastguard to inquire his opinion as to the state of the weather; and having carefully examined a threatening bank of clouds through his telescope, and ascertained that the objectionable little sailor was peeping from his barometer, she came home in rather low spirits, in spite of his assurances that "if it did splash a bit, it wouldn't be nowt." Luckily her fears proved groundless. Saturday turned out everything that could be desired in the way of sun and breeze, and two o'clock found a very excited group of children gathered outside Marine Terrace, where two yellow coaches, hired specially from Ferndale for the occasion, were in waiting to drive the party to the Tower.

Barton, Mrs. Stuart's maid, was busy packing the insides with baskets of tea-cups and hampers of provisions, and some of the smaller boys had already climbed to the top with a view of securing the box-seats, whence they were speedily evicted by the younger guard, who had his own notions about reserving the best places, and who, having already had a scuffle with Arnold Rokeby on the subject of the unauthorized blowing of his horn, was disposed to resent undue interference with his privileges. There were quite enough older people to keep the children in order, which seemed a fortunate thing, to judge from the effervescing nature of their spirits. Mrs. Stuart had invited several of her friends, among the number an athletic young curate named Mr. Browne, who tucked both Arnold and Bertie Rokeby easily under one arm, and held them there as in a vice, while he dangled Charlie Chester in mid-air with the other hand—a feat of prowess which so excited their admiration that they clung to him like burrs for the rest of the afternoon. The Wrights had turned up in full force, with the aunt and mademoiselle, and were commenting upon the horses and the general arrangements in their best English-French; while even the little Barringtons had been allowed, after all, to join the fun, though at the last moment, much to Ruth's disgust, their mother had decided to accompany them, to see that they did not race about in the sun or eat indigestible delicacies.

It took a long time to settle all the guests in their seats, and to stow away the lively members of the party where they could not get into mischief, yet would not interfere with the comfort of their more sober-minded elders, was as difficult a problem as the well-known puzzle of the fox, the goose, and the bag of corn; but eventually things were arranged to everybody's satisfaction. Bertie Rokeby, who had announced his intention of taking the journey hanging on to the leather strap at the back beside the guard, was safely wedged between his long-suffering mother and the jovial curate; while Charlie Chester had been allowed to screw into a spare six inches of box-seat next to the driver, who held out a half-promise that he might hold the reins going uphill. The whole company seemed in the gayest of spirits and the most sociable of moods. Mr. Chester, who was something of a wag, kept both coaches in a roar with his jokes, and a fashionably-dressed young lady in pince-nez, who had looked rather unapproachable at first, proved to have her pockets overflowing with chocolates, which she distributed with a liberal hand, and was voted by the boys in consequence a "regular out-and-outer."

The last comers being at length seated, and the last forgotten basket put inside, the guards blew their horns, the drivers whipped up, and the two coaches set off with a dash, to the admiration of all the visitors in Marine Terrace, and the rejoicing of a small crowd of barefooted boys from the town, who had assembled to watch the start, and who ran diligently for nearly half a mile behind them shouting, "A 'alfpenny! Give us a 'alfpenny!" with irritating monotony, and eluding the skilful lashes of the coachmen's long whips with considerable agility. It was not a very great distance to the Tower, and the children thought the drive far too short, and were quite loath, indeed, to come down when the horses stopped before the gray old gateway, and the guards, who had been rivalling one another in solos on the horn, joined in a farewell duet to the appropriate air of "Meet me again in the evening."

The ruined castle made a charming spot for an out-door party. Situated at the foot of a tall wooded hill called the Scar, its battered walls faced the long valley to the north, up which in the olden days a strict watch must have been kept for Border raiders. The ancient turreted keep, with its tiny loophole windows, was still standing, half covered with ivy, the hairy stems of which were as thick as small trees, and a narrow winding staircase led on to the battlements, from whence you might see, on the one hand, the green slopes of the woods, and on the other the yellow cliffs which bounded the blue waters of the bay. Inside the keep was a large square courtyard, where in times gone by the neighbouring farmers would often drive their cattle for safety when the gleam of the Scottish pikes and the smoke of burning roofs were seen to northward. The heavy portcullis hung yet in the gateway, and though the drawbridge was long ago gone, and the moat was dry, the fragments of an outer wall and a portion of a barbican remained to show how powerful a protection was needed in the days when might was right, and each man must guard his goods by the strength of his own hand. The courtyard now was covered with short green grass spangled with daisies, where a pair of tame ravens were solemnly hopping about, while the ivy was the home of innumerable jackdaws that flapped away at the approach of strangers, uttering their funny spoilt "caw," as if indignant at having their haunts disturbed.

Visitors were admitted to the castle by an old woman, who looked almost as ancient as the ruin itself, and who insisted upon giving a full account of the dimensions, situation, and history of the place, which she had learnt from the guide-book, and which she repeated in a high, sing-song voice, without any pauses or stops, as if she were saying a lesson. She followed the various members of the party for some time, trying to make them keep together and listen to her explanations; but as they much preferred to explore on their own account, she was obliged to subside at last to her little kitchen under the archway, and employ herself in the more practical business of boiling the water for tea. All the guests were very soon distributed about the ruins, some admiring the view from the battlements, some peering into the darkness of the dungeons, and others trying to re-people the guardroom and the banqueting-hall with knights and dames of old, and to imagine the clink of armour and the clash of swords in the courtyard below. The Rokeby boys were imperilling their limbs by a climb after jackdaws' nests, oblivious of the fact that it was long past the season for eggs, and the young birds, already in glossy black plumage, were flying round as if in mockery at their efforts. Austin Wright, after a vain attempt to establish an acquaintance with the ravens, had been seen racing as if for his life with the pair in hot pursuit of his small bare legs; while Charlie Chester, in an essay to investigate the interior of the well, very nearly fell to the bottom, being only saved by the tail of his jacket, which luckily caught on a prickly bramble bush, and held him suspended over the dark gulf till he was rescued by his indignant father.

In the meantime tea had been spread in the courtyard. Two great hissing urns were carried from the kitchen and placed upon the grass, and both grown-ups and children, abandoning the study of mediæval history or the pursuit of jackdaws, collected together to discuss sandwiches, cakes, and jam puffs, in spite of Mr. Chester's laughing protestations that such modern luxuries were out of place, and an ox roasted whole or a red deer pasty would have been a more appropriate feast for the occasion. Even the ravens came hopping round at the sight of the cups and plates, and waxed quite friendly on the strength of sundry pieces of bun and bread and butter, which they snapped up with voracious bills, growing too forward, indeed, as the meal progressed, for they stole the curate's tartlet, which he had laid down in an unguarded moment on the grass, and shamelessly snatched Bertie Rokeby's sponge-cake out of his very hand.

"I'm sure the Wrights enjoyed themselves," Isobel told her mother afterwards. "Harold had seven rice buns and ten victoria biscuits, and Charlotte and Aggie ate a whole plateful of cheese-cakes between them. Belle says they always have the most enormous appetites, and at her last party Eric took four helpings of turkey; he just gulped it down, and kept handing up his plate while the others were eating their first serving, and after that he tasted every different dish on the table. It's a great trial for the Wrights to go to parties at the Barringtons; they never get half enough supper, though they have the most delightful magic lanterns and conjurers. Ruth and Edna were scarcely allowed to eat anything at tea. Mrs. Barrington picked all the raisins out of Edna's bun, and made Ruth put back the jam tart she'd just taken. She said if they were really hungry they might eat some plasmon biscuits she had brought with her, but they mustn't touch pastry; and Ruth was so savage, she filled her pocket with queen-cakes when her mother wasn't looking—she said she didn't mean to come away without having tasted anything nice after all."

If the Barringtons were obliged to rise with unsatisfied appetites, the same certainly could not be said of the other guests; the piles of good things disappeared with much rapidity, and at last even the insatiable Eric Wright declined another bun. It was at this point that Mrs. Stuart produced a special basket, which she had reserved for a final surprise, and raising the lid, disclosed a row of marvellous little cakes, each made in the exact form of a sea urchin, with spines of white sugar, and the inside filled with vanilla cream.

"It's a delicate compliment to the Sea Urchins' Club," she said. "It was my own idea. I sent to my confectioner at home, and asked him what he could manage in the matter. I think he has carried it out very well. The cakes look so natural, you could almost imagine they had been fished out of the water."

Quite a howl of delight went up from the young guests, who had never seen such appropriate confectionery before, and the basket was handed round by Belle amid a chorus of thanks, the United Sea Urchins consuming their own effigies with much appreciation, even Ruth and Edna, at the special request of Mrs. Stuart, being allowed for once to share the treat, though only on the distinct understanding that they submitted peaceably to a dose of Gregory's powder if the unwonted dainties disagreed with them.

Tea being over, the party broke up to amuse itself in various ways, most of the children playing at hide-and-seek among the crumbling walls, or chasing each other up the winding staircase, while a few more adventurous spirits took the opportunity of exploring the dungeons with a candle. It was deliciously creepy down there; you could still see the iron stanchions by which the wretched prisoners had been chained to the wall, and the little hole through which their daily portions of food had been handed in to them, and could imagine, if you were fond of recalling the past, how from their beds of straw they would watch the light fading from the tiny barred window, and shiver as they heard the rats gnawing at the stout oak door, or felt a toad crawl over their feet in the murky darkness. Some of the grown-ups had been busy marking out bounds in the courtyard, and soon enlisted every one in an exciting game of prisoner's base. Mr. Chester and the curate made the most successful captains, directing the proceedings with great spirit, and sometimes by a bold dash rescuing the more important of their prisoners, and Bertie Rokeby covered himself with glory by quietly walking to the "prison" while the opposite side was occupied in a hardly-contested struggle, and unsuspectedly freeing all the captives one by one. It was warm work, however, on a hot August day, and after a time the Wrights, never good runners, subsided, panting, on to a piece of ruined wall, and even the enthusiastic curate, who had pulled off his coat, and was prosecuting the game in his shirt sleeves, began to show signs of flagging zeal.

"I'm done up!" cried Mr. Chester at last, flinging himself under the shade of a small elder tree near the banqueting-hall. "I haven't a leg left to stand on, and I'm hoarse with shouting orders. You'd better give in, and do something quiet. I don't want to see another boy or girl for the space of the next half-hour, so scoot, all of you, anywhere, and leave Mr. Browne and myself to enjoy a smoke in peace."

CHAPTER X. WILD MAIDENHAIR.

"On our other side is the straight-up rock,
And a path is kept 'twixt the gorge and it
By boulder stones, where lichens mock
The marks on a moth, and small ferns fit
Their teeth to the polished block."

SOMEWHAT hot and tired with their exertions, the children dispersed in small groups to lounge about or amuse themselves in any way they happened to feel inclined. As there was still plenty of time before the coaches returned at seven o'clock, Belle and Isobel, together with four of the Rokebys, decided to stroll up the Scar, from the top of which they expected to obtain a very good view of the distant moorland, together with a wide stretch of sea. A narrow path led steeply by a series of steps through the wood, a delightful, cool, shady place, with soft moss spreading like a green carpet underfoot, and closely-interlacing boughs shutting out the sunlight overhead. Trails of late honeysuckle still hung in sweet-scented festoons from the undergrowth, and an occasional squirrel might be seen whisking his bushy tail round the bole of an oak tree in a quest for early acorns. There was an interesting little pool, too, where a number of young frogs were practising swimming; and the children thought they saw an otter, but they could not be quite sure, for it scurried off so quickly up the bank that they had not the chance to get more than a glimpse of it. The hazel bushes were covered with nuts, a few of which already contained kernels, and clumps of ferns grew luxuriantly under the shadow of the trees.

Pleasant as it was in the wood, it was even more enjoyable when they reached the top of the hill, and seating themselves upon a thick patch of heather, looked down the other side of the Scar over the rich undulating silvan slope, where among great round boulders they caught the glint of a stream, and heard in the distance the rushing noise of a waterfall. At the foot of the incline, in a narrow valley between the Scar and the cliffs which bounded the sea, rose the gray-brown stone roof of a quaint old Elizabethan house. The richly-carved timbers, the wide mullioned windows, and the ornamental gables were singularly fine, and told of the time when those who built put an artistic pride into their work, and thought no detail too unimportant to be well carried out. The south side was covered with a glorious purple clematis, which hung in rich masses round the pillars of a veranda below, and even from the distance the flaming scarlet of the Scotch nasturtium clothing the porch arrested the eyes by its brilliant contrast with the delicate tea-roses that framed the windows.

"What a splendid place!" cried Belle, glancing beyond the twisted chimneys to where the smooth green lawns and gay beds of a garden peeped from between the trees of the shrubbery. "Just look at the beautiful conservatories and greenhouses, and such stables! There's a tennis lawn on the other side of the flagstaff, and a carriage drive leading down towards the road. It's the nicest house I've seen anywhere about Silversands. I wonder to whom it belongs, and what it's called."

"It's the Chase, and belongs to Colonel Smith, I believe," said Cecil. "There's a huge 'S' on the gates, at any rate, and one day when we were passing I saw an old buffer going in with a gun, and Arthur Wright said he was sure it was Colonel Smith, who has all the shooting on the common. Lucky chap! If it were mine, wouldn't I have a glorious time! I'd keep ever so many ferrets and dogs in those stables, and go rabbiting every day in the year."

"I'd have a very fast pony that could fly like the wind," said Winnie, "and I'd gallop all over the moors and the shore with my hair streaming out behind in ringlets like the picture of Diana Vernon on the landing at home."

"You'd very soon fall off," remarked Bertie unsympathetically, "seeing you can't even stick on to a donkey on the sands. The little brown one threw you twice this morning."

"That was because the saddle kept slipping," said Winnie indignantly. "And that particular donkey has a trick of lying down suddenly, too, when it's tired. It wants to get rid of you—I know it does—because it rolls if you don't tumble off. It did the same with Charlie Chester the other day, and shot him straight over its head; then it got up and flew back to the Parade before he could catch it. The pony would be quite a different thing, I can tell you, and I'd soon learn to ride it. What would you do, Belle, if you owned the Chase?"

"I'd give the most wonderful parties," said Belle, "and invite all kinds of distinguished people—dukes and duchesses, you know, and members of Parliament, and admirals, and generals, and perhaps even the Prince and Princess of Wales; and I'd send to Paris for my hats, and have my clothes made by the Court dressmaker."

"I'd give a cricket match on that lawn," said Isobel, "and ask all the Sea Urchins to tea. We'd have loads of lovely fruit from those gardens and greenhouses, and when we were tired of cricket we could get up sports, and let off fireworks in the evening just when it was growing dark. That's what I'd like to do if I lived there."

"Pity you don't," exclaimed Bertie; "we'd all come. But what's the use of talking when you know you'll never have the chance. I say, suppose we go down the wood on this side and try to find the waterfall? It must be rather a decent-sized one to make such a thundering noise."

The others jumped up very readily at the suggestion, and leaving the path, they slid through the steep wood, and climbing a high wall, found themselves at the rocky bed of a stream, which rushed swiftly along under the overhanging trees, forming little foaming cascades as it went. At one point the water, dashing between two steep crags, descended in a sheer fall of about thirty feet, emptying itself at the bottom into a wide and deep pool overhung by several fine mountain ashes, the scarlet berriesof which made a bright spot of colour against the silvery green of the foliage behind. The Rokebys instantly rushed at these, and began tearing off quite large branches, breaking the boughs in a ruthless fashion that went to Isobel's heart, for she always had been taught to pick things carefully and judiciously, so as not to spoil the beauty of tree or plant.

"It's grand stuff," said Cecil, descending to the ground with a crash, and switching at the ferns by the water's edge with his stick as he spoke. "I've got a perfect armful. Hullo! what's that all down the side of this overhanging rock? It's actually maidenhair fern growing wild in the open air! I'm going to have some. We'll plant it in pots, and take it home."

It was indeed the true maidenhair, flourishing on the damp crag under the spray of the waterfall as luxuriantly as though it had been in a conservatory, its delicate fronds showing in large clumps wherever it could obtain a hold on the rocky surface. I grieve to say that the Rokebys simply threw themselves upon it, pulling it up by the roots, and destroying as much as they gathered by trampling it in their frantic haste.

"O Cecil!" cried Isobel, in an agony, "you're spoiling the ferns. They looked so lovely growing there by the waterfall. Please don't take them all. Haven't you got enough now?"

"But he hasn't given *me* any yet," protested Belle. "And I must have some."

"One doesn't often get the chance to find maidenhair," declared Cecil, "so I shall make the most of it, you bet.—Here, Belle, you may have this piece. Catch! If I climb a little higher I can reach that splendid clump under the tree. I'll take that to the mater."

"I think, on the whole, you will not, my boy," said a dry voice from the bank behind; and looking round, the children, to their horror and astonishment, saw the tall figure of an elderly gentleman who had stolen upon the scene unawares. He spoke quite calmly, but there was a twitch about his mouth and a gleam in his gray eye which suggested the quiet before a thunderstorm, and he stood watching the group in much the same way as a detective might have done who had made a sudden successful capture of youthful burglars red-handed in the act of committing a felony.

"May I ask," he observed, with withering politeness, "by whose invitation you have entered my grounds, and by whose permission you have been destroying my trees and uprooting my ferns? I was under the impression that this was my private property, but you evidently consider you are entitled not only to annex my possessions, but to exercise a cheap generosity by presenting them to others. I shall be obliged if you will kindly offer me some explanation."

Cecil was so absolutely transfixed with amazement that for a moment he remained with his mouth wide open, staring at the newcomer as though the latter had dropped from the skies. The Rokebys were not well-trained children; they did not possess either the moral courage or the good manners which Charlie Chester, madcap though he might be, would undoubtedly have displayed in the same situation, and instead of meeting the matter bravely and making the best apology he could, Cecil flung down the ferns, and without a word of excuse took to his heels and ran back up the wood at the top of his speed, closely followed by Winnie, Bertie, and Arnold.

Belle for an instant wavered, but recognizing the old gentleman as the same whose acquaintance she had cultivated on the beach with such unsatisfactory results, she decided that discretion was the better part of valour, and turning away, vanished through the trees like a little white shadow.

Isobel, the only one of the six who stood her ground, was left to bear the whole brunt of the matter alone. She looked at the broken branches of mountain ash and the damaged ferns which the Rokebys had dropped in the panic of their flight, and which surrounded her like so much guilty evidence of the deed, then screwing up her courage, she faced the outraged owner in a kind of desperation.

"I'm *very* sorry," she began, twisting and untwisting her thin little hands, and colouring up to the roots of her hair with the effort she was making. "We oughtn't to have come. But, indeed, we didn't know it was your ground; we thought it was only just part of the Scar. And I don't believe the others would have taken the ferns if they'd thought for a moment, because they would have known maidenhair doesn't grow wild out of doors like bracken or hart's-tongue."

"But it *was* wild," said the colonel—"that's the unfortunate part of it. It wouldn't have distressed me if I could have replaced it from the conservatory. This happens to be one of the few spots in the British Isles where *Adiantum Capillus-Veneris* is found in an undoubtedly native situation."

"Oh, then that's worse than ever!" cried Isobel, with consternation. "I know how very, very rare it is, because mother and I once found a little piece in a cave in Cornwall."

"Did you? Are you sure it was an absolutely genuine specimen and not naturalized?" asked Colonel Stewart, with keen interest.

"No; it was quite wild, for it was in a very out-of-the-way place by the seashore."

"I hope you didn't take it?"

"Oh no! we didn't even pick a frond; and mother made me promise never to tell any one where it grew, she was so afraid some one might root it up."

"A sensible woman!" exclaimed the colonel. "Pity there aren't more like her! Why people should want to grub up every rare and beautiful thing they find in the country to plant in their miserable town gardens, I can't imagine. It's downright murder. The poor things die directly in the smoke. Look at these splendid roots that have been growing here since I was a boy! I would rather they had destroyed every flower in my garden than have worked such wanton havoc in the spot I value most in all my grounds."

"It's most unfortunate we came this particular walk," said Isobel, almost crying with regret. "You see, the Rokebys aren't used to the country, so they don't seem to think about spoiling things. I believe I could manage to plant these roots again; they're not very bad, and if I tucked them well into the crevices of the rock I really fancy they'd grow."

She picked up some of the ferns as she spoke, and began carefully to replace them in the little ledges on the side of the rock, moistening the roots first in the stream, and scraping up some soil with a thin piece of shale which she made serve the purpose of a trowel.

"They haven't taken quite all," she said. "That beautiful clump up there hasn't even been touched, and it may spread. I wish I could put back the mountain ash. I simply can't tell you how sorry I am we ever came."

The colonel smiled.

"I don't blame *you*," he said. "It was those young heathens who ran away. Their methods of studying botany were certainly of a rather rough-and-ready description. I should have thought better of them if they had stayed to apologize. Your friend with the light curls, whom, by-the-bye, I have met before, seemed also unwilling to enter into any explanations. In fact, to put it plainly, she left you in the lurch."

"I think she was frightened," said Isobel, wondering what possible excuse she could frame for Belle's conduct. "You came so—so very suddenly. There! I've put all the ferns back. They're rather broken, I'm afraid; but there are plenty of new fronds ready to come up, so I hope you'll find that, after all, we haven't quite spoilt everything."

"Think I'm not so much hurt as I imagined?" said the colonel, with a twinkle in his eye.

"Oh, I didn't mean that!" replied Isobel quickly. "I know we've done a great deal of harm. Please don't think I wanted to make out we hadn't."

"All right; you've done your best to repair the damage, so that's an end of the matter."

"I ought to be going now," continued Isobel. "The Rokebys and Belle will be wondering what has become of me, and the coaches were to start at seven o'clock. It must be after six now."

"Exactly half-past six," said Colonel Stewart, consulting his watch. "If you follow that footpath it will take you through a side gate and straight up the hillside; I expect you will find the others waiting for you on the top of the Scar. Good-bye. Give my compliments to your friends, and tell them to learn to enjoy the country without spoiling it for other people; and the next time they get into a tight place to show a little pluck, and not to run off like a set of cowardly young curs."

CHAPTER XI. THE ISLAND.

*"Oh! had we some bright little isle of our own,
In a blue summer ocean, far off and alone."*

THOUGH the United Sea Urchins were still very faithful to their cricket ground under the cliffs, the older and more daring spirits were always ready to ramble farther afield in quest of new scenes and adventures. Every day seemed to bring with it some fresh delight, whether it were a shrimping expedition among the green sea-weedy pools of the rocks on the far shore, or a cockle gathering on the gleaming banks left by the ebb-tide, where the breath of the salt wind on their faces or the feel of the wet, oozing sand under their bare feet was a joy to be garnered up and held in memory. Sometimes it was a scramble over the moors, between thickets of golden gorse and stretches of heather so deep and long that to lie in it was to bury oneself like a bee in a bed of purple fragrance, or a hard climb would take them to the summit of some neighbouring hill, where, watching the sun sink from a primrose sky into a pearly, shimmering sea, they would all grow a little silent and quiet, even the roughest spirits restrained in spite of themselves by the sight of that indescribable majesty and calm which marks the parting of the day. It is hours such as these—glad, exhilarating, glorious hours, when the world seems as young as ourselves, and merely to live and breathe is a delight— that lay up in our hearts a store of sunshine to be drawn upon in after life as from a treasure-house of the mind, and to brighten dark days to come with the rapture of the remembrance.

It was, perhaps, somewhat against her natural tastes that Belle found herself included in the many and various excursions of the Sea Urchins. She was no country lover, and the stir of a promenade in a fashionable watering-place gave her more pleasure than the dash of waves or the scent of wild flowers. She did not enjoy splashing her pretty clothes with sea-water among the rocks, or tearing them in search of blackberries on the hedgerows; and it was only her love of society, and a dislike of being left behind, which induced her to follow where the others led. The rough walks and hard scrambles were often a real trial to her, though with Isobel to tow her up steep hills, help her across stiles, disentangle her laces from insistent brambles, jump her over pools, and take her hand in dangerous spots, she managed to keep up fairly well. Isobel, to whom these excursions were the topmost summit of bliss, and who was apt to measure others' standards by her own, never suspected for a moment that Belle was beginning to grow tired of it, and received an occasional outburst of petulance or fretful complaint with such amazement that the latter would, for very shame, desist, and for a time the friendship continued to remain at high-water mark. That Belle was selfish and exacting never once crossed Isobel's mind, and though she could not help frequently detecting in her certain little meannesses, exaggeration, or even occasional wanderings from the truth, there always seemed to be some exonerating circumstance which would in a measure either clear her from blame or give her the benefit of a doubt. It is often so difficult to find fault with those for whom we care very dearly: we are ready to make excuses, condone their mistakes, overlook their shortcomings, anything but allow to ourselves the unfortunate and yet unmistakable fact that our idol has feet of clay; and so Isobel went on from day to day blinding her eyes with her adoration for her namesake, and investing Belle with a halo of virtues and attractions which certainly did not exist except in her own imagination.

Apart from Belle, I think that among the various members of the Sea Urchins' Club Isobel found the Chesters the most congenial. They had all the dash and daring of the Rokebys without the over-boisterous manners which characterized that rough-and-tumble family, whose friendship at times was apt to prove a trifle wearing. Little Hilda had taken a great affection for Isobel, and Charlie, since the adventure in the *Stormy Petrel*, was disposed to consider her in the light of a chum, and to cultivate her acquaintance. As knowing Isobel meant including Belle, the four children therefore might often be found in each other's company, and it was at Charlie's suggestion that they determined one afternoon to pay a visit to a certain small island which lay a short distance along the coast, at the other side of the rocky headland that jutted out at the far side of the bay.

"I've not been close to," said Charlie, "but you can see it very well from the top of the Scar. It looks a regular Robinson Crusoe desert island kind of a place, just given up to sea-gulls and rabbits. I don't believe a soul ever goes there."

"It would be grand if we were the first to set foot on it," said Isobel. "It would be our own island, and we'd claim it in the name of the club, like travellers do in Central Africa when they run up the Union Jack, and then mark the place pink on the map, to show it's a British possession."

"And then all the others could be settlers," added Hilda, "and we'd light a fire and cook fish and have *such* fun!"

"It would be exactly like the coral island in 'The Young Pioneers,'" said Belle. "Perhaps I might become the queen, like the mysterious white lady they found living among the natives, and have a throne made out of sand and shells, and wear a garland of flowers for a crown."

"Oh, we won't go in for nonsense like that!" declared Charlie, who was not romantic, and, moreover, enjoyed squashing Belle on occasion. "But we might build a hut there, and rig up a sort of camp, and then, if the whole lot of us came, we could have a regular ripping time. It's worth while going to see, at any rate."

Armed with a mariner's compass, a tin pail full of biscuits, Isobel's botanical case for specimens, and a stout stick apiece, the four friends set out on their pioneering expedition with all the enthusiasm of a band of explorers penetrating into the heart of an unknown continent, or a Roman legion bent on the conquest of some distant Albion. As the geography books determine an island to be "a piece of land surrounded by water," the particular spot in question could only claim to justify its name at high tide, since at low water it was joined to the mainland, and by scrambling over the rocks and jumping a few channels which the sea had left behind, any one could reach it quite easily dry shod. The children marched sturdily along over the wet sands, with a pause here and there to dive after a particularly interesting crab, or to float a jelly-fish left stranded by the tide, in the deeper water. Charlie, however, would not allow many digressions, and hurried them as fast as possible towards the object of their journey. The island, on a nearer view, proved to be a bare, craggy spot, about half a mile in length by a quarter in breadth, bounded by steep cliffs which supported a rocky plateau covered with short rough grass and sea pinks, and honeycombed in every direction with rabbit burrows. It seemed the haunt of innumerable gulls, guillemots, and puffins, for whole flocks of them flew away, wheeling overhead in wide circles, and uttering loud, piercing cries in protest at the invasion of their rocky stronghold.

"We'd better do the thing thoroughly. Suppose we start from this big rock and walk right round the island," suggested Isobel. "I have a piece of paper and a pencil in my pocket, and I'll draw a map of it as we go along, and we'll give names to all the capes and bays and headlands."

"Stunning!" agreed Charlie. "This rock can be 'Point Set-Off,' and we can take it in turns to christen the other places. I don't believe the island itself has a name; we shall each have to suggest something, and then put it to the vote. I'm for 'Craggy Holme' myself, but we won't decide anything yet until we have been completely over it."

Thrilled with the excitement of the occasion, the pioneers started on their tour of inspection, noting with approval that the pools at the foot of the cliff were full of sea anemones, star-fishes, hermit crabs, periwinkles, whelks, pink sea-weed, and a wealth of desirable treasures; that the brambles which grew on the slopes above were already covered with fast ripening blackberries; that there were flukes quite seven inches long in the narrow channel on the north shore; and that the sands beyond showed a perfect harvest of cockles and other shells. They had gone perhaps halfway round the coast, and were on the south side, facing the open sea, when suddenly, turning a corner, they found themselves in a spot which made them stand still and look at one another with little gasps of delight. Surely it was the ideal place for a camp. They were in a small creek between two great overhanging crags, where brambles and wood vetch hung down in delightful tangled masses, the fine white sand under their feet alternated with soft green turf, spangled with tiny sea-flowers, and there was quite a bank of small delicate shells left by the high spring tides. Close under the rocks lay the wreck of a schooner, driven ashore by winter storms, and stranded upon the shingle, the broken spars and a fragment of the hull lying half buried in the silvery sand, surrounded by a forest of sea-weed and drift-wood.

"Why, it just beats 'The Swiss Family Robinson' or 'The Boy Explorers' hollow!" said Charlie, turning to his companions with something of the look that Christopher Columbus may have worn when he stepped with his followers on to the shores of the New World. "Here's the very place we were hoping for! We'd soon get that old trail tilted out of the sand; she only needs propping against the cliff, and she'd make a regular Uncle Tom's cabin. With the Wrights and the Rokebys to help, we'd haul her up in a jiffy. Some of these spars and planks would do for seats and tables, and we could light fires with the drift-wood. It's a camp almost ready made for us, I declare."

"And look!" cried Hilda, pointing to a sand-bank which lay at the mouth of the creek; "the tide seems to have thrown up a great many things down there." And she hurried to the water's edge, where the drifting current had lodged a variety of miscellaneous articles—walking-sticks, tin cans, a child's boat, a straw hat, several baskets, glass bottles, and even a lady's parasol, all lying tangled among the sea-weed, washed across the bay no doubt from the beach at Ferndale. "I've fished out a little horse and cart, and there's something here that looks like the remains of a gentleman's top hat. We can use the tins for the cabin. They'll do for flower-pots. O Charlie! aren't you glad we came?"

"It's quite romantic," said Belle, sitting down on a spar, and twisting some pink bindweed round her hat. "We could have tea here, and get up a dance on the sands afterwards. I've found such a pretty pencil-case among the drift-wood. I mean to keep it."

"I don't think any one else has discovered the island," said Isobel. "So we've quite a right to take possession, haven't we?"

"It's the very thing we want, and we'll annex it at once," said Charlie; and drawing the empty shell of a sea urchin from his pocket, he slipped it on to the top of a stick, which he planted firmly in the sand as an ensign; then climbing on to the summit of a rock close by, he waved his handkerchief to north, south, east, and west, exclaiming, "We hereby take solemn possession of this island in the name of the United Sea Urchins' Recreation Society, and are prepared to hold the same in legal right against all comers. If any one has just cause or impediment to offer why the said society should not occupy this territory in peace and prosperity, let him speak now, or hereafter for ever hold his peace. Rule, Britannia! God save the King!"

With a burst of cheers the others unanimously declared themselves witnesses to the deed, and decided that possession being nine-tenths of the law, the island, for the time at any rate, was undoubtedly their own, and until any one appeared to dispute their claim they would make what they pleased of it.

"To-morrow we'll rig out a real pioneer party of settlers, and come with hammers and nails and axes and all the rest of it," said Charlie. "Then we can put up a flag and decide on names and everything. We haven't time to explore the top now, though it looks jolly upon those cliffs; we must get back before the tide turns. It's a ripping place, but it would be no joke, all the same, to be surrounded and have to spend the night here."

The Sea Urchins took to the idea of a camp on a desert island with the greatest enthusiasm, and next day the elder portion of them started off with any tools which they could buy, beg, or borrow, anxious to set to work at once upon the task of constructing a dwelling from the wreck of the old schooner. By fastening a rope to the hull, they contrived to tug it out of the sand and tilt it on end against a rock; then with the aid of the broken planks which were lying near they propped it up securely and repaired any damaged or broken pieces, so that it made the most successful hut, a kind of combination of a Viking's hall with a pirate's cave or an Indian wigwam. The face of the cliff which formed the wall on one side was full of ledges and crevices which served admirably for cupboards, a few nails driven into the boards answered for hat pegs, and it was no difficult matter to put up shelves from odd pieces of drift-wood.

It was amazing how the work brought out the varying capacities of the settlers. To every one's surprise, Arthur Wright developed a perfect genius for carpentry. He had borrowed a few tools from a friendly joiner in the town, and constructed quite a tidy little table, forming the legs from broken masts; and he managed to make a door for the fortress of the best portions of three rotten planks, fastening it on with hinges cut from an old leather strap, and even putting a latch which would open with a string pulled from the outside.

While the boys did the harder part of the work, the girls contented themselves with the more feminine element of artistic decoration. They thatched the roof elaborately with masses of brown bladder-wrack seaweed, tying it securely with pieces of cord; they fixed a row of twenty-one sea urchins, with the spines on, over the door as a coat of arms, one to represent each member of the club; and pink and white fan shells were nailed alternately round the window, with yellow periwinkles wedged between. A little garden was carefully laid out, a wall being made of stones and sand, and a path of fine gravel leading up to the door. Green sea-weed was put down to represent grass, the most wonderful arrangements in the way of cockles, mussels, and limpets took the place of flower-beds, and a few sea-pinks and harebells planted in tins rescued from the sand-bank adorned the window-sill. Inside, a fireplace had been built with stones at the rocky end, a hole being made in the roof to let out the smoke, and seats were dug from the sand sufficient to accommodate the whole party. A tin kettle and a frying-pan, purchased by subscription, constituted the cooking utensils of the camp, and the members waxed so eager over the domestic arrangements of their hut that they spent all their pennies at the cheap stalls in the market on tin mugs and plates and other articles likely to be of service to the community. Eric Wright denied himself toffee or caramels for three whole days—a heroic effort on his part—that he might contribute a certain gorgeous scarlet tea-tray on which he had set his young affections; the Rokebys clubbed together to buy muslin for window curtains; Belle presented a looking-glass as a suitable offering; and Mrs. Barrington, who was always generous when it was not a question of diet, allowed Ruth and Edna to purchase a dozen pewter teaspoons, a bright blue enamelled teapot, and a bread-and-butter plate with a picture of the

Promenade at Ferndale upon it. The sand-bank was rummaged for anything that would come in handy, and though it did not yield such wonderful treasures as the wrecked ship generally contains in desert-island stories, they found several empty bottles, an old lantern, a dripping-tin, a wooden spoon, and a battered bird-cage, all of which they decided might come in useful in course of time and were carefully put by in a safe place among the rocks.

Isobel, who toiled away at the camp with untiring zeal, had drawn and painted a very nice map of the island on a sheet of cardboard, all the various places being neatly marked, and had nailed it on the wall inside. After a good deal of discussion it had been decided to call the domain "Rocky Holme," the crag on the extreme summit was "Point Look-Out," the tall cliff to the north, "Sea-Birds' Cape," while the one on the south was "Welcome Head." The creek where they had established their headquarters was christened by the appropriate name of "Sandy Cove," and the hut bore the more romantic title of "Wavelet Hall." They had fixed a broken mast at the end of the little garden for a flagstaff, and ran up an ensign specially designed and executed for them by Mrs. Stewart, consisting of a large sea urchin cut out of white calico, and stitched upon a ground of turkey-red twill, with the initials "U.S.U.R.S." below; so that, with their colours floating in the breeze and the smoke of their fire rising in a thin white column among the rocks, no band of colonists could have felt that the country was more really and truly their own.

CHAPTER XII. A FIRST QUARREL.

"The little rift within the lute,
That by-and-by will make the music mute,
And ever widening slowly silence all."

IT had become an almost daily programme for the Sea Urchins to jump across or even to wade through the channel the moment the tide was sufficiently low to enable them to do so with safety, and to establish themselves upon their desert island. The joys of pioneering seemed to have quite put cricket in the shade; the hut had still the charm of novelty, and to fry the flukes which they had themselves speared or to concoct blackberry jam or toffee in an enamelled saucepan over the camp fire was at present their keenest delight. The only regret was that they did not possess a boat in which they could row over to their territory whenever they wished, and the boys had tried to provide a substitute by constructing a raft from some of the old planks left lying about from the schooner, lashing them together with pieces of rope in the orthodox "shipwrecked sailor" fashion, and making paddles out of broken spars. It looked quite a respectable craft—as Charlie Chester said, "most suitable for a desert island"—and they had anticipated having a good deal of fun with it, and being able to take little sea excursions if they could only manage to steer it properly; and Charlie even had ideas of rigging up a sail, and perhaps getting across the bay as far as Ferndale with a favourable wind. Its career, however, was short and brilliant. It was launched with much noise and nautical language by Charlie and the other boys, and started gaily off, greatly to the admiration of the feminine portion of the Sea Urchins, who ran along the shore shouting encouragement. But it had hardly gone more than a hundred yards, and was still in shallow water, when the too enthusiastic efforts of its amateur oarsmen caused it suddenly to turn a somersault, and upset the crew into the briny deep; then floating swiftly away bottom side up, it was caught by the current, much to the regret of its disconsolate builders, who, wet through with their unexpected swim, watched it drift in the direction of Ferndale, where the tide probably carried it over the bar, to wash about as a derelict in the open sea till the water had rotted the ropes that bound the planks.

After the raft proved a failure, the boys took to carving miniature yachts out of pieces of drift-wood, and sailing them in a wide pool which was generally left at the mouth of the creek. The girls hemmed the sails, and provided the vessels with flags in the shape of tiny coloured pieces of ribbon stitched on to the masts, and would stand by to cheer the particular bark in which they were interested, as the ladies in olden days encouraged their knights in the tourney. There was great competition between the various boats, and it seemed a matter of the utmost importance whether Charlie Chester's *Water Sprite*, Bertie Rokeby's *Esmeralda*, or Arthur Wright's*Invincible*, should reach the opposite shore in the shortest space of time. Occasionally a good ship would get becalmed in the middle of the pool, in which case its owner would have to wade to the rescue, probably finding it caught in a mass of oar-weed, or even entangled in the floating tentacles of a huge jelly-fish. The children had made a nice aquarium not far from the hut, and in this they put specimens of every different kind of sea-weed on the island, as well as crabs, anemones, limpets, sea cucumbers, star-fishes, zoophytes, or any other treasures of the deep that they might be lucky enough to collect; while the boys, I regret to say, took a keen delight in securing a couple of hermit crabs, and setting the pugnacious pair to fight in a small arena of sand which they prepared specially for the purpose, somewhat in the same manner as our unregenerate forefathers devoted certain portions of their gardens to the formation of cock-pits.

Another favourite amusement was to divide into two regiments, each under the leadership of suitable officers, and, armed with pea-shooters, to conduct a series of Volunteer manœuvres upon the shore. The defending party would throw up ramparts of sand, and duly garrison their stronghold, while the enemy would attack with the ferocious zeal of a band of North American Indians or a gang of Chinese pirates, being greeted by a volley of fire from the pea-shooters, and missiles in the shape of whelks' eggs, the dried air-vessels of the bladder-wrack, little rolled-up balls of slimy green sea-weed, or anything else which could be flung as a projectile without injuring the recipients too severely. Very exciting struggles sometimes took place for the possession of a fortress or the securing of an outpost; and I think the girls were really as keen as the boys in this amateur warfare, Letty and Winnie Rokeby proving deadly shots with their pea-shooters, and Aggie Wright becoming quite an admirable scout.

Isobel undertook the ambulance department, and made a delightful hospital with beds dug out of sand, and a dispensary fitted with empty bottles collected from the sand-bank. She installed herself here as a Red Cross Sister, with Ruth Barrington for a helper, and was ready to doctor the combatants, who were carried in suffering from various imaginary wounds, the sole flaw in her arrangements being that the invalids insisted upon getting well too quickly, and leaving their pills and potions to rush back and rejoin the fray.

The only one of the Sea Urchins who did not thoroughly enjoy the charms of the desert island was Belle. She was not suited for camp life, and though she tolerated the tea-parties when she brought her own china cup with her, she took no interest in the boat-sailing, and frankly disliked the manœuvres. She would not have come at all, only she found it so dull to remain behind, as her mother was mostly occupied in reading, writing letters, or entertaining friends, and not inclined to devote much attention to her little daughter. Poor Belle was expected to find her own amusements, and having no resources in herself, she sought the society of the other children in preference to being alone, though she grumbled incessantly at the boyish games, and longed for a different sphere, where pretty frocks and trinkets would have a better chance of due appreciation.

Towards Isobel the fever-heat of her first affection had cooled down considerably, and she had begun to treat her friend with a rather patronizing authority, ordering her about in a way which would have provoked any one with a less sweet temper to the verge of rebellion. She had quarrelled more than once with the Wrights and the Rokebys, since those outspoken families had given her their frank opinion of her behaviour on several occasions, and as it was not a flattering one, she had been far from pleased. So long as Belle's pretty pleading manners secured for her the best of everything she was a charming companion, but she could prove both pettish and peevish when she considered herself neglected. Her light, pleasure-loving nature depended for its happiness on continual attention and admiration, and if she could not have these she was as miserable as a butterfly in a shower of rain.

One afternoon the question of the possession of a certain basket, supposed to be common property among the settlers, resulted in a war of words between Belle and Letty and Winnie Rokeby—a quarrel which waxed so fast and furious that Isobel, who fought her friend's battles through thick and thin, was obliged to interfere (not without an uneasy consciousness that the Rokebys had right on their side), persuaded Letty to relinquish the disputed treasure, and bore Belle away up the hill to soothe her ruffled feelings by picking blackberries. Micky, the little pet dog, followed close at their heels. As a rule he preferred the society of Mrs. Stuart, and rarely accompanied the children on their rambles, but to-day they had brought him with them to the island.

"It *is* my basket," grumbled Belle, threading her way daintily between the brambles with a careful regard for her flowered delaine dress. "Mrs. Barrington lent it to me first. The Rokebys are so selfish, they want to keep everything to themselves. I don't know whether they or the Wrights are worse. It's such a pretty one, too—quite the nicest we have at the hut."

"Never mind," said Isobel hastily, anxious to dismiss the subject. "Let us fill it with blackberries. There are such heaps here, and such big ones."

It was indeed a harvest for those who liked to gather. Brambles grew everywhere. Long clinging sprays, some still in blossom and some covered with the ripe fruit, trailed in profusion over the rocks, their reddening leaves giving a hint of the coming autumn, for it was late August now, and already there was a touch of September crispness in the air. It was delightful on the headland, with sea and sky spread all around, the sea-gulls flapping idly below just on the verge of the waves, and banks of fragrant wild thyme under their feet, growing in patches between the great craggy boulders, which looked as though they had been piled up by some giant at play. The picking went on steadily for a while, though it was a little unequal, as Belle had a tender consideration for her spotless fingers, and gathered about one berry to Isobel's dozen.

"We shall soon have the basket full," said Isobel. "Hold it for a moment, Belle, please, while I get to the other side of this rock; there are some still finer ones over here."

"I should think we have enough now," said Belle, upon whom the occupation began to pall. "We don't want to make any more jam; the last we tried stuck to the pan and burnt, and wasted all the sugar I had brought. Mother says she won't let me have any more. Come back, Isobel, do, and take the basket. Why, what are you staring at so hard?"

"At this stone underneath the brambles," replied Isobel. "It's most peculiar. It has marks on it like letters, only they aren't any letters I know. Do come and look."

She pulled the long blackberry trails aside as she spoke, and disclosed to view a large stone, something like a gate-post, lying on its side, half sunk into the soil. It was worn, and weather-beaten, and battered by time and storms, but on its smooth surface could still be traced the remains of a rudely-carved cross, and the inscription,—

(IMAGE)

"What does it mean?" asked Belle. "Are they really letters?"

"I can't tell," replied Isobel. "It looks like some writing we can't read. Perhaps it's Greek, or old black letter. I wonder who could have put it here?"

"I don't know, and I'm sure I don't care," said Belle. "What does it matter? Let us come along."

"Oh! only it's interesting. I want to tell mother about it; she's so fond of old crosses, and she may know what it means. I can copy it on this scrap of paper if you'll wait a minute."

Belle sat down with a martyred air. She was not in the best of tempers, and she did not like waiting. She put the basket of blackberries by her side, and took Micky on her knee. Then, for want of anything better to do, she began to tease him by pulling the silky hair that grew round his eyes.

"Don't do that, Belle," said Isobel, looking round suddenly at the sound of Micky's protesting yelps.

"Why not?" asked Belle, somewhat sharply.

"Because you're hurting him."

"I'm not hurting him."

"Yes, you are."

"I suppose I can do as I like with him; he's my own."

"He's not yours to tease, at any rate. Belle, do stop!"

"I'll please myself; it's nobody else's affair," said Belle, giving such a tug as she spoke to Micky's silken top-knot that he howled with misery.

Isobel sprang up. She could not bear to see an animal suffer, and her anger for the moment was hot.

"Let him go, Belle!" she cried, wrenching at her friend's hands. "You've no right to treat him so. Let him go, I tell you!"

Micky seized the golden opportunity, and escaping from his mistress's grasp, beat a hasty retreat towards the beach, yelping with terror as he went, and upsetting the basket of blackberries in his flight.

Belle turned on Isobel in a rage.

"Look what you've done!" she exclaimed. "I wish you would mind your own business, and leave me to manage my own dog. All the blackberries have rolled over the cliff where we can't get them, and it's your fault. I hope you're sorry."

Isobel stooped to rescue the empty basket, but she did not apologize.

"I think it was as much your fault as mine," she replied. "You shouldn't have teased him. Perhaps we can pick the blackberries up again."

"No, we can't. They've fallen among the briers, and *I* don't mean to scratch my fingers by trying. You can stay and fish them out if you like. I'm going home."

"But we haven't had tea yet."

"I don't care. I don't want tea out of a tin mug. I shall have it comfortably at the lodgings, with a nice clean tablecloth and a serviette. I'm tired of stupid picnics." And Belle flounced away down the hill with anything but a sweet expression or a "Parisian" manner.

Isobel did not try to stop her. As the proverbial worm will turn, so there are limits to the endurance of even the most devoted of friends, and I think this afternoon she felt that Belle's conduct had reached a climax for which no excuse could be made. The latter, who considered herself both hurt in her feelings and offended in her dignity, scrambled down to the shore, and calling Micky to her heels, set off promptly for home.

"Hullo, Belle!" cried Bertie Rokeby, catching at her dress as she hurried past the hut. "Look out, can't you! Don't you see that you're trampling all over the shells that I've just laid out to sort on the sand? What's the row? You look like a regular tragedy queen—Lady Macbeth in the murder scene, or Juliet about to stab herself!"

"Let me go," said Belle crossly, trying to pull herself free. "What horrid, rough things you boys are! Why can't you leave me alone, I should like to know?"

"Humpty-Dumpty! We *are* in a jolly wax," said Bertie. "You're as bad as a cat with her back up. All the same, I don't want my shells smashed, so please to mind where you're stepping."

"Bother your shells!" said Belle. "You shouldn't leave them lying about in people's way. There! you've torn a slit in my dress. I knew you would! Let me go, Bertie Rokeby, you mean coward!" And jerking her skirt with an effort from his grasp, she started at a run along the beach, and fled as fast as she could in the direction of Silversands.

She had reached the southern point of the island, where they generally crossed the channel, and was hurrying on, not looking particularly where she was going, her eyes half blinded with self-pitying tears, when, turning the headland sharply, she ran full tilt against her quondam acquaintance of the Parade, who was walking leisurely along the sands with a cigar in his mouth and a breechloader under his arm. The collision was so sudden and unexpected that Belle sat down swiftly in a pool of slimy green sea-weed, while the gun, knocked by the impact from its owner's grasp, struck the rock violently, and discharged both barrels into the air. The colonel, who had been almost upset with the shock, recovered his balance as by a miracle, and hastened to ascertain the extent of the mishap; but finding no harm done, he picked up his gun and surveyed Belle with considerable disfavour.

"You might have caused a very nasty accident, young lady," he said. "It's a mercy the charge didn't land in either your leg or mine. Why don't you look where you're going?"

Belle raised herself carefully from the pool, glancing with much concern at the large green stains which had reduced her dress to a wreck, and at the moist condition of her silk stockings.

"How could I know any one was round the corner?" she replied, somewhat sulkily. "I wonder what my mother would have said if you'd killed me. I'm not sure if my leg isn't shot through, after all."

"Let me look," said the colonel quietly. "No, that's not a wound, though you've grazed it a little, very likely in falling. There's no real damage, and I think you're more frightened than hurt."

"My dress is spoilt," said Belle, determined to have a grievance. "These green stains will never wash out of it. It's really too bad."

"Be thankful it's only your dress, and not your skin," said the owner of the Chase, with scant sympathy. "What are you doing here, so far away from the Parade? You had better go home to your mother, and tell her to take more care of you, and not let you wander about alone to get into mischief."

"I was going home as fast as I could," retorted Belle, not too politely, for she disliked the old gentleman extremely, and wished he would not interfere with her. "And I think my mother knows how to take care of me without any one telling her, thank you."

"I have no doubt she imagines she does," replied Colonel Stewart, rather bitterly. "I can't say I admire the result. I should certainly wish to teach you better manners if I had any share in your bringing up."

"I'm glad you haven't," said Belle smartly; and catching Micky in her arms, she put an abrupt end to the conversation by running away again at the top of her speed over the shallows towards the mainland.

"He's perfectly horrid!" she said to herself. "This is the third place I've met him, and each time he has been more disagreeable than the last. I can't imagine why, but I somehow feel as if he had taken quite a dislike to me."

CHAPTER XIII. READING THE RUNES.

"Words from the long far-away
Link the dim past with to-day."

ISOBEL descended from the headland in the lowest of spirits. To have quarrelled with Belle, even in a just cause, was a disaster such as she had never contemplated, and for a moment she was half inclined to run after her friend and seek a reconciliation at any cost. Her pride, however, intervened; she felt that Belle had really been very rude and unreasonable, while her treatment of Micky was quite unpardonable. She strolled along, therefore, in the direction of the hut instead, trying to wink the tears out of her eyes, and to make up her mind that she did not care. All the Sea

Urchins were rushing off to investigate some mysterious black object which they could see bobbing about in the water, and which they hoped might prove to be a porpoise. They called to her to join them, but even the prospect of capturing a sea monster had for the moment no charms, so she shook her head and volunteered instead to stay in the hut and get tea ready for their return. She filled the kettle from a little spring of fresh water, which always ran pure and clear in a small rivulet down the side of the cliff, threw some more drift-wood and dry sea-weed on the fire which the boys had already lighted, then set out the tea things, and taking a piece of chalk, began to amuse herself by drawing upon the wall of the hut the curious letters which she had copied from the stone. She was so absorbed in her occupation that she did not notice a tall figure, who stooped to enter the low doorway, and paused in some astonishment at the scene before him.

"Hullo!" said a voice. "Am I addressing Miss Robinson Crusoe, or is this the outpost of a military occupation? I see a flag flying which is certainly not the Union Jack, and as a late colonel in his Majesty's forces, and a Justice of the Peace, I feel bound to protect our shores from a possible invasion."

Isobel turned round hastily. She recognized the newcomer at once as the owner of the maidenhair fern and the beautiful grounds into which she had so unwittingly trespassed, and noticing his gun, concluded that he must without doubt be the Colonel Smith of whom Cecil Rokeby had spoken, and whom she had also heard mentioned by Mrs. Jackson as a keen sportsman and a magistrate of some consequence in the neighbourhood.

"I'm not Miss Robinson Crusoe," she replied, laughing, "and it's not a military occupation either."

"Perhaps I am in a prehistoric dwelling, then, watching a descendant of the ancient Britons conducting her primitive cooking operations. Or is it an Indian wigwam? I should be interested to know to what tribe it belongs," said the colonel, advancing farther into the hut, and looking with an amused smile at the sand seats, the shelves, the pots, and all the other little arrangements which the children had made.

"No, I'm not an ancient Briton," said Isobel, "and it isn't a wigwam. It's 'Wavelet Hall,' and it belongs to us."

"And who is 'us,' if you will condescend to explain so ambiguous a term?"

"The United Sea Urchins' Recreation Society," said Isobel, rolling out the name with some dignity.

"No doubt it's my crass ignorance," observed the colonel, "but I'm afraid I have never heard of that distinguished order. Will you kindly enlighten me as to its object and scope?"

"Why, you see, we're all staying at Silversands," explained Isobel; "so we made ourselves into a club, that we might have fun together, and called it the 'Sea Urchins.' Then we found this desert island that doesn't belong to anybody, so we took possession of it, and built this hut out of the wreck of the old schooner, and it's ours now."

"Is it?" said the colonel dryly. "I was under the impression that the island belonged to me. It is certainly included among my title-deeds, and as lord of the manor I am also supposed to have the rights of the foreshore."

"I don't quite understand what 'lord of the manor' means," said Isobel; "but does the island really and truly belong to you?"

"Really and truly. I keep it for rabbit shooting exclusively."

"Then," said Isobel apprehensively, "I'm very much afraid that we've been trespassing on your land again."

"Not only trespassing, but squatting," returned the colonel, with a twinkle in his eye. "The case is serious. This island has belonged to me and to my ancestors for generations. I arrive here to-day to find it occupied by a band of individuals who, I must say" (with a glance out through the door at the barefooted Sea Urchins yelling in the distance as they hauled up the dead porpoise), "bear a very strong resemblance to a gang of pirates. I am frankly informed by one of their number that they claim possession of my property. I find their flag flying and a fortress erected. The question is whether I am at once to declare war and evict these invaders, or to allow them to remain in the position of vassals on payment of a due tribute."

"Oh, please let us stay!" implored Isobel; "we won't do any harm—we won't, indeed. We're all going home in a few weeks, and then you can have the island quite to yourself again."

"Suppose I were to regard you as surety for the good behaviour of the rest of the tribe," said the colonel: "would you undertake that no rare or cherished plants should be uprooted or any damage inflicted during your tenancy?"

"We wouldn't touch anything," declared Isobel, "we've only taken the blackberries because there are so many of them. I know you're thinking of the maidenhair. Oh, please, is it growing? I do so hope it wasn't spoilt."

"Yes, it's growing. I really don't believe it has suffered very much, after all. I took a look at it this morning, and found the young fronds pushing up as well as if they had never been disturbed."

"I'm *so* glad!" said Isobel, with a sigh of relief; "I've often thought about it since. It's very kind of you to say we may stay here; it would have seemed so hard to turn out after we'd had the trouble of building the hut."

"But what about the rent?" inquired the colonel; "will you be answerable for its proper payment? I may prove as tough a customer as old Shylock, and insist on my pound of flesh."

"We've very little money, I'm afraid," said Isobel timidly; "we spent all the club funds on buying the kettle and the frying-pan—even what we'd saved up for a feast at the end of the holidays. I've only got threepence left myself, though perhaps some of the others may have more."

"I must take it in kind, then—the sort of tribute that is exacted from native chiefs in Central Africa—though you can't bring me pounds of rubber or elephants' tusks here."

"We could pick you blackberries, if you like them," suggested Isobel; "or get you cockles and mussels from the shore. Sometimes the boys spear flukes. They're rather small and muddy, but they're quite nice to eat with bread and butter if you fry them yourself."

"My consumption of blackberries is limited," replied the colonel, "and there seems slight demand for shell-fish in my kitchen. The flukes might have done; but if they are only edible when you fry them yourself, I'm afraid it's no use, for I don't believe my housekeeper would allow me to try. No! I must think out the question of tribute, and let you know. I won't ask a rack rent, I promise you, and I suppose I could distrain on these tea things and the kettle if it were not paid up. The latter appears to be boiling over at this instant."

"So it is!" cried Isobel, lifting it off in a hurry. "I wonder," she continued shyly, "if you would care to have a cup of tea. I could make it in a moment, if you wouldn't mind drinking it out of a tin mug."

"Miss Robinson Crusoe is very hospitable. I haven't had a picnic for years. The tin mug will recall my early soldiering days. I have bivouacked in places which were not nearly so comfortable as this."

He took a seat in a sand armchair, and looked on with amusement while Isobel made her preparations. Something in the set of her slim little figure and the fall of her long straight fair hair attracted him, and he caught himself wondering of whom her gray eyes reminded him. He liked the quiet way she went about her business, and her frank, unaffected manners—so different from Belle's self-conscious assurance.

"Why can't the other child wear a plain holland frock?" he thought. "It would look much more suitable for the sands than those absurd trimmed-up costumes. What a pity she hasn't the sense of this one! Well, it's no use; it evidently isn't in her, and I doubt if any amount of training at a good school will make much difference."

Isobel in the meantime having brewed the tea handed it to him upon the scarlet tray.

"I'm sorry we haven't a cream jug," she apologized. "We always bring our milk in medicine bottles. Do you mind sugar out of the packet? I wish I had some cake, but Mrs. Jackson didn't put any in my basket to-day, and I don't like taking the others' without asking them. I hope it's nice," she added anxiously. "I'm so afraid the water's a little smoked."

"Delicious," said the colonel, who would have consumed far more unpalatable viands sooner than hurt her feelings, and who tried to overlook the fact that the tin mug gave the tea a curious flavour, and the bread and butter was of a thickness usually meted out to schoolboys. "But aren't you going to have any yourself?"

"Not now, thank you. I'd rather wait for the others. I promised to have everything ready for them when they came back."

"I see. You're 'Polly, put the kettle on,' to-day, and 'Sukey, take it off again,' also, as they appear to have 'all run away.' No more, thanks. One cup is as much as is good for me. Why, in the name of all that's mysterious, who has been writing these?"

The colonel jumped up and strode to the other end of the hut, having suddenly caught sight of the quaint letters which Isobel had drawn upon the wall.

"I have," replied Isobel simply.

"Then, my dear Miss Robinson Crusoe, may I ask how you came to be acquainted with runic characters?"

"I don't know what they are," said Isobel. "It's very queer writing, isn't it? I was only copying it for fun."

"Where did you copy it from?"

"It's on a stone at the top of the headland."

"This headland?"

"Yes, just above here, but a little farther on."

"Do you mean to tell me there is a stone bearing letters like that on these cliffs?"

"Yes; it's a long kind of stone, something like a cross without arms."

"I thought I had walked over every inch of this island, yet I have never noticed it."

"It was quite covered with brambles," said Isobel. "I found it when we were picking blackberries. I had to pull them all away before I could see it."

"If you can leave your domestic cares, I should very much like you to show it to me," said the colonel. "I happen to be particularly interested in such stones."

"I'll go at once," said Isobel, putting the kettle among the ashes, where it could not boil over, and slamming on her hat. "It looks ever so worn and old, but the letters are cut in the stone, like they are on graves."

She led the way up the steep, narrow path which scaled the hill, on to the cliff above, and after a little hunting about, found the brambly spot which had been the scene of her quarrel with Belle.

The owner of the island knelt down and examined the stone intently for some moments.

"To think that I must have passed this place dozens and dozens of times and never have known of its existence!" he said at last. "I have searched the neighbourhood so often for some record of the Viking period. Strange that it should be found now by the chance discovery of a child!"

"Are they really letters, then?" inquired Isobel. "Is it some foreign language?"

"Yes; they are runes, very old and perfect ones. The runic characters were used by our Teutonic forefathers before they learned the Roman alphabet. This stone shows that long, long ago the Northmen have been here."

"The same Northmen who came in their great ships, and burnt the abbey, and killed St. Alcuin at the altar?" asked Isobel, keenly interested.

"Very likely, or their sons or grandsons."

"Why did they write upon a stone here?"

"It was set up as a monument—just like a grave stone in a churchyard."

"But if the Northmen were pagans, why is there a cross carved on the stone?"

"Many of them settled in this country, and became Christians, and turned farmers instead of sea-robbers."

"Perhaps the monks went back to the abbey afterwards and taught them," suggested Isobel. "I always thought they must have felt so ashamed of themselves for running away. They couldn't all be saints like St. Alcuin, but they might do their best to make up."

"No doubt they did. They were brave men in those days, who were not afraid to risk their lives. It is possible that a small chapel may have been built here once, though the very memory of it has passed away."

"Is some one buried here, then?"

"Yes. Put into English characters, the inscription runs: '*Ulf suarti risti krus thana aft Fiak sun sin.*' That is to say: '*Black Ulf raised this cross for Fiak his son.*'"

"I wish we knew who they were," said Isobel. "The son must have died first. Perhaps he was killed in battle, and then his father would put up this cross. How very sorry he must have felt!"

"Very," said the colonel sadly—"especially if he were his only son. It is hard to see the green bough taken while the old branch is spared."

"My father died fighting," said Isobel softly. "But his grave is ever so far away in South Africa."

"And so is my son's. Death reaps his harvest, and hearts are as sore, whether it is the twentieth century or the tenth. Customs change very little. We put up monuments to show the resting-places of those we love, and a thousand years ago Black Ulf raised this cross that Fiak his son should not be forgotten."

"And he's not forgotten," said Isobel, "because we've found it all this long time afterwards. I didn't know what it meant until you told me. I'm so glad I can read it now. I want to tell mother; she likes old monuments, or any kind of old things."

"She has evidently taught you to think and to use your eyes," said the colonel, "or you would not have copied the inscription, and then I might never have discovered the stone."

"What a pity that would have been!" returned Isobel. "I was very lucky to find it. Do you think it makes up a little for the maidenhair?"

"Completely; though, remember, I didn't blame you for that incident. It was your friends—the same young ruffians, I believe, who are racing up the sands now, dragging some carcass behind them."

"Oh! they're coming back for tea," cried Isobel. "And I forgot all about the kettle! I hope it hasn't boiled away. I ought to go. You haven't told me yet, please, what you would like us to bring you instead of rent for the island. I should like to know, so that I can tell the others."

"I'll take this discovery in lieu of all payment," declared the colonel. "You and your companions, the Sea Urchins, are welcome to have free run of the place while you are here. Good-bye, little friend! You always seem to turn up in exceptional circumstances. You and I appear to have a few interests in common, so I hope that some time I may have the pleasure of meeting you again."

CHAPTER XIV. A WET DAY.

"Oft expectation fails, and most oft there
Where most it promises; and oft it hits
Where hope is coldest and despair most sits."

THE estrangement between Isobel and her friend was of very short duration after all. That same evening they had met on the Parade, and Belle had run up with her former affectionate manner, so completely ignoring the remembrance of any differences between them that Isobel thankfully let the matter slide, only too glad to resume the friendship on the old terms, and hoping that such an unpleasant episode might not occur again. The two had arranged to make an expedition together to the old town on the following day, but the morning proved so very wet that it was impossible for any one to go out of doors.

"It's a perfect deluge of a day," said Isobel, looking hopelessly at the ceaseless drip, drip which descended from the leaden skies. "It doesn't seem as if it ever meant to clear up again. I think it must have rained like this on the first morning of the Flood. It couldn't have been worse, at any rate."

The back sitting-room of a lodging-house does not, as a rule, afford the most brilliant of views, so the scene which met Isobel's eyes was hardly calculated to raise her spirits. The paved yard behind was swimming with water, through which a drenched and disconsolate tabby cat, excluded from the paradise of the kitchen, was attempting to pick its way, shaking its paws at every step. Marine Terrace being a comparatively new row, the back premises were still in a somewhat unfinished condition, and instead of gardens and flower-beds, your eye was greeted by heaps of sand and mortar, bricks and rubbish, not yet carted away by the builders, which, added to piles of empty bottles and old hampers, gave a rather forlorn appearance to the place. After watching pussy's struggles with the elements, and seeing her finally seek refuge in the coal-house, Isobel took a turn to the front door, and stood looking over the Parade, where the rolling mist almost obscured all sight of the sea, and sky and water were of the same dull neutral gray. The road was empty, not even the most venturesome visitors having braved the wind and weather that morning; while Biddy herself, usually as punctual as the clock, had evidently decided it was too wet a day to vend her fish. There was absolutely nothing to be seen; nevertheless Isobel would have stood there watching the endless drops falling from the unkindly skies, had not Mrs. Jackson appeared from the kitchen, and declaring that the rain was beating into the hall, firmly closed the door and shut out any further prospect.

"You'd get cold too, missy," she said, "standin' in a full draught, for Polly will leave that back door open, say what I will, and it turns chilly of a wet day. One can have too much fresh air, to my mind. There was a gentleman stayed here last summer, now, just crazy he was on what he called 'hygiene;' bathed regular every morning before breakfast, no matter how the tide might be. I warned him it was a-injuring his health to go in the water on an empty stomach, but he didn't take no notice of what I said, and lay out on damp sand, and sat under open windows, till he ended up with a bad bout of the brown-chitis, with the doctor comin' every day, and me turned sick nurse to poultice him—Emma Jane bein' at home then, or I couldn't have found the time to do it. I've no opinion of these modern health dodges as folks sets such store by now. In my young days we never so much as thought about drains, and if the pig-sty was at the back door, no one was any the worse for it! I call it right-down interferin' the way these inspectors come round sayin' you mustn't even throw a bucket of potato skins down in your own yard. Nuisance, indeed! It's them as is the nuisance. Their nasty disinfectants smell far worse, to my mind, than a few cabbage leaves. My grandmother lived to ninety-four, and never slept with her bedroom window open in her life, not even on the hottest of summer days, and drew her drinkin' water regular from the churchyard well, which they tell you now is swarmin' with 'microbes,' or whatever they call 'em. I never saw any, though I've let my pail down in it many a time; and it was a deal sweeter and fresher, to my taste, than what you get laid on in lead pipes. Jackson may go in for this new-fangled 'sanitation' if he likes, votin' for all kinds of improvements by the Town Council, which only adds to the rates. I'm an old-fashioned woman, and stick to old-fashioned country ways, and I think draughts is draughts, and gives folks colds and toothaches, call 'em by what high-soundin' names you will."

Judging the weather to be absolutely hopeless, and without the slightest intention of clearing up, Isobel went back to the sitting-room, where Polly had just taken away the breakfast things, and looked round for some means of amusing herself.

"I don't believe the postman has been yet," she said. "What a terrible day for him to go round! I should think he feels as if he ought to come in a boat. Why, there's his rap-tap now. I wonder if there are any letters for us?"

"I don't expect there will be," said Mrs. Stewart; "my correspondence is not generally very large."

"I think I shall go and see, just for something to do," said Isobel; and running into the hall, she returned presently with a letter in her hand.

"It's for you, mother," she said. "The people in the drawing-room had five, and the family in the dining-room had seven and two parcels. Aren't they lucky? There was even one for Polly, but Mrs. Jackson told her to put it in her pocket, and not to read it till she had got the beds made. I'm sure she'll take a peep at it, all the same. I wish some one would write to me. I haven't had even a picture post-card since I came."

The appearance of the letter which had just arrived seemed to cause Mrs. Stewart an unusual amount of agitation. She turned it over in her hand, glanced at Isobel, hesitated a moment, and finally took it unopened to her bedroom, that she might read it in private.

"It is my long-expected reply at last!" she said to herself. "I thought he could surely not fail to send me an answer. I wonder what he has to say. I feel as though I scarcely dare to look."

With trembling fingers she tore open the envelope, and unfolding the sheet of notepaper, read as follows:—

"THE CHASE, SILVERSANDS,

August 24th.

"DEAR MADAM,—I have delayed replying sooner to your communication, as I wished to thoroughly inform myself upon the question which you put before me. Acting on your suggestion, I have, without her knowledge, noted the general disposition, demeanour, and tastes of your daughter, and finding they are of a nature such as would not make a closer intimacy congenial to either of us, I must beg to decline your proffered meeting. As I would wish, however, that my son's child should receive a fitting education, I am about to place to her credit the sum of £200 per annum to defray her expenses at any good school that you may select from a list which will be submitted to you shortly by my solicitor. He has full instructions to conduct all further arrangements, and I should prefer any future communication from you to be only of a business character.—Believe me to remain yours truly EVERARD STEWART."

Mrs. Stewart flung down the letter with a cry of indignation.

"What does he mean?" she asked herself. "Where can he have seen Isobel? To my knowledge she has spoken to nobody except this old Colonel Smith and a few of the townspeople. How can he have 'noted her disposition, demeanour, and tastes'? And if so, what fault can he possibly find with my darling? Is it mere prejudice, and a determination on his part to avoid any reconciliation? If I were not so wretchedly poor, I would not accept one farthing of this money for her. But I must! I must! It is not right that my pride should stand in the way of her education, and for this I must humble myself to take his charity. He is a stern man to have kept up the ill-feeling for so many years. Every line of his letter shows that he is opposed to me still, though he has never seen me in his life; and instead of loving Isobel for her father's sake, he is prepared to hate her for mine. We are so friendless and alone in the world that it seems hard the one relation who I thought might have taken an interest in my child should cast her off thus. Well, it makes her doubly mine, and if she can never know her grandfather's beautiful home, my love must be compensation for what she has lost. My one little ewe lamb is everything to me; and though I would have given her up for the sake of seeing her recognized, it would have nearly broken my heart to part with her."

She put the letter carefully away, and went down again to the sitting-room, where Isobel was standing by the window, gazing disconsolately at the streaming rain, with just a suspicion of two rain-drops in her eyes, for she did not like to be left alone, and Mrs. Stewart had been long upstairs.

"Never mind, my sweet one," said her mother, stroking the pretty, smooth hair. "It is a disappointing day, but we will manage to enjoy ourselves together, you and I, in spite of rain or any other troubles. Suppose we go through all your collections. You could write the names under the wild flowers you have pressed, arrange the shells in boxes, and float some of the sea-weeds on to pieces of writing-paper."

Isobel cheered up at once at the idea of something definite to do, and the table was very soon spread over with the various treasures she had gathered upon the beach. Silversands was a good place for shells, and she had many rare and beautiful kinds, from pearly cowries to scallops and wentletraps. She sorted them out carefully, putting big, little, and middle-sized ones in separate heaps; she had great ideas of what she would do with them when she was at home again, intending to construct shell boxes, photo frames, and various other knickknacks in imitation of the wonderful things which were sold at the toy-shop near the railway station.

"If I could make a very nice frame, mother," she said, "I should like to send it to Mrs. Jackson for a Christmas present, to put Emma Jane's photo in. I believe she'd be quite pleased to hang it up in the kitchen with the funeral cards. I might manage a shell box for old Biddy, too. It would scarcely do for a handkerchief box, because I don't believe she ever uses such a thing as a pocket handkerchief, but I dare say she would like it to put something in. Do you think the shells would stick on to tin if we made the glue strong enough? I could do a tobacco-box then for Mr. Cass the coastguard, one that he could keep in the parlour for best."

"I'm afraid you will have to collect more shells if you intend to make so many presents," said Mrs. Stewart. "I think, however, that we might manufacture some pretty pin-cushions out of these large fan shells by boring holes in the ends, fastening them together with bows of ribbon, and gluing a small velvet cushion in between."

"That would be delightful!" cried Isobel, "and something quite different to give people. I'm afraid they're rather tired of my needle books and stamp cases. I wish we could think of anything to do with the sea-weed."

"We're going to float them on to pieces of paper, and when they are dry we will paste them in a large scrap album, and find out their names from a book which I think I can borrow from the Free Library at home."

"I don't quite know how to float them."

"You must watch me do this one, and then you will be able to manage the rest. First I'm going to fill this basin with clean water, and put this pretty pink piece to float in it. Now, you see, I am slipping this sheet of notepaper underneath, and drawing it very carefully and gently from the water, so that the sea-weed remains spreads out upon the paper. I shall pin the sheet by its four corners on to this board, and when it is dry you'll find that the sea-weed has stuck to the paper as firmly as if it had been glued. It's not really difficult, but it needs a little skill to lift the sheet from the water without disarranging your sea-weed."

"This one's lovely," said Isobel. "I must try to do the green piece next. How jolly they'll look when they are all nicely pasted into a book! I wonder if it will be difficult to find out the names? It's rather hard to tell our flowers, isn't it?"

"Sometimes; but I think we are improving in our botany. How many different kinds have we pressed since we came here?"

"Forty; I counted them yesterday. And we have fifty-seven at home. We shall soon have the drawer quite full. Do you think I might look at the scabious that I put under your big box last night?"

"I'm afraid you will spoil it if you peep at it too soon. When I was a little girl my brother and I used sometimes to amuse ourselves by putting specimens to press under the leaves of an old folding-table, and pledging each other not to look at them for a year. It was rather hard sometimes to keep our vows, but the flowers were most beautifully dried when we took them out again. Some day we will start a collection of pressed ferns; they are really easier to do than wild flowers, because they keep their colour, while the pretty blue of harebells or speedwells always seems to fade away."

"I've done three sea-weeds already," said Isobel, successfully arranging a delicate piece of pink coralline with the point of a hat pin. "I'm afraid this next white one will be very difficult, it's so thick."

"You can't float that. It's a zoophyte, not a real sea-weed; and, indeed, not a vegetable at all, but the very lowest form of animal life. You must hang it up to dry, like you do the long pieces of oar-weed. We'll try to get the messy work done this morning, so that we can clear the table for Polly to lay dinner, and in the afternoon I thought you might finish your tea-cosy for Mr. Binks. There is not much to be done to it now, and then I can make it up for you."

"Oh, that would be nice! When can we go and see him?"

"I believe my foot will be strong enough by Thursday, so you shall write a letter to him after dinner, and say so."

"How jolly! I'm longing to see the White Coppice, and the balk, and Mrs. Binks. I hope she won't forget to bake the cranberry cake. I shall have to write a very neat letter. I want to copy out the runic inscription, too, on to a fresh piece of paper."

"Yes, do, dear. If my ankle bears me safely as far as the White Coppice, I shall certainly venture to the island afterwards, and take a sketch of the stone. It's a most interesting discovery."

"Colonel Smith said he was going to have it raised up," said Isobel; "half of it, you see, is buried in the ground. He wasn't sure whether he would leave it where it is, or take it to his house. He's so dreadfully afraid, if he lets it stay on the island, that horrid cheap trippers might come some time and carve their names on it. He says the brambles growing over it have kept it safe so far. I wish you knew him, mother, he's *so* kind. Belle says she doesn't like him at all, but I do."

"I think it's very good of him to let you have the run of his island; it has made a most delightful playground, and you and the Sea Urchins will have spent an ideal holiday."

"We have indeed. I'm so glad we came to Silversands. I wish we could come every year, and always have the island to play on. It would be something to look forward to through the winter."

"I'm afraid that isn't possible, dear," said Mrs. Stewart regretfully, thinking of what might have been if the hopes which prompted her visit had been fulfilled. "I doubt if we shall ever return here again. But we will have other happy times together; there are many sweet spots in the world where we shall be able to enjoy ourselves, and I have plans for the future which I will tell you about by-and-by."

"I've had quite a jolly day in spite of the rain," declared Isobel that evening, when, the deluge having ceased at last, the setting sun broke through the thick banks of clouds, and flooding the sea with a golden glory, brought out all the cooped-up visitors for an airing upon the Parade.

"I haven't!" said Belle. "It was perfectly detestable. I had absolutely nothing to do except throw balls for Micky, and even he got tired of that. Mother said we made her head ache, and she went to lie down. It's never any fun talking to Barton, she's so stupid; so I sat and watched the streaming rain through the window, and wished we'd never come to Silversands. I think a wet day in lodgings is just about the horridest thing in the world, and I simply can't imagine how you can have enjoyed it."

CHAPTER XV. TEA WITH MR. BINKS.

*"At many a statelier home we've had good cheer,
But ne'er a kinder welcome found than here."*

THE tea-cosy, when finished, was a thing of beauty, and Isobel packed it up in sheets of white tissue paper with much pride and satisfaction. Both the steaming teapot on the one side and the ecclesiastical-looking "B" on the other had given her a great deal of trouble, and she was not sorry that they were completed.

"Going to have tea with that vulgar old man we met in the train!" exclaimed Belle, raising her eyebrows in astonishment when Isobel told her of their plans. "You really do the *funniest* things! I thought him dreadful. I suppose, since he asked you, you couldn't get out of it, but I'm sorry for you to have to go. I shouldn't have been able to come to the island in any case to-morrow, because mother wants to take me to see the Oppenheims."

"Who are they?" asked Isobel.

"Oh, they're a family mother knows in London. They're ever so rich. They've taken a lovely furnished house near the woods, with a tennis-court and a huge garden. They're to arrive this evening, and they're bringing their motor car and their chauffeur with them. The Wilsons and the Bardsleys are coming by the same train. Blanche Oppenheim is six months older than I am, and mother says she's sure I shall like her. It will be nice to have some more friends here; Silversands is getting rather dull. There's so little to do in such a quiet place. There never seems to be anything going on."

Isobel thought there had been a great deal going on of the kind of fun she enjoyed, though it might not be altogether to Belle's taste, and even her friend's depreciation of poor Mr. Binks could not spoil the pleasure with which she anticipated her visit to the White Coppice. She was full of eagerness to start on Thursday afternoon, and was ready fully half an hour too soon, though her mother assured her they could not with decency arrive before four o'clock.

The White Coppice lay opposite to Silversands, at the other side of a narrow peninsula, and you could either reach it by going five miles round by the road, or by walking two miles across the hills. Mrs. Stewart and Isobel naturally preferred the short cut, and leaving the little town behind them, were soon on the bare wind-swept heights, following a track which led over the heather-clad moor. It seemed no-man's land here, given up to the grouse and plovers, though now and then they passed a rough sheep-fold, and once a whitewashed farmstead, the thatched roof of which was bound down with ropes to resist the autumn storms, and the few trees that sheltered the doorway, all pointing their struggling branches in the same direction, served to show how strong was the force of the prevailing wind. From the crest of the hill they could see the sea on either hand, and at the far end of the promontory could catch a glimpse of the pier at Ferndale, where a steamer was landing its cargo of excursionists to swell the already large crowd of cheap trippers, who seemed to swarm like ants upon the shore.

"I'm glad we're not staying there," said Isobel, who had been taken for an afternoon by Mrs. Chester in company with Charlie and Hilda; and though she had laughed at the niggers and the pierrots, and enjoyed watching the Punch and Judy and the acrobats on the shore, and had put pennies into the peep-shows on the pier, had returned thankfully from the crowded promenade and streets full of holiday-makers to the peace and quiet of Silversands.

"It's rather amusing just for a day, but the people are even noisier than those we met in the train; they were throwing confetti all about the sands, and shouting to one another at the top of their voices. I like a place where we can go walks and pick flowers, and not meet anybody else. We shouldn't have found a desert island at Ferndale."

"You certainly wouldn't," said Mrs. Stewart. "If 'Rocky Holme' were there it would be covered with swings and gingerbeer stalls, and your little hut might probably have been turned into an oyster room or a penny show. It is delightful to find a spot that is still unspoilt. Luckily the trippers don't appear to go far afield; they seem quite content with the attractions of the pier and band, and have not yet invaded these beautiful moors. How quickly we seem to have come across! We're quite close to the sea again now, and I believe that gray old farmhouse nestling among the trees below will prove to be the end of our journey."

The White Coppice was so called because it stood on the borders of a birch wood that lay in a gorge between the hills. It was protected by a bold cliff from the strong north and west winds, sheltered by a slightly lower crag from the east, and open only towards the south, where the garden sloped down to a sandy cove and a narrow creek that made a natural harbour for Mr. Binks's boat, which was generally moored to a small jetty under the wall. It was an ancient stone farmhouse, with large mullioned windows and hospitable, ever-open door, over which two tamarisk bushes had been trained into a rustic porch. The garden was gay with such hardy flowers as would flourish so near to the sea, growing in patches between the rows of potatoes and beans, and interspersed here and there with the figureheads of vessels, while at the end was a summer-house, evidently made from an upturned boat, and covered thickly with traveller's joy. Here Mr. Binks appeared to be taking an afternoon nap while awaiting the arrival of his visitors, but at the click of the opening gate he sprang up with a start, and advanced to meet them with brawny, outstretched hand.

"I'm reet glad to see you, I am!" he exclaimed cordially. "It's royal weather, too, though a trifle hotter nor suits me.—Missis!" (bawling through the doorway), "where iver are you a-gone? Here's company come, and waitin' for you!"

Mrs. Binks could not have been very far away, for she bustled into the front garden in a moment, her round, rosy, apple face smiling all over with welcome. She was a fine, tall, elderly woman, so stout that her figure reminded you of a large soft pillow tied in the middle. She wore an old-fashioned black silk dress, with a white muslin apron, and a black netted cap with purple ribbons over her smoothly parted gray hair.

"Well, now, I'm *that* pleased!" she declared. "Come in, and set you down. You'll be fair tired out, mum, with your walk over the moor, havin' had a bad foot and all. It's a nasty thing to strain your ankle, it is that.—Come in, missy. Binks has talked a deal about you, he has—thinks you're the very moral of our Harriet's Clara over at Skegness; but, bless you, I don't see no likeness myself. The kettle's just on the boil, and you must take a cup of tea first thing to freshen you up like. It's a good step from Silversands, and a bit close to-day to come so far."

Seated in a corner of the high-backed oak settle, Isobel looked with eager curiosity round the old farm kitchen. Its flagged stone floor, the sliding cupboards in the walls, the great beams of the ceiling covered with hooks from which were suspended flitches of bacon, bunches of dried herbs, strings of onions, and even Mr. Binks's fishing-boots—all were new to her interested gaze, and her quick eyes took in everything from the gun-rack over the dresser to the china dogs on the chimney-piece. The kitchen was so large that half of it seemed to be reserved as a parlour; there was a square of carpet laid down at one end, upon which stood a round table spread with Mrs. Binks's very best china tea-service, and a supply of dainties that would have feasted a dozen visitors at least. The long, low window was filled with scarlet geraniums, between the vivid blossoms of which you could catch a peep of the cove and the water beyond; and just outside hung a cage containing a pair of doves, which kept up an incessant cooing. Mrs. Binks made quite a picture, seated in a tall elbow chair, wielding her big teapot, and she pressed her muffins and currant tea-cakes upon her guests with true north-country hospitality.

"You ought to be sharp set after a two-mile walk," she observed. "Take it through, missy, take it through! You must have 'the bishop' with 'the curate,' as we say in these parts; the top piece is nought but the poor curate, for all the butter runs to the bottom, and that's the bishop! Is your tea as you like it? You must taste our apple jelly, made of our own crabs as grows in the orchard out at back, unless you'd as lief try the damson cheese or the strawberry jam."

Mr. Binks seemed much undecided whether his position as host required him to join the party, or whether his presence in such select company would be an intrusion, and in spite of Mrs. Stewart's kindly-expressed hope that he would occupy his own seat at the table, he finally compromised the matter by carrying his tea to the opposite end of the kitchen, and taking it on the dresser, from whence he fired off remarks every now and then whenever Mrs. Binks, who was a hard talker and monopolized the conversation, gave him a chance to put in a word. It was amusing talk, Isobel thought, all about Mrs. Binks's children and grandchildren, and the many illnesses from which they had suffered, and the medicines they had tried, and the wonderful recoveries they had made, interspersed by offers of more tea and cake and jam, or lamentations over the small appetite of her visitors, whom she seemed to expect to clear the plates like locusts.

"No more, missy? Why, you are soon done! And you haven't tasted my cranberry cake! You must have a bit of it, if you have to put it in your pocket. It's made by a recipe as I got from my great-aunt as lived up in Berwick, and a light hand she had, too, for a cake," laying a generous slice upon Isobel's plate, and seeming quite hurt by her refusal.

"You mustn't make her ill, Mrs. Binks," laughed Mrs. Stewart, "though she fully appreciates your kindness.—Isobel, would you like to open the parcel we brought with us?"

"You worked this for us, honey? Well, I never did!" cried Mrs. Binks, touching the gorgeous tea-cosy gingerly, as if she feared her stout fingers might soil its beauty.—"Peter, come hither and look at this.—Use it for tea every day? Nay! that would be a sin and a shame. It's a sight too pretty to use. I'll put it in the parlour, alongside of the cup Binks won at last show for the black heifer. You shall see for yourself, missy, how nice it'll stand on the sideboard, on top of a daisy mat as Harriet crocheted when she was down with a bad leg."

Mrs. Binks opened a door at the farther side of the kitchen, and proudly led the way into her best sitting-room. It was a close little room, with a mouldy smell as if the chimney were stopped up and the window never opened. One end of it was entirely filled by a glass-backed mahogany sideboard; a large gilt mirror hung over the fireplace, carefully swathed in white muslin to keep off the flies; the walls were adorned with photographs of the Binks family and its many ramifications, taken in their best clothes, which did not appear to sit easily upon them, to judge by the stiff unrest of their attitudes; and opposite the door hung a wonderful German oleograph depicting a scene that might either have been a sunrise on the Alps or an eruption of Vesuvius, according to the individual fancy of the spectator. The square table was covered with a magenta cloth, in the centre of which stood a glass shade containing wax fruit, while several gorgeously bound volumes of poems and sermons were placed at regular intervals each upon a separate green wool-work mat.

It was so hot and airless in there that Isobel was quite glad when Mr. Binks suggested they should adjourn to the garden, that he might show her the figureheads which stood among the flower-beds like a row of wooden statues. Each one was the record of some good ship gone to pieces upon that treacherous coast, and as he walked along pointing them out with his stick, the old man gave the histories of the wrecks, at many of which he had played an active part in saving the lives of the crews.

"That there's the *Arizona*—her with the broken nose; smashed up like matchwood she was, on the cliffs beyond Ferndale, and the captain drowned and the second mate. That there's the *Neptune*. The trident's gone, but you can see the beard and the wreath. She went down of a sudden on a sunken rock, and never a man left to tell as how it happened. This un's the *Admiral Seymour*, wrecked outside Silversands Bay; but we had the lifeboat out, and took all off safe. And this here's the *Polly Jones*, a coastin' steamer from Liverpool, as went clean in two amongst them crags by the lighthouse, and her cargo of oranges washed up along the shore next day till the beach turned yellow with 'em."

"You know a great deal about ships," said Isobel, to whom her host's reminiscences were as thrilling as a story-book.

"I should that. I've been sailin' for the best part of fifty year—leastways when I wasn't farmin'. I've not forgot as I promised to row you over to the balk. If your ma's willin', we'd best make a start now, whilst the tide's handy. It's worth your while to go; you'd not see such a sight again, maybe, in a far day's journey."

Mrs. Binks declined to join the expedition, so only Mrs. Stewart and Isobel stepped into the boat which Mr. Binks rowed over the bay with swift and steady strokes. Their destination was a narrow spit of land about a quarter of a mile distant, where the crumbling remains of an old abbey rose gray among the surrounding rocks. Long years ago the monks had fashioned the balk to catch their fish, and it still stood, a survival of ancient days and ancient ways, close under the ruined wall of the disused chapel. It consisted of a circle of stout oak staves, driven into the sand, so as to enclose a space of about forty yards in diameter, the staves being connected by twisted withes, so that the whole resembled a gigantic basket. It was filled by the high tide, and the retreating water, running through the meshes, left the fish behind as in a trap, when they were very easily caught with the hands and collected in creels.

"You wouldn't see more than a couple like it in all England," said Mr. Binks. "They calls it poachin' now, and no one mayn't make a fresh one; but this here's left, and goes with the White Coppice, and I've rented the two for a matter of forty year."

He drew up the boat under the old abbey wall, and helping his guests to land, led them down the beach to the enclosure, where the wet sand was covered with leaping shining fish, some gasping their last in the sunshine, and some seeking the temporary shelter of a deeper pool in the middle. Bob, Mr. Binks's grandson, was busy collecting them and putting them into large baskets, assisted by a clever little Irish terrier, which ran hither and thither catching the fish in its mouth, and carrying them to its master like a retriever, much to Isobel's amusement, for she had certainly never seen a dog go fishing before.

It was a pretty sight, and a much easier way, Isobel thought, of earning your living than venturing out with nets and lines; and she resolved to tell the Sea Urchins about it, so that they might make a small balk for themselves on their desert island, if the colonel would allow them. She and her mother wandered round the old abbey, while Mr. Binks was engaged in giving some directions to Bob; but there was nothing to be seen except a few tumble-down walls and a fragment of what might once have been part of an east window. They were lifting away the thick ivy which had covered a corner stone, when, looking up, Isobel suddenly caught sight of a familiar figure coming towards them across the rough broken flags of the transept.

"O mother," she whispered, "it's Colonel Smith!" and advancing rather shyly a step or two, she met him with a beaming face.

"Why, it's my little friend again!" cried the colonel. "Hunting for more antiquities? I wish you would find them. This is surely your mother" (raising his hat).—"Your daughter will, no doubt, have told you, madam, what an interesting discovery she made on my island. I feel I am very much indebted to her."

"She was equally delighted," replied Mrs. Stewart. "She has talked continually about this wonderful stone and its runic inscription. I am hoping to be able to take a sketch of it before we leave. I hear there is carving on the lower portion, as well as the runes."

"So there is, but it's half hidden by the soil. I'm taking some of my men to-morrow to dig it out of the ground and raise it up, and am sending for a photographer to take several views of it. It is of special value to me, owing to the particular Norse dialect employed, which is similar to that on several monuments in the Isle of Man, and shows that the same race of invaders must have swept across the north, and probably penetrated as far as Ireland."

"I have seen runic crosses in Ireland," said Mrs. Stewart. "There's a beautifully ornamented one near Ballymoran, though the carving is more like Celtic than Teutonic work—those strange interlacing animals which you find in ancient Erse manuscripts. I am very interested in old Celtic remains, and have a good many sketches of them at home."

"You couldn't take up a more fascinating study," said the colonel eagerly. "It's a very wide field, and one that has not been too much explored. I've done a little in that way myself, and I am collecting materials for a book on the subject of Celtic and runic crosses, but it needs both time and patience to sort one's knowledge. It's worth the trouble, though, for the sake of the pleasure one gets out of it."

"I am sure it is," replied Mrs. Stewart, with ready sympathy. "To love such things is a kind of 'better part' that cannot be taken away from us, however much the uninitiated may laugh at our enthusiasm."

"You're right," said the colonel. "We can afford to let them laugh. We antiquarians have the best of it, after all. I should have liked to have seen your picture of the Irish cross. I wish I could sketch. You are fortunate to have that talent at your disposal; it's a great help in such work, and one which I sadly lack. Why, here's Binks!—Do you want anything, Peter?"

"No, sir," answered Mr. Binks, touching his cap. "Only to say as how the tide's runnin' out fast, and we ought to be startin' back now, or I'll have to carry the boat down the sands; she's only in a foot of water as it is."

"We must indeed go," said Mrs. Stewart, consulting her watch. "It's time we were walking home again.—Thank you" (turning to the colonel) "for your kindness to my little girl and her companions in allowing them to play on your island. I hope they are careful and do no damage there."

"Not in the least. There's nothing to hurt. Good-evening, madam. It has given me great pleasure to meet one with whom I have such a congenial subject in common. You must come, by all means, and sketch the stone, and I wish you every success in your study of both Celtic and runic antiquities."

"What an interesting old gentleman!" said Mrs. Stewart, when, having bid many farewells to Mr. and Mrs. Binks, she and Isobel at last turned their steps homeward over the moors. "It was, as he said, quite a pleasure to meet. I suppose there's a freemasonry between antiquarians. I should like to have a copy of his book when it's published. I wonder if he would find my sketches of the Irish crosses useful. I think I must venture to send them to him when I return home. We don't know his address, but no doubt Colonel Smith, Silversands, would find him. We've had a delightful afternoon, Isobel, and not the least part of it, to me, has been to make the acquaintance of your friend of the desert island."

CHAPTER XVI. BELLE'S NEW FRIEND.

"How soon the bitter follows on the sweet!
Could I not chain your fancy's flying feet?
Could I not hold your soul to make you play
To-morrow in the key of yesterday?"

ISOBEL found Belle on the Parade next morning in the midst of quite a group of fashionable strangers. She was wearing one of her smartest frocks, and was hanging affectionately on the arm of a girl slightly taller than herself, a showy-looking child, with hazel eyes and a high colour, dressed in a very fantastic costume of red and white, with a scarlet fez on her thick frizzy brown hair, and a tall silver-knobbed cane, ornamented with ribbons, in her hand. Belle appeared to find her company so entrancing that at first she did not notice Isobel, and it was only when the latter spoke to her that she seemed to realize her presence, and said "Good-morning."

"We're just off to the island," said Isobel. "Charlie has got a fresh coil of rope, and the boys are going to try and make a new raft. The Rokebys are bringing some eggs, and we mean to fry pancakes and toss them, as if it were Shrove Tuesday. Are you coming?"

"Well, not this morning, I think," replied Belle. "I've promised Blanche to show her the old town. She doesn't know Silversands at all."

"Would she like to go with us to the hut?" suggested Isobel, looking towards the newcomer, who stood playing with the loops of ribbon on her cane, and humming a tune to herself in a jaunty, self-confident manner.

"Oh, I don't think so," replied Belle. "It's too far. She hasn't seen the beach or the quay yet. We're going now to buy fruit in the market, and then we shall have a stroll round the shops. You can take Micky with you to the island if you like. I'll put on his leash, so that he won't follow me."

"No, thanks; I should be afraid of losing him," replied Isobel. "I'd really rather not. Shall I see you this afternoon?"

"Blanche has asked me to play tennis in their garden," said Belle, drawing Isobel aside. "But I shall be home about six, because the Oppenheims dine at seven, and Blanche always has to dress. I'll come for a walk then, if you'll call for me. I must go now; the others are waiting."

Isobel went away with a rather blank feeling of disappointment. She had grown so accustomed to Belle that it seemed quite strange to be without her, and the morning passed slowly, in spite of the pancakes which she helped Letty and Winnie to mix and toss over the fire. She felt she was only giving half her attention to the raft that the boys kept calling her to admire, and that her thoughts were continually with Belle, trying to imagine what she was doing, and wondering if she were enjoying herself. Mrs. Stewart had found the walk to the White Coppice such a strain on her weak ankle that she would not dare to venture any great exertion for several days, so her intended expedition to the island to sketch the runic cross had perforce to be put off. She and Isobel carried their tea to the beach close by that afternoon, and drank it under the shade of a rock; but though it was pleasant sitting close to the lapping waves, and Mrs. Stewart had brought a new book to read aloud, Isobel's mind would wander away to the garden near the woods where Belle was playing tennis, and she would recall herself with a start, realizing that she had not taken in a single word of the story.

She went round, according to her promise, soon after six o'clock, to find Mrs. Stuart and her friend deep in patterns of dress materials, price lists, catalogues, and copies of the *Queen*, and other ladies' newspapers.

"The Oppenheims are giving a garden-party next Tuesday," explained Belle. "They have a great many friends staying in the neighbourhood who will drive over. They've asked me, and I haven't a thing fit to go in. My white silk's too short, the pink crape's quite crushed, the blue muslin won't look nice after it's washed, and my merino's hardly smart enough. I must have a new dress somehow."

"I don't generally like you in ready-made clothes, Belle," said Mrs. Stuart, "but really this embroidered silk in the advertisement looks very pretty, and Peter Robinson's is a good shop. I think I shall risk it. There will be just time, if I catch this post. Would you rather have the blue or the pink?"

"The blue," said Belle promptly, "because of my best hat. You'd better write for some more forget-me-nots at the same time; the ones in the front are rather dashed. I can wear my blue chain and the turquoise bracelet, and I have a pair of long white gloves not touched yet. But oh, mother, my parasol! It's dreadfully bleached with the sun. Do, please, send for another. There's a picture of one here with little frills all round, just what I want."

Belle's mind was so absorbed by the arrangement of her costume for the coming party that, until the letters were written and finally dispatched to the post, she could give no attention to Isobel, and in the short walk which they took afterwards on the beach her whole conversation was of the Oppenheims and the delightful afternoon she had spent at their house.

"Blanche has five bracelets," she confided, "and four rings, and a dressing-case full of lockets and chains and brooches. She took me upstairs and showed them to me. She's brought her pony with her, and some morning she's promised to borrow her sister's riding-skirt for me, and the coachman is to take us on to the common to ride in turns. Won't it be glorious? She's *such* an amusing girl! She knows all the latest songs, and you should just hear her take people off: it makes you die with laughing. She's been a year at a jolly school near London, where the girls are taken to *matinées* at the theatre, and have a splendid time. I mean to ask mother to send me there. It's dreadfully expensive, but I know she wouldn't mind that."

"We missed you at the island to-day," said Isobel. "The pancakes were delicious. We ate them with sugar and lemons."

"Did you?" said Belle inattentively. "Perhaps I may come to-morrow, if I have time."

"To-morrow's the cricket match at the old playground," said Isobel. "We always have it on Saturday, you know. Had you forgotten?"

"I suppose I had," replied Belle. "I'll bring Blanche, if she cares about coming. I don't know whether she plays cricket."

On Saturday morning Isobel called early at No. 12, only to find that Belle had already gone to the Oppenheims, and would not return until lunch.

"I'm sorry she's not in, dear," said Mrs. Stuart kindly, noticing Isobel's look of disappointment; "but she expects to see you in the afternoon, I'm sure. She told me she would be meeting all her friends upon the shore, so some of the others will no doubt know what has been arranged, if you ask them. I believe I saw the Rokebys pass a moment ago; you could soon overtake them if you were to run."

The matches on the small green common which had been their first playground were still an institution of the Sea Urchins' Club, and Isobel looked forward to them with considerable pleasure. She had not sufficient strength of arm to gain credit as a batsman, but she was a splendid fielder, and Charlie declared that no one made a better long-stop. This afternoon both boys and girls had assembled in full force punctually at the appointed time, and the game was nearly halfway through before Belle and her new friend came sauntering leisurely up to the pitch.

"Oh! we don't want to play, thank you," said Belle, "only to look on. Please don't stop on our account. We're just going to sit down and watch you."

The pair retired to the old boat, where they settled themselves under the shade of Blanche's parasol, and, to judge from their giggling mirth, found great entertainment in making merry at the expense of the others. Isobel, who was fielding, had not a chance to speak to Belle until the opposite side was out, but Arthur Wright having sent a catch at last, she was free until her own innings. She ran up with her accustomed eagerness, expecting her friend to kiss her as usual, and to make room for her upon the boat. To-day, however, Belle did nothing of the sort.

"That you, Isobel?" she said carelessly. "I should think you're hot. I don't know how you can tear about so. Blanche said your legs looked like a pair of compasses when you flew after the ball."

"Aren't you going to play?" asked Isobel. "We want one more on each side."

"No, thanks. I hate racing up and down in the sun. It takes one's hair out of curl."

"Oh, I don't think it would," replied Isobel.

"People with rats' tails can't judge," said Blanche, twisting one of Belle's light locks and her own dark ones together as she spoke, and looking at the combination with a critical eye. "If my brother were here, he'd be in fits over this cricket. I never saw such a game. That big boy holds his bat in the most clumsy way."

"He's a very good player," said Isobel. "He gets more runs than anybody else, and it's terribly hard to put him out."

"Jermyn would bowl him first ball!" returned Blanche scornfully. "Perhaps you've never seen Eton boys play? I always go to Lord's to watch the match with Harrow: it's as different from this as a first-class theatre is from a troupe of niggers."

"Why, but this is only a children's mixed team," said Isobel. "Of course some of the little ones scarcely know how to play at all. We just send them very easy balls, and let them try.—You're surely not going, Belle. Tea will be ready in a quarter of an hour. Mrs. Rokeby's boiling the kettle on a spirit lamp over by the rocks."

"We don't want any, thank you," said Belle, rising from the boat and brushing some sand off her dress. "Mrs. Oppenheim is going to take us to tea at the new café. I hear they've capital ices and a band. The Wilsons were telling me about it yesterday. They say you meet everybody there from four to five o'clock."

"Shall I see you on the Parade this evening?" called Isobel, as Belle strolled away in the direction of Silversands, her arm closely locked in Blanche's.

"I don't think so," replied Belle, without turning her head, and saying something in a whisper to Blanche, which evidently caused the latter much amusement, for she broke into a suppressed peal of laughter, and glancing round at Isobel, went along shaking her shoulders with mirth.

Isobel stood looking after the retreating couple with a lump in her throat and a curious sick sensation in her heart. She could not yet quite realize that Belle did not desire her companionship—only that somehow Blanche had carried off her friend, and that everything was completely spoilt. Between Blanche and herself she recognized there was an instinctive hostility. Blanche had been so openly rude, and had treated both her and the Sea Urchins with such evident contempt, that Isobel, not usually a quarrelsome child, had felt all her spirit rise up within her in passionate indignation.

"Why does she come here to make fun of us?" she asked herself hotly. "We had such jolly times before. None of the others were ever nasty like this—not even Aggie Wright or Hugh Rokeby. Why can't she keep with her own family? And why, oh, why does Belle seem to like her so much?"

Next day being Sunday, Isobel only saw her friend at a distance in church, Mrs. Stewart, who had a suspicion of what was happening, suggesting that they should pass the afternoon with their books on the cliffs, thinking it would be better to leave Belle severely alone, and give no opportunity for a meeting. On this account she spent Monday in Ferndale, asking Hilda Chester to accompany them, and taking the two children to hear the band play on the pier, and to an entertainment afterwards in the pavilion. The Rokebys came on Tuesday morning, inviting Isobel to join them in a boating excursion, from which they did not return until late in the evening, so that for the first time since the beginning of their acquaintance the namesakes had not spoken to each other for three whole days. Isobel had borne the separation as well as she could, but she longed to see Belle again with the full force of her loving nature. She invented many excuses for the conduct of the latter, who, she thought, was no doubt regretting her coldness, and would be as delighted as ever to meet. If only she could get Belle to herself, without Blanche, all would surely be right between them, and the friendship as warm as it had been before.

"May I ask her to tea, mother?" she begged, with so wistful a look in her gray eyes, and such a suspicious little quiver at the corners of her mouth, that Mrs. Stewart consented, somewhat against her better judgment.

Finding Belle on the cricket-ground next morning, Isobel broached the subject of the invitation at once.

"To-day?" said Belle. "I'm going to the Oppenheims'. I haven't told you yet about their garden-party. It was *such* a swell affair! They had waiters from the Belle Vue Hotel at Ferndale, and the Grenadier band from the pier. I never saw lovelier dresses in my life. My blue silk came just in time, and it really looked very nice, and the parasol is sweet. You can't think how much I enjoyed myself."

"Would to-morrow do?" suggested Isobel, "if you can't come to-day?"

"To tea? At your lodgings?" replied Belle, with a rather blank expression on her face.

"Yes, unless we carry the cups out on to the shore and have a picnic. Perhaps that would be nicer."

"Mother wants to take me to call on the Wilsons to-morrow."

"Then Friday or Saturday? It doesn't matter which to us."

"Really," said Belle, looking rather embarrassed, "I expect I shall be going to the Oppenheims both days. Blanche likes me to make up the set at tennis, and it's so cool and nice in the garden under the trees. There she is now, coming along the beach and beckoning to me. I wonder what she wants. I think I shall have to go and see." And Belle ran quickly off, as if glad to find an excuse for getting away; and meeting the Oppenheims, she turned back with them towards the Parade.

Left alone, Isobel felt as though some great shock had passed over her. She saw only too plainly that Belle did not want to come—did not care for her society or value her friendship; and the bitterness of the knowledge seemed almost greater than she could bear. She walked slowly to the cliff, and climbing part of the way up, sat down in a sheltered nook, hidden from sight of the beach; then putting her head on her hands, she let loose the flood-gates of her grief. God help us when we first find out that those we care for no longer respond to our love. The wound may heal, but it leaves a scar, and remains one of those silent milestones of the soul to which we look back in after years as having marked an epoch in our inner lives. At the time it appears as if all our affection had been wasted; but it is not so, for the very fact of loving even an unworthy object increases our power to love, and enlarges the heart, lifting us above self, and, as bread cast upon the waters, will return to us after many days in a greater capacity for sympathy with others, and a widening of our spiritual growth.

To Isobel it seemed as if the whole world had somehow changed. She had had few companions of her own age, and this was her first essay at friendship. Those who enjoy very keenly suffer, alas! in like proportion, and hers was not a disposition to take things lightly. She stayed for a long, long time upon the cliffs, fighting a hard battle before she could get her tears under sufficient control to walk home along the shore, as she did not care to face any of the Sea Urchins with streaming eyes. Perhaps a touch of pride came to her aid. She would, at any rate, not let Belle know how greatly she cared, and when they met again she would behave as if she too were not anxious about the acquaintance. So much she felt she owed to her own self-respect, and she meant to carry it out, whatever it cost her.

"I wouldn't break my heart, darling," said Mrs. Stewart, who, seeing Isobel's red eyes, soon discovered the trouble, and offered what comfort she could. "Belle isn't worth grieving for. I was afraid of this from the first, but you were so taken with her that it seemed of no use to warn you. I don't think she was ever half what you believed her to be, and she has proved herself a very fickle friend. Never mind. We shall be going home soon, and you will have other interests to turn your thoughts. We shall see little more of her at Silversands, and the best thing we can do is to forget her as speedily as we can."

CHAPTER XVII. THE CHASE.

"Tones that I once used to know
Thrill in those accents of thine,
Eyes that I loved long ago
Gaze 'neath your lashes at mine."

EXCEPT by Isobel, Belle was scarcely missed at the desert island, where the Sea Urchins had so many interesting schemes on hand that they did not trouble to spare a thought to one who had not taken the pains to make herself a general favourite. For the last few days all the children had been absorbed in the construction of another hut upon the opposite end of the island. It was built with loose stones, after the fashion of an Irish cabin, and they intended to roof it, when it was finished, with planks covered with pieces of turf. This new building was to surpass even the old one in beauty and ingenuity. It was to consist of several rooms, and both boys and girls toiled away at it with an ardour which would have caused the ordinary British workman to open his eyes in amazement.

Isobel worked as hard as any one, carrying stones, and mixing a crumbly kind of mortar made out of sand and crushed limpets, which Charlie fondly imagined would resemble the famous cement with which mediæval castles were built, and would defy the combined effects of time and weather. Since Belle's desertion she had been much with the Chesters. Hilda, though several years younger than herself, was a dear little companion, and Charlie was a staunch friend, standing up for her when necessary against the Rokeby boys, whose teasing was sometimes apt to get beyond all bounds of endurance. On the following Friday the whole party were busy upon the shore, collecting a fresh supply of shell-fish for their architecture, when Isobel, who had left the others that she might carry her load of periwinkles to the already large heap under the rocks, spied her friend the colonel in the distance, and flinging down her basket, hurried along the beach to greet him.

"Well met, Miss Robinson Crusoe!" cried the colonel. "I was just on the point of going up the cliff to take another look at the old stone. I'm like a child with a new toy. I find I can't tear myself away from it, and I want to keep going back to read the runes again, and to see that it is safe and uninjured. Will you come with me to keep me company?"

Isobel was nothing loath—she much enjoyed a chat with the owner of the island; and they sat for a long time on a large boulder near the cross, while he wrote the runic alphabet for her on a leaf torn from his pocket-book.

"Now I should at least be able to make out the words of another inscription if I found it," she said triumphantly, "even if I didn't know what it meant. I shall copy these, and then write my name in runes inside all my books. I think they're ever so much prettier than modern letters."

"With the slight disadvantage that very few people can decipher them," laughed the colonel. "You might as well sign your autograph in Sanscrit. How fast the tide is rising! I think we should warn your playfellows that they ought to be running home. I'm always afraid lest they should be caught on these sands."

He rose as he spoke, and walked to the verge of the cliff, where he could command a view of the shore below, just in time to see the last of the children hustled by Charlotte Wright (whose sensible practical head never forgot the state of the tide) up the beach at the Silversands side of the channel, which was already beginning to fill so quickly as to render any further crossing impossible.

"Oh, look! What shall we do?" cried Isobel, in some alarm. "We're quite cut off. We can't possibly get through that deep water even if we try to wade. We shall have to stay on the island all night."

"And sleep in the hut like true pioneers?" said the colonel. "It would certainly be a new experience. No, little Miss Crusoe, I don't think we are driven to such a desperate extremity as that yet. I left my boat at the other side of the headland, and my man is only waiting my signal to row round. I will take you across with me to the Chase, and land you in safety."

Mounting to the top of the hill, he waved his handkerchief, and a small row-boat which had been anchored in the bay put off immediately in their direction.

"It's not nearly so romantic as if we had been obliged to spend a lonely night shivering in the hut," said the colonel. "We've missed rather an interesting adventure, but it's much more comfortable, after all. By-the-bye, will your mother feel anxious if she sees the other children return without you?"

"She's gone to Ferndale this afternoon to buy some more paints and drawing paper," replied Isobel. "You can't get sketching materials in Silversands. She won't be home until seven o'clock, because there isn't a train earlier. I shall have to take tea alone."

"Better have it with me," suggested her friend. "I feel I owe some return for the hospitality you exercised in the hut. I haven't forgotten the nice cup of tea you made. You must see my flowers, and I can send you home afterwards in the dog-cart."

"That *would* be nice!" cried Isobel, her joy at the prospect showing itself in her beaming face. "We saw your garden from the top of the Scar that day we went into your grounds, and I thought it looked *lovely*."

"Well, I believe I have as good a show as most people in the neighbourhood," admitted the colonel; "but you shall judge for yourself. Here we are at the landing-place. Take care! Give me your hand, and I will help you out."

The Chase appeared to have a private wooden jetty of its own, which led on to a strip of shingly beach, at the other side of which an iron gate admitted them into a small plantation of fir trees, and through a shrubbery into the garden. Isobel could not restrain a cry of pleasure at the sight of the flowers, which were now in the prime of their early autumn glory, and she did not know whether to admire more the little beds, gay with bright blossoms, which dotted the smoothly mown lawns, or the splendid herbaceous borders behind, full of dahlias, sunflowers, gladioli, hollyhocks, torch lilies, tall bell-flowers, and other beautiful plants.

"I must show you all my treasures," said the colonel, pleased with her appreciation, as he took her to the pond where the pink water-lilies grew, and the bamboo and eucalyptus were flourishing in the open air.

"You don't often find subtropical plants so far north," he explained, with a touch of pride as he pointed them out; "but this is a very sheltered situation, and we protect them with matting during the winter. You should see the irises in the spring and early summer; they are a mass of delicate colour, and thrive so well down by the water's edge."

The rock garden, with its pretty Alpine blossoms; the rosery, where the queen of flowers seemed represented by every variety, from the delicate yellow of the tea to the rich red of the damask; the fountain, where the water flowed from the pouting lips of a chubby cherub, astride on a dolphin, into a basin filled with gold and silver fish; the terraced walk, covered by a fine magnolia; and the summer-house on the wall, containing a fixed telescope through which you could look out over the sea—all were an equal delight to Isobel's wondering eyes, for she had never before been in such beautiful grounds. Nor was the kitchen-garden less of a surprise, with its peaches and apricots hanging on the red brick walls, carefully netted to preserve them from the birds; its beds of tall, feathery asparagus, and its ripe greengages and early apples. The trim neatness of the vegetable borders was enlivened by edgings of hardy annuals, and here and there a mass of sweet peas filled the air with a delicious fragrance, while in a corner stood a row of bee-hives, the buzzing occupants of which seemed busily at work among the scarlet runners. Isobel thought no enchanted palace could rival the greenhouses, gay with geraniums and fuchsias and rare plants, the names of which she did not know, or the vinery with its countless bunches of black grapes hanging from the roof. It was so particularly nice to be taken round by the owner, who could pluck the flowers and fruit as he wished, and so different from the park at home, which was her usual playground, where you might not walk on the grass, and hardly dared to admire the flowers, for fear the policeman should suspect you of wanting to touch them.

"You will be quite tired now, and hungry too, I expect," said her host, as he led the way on to a long glass-roofed veranda in front of the house, where two chairs and a round table spread for tea were awaiting them. "I must show you my horses and dogs afterwards. I have five little collie pups, which I am sure you will like to see, and a brown foal, only a fortnight old. My coachman has some fan-tail pigeons, too, and a hutch of rabbits."

It seemed very strange to Isobel to find herself sitting in the comfortable basket-chair, talking to the colonel while he poured the tea from the silver teapot into the pretty painted cups. She could scarcely believe that only three weeks ago she had trespassed in his grounds, and had almost expected him to send her to prison for the offence, while now she was chatting to him as freely as if she had known him all her life. That her holland frock was not improved by an afternoon's play on the island, that her sand shoes were the worse for wear and her sailor hat was her oldest, and that the wind had blown her long hair into elf locks, did not distress her in the least, though I fear Mrs. Stewart would hardly have considered her in visiting order. Certainly the colonel did not seem to mind, and whatever he may have thought of the appearance of his young guest, her good manners and refined accent had shown him from the first that she was the child of cultured people.

"Mother means to sketch the runic cross on Monday," volunteered Isobel, as the talk turned on the subject of the island. "She went to Ferndale to-day on purpose to buy a new block; her old one was too small, and not the right shape."

"I shall hope to see her picture," replied the colonel. "I must show you the photos of the stone, which arrived this morning. They are in my study; so, if you really won't have any more tea, we will come indoors and look at them now."

He led the way through an open French window into a large and pleasant drawing-room, which appeared so filled with beautiful cabinets of curiosities, old china, rare pictures and books, that Isobel would have liked to linger and look at them if she had dared to ask; but the colonel strode on into the panelled hall, and passing the wide staircase with its carved balustrade and its statue of Hebe, holding a lamp, at the foot, took her into a long low library at the farther side of the house. It was a cosy room. Its four windows overlooked the rose garden, and had a peep of the cliffs and the sea; a large writing-table strewn with papers stood in a recess; and various padded morocco easy-chairs seemed to invite one to sit down and read the books which almost covered the walls from floor to ceiling. Over the fine stone chimney-piece hung two portraits, the only pictures to be seen—one an enlarged photograph of a handsome young officer in a Guards uniform; the other a small oil painting of a little girl with gray eyes and straight fair hair, parted smoothly in the middle of her forehead, and tied by a ribbon under her ears.

"I only received the prints this morning," said the colonel, taking an envelope from his desk. "There are four views altogether, as you will see; but I think you will like this the best, for it shows the runes so plainly."

He held out the photo of the ancient cross, but Isobel did not notice it. She was standing with parted lips, her eyes fixed in amazement upon the two portraits over the fireplace.

"Why," she cried, in an eager voice, "that's father—my father!"

"Your father, my dear?" said the colonel, astonished in his turn. "Impossible! This is a portrait of my son."

"But it *is* father!" returned Isobel. "It's the same photo which we have at home, only larger. That's the V.C. he won in India, and his Guards uniform. And the other picture is little Aunt Isobel!"

"What do you mean?" asked the colonel hastily. "How could it be your Aunt Isobel?"

"I don't know, but it *is*!" replied Isobel. "I have a tiny painting exactly like it, done on ivory, inside a morocco case. It belonged to father, and he left it to me. She was his only sister, and she died when she was eleven years old—just the same age as I am."

For answer the colonel took Isobel by the shoulders, and holding her beneath the portrait, looked narrowly at her face. The evening sunshine, flooding through the window, fell on the fair hair, and lighted it up with the same golden gleam as that of the child in the picture above; the gray eyes of both seemed to meet him with the same half-wistful, half-trustful gaze.

"The likeness is extraordinary," he murmured. "I wonder I have never noticed it before. Is it possible I could have made so great a mistake? In what regiment was your father?"

"He was in the Fifth Dragoon Guards."

"You have told me he is dead?"

"Yes; he was killed in the Boer war."

"How long ago?"

"Six years on my birthday."

"Was it near Bloemfontein?"

"Yes, in a night skirmish. He is buried there, just where he fell."

"Had he any other relations besides yourself and your mother?"

"Only my grandfather, whom I have never seen."

"And your name?—your name?" cried the colonel, white to the lips with an emotion he could not control.

"Isobel Stewart."

CHAPTER XVIII. GOOD-BYE.

"We say it for an hour, or for years;
We say it smiling, say it choked with tears;
We say it coldly, say it with a kiss,
And yet we have no other word than this—Good-bye!"

COLONEL STEWART'S very natural mistake in confusing the namesakes, and Isobel's equal error in believing her grandfather to be Colonel Smith, were soon explained. The former, full of relief at this unexpected turn of affairs, paid a visit to Marine Terrace that same evening, and in the interview with his daughter-in-law which followed he begged her pardon frankly and freely for his prejudice and injustice.

"It seems late in life for a gray-haired old man to turn over a new leaf," he said, "but if you can overlook my misconception and neglect of you in the past, I trust we may prove firm friends in the future. And as for Isobel, she is a granddaughter after my own heart. Will you forget that miserable letter which I wrote (it was intended not for you, as I know you now, but for the mother of that other child), and show your forgiveness by coming to cheer my loneliness at the Chase? Now that we understand each other, I think we need have no fear of disagreements, and our mutual love for the one who is gone and the other who is left will make a bond of sympathy between us."

Isobel's joyful astonishment may be pictured when she discovered that her friend of the island was in very truth her own grandfather, and her happiness when she and her mother removed the next week from Marine Terrace to the Chase can scarcely be described.

"It's just like a fairy tale!" she declared. "I never thought when I sat on the top of the Scar that afternoon, looking down at the lovely house and garden, and saying what I would do if I lived there, that it could ever really come to pass. It's almost too good to be true, and I shouldn't be in the least surprised if it were only a dream after all."

It soon proved to be no dream, but a most satisfactory reality, when she saw herself installed as her grandfather's favourite companion in the very surroundings which she had so much admired. To Colonel Stewart she filled the vacant place of the little daughter he had lost in former years; and so keen was his pleasure in his newly-found grandchild, that if Isobel had not been of a thoroughly sensible nature I fear she would have run a very great risk of becoming completely spoilt. Her mother's influence and her own naturally unselfish disposition saved her from that, however, and the wholesome discipline of school life afterwards taught her to be able to take her grandfather's kindness without acquiring an undue idea of her own importance. She was very happy at the Chase, and especially delighted when Colonel Stewart made her a formal present of the desert island.

"It shall be yours, to do what you like with," he declared. "I promised to lease it to you when you found the runic cross, and I think you deserve to have it for your own. It shall be one of my presents to you on your eleventh birthday."

That happy event was to take place in the course of a few days, and to celebrate the occasion all the Sea Urchins had been invited to a garden *fête* at the Chase, as a winding up of the club before the various children left Silversands; for it was September now—governesses were returning, schools were reopening, and the holidays were over at last.

It was a lovely autumn morning when Isobel, with a bright birthday face, looked out of the open window of her pretty bedroom, to see her island shining in the early sunshine against the sea, and the shadows falling over the lawns and gardens of the beautiful spot which was now her home.

"I'm the luckiest girl in the world!" she thought, as she ran down to the breakfast table, to find her plate filled with interesting-looking packages, and the prettiest white pony waiting for her outside the front steps, with a new side-saddle, quite ready for her to learn to ride.

"I want you to be a good horsewoman," said the colonel. "I think you are plucky enough, and when you've had a little practice I hope you'll soon enjoy a canter with me across the moors. The Skye terrier I spoke of will be coming next week; I had to send to Scotland for him, so he could not arrive in time for your birthday, but you will be able to make his acquaintance later."

To have a pony of her very own had always been one of Isobel's castles in the air, and she spent the morning trying her new favourite in a state of rapture that was only equalled by her joy at receiving her friends in the afternoon. All the Sea Urchins were there, from tall Hugh Rokeby to the youngest Wright; and though they seemed somewhat shy and on their best behaviour at first, their restraint soon wore off at the sight of the splendid cricket pitch, the archery, and the other games which the colonel had prepared for them. After some hesitation it had been decided to include Belle in the invitation, and she appeared with the others dressed in one of her daintiest costumes and her most becoming hat, not in the least abashed by any remembrance of her former behaviour.

"So you're really living at this splendid place, darling!" she cried, clasping Isobel's arm close in hers, with quite her old clinging manner. "It's *ever* so much nicer than the Oppenheims', and I suppose it will all be yours some day, won't it? The pony is simply a beauty. I'm *so* delighted to come this afternoon! Somehow I haven't seemed to see very much of you lately, though I don't think it has been my fault. You always were my dearest friend, and always will be."

"I am pleased to see all my friends here to-day," replied Isobel quietly, then very gently she drew her arm away.

She knew Belle's affection now for what it was worth; the old love for her had died that day on the cliff, and however much she might regret the loss, nothing could ever bring it back to her again. Other and truer friendships might follow, but this was as utterly gone as a beautiful iridescent bubble when it has burst.

It was the first time that the Rokebys had met Colonel Stewart since they had uprooted his cherished maidenhair, and with a good deal of blushing and poking at each other they blurted out an apology for their conduct on that occasion.

"We won't speak of it," said the colonel. "You wouldn't do it again, I'm sure, nor shirk the matter afterwards. Certainly" (with a twinkle in his eye) "you vanished like the wind, and I shall expect to have a wonderful exhibition of such running capabilities on the cricket-ground. It's an excellent pitch, and if you don't make a record I shall be surprised."

With both Charlie and Hilda Chester he was more than pleased, and hoped they might be frequent visitors at the Chase if they returned to Silversands, while he extended a hearty and kindly welcome to all the young guests, who echoed Bertie Rokeby's opinion that it was "the most ripping party that ever was given."

The first half of the afternoon was devoted to cricket, which, I really believe, the colonel enjoyed as much as his visitors; it recalled his old school days, and he had many a tale to tell of matches played fifty years ago on the fields at Eton by boys who had since made their mark in life. Tea was served in the large dining-room, which looked cool with the light falling through the stained-glass window at the end on to the white marble statues which stood in recesses along the walls. It was "a real jolly tea— not one of those affairs where you get nothing but a cucumber sandwich and a square inch of cake, and have to stand about and wait on the girls!" as Bertie Rokeby ungallantly observed, but a sit-down meal of a character substantial enough to satisfy youthful appetites, and lavish in the matter of ripe fruit and cakes. Mrs. Stewart took care that Ruth and Edna Barrington, who, for a wonder, had come unattended, were well looked after, and provided with such few dainties as they permitted themselves to indulge in, being under a solemn pledge to their mother to abstain from all doubtful dishes. There were crackers, although it was not Christmas time, and a pretty box of bon-bons laid beside every plate; but I think the leading glory of the table was the birthday cake, which, according to Charlotte Wright, reminded one of a wedding or a christening, so elaborate were the designs of flowers and birds in white sugar and chocolate on its iced surface, while the letters of Isobel's name were displayed on six little flags in red, white, and blue which adorned the summit.

After tea came a variety of sports for prizes—archery, quoits, jumping, vaulting, and obstacle races, in the latter of which considerable ingenuity had been shown. It was an amusing sight to watch the boys clumsily trying to thread the requisite number of needles before they might make a start, and toilsomely sorting red and white beans in the little three-divisioned boxes supplied to them, or the girls picking up marbles and disentangling coloured ribbons with eager fingers. The potato races were voted great fun, for it was a difficult matter to run carrying a large and knobby potato balanced upon an egg spoon, and it was almost sure to be dropped just as the triumphant candidate was on the point of tipping it into the box at the end, giving the enemy an opportunity of making up arrears, and of proving the truth of the proverb that the race sometimes goes to the slow and sure instead of to the swift. Three-legged races were popular among the boys, and Bertie Rokeby and Eric Wright, with their respective right and left legs firmly tied together, against Charlie Chester and Arnold Rokeby similarly handicapped, made quite an exciting struggle, the former couple winning in the end, owing to Charlie's undue haste upsetting both himself and his partner. The jumping and vaulting were mostly appreciated by the older children, but both big and little exclaimed with delight when one of the gardeners brought out a famous "Aunt Sally," which he had been very busy making, with a turnip for her head, carved with a penknife into some representation of a human face, over which reposed an ancient bonnet, a shawl being wrapped round her shoulders, and a large pipe placed between her simpering lips. She was tied securely to the top of a post, and the children threw sticks at her, the game being to see who could first knock the pipe from her mouth, a feat which proved to be more difficult than they had at first supposed, and which caused much merriment, the prize being won in the end by Letty Rokeby, whose aim was as true as that of any of the boys.

The sun had set, and the September twilight was just beginning to deepen into dark, when the young guests were arranged in rows on the terrace steps to witness the final treat—an exhibition of fireworks, which the colonel had sent a special telegram to London to obtain in time. It was a very pretty display of Catherine wheels, Roman candles, rockets, and golden rain, finishing with the Royal Arms in crimson fire; and it made such a splendid close to the day that twenty pairs of hands clapped loudly, and twenty voices joined in ringing cheers, as the little red stars winked themselves out into the darkness. The party was at an end, and an omnibus was in waiting to drive the visitors, all unwilling to go, back to their lodgings at Silversands. Isobel kissed Belle with a feeling that it was a last farewell; their ways for the future lay apart; they had different ideals and different hopes in life. Alike in name, they had been so unlike in character as to render any true friendship impossible, though their chance meeting had been fraught with such unforeseen consequences. It was little more than six weeks since Isobel had first arrived at Silversands, yet so much seemed to have happened in the time that, as she stood upon the steps holding her grandfather's hand, she could scarcely realize the strange things which had come to pass.

"Good-bye! good-bye!" sounded on all sides, as the reluctant Sea Urchins at length took their departure. To-morrow most of them would be scattered to their own homes, and the club would be a thing of the past.

"I shall never forget any of you, never!" said Isobel. "We've had glorious fun together, and it's been the very jolliest holiday I ever remember in my life. I can't tell you how much I've enjoyed your coming here to-day, and I wish every one of you as happy a birthday as mine. Good-bye!"

THE END

BOOK SIX.
THE MANOR HOUSE SCHOOL

CHAPTER I. NORA'S NEWS

It was the first week of the summer term at Winterburn Lodge. Afternoon preparation was over, and most of the girls had left the classroom for a chat and a stroll round the playground until the tea-bell should ring. From the tennis court came the sounds of the soft thud of balls and a few excited voices recording the score; while through the open windows of the house floated the strains of three pianos, on which three separate pieces were being practised in three different keys, the mingled result forming a particularly inharmonious jangle.

On a bench in the corner by the swing two yellow heads and a brown one might be seen bent in close proximity over a rather dilapidated atlas. Their respective owners were apparently making a half-hearted endeavour to hunt out a list of towns upon the map of England, and were amusing themselves between whiles with the pleasant, though somewhat unprofitable pastime of grumbling.

"I hate geography!" declared Lindsay Hepburn. "If we could be taken a picnic to each of the places, there'd be some sense in it; but to have to reel off a string of tiresome names that don't mean anything at all to you—I call it stupid!"

"It's such a fearfully long lesson, too!" agreed Cicely Chalmers dolefully. "Miss Frazer might have set us a shorter one for the first! It's really too bad of her to make us begin with two pages and a half in a new book! I'm sure I shall never get it into my head, if I try till midnight."

"I wonder why things always seem so much harder to learn when one's just come back after the holidays?" propounded Marjorie Butler with a melancholy yawn.

"I don't know. I suppose because it all feels so horrid. It's perfectly dreadful to think what a huge time it is until we can go home again."

"Thirteen whole weeks! And every one of them will be exactly the same: lessons with Miss Frazer or Mademoiselle, an hour's practising, a walk in the park or along the Surrey Road, and a game of tennis when you can manage to get hold of the court. There's never anything different, unless Miss Russell takes us to a museum or a concert, and that doesn't happen often, worse luck!"

Lindsay's picture of the forthcoming term certainly did not seem a remarkably enlivening one, and the other two groaned at the prospect.

"I wish one wasn't obliged to go to a boarding school," said Cicely in an injured tone.

"Girls! Girls!" cried a fourth voice, breaking abruptly into the conversation, "I've been hunting for you everywhere. I thought you were in the house or the gymnasium. Oh! I've such a piece of news to tell you!"

"What's the matter, Nora?" enquired Marjorie, for the newcomer was out of breath, and looked as excited as if it were breaking-up day.

"Come here and sit between us," added Lindsay, pushing the others farther along the seat to make room.

"Is it anything really nice?" asked Cicely.

"It depends on what you call 'nice'. I'll give you each six guesses, and even then I don't believe one of you'll be right."

"Miss Frazer doesn't mean to take geography to-morrow?"

"Absolutely wrong, though I wish she wouldn't."

"Somebody has broken another window with a tennis ball?"

"Don't be silly! It's much more interesting than that."

"Miss Russell's going to give us a holiday?"

"You're getting warm! Try again."

"Oh, we can't!"

"We give it up!"

"Go on and tell!"

"Do you remember that just before Easter a gentleman came with Dr. Redford, and they both went over the school, peeping and poking about in such a mysterious manner?"

"Yes, we wondered what they were doing."

"Well, it turns out that he's a sanitary inspector, and he's sent a report to Miss Russell to say that the drains are wrong, and must be taken up immediately."

"Is that your grand news?"

"No, it's only the first part of it. Let me finish, and then you'll see. Dr. Redford says the drains can't possibly be touched while we're all in the house, and yet they must be opened at once. Can't you guess now?"

"Miss Russell never means to send us home when we've only just come back?" gasped Lindsay hopefully.

"No, not that, though it's nearly as jolly. She's taken a beautiful old manor house in the country, and it's to be our school for the whole of the summer term. We're to go there in a body—girls, and teachers, and servants, and everyone."

If Nora had hoped to astonish her companions she had certainly succeeded. They were wild with curiosity, and fired off questions all three together.

"Where is it?"

"When are we going?"

"How did you get to know?"

"One at a time, please," said Nora, enjoying her importance. "I met Mildred Roper in the hall just now. Miss Russell has been explaining it to the monitresses, and said they might tell us as soon as they liked. It's a lovely Elizabethan house, at a place called Haversleigh, a long way from here. We're to start next Tuesday."

Such a tremendous event as the removal of the school from town to country was without precedent in the annals of Winterburn Lodge.

"It's almost too good to be true," cried Cicely rapturously.

"It will be like the last day and setting off for the seaside both together," declared Lindsay, waltzing round the seat in the exuberance of her spirits.

"Not quite, because we shall have lessons when we get there," corrected Nora.

"Well, at any rate it'll be ever so much nicer than being in London."

"Hurrah for the old Manor!" shouted Marjorie Butler, clapping her hands.

Miss Russell had indeed been much alarmed by the sanitary inspector's report. She was determined to make the change without delay, and hurried on the preparation as speedily as possible.

Boxes were brought down from the attic, and teachers and monitresses were kept busy superintending the packing of clothes, linen, schoolbooks, and numberless other articles. For the few days that remained work was relaxed, the headmistress's chief anxiety seeming to be the health of the girls, and her one object to take them away before any sign of illness should break out amongst them.

"Miss Russell looked so worried when I told her my head ached," said Nora Proctor. "She asked every one of us afterwards if we had sore throats."

"I was silly enough to say I thought mine felt a little scrapy," said Lindsay ruefully. "I soon wished I hadn't, because she gave me a horribly nasty disinfectant lozenge, and told me to suck it slowly until I'd finished it. Ugh! I can taste it yet!"

"I'm absolutely sick of the smell of carbolic. There's a jar full in every room," said Cicely.

"Never mind! You'll only have to endure it for one day more. We're actually off to-morrow."

Those in authority might certainly be excused if they looked worried, for it was no light task to accomplish so much in such a short space of time. By Tuesday morning, however, the final arrangements were completed; the rows of boxes were locked, strapped, and piled on railway carts; while the girls, an excited, chattering crew, were ready and waiting for the omnibuses which were to take them to the station.

"Good-bye to poor old Winterburn Lodge!" said Cicely, giving a last peep into the familiar classroom. "We shan't see these maps and desks again until next September."

"I wonder how many things will have happened before we come back here?" said Lindsay thoughtfully.

It was a long journey into Somerset, but Miss Russell had engaged saloon carriages, and taken large baskets of lunch; so, in the opinion of her thirty pupils at least, the expedition felt like a picnic.

"How I wish we could go every year, or that Miss Russell would remove into the country altogether," said Beryl Austen, who had secured a corner seat, and was in raptures over the view.

"Then it wouldn't be town, and we shouldn't be able to have visiting masters," said Mildred Roper, one of the monitresses.

"Who wants them? I'm sure I should be only too delighted never to see any of them again!"

Mildred smiled.

"I suppose, after all, we're sent to school to learn something," she remarked dryly. "I'm afraid you'll find Miss Frazer will give you plenty of work to make up for the loss of Herr Hoffmann and Monsieur Guizet."

"I don't care a scrap, so long as there's fun when lessons are over. We're going to have a glorious time, and I mean to thoroughly enjoy myself."

Beryl only expressed the sentiments of the rest of the girls, most of whom regarded the coming term in the light of a holiday. As the train steamed through green meadows and woods just breaking into leaf, it indeed seemed as if London and professors had been effectually left behind, and their spirits rose higher with every mile.

By afternoon they were all impatience to arrive. For fully an hour before they reached their destination they kept enquiring whether they must get out at the next station, and were sure that each ancient house visible from the carriage windows could not fail to be the Manor.

"Here we are at last!" announced Miss Russell, when, after many false alarms, the welcome word "Haversleigh" made its appearance in plain letters, and a porter's voice was heard pronouncing something which bore a faint resemblance to the name. "Steady, girls! Steady! Remember each is to take her own bag, and file out in proper order. Nobody is to move until I say 'March!'"

Miss Russell first held a review on the platform, to make sure that none of her pupils or their belongings had gone astray.

"I am quite relieved we have all arrived safely," she said. "I think we may congratulate ourselves that not even an umbrella is missing. It is only half a mile from here to the house, quite an easy walk, so we will start at once, and leave our luggage to follow."

In a few minutes more they had passed the ticket collector, and found themselves on the leafy high road. It seemed as different from London as a fairy tale from a Latin grammar. There had been a slight shower of rain, which had brought out the scent of growing grass and budding leaves; the ground was white with the fallen blossom of blackthorn hedges; and a thrush, seated on the summit of an apple tree, was pouring forth a volume of song that sounded almost like a welcome to the country.

With so many new sights to gaze at, it was difficult to walk primly two and two, and the line proved a straggling one, in spite of Miss Frazer's efforts in the rear. At a pair of great iron gates Miss Russell stopped and turned to her girls.

"This is our first glimpse of the Manor," she said, with a touch of pride in her voice. "I want you to take a good look at your new school."

It was nicer even than they had expected—a glorious old place, built partly in Tudor fashion of grey stone, and partly of black and white timbers. There were latticed windows, and a porch ornamented with stone balls, and curious twisted chimneys, and picturesque gables at odd angles.

"It's like a house out of one of Sir Walter Scott's novels," said Marjorie Butler.

"It looks as if one might have all kinds of adventures there," added Lindsay Hepburn gleefully.

The inside proved just as satisfactory as the outside. It was delightful to sit down to tea in a great dining-hall, with a carved roof, and walls hung with spears, shields, and stags' antlers.

"I feel we oughtn't to be drinking tea," said Cicely Chalmers. "I'm sure they didn't have it in Queen Elizabeth's times. It was tankards of ale or mead in those days."

"Don't finish your cup, then, if you wish to imagine yourself entirely in the past," said Mildred Roper. "I'm afraid you'll have to leave the marmalade too. That's quite a modern invention, and so are the Bath buns."

"Don't be horrid!" said Cicely. "It really is an old-fashioned place. Lindsay and I have got the quaintest panelled bedroom you could possibly imagine. There's a great four-post bed, with yellow brocaded curtains; it's big enough to hold six, instead of only two."

"And there's a lovely library, and a picture gallery, and ever so many queer rooms and long passages upstairs," put in Nora Proctor. "I got quite lost, and couldn't find my way down at first."

"So did I," said Beryl Austen. "I tried to explore a little, but it looked so dim and dark I didn't dare to go alone, so I turned back. I thought I might meet a Cavalier or a Roundhead on the landing!"

Beryl was not the only one to whom their new quarters seemed rather weird and strange on this first evening of their arrival. After being accustomed to electric light and modern bedrooms, it was a great change to walk upstairs with candles to antique chambers that might have belonged to the Middle Ages.

"Don't be silly, girls!" exclaimed Miss Russell indignantly, as they scurried past the suits of armour in the picture gallery. "I shall not allow any absurd nonsense of this kind. You have no more to be afraid of here than you had at Winterburn Lodge. I will take you over the house to-morrow and show you everything, and when you study the real history of the place you won't want to concern yourselves with silly superstitions."

Though the old Manor might look ghostly by night, it wore a bright and cheerful aspect in the sunshine of next morning, and not even the most ardent of Cockneys would have wished herself back among streets and squares. It certainly seemed more interesting to learn lessons sitting on tall-backed oak chairs at a carved table, than at desks in an ordinary schoolroom, furnished with maps and blackboard. The teachers enjoyed it as much as the girls, and everybody had a delightfully romantic feeling of being transferred to the reign of Queen Elizabeth.

"We oughtn't to have science, or physiology, or anything up-to-date here," said Cicely, as, in company with the rest of the third form, she took possession of the panelled parlour that was to be their temporary classroom.

"No, indeed," said Lindsay. "Girls in those days didn't have half our work."

"You forget Lady Jane Grey," said Miss Frazer. "In the matter of knowledge she would easily have put you to shame. If you want her sixteenth-century studies you will have to begin Greek as well as Latin, French, Italian, and some Hebrew and Arabic!"

"Oh, dear!" exclaimed Lindsay, aghast at such a list of accomplishments. "I'd rather stick to our own century."

"I thought ladies did nothing but go hunting and hawking then," said Marjorie Butler. "Did they all know Greek and Latin?"

"Probably not, but they could make preserves, and perfumes, and other secrets of the still-room; and they embroidered the most beautiful tapestries, if we are to judge from the specimens in the big drawing-room. Young people were very severely brought up. They might never sit without permission in the presence of their parents orteachers, and they were beaten for the slightest offences. Don't you remember that even poor Lady Jane Grey was punished with 'nips, bobs, and pinches'; and little Edward VI had his whipping-boy, to receive the blows which it was not considered seemly to bestow upon his own princely person!"

"Had the other boy to be whipped for what the king had done? How horribly unfair!" said Beryl Austen.

"Yes, their ideas of justice were rather different from ours. They would have thought present-day children absolutely spoilt. The girls who perhaps may have done lessons in this room three hundred years ago would not learn them so easily and pleasantly as you are going to do this morning. Fetch the geology books, Beryl. We must go on with modern work, in spite of our ancient surroundings."

CHAPTER II. AN INTERESTING STRANGER

Among all Miss Russell's thirty pupils you could not have found two stancher friends than Lindsay Hepburn and Cicely Chalmers, both of whom were members of the third, or lowest, class.

Lindsay was a short, plump, fair, jolly-looking girl of twelve, with a very energetic disposition; apt, according to Miss Frazer, to be inconveniently lively and irrepressible in school, but a general favourite in the playground.

Cicely, six months younger, was much more quiet and steady on the surface, though her twinkling brown eyes belied her demurer manners, and proclaimed her ready for anything in the shape of fun. She admired Lindsay immensely, and copied her absolutely, being generally ready to follow her through thick and thin, whatever scrapes might be the consequence.

The pair shared a bedroom, and were so inseparable that Cicely was often called Lindsay's shadow. That was an injustice, however; she had a character of her own, though she might choose to merge it in her friend's stronger personality. It is with these two, and their strange experiences at the Manor, that my tale is chiefly concerned, for if it had not been for Lindsay's enquiring mind, backed by Cicely's persistent efforts, there might have been no story to tell.

This is how it all began.

On the second morning after their instalment at Haversleigh the whole school was assembled ready for a history class in the big dining-hall. Miss Russell, for a wonder, was late, and when she entered at last she brought with her a new pupil. The stranger was about sixteen, a pretty, graceful girl, with hazel eyes, long chestnut hair, and a rather distinguished air. She was given a seat in the first form, and replied to the few questions asked her in a quiet voice; then, at the close of the lecture, she took her books and went away alone, without waiting to join in the next lesson.

Naturally her sudden appearance and departure excited much curiosity. The moment work was over, Lindsay and Cicely seized upon

Kathleen Crawford, who was rather a friend of theirs among the monitresses.

"Who's the new girl?" they asked. "We hadn't heard anybody was coming."

"She's only a day pupil for a few classes," answered Kathleen. "Her name's Monica Courtenay. She lives here, but of course not just now."

"What do you mean?" enquired Cicely.

"Why, surely you knew Miss Russell has taken the Manor for the summer from Mrs. Courtenay?"

"I never thought about whom it belonged to," confessed Lindsay.

"Well, at any rate, Mrs. Courtenay and Monica are staying in rooms in the village while their house is let, and Monica is to come three times a week for French and history."

"So this is really her home?"

"Yes, and I heard someone say it is all her own. She's an only child, and her father is dead."

"It must seem funny for her to see a whole school here!"

"I expect it does. I shouldn't like it if the place were mine."

"Is she nice?"

"How can I tell? I saw no more of her than you did yourselves."

Everybody was greatly interested in the newcomer, and ready, at the end of a week's acquaintance, to decide heartily in her favour. Monica was rather dignified and reserved in her manners, and evidently not much accustomed to mix with companions of her own age; but when her shyness began to wear off she proved most attractive.

"She's not at all conceited, although she's mistress of the Manor," said Lindsay.

"No, I can't say she gives herself airs in the least," agreed Cicely.

"I think she behaves beautifully," said Mildred Roper. "She never so much as hints that it's her own house, or tries to take the lead, as some girls would certainly have done. She doesn't go anywhere without leave, nor even stop to play tennis unless she's asked. I heard her apologizing to Miss Russell yesterday for giving an order to the gardener. Mademoiselle says she is 'bien elevée' and 'très gentille', and that's a great compliment, for she doesn't admire English girls as a rule."

"No one could help liking Monica," said Kathleen Crawford. "She's charming. I call her one of the nicest girls I've ever met. And she's had such hard luck! I've just been hearing all about her from Irene Spencer."

"How does Irene know?" asked Lindsay.

"She stays sometimes with an uncle who is vicar of the next parish, and her cousins are friends of Monica's. It's a most extraordinary story—it might have come out of a book."

"Oh, do tell us!" said the others eagerly.

Kathleen's tale was in scraps, and missed out several points of which she was not aware at the time, so it will be better to set it down here as the girls learnt it more fully afterwards, for it was of great importance, and formed the basis of much that was to follow.

The Courtenays, it appeared, were a very ancient family, and had inherited the Manor from an ancestor who had fought bravely on the Yorkist side in the days of the Wars of the Roses. In the present generation there was no male heir, and Monica was the last of her race.

Until a few years ago the old house had been in the possession of her great-uncle, Sir Giles Courtenay, a most eccentric man, so odd and peculiar, indeed, that many people had considered him to be out of his mind. He was reputed to be extremely wealthy, yet lived in a miserly fashion, entertaining no visitors, and never spending a penny which it was possible for him to save. He never married, but passed his days as a recluse, shut up among the books in his library, seeing only a few old servants whose services he had retained. Sometimes in the early morning he would wander about the woods and fields in the neighbourhood, seeking for wild flowers, but on such occasions he seemed much annoyed if spoken to, and evidently preferred to take his rambles unnoticed.

At his death he left everything to his great-niece, Monica.

"Both the Manor", so ran the will, "and all that it may contain, especially commending to her the volumes in my library, and advising her to pursue the study of botany, which has ever been a solace and a distraction to me amidst the various ills and disappointments of life."

At first it was supposed that Monica must be a great heiress, but when Sir Giles's legacy came to be investigated nothing could be found beyond the ordinary furniture in the house and a few pounds in the local bank. No one knew anything about his affairs, and neither papers nor documents were forthcoming to give the slightest indication as to what had become of the fortune he was known to have inherited.

Not only was all trace of the money lost, but the valuable silver plate and jewellery that had been handed down from generation to generation of the Courtenays were also missing, and there was no clue to their whereabouts. It was generally believed that Sir Giles must have concealed the whole of his wealth somewhere in the old house, but, though a minute search had been made from cellar to garret, the hiding-place had not yet come to light.

Instead, therefore, of owning a fortune, Monica had received nothing but the Manor, in itself a very barren heritage. She and her mother had taken up their residence there, but they possessed only a small income, quite insufficient to maintain the former traditions of the family. It was on this account that they had been glad to let the house to Miss Russell for the summer, and to retire themselves into quiet lodgings close by.

"Hasn't Monica ever tried to hunt for the treasure?" asked Lindsay, when Kathleen had finished her narrative.

"Oh, yes—often! I believe she has gone systematically through each room, but it's so well hidden that it seems quite impossible to find it."

"Yet it must be there!"

"No doubt. It may never turn up, though, until the place is pulled down. The whole thing is a complete mystery, and so far nobody has been able to solve it."

"Have you asked Monica where she has looked?"

"Certainly not. Irene says she's very sensitive about it, and can't bear to hear it spoken of. Naturally it must have been a most terrible disappointment. I don't wonder she avoids the subject. Please be careful never to mention it to her, or you'll offend her dreadfully, and I shall be sorry I told you."

"I'm sure both Lindsay and Cicely would have too nice feeling to question Monica on such a personal matter," said Mildred Roper.

"Of course we shan't say anything—we wouldn't for worlds," promised the two younger girls.

That Monica should be the heroine of so romantic a story made her doubly interesting in the eyes of Lindsay and Cicely. They were much impressed by Kathleen's account, and retired to the privacy of the summer-house to talk it over together.

"It must be dreadful to be so poor when you know you ought to be so rich!" said Lindsay.

"And so tantalizing, when perhaps the fortune is actually in the house," said Cicely.

"I could never be happy for thinking about it."

"No more could I."

"Look here! Why shouldn't you and I set to work? So long as this treasure is hidden away somewhere, I suppose it's possible to find it."

"Oh, don't I wish we could!" cried Cicely, her eyes round at the idea.

"Well, I can't see why we shouldn't have as good a chance as anybody else. I expect it's chiefly a matter of careful hunting."

"How splendid it would be if Monica really turned out an heiress after all!"

"Glorious! It's worth trying for. Those panelled walls might be full of hiding-places. We don't know what we may discover when once we begin."

"We shan't have to let Miss Frazer catch us looking about."

"Rather not! Nobody must know what we intend to do."

"Not even Marjorie Butler?" pleaded Cicely.

"No," said Lindsay firmly. "Marjorie couldn't help whispering it to Nora, and then it would be all over the school. The big girls would make dreadful fun of us, I'm sure. They'd call us 'The Gold Seekers', or some other stupid name, simply for the sake of teasing. Besides, if it were talked about among the rest, it would be sure to get to Monica's ears, and we particularly don't want that."

"No, she mustn't hear a word of it."

"Very well, then, we had better keep it to ourselves. Will you promise faithfully that it shall be a dead secret just between you and me?"

"Absolutely dead!" agreed Cicely.

The two girls were determined to institute a thorough search for the lost legacy, but they foresaw many difficulties in the way. In the first place, it was hard even to make a start without letting anybody suspect what they were doing. Although the term at the Manor seemed like a holiday, it was nevertheless school: there was a certain amount of supervision by the mistresses, and there were rules and regulations to be obeyed, the same as at Winterburn Lodge. The girls were not allowed to wander about alone exactly when and where they wished, and even during recreation time they were expected to play games in the garden.

One of the greatest hindrances to their plan was Mrs. Wilson, an elderly servant who had been left in charge by Mrs. Courtenay, and who seemed to consider herself responsible for her mistress's property. She evidently much resented the presence of thirty schoolgirls in the Manor, and kept a keen eye upon them to see that they did no damage. She was continually watching to satisfy herself that they were not scratching the furniture, nor spilling candle-grease upon the stairs; and was loud in her complaints to Miss Russell over the most absurd trifles.

If she had had sufficient authority, I believe she would have limited the girls entirely to their bedrooms and schoolrooms, but as that was impossible, she did her best to frighten them away from the rest of the house by being as disagreeable as she could. As a natural consequence they detested her. They nicknamed her "The Griffin", and took a naughty pleasure in defying her as far as they dared.

"She's as sour as a green gooseberry!" grumbled Effie Hargreaves. "If we only take a stroll along the portrait gallery, she thinks we're going to knock down the armour, or poke our fingers through the pictures."

"Yes, she seems to imagine we can't look at a thing without breaking it. It's perfectly ridiculous!" declared Beryl Austen.

"She's an absolute nuisance. It's a pity she was left behind," said Nora Proctor; and that was the general verdict in the old housekeeper's disfavour.

With such a dragon continually on the alert, it was almost impossible for Lindsay and Cicely to find the slightest opportunity of beginning their treasure hunt, and they were reduced to very low spirits on the subject. One half-holiday afternoon, however, Lindsay reported that Mrs. Wilson, dressed in black bonnet and mantle, had been seen to leave the back door and walk away in the direction of the village.

"Now is our chance!" she assured Cicely. "Miss Russell is lying down in her bedroom with a bad headache, Miss Frazer is playing tennis, and Mademoiselle is sitting reading in the arbour. Everyone else is in the garden, and if we run indoors at once nobody will notice, and we shall have the place practically to ourselves."

Could anything have been more fortunate? They lost no time in hurrying into the Manor, feeling almost as desperate conspirators as Guy Fawkes and his confederates; and commenced immediately to make a careful tour of investigation. They stole round the hall, the dining-room, and the library, scrutinizing every nook and corner, tapping the panels to hear if they sounded hollow, and peeping up the old wide chimneys, but all with no success.

"I'm afraid we shan't find anything down here," said Lindsay at last. "I expect people made hiding-places where they wouldn't be so easy to get at. Let us go and explore the attics. We've never been up there yet."

They reached the top storey without encountering even a servant. Somehow it felt a little eerie to hear nothing but the echo of their own footsteps, and to find themselves quite alone in such an out-of-the-way part of the house. The Manor was very large, and nearly the whole of the left wing was unoccupied. They passed door after door, all leading to more and more empty rooms, till Lindsay began to grow almost dismayed at the bigness of their undertaking.

"I didn't know the place was so huge!" she sighed. "I'm afraid one might spend years looking round and examining it thoroughly. I don't wonder Monica lost heart. There isn't the faintest clue to go upon, either, to give one a hint where to hunt."

"Hadn't we better be turning back?"

Cicely was growing rather tired of the fruitless attempt.

"In a minute. Let us go to the end of this landing."

The passage in itself was like the others, but it differed in one particular, for it terminated in a narrow, winding staircase. This looked tempting—just the sort of thing, in fact, that they felt ought to lead to somewhere interesting and important.

"It's like the way to the turret chamber where Sir Walter was imprisoned, in *Tales of the Middle Ages*," said Lindsay.

"Or where Katherine was dragged when Sir Gilbert found she had overheard the secret plot," said Cicely.

They scrambled almost on hands and knees up sixteen steep steps. At the top was a small landing, and exactly facing them, up three steps more, stood a closed door. The girls paused for a moment to consider what to do next.

"Listen!" said Cicely suddenly. "I thought I heard a queer noise."

There certainly was a most extraordinary sound issuing from the room opposite. It resembled somebody groaning, or giving long-drawn, sighing breaths. It went on for a few moments and then stopped, then commenced louder than before, and finally died away altogether.

"What is it?" whispered Cicely, rather nervously.

"I don't know, but I'm going to look and see."

"Oh! Dare you? I hope it's nothing that will bounce out!"

"Nonsense! Why should it?"

"It might. Do be careful!"

"Don't be silly!" said Lindsay. "We came up here on purpose to discover things, and help Monica. If there's a noise in that room, we certainly ought to find out what's making it."

And with this plausible excuse for satisfying her curiosity, she opened the door cautiously, and peeped inside.

CHAPTER III. A STRONG SUSPICION

If Lindsay and Cicely had counted upon finding something interesting behind the closed door, they were much disappointed. The room was absolutely bare and unfurnished. It was not panelled, as mysterious rooms ought to be, but had an old-fashioned and rather ugly wallpaper, adorned with big bunches of grapes and flowers; and there was a plain, whitewashed ceiling. At one side a window overlooked the garden, and at the other was a shallow store cupboard, the open door of which revealed rows of empty shelves, probably intended for jam or linen.

There was nothing to give the least suggestion of romance, or the possibility of any concealed hiding-place. There was no carved overmantel nor four-post bed; in fact, the only article of any description to be seen was a large horn lantern that hung from a hook in the ceiling. The curious noise had ceased, and although the girls looked round most carefully, they were not able to find anything which would account for it.

"There isn't a corner that even a cat might hide in," said Lindsay. "It was so loud, too! I can't understand it in the least."

"I call it rather uncanny. Let us go!" said Cicely.

She was stepping down on to the little landing again, when, to her dismay, she almost ran into the arms of Mrs. Wilson, who, still in black bonnet and mantle, had returned from the village sooner than they anticipated, and must have come unheard up the winding staircase.

"The Griffin's" surprise at seeing them seemed as great as their own. She gave a gasp of consternation, peeped hastily inside the empty room, then turned to Lindsay and Cicely with a look of mingled relief and wrath.

"What were you doing in the lantern room?" she asked sharply. "You know perfectly well you've no right to be up here. You must mind your own business, and keep to your own places, instead of poking and ferreting about into matters that don't concern you. I can't have you rambling about wherever you please, and the sooner you understand that the better. It was sorely against my advice that the Manor was let for a school!"

She spoke rudely, and seemed more upset and annoyed than the occasion warranted. She swept the two girls downstairs before her, muttering angrily as she went, and did not let them out of her sight until she had watched them safely into the garden.

"How horrid she was!" exclaimed Cicely, when they were alone, and able to talk things over. "Miss Russell never said we weren't to go on to that top landing."

"What was Mrs. Wilson doing there herself—in an empty room, in such a deserted part of the house?" asked Lindsay meditatively.

"I don't know. She looked quite aghast at seeing us."

"I believe there's something about it we don't understand. Perhaps she has some reason beyond mere fussiness and nastiness for wanting to keep us away from that particular room."

"What kind of a reason?"

"Well, suppose she had discovered the hiding-place?"

"Wouldn't she tell Monica?"

"She might intend to take some of the money."

"Oh, how dreadful! It's quite possible, though, that she knows where it is. She was housekeeper to old Sir Giles for ever so many years."

"It seems to me most suspicious," said Lindsay. "We must watch her, and find out everything we can, for Monica's sake."

The idea that Mrs. Wilson was concealing the treasure for her own ends was a thrilling one. The more they thought about it, the more probable it appeared. Who had a better opportunity than she of searching the old house? She might even have been present when her eccentric master stowed his fortune so carefully away. If this were really the case, the greatest caution was necessary, for to allow "The Griffin" to see that they had noticed anything might entirely spoil their plans.

"We must treat her just as usual," said Lindsay, "only we must keep our eyes and ears open, in case something should turn up to give us a hint."

For the next few days they behaved with what they considered the greatest diplomacy. They took care not to aggravate Mrs. Wilson, nor in any way to attract her special attention; but they looked out for the slightest chance of following her movements, dodging round corners, and stalking her along passages with the zeal of detectives. Unfortunately their efforts were not so unobserved as they supposed, and drew down a reproof from headquarters.

"Lindsay and Cicely! how is it that you are continually loitering about the landing when you ought to be in the garden?" said Miss Russell. "I shall have to make a new rule, that nobody is to come upstairs until ten minutes before meals. In this lovely weather I expect you to be out-of-doors. It is a shame to waste a minute in the house. Don't let me find you here again during recreation time."

This was a blow, as it brought the great scheme temporarily to a standstill. The girls could not venture to disobey openly, and judged it wiser to let things rest for the present, until the mistress should have forgotten the matter, and they might once more quietly begin to renew their investigations.

"We'll play cricket hard, and put our names down for the tennis handicap," said Lindsay. "We mustn't on any account let Miss Russell think we'd a special motive in what we were doing."

"Rather not! We'll 'lie low and say nuffin", like Brer Rabbit," agreed Cicely.

There was no lack of liveliness or occupation at the Manor to justify anybody in idling about the passages, and there were certainly many small excitements, apart from mysterious chambers or hidden treasures. All kinds of funny events kept occurring which had never disturbed the prim atmosphere of Winterburn Lodge.

Nora Proctor and Marjorie Butler awoke half the school one night by loud and repeated screams, and when Miss Frazer rushed into their room, imagining fire or burglars, she found them cowering behind the bed curtains, in mortal terror of a large bat that had made its way through the open casement. Earwigs were a constant nuisance, and everyone grew almost accustomed to catching green caterpillars, which crept in from the roses that surrounded the windows, and would turn up in the most undesirable spots.

Naturally so old a house was infested with rats and mice. They scuttled inside the walls, and squeaked behind the wainscots, and seemed to hold carnival at the back of the oak panelling, often disturbing the girls at night with the noise. This was particularly noticeable in the room where Lindsay and Cicely slept. They were sometimes awakened by sounds like the rolling of barrels overhead, as if heavy objects were being clanked about up in the ceiling.

"You've no need to be afraid of them," said Mrs. Wilson, who made light of all complaints, "they never venture out of the walls, to my knowledge."

The fear, however, that a rat might possibly gnaw its way into her bedroom afflicted Cicely continually.

"If it ran across my pillow I should die of fright, I know I should!" she wailed. "I wish Mrs. Wilson would let us have the cat to sleep with us. I should feel far safer."

"I wish we could send for the Pied Piper, and get rid of them all. They woke me twice last night," said Lindsay.

Poor Cicely never dared to retire without first having a thorough examination to assure herself that no lurking rodent was lying hidden behind the wardrobe, or in any other obscure corner. One evening she was making her usual round, armed with a tennis racket for protection, and was peeping under the bed, when she suddenly let the valance fall hurriedly, and drew back with a shriek.

"There's a rat there! I saw it quite plainly; its great big eyes were glaring at me!" she announced in a trembling voice.

"What are we to do?" exclaimed Lindsay, in equal consternation.

"Call for Miss Frazer this instant. She hasn't gone downstairs yet."

"Don't disturb it on any account!" decreed Miss Russell, who was fetched from the drawing-room to cope with the emergency. "I shall send at once for Scott, the gardener, and ask him to bring his terrier dog. We must really take some measures to destroy these pests."

It was not very long before Scott arrived. He clumped solemnly up the stairs with a thick stick in his hand, and Bill, his sharp little fox terrier, at his heels. Mrs. Wilson accompanied him, bearing the kitchen poker; and the parlour-maid followed, holding the yard dog by the collar, in case Bill should miss his prey. Miss Frazer and Miss Humphreys were there to support Miss Russell; while Mademoiselle and a great many of the girls hovered outside in the passage, half-frightened and half-excited over the coming fray.

"If you'll please to tell me where the young lady saw it, mum," said Scott, "I'll let Bill on it sudden. He's death on rats."

"It was just at the foot of the bed," quavered Cicely. Scott stooped, and raised the valance with the greatest precaution. Bill sniffed eagerly, but he did not pounce upon any concealed victim.

"There's nothing there, mum—leastways no rat," said Scott, straightening his back.

"Are you sure?" gasped Miss Russell. "It couldn't possibly have escaped."

"I think it's been a little mistake of the young lady's, mum," said Scott, suppressing a grin. "If you'll kindly take a look under the bed, you'll see for yourself."

Miss Russell hastened to comply, and, bending down, gave an exclamation as she drew out one of Lindsay's best Sunday gloves.

"What an extraordinary illusion!" she cried. "I don't wonder Cicely took it for a rat. The soft doeskin is exactly the same colour, and the buttons were gleaming just like two bright eyes. I never saw a more perfect resemblance. I should certainly have been deceived. Well, I'm glad our chase has been a case of much ado about nothing. I think you may go to bed with easy minds to-night, girls. If we have any more alarms, we must send for Bill to protect us. Good dog! Can you find some scraps for him in the kitchen, Mrs. Wilson?"

Cicely's rat was of course a great joke in the school, and a subject of teasing for several days afterwards.

"You'll imagine your dressing-gown is a tiger next," said Effie Hargreaves.

"Some people scream at nothing. I'd have been sure about it first, before making such a fuss," said Beryl Austen.

"She thought it was a wily rat, and watched to see it move,

She looked again, and saw that it was nothing but a glove!"

improvised Nora Proctor, who was fond of *Alice*, and had rather a taste for parody.

"It was such a disappointment to us, when we were waiting to hear the scuffle," said Marjorie Butler.

"We shan't believe in your scares next time," said Effie.

"It's all very well, but I'm sure you'd have been just as frightened yourselves," retorted Cicely. "You've no need to make so much fun of me."

"It's too bad. I vote we pay them out, and have the laugh on our side," sympathized Lindsay, leading her friend away. "I've thought of such a capital idea. Come to the summer-house and we'll talk it over."

As the result of Lindsay's cogitations, the two girls went boldly to Mrs. Wilson, and begged an old cardboard box.

"It's half to pieces," said "The Griffin", quite amiably, for a wonder. "It's not much good you'll do with it, I'm afraid."

"Never mind, it's enough for what we want, thank you. We're not going to put anything very heavy in it, are we, Cicely?"

Cicely's reply was such a wildly hysterical giggle that Mrs. Wilson stared at her in offended surprise.

"She's only silly!" explained Lindsay hurriedly. "Please, could you let us have some scraps of dark cloth? Perhaps there'd be something in the rag bag. Be quiet, you stupid!"

The last remark was aside to the irrepressible Cicely, who straightened her face with an effort. "We're going to do some sewing," she volunteered, choking back her mirth.

"You're not generally so industrious," said Mrs. Wilson grimly. "I should be glad to see you using your needle for once. It seems all tennis and croquet with you young ladies."

She produced the rag bag, however, and allowed the girls to take their choice of the various odds and ends which it contained. They selected a piece of rough, hair-brown serge; then, fetching their work-baskets, they retired to a remote part of the garden, where they were not likely to be disturbed. If Mrs. Wilson had imagined they were about to engage in some fine and delicate needlework, she was much mistaken. They confined themselves to cutting and snipping, and to a few big, cobbling stitches that would have caused her to exclaim in righteous horror.

At the end of half an hour all was finished, and Lindsay proudly held up the result of their labours. It really was not a bad imitation of a rat. It had a nice round, plump body, four squat legs, a pointed nose, and a long, thin tail.

"We can't make whiskers," said Lindsay, "but that doesn't matter in the least. They wouldn't notice them. What a good thing it's light until so late now! They'll be able to see it perfectly well."

"We couldn't manage if the bed weren't a four-poster," said Cicely, chuckling in anticipation of the fun to come.

Beryl Austen and Effie Hargreaves slept in a room almost opposite to Lindsay's and Cicely's. Before eight o'clock arrived the two latter contrived to make an excuse to go upstairs, and hastily completed their preparations. The arrangements were ingenious. They fastened their rat very lightly by two pieces of thin sewing cotton to the middle of the piece of tapestry that formed the roof of the great four-post bed. To the cotton was attached a long strand of string, which passed through the curtains and out at the door (conveniently near the bed), the end being hidden under the mat on the landing.

"You'll see, when we jerk the string, the cotton will break, then down will plump the rat right on to their chests," said Lindsay, justly proud of her inventive powers. "Poke the box under the valance, Cicely, quick! I thought I heard someone coming."

The cardboard box contained a bobbin, to which a second string was tied, and concealed in the same manner as the first.

"I don't believe they'll suspect anything," said Cicely. "Won't it be lovely to give them a scare!"

At bedtime the conspirators retired innocently as usual, having wished Beryl and Effie good night in the passage.

"I nearly said I hoped nothing would disturb them," laughed Lindsay, "but I thought it would be wiser not. How long must we leave them to go to sleep?"

"About half an hour, I should think. Let us get up as soon as we hear the clock in the picture gallery striking nine."

The twilight lasted long, so it was still quite possible to distinguish objects as two nightgowned, barefooted figures stole gently across the landing. Fortunately everything was perfectly quiet in the upper portion of the house. The younger girls were in bed, and the elder ones were with the teachers downstairs.

"We must be sure to work the right strings," breathed Lindsay. "Have you got yours? This was mine, with a knot at the end."

She gave a smart pull, and the bobbin rattled loudly inside the box. They could hear it plainly, even through the closed door.

"What is that?"

The question came in an anxious and wideawake tone from within the room.

"I don't know. Oh, there it is again!"

The voice this time was Effie's.

"It sounds as if it were under the bed!"

"Oh, surely it's not a rat!"

"Now for it!" whispered Cicely, pulling the second string.

The result was all they could have desired. A series of yells proceeded from the four-post bed, sufficient not only to rouse the occupants of the other rooms on the landing, but to bring Miss Frazer hurrying up from the library. Lindsay and Cicely dropped their strings and fled, not a second too soon. They could hear Miss Frazer striking a match to light the candle, and her exclamation when she discovered the cause of the uproar.

"All the girls have turned out to see what's the matter," said Cicely. "If you and I don't go too, they'll know who's done it."

"I think we shall have to own up, in any case," replied Lindsay.

"It was worth the scolding," she declared afterwards, when Miss Frazer had administered a due homily on the danger of practical jokes. "I only wish I could have seen their faces when the rat plumped on to them. They needn't talk of screaming at nothing, and if they ever begin to tease us about anything again—well, we'll just say 'Rats!'"

CHAPTER IV. HAVERSLEIGH

There never was such a glorious place as the Manor. Upon that point the whole school perfectly agreed. The garden was as fascinating as the house, and proved an absolute dream of delight, with its smooth bowling-green, its winding paths, its charming little arbours overgrown with creepers, its clipped yew hedges, and its unexpected flights of steps. It might have been designed as a kind of terrestrial paradise for girls. The big lawns afforded space for so many tennis courts that there was no need for the younger ones to hover about, waiting enviously until their elders had finished before they could get a chance of a game; and there was plenty of room left for croquet and clock golf. The shrubbery and the plantation were ideal spots for hide-and-seek (almost too good, Lindsay said, because it was so very difficult to find anybody); while the various rustic seats scattered under the trees made sewing and reading a luxury on hot days, when no one felt inclined for violent exercise. A stone-flagged terrace ran the entire length of the front of the Manor, proving an invaluable playground when the grass was too wet for games in the garden; and a roomy summer-house stood near the bowling-green, so big that it was capable of sheltering all the school during a thunder shower.

Beyond the avenue, and at the farther side of the shrubbery, was a maze. Marvellous little narrow, twisting paths, with high hedges of clipped box, wound round and round in an utterly bewildering manner, most of them either ending blindly or turning back to the original entrance, and only one of the number leading to the arbour in the centre. For a long time the girls amused themselves with trying to discover the proper clue. Cicely, like Hansel, dropped pebbles to show which paths she had already traced; Lindsay essayed to cut the Gordian knot by creeping through the hedge; and it was only after many and repeated trials that they were at last able to solve the puzzle.

In the midst of one of the lawns grew a grand old yew tree, the lower branches of which were easy to climb. It was a favourite haunt of the younger girls, each having her special seat, and here they might often be seen perched like birds, and certainly chattering enough to suggest a flock of magpies. A stalwart oak close by supported a swing that was far more romantic than the swing in the playground at Winterburn Lodge, because a strong push would send the happy occupant high up among the green leaves, and give her a flying peep into a missel-thrush's nest on the topmost bough, where four gaping yellow mouths were clamouring for food. In a corner, down a flight of steps, there was a pond where grew marsh marigolds, and irises, and forget-me-nots, and other water-loving plants. A pair of ducks lived here in a wooden hutch, and would come waddling up to be fed with bread, which the girls saved from breakfast for them. Great was the delight of the whole school when one morning a brood of seven small ducklings appeared on the water, each as yellow as a canary, and seemingly quite at home already in its native element.

Then there was the rose garden, where every variety of the queen of flowers seemed to flourish, from the delicate Maréchal Niel to the sweet, oldfashioned, striped York and Lancaster. Archways and pillars were covered with climbers and ramblers, a little untrained, but hanging down in such glorious profusion that one almost approved of the neglect. Round this garden was a high hedge of clipped holly, so that it was sheltered from every wind, and the roses bloomed as if in a greenhouse. Nor must we forget the peacocks, which were as much a feature of the old house as the twisted chimneys, or the stone balls on the porch. There were six of them, and the gorgeous sheen of their feathers as they spread their tails in the sunshine was a sight worth remembering. In fact, as Miss Russell often remarked, they gave a finishing touch to the whole scene, and made the Manor look more than ever like a medieval picture.

The village of Haversleigh was only ten minutes' walk from the lodge gates. It consisted of one long row of quaint black-and-white cottages, with thatched roofs, and gardens so gay with flowers that they seemed to be overflowing into the road, and pinks and pansies were coming up between the cobblestones of the street. At the end stood the beautiful ancient church, built in days when each artisan was a master of his craft, and made his work a labour of love. Strangers often came from a distance to admire the delicate tracery of the windows, the exquisite carving of the pillars, and the splendid old oak choir stalls that had formed part of a tenth-century abbey. At the west end hung a collection of banners, won by Monica's ancestors in many a hard-fought battle, and, all tattered and faded as they were, still bearing tribute to the glories of the past. There were monuments, too, in memory of the Courtenays: stone effigies of knights in armour, lying under carved canopies emblazoned with their coats-of-arms; stiff ladies and gentlemen of Tudor times, with starched ruffs and buckled shoes; and one lovely marble figure, by a forgotten sculptor, of a young daughter of the house who had perished during the Great Plague. The ruthless hands that had chipped and spoiled many of the other monuments had spared this one, and the beautiful, calm face seemed to be resting in tranquil sleep, patiently waiting for the summons to arise to immortality.

The Manor pew, though large, could not accommodate the school. The girls sat in the left aisle, and made quite an important addition to the little congregation of villagers. They certainly helped to swell the singing, and I think even the most thoughtless among them learned to love that dear old church, and carried its remembrance into after years.

The Rectory marked the last boundary of the village, then the road passed over a bridge straight into the open country. The scenery was pretty without being grand. Picturesque farmhouses stood in the midst of rich pastures, behind which rose wooded slopes leading to a higher peak, called Pendle Tor, that stood out as a landmark for the district. Naturally the girls were very anxious to explore the neighbourhood, and delighted when Miss Russell allowed walks on half-holidays. The whole school was not often sent out together, but each form would go in turn, separately, with its own teacher—an arrangement that all much preferred, as they could then ramble about in an informal manner, instead of keeping to the prim file which was the general rule.

One Wednesday afternoon, at the end of May, it was the turn of the third class, and its six members were standing by the gate, impatiently awaiting the arrival of Miss Frazer, who, to do her justice, was not often at fault in the matter of punctuality.

"I hope she isn't telling Miss Russell what bad marks I got this morning," said Effie Hargreaves dismally. "She threatened last week to report me if I had another cross for history, and I missed five times, and four times in literature, and all my problems were wrong in arithmetic too."

"I believe they're planning to hire another piano," said Beryl Austen, "so that we can all get in the same amount of practising as we did at Winterburn Lodge."

"Oh, what a shame! I'm sure half an hour a day is enough for anybody," came in a chorus from the others.

"Especially now, when we haven't a music master," added Cicely.

"That's the very reason," explained Beryl. "Miss Russell says she wants us to keep up what we've learnt, so that we won't seem to have fallen back when we begin with Mr. Nelson again."

"Don't talk of Mr. Nelson! We shan't see him for ages."

"You will, in September."

"Well, it's not September yet, it's only May, and in the meantime we're learning from Miss Frazer. Here she is, by the by, hurrying down the drive as fast as she can."

"I'm sorry to have kept you waiting, girls," said the teacher, "but Miss Russell has been giving me a commission to transact while we are out. She wants us to go to Monkend, a farm about a mile and a half from here."

"A new walk?" asked Beryl.

"Yes, we have never been there before, but I don't think we can miss the way."

A perfectly fresh walk was a pleasant prospect. Everyone set off, therefore, in the best of spirits. It was a beautiful afternoon, one of those glorious days when summer seems to clasp hands with spring and join the delights of both seasons. The newly unfolded leaves were still a tender green, and the sycamores were covered with pendent blossoms, in the golden pollen of which the bees revelled like drunkards. The larches had opened all their tassels, and the young cones on the firs glowed with such a pink hue that they resembled candles on a Christmas tree. The hawthorns were almost over, but here and there a crab apple showed a mass of pink bloom, or a guelder rose made a white patch in the hedge;

and all the stretches of grass by the roadsides were carpeted with bluebells and starry stitchwort.

Miss Frazer was indulgent, and would wait for a few minutes while the girls gathered handfuls of flowers, or climbed up to the top of a bank to admire the view. She was as interested as they were in the finding of a robin's nest; and quite as excited when a hawk swooped suddenly into a bush, and flew away with a young thrush in its claws. The cuckoos were calling persistently from the woods, the larks were singing up in the air above, and all the hedgerows seemed to teem with busy bird life.

Their way soon left the high road, and, striking across a field, led them through a copse where there was an interesting pond, swarming with tadpoles. The girls would have lingered here, trying to catch the funny, wriggling, little black objects, but Miss Frazer's patience gave way at last, and she hurried them on, declaring that if they were not quick they would never get to the farm and back before tea-time.

Monkend was a quaint old house, built in the midst of cherry orchards. Its timbered walls were grey and weather-stained, and its tiled roof yellowed with lichens. By the side of the open barn door the cows were standing lowing to be milked, and the dairymaid, a rosy-faced young woman in a blue apron, was coming from the kitchen, singing as she swung her bright pails. She stopped in astonishment at the unwonted sight of visitors to the farm, and ran to call her mistress to the scene.

"You may wait for me here, girls, while I do my business with Mrs. Brand," said Miss Frazer; "or if you like you may walk back to the stile, and I will overtake you in the wood."

Mrs. Brand insisted that Miss Frazer should come into the best parlour to transact her errand, so, left alone, the girls began slowly to retrace their steps towards the copse.

"I wonder how long she'll be," said Lindsay, who with Cicely had lingered a little behind.

"I believe she has to pay a bill and order more butter and eggs and things, so I don't expect we shall see her for five or ten minutes at least," replied Cicely.

"Then there'll be just time to run round the farm. I want to peep inside those barns, and see what is at the other side of those haystacks. It looks interesting. Come along! The dairymaid is busy milking, and won't see us, and I don't suppose it matters if she does. We'll soon run after the others."

Feeling rather adventurous, the pair fled away down the yard, and dived through an open doorway into the depths of a big barn. How fragrant it smelled—such a delicious, sweet scent was in the air! Surely it must come from that great heap of hay in the corner. The girls ran across, and jumping on to the pile, were soon burying each other with armfuls of the hay, and scooping out nests to sit in. It was dark inside the barn—the beautiful brown gloom that one sees only in old castles or churches, or ancient buildings, and is quite different from the black of ordinary darkness. Through the open door came just one shaft of sunshine, in which the specks of dust seemed to float and flutter like living things. Overhead the great beams of the roof were lost in dim obscurity; very old and rough they were, and covered with a mass of cobwebs, among which Cicely declared she could see bats hanging head downwards, with folded wings, though Lindsay said it was all her imagination.

It was so nice sitting perched on the hay that neither was in a hurry to move. I believe they quite forgot about the time, until at last they heard Miss Frazer's voice in the distance bidding good-bye to Mrs. Brand.

"We shall have to go," groaned Cicely. "What a nuisance! I could stay here for hours."

"So could I," said Lindsay, getting up with a yawn, and brushing loose stalks from her dress. "Let us jump down on the other side of the hay."

I do not know why it should have occurred to Lindsay to get off the stack by the back instead of the front. If they had gone out of the barn by the way they came, they could have overtaken Miss Frazer in a moment, and the adventure which followed would never have happened at all. As it was, fate decreed that Lindsay, in her flying leap through the dusk, should knock her shins against something decidedly hard. She stood rubbing them ruefully, and put out her hand to feel what had been the cause of her bruises. It was a ladder, standing against the wall, and through the gloom of the barn she could just distinguish its upper end, which seemed to communicate with a doorway in the angle of the roof. This looked attractive. She pointed it out at once to Cicely.

"Where does it lead, do you think?" asked the latter.

"To some granary above, I expect. I wonder what's up there! Shall we go and explore?"

Without even waiting for an answer, Lindsay had begun to ascend, and as she was six rungs up before Cicely ventured a half-hearted remonstrance, she did not see fit to come down again.

"Oh! we shan't be a minute," she declared. "Miss Frazer will wait for us in the wood, and we can run all the way from the farm."

Where Lindsay went Cicely always felt bound to follow; accordingly, she clambered up the ladder behind her friend, and in due course both arrived at the top. As Lindsay had supposed, they found a granary half-filled with sacks of corn and a pile of loose barley. A door at the farther end appeared to open on to a flight of steps leading outside, while opposite was a small lattice window overlooking the fields.

"There's really nothing to see," said Cicely. "It was hardly worth while coming, after all."

"We might go out through that door, instead of climbing down the ladder again," suggested Lindsay, beginning to walk round the sacks. "Why, look! Somebody has left his lunch here."

On the top of the barley was a tin can, and also a red cotton pocket-handkerchief, evidently containing slices of bread. From sheer idle curiosity Lindsay seized them, and showed them laughingly to Cicely.

"Will you have some afternoon tea?" she exclaimed in joke.

At that moment she was startled by a low growl behind her. From a corner of the room sprang a collie dog that, unobserved by them, had been lying among the sacks, and keeping a watch over its master's property.

Lindsay promptly replaced the tin and the handkerchief on the barley.

"Good dog! Poor fellow!" she said encouragingly, holding out her hand.

The dog, however, did not make the least response to her friendly advances. It came a little nearer, growling again, and showing its teeth in an ugly fashion.

"Come here, silly fellow! Does it think I want to steal something?" said Lindsay.

"I expect it does," replied Cicely, in rather a shaky voice. "Don't try to touch it! It'll certainly bite you."

Even Lindsay, fond of animals as she was, could not deny that the gleaming eyes and snarling mouth looked the reverse of friendly.

"Perhaps we'd better be going," she said, turning towards the door.

Directly she moved, the dog growled louder, and would have flown at her if she had not instantly stopped.

"What are we to do?" she exclaimed, looking at Cicely with a terrified face.

They were indeed in a most awkward and dangerous position. The dog, deeming itself guardian of the granary, and doubtless considering the two girls intruders for dishonest purposes, would let neither of them beat a retreat. It stood looking vigilantly from one to the other, snarling so fiercely if they stirred even an inch that they did not dare to put its intentions to the test. Oh! why had they come? If they had only gone back down the ladder before they had roused the dog, or if Lindsay had not been inquisitive enough to peep inside the handkerchief, they might have been across the yard and following Miss Frazer to the wood. How were they ever to escape? Would they be obliged to remain there until the dog's master returned?

"Perhaps Miss Frazer'll come to hunt for us," quavered Cicely, in a very small voice, and with a timid eye on the collie lest it should spring. Evidently it did not object to conversation, so long as they kept still, for though it looked at her it did not growl. That was one comfort, at any rate. The situation was terrible enough, but to endure it in silence would have been ten times worse.

"I don't believe anybody knows where we are," said Lindsay. "I wonder if the dairymaid noticed us go into the barn. They wouldn't dream of our climbing the ladder. They'd look all round the stackyard, and perhaps think we'd taken a short cut and gone home."

Would nobody ever arrive to release them? The minutes seemed long as hours, and they felt as if their trembling knees could scarcely support them. Cicely, from the place where she was standing, could fortunately look through the window and command a view of the field below. Though she gazed with as keen anxiety as Sister Anne in the story of Bluebeard, she did not see anybody hurrying to their rescue. The dog apparently grew a little tired, for it threw itself down on the floor, but without relaxing any of its former vigilance.

"I believe it's going to stop here all night," groaned Cicely, almost in tears.

The case was waxing desperate. So weary were the poor girls that they were ready to drop with fatigue. Unless something happened, and that speedily, there was bound to be a catastrophe. At the moment, however, when Cicely felt that she simply could not endure any longer, deliverance came. Through the little squares of the wooden lattice she saw a figure strolling leisurely across the field. It was Monica Courtenay, and she was walking in the direction of the farm. Cicely shouted at the very pitch of her voice:

"Monica! Monica! Help! Oh, do come!"

Monica stopped in much astonishment, and looked round as if to ask who was calling her by name; then, deciding that the screams came from the direction of the granary, she hurried as fast as she could up the steps, and opened the door. Her amazement was only equalled by her distress at the girls' plight.

She did her best to call off the dog, but as that proved impossible she ran to fetch the first person she could find. In less than a minute she had returned with Mr. Brand, whose stout boot and stick soon sent the collie yelping disconsolately into a corner, to realize that it had exceeded its duties.

"He's a good watchdog, is Pincher," said the farmer, "but he's been a bit too clever to-day. You silly hound! You ought to know better than to set on two young wenches. You may well slink off! You'd better keep out of reach of my stick, I can tell you!"

Lindsay and Cicely were much upset and shaken by their terrifying experience. They never forgot how kindly and considerately Monica behaved. She did not tell them it was their own fault, and that it served them right for prying into places where they had no business (as Mildred Roper or any of the other monitresses would certainly have done); she only sympathized in her gentle way, and offered to escort them to the Manor by a short cut, so that they should not be so very late after all.

"It was a lucky thing I happened to be taking a walk this way," she said. "It might have been hours before any of the farm people went into the granary. I wouldn't keep such a savage dog if it were mine."

As Lindsay supposed, Miss Frazer was not aware that she had left two of her pupils behind at Monkend, and imagined that the missing pair must have walked home in front of the others. Their absence had only just been discovered when they arrived to explain the cause. The teacher was hardly so tender with them as Monica, and they received more scolding than sympathy.

"Though it wasn't such a very dreadful crime to go into the barn," said Lindsay afterwards to her companion in misfortune. "Miss Frazer needn't say we are the two who are always in mischief, because it might have happened just as easily to any of the others. I saw Beryl and Effie peep into the cowhouse as they passed, though they didn't climb up a ladder. Wasn't Monica nice? I believe the old farmer would have been cross with us if she hadn't been there. He evidently knows her very well. So do all the people in the village. She seems to know each man, woman, and child there, and to be a favourite with everybody."

CHAPTER V. AN UNEXPECTED DEVELOPMENT

Lindsay and Cicely had by no means forgotten either their quest for the treasure or their curiosity about the lantern chamber. In spite of several small efforts, nothing fresh had occurred to elucidate matters, and they were almost beginning to despair of ever making any further progress, when quite unexpectedly something important happened.

One afternoon, as they were sending tennis balls to each other along the terrace, they heard a voice calling to them from overhead. They looked up, and saw Merle Hammond, a second-form girl, leaning out of one of the upper windows of the house and beckoning to them violently.

"Lindsay and Cicely, is that you?" she cried. "Come up here; I've made such a discovery!"

"Where are you?" asked Cicely, for the old Manor had so many windows, it was impossible to identify any particular one from the outside.

"In a room up a funny winding staircase, on the top landing. It's empty, but there's a big kind of lamp hanging from the ceiling. Oh, you'll never guess what I've seen!"

"The lantern chamber!" gasped both the girls, and, dropping their rackets, they raced into the house in a state of the wildest excitement.

Were they actually on the brink of solving the mystery? How had Merle found it out? It was good of her to call to them. Had she accidentally come across the hiding-place? or was it some other secret still?

The answer to all these questions lay in that attic room, and they fled upstairs as if their feet were wings.

They were halfway along the passage, and a few seconds more would have seen them safely on the top landing, when (oh, the bad luck of it!) they almost knocked down Miss Frazer, who emerged at exactly the wrong moment from her own bedroom door.

"Gently, girls, gently!" she remonstrated. "Where are you going in such a hurry?"

It was impossible to explain. How could they tell the teacher the nature of their errand? They both stood still, looking very "caught" and dismayed, and said nothing.

"As you have come indoors so early, you had better tidy your drawers," continued Miss Frazer dryly. "I looked at them just now, and found them in terrible disorder. You will have nice time to do it before tea."

Could anything have been more aggravating? The poor girls were nearly crying with vexation. There was no appeal, however. Miss Frazer escorted them into their bedroom, and stood over them, giving directions, until each pair of stockings or pocket-handkerchief was disposed according to her ideas of neatness. They might chafe and fret inwardly at the delay, but outwardly they were obliged to behave with due decorum.

The governess was certainly justified in her disapproval, for Cicely's best coat and hat were lying jumbled together at the bottom of the wardrobe, and Lindsay's belongings looked as if they had been stirred up with a stick.

"If I notice any of your places in such a condition again, I shall be obliged to give you each a punishment," she said gravely. "Wash your hands now, and comb your hair. There's the first bell."

Would Miss Frazer never leave them alone? If only she would take her departure at once, they could perhaps manage to rush up to the lantern room before the second bell rang. Merle must be waiting for them, and wondering why they did not come. And the secret was waiting too! Lindsay looked at Cicely, almost meditating a bolt. Possibly the mistress read her intention in her face; at any rate, she waited until both were ready, then marched them downstairs to the dining-room like a female policeman, without giving them the slightest chance to escape.

"Of all jolly sells this is the biggest!" whispered Cicely.

"I wish Miss Frazer had been at the bottom of the sea!" groaned Lindsay.

Merle came in rather late and took her place at table, looking a little red and self-conscious. Lindsay tried to meet her eyes, but she avoided the gaze, and went on stolidly with her bread and butter as if nothing had happened. When Cicely made a like effort she fared the same. What had Merle seen? How they longed for tea to be over, that they might hear of her discovery! They hoped she would not reveal it to any of the other girls first, and they looked on in quite a fever of anxiety whenever she spoke to Elsie Ryder or Marjorie Butler, who sat one on either side of her.

"She doesn't know what we suspect about Mrs. Wilson," whispered Lindsay. "She may be letting out something it would be far better, for Monica's sake, not to tell."

The moment the meal was finished the two girls followed Merle into the garden, but, greatly to their surprise, she took no notice of them, and began to play tennis.

"I expect she's waiting for a safer time. Of course it wouldn't do for her to be seen talking to us so particularly. We'll stay here while she finishes her set," said Cicely.

The game lasted until preparation, and then Merle walked away with such an evident intention of escaping from them that the two were most indignant.

"What does she mean?" burst out Lindsay.

"Do you think she's offended because we didn't go up at once?" returned Cicely. "She doesn't know yet that Miss Frazer stopped us. We must explain it as soon as we can."

They tried to get hold of Merle after supper, but she kept persistently to Elsie Ryder's company, and would not give them any opportunity of speaking to her in private, so they were obliged to go to bed in a horrible state of suspense. Next morning things were just as bad. There was no mistaking the fact that Merle wished to avoid them, and it was only with the greatest difficulty that they succeeded at last in catching her alone.

"What do you want?" she enquired abruptly. "Please don't go chasing me about like this all over the school."

"We want to know what you saw in the lantern room, of course," replied Lindsay.

"Well, I'm sorry, but I can't tell you."

"Not tell us!"

Lindsay and Cicely could scarcely believe the evidence of their own ears.

"No, it's quite impossible."

"But why?"

"Simply that I can't."

"Were you offended, Merle, because we didn't come when you called us?" asked Cicely.

"We were hurrying up as fast as we could, only Miss Frazer stopped us and made us tidy our drawers. It wasn't our fault," added Lindsay apologetically.

"No, I'm not offended in the least. I'm very glad you didn't come."

"But you shouted to us to be quick."

"I know I did."

"Was it something or somebody you saw in that room?"

"Please don't ask me."

"But look here, Merle, this is too bad," protested Lindsay. "You're playing a very nasty trick upon us."

"It can't be helped. I've said I am sorry," returned Merle doggedly.

"Well, you are a fraud," cried Cicely. "I like people who keep their promises."

"So do I," said Merle, in rather a significant tone. "It's exactly what I intend doing, too."

"You don't mean to say you've promised not to tell!" exclaimed Lindsay.

"I didn't say anything at all."

"Have you told Elsie Ryder or Marjorie Butler?"

"Certainly not. I haven't mentioned the matter to anybody, and I hope you won't either."

"But why shouldn't you whisper it just to Lindsay and me? We wouldn't let a soul know," pleaded Cicely reproachfully.

"I can't explain why. Do let us drop the subject."

Here was indeed a deadlock. They had been afraid lest Merle should betray her secret indiscreetly, but they had certainly never contemplated being kept out of it themselves. The more they pressed her, the more obstinately she refused, and neither scolding nor coaxing would induce her to disclose even the least hint. They gave it up at last, feeling very baffled and rather out of temper.

"We do know something about your old room, all the same," said Lindsay crossly, as a parting shot.

"Oh, Lindsay, you don't really!"

There was an anxious note in Merle's voice.

"More than you think."

"Then, whatever it is, you had better keep it to yourselves, and not let it go any farther."

Merle's extraordinary behaviour seemed to make the mystery even deeper than before. She had evidently been exploring the Manor on her own account and had made some discovery, which she undoubtedly had intended to share with them when she called from the window. Then something must have occurred afterwards which caused her to change her mind.

To whom had she given a promise of secrecy? Surely not to Mrs. Wilson? That would be aiding and abetting one whom they strongly believed to be Monica's enemy. If only Miss Frazer had not such a tiresome love of tidiness, they might have reached the lantern room in time, and be now in possession of the information they wanted. It was too tantalizing to feel that they had been so near a solution of the problem, and had missed it by a few moments.

Events never happen singly. For a whole fortnight they had been able to find out nothing, yet on the very day following this disappointment something occurred which seemed to add another link to their chain of strange circumstances. They had managed to escape Miss Frazer's vigilance, and were indulging in a surreptitious game of "tig" along the forbidden ground of the picture gallery, when one of the bedroom doors opened, and Mrs. Wilson appeared in the distance, carrying a pile of clean towels in her arms.

"There's 'The Griffin'!" exclaimed Lindsay. "She mustn't catch us here, on any account. She'll tell Miss Russell, and we shall each lose a conduct mark. Quick! Let us hide somewhere till she's gone by."

The ancient arras seemed to offer a safe retreat. As fast as possible they whisked behind it, and stood flattening themselves against the wall, hoping Mrs. Wilson would notice nothing lumpy or unusual as she passed.

At the same time came a sound of heavy tramping footsteps from the other end of the gallery, and Cicely, peeping through a hole in the tapestry which happened to be on a convenient level with her eyes, saw Scott, the gardener, coming down the flight of stairs which led from the upper landing. He met Mrs. Wilson exactly opposite the hiding-place where the girls were concealed, and the two stopped to speak, quite unaware that listening ears were eagerly following their conversation.

"Have you been in the lantern room?" began the old housekeeper uneasily. "I'd no idea you were going up this afternoon."

"Thought I'd best take a look," returned Scott.

"There wasn't any need. I was there myself this morning, and things were all right."

"I don't know what you may call all right," grunted Scott. "There was far too much noise going on to satisfy me."

"You don't think there's any danger——?" burst out Mrs. Wilson, in an anxious voice.

"No, no!" interrupted Scott quickly. "Not for the present, at any rate. Don't upset yourself. Still, it needs care, especially with all this crew in the house."

"Yes, it's that that's worrying me. I shan't breathe freely till they're gone. And such an inquisitive, meddlesome set they are, too! You'd scarcely believe the trouble they give me. Two of them took it into their heads one day to go wandering on the upper landing. I actually found them inside the lantern room!"

Scott gave an exclamation of something like alarm.

"That'll never do!" he said. "You mustn't let them go poking about there; it would be most unsafe. Can't you lock the door?"

"No, the key's lost."

"I must try if I can find a padlock for it."

"I wish you would. It would take a load off my mind. By the by, I wanted to warn you——"

But here one of the housemaids came along the landing, Mrs. Wilson's voice sank to a whisper, and the only words audible were "Miss Monica", "evening", and "wouldn't trust".

"I'll be extra careful," said Scott, as he clumped away.

Lindsay and Cicely waited several moments after the gallery was empty before they ventured to emerge from behind the tapestry. They had the great satisfaction of having learnt something. They now knew definitely that there was a secret in connection with the lantern room which both Mrs. Wilson and Scott were anxious to keep from them.

"What can it be?" speculated Cicely. "Did you notice what he said about the noise? It must have been that dreadful groaning we heard."

"I've been thinking about that," replied Lindsay. "There may be a hidden room, and someone shut up in it."

"As a prisoner, do you mean?"

Lindsay nodded.

"But who could it be?"

"I can't imagine, unless—could it possibly be old Sir Giles Courtenay? Perhaps he didn't really die, after all. Don't you remember, in *Ivanhoe*, how Athelstane of Coningsburgh was supposed to be killed, and he was really only stunned; and the monks of St. Edmunds put an empty coffin in the chapel, and kept him in a dungeon and pretended he was dead, because they wanted his property? Mrs. Wilson may be doing the same."

"How dreadful!" Cicely looked quite appalled at the idea. "I suppose she goes up, then, to feed him. Scott must know too. I shouldn't have thought it of Scott. I rather liked him. I expect they'll share the money between them. I wonder what 'The Griffin' was warning him about. I hope they're not hatching a plot against Monica!"

"It looks bad," said Lindsay, "decidedly bad. It's evidently something shady, or they wouldn't want to keep it so quiet. It may be a very good thing for Monica that we've taken the matter up."

"What shall we do?"

"We must stalk 'The Griffin' again, and try to follow her to that room, and see what she does there."

"She's as wary as a weasel."

"Then we must be clever and outwit her. I'm positive she has some scheme on hand that ought to be watched. One doesn't know how much may depend upon it."

It was certainly very exciting to feel that dark deeds might be taking place in the attic, and that they were the fortunate instruments selected by fate for the purpose of bringing the wrongdoers to justice. It gave them a delightful sense of superiority over the other girls, whose heads were full of nothing but tennis and croquet, and who never troubled themselves with a thought about the missing treasure.

"Merle is the only one who knows anything," said Lindsay, "and I verily believe 'The Griffin' must have bribed her."

Mrs. Wilson evidently used the utmost precaution in her visits to the top landing. In spite of the pains they took to watch her movements, it was some days before they found the propitious moment. "All things come to those who wait," says the old proverb, however, and it proved true in this case.

One afternoon, through the chink of the bathroom door, they saw her walk into the gallery as if she were going to the upper story. As stealthily as Indians they crept after her. They tiptoed along the passages, and just caught a glimpse of the tail of her skirts as she passed up the winding staircase and entered the lantern room. Very quietly they followed on to the little landing, and listened for a moment outside the closed door.

"What is she doing?" whispered Cicely.

"That's what I want to find out."

They both tried to peep through the keyhole, and bumped their heads together in the attempt.

"I can hear her moving!"

There was a slight noise inside, almost like the clicking of a latch, then all was perfectly silent.

Lindsay could bear it no longer.

"Here goes!" she cried boldly, and flung open the door. To her utter amazement, the room was absolutely empty. Mrs. Wilson had vanished as completely as if she had been a ghost.

CHAPTER VI. MONICA

The two girls rushed into the empty room and examined every corner minutely. There was not a trace of any secret exit to be found. The opening through which Mrs. Wilson must have disappeared was evidently marvellously well concealed.

"Where can she be? It's like magic!" whispered Cicely.

"Wherever she's gone, I suppose she'll have to come back," replied Lindsay.

"Listen!" said Cicely, with a start.

It was the same strange sound again which they had heard on their former expedition—a low, long-drawn-out moaning, as of someone in pain, feeble at first, then growing louder, and suddenly ceasing.

"Oh! I wonder if she's hurting anybody?" cried Cicely, shuddering with horror.

"I'd give a great deal to find out what's going on. I'm afraid it's something that won't bear the light of day," said Lindsay uneasily.

"Dare we wait till she comes out of her hiding-place?"

"Yes, but we mustn't stay here. It would spoil everything if she caught us. Let us go outside and close the door again, and watch through the keyhole; then, if we see her coming, we can rush."

Mrs. Wilson's errand was evidently a long one. Though they relieved each other more than once in mounting guard over the keyhole, she did not return.

"Perhaps she knows we're here, and won't come out till we've gone," suggested Lindsay at last.

"How could she know?"

"She may have been looking at us all the time through some little spy place."

"Oh, how horrid! It makes me feel quite creepy to think of it."

The fact that they were doing exactly the same did not strike either of the girls. Circumstances alter cases, and they considered they were justified in their plan of action. They grew extremely tired of waiting, but they were determined not to give in.

"There's that noise again!" said Cicely. "She must have a prisoner shut up there; I'm perfectly certain about it."

Both put their ears to the door, and were so absorbed in listening to the queer sounds inside the room that they did not hear footsteps sounding up the winding staircase. An exclamation behind them caused them to turn hastily round.

There was Monica!—the last person in the world whom they had expected to see, and who was looking as astonished as themselves at the meeting. Lindsay and Cicely felt decidedly embarrassed. Monica must have seen them peeping through the keyhole, and they knew they had been discovered in a somewhat doubtful and discreditable occupation. They could not possibly begin to explain that it was entirely on her account and for her benefit, so they simply turned very red and said nothing. It was a most uncomfortable situation.

There was a painful pause, and then Monica recovered her presence of mind.

"Why, Lindsay and Cicely, I thought you were with the others in the garden!" she said.

"We were only exploring the house a little," replied Lindsay, trying to pass the matter off carelessly. "Miss Russell said there were interesting things all over it."

"I'm afraid you won't find much to interest you among empty bedrooms," said Monica, in her calm, quiet voice. "If you like to come downstairs with me I'll show you some of the curiosities in my cabinet.

I've a great many old coins and a few daggers that were dug up when the moat was drained."

Looking rather shamefaced, the pair went with Monica to the library, where she unlocked an oak cupboard, and spent quite twenty minutes in explaining her various treasures. She was most kind, and spared no trouble, but the others could not get over their confusion. They had the guilty sensation that they had been caught like naughty children, and were being amused to keep them out of the way.

"Why was Monica going into the lantern room?" demanded Lindsay, the moment they were alone.

"Does she know the secret?" ventured Cicely.

"Either she knows, or she's trying to find out. Perhaps she's stalking Mrs. Wilson too!"

This was a new idea, and required consideration.

"Then that would perhaps be what 'The Griffin' was warning Scott about," said Cicely reflectively. "Ought we to tell Monica?"

"Not yet—not till we've something more definite to go upon. We've only suspicions at present, and one can hardly speak about those. She might be offended, and think us meddlesome, especially as she doesn't like to talk of her affairs."

"I'm afraid she'll think us sneaky and underhand, in any case. I'm so sorry she saw us spying like that."

"Well, we couldn't help it, and we can't explain."

"Mightn't we just say why——?"

"It's no use," interrupted Lindsay decidedly. "We'd better not breathe a word."

And Cicely, as usual, gave way.

It was gratifying to feel that they were Monica's champions, though she might not yet be aware of what she owed them. They must be content to be misunderstood for a little while; afterwards she would appreciate what they had been doing for her, and would thank them accordingly. They often looked at her in school with the satisfactory sensation that they knew something of which everyone else, even Miss Russell, was ignorant.

I fear the lessons suffered sometimes while they indulged in daydreams, for it was hard to recall such mundane matters as the capital of Mexico, or the date of Magna Charta, when their thoughts were far away in the lantern room, busy with concealed prisoners or supposed plots.

"You're the two most inattentive girls in the class!" cried Miss Frazer indignantly one day, after a specially bad lapse of memory. "You both did far better at Winterburn Lodge. I cannot understand why your work should have fallen off so much lately. This is the third time this week you have had bad marks. If it occurs again, I shall be obliged to report you to Miss Russell."

Apart from their interest in her as the owner of the hidden treasure, Lindsay and Cicely regarded Monica with the worship which schoolgirls are sometimes fond of bestowing upon a companion who happens specially to attract them. They admired the shape of her nose and her long chestnut hair, and considered her dignified manner absolute perfection. They used to follow her about at a respectful distance, longing to improve the acquaintance; but they received so many snubs from the elder girls, who also wished to monopolize her, that matters did not advance much further than an occasional "Good morning" or "Good afternoon".

"The big ones are so jealous, they like to keep her all to themselves," grumbled Cicely. "Eleanor Wright was quite rude when I offered to lend Monica a pencil yesterday. She said I was 'officious'."

"They're horribly mean," agreed Lindsay.

Monica had certainly become a great favourite at the Manor with both teachers and pupils, and, had she been of a less steady disposition, might have run considerable danger of being spoilt. She took her sudden popularity, however, very serenely, and scarcely seemed to notice that her schoolfellows were quarrelling over who should sit next her in class, or take part with her in a game of tennis.

"She always seems so calm and superior, like a nightingale among sparrows," remarked Irene Spencer sentimentally.

"Or a swan among a flock of geese," laughed Mildred Roper. "You've all grown really quite silly over Monica. I admire her very much myself, but I don't go and kiss her jacket when it's hanging in the vestibule, or beg her old torn exercises for keepsakes."

"Oh, well, you're a monitress!"

"I've got a little common sense left, I'm thankful to say."

The pretty rose-covered cottage where Monica and her mother had established themselves for the summer was only a few minutes' walk away from the Manor. One afternoon Miss Russell, happening to meet Lindsay and Cicely in the hall, gave them a note, and told them to take it at once to Mrs. Courtenay, and bring back an answer.

The two girls ran off in high glee, delighted to have this opportunity of seeing their idol in private. They found Monica preparing her French lesson in the small strip of front garden, but she put her books aside as they opened the gate.

"Come to Mother," she said, when they had explained their errand, leading the way through a French window into a low, old-fashioned sitting-room.

Mrs. Courtenay was a sweet, delicate-looking lady, with a gentle, refined face, and hair slightly streaked with grey. She did not rise from her sofa when they entered, but held out her hand instead, and asked them to come and speak to her.

"I am somewhat of an invalid, you see," she said. "The doctor is very strict, and has told me to lie still. It's rather hard, but I am trying to obey. So you are two of Monica's little friends? Well, now you are here, you had better stay for tea. The letter? Oh, I'll send Jenny, our maid, with the answer, and she shall tell Miss Russell that I'm keeping you. We'll take care that you go back in plenty of time for preparation."

This was indeed a most unexpected treat. Both Lindsay and Cicely beamed with smiles. They were the only girls in the school who had been thus favoured, and they felt that their present enjoyment would be equalled by the envy which they would excite among the others on their return.

"I am glad to hear you are all so happy at the Manor," continued Mrs. Courtenay. "Isn't it a dear, interesting old place? I expect Monica will have told you most of the legends. No! Why, Monica, what have you been thinking of? Do you mean to say they haven't heard yet about your ancestress and Sir Humphrey Warden in the rose avenue?"

"There really hasn't been any time for telling stories, Mother," declared Monica, "we've been so busy playing tennis when we were not at lessons. I'm never very good at remembering them, either—not like you are."

"I suppose I must consider myself the family chronicler," said Mrs. Courtenay. "We certainly ought to let Lindsay and Cicely hear the tale of the picture. Ah, here comes tea! Monica, you must look after our guests."

Monica evidently loved to be her mother's nurse. She placed a small table by the side of the sofa, and busied herself in arranging cushions and seeing that everything was placed for the invalid's greatest comfort. She did not neglect the visitors either, and brought out a jar of honey for their special benefit.

"I know you'll like it, because you were so interested in the bees," she said. "Do you remember the day when you went too close to the hives, and nearly got stung?"

"Yes; we had to run the whole length of the walk where the roses grow. I shan't forget it in a hurry," answered Cicely.

"That is the rose avenue where my namesake outwitted Sir Humphrey Warden. I wish you would tell them the story, Mother."

"Oh, do, please," pleaded Lindsay and Cicely; "we'd like so immensely to hear it!"

"I believe I shall just have time while we finish tea," said Mrs. Courtenay. "I suppose you need not be back in school until half-past five? Have you been in the long gallery at the Manor, and looked at the pictures?"

"Yes, often," said Cicely.

"Then you will remember one, at the far end, of a girl in a white dress, holding a bunch of roses in her hand?"

"Yes; it's the prettiest of them all. We always say it's the exact image of Monica."

"It is the portrait of a Monica Courtenay who lived here in the time of the Civil War. Her father was killed fighting for the king at Marston Moor, and her only brother, Sir Piers, was also one of the hottest supporters of the crown. When Cromwell came into power, Sir Piers had to flee for his life. He was chased from one hiding-place to another. Sometimes, like Prince Charles, he had to clamber up a tree until the soldiers had passed by, and once he spent a night in a fox's hole.

"At length, one summer evening, hunted almost to desperation, he returned to his old home. He met his sister in the garden, and though she exclaimed with joy at seeing him, she immediately made a sign for silence, and motioned him to conceal himself under a large box tree which stood near.

"It was not safe, so she whispered, to go to the Manor. There were spies about, and Sir Humphrey Warden, the most zealous Roundhead in the district, had set a watch upon the house. At any moment they expected he might arrive with a troop of soldiers. Piers must stay where he was, and she would run and bring him the key of theboathouse; then, under cover of the darkness, he might creep away to the river, get out the boat, and drop with the current until he reached the sea, where possibly he might find a ship to take him over to France.

"She hurried indoors at once to fetch the small key that unlocked the boathouse, but as she was returning down the avenue she found she was just too late. There was a tramp of horses' hoofs, and Sir Humphrey Warden came riding up at the head of a band of men.

"'Good even, fair neighbour,' he said. 'I must needs make an inspection of your house, and with your permission I will give myself the honour of supping with you to-night. What brings you hither?'

"'I do but take the air, and pluck a few of these fragrant blossoms,' replied Monica hastily. 'I will presently conduct you to the Manor myself, and entertain you.'

"She was in a desperate strait. How could she manage to save her brother? Now that Sir Humphrey had come, she knew her every movement would be watched. No one could be trusted, for the servants (so she feared) had all been bribed. Gathering a bunch of roses, she contrived unnoticed to slip her little key inside the heart of one of them.

"'I would fain crave the favour of a flower, madam,' said Sir Humphrey, who was an admirer of fair dames, in spite of his Puritan dress.

"'Take your choice, sir,' replied Monica, boldly holding out her bunch. 'Nay, not this red one; it is overblown, and will fall directly. 'Tis but fit to be flung away. This pink hath the sweeter scent, an you will wear it for me.'

"As she spoke she tossed the rose containing the key with apparent carelessness over the hedge to the foot of the box tree where her brother was lying concealed; then, leading her unwelcome guest to the house, she gave orders for his due entertainment.

"Sir Humphrey and his men searched the Manor in vain, but they never thought of looking in the garden, where the fugitive was waiting till the darkness should be black enough to hide him. Sir Piers got safely away to France, and returned in triumph to his estates when Charles II came to his own again. As a remembrance of his wonderful escape, he caused his sister's portrait to be painted, with the bunch of roses in her hand. Ever since the Courtenays have had an almost superstitious reverence for the picture. There is an old saying that it guards the safety and fortunes of the family."

"And what became of Monica?" asked Lindsay, who had been deeply interested in the story.

"She married a cavalier friend of her brother's, and went to live in Devonshire. I believe she kept one of the roses treasured away in a box, and it was buried with her when she died."

"I suppose Monica was christened after her?" said Cicely.

"Yes; that has always been a favourite name with the Courtenays, though I do not think any of them can have more closely resembled the portrait."

"How can the picture guard your fortunes?" enquired Lindsay.

"I don't know. It is one of those quaint ideas that sometimes linger in families. Of course it is only a tale, and I am afraid I have been a long while in telling it. Monica, dear, it is twenty minutes past five. Lindsay and Cicely must hurry back to school at once, if they are to be in time for preparation. We shall get into sad disgrace with Miss Russell if we allow them to be late."

"I think your mother is perfectly sweet," said Lindsay, as Monica walked with them along the road to the Manor gates.

"She's just everything in the whole world to me," replied Monica. "I wish she were stronger, though. She has been ill for such a long time. The doctor says it would do her good to spend next winter in the south of Italy, but that, I'm afraid, will be quite impossible. She ought to go, it might make all the difference," she continued, almost as if talking to herself; "yet we can't manage it, however much we try, unless, indeed——"

But here she seemed to recollect the presence of her companions, and wishing them a hasty good-bye, she turned back to the cottage.

"I know what Monica was going to say," remarked Cicely, as they walked up the drive.

"She meant her mother would be able to go away if the treasure were found," replied Lindsay. "Oh! it does seem hard, when they need it so badly, that it should be shut up somewhere, and doing no good to anybody at all."

"I think Monica is frightened lest Mrs. Courtenay should grow worse and die, if they have to stay in England for the winter. I don't believe she would enjoy a penny of her fortune if it were to come too late for her to share it with her mother."

CHAPTER VII. LINDSAY'S LUCK

One day, shortly before Whitsuntide, Irene Spencer walked into the third-class schoolroom with a letter in her hand, and a look on her face which proclaimed news of some importance.

"I don't believe any of you will ever guess what I've come to tell you," she announced. "I've heard this morning from my aunt at Linforth Vicarage. She writes asking me to spend a few days there at Whitsuntide (we are to have a short holiday, you know), and she says: 'We have asked Monica Courtenay, and we should be very pleased if Miss Russell would also allow you to bring one of your younger schoolfellows who would prove a nice companion for Rhoda.' My cousin Rhoda is twelve, so I have to pick out one from among you six. Whichever it is will have an uncommonly jolly visit, because we always have glorious times at Linforth."

"How delightful! Oh, do take me!" exclaimed the six in chorus, each enchanted with such a tempting prospect, and anxious to be the chosen favourite.

"I wish I could take you all," replied Irene, "but unfortunately the invitation is only for one. Miss Russell says this will be the best way to arrange it. The girl who is nearest to Rhoda's age must go. Will you each tell me the date of your birthday, and then I shall be able to decide. Rhoda's is on the twentieth of March."

It certainly seemed the fairest way of settling the question, and one against which there could be no appeal.

"Miss Russell is a modern Solomon," declared Cicely. "I'm afraid I haven't the slightest chance, because I'm only eleven and a half, and so is Nora."

"I'm almost thirteen," wailed Beryl. "I wish I were a few months younger. Effie, I shall be horribly jealous if the chance falls to you."

"No such luck! I am a Christmas child," returned Effie. "I believe Marjorie is nearer."

"The twenty-seventh of February. Can anybody do better than that?" asked Marjorie hopefully.

"Mine is the sixth of April," said Lindsay.

"About as much after Rhoda's as Marjorie's is before," said Irene. "We must count it up exactly. Somebody give me a pencil and a piece of paper. Let me see, the twenty-seventh of February to the twentieth of March is twenty-one days, and the twentieth of March to the sixth of April is only seventeen. Then Lindsay is nearer by four days."

"Hurrah!" cried Lindsay, clapping her hands, "I'm glad I wasn't born a week later. How dreadfully sorry I am for you all, especially Marjorie!"

"My aunt says she will send the trap for us on Friday afternoon," continued Irene. "And we are to stay until Tuesday morning, so that will give us three whole days at Linforth. I'm sure you'll like Rhoda, and my other cousins too. There are eight of them altogether. Meta, the eldest, is seventeen; she's going to study music in Germany next September. Ralph and Leonard are fifteen and fourteen; they go to the Appleford Grammar School, and ride there every day on their bicycles. Then comes Rhoda, and there are four little ones. They do lessons with a governess, but perhaps some time Rhoda is to be sent to Winterburn Lodge. Aunt Esther says she shan't treat us as visitors; we must make ourselves at home amongst the others."

The visit seemed an event worth looking forward to, not only on its own account, but because Monica was to be one of the party. Lindsay could hardly believe her good fortune, and rejoiced again and again over the happy date of her birthday. She was in a state of great excitement on the Friday afternoon, when the phaeton arrived with Monica already installed on the front seat. To drive away in such company was indeed a matter for congratulation, and she felt much sympathy for the disconsolate five who were perforce left behind, especially for poor Cicely, who would miss her more than anybody, and whose eyes were full of tears at the parting.

"Never mind," she whispered to the latter, "perhaps it will be your turn next time for something nice. At any rate, I shall have heaps to tell you when I come back."

Linforth Vicarage was a long, rambling stone house, the flagged roof and mullioned windows of which proclaimed it as belonging, equally with the Manor, to a period of the past. It was a delightful, roomy, almost medieval kind of a place, so picturesque, in its old-world fashion, that one could forgive the lowness of the rooms, the narrowness of the passages, the steepness of the stairs, and the inconvenience of the fact that the front door opened directly into the dining-room, and the bedrooms nearly all led into one another. None of these drawbacks seemed to distress the young Greenwoods, who thought their home the nicest spot in the world. They were a particularly jolly, merry, happy-go-lucky family, full of jokes and noise. Rhoda, for whose benefit Lindsay had been invited, received her visitor with enthusiasm.

"I'm so glad Miss Russell let you come!" she said. "You see, Meta will monopolize Irene and Monica, and I should have been left out altogether. I'm delighted to have someone of my own age."

Monica was a great favourite in the household, and held in request by all, from Mr. and Mrs. Greenwood to Cyril, the baby. As Rhoda had prophesied, however, she disappeared after tea with Meta and Irene, the three elder girls evidently wishing to have a chat in private. Rhoda made an effort to secure Lindsay to herself, but the four little ones—Wilfred, Alwyn, Joan, and Cyril—begged so piteously not to be banished from the society of the interesting visitor that in the end she yielded, and allowed them to help to exhibit the various treasures in the garden which she wished to show to her new friend.

The Greenwoods had quite a menagerie in the way of pets. They kept them in a disused stable, in neat cages with wire fronts, most of which had been made by Ralph and Leonard. There were silky-haired, lop-eared rabbits, that could be hugged in small arms without offering any remonstrances; bright-eyed little guinea-pigs, which often caused exciting chases by escaping from their owners' embraces and hiding away behind the cages; a family of piebald mice, consisting of a mother and five young ones, which generally went to bed in the daytime, and had to be poked out of their sleeping quarters with a lead pencil to make them show themselves; a morose-looking tortoise that would allow Wilfred to scratch its head, but spat indignantly at the others; and a whole box full of silkworms in various stages, from tiny, wriggling black threads to chrysalids in cocoons. The children were accompanied to the stable by a sharp little black Pomeranian; but they were obliged to leave him outside in case he might hurt the rabbits, and he sat howling dolefully on the doorstep until they came out again. He escorted them into the garden afterwards, however, and so did a large nondescript kind of yard dog, which was called Bootles, and which allowed itself to be harnessed to a mail-cart, and drew Cyril up and down the path.

"I want to show you our fruit trees," said Rhoda, leading the way to the orchard. "We each have one of our very own, planted as soon as we were born. Meta, Ralph, and Leonard have apples, Wilfred and Alwyn pears, mine is a Victoria plum, Joan has a greengage, and Cyril a black cherry. You see, they stand in a row, away from the other trees, so we call this our part of the orchard."

"Whose is the ninth?" enquired Lindsay, looking at a fine pear tree which headed the line.

"That belonged to our eldest brother," said Rhoda. "He died before I can remember, but we still call it 'Herbert's tree'. The pears are always ripe every year on his birthday, so we pick them all and pack them carefully in a box, and send them to a children's hospital in London. Mother sends the money she would have spent on his birthday present too. They're the most beautiful pears, the best we have, and we thought that was the nicest thing we could do with them."

The Greenwoods' little gardens were as interesting as their fruit trees. Each child appeared to have been trying a different experiment. Wilfred had made a pond in his by sinking an old wooden tub in the ground, and was trying to persuade a water-lily to grow in it. He had planted a clump of iris and some forget-me-nots at the edge, which hung over rather gracefully, and really looked quite pretty. He kept several frogs to swim about in the water, though the constant catching of these rather interfered with the wellbeing of the struggling lily. Alwyn had built a miniature house in her plot out of old bricks and stones, and had thatched it neatly with straw. She had made a gravel path up to the front door, and had sown grass to represent lawns, and cut a round flower bed in the middle of each. Joan's garden was subject to violent changes. Last year it had been a potato patch, but as she dug up those useful vegetables every day to see how they were sprouting, it was not surprising that they refused to make much growth. Lately she had converted the whole into a dolls' cemetery, and, with Cyril's aid, keenly enjoyed conducting the funerals of various headless favourites, waxing so enthusiastic over the obsequies that she even buried several quite respectable wax babies, though, regretting their loss afterwards, she was eventually forced to dig them up again. She put tombstones at the heads of the graves, made of slates from the roof of a tumble-down shed, and carefully wrote names, dates, and epitaphs upon them in slate pencil, being greatly distressed when the inscriptions were invariably obliterated by every fresh shower of rain.

Cyril had sown the letters of his name in mustard and cress, which were just coming up fresh and green, and would soon be ready to cut. He also had some bulbs under pieces of glass in a corner which he called his hothouse. Ralph and Leonard were so busy at school that their gardens appeared to be mostly cared for by Rhoda, who had a very ambitious scheme for her own.

"I want to make a floral clock," she explained. "You see, I've dug a round face and marked it out into twelve parts, and I'm going to put each figure in different-coloured flowers. Then I thought if I could fix a pole in the middle it ought to cast a shadow, and tell the time like a sundial. I've made it north, south, east, and west by my compass, and it will be most delightful if I can only get it to work."

Rhoda had almost as much to show Lindsay in the house as out-of-doors. There was her bedroom, a tiny sanctum where she kept all her special treasures out of the way of the children's meddlesome fingers. It was a very old-fashioned little room, with a low, black-beamed ceiling, and a window that opened on to a small balcony, where she could grow nasturtiums and other trailing plants in pots. The walls were covered with pictures in home-made frames, wonderful arrangements of corks, acorns, shells, or plaited straw; and there were quite a nice writing-table and some wonderful bookcases.

"The boys made these out of old boxes," said Rhoda. "They learn how in their carpentry class at school, and they did them to surprise me on my birthday. I keep all my books here. Father is giving me the poets now as Christmas presents. I have Longfellow and Shakespeare and Wordsworth, and I expect it will be either Cowper or Goldsmith next time. This is my paint-box. I daren't leave it in the schoolroom for fear of the little ones getting hold of it. Isn't it a beauty? Miss Johnson, our governess, gave it to me as a prize for passing the Trinity College exam. in piano and theory."

"Do you like music?" asked Lindsay.

"Yes, I think I'm rather fond of it. Miss Johnson wanted me to go in for this exam.; she said it would be something to practise for. We had to go to Bridgend to take it. It was rather fun, for we were the whole day in getting there and back, and luckily I wasn't a scrap nervous. Do you play?"

"A little," replied Lindsay. "I'm learning the violin, but I can't have any lessons at the Manor."

"I wish you could come over and help us at one of our temperance concerts."

"Oh, I should be much too frightened!" exclaimed Lindsay, in horror.

"You needn't mind in a little village like this," declared Rhoda. "The people would think whatever you did was splendid. They clap at everything, even when Ralph gives nigger songs; and he's got no voice, and the banjo's generally out of tune, so that he's singing away in one key and playing in another."

"I don't know whether I could promise to keep in tune," laughed Lindsay. "Do you play at these concerts?"

"Yes, nearly always. It was a little awkward last time, because something had gone wrong with the keys of the piano. They stuck down, and I had to get Wilfred to sit underneath and keep poking them up as fast as I played on them, or else half the notes wouldn't sound; and it seemed so queer to only get part of a chord, and to miss the middle of a run. It quite put me out. I suppose it was the damp that caused it. We must get a tuner to come and see to it."

"Did the people applaud?"

"Yes, tremendously. I think it amused them to see Wilfred sitting underneath. They simply roared every time he pushed up the keys. It was as good as a comic song. It really is tiresome, though, to have a piano like that at the school. John Crosby, the stonemason's little boy, sings very nicely, and I went so wrong in playing his accompaniment, through losing so many of the notes, that he finished half a verse ahead of me. I apologized to him afterwards, but he said he didn't think anyone had noticed it!"

Lindsay found it quite a novel and entertaining experience to stay in the midst of such a large, enterprising, lively family as the Greenwoods. From Meta, the eldest, to Cyril, the baby, hardly out of petticoats, all had very decided opinions of their own, which they urged and argued with considerable force of character, but an amount of good temper which spoke well for their training. Mrs. Greenwood, who thought quarrelling greatly a matter of habit, insisted upon a certain standard of home politeness being maintained, and would tolerate neither domineering in the elder ones nor whining amongst the younger.

"You can discuss a subject perfectly well without being rude to each other when you differ," she declared. "You must take it in turns to have your own way. It is not fair that the eldest should always arrange everything, but on the other hand Joan and Alwyn will get nothing at all if they begin to wail and complain in that most grumbling and unpleasant tone of voice. I think it is a disgrace if you're all so selfish that you can't agree. You must each be prepared to give up a certain amount, for among eight children it is quite impossible for every one to be first and foremost."

Irene, being the Greenwoods' cousin, was accustomed to their tempestuous ways, and ready to hold her own amongst them; while Monica looked on with an amused smile, without taking part in any arguments or disputes. There was certainly plenty to do at the Vicarage, and none of the three guests could complain that the holiday was dull.

On Saturday afternoon Meta, Rhoda, and the two eldest boys arranged that they should make an expedition to a large lake about a couple of miles away. They had been promised the loan of a boat there, and they proposed to take their visitors for a trip on the water. They started off with baskets of provisions, intending to land and have a picnic tea, if they could find sufficient dry sticks upon the banks to light a fire and boil their kettle. Both Meta and her brothers could row well, so the boat was soon skimming over the lake in a delightfully smooth and satisfactory fashion.

"We daren't anchor anywhere near the woods," declared Meta, "Sir Percy Harwood, the owner, is so very strict about trespassing."

"Yes, the keepers are down on you if you even go a few yards into the preserves," agreed Ralph. "Look here! What do you say to camping out on that little island? There can't be any pheasants there to scare, and we ought to get plenty of sticks."

The island in question was a small, green-looking collection of hazel bushes and birch trees, well out in the middle of the lake. It had an attractive appearance, so they rowed through the quiet stretch of water that separated them from it, and ran the boat in among the reeds that grew at the edge.

"It seems rather jolly," said Rhoda. "Suppose we leave the baskets here, and go and explore first to find a good place?"

"It's quite romantic," declared Irene, "like Ellen's Isle in the *Lady of the Lake*. We ought to find a hunting-lodge among the trees, and an interesting outlaw living there."

"More likely to find a poacher!" laughed Ralph; "though there'd be nothing for him to trap here, unless he kept a boat stowed away in the reeds, and took midnight excursions into the woods."

"I think it's the kind of place for a hermit," said Monica. "He could have had a little cell and told his beads without being disturbed by anybody, except an occasional knight-errant who would blow a horn from the opposite bank. I wonder if one ever lived here?"

"The landlords couldn't have been so particular about trespassing in those days, then, if he did," replied Leonard. "I don't believe Sir Percy Harwood would let anybody settle so near his pheasants; he'd suspect steel traps or wire snares under the cassock, and expect to hear a shot in the woods instead of a vesper bell."

"We'll tie the boat to this old stump," said Ralph. "Be careful where you step in getting off—the ground seems fearfully soppy. Perhaps it may be better higher up. Let us come on a little. I say, there's something rather queer about it, isn't there?"

There certainly was something decidedly queer. The green mossy earth under their feet gave way as if they were treading upon a feather bed. At each step it sank with a curious squelching sound, and rose behind with the elasticity of a cork, so that as they sprang here and there the whole of the little island appeared to be bounding up and down beneath them, as Leonard expressed it, "just like a spring mattress when you jump on it".

"The ground is so funny, too," said Meta, poking about with a stick; "it doesn't seem proper soil, only roots and moss and grass growing through it. Why, this stick goes down ever such a long way, and there's actually water coming up!"

The others all came to investigate, and standing close together began to dig their sticks into the curious heaving surface. It bore their combined weight for a moment or two, then sinking suddenly, like a punctured indiarubber ball, it collapsed, and they found themselves struggling nearly up to their waists in water. Luckily they were able to clutch at the hazel bushes above, and, by swinging themselves along the branches, to arrive at a firmer foothold, though even there the ground felt very insecure and spongy, and little dark pools came oozing up with every step.

"We must keep as far apart from each other as we can," shouted Ralph; "the wretched place has no solid foundation, it's only a collection of sticks and leaves. Cling to the trees, and try to get back to the boat before you go in any deeper. Don't put your weight on it! It's like walking on thin ice."

Very wet and muddy, and somewhat frightened, the explorers picked their way carefully back, treading as much as possible on the roots of the trees, and never letting go their hold of the boughs. They scrambled into the boat again with considerable relief, and held a review of their damaged garments.

"I'm soaked to the skin!" declared Rhoda. "It's a horrible nuisance. Look at Lindsay!"

"I don't mind my clothes so much, if it weren't so uncomfortable. My dress will wash," said Lindsay.

"Mine won't though, I'm sorry to say!" groaned Irene.

"I was carrying the cakes, and they're wet through, and not fit to eat," announced Leonard.

"The island is a perfect trap," said Meta, trying to squeeze the muddy water from her own dress and Monica's. "I believe it's nothing but a kind of raft, made out of all the dead wood and rubbish that have accumulated in the lake. I expect seeds have blown on to it, and then trees and bushes have sprung up. Now I think of it, I don't believe it was in the same place last year, so it must be able to float. We shall have to go home; we can't stop and picnic when we're drenched like this."

"I wonder how the hermit managed, if he ever lived there?" said Monica.

"It must have been an excellent penance, with a chance of martyrdom at the end of it," returned Ralph. "Well, I must say we have given our visitors a pleasant afternoon! They won't want to take this as a specimen of our picnics. No good offering tea and cake in this condition!"

"I'd rather have a cake of soap and a can of hot water!" said Irene.

"Never mind!" said Leonard consolingly. "I vote we go up Pendle Tor on Monday. We can boil a kettle there, and have no end of fun. If you've never been before, I expect you'll say it makes up for this."

CHAPTER VIII. PENDLE TOR

It was with much pleasurable anticipation that the picnic party set out on Whit Monday for Pendle Tor. The four younger Greenwoods were left at home, as the walk would be too far for them, but they announced their intention of climbing a small hill behind the Vicarage in the afternoon, and having an alfresco tea on their own account, which was to be equal, if not superior, to that enjoyed by their elders—"because Mary will just have finished baking, and she has promised to bring us some buns straight out of the oven, and you certainly won't get those on Pendle Tor," said Joan.

Although they might be debarred from the pleasure of hot tea-cakes, the mountaineers nevertheless did not mean to starve on their journey, to judge from the baskets full of provisions which they bore with them. Leonard had taken a milk-can that would serve to boil the water in instead of a kettle, it being lighter to carry, and having the added advantage that they could pack the teacups inside.

"You see, an iron kettle is such a weight", he explained, "and the last time we took one of those rubbishy sixpence-halfpenny tin ones the solder all melted directly we put it on to the fire, and the spout dropped off. We can sling the milk-can on a stick and prop it over the fire, and it does splendidly."

"Mind you don't break the cups!" said Irene, expecting to hear a smash after the reckless way in which the can was being swung about.

"Couldn't do it if I tried; they're all enamel ones. The Mater wouldn't trust us with her best china, I assure you."

"There are ever so many trout up in the stream by Inglemere," remarked Ralph. "If we could manage to tickle a few, we might fry them in the lid of the milk-can."

"It's rank poaching!" declared Meta.

"I don't care in the least," returned Ralph. "If Sir Percy complains that any are missing, you can give him the bones, with my compliments."

"I don't think he would mind your catching one or two," said Monica. "I know Sir Percy rather well, and it is only real poachers that he's so hard on, and excursionists who come sometimes and try to fish. You see, as he says, if everyone were allowed to take fish, there would soon be none left, and people would begin to do it for the sake of selling them, and not for the sport. He allowed Mr. Cross's nephews to fish last summer when they were staying at the Rectory, and he said I might too, if I ever felt inclined."

"I've never seen trout tickled," said Lindsay.

"It will be a case of 'First catch your fish, then cook it'," laughed Rhoda. "It isn't at all easy to whisk them out—they're the most slippery things you can imagine. I'm glad we don't have to depend on Ralph's skill for our dinner. I was hoping we might find some mushrooms, and stew them in part of the milk we've brought. We could put the can down among the ashes of the fire, and they'd be cooking while we ate the first course."

"Well, it is certainly a case of 'First pick your mushrooms', for you don't even know whether there'll be any," retorted Ralph. "The trout are always there, at any rate."

It was a long walk to Pendle Tor, and appetites, sharpened by the fresh air of the hills, began to grow rather keen; but as they had all resolved not to have their picnic before they had reached the summit, they staved off the edge of their hunger with a few biscuits, and, trudging on, covered the last mile in such quick time that Leonard declared it reminded him of a paper-chase. It was rather a steep pull to gain the highest point, yet they were well rewarded when they reached it by the bird's-eye view of the landscape around them, farms, churches, and distant village looking like so many toys, and the fields like the divisions in a map.

"I hope it doesn't mean to rain," said Monica, pointing to some rather threatening clouds that were rolling up from the west.

"We shall get a nice wetting if it does, for we haven't an umbrella amongst us!" returned Irene.

"Rain? Not it! Don't distress yourself; the glass was up to 'Fair' this morning. It's only a little scrap of mist blowing over. I don't mind giving you a butter-scotch in exchange for every drop of rain you get on your hat to-day," declared Ralph, whose prophecies were generally in exact accordance with his hopes, and who was apt to shut his eyes to unwelcome truths.

"Better not promise too much, old chap, or you may have to pay up," said Leonard. "I don't like the look of the sky myself. But what's the odds? It won't be the first time we've been wet through, by a long way, and I suppose we shan't melt."

"What about the lunch?" asked Rhoda. "I'm getting so famished, I can't wait much longer."

It was decided that the extreme top of the Tor was hardly a suitable place—the wind was strong, and no water was available; so they climbed some little distance down the cliff on the farther side, and at last hit upon a sheltered spot among the rocks, where a small surface spring, bubbling up from the ground, enabled them to fill the milk-can which was to serve as a kettle. The boys cut large bundles of dry heather, and, stacking it well together, soon had a good fire burning. They found it after all impossible to suspend the can, for the flames burnt directly through any stick that they tried to hang over the blaze; so they were obliged to set it securely on an arrangement of stones, and rake the fire round it. They had brought the tea in a muslin bag, which they dropped into the can, to save a teapot; and though pouring out was rather difficult, owing to the tin being so extremely hot, Meta managed to dispense the cups without burning her fingers.

"You haven't provided the fish course yet," said Rhoda to Ralph. "I thought we were to have fried trout as part of the feast."

"And I thought you were to give us mushrooms," retorted Ralph.

"Shouldn't care to wait while she cooked them," declared Leonard. "Ham sandwiches and hard-boiled eggs are quite good enough for me. Did you bring any salt? Another cup of tea, please, and don't be stingy with the sugar, Meta. I like three lumps."

"I wonder why things always taste so different out-of-doors," said Lindsay, looking reflectively at the three-cornered strawberry jam pastry she was eating.

"Why, I saw you swallow an ant on your tart just now," said Ralph, "so perhaps that has given it a flavour. Oh, you needn't distress yourself! Ants are quite wholesome, I assure you. There are a frightful lot of them crawling about here, though. I think we shall have to move on a stave."

"Ugh! Yes. They're stinging me already!" agreed Lindsay.

They were all a little tired after their long walk, so they were glad to sit and rest after lunch, asking riddles, cracking jokes, and listening to the boys' school tales of exciting cricket matches, private feuds, combats between class champions, and the punishments that had been meted out to certain sneaks and bullies—accounts which were as thrilling in their way as the doughty deeds of mail-clad knights of old, the warlike sentiments being just the same, though the setting of the century might differ. It was so interesting that nobody gave a thought to the time, or remembered the ominous clouds that had been stretching themselves out like long ribbons over the moor.

"Why, where's the view gone to?" cried Monica at last. "I thought we could see Linforth and the lake from here, and the tower of Haversleigh Church."

She might well exclaim in astonishment. Instead of the landscape which had met their eyes before, there was nothing to be seen but a great white wall of mist that seemed to close them in on every side, as if some giant hand had suddenly drawn down a blind between them and the distance.

"Whew!" exclaimed Ralph, starting to his feet, and indulging in a long-drawn-out whistle. "This is a nice fix! We're in the middle of a cloud. I never saw it coming up. It will be uncommonly awkward to get out of it. What a shame of old Pendle Tor to play us such a trick!"

"Will it soon blow over, do you think?" asked Irene.

"I don't know," replied Meta rather gravely. "Sometimes the clouds stay on these moors for days and days together. I wish we had noticed it sooner, and gone down to the road again before we were surrounded. I'm afraid it may be very difficult to find our way now."

"I don't think it's any use waiting," said Leonard, "it mayn't clear for hours. We'd better pack up our traps, and make the best push we can to try to strike the path."

"We must all stick close together," remarked Ralph. "It won't do to get divided, or we might never find each other again. We'd better keep well to the right; there's an old quarry on the left, and it wouldn't be exactly pleasant to walk into it. Luckily I've a pocket compass on my watch chain."

Very much sobered in spirits, the picnic party hastily packed up the baskets, and, choosing Ralph as guide, set off down the hillside, hoping to find some track that would lead eventually into the road below. It was a strange walk, groping their way through what Monica described as "white darkness". The heavy mist hung in the air like a blanket, so completely shutting them in that they could scarcely see each other at a distance of even a few feet, and it was only by keeping near enough to touch one another that they managed to avoid being separated. Though they had some general idea of their direction, they did not really know where they were walking, and stumbled blindly on through heather and bilberry bushes, over stones and rocks, only feeling that they were going downhill. It was very slow progress. Ralph stopped continually to consult his compass, and occasionally gave a loud "cooee", in case they might find some wandering shepherd or countryman who would be able to help them. There was no answer to his calls, however—only the occasional bleat of a sheep that sounded far off and muffled through the mist. They knew there was neither cottage nor farm within hail, and unless they could strike the road they might wander on hour after hour over the moors, only getting farther and farther out of their way. Tired out with the rough trudge, the girls at last declared they must sit still for a few minutes and rest.

"I'm awfully sorry to have landed you in such a hole," said Ralph, "but who would have thought those innocent-looking clouds would have come down on us like feather beds? You really never know what to expect on these hills."

"I wonder what we'd better do?" said Monica.

"Stay where we are," suggested Irene.

"It would be too cold to spend the night here," replied Meta.

"We haven't even our jackets with us," added Lindsay.

"Unless we're quite dead beat, we'd better push on," said Leonard. "I'm hoping we may come to the stream, because we could find our way along the banks to Whitcombe, at any rate. I've been listening for it all the time, but I haven't heard a sound."

"I wish we had a divining rod!" groaned Rhoda. "That would tell us in what direction the water lay. We've been going south-east all the time, haven't we?"

"Yes, I believe the stream lay due south from where we started," answered Ralph, "but I didn't dare to turn that way, because of the quarry. Perhaps we may strike it higher up. If you're rested, girls, we'll be going."

The damp, clinging clouds appeared to have settled down to stay. The wind that had been blowing earlier in the day, when they ascended Pendle Tor, had ceased, and there was not even the breath of a breeze to blow away the clammy mist that was already drenching their clothes with a chilly dew. It was now half-past five o'clock, and they had been wandering for more than an hour.

"I haven't an idea where we are, nor how far we've come," said Ralph. "I only know I've been steering east by the compass. Of course we've been going very slowly, but I think we shouldn't be far from the brook. If we could find that, it would be an enormous help."

"I believe I hear water now," said Rhoda, pausing a moment. "I'm sure I do: to our left. Listen!"

All stood still, with every sense on the alert, straining their ears intently for the faintest murmur. In the far distance it seemed to them that they could certainly catch the unmistakable rush of a stream flowing swiftly over a rough, stony bed. Guided by the sound, they stumbled on, till at length, after climbing over a number of rocks, they reached the welcome brook that was to be their path to home and safety.

"I'm uncommonly glad to see it!" said Ralph, stooping to take a drink. "I began to think we should never get back again. If we follow it down, it will lead us straight into Whitcombe. Of course, that's far enough out of our way, but we might get a trap there, and drive home."

It was a most terrible scramble down the bed of the stream, over jagged rocks, among briers and bushes, and through rushes and reeds. The mist still wrapped them round, and they did not dare to venture away from the water to find smoother walking. The three visitors, who were not accustomed to such exploits, were nearly exhausted, while even sturdy Meta and Rhoda showed signs of giving in.

"We're at the old bridge now," said Ralph, trying to encourage them. "We can climb up and get on to the road. It's only about three miles farther to Whitcombe village. We're bound to find a trap of some sort there, and then you'll be all right."

"I think the mist is lifting a little," said Leonard; "it isn't half as thick as it was. Look at the sun trying to get through!"

"I believe we're walking straight out of the edge of the clouds. That's what it is!" declared Ralph. "I begin to see the trees. Hurrah! It's clearing ever so. We'll scramble up the bank, and we shall get along much faster on the road than down here on these wretched stones. Cheer up, girls! You'll soon be in Whitcombe now."

An hour afterwards, very footsore and weary, the party limped into Whitcombe, a small hamlet consisting of a wayside inn and a handful of cottages. It was eight o'clock, and the sun, behind long bars of crimson and grey, had already begun to sink below the horizon. They were nine miles away from home, as the stream had led them in quite a different direction from Linforth, and, as Leonard expressed it, they had "altogether landed themselves in a jolly pickle". Just at present tea seemed the most pressing necessity, so a council of war was held to see what funds could be mustered for the purpose. These did not amount to very much. Lindsay and Rhoda were penniless, Monica also had left her purse at the Vicarage. Irene and Meta mustered a shilling between them. Ralph had a sixpence, while the contents of Leonard's pockets proved to be exactly those of the traditional schoolboy's, twopence-halfpenny and an old knife.

"I'm afraid it won't go very far," said Ralph. "We shall have to ask them to give us tick. Come along! We'll try the inn, and see what they will do for us."

"We must tell them who we are," added Meta, "and say Father will pay afterwards."

The sight of seven such *bona fide* travellers appeared to occasion much surprise, to both the good woman at the bar and the few villagers who, with pipes and glasses, were sitting discussing local politics and the chances of the harvest. Tea at the unwonted hour of eight seemed an unprecedented request, and the landlady was not content until she had satisfied her curiosity as to who her guests were, where they came from, and what they wanted at Whitcombe at that time in the evening.

"What we want is some tea," said Ralph, after a brief explanation of their adventure, "and anything in the shape of a conveyance that can take us back to Linforth to-night. We've only one and eightpence-halfpenny amongst us, but my father will pay the rest when we get home. If you like, I'll leave you my watch and chain."

"You've no need to do that!" laughed the landlady. "I'm sure I can trust you. Come into the little parlour, and have your teas there. The young ladies look ready to drop, and this is no fit place for them to sit down in. Those mists be nasty things up Pendle Tor. It's a mercy as you've got down at all. There was a gentleman from London caught there last autumn, and he wandered round and round in a circle for two days before it cleared and they found him. He was nigh dead, too, with the cold and the damp. My son Albert shall put the horse in the trap and drive you home. I dare say you'll manage to cram in somehow."

No tea was ever so acceptable as the large, steaming cups which they drank in the stuffy little parlour, and no carriage and pair could have been more welcome than the old market cart that came round to the door afterwards. It was rather a problem how to pack themselves and the driver into it, but Lindsay sat on Meta's knee, and Rhoda squeezed herself between her two brothers on the front seat. The horse walked up and down hill, and only rose to a measured trot on level ground, so it took a considerable time to accomplish the nine-mile journey, and it was nearly eleven o'clock before they reached the Vicarage. Very tired and cold and cramped, they rushed into the house, where Mrs. Greenwood, in an agony of suspense, had been imagining all the accidents which could possibly have happened to them, and was preparing herself for the worst. The Vicar and some of the neighbours, it appeared, were out searching for them with lanterns, so a messenger was quickly sent through the village to spread the good news of their safe arrival.

"You can't complain you've had no excitement here," said Ralph to the three guests. "We almost drowned you on Saturday, and to-day we nearly lost you on the moors. You're going to-morrow, or we might have had some more hairbreadth escapes. At any rate, I don't think you'll forget Pendle Tor in a hurry!"

Lindsay had certainly plenty of news to relate when she returned to the Manor. Her classmates were quite envious, and poor Cicely was a little wistful lest Rhoda should have usurped her place in her friend's affections. Of that, however, she need not have been afraid. Lindsay was faithful to her chosen chum, and had so many things to ask about, as well as adventures to tell, that the two were soon chattering as fast as usual. Cicely had made no further important discoveries during the few days, though she had kept a careful watch on Mrs. Wilson, and had once noticed her go up to the lantern room carrying a jug in her hand. Scott had not been in the house again, but he had been seen talking earnestly with "The

Griffin" in the garden. He had gone hastily away when Cicely approached, so he evidently did not wish the conversation to be overheard. Whether it had anything to do with the mystery or not, it was of course impossible to say.

"I'm rather glad, on the whole, that nothing particular happened while you were away," said Cicely. "I should have wanted so dreadfully to tell somebody, I'm afraid Marjorie Butler might have wormed it out of me. As it is, they none of them know, and we still have the secret to ourselves."

CHAPTER IX. THE PLOT THICKENS

After hearing the story of Monica Courtenay, their friend's ancestress, Lindsay and Cicely felt a special interest in her portrait. They strolled one afternoon along the picture gallery to take another look at it. There were the pretty smiling face—so like Monica's—and the bunch of red roses that had saved the life of Sir Piers Courtenay. Was all the good fortune of the race to be hers, and would none of it descend to the namesake who so closely resembled her?

"If she could only come back and be of some use again!" sighed Lindsay. "She ought to know every secret of this house."

"I wish we could make her speak and tell us," said Cicely.

At that moment a distant door banged, and a great gust of wind blew along the gallery. Cicely started violently.

"Lindsay, did you see?" she exclaimed. "The picture moved in its frame!"

"Nonsense! How could it?" said Lindsay, who had been looking the other way.

"I tell you it did!"

"You must have imagined it."

It certainly seemed rather improbable. The portraits were all firmly fixed in the panelled walls, and no breath of air could be expected to penetrate behind them.

"It's almost as if she were alive," continued Cicely, "and just when we were wishing she could talk! No wonder people make up tales about her. I don't think I quite like it."

"How silly you are!" said Lindsay scornfully. "You might have seen a ghost!"

"Well, it is queer! You needn't laugh at me so. I'm not going to stay here any longer; I vote we go out into the garden."

Pictures that moved were rather more than Cicely had bargained for. Mysteries were all very well in their way, but she began to feel it was possible to have too much of a good thing. It was a distinct relief to her to leave the gloomy old gallery, with its armour and tapestry, and walk out into the fresh air and sunshine. There was still half an hour to be disposed of before tea, and the two girls sauntered leisurely in the direction of the kitchen-garden.

"I wish I knew where the boathouse used to be that Sir Piers wanted the key for," said Lindsay.

"It was not very far away, I dare say. The river runs somewhere at the bottom of those fields."

"I wonder if there's a path."

"I believe there's one at the end of the orchard. I saw Scott walking down there once."

"Shall we go and see?"

"All right!"

The orchard was forbidden ground. Perhaps, though, the fact that they risked a scolding, or even a mark for bad conduct, only made the adventure more interesting. They ascertained first that Scott was safely attending to his tomatoes in the greenhouse, then they dived hastily between the rows of young apple trees. Cicely was right. At the far end there was a small gate that led into a meadow.

"The river must be over there, hidden by those willows," said Lindsay.

"I hope we shan't meet a bull," said Cicely, looking nervously at a group of cattle in the distance.

"Oh, come along! You're surely not afraid of cows!"

They had soon crossed the field and reached the shade of the willows by the water's edge. The low bank was covered with reeds and rushes. Tall purple flowers were growing on a green, boggy island close by. It was a very pleasant place, just the kind of spot to choose on a hot summer's afternoon.

"Far nicer than the garden, because we have it all to ourselves," declared Cicely.

"Oh, look what I've found!" exclaimed Lindsay ecstatically.

She had been poking about among the reeds, and now pointed in triumph under the branches of a big willow to a smooth little pool, where there actually floated a punt, anchored by a long chain to the trunk of the tree.

It was a most attractive-looking boat, nicely polished, and with the name *Heatherbell* painted in neat white letters on the prow. It came quite easily to the edge of the bank when Lindsay pulled the chain, and seemed deliberately to invite them to step into it. Such a temptation was not to be resisted. In a moment they were both inside.

"If I can manage to untie it, I'm sure I could punt us out on to the river," said Lindsay.

"Oh, do! And then perhaps we could find some water-lilies," agreed her ever-willing friend.

Lindsay leaned over to reach the chain. It was wound tightly round the tree, and was very difficult to unfasten.

"I'll come and help you!" cried Cicely, and without a thought of the consequences she bounced up, and stepped to the other end of the boat.

Her sudden change of position utterly upset the balance of their small craft. There was a splash, a succession of squeals, and both girls were floundering in the water. Luckily the pool was shallow, and they were in no danger of drowning; but by the time they reached the bank they were wet through, and in an extremely draggled condition.

"What are we to do?" said Cicely blankly, trying to wring the water out of her skirts.

"Go back, I suppose, and put on dry things," replied Lindsay. "We shall get into a fearful scrape, I expect."

"Yes! What will Miss Frazer say?"

Miss Frazer was on the point of collecting her flock in preparation for tea, when two dejected, dripping figures came creeping along the terrace. If they had hoped to reach the side door unobserved, they were soon undeceived; the governess's sharp eyes spied them at once.

"Lindsay and Cicely!" she burst out wrathfully. "You naughty girls! Where have you been? Come at once into the house and change your clothes. You give more trouble than all the rest of the class put together. Miss Russell will have to be told about this."

Miss Russell was angry—really angry. She lectured them both severely, and stopped their recreation for the whole of the next day. This seemed only a very small circumstance in itself, but strangely enough it led indirectly to something of much more consequence.

The two delinquents looked decidedly rueful when, instead of going into the garden as usual, they were obliged to sit in the classroom, and copy out a passage from "Lycidas" in their best handwriting. It was trying, certainly, particularly as the other girls were playing a tennis handicap, and they could hear the soft thud of balls, and the cries of "'Vantage!" or "Game!" It was possible to see a few heads bobbing over the wall, but they could not gather how the tournament was progressing, nor which was the winning side.

Long before tea-time they had finished their allotted portions, and going to the window they leaned out, to try to catch a glimpse of what was happening on the lawn. The classroom was at the back of the house, and overlooked a small paved courtyard. Below, on a wooden bench in the sunshine, sat Scott, leisurely blacking boots, and humming to himself in a voice that had little tune in it. The cat, purring loudly, was rubbing herself vigorously against his trousers.

The girls were just going to call to him, and beg him to peep through the door in the wall and give them some news of the tennis players, when they suddenly changed their intention. Mrs. Wilson had appeared in the porch. She brought out a flower vase, flung the stale water away, and refilled it from one of the butts that stood near.

Scott had evidently seen her too, for he gave a short whistle to attract her attention, then, throwing down his blacking brush, he crossed the courtyard to speak to her. In spite of his lowered tone, his voice rose up clearly to the classroom window above.

"About what we were talking of this morning," he began. "It had best be done as soon as possible. I'll do it to-night."

"I've marked the place," replied Mrs. Wilson, "but I'll come with you to make sure. You'll want a helping hand. It's too much for one."

"You can hold the lantern, at any rate. It's a job that will need some caution. We mustn't attempt it till it's quite dark."

"No, not till everything's quiet," said Mrs. Wilson, as she re-entered the house.

Lindsay drew Cicely back quickly into the room, as Scott returned to his rows of boots on the bench. She did not wish him, at any cost, to see them at the window, or to know that they had overheard the conversation.

"What are they going to do?" asked Cicely breathlessly.

"I don't know. It must be something dreadful if they want to keep it so quiet."

"And do it in the dark, too!"

"I'm afraid both Mrs. Wilson and Scott are bad characters," said Lindsay in an impressive voice. "I expect they've stolen the treasure, and they're going to hide it in the garden. Perhaps even it may have something to do with the prisoner in the lantern room."

"You don't think they've killed him?" gasped Cicely.

"I can't tell. I believe they're capable of anything. I'm quite uneasy for fear they intend to harm Monica. We'll watch to-night, and find out what they're about. I shouldn't wonder if we're on the verge of a great discovery. It was most fortunate we were kept in this afternoon; if we hadn't happened to be at the window just then, we shouldn't have heard their plans."

Cicely's face had lengthened considerably at the idea of the black doings which it was evidently their duty to investigate.

"I don't know how we're to follow them in the dark," she said, after a moment's hesitation.

"We must," declared Lindsay emphatically. "I feel it all depends on us. Monica may be in the greatest danger, and we are the only ones who know anything about the matter, and can save her."

The tea-bell ringing at that moment sent them down to the dining-hall. The meal had been delayed half an hour on account of the tournament, so preparation followed immediately afterwards, and Lindsay and Cicely were obliged, with their thoughts still running on possible tragedies, to endeavour to apply their minds to the unromantic details of parsing.

It seemed of such minor importance whether a verb were transitive or intransitive, weak or strong, compared with whether Mrs. Wilson and Scott were really going to meet in the garden to carry out some fell intention. The time seemed endless until the books were at last put away, and they could snatch a few moments for private talk.

"There's one comfort," said Lindsay, "they won't begin until it's dark, so they can't have been doing anything while we've been in prep."

"It's generally light for quite half an hour after we're in bed," said Cicely. "I don't see yet how we're to know when they're starting."

"We shall find out," returned Lindsay confidently. "I have a kind of feeling that something is going to happen to-night."

"What are you two whispering about?" asked Nora Proctor curiously.

"Oh, only a joke of our own!"

"You've got some secret, I'm sure," said Beryl Austen; "you're always looking at each other and making signs. I noticed you yesterday during arithmetic."

"Do tell us, Cicely," begged Marjorie Butler. "You and I used to be friends, but we never have a secret together now."

"There's really nothing worth telling," declared Cicely, much embarrassed.

"We shall have to be careful though," said Lindsay afterwards. "We don't want the others to hear, and then go poking about and making discoveries."

"Certainly not; if there's anything to be found out, I'd rather we found it out ourselves."

Cicely was tired when bedtime arrived, and ready to curl herself up and forget what might be happening outside. Lindsay, on the contrary, lay with wide-open eyes, watching the room grow darker and darker. When the wardrobe and the chest of drawers and the washstand had at last all merged together into one deep mass of shadow, she got up and peeped through the open window. What she saw there caused her to run hurriedly and shake her sleepy companion.

"Cicely! Do wake up! There's a light moving in the garden."

It took a second or two for Cicely to recover her senses, but when she realized the nature of the news, she hopped out of bed in frantic excitement.

"Is it Mrs. Wilson and Scott?" she asked eagerly.

"I expect so, but of course I can't tell. Be quick! We must go at once and see what they're doing."

The two girls hastily scrambled into their clothes, and tiptoed downstairs to the side door. The servants had not yet locked up, so it was still standing ajar.

"Suppose we were to meet Miss Russell or Miss Frazer!" shivered Cicely, with a nervous glance down the corridor.

"Don't think about it. They're both safe in the drawing-room."

In another minute they had closed the door gently behind them, and were running softly across the lawn. It was a cloudy night, with neither moon nor stars in the sky. The outlines of the trees and shrubs were just visible, but it was very dark indeed under their shade.

"The light seemed to be going through the shrubbery towards the arbour," said Lindsay, feeling her way along the rose avenue.

"There it is!" replied Cicely, as a faint gleam shone in the distance.

"We must be very, very careful," said Lindsay, "not to disturb them on any account. We must stop somewhere near, and just look and listen."

As quietly as ghosts they stole down the path, trying not to rustle so much as a leaf. They were close now to the lantern. They could see it quite clearly, set on the ground, and two figures bending over it.

Skirting round under the bushes, they reached the shelter of an oak tree that grew on the side of a bank, and peeped cautiously round the trunk. Yes, it was certainly Scott and Mrs. Wilson who were in the shrubbery below. Every now and then a glint of light revealed their faces unmistakably. They were talking together in low tones, unfortunately too low for their conversation to be overheard. Scott held a spade in his hand, and was stooping to watch Mrs. Wilson, who, kneeling on the grass, was fumbling inside a large sack.

"Can you see if she's counting money?" breathed Cicely into Lindsay's ear. "I believe they're going to bury it."

"It looks like something bigger and heavier," whispered Lindsay, trying to crane her neck farther forward.

"Is it silver plate?"

"It might be anything in that huge sack."

"Oh! Not a body!"

I believe Cicely would have fled precipitately if Lindsay had not held her tightly by the hand. The fear that old Sir Giles Courtenay was being finally disposed of oppressed her like a nightmare.

"No! I expect it's the treasure. We must notice exactly where they're putting it."

Lindsay took a step nearer, to gain a better view of the proceedings, but as she did so her foot trod noisily on a dead twig.

"What's that?"

The question was in "The Griffin's" well-known voice.

There was a growl in reply from Scott.

"Best take a look, anyhow," came from Mrs. Wilson.

Scott seized the lantern, and began to flash it round in every direction. Then, oh horrors! he walked straight towards the oak where the two girls were hiding. Nearly paralysed with fear, they did not dare to run away, and could only hope that, after all, under cover of the darkness, he might chance to overlook them.

In her desperation, Lindsay tried to draw farther behind the trunk of the tree. To do so she perforce pushed Cicely back. The latter was not quite prepared for the sudden movement, the ground was uneven, she swayed, clutched violently at her companion to save herself, and over they both rolled down the bank, almost to the very feet of Scott himself.

As Lindsay and Cicely came crashing down the bank, Scott uttered a cry of consternation. In the suddenness of his dismay, the lantern dropped from his hand, extinguishing the light in its fall.

Instantly the two girls were on their feet, and rushed helter-skelter across the garden through the darkness. They plunged anyhow through bushes and over flower-beds, scratching their faces on overhanging boughs, and tearing their dresses on thorns, their one fear lest Scott should be pursuing them, and their one anxiety to gain the safe shelter of the house.

They reached the side entrance without hearing any footsteps behind them. If Scott had tried to follow them, they had evidently managed to elude him, and he must have given up the chase. The door was still unbolted, and they hurried breathlessly upstairs, luckily meeting nobody on the way. What a harbour of refuge it seemed to be, back in their own room! Without daring to light the candle, they went back to bed again with all possible speed.

"Well, we have had an adventure!" began Lindsay, when they were once more comfortably ensconced between the sheets.

"Do you think Scott noticed who we were?" whispered Cicely.

"I can't tell. He had just time to catch a glimpse of our faces before the lantern went out."

"I'm sure they were doing something dreadful that they wanted to keep secret, he looked so utterly horror-stricken at seeing us."

"There's no doubt about it. The unfortunate part is that now they find they've been discovered, they'll bury the treasure somewhere else instead."

"What a pity we fell just at that moment!"

Cicely's voice was very doleful.

"It will have aroused their suspicions, too, and will make them extra careful," lamented Lindsay. "If Scott recognized us, he and Mrs. Wilson will know we're watching them. They'll owe us a grudge. 'The Griffin' was bad enough before, but she'll be worse than ever now."

They scanned the old housekeeper's face narrowly next morning, as she carried the coffee into the dining-room, but her countenance wore its accustomed aspect of grim inscrutability. If she connected them with last night's happenings, she certainly did not betray the knowledge; it was impossible to tell whether she mistrusted them or not, or what feelings lay concealed under her forbidding exterior.

The moment breakfast was over, they rushed into the garden to renew their acquaintance with the scene of their adventure. Somebody had plainly been digging in the bank, though the traces had evidently been tidied carefully up, and the sods replaced.

"Do you think there could be anything here?" said Cicely wistfully, poking a stick into the loosened soil.

"Oh, dear me, no!" replied Lindsay. "Why, the first thing they'd do would be to rush off with that sack to some safer spot. Even the very stupidest persons wouldn't have gone on burying valuables in a place where they knew they'd been watched. 'The Griffin' and Scott are certainly not idiots!"

"If we could only guess where they'd put it!" sighed Cicely.

For the present they had had such a fright that, though neither would confess it, both were a little inclined to let the matter rest in abeyance. It needed courage to risk the anger of Mrs. Wilson and Scott if they were once more caught meddling. It had seemed pleasant enough to search for the treasure themselves in the house, but the affair was now beginning to assume a graver aspect.

"I sometimes wonder if we ought to tell Monica or Miss Russell," said Cicely, who occasionally had uneasy scruples as to the wisdom of their plan of secrecy.

"It wouldn't be of the slightest use," declared Lindsay. "'The Griffin' and Scott would simply deny everything. They'd make out it was all nonsense on our part, like grown-up people generally do. And how could we prove we were right? Miss Russell would tell us to mind our own business, and we should only get into a scrape for our pains. No, we shall just have to let things take their course, and trust to luck."

CHAPTER X. UNDER THE HAWTHORN TREE

It was high summer at Haversleigh. The trees, now in full leaf, cast rich shadows over the landscape, the wild roses were in bloom on the hedgerows, and tall foxgloves stood like crimson sentinels at the margins of the woods. The fields were white with moon-daisies, growing among the long, lush grass; and all the roadsides were a tangle of vetches, campion, bugle, trefoil and speedwells. The wind was fragrant with the scent of newly turned hay; everywhere the mowers were busy, and the daisies were falling fast beneath the swinging scythe or the blades of the reaping-machine. In the Manor garden the roses had reached perfection, and the flower-beds were a mass of colour. The girls spent every available moment out-of-doors, making the most of the bright days, and enjoying their country visit to the full.

One blazing half-holiday afternoon Lindsay and Cicely, allowed for once in the select company of a few of the elder girls, were lounging blissfully under the shade of a big hawthorn tree. The air seemed dancing for very heat; the grasshoppers were chirping away at the edge of the lawn, a lizard lay basking on the stones of the terrace wall, and the sparrows for once were silent.

"It's far too hot to play tennis," said Irene Spencer. "One just wants to sit somewhere where it's green and cool."

"I'm glad we're here, then, instead of at Winterburn Lodge," said Mary Parkinson.

"So am I; and yet Winterburn Lodge is nicer than many other schools," remarked Mildred Roper.

"It's not half bad," assented Mary. "I like it better, at any rate, than the French school I was at in Brussels."

"I didn't know you'd ever been in France," said Lindsay, idly picking a dandelion clock and blowing it to find out the time.

"No more I have, goosey."

"Then why did you say you'd been at a French school? You're telling fibs."

"No, I'm not, because Brussels doesn't happen to be in France—it's in Belgium."

"I thought you were supposed to learn geography in the third class," laughed Irene Spencer.

"She said a French school, not a Belgian one," objected Lindsay.

"Well, everybody speaks French in Brussels."

"Don't they speak Flemish?"

"Only the poor people, and even they can generally talk French as well."

"How long were you there, Mary?" put in Mildred Roper.

"Only one term. I got ill, and had to come home."

"Was it nice?"

"Oh, just tolerable!"

"Had you to talk French all the time?"

"I had to try, because none of the girls knew anything else. They used to laugh at me if I spoke English."

"How nasty! I shouldn't have cared to be you," said Cicely.

"Yes, it was horrid, when I was sure they were saying things about me and I couldn't understand them. I used to get quite cross, and that made my head ache."

"Was the school in the country?" asked Lindsay.

"No, I've told you already it was in Brussels, and that's a big city. It was a large building, with a great high wall all round it, with spikes on the top, as if it were a prison. Inside there was a courtyard where we used to play games. It had orange trees and oleanders in big green tubs, but no grass nor flowers. You couldn't possibly have called it a garden. We hardly ever went out for proper walks. Sometimes we were taken to the park, but even there we had to go very primly, two and two, with the teachers looking after us most sharply."

"Were the teachers nice?"

"Yes, pretty well. I liked them better than the girls, at any rate. There were two sisters in my class, called Marie and Sophie Beauvais, who were always making fun of me because I was English. I had a horrid time until a German girl came to the school, and then they teased her instead of me. The best thing of all was the coffee. It was perfectly delicious—nicer than any I've ever tasted in England."

"Why didn't you stay in Brussels?"

"I was ill, and my mother had to come and fetch me. She declared she would never let me go so far away from home again; so she sent me to Winterburn Lodge instead. Miss Russell is very kind if one's not well, and Mother said she would rather have me properly looked after, even if I didn't learn French."

"Yes, Miss Russell does take care of us," said Irene. "I used to be at another school, and the teachers never noticed if we had headaches, or couldn't eat our meals. We had to work most fearfully hard for exams, too. The headmistress made a point of getting a certain number of passes each year, and one was obliged to prepare and goin whether one was clever or not. Give me good old Winterburn Lodge!—especially when one's at the Manor instead. By the by, there's Monica. She's surely not come to play tennis? It's too hot."

"Fifteen degrees too hot," agreed Monica, throwing herself down on the grass beside the others and fanning herself with her hat. "Out on the road the heat's at simmering-point. I came to bring a message to Miss Russell, and I hear she's gone to Linforth and won't be back until half-past four. I think I shall wait for her."

"Oh, do!" cried the others. "We'll have a 'palaver' here under the trees."

"What's a 'palaver', please? I hope it's something cool and fizzy to drink."

"No, it's nothing of the sort. It's a kind of meeting, where everybody has to tell a story in turn."

"But I'm rigidly truthful!" objected Monica, with a twinkle in her eye.

"You naughty girl! You know we don't mean telling falsehoods. It's telling tales," said Irene.

"I'm no tell-tale either!"

"Don't be too funny. Your story will have to be longer than anyone else's to make up for this. Mildred, you explain, as I don't seem able to express myself properly."

"It can either be a story you have read, or one of something that has happened to yourself," said Mildred. "We prefer people's own adventures if we can get them."

"So few people have any adventures in real life!" said Monica.

"Then you can tell something out of a book."

"Suppose I can't remember anything?"

"You must. It needn't be grand; we're not a critical audience."

"I'm very stupid at telling things," said Monica; "might I read you something instead?"

"If you've got it here."

"As it happens, I have," replied Monica, opening a bound volume of a magazine which she held in her hand. "I brought this book to lend to Miss

Russell, as I knew it would interest her. It has a story about the old Manor in the times of the Wars of the Roses, and how Sir Roger Courtenay came to win it for his own. I dare say you might like to hear it."

"If it's about the Manor I'm sure we shall," said Irene. "Who wrote the tale?"

"A gentleman who stayed in the village a year or two ago. He was very enthusiastic about Haversleigh. I suppose he made it up from the short account in the guide-book. All the facts are quite true, though he must have used his imagination for the details. The worst of it is that it's a fairly long story, and if I read it I'm afraid there won't be any time left for you to tell yours."

"Oh, we don't mind that!"

"So much the better!"

"Fire away!"

"Do go on!"

Thus encouraged, Monica found her place and, the girls having clustered round her in a close circle so as to hear the better, she began her tale:

SIR MERVYN'S WARD

The middle of the fifteenth century was one of the most stormy periods that the pages of English history have ever recorded. The rival claims of the houses of York and Lancaster had led to those disastrous Wars of the Roses that wiped away the flower of chivalry and made the fair land one bloody battlefield. In the autumn of 1470 Edward IV had been driven from his throne by the powerful Earl of Warwick, known as the Kingmaker, and Henry VI had been once more restored to power, though for how long a period none could venture to guess. They were hard times to live through, especially for those lesser gentry and yeomen who had not placed themselves definitely under the protection of any of the greater barons, and still strove to keep their estates in peace and quiet. The turmoil of the great struggle had not spared even the obscure village of Haversleigh. The inhabitants went about their tasks with an air of unrest. It seemed scarcely worth while to plough the fields, and sow corn which might be trampled underfoot by the soldiery before there was a chance to reap it. There were loud and deep murmurs among the villagers at the many exactions and tyrannies of Sir Mervyn Stamford, the then occupant of the Manor, the estates of which he administered on behalf of his ward, Catharine Mowbray. Catharine's father, Sir John Mowbray, had fallen in battle on the side of the Yorkists, but with the return of Henry VI to power, Sir Mervyn, a stanch Lancastrian, had bought the rights of her guardianship from the half-imbecile king, and had not only assumed control of her property, but had announced his intention of wedding the maiden, either with or without her consent.

This was a state of affairs which, however satisfactory to Sir Mervyn himself, was by no means pleasing either to Catharine or to her lover, Roger de Courtenay, a young gentleman of high lineage though broken fortunes. Sir Mervyn was indeed a man whom any girl might have dreaded. Dark, stern, and forbidding, his face seamed with scars, he was a harsh master, a relentless foe, and a cruel tyrant to any who dared not resist his authority. He was cordially hated in Haversleigh, the inhabitants of which were Yorkists to a man, but he had garrisoned himself so strongly in the Manor, with so formidable a band of retainers, that the wretched villagers could do no more than groan under his oppressions, and bewail the advent of the day when, by his marriage with the unwilling Catharine, he would become their legal lord.

Matters were at this crisis one April morning in the year 1471 when Diccon of the Moat Farm came slowly down a path through the forest from Torton. He led a horse laden with a sack of flour, which he had taken to be ground at the mill of the convent of St. Agatha, to avoid the heavy dues imposed by Sir Mervyn on every sack ground within the jurisdiction of the Manor. In consequence he looked warily about him, since, should he chance to meet any of Sir Mervyn's retainers, not only would his flour be confiscated, but his own back would receive such a cudgelling as would lay him up for a month or more. For this reason he had avoided the main road, and chosen a little-used bridle path; and he glanced cautiously up and down each green alley, and listened for every sound that might give a hint of approaching footsteps. It was with a sense of swift alarm, therefore, that he saw a figure suddenly step out from behind the shelter of an oak in front, and heard himself challenged by name. The newcomer was a young man, tall and of fine build, and his commanding presence belied the shabbiness of his poor and travel-stained attire.

"I am an honest man minding mine own business, and sith ye are the same, seek not to hinder me," replied the owner of the Moat Farm.

"Nay, Diccon! Hast thou forgot thine old friend? Come hither, I pray thee, for in good sooth I have tidings of great import."

So saying, the stranger dropped the cloak with which he had so far partly concealed his face, and showed his features more fully.

"Master Roger!" gasped Diccon. "This is indeed a rash venture. An Sir Mervyn find you within a five mile of the Manor there will be an arrow through you ere nightfall."

"I am more like to send an arrow through him," replied Roger fiercely. "He hath done me ill enough already, and now to crown it all he purposes to wed my betrothed. Catharine is mine, not only by her choice, but by the law of the land. She was affianced to me by King Edward himself. Have her I will, or leave my body for the crows!"

"Brave words, Master Roger, brave words!" said Diccon, shaking his head. "'Twill need more than a single sword to cross Sir Mervyn in the matter."

"Where a sword can naught avail, craft and guile must find a way," returned Roger. "List you, I have brought tidings. Edward has come to his own again. But two days since did his arms meet those of Lancaster at Barnet. The Red Rose is trampled under foot, and Warwick and Montague lie dead upon the field."

"In sooth if this be true it were news of great import."

"I met one who carried a letter from my lord of Gloucester. He rode to gather the supporters of York in the West. Margaret the Queen hath landed at Weymouth, and is calling the men of Devon and Cornwall to the standard of the red rose. I hied me in all haste to my lord of Norfolk, and he hath given me a band of stout fellows that are even now hid under the brushwood yonder. An I can surprise Sir Mervyn ere he hears that the emblem of Lancaster is raised in the west it will strike a blow for York in Somerset, and moreover I shall win me my bride. I must myself to the Manor. I would see how it is garrisoned, and convey a message to Catharine alone."

"You are a dead man first!" exclaimed Diccon. "This were folly, Master Roger. A lion's den were safer than the Manor."

"None shall pierce my disguise if you, good Diccon, will but aid to trick me out for the part I fain would play. I wot I could count on your faith!"

"To the last drop of my blood. Yet it is a rash venture, and one that ill pleases me," replied the old man sadly.

Late that same afternoon the golden shafts of the warm spring sunshine were finding their way through the narrow windows of an upper room in the Manor. The house in those days was but a quarter of its present size; it was strongly fortified, and bore more resemblance to a medieval keep than to the Tudor mansion of later times. Strength and defence had been considered before beauty and elegance, and there was little even of comfort to be found inside the stern, forbidding walls. In the apartment in question some rude attempt had been made to render things more habitable than in the rest of the grim establishment. A few pieces of tapestry covered the rough masonry, and the floor was strewn with fresh rushes. On a carved wooden bench by the window sat a fair and beautiful girl of seventeen, who was occupying herself with a piece of needlework, and talking earnestly meanwhile to her attendant, a maiden of her own age, busy also with her tambour frame.

"I tell thee, Anne, I will not wed him—not if he drag me by force to the altar! Verily, it is a pretty case. Here be I a prisoner in mine own manor, my estates squandered, my tenants oppressed and robbed, my retainers dismissed, save only thee, my poor faithful Anne; and in return I am to wed him to boot! Nay! Rather will I take the veil and give all my goods to the convent of St. Agatha at Torton; though thou knowest I have scant mind to be a nun."

"It wants but five morns now to the bridal day," sighed Anne. "If I mistake not, lady, Sir Mervyn will wed you even against your will and despite the convent."

"Then I will die first! Oh, Roger, Roger!" she added softly to herself, "only a year agone, and I was thy betrothed! It is six months since I had tidings of thee, and whether thou art alive or dead I know not."

"Nay, weep not, sweet lady—weeping cures no ills," said Anne; then, wishful to divert her mistress's sad thoughts, she directed her attention to a commotion which was going on in the courtyard below. "Some stranger hath arrived. If I mistake not, 'tis a huckster come to spread out his wares. An it be your pleasure, I will hie me down and bring you tidings of what he hath."

Receiving a half-hearted consent, she hurried to the great courtyard, where many of the servants and retainers were already gathered to look at the contents of the pedlar's pack. At that period the arrival of a travelling merchant was an event at a remote country house, and even Sir Mervyn himself did not disdain to examine the cloths and buy an ell or two of velvet for a doublet. The pedlar, a white-haired man, much bent, and with a strange hood of foreign fashion drawn over his face, wasproclaiming the virtues of his goods in a lusty voice.

"What do ye lack? What do ye lack?" he cried. "I have here hosen, shoon, caps, gloves, girdles, such as ye never might see out of London town. Here be beside cloth of silk and damask fit for the Queen. Is there no worshipful lady of this noble lord before whom I might spread forth my choicer wares?"

"My mistress would gladly have silk for a kirtle, an I may summon her to the courtyard," Anne ventured to whisper to Sir Mervyn.

Receiving a grudging permission, she hurried panting up the stairs with her tidings. Catharine at first would hardly be persuaded to descend from her chamber into the hated presence of Sir Mervyn, and it was finally more to please her maid than herself that she assented.

"Fair apparel is of scant use to one who hath a mind to wed the Church," she said, "but thou shalt have a riband for thyself, Anne, and a silk girdle withal."

No one remarked the swift, eager glance that the pedlar bestowed upon Catharine as she appeared in the doorway, nor how his hand shook as he untied his second pack. With apparent lack of intention he managed skilfully to draw her a few steps away from the rest, under pretence of exhibiting his silks in the best light; then,whispering: "Keep secret! Betray not that you receive this!" he rapidly thrust a small piece of parchment into her hand. Full of surprise, Catharine yet had the presence of mind to utter no exclamation, and to conceal the parchment in the folds of her gown. Hastily completing her purchases, she retired again to her chamber, where, dismissing Anne, she was able to examine the letter in private. It contained but a few lines:

"Right dear and well beloved,

"The White Rose musters again in the west, and I have hope of your release. Ope the west postern ere sunrise. Till then God keep ye.

"Written in great haste this eve of St. Withold by the hand of him who would remain ever yours,

"ROGER COURTENAY."

Catharine's wild excitement on the perusal of this missive can be more readily imagined than described.

"He is alive! He comes to my rescue!" she exclaimed. "Perchance it was even Roger himself disguised as the pedlar. He was ever one to venture a bold deed. Alack! that I should have been so near, and not have known him!"

She did not dare to confide her secret even to her faithful maid, Anne, but retiring as usual at nightfall she lay awake, waiting in burning anxiety for the earliest peep of dawn. When the first faint glimmer of light stole into her room she rose and crept softly down the stairs. She was obliged to make her way through the great hall, where the men-at-arms lay sleeping on the rushes. A dog sprang up and growled, but she managed to quiet it with a caress, and passed on without disturbing the sleepers. The little west postern door was heavily barred, and it took all the strength of her white hands to pull back the bolts. Cautiously she peered out into the half-darkness. At the same moment a tall figure stepped from the shadow and clasped her in his arms.

"Sweet, you must fly! This is no place for ye now," whispered Roger. "Diccon waits with a trusty steed to conduct ye to Covebury. Take sanctuary at the convent of the Franciscans till I come to claim ye. I have stern work to do here."

Wrapping her hastily in a cloak, and helping her to mount, Roger waited till he judged the fugitives to be at a safe distance; then, giving the word of command to his followers, he commenced his attack on the Manor. Sir Mervyn and his retainers, surprised in their sleep, nevertheless offered a determined resistance. A fierce combat was waged in the great hall and in the courtyard, till, pressed from one point of vantage to another, the defenders made a desperate sally, and rushing helter-skelter down the village sought refuge inside the ancient church. It was of no avail; the villagers, hastily armed with swords and pikes, had joined in the fray. Determined to avenge themselves upon Sir Mervyn for his many acts of tyranny and injustice, they set upon him without mercy, and without respect even for the sacredness of the edifice. Chased from the choir to the Lady Chapel, and from the Lady Chapel to the tower, he fled up the narrow steps to the belfry, where he turned at bay, and held the staircase with the courage of despair. Driven from this last standpoint, he climbed yet higher to the rafters where hung the bell, and slew six men in succession before he fell, at length, shouting curses upon his foes.

Roger Courtenay had scant time to enjoy his triumph. The Yorkist army was mustering for a great struggle; so, having left a small garrison in charge of the Manor, he rode away immediately with the rest of his followers to join the adherents of the White Rose. The result of the battle of Tewkesbury is a matter of history. The unfortunate remnant of Lancaster took to flight, and York gained a final and triumphant victory. Roger, whose bravery was conspicuous throughout the day, worthily won his spurs, and was knighted on the field by Richard of Gloucester. His forfeited estate was restored to him, and King Edward himself forwarded his union with Catharine Mowbray, so that before the summer was over the ancient parish church of Haversleigh, which but lately had rung to the clash of arms, now echoed instead to the merry peal of wedding bells.

CHAPTER XI. SIR MERVYN'S TOWER

"Is that all?" asked the girls, as Monica finished her story and closed the book.

"Why, yes. It's a fairly long tale, I think."

"Not long enough. I want to know so much more about them," said Irene.

"Is it perfectly and absolutely true?" enquired Cicely.

"Yes, it is quite true. It was Sir Roger Courtenay who began to build the Manor as it stands to-day. All the central portion was put up in his time, and the coats of arms over the porch are those of himself and his wife, Catharine Mowbray. Their tomb is in the church too—that big carved monument in the side chapel. They had seven children—five sons and two daughters. The eldest son, Sir Godfrey Courtenay, married a relation of Sir Thomas More. Her name is mentioned in one of the Paston Letters."

"Was it really in Haversleigh Church that Sir Mervyn climbed into the belfry and was killed?"

"Or did the writer make that up?"

"No, that is true too," replied Monica. "The tower is still called 'Sir Mervyn's Tower', and it is said there is the stain of his blood on the great bell, and that nothing can ever take it off."

"Have you seen it?"

"Yes, once. It's only a patch of rust."

"Was Sir Mervyn buried in the church too?"

"There's no monument to him, and no record in the old church documents of his grave. I should think it was much more likely that his followers were allowed to carry him to his own estate near Appleford, and bury him in the church there. The story runs that his ghost haunts Haversleigh Tower and walks up the belfry stairs, but of course that's nothing but superstition and nonsense."

"Don't you believe in ghosts?" asked Cicely, who was sometimes a little afraid of the dark passages at the Manor.

"No: when people are dead, I think if they were good they are either resting until the resurrection, or have something so much better and nobler to do in another world that they could not revisit this, any more than a butterfly could turn again into a chrysalis; and if they were bad, I am sure they would not be allowed to come back simply to terrify the living."

"Quite right," agreed Mildred. "In most of the stories one reads about ghosts, they never return for any useful purpose, only to make silly people run and scream."

"There was one thing that didn't seem perfectly clear in the story," said Lindsay. "Was it really Roger who came to the Manor disguised as an old pedlar?"

"Evidently it was. He couldn't trust anyone else to give the letter to Catharine, and he wanted to see for himself how Sir Mervyn was prepared to defend the Manor. There is still part of a ruin left of the old Franciscan Convent near Covebury, where Catharine took sanctuary. It's not much though—only a few pillars and a tumble-down wall."

"Why didn't she go to the Convent of St. Agatha at Torton? It was so much nearer to ride."

"Because the nuns there wished to persuade her to take the veil, and she wanted to marry Roger."

"Were they very angry with her?"

"How can I tell, Cicely? You must ask the writer of the romance; he has a better imagination than I have. I wonder if Miss Russell has come back yet? I'm going indoors to see. By the by, I want to ask a favour. I practise the organ every Wednesday evening at the church, and to-night Judson, the old clerk, will be too busy to blow for me as usual. Would anybody be charitable enough to volunteer? And would Miss Russell allow it, do you think?"

"I expect Miss Russell wouldn't mind," said Mildred. "I'd go with pleasure if I could, but I have an hour's practising to do myself to-night, as well as preparation, and so have Irene and Mary."

"Oh, Monica, could we blow the organ?" cried Lindsay. "Cicely and I have both finished our practising, and if we were to learn our French at once, before tea, I believe Miss Frazer could be persuaded to excuse us from prep. We'd simply love to come."

"Thank you, Lindsay. I'll ask Miss Russell. If she says 'Yes', will you meet me at the church at seven?"

Miss Russell was lenient enough to give the required permission, having ascertained that all lessons for next day were duly prepared; so

Lindsay and Cicely, much envied by the rest of their class, betook themselves with zeal to try their 'prentice hands at the task of organ blowing. The church was open, and Monica was already waiting for them in the porch. She soon showed them how to work the bellows, and after telling them to stop and rest as soon as they were tired, seated herself at the keyboard and began her practice. Both the younger girls felt it a decidedly novel and interesting experience to be in the little space behind the pipes, working away at a long handle. As they took it in turns they were able to keep the organ going fairly steadily, and only once left Monica without wind in the middle of a piece. As a reward she allowed them to try the instrument before she locked it up, showing them the various stops and pedals, and how they were to be used.

"It's much more difficult than the piano," sighed Cicely, after a rather unsuccessful attempt, "and yet it's simply grand to hear the lovely big notes sounding through the church. I should like to learn myself sometime when I'm older."

"Saint Cecilia was the patroness of music, and is always represented playing the organ, so you might very well justify your name by following in her footsteps," said Monica. "Now I simply must go, because my mother will be wanting me. I've been far longer than usual to-night."

"It's our fault, I'm afraid," said Lindsay. "We kept making you pull out the stops."

"No, you were dears to come. Perhaps Miss Russell will let you blow for me some other evening; then we'll start earlier, and I shall have time to let you both try again."

They had passed under the old yew trees of the churchyard and out through the lich-gate into the road, when Monica suddenly looked over her music and exclaimed:

"How stupid! I've left my little copy of *Lux Benigna* behind. It doesn't really matter much, only I don't care to get my pieces mixed up with the organist's, and he will be there at a choir practice to-morrow."

"Shall we go back?" suggested Cicely.

"No, I'm in too great a hurry. I want to get home at once."

"Then we'll fetch it for you," said Lindsay.

"Oh, thanks so much! Will you take it to school, please, and give it to me to-morrow, so that I needn't wait now? Good-bye!" and Monica hastened away as fast as possible in the direction of the cottage.

Lindsay and Cicely walked leisurely into the church again, and found the missing piece of music lying on a seat near the organ. They were returning down the aisle when Cicely said:

"Which is the tomb of Sir Roger Courtenay and Catharine Mowbray?"

"Monica said it was the one in the small side chapel," replied Lindsay. "Shall we go and look at it?"

What an old monument it was! Four centuries had passed away since it was placed over those who slept beneath. The carving was chipped and the marble scratched; part of Sir Roger's head was broken away, and one of poor Dame Catharine's clasped hands; and the letters of the inscription were so worn and effaced that it was with difficulty the girls could make out even a few words.

"It's in Latin, so we couldn't have understood it in any case," said Lindsay.

"How funny her costume is!" said Cicely. "She has a coif on her head, and very long sleeves; and he is in full armour. It makes them seem much more real people when we know their story."

"Can you imagine them living at the Manor?"

"I can hardly believe there was ever a fight going on inside this church."

"And people killing one another!"

"I suppose Sir Mervyn ran through this door up into the tower."

"I wonder if the stain is still on the bell?" said Lindsay.

"The story was that nothing could ever take it off."

"Shall we go up and see if it's really there?"

"What! Up into the belfry?"

"Yes. Why not?"

"Well, isn't it getting too late, and a little dark?"

"Not yet."

"All right, then," assented Cicely, agreeing as usual with Lindsay's proposal.

The small, nail-studded oak door leading to the tower stood open, and they could see that there was a winding staircase inside. There was nobody to forbid them to explore, and though they knew they were due back at the Manor they considered they might allow themselves a little latitude in the way of time. It was rather dark up the corkscrew stairs, though there was a slit every now and then in the wall to admit air and light. At the top they found themselves in a square room, where the clerk evidently pulled the bell on Sundays, for the rope was hanging within easy reach. The roof was made of enormous oak rafters, and through it ran a ladder reaching higher than they could see.

"That will be the way up to the bell," said Lindsay.

"What a horrible place for Sir Mervyn to climb!" commented Cicely. "I can imagine him rushing up with a dagger in his hand, and the others swarming after him. I'm almost sorry they killed him. He was very brave, although he was so bad. You go first, Lindsay."

Up and up they toiled, till they thought they should never reach the top.

"The bell's hung very high," panted Cicely.

"We're nearly there now," replied Lindsay.

The ladder ended in a rough platform which was built round the bell, probably to allow workmen to attend to it now and then in case it were not hanging safely. It looked a great mass of metal, so large and heavy that even the clapper must be an enormous weight.

"There's a very queer mark on it here," said Cicely, in rather an awed voice.

Lindsay walked round to the other side of the platform. There was a most curious stain running along a portion of the bottom of the bell—a dull, irregular mark that might well have had its origin in some dark and dreadful deed. Cicely touched it cautiously, and then looked at her finger as if she expected to find the traces red on her hand.

"I think we'd better go down again," she said, with a shiver.

"All right, only I want to look out of the window first. Oh, what a glorious view!"

There was indeed a splendid prospect to be seen from the old church tower—a vista of village roofs, and tree tops, and fields, and winding high road, and distant woods and hills, all bathed in the beautiful, rosy light of sunset. It was so lovely that the girls stood for some time watching the sky turn from pink to crimson, and great bands of dappled clouds catch the reflection from the glow beneath. They quite forgot that supper would probably be over at the Manor, and that Miss Russell would be wondering why Monica had kept them so long, and wishing she had not allowed them to go without Miss Frazer or one of the monitresses to escort them back.

At last they tore themselves reluctantly away. It was much harder to come down the ladder than it had been to climb up. Cicely turned quite giddy, and they were both glad when they reached the square room where the bell rope was hanging. It was very dark on the winding staircase; they had to feel their steps most carefully, and keep a hand on the wall as they went. The church looked dim and gloomy as they found themselves once more in the nave. Cicely turned her back upon the monuments. She did not want to give even a glance in their direction just then. Perhaps Lindsay felt the same, for she also hurried quickly towards the door. To their utter amazement it was closed, shut tight and firm; and though they lifted the latch, and tugged and rattled and pulled with all their might, they could not open it. They stared at each other with blank, horror-stricken faces. They were locked up alone in the empty church!

"Let us call," quavered Cicely.

"Perhaps someone may be in the churchyard. I can't believe they've really left us shut up here. Somebody must be coming back," said Lindsay.

She knew in her heart of hearts all the same that it was a forlorn hope. The old sexton had probably seen Monica walk through the village, and had come to lock the church as usual after her practice, quite unaware that anyone was exploring the belfry. By this time he would be at home again, with the keys in his pocket. The two girls shouted themselves hoarse, and kicked and beat against the door, but there was no reply except hollow echoes that resounded from the vaulted roof. The church was just out of earshot from either the village on one side or the rectory on the other, and it did not seem likely that anybody would happen to pass through the churchyard at that hour in the evening. No doubt they would soon be missed at the Manor, but Miss Russell would be sure to go first to Monica to enquire about their absence, and it might therefore be some little time before anyone came to look for them inside the church.

"What are we going to do?" asked Cicely.

"We must get out somehow," replied Lindsay desperately. "Let us walk all round, and see if there is any window it would be possible to climb through."

They went up the aisle, looking carefully at the windows; but all were equally impracticable, being built high up in the walls, and the only panes that opened were at the top.

"There may be a lower one in the vestry," said Lindsay, after they had examined the side chapels and transepts. "Here's the door, and fortunately it's not locked."

Again they were doomed to disappointment. The vestry was one of the oldest portions of the building, and the tiny diamond-paned casement was fully ten feet above their heads. Plainly it was useless to think of escape there.

"We'd better go back to the door," said Cicely, "just in case anyone should be coming down the road, and might hear us."

The light was rapidly growing dimmer and dimmer, the pillars cast long shadows, and the corners were already wrapt in darkness, through which here and there a figure on a monument stood out white against the gloomy background. Once more the girls thumped at the door and shouted, though they feared it would be of no avail.

"There's only one thing left to be done, Cicely," said Lindsay at last.

"And what's that?"

"Go up into the belfry again and ring the bell. Everybody in the village would hear that, and Judson would come to see what was the matter."

"Yes," replied Cicely with some hesitation, "I suppose we must—but——"

"But what?"

"We should have to walk up the belfry stairs."

"Well?"

"Oh, Lindsay, Sir Mervyn! Suppose we were to meet him on the staircase? The village people say he walks!"

"And Monica said it was nothing but nonsense and superstition."

Lindsay tried to sound brave, but she held Cicely's arm tightly notwithstanding.

Poor Cicely felt "'twixt Scylla and Charybdis". To toll the bell seemed their only chance of escape, and to do so they must certainly mount into the square room where the rope was hanging. On the one hand was the prospect of spending some time in a building which was rapidly growing darker and darker, and on the other, there was a quick dash up the winding staircase, which was the centre of all her nervous fears.

"We must do it," urged Lindsay. "Come along! Let us go now, before you think about it any more."

It was very dark when they went through the small door and began groping their way up the narrow steps. There was not room for both to walk abreast, so Lindsay went first and Cicely clung tightly on to her skirt behind, ready to turn and flee precipitately if she heard the slightest sound from above. The stairs seemed twice as long as when they had mounted them before, and far narrower and steeper.

"Here we are!" exclaimed Lindsay, when at last they found their feet on the flooring of the tower room. There was just light enough to faintly distinguish objects, and they were making straight for the bell rope when Cicely grasped Lindsay's arm in a panic of fear.

"What's that noise?" she whispered breathlessly.

"Where?"

"There! Up the ladder in the roof!"

Both girls listened, their hearts beating in great thumps. Cicely was not mistaken. There was a faint rustling, as if someone were moving softly about in the tower above. Too terrified even to run away, they stood with their eyes fixed on the open trapdoor that led up to the bell.

"He's coming!" shrieked Cicely, as something large and white appeared silently through the aperture and glided down into the room. There was a sudden weird, uncanny cry, like a mournful, despairing wail, and a large pair of wings flapped through the open lattice that served for a window out into the thickness of the yew trees beyond.

"It's an owl—a big white owl! That's your ghost, Cicely!" cried Lindsay, with intense relief.

"It's gone, at any rate. Oh, what a fright it gave me! I thought it was Sir Mervyn himself."

"I expect it sleeps up there during the day, and then goes out hunting at night for birds and mice. What a fearful screech it gave!"

"Let us go and ring the bell before we have any more scares."

They dashed across the room and seized the rope. Surely since the day it was first hung the poor old bell had never been tolled with such frantic, hurried jerks. It was like an alarm of war or fire as the swift, short strokes went echoing from the tower. The girls pulled and pulled until they were both nearly exhausted.

"Somebody must have heard us by this time," said Lindsay. "Let us go down into the church and wait by the door."

"I don't feel so afraid of Sir Mervyn now I know he's only a white owl," declared Cicely.

They stumbled down the stairs and across the dark nave, then stood waiting anxiously for some sign of coming relief. Was that a distant footstep? Yes; they heard the creaking of the lich-gate, the sound of voices, and the crunching of boots on the gravel path. They sprang at the door, knocking and shouting for help with all their might. In another moment the great key turned in the lock. It was Judson, the sexton, who stood outside, with quite a number of people from the cottages behind him. All the village had been roused by the tolling of the bell, and everyone expected to find either a gang of thieves at work or the building on fire, instead of only two frightened little schoolgirls from the Manor.

At that moment both Miss Russell and Monica came hurrying up, the latter reproaching herself keenly for not having seen her companions safely home, and the former very angry at their escapade. As Lindsay had supposed, they had been expected back more than an hour ago, but Miss Russell thought Monica must have had an unusually long practice. When their bedtime arrived, and still they were missing, the headmistress had grown uneasy, and started in search of them. She had gone first to the church and found the door locked (it must have been while they were in the vestry), so concluded that they had returned with Monica to the cottage. She had been seriously alarmed to find they were not there, and her anxiety was shared by the Courtenays; and both she and Monica were on the point of rousing the whole village to aid in discovering their whereabouts when the sudden clanging of the bell made them hasten to the church. The girls gave a brief account of their adventure in reply to the many enquiries of their rescuers.

"I thought I could have trusted you to return straight home," said Miss Russell reproachfully. "No, Monica, it is not in any way your fault. Lindsay and Cicely knew perfectly well they had no right to linger behind, nor to enter the tower. I am disappointed in them, for I certainly should not have allowed them to go and blow the organ if I had believed there was the slightest opportunity for such behaviour. They have only themselves to blame, and I consider they thoroughly deserved the fright they have had."

CHAPTER XII. AN ENIGMA

Though most of the delights of the summer term at the Manor consisted of outdoor amusements, other interests were not entirely lacking. In a magazine which Miss Russell took in for the school library there was an announcement of a competition which offered a prize to children under thirteen for the largest number of poetical quotations descriptive of wild flowers. Both Lindsay and Cicely were anxious to try, and ransacked all the volumes of poetry they could get hold of for suitable extracts.

"I think it's too much bother," said Nora Proctor. "It means looking through such a heap of books, and then copying out the pieces so neatly afterwards. It would take one's whole recreation time."

"And probably one wouldn't get anything for it in the end," said Marjorie Butler.

"I began," said Effie Hargreaves, "but, as Nora says, it's far too great a fag. I got ten quotations from Shakespeare, and six from Tennyson. I'll give them to you, Cicely, if you like."

"Oh, thanks, if they're not the same as I have already!"

"I tried for a prize once in a magazine," said Beryl Austen, "but I only got highly commended. I'm afraid my writing wasn't good enough."

Though the other girls did not care to compete themselves, they were interested in Lindsay's and Cicely's lists, and gave them any assistance they could in hunting out fresh quotations.

"I'll tell you what," said Beryl, "you ought to ask Monica. She reads a great deal, and I believe she's rather clever at botany. I heard her talking about the wild flowers of the neighbourhood to Miss Russell."

"Yes, I believe she has a nice pressed collection," said Effie. "She promised to show it to us some day."

Lindsay and Cicely took Beryl's advice, and waylaid Monica as she came to the French class next morning.

"I'm glad you asked me," she replied. "I've no doubt I shall be able to help you; I have a good many beautiful books on botany in the library. I'll bring the key this afternoon, and unlock the case for you."

Monica always kept her promises. She arrived about four o'clock, and opened the large glass doors that preserved the handsome calf-bound volumes from dust and dirt.

"Here they are," she said. "Some are very dry and scientific, and some are popular, and have coloured pictures. There are catalogues of plants, and schedules of species, and old herbals, and every kind of book you can imagine that has a bearing on the subject. Some are about British flowers and some about foreign ones, and there are others on mosses and ferns and fungi. They used to belong to my uncle; he was extremely fond of botany."

"Have you read them all?" asked Cicely.

"No, I'm afraid I have rather neglected them. You see, I have had so many lessons to learn. One can't study everything at once, and Mother particularly wants me to work hard at French. Perhaps some day I may attack the natural orders. It will take you a long time to look through every one of these books. I'll leave the case unlocked, so that you can get them out when you like. I know I can trust you not to spoil the covers, and to put each back in its proper place."

"We'll be very, very careful of them," Lindsay assured her. "We won't carry them into the garden. We'll sit and read them here at the table."

"That will be all right, then," said Monica. "I feel they are rather a particular charge, because they were left to me as a special legacy. I believe my uncle valued them more than anything else in the world. I often think I don't appreciate them as much as I ought."

As Monica had said, it took considerable labour to thoroughly examine all the books and search for extracts. Some merely contained long lists of Latin names, and others were far too learned and scientific to interest schoolgirls. A few, however, treated the subject from its romantic side, and quoted passages of poetry such as they wanted. Miss Russell, who had encouraged them to try for the prize, gave them permission to use the library when they pleased; so for the next few days they spent most of their spare time there.

It was a pleasant occupation, and one that seemed to bring them into touch with the old poets who had loved Nature so dearly, and sung so charmingly about her blossoms. It was quite wonderful to think that nearly six hundred years ago Chaucer had noticed and recorded the little golden heart and white crown of the daisy; and that King James I of Scotland, while pining as Henry IV's prisoner in Windsor Castle, could remember and write of—

"The sharpë, greenë, sweetë juniper,

Growing so fair with branches here and there".

The competition proved most interesting, and, as it happened, was to be connected with unforeseen occurrences.

One afternoon, Cicely, who was trying to work her way systematically along the shelves, brought down a thick, bulky volume, bound in brown leather, with metal corners, and entitled *Floral Calendar*.

"This must be an old one," she remarked. "Look how yellow the paper is, and there are actually long S's. Someone has scribbled notes all round the edges of the pages."

"I wonder if it was Sir Giles Courtenay?" said Lindsay.

Cicely turned to the flyleaf at the beginning. Yes, in exactly the same rather straggling hand was the inscription:

"GILES PEMBERTON COURTENAY,

HAVERSLEIGH MANOR,

SOMERSET."

"He seems to have been fond of writing in his books," said Lindsay. "What's this opposite his name?"

On the inside of the cover quite a long piece of poetry had been copied. It appeared to be something in the nature of an acrostic or charade, and it ran thus:—

ENIGMA

My *First*, among flowers you can't find a better,
'T was used by a king for securing a letter.
My *Second*, whose blossoms of yellow soon fade,
Comes out every night in the calm evening shade.
My *Third*, oft called Iris, is much in demand,
It grows on an island named Van Diemen's Land.
My *Fourth*, a wild flower with sweet golden eye,
Is more blessing than "torment" to all who pass by.
My *Fifth*, with great trusses of lavender hue,
Is the sweetest of shrubs that the spring brings to view.
My *Sixth*, an old blossom in medicine once famed,
Was good for the eyesight, and thus it was named.
Now if you have guessed all these flowers that I prize,
Please take my initials and finals likewise:
The former you'll find to be hiding the latter;
If you've solved the enigma you'll see 'tis a matter
Perchance may provide you with just a lost link,
And bring you a greater reward than you think.

G. P. C.

Both Lindsay and Cicely were particularly fond of any kind of riddle. They seized upon this floral enigma with delight, and began to puzzle it out with the help of the illustrated catalogue of plants given in the old volume.

"How funny of Sir Giles Courtenay to have written it inside a botany book!" said Cicely.

"I suppose he was quite mad," replied Lindsay.

"He must have made it up himself, as it's signed with his initials," continued Cicely. "It was rather clever of him, wasn't it?—especially if he was mad. I'm sure I couldn't invent verses, however hard I tried."

"'My *First*, used by a king for securing a letter', is evidently 'Solomon's Seal'," said Lindsay. "Give me that spare piece of paper, and I'll put it down."

"'My *Second*' must be 'Evening Primrose'," said Cicely. "I can't think of any other yellow flower that comes out at night."

The third for a long time baffled the efforts of both girls to discover it. They searched through the lists of wild and garden flowers in vain.

"Irises are sometimes called 'flags'," ventured Cicely at last, turning to the page of 'F' in the index. "Why, here are quite a number. There are Asiatic flag, and corn flag, and dwarf flag, and Florentine flag, and German flag. Oh! and a heap more, too—golden flag, and Iberian flag, and Japanese, and Persian, and Missouri, and Tasmanian."

"That's the one!" said Lindsay. "Van Diemen's Land is the old name for Tasmania. 'My *Third*' must be Tasmanian flag."

"Why, of course. We're getting on, aren't we?"

The fourth, as it was stated to be a wild flower, was sought for in the list at the end of *British Flora*. It did not take a very large amount of penetration to fix it as 'tormentilla', especially as they could identify its golden eye in the coloured picture.

"The great trusses of lavender hue, growing on a shrub in spring, will mean lilac. I'm getting quite proud of our guessing," declared Lindsay.

"We've only one more left now," said Cicely.

The last proved the most difficult of all. I doubt if they would have been able to solve it, had not Lindsay chanced to take down an ancient herbal, and found a list of plants once employed for medicine.

"Amid all herbes that do grow, and are of greatest comfort and solace to mankind," so ran the passage, "a foremost place hath the euphrasy. Though it be but an humble plant scarce an inch in height, yet it maketh an ointment very precious for to cure dimness of sight. Thence it hath been called in the vulgar tongue 'eye-bright', nevertheless its true name is euphrasy, and thus it is known among apothecaries."

"It must be right," said Lindsay. "It's the only one that is said to do any good to the eyesight. The others seem to be for toothaches or agues."

"Or to heal wounds or sores," said Cicely. "People must have been continually hurting themselves in those days, if they needed so many 'salves' and 'unguents'."

They had now discovered all the six flowers, and wrote the result neatly down on a piece of paper.

S	olomon's Sea	L
E	vening Primros	E
T	asmanian Fla	G
T	ormentill	A
L	ila	C
E	uphras	Y

"The initials read 'settle' and the finals 'legacy'," said Cicely. "How very queer! That hasn't anything to do with flowers."

"Let us look at the end lines again," said Lindsay, and she read aloud:

Please take my initials and finals likewise:
The former you'll find to be hiding the latter;
If you've solved the enigma you'll see 'tis a matter
Perchance may provide you with just a lost link,
And bring you a greater reward than you think.

"The initials hide the finals. 'Settle' hides 'Legacy'," repeated Cicely meditatively.

"Why, I see it now!" burst out Lindsay suddenly. "Oh, Cicely, I believe it means a great deal more than an ordinary riddle! It has something to do with the lost treasure. Don't you understand? The settle is hiding the legacy—Monica's legacy!"

"Oh, surely not!" exclaimed Cicely, bouncing up in great excitement.

"But I really think so. The poetry says the enigma is 'to provide the lost link' and 'bring a greater reward than you think'. This is indeed a discovery! It's evidently intended to tell Monica where her money is to be found."

"Can we be quite, quite certain?" hesitated Cicely.

"Well, everything seems to point to it. Don't you recollect Irene Spencer said that in old Sir Giles' will he left 'the Manor and all that it may contain to my great-niece Monica, especially commending to her the volumes in my library, and advising her to pursue the study of botany'? I remember those were the exact words. This must have been the reason. He had written the secret of the hiding-place inside the *Floral Calendar*, and he thought she would find it there. Perhaps he wasn't so very mad after all."

"I wonder if Monica has seen it and puzzled it out?"

"I don't know. She said she didn't often trouble about the books."

"Then is the treasure hidden inside some old settle in the house?"

"It seems likely."

"In that case we must be wrong about the lantern room."

"Perhaps we are. Well, at any rate this throws new light on the subject, and gives us a clue as to where to hunt. We'll go over the Manor again, and look carefully at every settle."

"I hope we're really on the right track at last," sighed Cicely. "What a glorious day it would be if we could actually say to Monica: 'Here's your fortune!'"

CHAPTER XIII. LINDSAY MAKES A RESOLVE

Lindsay and Cicely thought they understood what a settle was, but, to avoid the possibility of any mistake, they looked the word up in the dictionary. "Settle—a long bench, with high back, for sitting on," was the explanation given by that authority.

"So it 'settles' the matter," said Cicely, trying to make a pun.

"Well, it shows us it's not a chest, anyhow," replied Lindsay, "though the oak bench in the passage near the top of the stairs has a kind of box under it. The seat lifts up like a lid."

There were four pieces of old furniture in the Manor which might claim to answer to the description given in the dictionary. Two were in the dining-room, one in the picture gallery, and another, as Lindsay had said, at the head of the stairs. The girls made a most lengthy and careful inspection of them all, but without the slightest result. Neither their backs nor their seats were hollow, or capable of containing anything. Three of them stood upon carved oak legs, like chairs, and though the last was made in the fashion of a chest, it proved on investigation to be absolutely empty. It was a bitter disappointment.

"Can we have been mistaken about the enigma?" said Cicely, almost in tears.

"I don't believe so. What I think is, that Mrs. Wilson and Scott have been clever enough to find the money and carry it off. Perhaps there was another settle somewhere in the house, and they took it bodily away."

"Wouldn't Monica have missed it?"

"It may have been done just after Sir Giles died, and before she came to the Manor."

"Where would they put it?"

"Possibly in the lantern room, inside some hiding-place they know of."

"Then, until we can find out the secret of the lantern room, it seems to me we can't get any farther."

"And we don't even know that the treasure is still there, because it may be buried in the garden," groaned Lindsay.

The whole affair of the lost legacy was most aggravating and tantalizing. They seemed so continually on the point of unravelling the mystery, only to find themselves again defeated and baffled. Cicely was tempted to throw it up altogether in despair, but Lindsay had a native obstinacy of disposition that could not bear to be beaten.

"I shall go on trying as long as we're at Haversleigh, on that I'm entirely resolved," she declared. "I don't mean to give up until we're actually on our way to the station on breaking-up day."

"And that's only three weeks off now," said Cicely.

The summer term at the Manor had proved so enjoyable that the girls were not nearly so enthusiastic as usual for the advent of the holidays. Most of them felt a keen regret at leaving the beautiful old place, and bewailed the fact that the alterations at Winterburn Lodge were reported to be progressing favourably, and that the drains there would be in perfect order long before they need return in September.

"Couldn't we have school here always instead of in London?" they suggested hopefully to Miss Russell.

"No," said the headmistress; "there are many considerations which would make it impossible. Mrs. Courtenay and Monica will want to live in their own home again, and Haversleigh is too inconvenient a place for a permanency. We have managed wonderfully well for a few months with only Mademoiselle, but we certainly miss Herr Hoffmann's and Monsieur Guizet's classes, to say nothing of drawing and dancing lessons. Visiting masters cannot arrange to come so far away from town. There are no proper educational advantages to be had in the depths of the country."

"We shall be sorry when it comes to good-bye," declared the girls.

"We must make the most of our remaining time here then," said Miss Russell, "and try to see all we can in the neighbourhood before we go."

The mistress's birthday, falling on the following Wednesday, offered a propitious opportunity for an excursion such as she suggested. The girls were accustomed to celebrate the occasion with some little festivity, and were delighted when it was arranged that they should visit the town of Appleford, about ten miles away.

"There is the Dripping Well to see, and a fine old church," said Miss Russell. "I am sure we shall be able to spend a very pleasant afternoon there. We must ask Monica to come with us."

There was some doubt at first as to whether Monica would be able to accept the invitation. She had missed her French lesson one day, and arrived at school late on the next, looking pale and upset. Mrs. Courtenay had been very ill, so she explained. The doctor had been sent for, and had given an unfavourable report. Naturally extra care and attention were needful, and who could give these so well as her own daughter?

On the day of the picnic Monica turned up with rather an anxious face.

"I scarcely like to leave Mother," she said, "but she wants me so much to have this treat that she would not rest content until she had seen me put on my hat and start off. Fortunately Jenny is a good nurse, and will look after her nicely. Still, I always feel uneasy when I am long away from her."

The girls were to drive the whole distance to Appleford, and the prospect was so exhilarating that everyone was at the high-water mark of enjoyment. Even poor Monica caught the prevailing spirit, and for the moment, at least, began to forget her cares. There was just room to pack both teachers and pupils into the four wagonettes which arrived from the George Inn, but nobody seemed to mind crushing, and even Mademoiselle was in a good temper.

"I smile because I shall again see shops and streets," she declared.

"I believe Mademoiselle will be delighted to go back to Winterburn Lodge," said Marjorie Butler, who was in another wagonette, but overheard the remark.

"Yes, I think she's absolutely yearning for pavements and lamp-posts," said Cicely. "She'll weep with joy at the sight of a tramcar. She says it is terribly 'triste' here."

"Mademoiselle is French," observed Effie Hargreaves scornfully.

"What a very original remark! You didn't suppose we took her for a German?"

"Well, I mean she's a foreigner at any rate, so we can't expect her to like the country," replied Effie, with true British prejudice.

There were several small excitements on the journey. Beryl's hat was blown by a sudden puff of wind over a bridge, and was in great peril of descending into the river when it was rescued by the driver; the door of the second wagonette burst suddenly open, and nearly precipitated Irene Spencer into the road; while the whole cavalcade was brought to a standstill at a narrow turning by finding a broken-down motor-car blocking up the way.

Appleford proved to be a delightfully quaint old country town, with twisting streets and black-and-white houses.

"I'm afraid Mademoiselle will be very disappointed with the fashions. She certainly won't find Paris modes here," laughed Marjorie Butler, looking at the one row of small shop windows that appeared to satisfy the wants of the population.

"I'm glad there's a confectioner's, anyhow," said Effie Hargreaves, who was burning to spend her pocket-money on chocolates.

"And a place for picture postcards," added Nora Proctor; "I can see a whole tray full of them standing outside that door."

The arrival of four wagonettes containing so many schoolgirls evidently caused quite an excitement in the usually quiet street. Heads were popped out of windows, shopkeepers came to their doors, and people began to collect at corners and stare.

"Almost as if we were a wild-beast show!" said Cicely.

"I believe they hope we're going to march in procession round the market square and sing, or play as a band," declared Nora Proctor.

"Come along, girls! I am afraid we are attracting too much attention," said Miss Russell. "Let us set off for the Dripping Well as fast as we can. You must make any purchases you want when we return; I cannot let you wait now."

Effie Hargreaves had already dived into the toffee shop, and issued with several paper packages in her hand; so she went on her way rejoicing that she had seized the opportunity while there was yet time. Fortunately for the others, she was of a generous disposition, and ready to share her sweets.

"We'll pay you back when we get some of our own," said Marjorie Butler, blissfully sucking a caramel.

The Dripping Well was situated in a wood, about a mile from the town, and was, as the guide-book described it, "a most curious natural phenomenon". The water trickled slowly over a large rock, and was so charged with lime that it left a thin deposit over everything it touched. Articles hung up there, after a short time bore the appearance of having been turned to stone. All kinds of objects were suspended from the rock, in the process of being encrusted by the lime—top hats, boots, stockings, gloves, loaves of bread, and even bunches of flowers.

"It looks just as if the Gorgon had stared at them and petrified them with a glance," said Nora.

"I wonder, if we were hung up, should we turn solid too?" said Lindsay.

The caretaker of the well had many specimens to show them which he had polished, and was anxious to sell. There was quite a large collection in his cottage. The girls, after hastily conferring together, bought a stone bouquet as a birthday present for Miss Russell, an offering which she declared should grace the school museum when they returned to Winterburn Lodge.

"I thought she'd have put it in the drawing-room," said Beryl Austen, rather disappointed.

"Well, of course it is more of a curiosity than an ornament," said Mildred Roper. "It wouldn't have looked very beautiful decorating the mantel-piece, I'm afraid—not nearly so nice as a real bunch of flowers."

Close to the well was a cave in the cliff which a hermit had once used for his cell—a very picturesque spot to have chosen for his meditations, so the girls decided.

"But horribly damp; the poor man must have been racked with rheumatism," said Miss Frazer, who was of a practical mind.

"Perhaps, like Friar Tuck, he didn't often use it, and preferred to hunt venison in the woods," suggested Kathleen Crawford.

"No, he was a really devout hermit, who told his beads, and lived on bread and water," said Monica. "He dug his own grave in the rock about a hundred yards from here. You can see it still, though his bones have long ago been taken away for relics."

"I wonder if they petrified them first in the well," said Nora Proctor, "and how much they sold them for? There are more than two hundred bones in the human body, so a hermit ought to have been worth a good deal when he was properly divided."

"You naughty, irreverent girl!" said Monica.

Tea had been prepared at the old-fashioned inn in the market square. Afterwards they went to look through the church, where there were some fine examples of Gothic carving, and several beautiful stained-glass windows. One in particular, which Monica pointed out, was in memory of a member of the Courtenay family. There was achained Bible, besides a black-letter Prayer Book, a pair of tongs for turning dogs out of church, and several other curiosities shown by the old verger; so time passed rapidly, and everyone was quite surprised when Miss Russell looked at her watch, and announced that they must be returning home.

"Will someone fetch Monica? I believe she is in the churchyard with the Rector's wife," she said.

Lindsay and Cicely volunteered to go, and found their friend under a big yew tree, engaged in talking to a lady who was evidently making enquiries about Mrs. Courtenay. Not liking to intrude and interrupt the conversation, they stood waiting until they should be noticed.

"The doctor was over yesterday," Monica was saying, with a choke in her voice. "He told me our only chance is to send to London for Sir William Garrett. And how can we? His fee is a hundred guineas."

"That is a heavy amount."

"Impossible for us. You know how gladly I would sell even the Manor to raise the money, but I cannot touch a penny of my property until I come of age, and that won't be for more than four years. I try not to blame Uncle Giles, yet sometimes——"

Here Monica broke down altogether, and wiped her eyes.

"You mustn't give up hope, my dear child," said the Rector's wife kindly. "Perhaps your mother may be spared to you after all. Strange things come to pass sometimes, and good can often result from evil."

"I wish I could believe so," sobbed Monica. "I don't care in the least about the fortune for myself; I only want it when I think of what it might do for her!"

"Cicely!" said Lindsay solemnly the next morning, as she tied her hair ribbon before the looking-glass, "we simply must have another try to find that treasure."

Cicely paused with her brush in her hand.

"It's dreadful that Mrs. Courtenay may die because they can't scrape together a hundred guineas," she agreed.

"And Monica is breaking her heart over it," continued Lindsay. "She goes about looking so unhappy, it makes me quite miserable too. I'd give everything in the world I have to help her."

"I don't know where we're to hunt next. We seem to have explored every corner, and we never have any luck."

Cicely's voice sounded utterly despondent.

"We can only go to the lantern room again. It's the one place where we're sure there's a secret. If Merle could discover something there, why shouldn't we?"

It appeared a forlorn hope, but anything was better than just sitting down and making no effort at all. Monica's troubles weighed much on Lindsay's mind. The idea that the invalid must slip out of life for lack of the money that might save her seemed too cruel to be endured.

"I wish I had a hundred guineas of my own to give them," she thought sorrowfully. "Oh dear! it's such a big sum—one might as well wish for the moon. I'm afraid there's not the slightest chance for poor Mrs. Courtenay unless the legacy turns up."

It was in rather a dejected mood that the girls betook themselves to the upper landing that afternoon, and once more climbed the now familiar winding staircase. The lantern room looked exactly the same as on their two former visits. There was nothing in it to excite interest or arouse curiosity. A more unromantic chamber could not be conceived.

The window was closed, the rusty firegrate contained only a few ashes, and the door of the cupboard stood open, revealing rows of empty shelves. The one object worthy of notice was the ancient lantern, which hung from a hook in the middle of the ceiling. That, at any rate, was curious. It was of a quaint, medieval pattern, and the sides, instead of being of glass, were of thin pieces of horn.

"It's a funny old thing," said Lindsay. "I suppose they used a dip candle for it. I wonder if there's a piece left in it still?"

She stood on tiptoe, and made an effort to open the lantern, but it was hung too high to allow her to peep inside. Reaching up as best she could, she gave it a jerk, to try to lift it down. Quite suddenly and unexpectedly the lantern and hook descended by a chain from the ceiling. There was a strange grating sound, and, turning round, the girls saw a sight which made them gasp with amazement.

CHAPTER XIV. THE LANTERN ROOM

Lindsay and Cicely might well cry out with surprise. A most peculiar thing had happened. A part of the back of the cupboard had opened like a door, revealing a narrow passage behind. Here at last was the hiding-place for which they had sought so long in vain.

They had never suspected the cupboard. It looked so ordinary, with its rows of shelves, that no one would have dreamt it concealed a secret exit. By a clever arrangement the lantern evidently worked a spring, and when pulled down caused the door to unclose automatically. Somebody in days gone by had no doubt constructed it thus to form a refuge in time of danger. The girls were in raptures of delight.

"This, of course, was where Mrs. Wilson vanished," said Lindsay.

"And what Merle saw," added Cicely.

It was an intense satisfaction to have found it out for themselves, especially when they had come upstairs with such small expectation of success. Where did the passage lead? That was naturally the first question they asked each other.

"It looks very dark," said Cicely, peering rather nervously into the opening.

"I wish we had a candle," said Lindsay. "There isn't even an end left inside the lantern, and we've no matches either."

"Shall I go downstairs and fetch some?" suggested Cicely.

"No, no! You might meet 'The Griffin' on the way. We'd better explore now, as quickly as we can, while the coast is clear."

It needed a little screwing up of courage to plunge into the dim obscurity before them. Lindsay went first, with Cicely clinging particularly closely on to her arm behind. The passage seemed to lead along the inside of the wall for about two yards, then took a sharp turn, and ended at the foot of a kind of ladder stairway.

One gleam of light fell from above, as if through some small chink in the roof, just sufficient to allow them to distinguish their surroundings and enable them to scramble up the rough steps. At the top they found themselves in a huge garret, how big they could not tell, for the corners were completely lost in black nothingness. The floor was thick with dust (such old dust!), and was so worm-eaten and rotten that it felt quite soft and crumbling under their feet.

They were close beneath the tiles, to judge from the rafters overhead. The air was hot and stifling, and had that stale, mouldy smell noticeable in places long shut up. They began to walk cautiously along, peering on all sides as their eyes grew more accustomed to the darkness.

"It's just the place for them to have put the treasure," said Cicely.

"If we only had a light!" sighed Lindsay. "I want to go nearer the wall, and see if I can find any heaps of money or silver tankards."

She groped her way a little more boldly across the room, and, putting out her foot, began to feel about.

"Do be careful!" begged Cicely.

It was a most necessary warning. The ancient, rotten boards could not stand the strain of Lindsay's weight, and down went her leg, making a great hole in the floor. Luckily she was not seriously hurt, only scratched and considerably frightened. With Cicely's help she managed to extricate herself, and withdrew to the safer middle of the garret.

"The old house must be almost ready to tumble down," she declared.

"Monica said parts of the Manor were very much out of repair," replied Cicely. "Besides, if this is a secret place, no one could ever come up to mend it."

"I wonder where my leg went to?" said Lindsay.

"Perhaps into some room below."

"In that case Mrs. Wilson will notice a hole in the ceiling, and will know somebody has been up here."

It was not an encouraging incident, but they were determined to venture farther all the same.

"We couldn't think of turning back now," said Lindsay.

At the far end of the room there was a door that seemed to lead into an attic even darker than the first.

"It's not much use going in there without a light," said Cicely.

"Just a few steps," said Lindsay.

She entered, and put up her hand to feel the height of the roof above. Instantly there was a tremendous rushing sound around them. The air seemed filled with flapping, shadowy forms, which brushed lightly against their cheeks. In an agony of fear poor Cicely shrieked and shrieked again, and clung to Lindsay desperately, as to the one substantial and human thing in the midst of what was horrible and unknown.

"All right, they're only bats," gasped Lindsay, in a rather quavering voice. "We've disturbed them, I expect."

Slightly reassured, Cicely dared to raise her head from her friend's shoulder and look round. They were surrounded by the fluttering wings of the bats. These little denizens of the darkness must have been hanging in numbers from the ceiling, and Lindsay's entrance had disturbed them. With strange squeaks and hisses they flitted to and fro for a few moments, then flew off to seek some safer retreat.

"I hope they've really gone," said Cicely, heaving a sigh of relief. "Don't go any farther in there, Lindsay. You can't see an inch before your face."

"But it may be the one important place," said Lindsay, yielding reluctantly as Cicely pulled her back into the outer garret. "I'd exchange all my next birthday presents for a candle."

"Hush! I want to listen. I thought I heard something."

"What?"

"A kind of rustling."

"I expect it was the bats, or a rat."

Cicely gave an apprehensive glance behind. Her nerves were not so strong as Lindsay's. Though she had had time to grow accustomed to scratchings inside the wainscots at the Manor, she could not overcome her dread of rats. Perhaps Lindsay was less valiant in her heart of hearts than she would have liked to confess. After all, it was little satisfaction to explore a room where she could see nothing.

She was just deciding to go, when Cicely once more clutched her arm.

"Oh, what is it?"

The exclamation burst simultaneously from the lips of the two girls. Close, almost, as it seemed, in their ears, echoed that horrible low groan which had so terrified them twice before. Heard amidst such strange and dim surroundings, it was more than flesh and blood could stand. Without waiting to make any further investigations, they turned and fled.

They hardly knew afterwards how they had stumbled across the rotten floor and scrambled down the ladder. With blinking eyes they looked into each other's scared faces as they emerged from the dark passage into the bright daylight of the lantern room again.

"What a dreadful place!" shuddered Cicely. "I'm thankful we've got safely away from it. I don't believe I'd venture up there again for all the fortunes in the world."

"We must close the entrance," said Lindsay anxiously. "We must take care to leave everything as we found it."

The secret door shut with a spring, and in a moment there was nothing to be seen again but the innocent-looking cupboard. The lantern had ascended to its former place in the ceiling; the chain worked on a pulley, and, as it ran up or down, it fastened or unloosed the lock.

Cicely, at any rate, was not sorry to descend to the more civilized portions of the house.

"I wonder if Merle explored as far as we did," she said.

"I hardly think so," returned Lindsay. "She couldn't have had time. I believe she must have met 'The Griffin' coming out, and have been frightened into not telling."

The more the girls talked the matter over, the more complicated seemed the mystery. Though they had found Mrs. Wilson's hiding-place, they were no nearer ascertaining whether the treasure was concealed there or elsewhere. Out in the sunshine Lindsay's courage returned, and she began to reproach herself for having given up the search so soon.

"We'll go some other day, and take two candles and a box of matches with us," she announced.

"Is it really any good?"

Cicely's spirit quailed at the prospect of once more encountering the unknown horrors that might be lurking in that dark attic. She could not forget the groans she had heard there.

"Of course it is! I didn't think you'd be the one to draw back," said Lindsay reproachfully. "We've both pledged ourselves to do everything in our power to help Monica. It would be mean and cowardly to give in just because we felt afraid. If you don't care to come with me, I shall have to go alone. I'm only waiting for a good opportunity."

For several days the opportunity tarried. Mrs. Wilson was too often about the passages to make the expedition safe. On one occasion Cicely went to act scout, but found the housemaid sweeping the top landing, and had to beat a hasty retreat.

They were not able to discover where Lindsay's leg had descended so suddenly through the rotten floor, or whether any of the ceilings in the upper rooms had suffered in consequence. If Mrs. Wilson had found out the damage, she kept her own counsel. When at last they managed to seize a favourable chance, and to steal up the winding staircase, a sad checkmate awaited them. The door of the lantern room was securely fastened with a padlock.

"Scott said he was going to put one on," said Lindsay, after staring blankly at the unwelcome impediment. "Don't you remember, when he was talking to 'The Griffin' in the picture gallery, and she told him we had been here?"

"I'm certain they suspect us," returned Cicely. "Perhaps they only took part of the silver or jewellery away in that sack, and the rest is still up in the garret."

The sole plan of action they could think of after this last disappointment was to keep a watch upon Scott. If he had really concealed a portion of the treasure in the garden, he would probably go to look at it occasionally, to make sure of its safety. At Cicely's urgent request they had already made a careful examination, with a trowel, of the bank where Scott had been digging when they surprised him in the dark. It was fruitless work, however; nothing was there.

"I told you beforehand they wouldn't be so foolish," said Lindsay.

"I thought they might have dropped a piece of money, or an ear-ring perhaps, in their hurry—just something to show us what had actually been here," said Cicely, grubbing about in the loose soil.

"Trust Scott and Mrs. Wilson! They're an uncommonly clever couple. You may be sure they'd take care not to leave even a sixpence behind them."

"I've heard that criminals can't keep away from a place where they've buried anything," continued Cicely. "They always haunt the spot."

"Then we must notice where Scott goes most frequently," replied Lindsay.

For the present, Scott seemed to be particularly attracted to the cucumber frames.

"He's there constantly," said Cicely.

"Far oftener than is necessary, I'm sure," agreed Lindsay.

"It might be a likely place, too," added Cicely meditatively.

Several small incidents seemed to confirm their surmises.

"He was so cross last night when Marjorie Butler sent her ball over the hedge into the kitchen-garden, and went to fetch it," said Lindsay.

"Yes, he said she might have broken the glass in one of the frames; but I don't suppose that was the real reason. She may have gone near him just when he was putting something back."

"I heard Miss Russell asking him when the cucumbers would be ready, and he answered in a great hurry: 'Not for ever so long yet'. And then he said it was 'best not to be lifting the frames, and disturbing them more than needful'."

"He was evidently afraid she was going to ask to see them."

The idea that silver cups, jewels, or spade-guineas might be lying hidden under the glossy leaves of the cucumber plants began to obtain possession of the girls' minds.

"If we could only manage to look while he's out of the way," suggested Cicely eagerly.

Scott's close attention to his duties was most annoying. There really appeared to be something in Cicely's theory of criminals haunting a particular spot. He seemed never absent from the kitchen-garden, at any rate when they were in its vicinity. They could hear him mowing the lawn during lesson hours, but when recreation arrived, and they ran out hopefully to reconnoitre, he would be weeding the strawberries, or gathering peas within a few feet of his cherished hotbeds.

"There's only one way for it," said Lindsay. "We shall have to make a plot. You must hide near the kitchen-garden, and I'll do something to take him off; then, while he's gone, you must rush to the frames and open them."

"That would be grand! What will you do?

"I shall have to think it over. I know! We'll wait till this evening, when he's watering the cucumbers. I'll stand on the pipe of the hose; that will stop the water, and he'll go to see what's the matter."

"Capital!" agreed Cicely.

It took a little scheming to arrange their plan satisfactorily. They were much afraid lest Scott should do his watering earlier than usual, and greatly relieved when they ran out after preparation to find him only just beginning to uncoil his hose. He used a small tank on wheels, which he generally left on the gravel walk outside the kitchen-garden, bringing the indiarubber tubing through the hedge.

To the girls' extreme annoyance, Marjorie Butler spied them, and, coming up, insisted upon reading aloud to them a letter she had received that morning from a sailor cousin. Would she never go away? It was too tiresome of her to confide in them at such an inappropriate time.

"Don't let us keep you, if you want to play tennis," begged Lindsay, with cold politeness.

"Oh, I don't mind at all, thank you! I thought you'd be interested to hear about Cousin Cyril," replied Marjorie.

Lindsay wished sincerely that Cousin Cyril had been at the bottom of the sea, instead of sailing over it and writing long descriptions of its charms. The precious moments were passing by. She could hear the gentle swish of the water as Scott applied the hose; if they were not quick, he would have finished, and the opportunity would be gone.

"I believe Miss Russell is coming out to play croquet to-night," she ventured desperately.

"Is she? Oh! she promised I might be on her side next time. I wonder if she's there yet? I must go and see at once."

"Thank goodness!" ejaculated Lindsay, as their classmate's blue-linen dress disappeared along the avenue. "Now, I'm going to put this heavy stone on the hose pipe, just where it goes through the hedge. Then we'll both creep through that hole into the kitchen-garden."

Without wasting another minute, Lindsay hastily did as she had said, concealing the stone among the long grass, after which both girls crawled through the hedge into the midst of a bed of Jerusalem artichokes. As they had expected, their plot answered admirably. Scott gave a grunt of vexation, and looked at his hose. His water supply had undoubtedly failed him. He stumped away, grumbling, to examine the tank.

"I don't believe he'll ever look amongst the grass. He'll think something's wrong with the tap," chuckled Lindsay.

The moment Scott had vanished through the gate, they dashed (regardless of the artichokes!) in the direction of the frames. Lindsay slid her hands rapidly in a search under the large, vine-like leaves; and Cicely, armed with a trowel, began to dig furiously. All in vain! Though they prodded the soil with sticks they could not feel anything particularly solid underneath, and there was no time to make very deep excavations.

"He's coming back!" panted Lindsay. "Smooth the earth over in that corner, and place that leaf to hide it. Quick, or he'll catch us! Don't go through the artichokes; we must run the other way!"

CHAPTER XV. HIDE-AND-SEEK

The July days literally flew, and the term was drawing rapidly to a close. Miss Russell seemed determined to make the very most of the last weeks at the Manor, and arranged something fresh for nearly every afternoon. On one day there was a cricket match, on another a putting contest, and on a third a tennis tournament, all of which caused much excitement in the small world of the school.

Both Lindsay and Cicely were fond of games, and anxious to win their share of distinction, so by mutual consent they decided to relax their watch on Scott until after the athletic sports. These were always considered a great event, and this year were to be on a larger scale than usual.

"It's so splendid to be able to have them in these lovely grounds," said Mildred Roper. "There never seemed half enough room on the lawn at Winterburn Lodge."

"I hear Miss Russell is going to give quite a party," volunteered Nora Proctor. "She's invited the Rector and Mrs. Cross and all the people who have called on her at Haversleigh, so we shall have plenty of spectators."

"I wish Mrs. Courtenay could come," exclaimed Cicely.

"I wish indeed she could. I'm afraid she must be worse to-day, as Monica was not at the history class," said Mildred.

All the girls were busy "getting into good form", as they expressed it. The elder ones worked untiringly at tennis, while the younger ones practised running with a zeal worthy of candidates for a Marathon race.

"Miss Russell says there'll be several handicaps, but she won't tell us what they are," remarked Beryl Austen.

"Well, it's much more fun if you don't know beforehand," returned Effie Hargreaves. "They wouldn't be handicaps if we could do them too easily."

"I found a piece of four-leaved clover yesterday," observed Cicely, "so I ought to be lucky. I showed it to Mademoiselle, and she was quite envious. 'Vous aurez la chance!'" she said.

"How jolly! Have you kept it?"

"Rather! I've left it to press between two pieces of blotting-paper, under a pile of books. I'm going to have it put in a locket when I go home."

"I don't believe in luck," declared Nora. "I'm sure all the four-leaved clovers in the world wouldn't make Marjorie Butler win a race. She's out of breath before she's run ten yards."

"Is Monica going to take part?" asked Beryl.

"I don't know. She said she had put her name down provisionally. If she does, I expect she'll astonish us all. She can jump most beautifully—she's as light as a feather."

The afternoon of the sports was brilliantly fine. By half-past two the guests had assembled on the big lawn. They looked quite a small crowd. The school had aroused interest in the neighbourhood, and people had come from several miles' distance in response to Miss Russell's cards of invitation. Irene Spencer was the only girl who could boast of having any relations present, her uncle, aunt, and several cousins having driven over from Linforth Vicarage. The visitors were evidently prepared to enjoy everything.

"It is not often we have an opportunity in the country of witnessing Olympic games. I am looking forward to seeing so many young Atalantas run races. Where are the wreaths of laurel and parsley that are to grace the occasion?" said Mr. Cross, the genial rector, who was fond of a joke, and at home among schoolgirls.

"There aren't any," laughed Cicely. "Miss Russell uses the laurel leaves to flavour the custards, and the parsley to garnish the hams."

"I'm astonished at her putting such classic plants to such ignoble purposes. She has asked me to distribute the prizes, and I thought I should be expected to place green chaplets upon the brows of the victors. It's too bad, when I had composed a speech on purpose. You suggest I should make up another? Not so easy, my dears. I shall come to some of you for assistance. I wonder if Miss Frazer would be equal to the occasion?"

"I'm sure she couldn't think of anything funny," declared Cicely.

"Then I shall have to trust to what I can say on the spur of the moment. If you notice I'm breaking down, please begin to clap, and then everybody will suppose I have finished. Here comes Miss Russell. I believe she wants me to act umpire too. Greatness is being thrust upon me. I hope I shan't disgrace my high position."

In spite of the Rector's mock protestations, he seemed very capable of managing the sports, and reviewed the rows of waiting girls with the eye of a general.

"It takes me back to my own schooldays," he said. "I used to think then I would much rather win the long jump than be made Archbishop of Canterbury; and I considered the captain of our cricket club a far bigger fellow than the Prime Minister. Where's Monica? Isn't she joining in to-day's doings?"

Monica arrived at the last moment, just when everybody had given her up, and took her place quietly among the members of the first form.

"I was afraid I couldn't come at all," she explained; "but Mother is asleep now, so I can leave her for an hour, at any rate. I have told Jenny to send for me if she wakes."

The first item on the programme was a tennis contest, limited to the elder girls. It was a hard-fought battle, as the competitors were evenly balanced, and it ended in a victory for Mildred Roper and Kathleen Crawford. Monica played well, but she had not been able to spend so much time at practice as the others, and she missed several balls.

"It was very stupid of me," she apologized. "I never seem to grow accustomed to Mildred's fast serves."

A race followed for the second class, which Irene Spencer, much cheered by her cousins, nearly succeeded in winning, though she was beaten at the last by Merle Hammond, who made a sudden and unexpected spurt. It was now the turn of the third-form girls. They were to run a handicap, and awaited particulars with much eagerness.

"Miss Russell seems to set as severe tasks as the wicked stepmother in the fairy tales," said Mr. Cross. "She decrees that you are each to be given a small box of peas and beans and buttons mixed together, and that you are to sort them before you start to run the race. Will you please all kneel on the grass with your boxes in front of you. Are you ready? One—two—three—off!"

It was a question of deftness of fingers. Effie Hargreaves justified the old proverb, "More haste, less speed", by upsetting her box; and Marjorie Butler got her piles mixed in her agitation. Cicely finished first, and was halfway across the lawn before Nora Proctor overtook her. It was a keen struggle between these two. All the others were some distance behind, for Lindsay was not so fleet of foot, and Beryl Austen slipped and fell on the dry grass.

"It's Nora! No, it's Cicely!" cried the girls. "Well done, Cicely! Go on, Nora! She's gaining! No, she isn't! Why, it's Cicely after all!" as the latter reached the winning-post a couple of yards in advance of her opponent.

"Well run!" said the Rector. "You got over the course like young greyhounds. If you learn lessons at the same speed, you will turn out prodigies. Why is Miss Russell shaking her head? She says there is no danger of that. Really, I feel quite relieved to hear it. I was beginning to be almost afraid of you. I believe you are expected to pick up the beans before we continue our proceedings."

The programme was arranged so as to be as varied as possible. There were a round at clock-golf, a skipping tournament, an egg-and-spoon race, and an archery contest.

"It's jumping next," said Lindsay, as Miss Frazer and Miss Humphreys came forward, carrying a rope; "the first-form girls are to begin. I particularly want to see Monica."

Monica had taken her place modestly at the very end of the line, so that at each trial she was the last to compete. Her movements were very light and graceful, and the girls watched her with approval. One by one, as the rope was raised higher, the competitors began to thin, till at length their number was reduced to three—Kathleen Crawford, Bertha Marston, and Monica.

All looked eagerly to see the next attempt. Kathleen just managed to scramble over, Bertha failed utterly, but Monica took the jump with absolute ease.

"This will be the final test, I expect," said Miss Russell, when the two successful ones returned to the starting-point.

"I don't think they can do that!" murmured Lindsay, gazing with awe at what was to her the impossible height required.

It was too much for Kathleen. She ran, balked, and made another vain effort, to give it up.

"Now, Monica!"

The name was on everybody's lips.

Monica appeared to be perfectly cool, far less excited, indeed, than the spectators.

"Rest a moment, my dear, if you are out of breath," suggested Miss Russell.

"No, thank you. It would hardly seem fair to Kathleen. I'll try now."

"Took it like a bird!" cried the Rector, clapping his hands, as the rope was once more successfully cleared.

The girls raised a storm of cheering, to show partly their admiration for the skilful deed, partly their appreciation of Monica herself.

"She is a great favourite in the school," Miss Russell explained to Mr. Cross.

"I am delighted to see her mixing with other young people," he replied; "she has a dull time, poor child, as a rule, and has felt the disappointment about her uncle's property more than she cares to confess. Mrs. Courtenay's illness is very distressing. My wife was speaking to the doctor yesterday: he considers Sir William Garrett ought to be sent for at once; in a few weeks it may prove too late."

"You have known the family a long time?" asked Miss Russell.

"Since Monica's birth. I was as well acquainted with old Sir Giles as he would allow anyone to be. I used to call and see him sometimes, and discuss botany, the only subject in which he showed any interest. He lived so penuriously that his income must have accumulated for many years. He rarely spoke of business matters, but on one occasion he requested me to sign my name as witness to some document, the contents of which he did not tell me.

"He referred, however, to Monica as if she were to benefit substantially under his will, and asked me if I considered it harmful for a girl to be left an heiress. I assured him it would not be so in her case; both her disposition and upbringing were such that money could not spoil her.

"'A season of adversity is often the best preparation for prosperity,' he replied.

"I have remembered his words ever since.

"He sent for me on his deathbed, and I have sometimes wondered if there were any secret he wished to confide to me. Most unfortunately I was visiting a sick parishioner several miles away, and did not get the message in time. When I arrived at the Manor he was past speech. He tried to scrawl a few lines on a piece of paper, but the writing was quite undecipherable. If he regretted any earthly act, it was too late then to alter it; he was going to settle his great account."

While the Rector and the headmistress were talking, tea had been carried into the garden, and the girls now busied themselves in attending on the guests.

"I think the competitors must need refreshment more than we do," said Mrs. Cross, as Cicely handed her the cream.

"They are not forgotten," said Miss Russell, "but they are only too pleased to make themselves useful first."

Certainly the girls could not complain of being neglected; both cakes and strawberries were waiting for them on a separate table, where Miss Frazer was presiding.

When tea was over, the prizes were brought out, and the Rector, with a few appropriate remarks, began to distribute the awards. Cicely went up proudly to receive a pencil-case, and Nora Proctor, who had won the egg-and-spoon race, was presented with a box of chocolates.

"First prize for high jump, Monica Courtenay," announced Mr. Cross.

Everyone looked round for Monica, but she was nowhere to be found.

"She was here just before tea," said Miss Humphreys.

"I saw their maid come and speak to her during the archery competition," said Beryl Austen. "She went away immediately."

"She was obliged to go to her mother, no doubt, and did not wish to interrupt the shooting by saying good-bye," commented Miss Russell. "We must keep her prize for her."

"She won't get the clapping, though," lamented Lindsay.

"I think Monica will be rather glad to avoid that," said Mildred Roper. "She's so shy and retiring, she doesn't like to be made a public character."

The day following the sports was hopelessly wet. Lindsay and Cicely were awakened in the morning by the drip, drip of the rain on the ivy outside, and the splashing of water as it fell from the spout into the butt underneath. It was an absolutely drenching downpour, coming from a leaden sky that showed no prospect of clearing.

The weather had been so glorious during their stay at the Manor that they felt aggrieved at the change. It was particularly annoying, because Irene's uncle and aunt had invited all the girls to walk over to Linforth that afternoon, promising to show them the church, and to regale them with cherries afterwards in the Vicarage orchard.

"Wet at seven, fine at eleven!" said the sanguine Cicely.

"Not to-day, I'm afraid," replied Lindsay. "The glass was dropping last night. It's set in for a deluge."

The whole school seemed slightly depressed in spirits in consequence of the rain. No doubt it was a reaction from the excitement of the afternoon before. All their favourite occupations lay outside, and it was so long since they had been weather-bound that they seemed scarcely able to amuse themselves in the house. Everybody lounged about idly during afternoon recreation, looking dismally out of the windows at the lawns, where the markings of the tennis courts were being rapidly washed away.

"It's no use staring at the puddles," said Lindsay. "We can't possibly go to Linforth. It's just a piece of abominably bad luck. Everything's horrid!"

Lessons had not been a success that morning. Perhaps Miss Frazer also felt the influence of the gloomy day. Her pupils, at any rate, had been unusually stupid and inattentive; Lindsay, in particular, had merited a sharp scolding, and was dejected in consequence.

"We must do something," said Cicely. "I vote we hunt up the rest of our class, and go upstairs and have a really good game of hide-and-seek."

As anything seemed better than sitting still, the other girls agreed readily to come and play.

"Two can hide and four can look," said Marjorie. "Only, we'll keep on this landing."

The old Manor offered a splendid field for the purpose; it was so full of cupboards and crannies and odd nooks that it was quite hard to find anybody. The dull day improved the fun, for twilight reigned in most of the passages, and rendered many hairbreadth escapes possible. Nora actually had her hand on Beryl's foot without discovering the fact; Effie crept inside a suit of armour, and baffled pursuit for ever so long; and Marjorie was almost given up, but at length was discovered crouching in a dark angle which the others had passed several times without noticing her.

It was now the turn of Lindsay and Cicely to hide. They were determined to choose a specially good place, and debated the point until the latter grew impatient.

"Do be quick!" she exclaimed. "They'll soon have finished counting a hundred."

"I can't make up my mind whether it's better behind the tapestry or under the ottoman," deliberated Lindsay.

"Cuckoo!" cried Beryl's voice.

"They're coming! We've no time for either. We must get into the old box-settle."

It was the only possible retreat near at hand. Already they could hear the girls' footsteps creaking along the oaken boards of the picture gallery;

in another moment they would have turned into the passage, and reached the top of the stairs. Without more ado both hiders scrambled inside the settle, and pulled down the lid over their heads.

It was a very tight fit indeed for two, and most uncomfortable.

"Could you let me have an inch more room?" begged Cicely in an agonized whisper.

"I'll try," returned Lindsay.

It was difficult to stir in such narrow quarters. To move at all, she was obliged to make a vigorous heave towards her end of the chest. The effect was as unexpected as extraordinary. Lo and behold! the entire bottom of the settle seemed to give way, and without any warning the two girls were precipitated into some unknown place below.

CHAPTER XVI. A SURPRISE

So sudden was their descent that Lindsay and Cicely had no time even to cry out. They evidently had not fallen far, and though for a moment they both thought they were killed, they soon found that beyond a few bruises neither was hurt. They picked themselves up in a state of bewilderment, and stared around them as if hardly realizing yet what had happened.

They were in a little low chamber about eight feet square. The walls were of unpolished oak timbers, roughly plastered in between, and the floor also was of oak beams. In one corner there was a tiny window, covered with a mass of cobwebs, through which nevertheless came sufficient light to enable them to see their surroundings. The trapdoor in the ceiling, through which they had dropped so unexpectedly, must have worked on a swivel, for it had righted itself again, and was once more closed above them.

Still half-dazed, the girls stood for a moment trying to recover their scattered wits, too shaken and amazed even to speak.

"Well!" exclaimed Lindsay at last, with a volume of meaning in the monosyllable.

"This is a house of surprises!" cried Cicely.

"Where are we?"

"How can I tell?"

"We seemed to tumble through the bottom of the settle."

"Yes, after you gave that great lurch to your end."

"We must be in another secret hiding-place."

"Then I vote we hunt about, and see what's in it."

One side of the small room was completely filled, as high as the ceiling, with a pile of boxes. They seemed a very miscellaneous collection. There were ancient hair trunks, such as were in use seventy or eighty years ago, made of wood covered with cow hide, with the hair left on; there were leather portmanteaux with strong brass corners, tin trunks, and even plain wooden packing-cases. On the floor, and leaning against the boxes, stood a row of fair-sized linen bags, and a couple of larger sacks.

It seemed to the girls as if they must have penetrated to some forgotten lumber room. Everything was thickly covered with the accumulated dirt and cobwebs of years. They could have written their names in the dust. As if she were moving in a dream, Lindsay stooped, and picked up one of the linen bags.

"How heavy it is!" she said. "I wonder what's inside?"

"It feels like something hard," replied Cicely, pinching it critically with her finger and thumb.

The mouth was secured by a cord, and Lindsay fumbled long trying to untie the knot.

"Oh! don't bother over it; here's my penknife," cried Cicely, waxing impatient.

In another moment she had cut the string, and a shower of golden sovereigns came pouring out on to the floor. The two girls looked at each other, with faces that were almost awe-stricken.

"Cicely!" said Lindsay solemnly. "I verily believe we have found Sir Giles's fortune!"

A further examination established the matter beyond any doubt. The bags were filled to the brim with gold pieces. In a state of intense excitement the girls continued their investigations. The two large sacks contained salvers, tankards, and goblets, dull and tarnished indeed, but unmistakably of silver. It was difficult to get at the boxes, but they managed to clamber up and open one at the top of the pile, disclosing more silver articles and some ornaments of gold.

"Don't let us pull out too many things, or we shan't be able to stuff them back again," said Cicely, trying to close the lid of the overflowing hair trunk.

"No doubt these underneath are filled with money or jewels," said Lindsay rapturously.

"This little box seems made of silver," remarked Cicely, taking up a small antique casket that specially claimed her attention. Its sides were beautifully chased in classic designs, and it bore the Courtenay arms on the lid.

"It's full of pieces of paper, with figures on them," she continued.

"Let me look!" cried Lindsay. "Why, don't you see?—they're bank notes!"

They were certainly in the midst of treasures. The extent of Sir Giles's hoard had evidently not been exaggerated. At the bottom of the casket lay a letter addressed:

"TO MY GREAT-NIECE MONICA COURTENAY."

"The writing on the envelope is exactly the same as in the *Floral Calendar*," said Cicely. "I remember those funny flourishes, and the 'a's' not closed at the top."

"So it is; I should know the sprawling look of it anywhere."

"It's such funny, old-fashioned writing, as if it were done with a quill pen. I think we had better put this away again."

Lindsay replaced the letter carefully with the bank notes inside the silver box.

"Then Sir Giles did intend the enigma for a guide," she observed. "The last lines were right.

'... you'll see 'tis a matter

Perchance may provide you with just a lost link,

And bring you a greater reward than you think.'"

"And the settle concealed the legacy after all!"

"Yes, a great deal more safely than we supposed."

"I never imagined the treasure would be in a place like this, all stowed away in old boxes! I thought we should press a secret spring, and a panel would fly open in the wall, and then we should see money and jewels lying together in a big heap!"

"I don't mind how we've found it, so long as it's here."

"Still, it's a surprise!"

"It will be a splendid surprise for Monica. This is actually her very own."

236

"She would have been content with a hundred guineas, and there are more than a hundred guineas here," said Cicely, letting some of the sovereigns slide through her fingers with a sigh of satisfaction.

"She ought to know about it at once," returned Lindsay. "If you can tear yourself away from these money bags, we'd better be thinking of going."

"Yes, I suppose it's time we went back. By the by, how are we to get out of this place?"

Ah! How to go back?—that was the question! The trapdoor had shut itself high above their heads.

"I expect if we stand on one of the boxes, we can push it up!" said Lindsay.

With much difficulty they dragged a heavy chest across the floor and climbed upon it. It was a fruitless effort. However hard they might try, the trapdoor would not budge an inch.

"There may be a secret spring," faltered Cicely, feeling in every direction to find some bolt or knob, but all in vain. Then the horrible truth broke upon them. They were locked up as securely as the legacy!

"What are we to do?"

Lindsay's pink cheeks were white with alarm.

"Let us call. Perhaps the girls are hunting for us still in the passage, and they may hear."

Both shouted until they were hoarse, yet there was no reply. This was indeed hide-and-seek with a vengeance. Their game had turned out more than they had bargained for.

"I'll bang on the ceiling. It may sound louder than calling," said Lindsay. "The girls must have given us up, and gone downstairs, for nobody seems to hear," she continued, after belabouring the trapdoor for several minutes.

"Perhaps they're at tea," suggested Cicely.

They examined the little window in the corner, but the fastenings were so rusty from long disuse that, tug as they would, they could not open it. They wiped away the dust and cobwebs from it, and peeped out.

"If it overlooks the garden, we could smash the glass and wave a handkerchief, at any rate," proposed Lindsay. "Scott would be almost sure to notice it, even if nobody else were out in the rain."

Alas! the window appeared to be securely hidden away among the gables, and absolutely out of sight from below.

"Would it be possible to crawl on to the roof?"

Lindsay shook her head in reply. The frame was too small for even the slim Cicely to squeeze through. The girls sat down and surveyed the piles of treasure around them with dismay. If they had required a sermon on the vanity of riches, it was there without any need of words.

"We can't eat bank notes, nor sleep on beds of sovereigns," remarked Lindsay at last.

"We may be shut up here for days and days before they find us," said Cicely blankly.

"They'll miss us directly, of course; but they won't know where to look. Even if they peeped inside the settle, they wouldn't be any the wiser."

"Do you remember the piece of poetry we read last week about Ginevra? She hid inside a chest on her wedding day, when they were playing hide-and-seek, and the lid snapped with a spring lock. They never found her—only her bones, years afterwards!"

"Don't talk of such horrible things."

"How long does it take people to starve?" continued Cicely in a tremulous voice.

"About ten days, I believe. They grow gradually weaker and weaker."

Cicely groaned.

"There isn't anything to drink either, and I'm getting so thirsty," she said, her eyes filling with tears.

"We must try again," declared Lindsay, jumping up. "Let us pull out another trunk, and manage to lift it on to the chest. I believe if I were nearer the ceiling I should be able to push harder."

The boxes were arranged in a rather random fashion, so that as the girls dragged one from the bottom, the whole pile came tumbling down in confusion. They had to jump aside to avoid being hurt. When the upset was over, Cicely pointed silently to the wall opposite. In the part which before had been hidden was a small, low door. Here, surely, was a chance of escape.

They scrambled over the packing-cases and trunks without troubling to look inside them, though some had burst open in the fall. To find a way out seemed at present far more important than more silver tankards and salvers.

Was this exit also secured? With trembling hands Lindsay raised the latch. To her intense relief the door opened, showing a very narrow, unlighted passage.

After their experience in the garret it was not encouraging to find themselves once more obliged to explore in the dark, but there seemed nothing else to be done.

"It must lead somewhere," said Cicely. "I'd rather go anywhere than stay here."

"We'd better step carefully, in case the floor is as rotten as it was in the other place," cautioned Lindsay. The passage smelled dank and close. The air in it had probably been unstirred for many years. The faint light which entered it from the treasure room was soon lost, and they were obliged to grope their way by feeling along the walls. On and on they went for what appeared to be a considerable distance, sometimes turning sharp corners, and sometimes going up or down rickety steps.

"It must run half round the house," said Cicely. "Shall we never get to the end?"

Suddenly Lindsay, who was walking first, came to a halt.

"I can't go any farther," she faltered; "there's a wall in front."

The poor girls were almost in despair. They had been so confident that the passage would surely be taking them to the outer world; to find themselves once more at a full stop was a terrible blow.

"Must we go all that dreadful long way back?" wailed Cicely.

"I expect there is some door that we've passed without knowing it," replied Lindsay, rather chokily.

"Then we can never find it in the dark. It's no use. We shall both starve to death here, and they'll discover our skeletons a hundred years afterwards."

Cicely had utterly broken down, and was sobbing bitterly.

"We won't give up too soon," said Lindsay, whose sturdy courage stood her in good stead on this occasion.

She had been feeling about here and there on the blank wall that faced them, and her fingers at last encountered something that seemed like a sliding bolt. She pushed it back eagerly. A door opened outwards, letting in a blaze of light. To their utter amazement they were gazing down into the picture gallery!

It did not take them many seconds to spring to the floor and turn round to look through what aperture they had made their escape. It was the portrait of Monica Courtenay that formed the secret exit. It had swung out, frame and all, into the gallery, and appeared to be fitted with hinges so as to close and unclose quite easily.

"Now I see why the picture shook in its frame that day!" exclaimed Cicely. "I wonder we never thought of this before."

"And of course that was why she was supposed to guard the fortunes of the Courtenays. No doubt they always kept their valuables in this hiding-place, and only the head of the family would know the way to it."

"So old sayings do generally mean something, and aren't just nonsense."

"Let us go and tell at once. Everybody'll be wondering where we are. They must be doing prep. now, and Miss Russell will be sitting with the first class."

The headmistress's tranquil demeanour was not usually easily ruffled, but she sprang up in excitement as her two missing pupils burst into the library proclaiming the glorious news.

"Lindsay and Cicely! Where have you been? I was growing most uneasy at your absence. You say you have actually found Sir Giles's treasure? It is hardly to be credited. Girls, girls, try to calm yourselves and give me an intelligible account!" as first one and then the other took up the tale in disjointed sentences.

"We played hide-and-seek—and fell through the bottom of the settle—there were great bags of gold—and boxes of silver things and bank notes—won't she be rich? And he'd written it in an enigma—we thought we were going to starve there like Ginevra—and we climbed down through the portrait—oh, may we go and tell Monica about it now?"

"This is indeed a most extraordinary discovery," said Miss Russell, when at length she had drawn from them a more lucid statement of affairs. "Monica must certainly know, but no one is to tell her except myself. I will go down presently to the cottage and see her, and warn her to break the news very gently to her mother. If Mrs. Courtenay were to hear of it suddenly, the shock might be exceedingly dangerous, in her weak state of health."

The news that something of great importance had happened seemed to spread like wildfire through the school. Both teachers and pupils, abandoning their books, came crowding into the library to hear particulars. Even the servants hurried to the spot.

"Oh, bless you, bless you!" cried Mrs. Wilson, who had pushed her way among the girls to the central source of information. "This is indeed a day of rejoicing—a day to remember and give thanks for to the end of one's life!"

Lindsay and Cicely stared at her in amazement. Was it actually "The Griffin" who was speaking? And were those tears that were trickling down her hard cheeks? What did it mean? Was she acting a part? Or had they after all misjudged her? There was no time then for either surmises or explanations. They were the heroines of the hour, and had to repeat their story afresh to those who had not yet heard it at first hand.

"We couldn't imagine where you were hidden," said Marjorie Butler. "We were hunting in the picture gallery for ever so long. Beryl peeped inside the settle, and said it was empty."

"We were still more puzzled when you didn't turn up for tea," said Nora Proctor. "Do tell us again about the bags of money!"

Miss Russell, however, thinking the excitement had lasted long enough, interfered and put a stop to the recital.

"Everybody must go back to preparation at once," she decreed. "Lindsay and Cicely have had no tea. Are you hungry?" she added, turning to the adventurous pair.

"Starving," they replied laconically.

"Then I will excuse your preparation to-night, and you may come with me to the dining-room. It would be rather hard to expect you to set to work upon lessons immediately after such an experience."

CHAPTER XVII. GOOD-BYE TO THE MANOR

Monica's agitation, when she heard that her uncle's legacy had been found, was extreme. At first she refused to believe it; but when she was told the story of Lindsay's and Cicely's strange adventure, she began slowly to realize that it was no fairy tale, and that the fortune, so sorely needed and so much longed for, was lying awaiting her disposal.

"The money is there, and I can have some of it now?" she asked, still almost incredulously. "Will there be as much as a hundred guineas?"

"Far more than that, my dear, from the girls' account."

"Then we can send for Sir William Garrett!" she said, with a sigh of intense relief.

Miss Russell, who did not like the responsibility of being even a temporary custodian of such riches, had informed the Rector of what had occurred, and requested him to come to the Manor and help her to investigate the matter. As he was Monica's guardian, he seemed the proper person to take charge of her affairs. He arrived next morning, and, accompanied by Miss Russell and Monica, made a careful examination of the hiding-place and its contents. At the mistress's urgent request, he promised to arrange that all the valuables should be removed as speedily as possible to the bank.

"I could not sleep with them in the house, I should be so afraid of burglars, now the news of the discovery has been spread abroad," declared Miss Russell.

"They were only too safe here," said Monica.

"Yes, when their whereabouts was a mystery. It is different when everyone knows."

The wealth which old Sir Giles had stored in the secret room was considerable. He had evidently distrusted investments, and, following his own singular whim, had hoarded his money in gold and bank notes. There were precious stones also, in themselves worth a small fortune, which he must have collected, in addition to the family jewels and the old silver plate that had been handed down through generations of Courtenays.

After looking through some of the boxes, the Rector picked up the casket, and made a short scrutiny of its contents.

"This envelope is addressed to you, Monica," he observed.

The girl took it hesitatingly, then passed it back to her guardian.

"It seems like a message from the dead," she said. "I think, please, I would rather that you should read it aloud."

The letter was well in keeping with its writer's eccentric and morbid character. It ran thus:—

"MY DEAR MONICA,

"Gold, silver, and precious stones are but vanity of vanities, a snare to many, and the root of all evil. By the time you claim these, I trust you will have found how easy it is to dispense with them, and that you will despise them as much as I do.

"They have never brought me any happiness, and I am uncertain whether it is a kindness to bequeath to you what to me has been but an irksome encumbrance. After giving long and earnest thought to the matter, I have decided to leave it in the hands of destiny.

"I shall lay by these possessions in the hidden chamber, the existence of which was told me by my grandfather, and now is unknown to any except myself. I have concealed the secret, however, in an enigma, which, if you have followed my advice concerning the study of Botany, you will have found written inside the cover of the *Floral Calendar*.

"Should Heaven ordain that you are to take up this burden, then you will read my riddle aright. Should it be otherwise decreed, this message will never meet your eyes. Believe me that I have striven to act for your best good.

"From your uncle and well-wisher,

"GILES PEMBERTON COURTENAY."

"He seemed quite afraid for me to have this money," faltered poor Monica, on whom the letter had left a deep impression. "Shall I regret it? Is it really such a dangerous thing?"

"Not if you make a wise use of it. In your hands I hope it may prove a blessing instead of a curse," answered the Rector.

"It does not seem to have brought any happiness to Uncle Giles. He calls it a burden."

"Riches can never bring happiness unless they are being employed for the benefit of others."

"It is sad to think how long these have lain idle," remarked Miss Russell. "Monica will be able to do much good with them."

"Then you are sure I may take them?" asked Monica, turning to her guardian. "I didn't find out the enigma myself, you see."

"I am certain you may receive the legacy without scruple, my dear child! Your uncle himself said he had left matters to the disposal of destiny. It appears to me as if Lindsay and Cicely had been led just at the right time to this happy discovery. You must accept your fortune as a special gift of Providence. So far it has been a talent laid up in a napkin; it can now be your care to let it yield ten talents in return."

Though Lindsay and Cicely had satisfactorily accomplished their quest, they felt there were many points in connection with their adventure at the Manor that still puzzled them. The mystery surrounding the lantern room had not yet been cleared up, neither had the strange behaviour of Mrs. Wilson and Scott been accounted for.

So anxious were they to decide these perplexing points that they determined to confide the whole affair to Monica, and see if she could offer any explanation. A month ago it would have been impossible to get her for half an hour to themselves, but since their finding of the treasure the other girls were ready to allow them a special claim to her society, and took it as a matter of course when they carried her off to the summer house for a private chat.

Monica listened attentively to the story of their various experiences and suspicions. At the end she laughed heartily, then suddenly looked grave.

"You dear silly children!" she exclaimed. "It was a case of much ado about nothing, and yet you nearly ran into such great danger that it makes me shudder even to think about it. There certainly was a reason for visiting the attic, though not at all of the kind you imagined. It contains a large cistern, which supplies the water for the bath and the kitchen boiler. This is fed by a tank on the roof that catches the rain, and in dry weather it is apt to get out of order. If it is not working properly, it makes a curious blowing noise."

"Like groaning?" asked Cicely.

"Yes, very like groaning, though it would need a gigantic prisoner to utter such fearful moans of distress. No wonder you thought somebody was being tortured!" and Monica laughed again.

"You can understand," she continued, "that with so many girls in the house requiring baths, we were afraid lest the tank should run dry, and were continually examining the cistern, to make sure that the water was flowing properly. If it had stopped even for an hour, it might have caused the kitchen boiler to burst."

"Did Mrs. Wilson go to look, then?" enquired Lindsay.

"Either Mrs. Wilson or Scott went every day. My mother was so anxious about it that I several times ran up myself, so that I could tell her all was perfectly safe. Mrs. Wilson was equally nervous. We had so little rain in June that she was sure the tank must be nearly empty."

"Then that was what she and Scott meant about the noise and danger, when they were talking in the picture gallery!" interposed Cicely.

"Yes," replied Monica. "When people try to overhear conversations, and put two and two together for themselves, they rarely succeed in coming to a right conclusion."

Lindsay and Cicely blushed. They had known from the first that Monica would not approve of either eavesdropping or peeping through keyholes. This was the part of the business of which they both felt rather ashamed; they were conscious that there had been a great deal of curiosity mixed up with their efforts on her behalf. Monica, however, took no notice of their heightened colour, and went on:

"Both Scott and Mrs. Wilson were quite right in wishing to keep you away from the attics; you will understand when I explain why. The hiding-place in the lantern room is a relic of the times of King James I. Have you learnt yet in your history books what severe penal laws were made against Roman Catholics in those days? Any priest found celebrating Mass might be executed, and often he was tortured first to make him tell the whereabouts of his companions. Our ancestors, who lived then at the Manor, still belonged to the old faith, and they needed some spot where they could worship without fear of being disturbed; so they made the secret entrance through the cupboard, and private services were held in the great garret. Even with such precautions it was a very dangerous thing for a priest to remain long in a country house. If his presence were suspected, and information given, a party of soldiers would at once come with a search warrant to hunt for him.

"Then he would have to be ready to hurry away into some safer retreat still, in case his first place of concealment were discovered. At the end of the farther attic there is a small cupboard most cunningly hidden in the wall. In front of it there is a shaft, a great, horrible, yawning chasm, several feet wide and very deep, going quite to the basement of the house. It was intended as a trap to baffle pursuers, who would fall down it in the dark when chasing their fugitive."

"Is the shaft still there?" asked Cicely.

"Yes, it is quite untouched and open. It is in such a far-away part of the attic that nobody has considered it worth while to go to the trouble of having it covered in. Now you can understand how alarmed Mrs. Wilson was when she found that some of you had been in the lantern room. She didn't believe you would really be able to find your way through the cupboard; still, she was never easy when she thought of the danger you might perhaps run into. She couldn't rest until Scott had padlocked the door."

"We were very near it," said Cicely, with a shiver.

"It was the greatest mercy you didn't venture any farther. I can't be too thankful that the cistern made a noise just at that moment, and frightened you down again."

"Then you knew of this secret door, though not of the one in the picture gallery?" said Lindsay.

"Yes; it was discovered two centuries ago, in the reign of Queen Anne, I believe. In many old manor houses there are equally clever contrivances for hiding-places. They are often called 'priests' holes'. I've heard of one under the steps of the stairs, and another in a window-seat, or up a chimney, or even behind a picture."

"Like ours," said Cicely.

"No doubt the one under the settle may have been a 'priests' hole' too, and perhaps had the second entrance for extra security. Very sad stories are told about some of the hiding-places. Sometimes the poor fugitive couldn't find an opportunity to get away, and the person who knew the secret, and should have brought him food, was killed or taken prisoner. Then he either had to come out, and deliver himself up to the soldiers, or to remain and die a slow, lingering death of starvation."

"I thought we were going to do that when we were locked in with the treasure," remarked Cicely.

"How much did Merle find out in the lantern room?" interposed Lindsay.

"She happened to pull at the lantern, and had just the same surprise as you," replied Monica. "She had gone a few steps into the passage when I came down from looking at the cistern, and met her, much to her astonishment. Of course I explained everything, and begged her not to tell, because we didn't want any more schoolgirls to start exploring."

"Then it was to you she gave that mysterious promise?"

"Certainly it was to me. I'm glad to hear she kept it so well."

"But I still don't half understand," said Lindsay. "We thought Mrs. Wilson and Scott were hiding the treasure up there. We saw them take a sack into the garden one night and bury something."

"You managed to give poor Scott a great fright," laughed Monica. "He told me about it the next day. He was doing nothing more dreadful than digging out a wasps' nest. Mrs. Wilson had discovered it in the bank, and she went with him to show him the place and help him. Of course it could not be done by daylight, when the wasps were flying about; but at dark, when they were all safely inside their hole, Scott burnt tobacco to stupefy them, and then took the nest. He said two of the young ladies had suddenly tumbled down the bank while he was at work, and startled him terribly."

"So he and Mrs. Wilson weren't burying the treasure after all? They didn't even try to steal it?"

"No, indeed! I feel sorry to think they should have been suspected for a moment of such bad intentions. Mrs. Wilson may be rather gruff and blunt in her manners, but she is a faithful old soul, and devoted to Mother and me. I believe she would have starved rather than touch a penny that belonged to us. And Scott too is absolutely honest. I assure you he keeps nothing stowed away inside the cucumber frames! Naturally Mrs. Wilson had often looked for the hiding-place, but it was all on my behalf, and nobody rejoiced more heartily than she did when it was found."

"We were on a completely wrong track," said Lindsay. "The only right clue was the enigma. I'm glad we puzzled that out, though we didn't win any prizes in the competition."

"And yet the enigma was no real use," put in Cicely. "We shouldn't have gone through the bottom of the settle if we hadn't been playing hide-and-seek. Isn't it queer that when we tried so hard to find the secret room we couldn't, and then that we should come across it just by accident?"

To Monica the affair seemed no accident, but, as the Rector had said, a merciful arrangement of Providence. It enabled her to send for Sir William Garrett, and the great specialist arrived in the course of the next few days. After examining Mrs. Courtenay, he gave a more favourable report on her case than her own physician had dared to hope.

"You have consulted me in the nick of time," was his verdict. "I trust to be able to effect a complete cure. A winter in the south would work wonders, and, if my treatment is thoroughly carried out, she should return to Haversleigh in the spring with restored health."

It was an intense relief to be thus reassured. Monica felt as if a heavy weight had been lifted from her mind. When the doctors had finally taken their departure, she ran to share her good news with her friends at the Manor. "Of course," she explained, "Mother will require the greatest care, but we can give her anything now that she needs. Sir William Garrett has promised to send a nurse from London who understands his special treatment, and who could go with us to Italy in the autumn. Oh, how splendid it will be when I can bring her back absolutely strong and well! I can hardly feel thankful enough. And it is all owing to you," she added, kissing Lindsay and Cicely with tears in her eyes.

It had come at length to the very end of the term; the girls were making up their minds to bid a reluctant good-bye to the beautiful old house where they had spent such a pleasant and eventful twelve weeks.

"If we weren't going home, I couldn't bear to leave it," said Cicely. "I've grown so fond of everything. Our dear bedroom, with its big four-poster (I love those yellow brocaded curtains), and the roses round the window that smell so delicious first thing when one wakes in the morning, and the dining-hall, and the picture gallery, and the library, and the oak parlour where we have lessons, and, above all, the garden. Oh dear, it makes me quite sad to think perhaps I may never see them again! What a change to settle down at Winterburn Lodge in September!"

"I suppose life can't be all honey; we shall have to go back to plain bread and butter now," replied Lindsay philosophically. "But I'll tell you a secret to cheer you up. Monica says her mother has promised that when they return from Italy she'll ask you and me to spend part of the summer holidays at the Manor. But she doesn't wish us to let any of the other girls know of the invitation just at present."

"How perfectly delightful!" exclaimed Cicely, with shining eyes.

"It's a whole year off yet."

"I don't mind, so long as I can think of coming here again some time, and being Monica's visitor. It's something to look forward to."

The last day arrived, as last days invariably do, whether one is longing for their advent or the reverse. Boxes had been brought down and packed, and Miss Russell's linen and silver had been collected and stowed away in great wicker baskets, which were already dispatched on their road to London. The girls, marshalled in order on the drive, were only waiting for the word "March!" to start for the railway station.

Monica stood on the steps to see them off, her pretty, fair face and rich chestnut hair framed in the oak doorway.

"I shall miss you all dreadfully," she said. "It has been a great pleasure for me to have you here. Please don't forget me."

"We're not likely to do that," replied Mildred Roper, speaking for herself and the rest. "We've spent a glorious three months. It's been more like holidays than school. I think every one of us, to the end of her life, will remember this summer term at the old Manor. Good-bye!"

THE END

BOOK SEVEN.
A FOURTH FORM FRIENDSHIP

A School Story

CHAPTER I. ALDRED'S SKETCH

"Two pencils, an india-rubber, a penknife, camp stool, easel, paint-box, a tube of Chinese white, a piece of sponge, paint rag, and water tin," said Aldred Laurence, checking each item off on her fingers. "Let me see! Can I possibly want anything else? It's so extremely aggravating to get to a place and find you've left at home what you most particularly need. My block, of course! How could I be so stupid as to forget it? It's no good taking pencils and paints if I've nothing to draw upon!"

"Hello, Aldred! What a spread!" exclaimed Keith, rousing himself from the luxuries of a comfortable chair and an absorbing book to notice that his sister had put on her hat, that her gloves lay on a chair, and that she was already beginning to pack some of the articles in question inside a home-made portfolio of dark-green American cloth. "The table looks like an art repository!" he continued. "Have you suddenly turned into a Rubens, or a Raphael? Where are you going with all those traps?"

Aldred paused to count her paint brushes, fitted the spare tube of Chinese white into a vacant corner of her paint-box, and slipped the penknife into her pocket.

"I want to make a sketch of old Mrs. Barker's cottage," she replied. "The clematis is out over the porch, and it looks lovely. I heard Mr. Bowden say yesterday that it was a splendid subject. Don't you remember, he made a picture of it last year?"

"So he did, and a jolly good one too. Yours won't be anything like up to that, Sis!"

"I dare say not, but you needn't discourage me from trying, at any rate."

"Oh, I'm not discouraging you. Go by all means, and good luck to your efforts! You can show me the masterpiece when you come back;" and the boy, flinging his legs over one arm of the chair, settled himself in an even more inelegant and reposeful attitude than before, and plunged again into the fascinating adventures of Captain Kettle.

That, however, did not at all content his sister.

"I thought you were coming with me," she said reproachfully. "I was counting upon you to hold my water tin while I painted."

Keith detached his mind from tropical Africa with an effort.

"Then you counted without your host, my dear girl!" he responded. "I'm extremely comfortable here, and I assure you I haven't the smallest intention of pounding half a mile down the dusty road, on a baking afternoon, to look at a picturesque cottage and act water-carrier when I get there!"

"The tin upsets when I hold it on my paint-box," said Aldred, in a rather aggrieved voice, "and if I put it on the ground I have to stoop every time I want to dip my brush."

"Then make a hole in each side, tie a piece of string across, and hang it on the peg of your easel. I'll fix it up for you in half a second, if you'll find me the hammer and a nail. Girls have no invention! The thing's as simple as possible. I wonder you couldn't think of it for yourself. Where's a piece of string? Now, isn't this A1? Put it inside your case. There! Off you go!"

Aldred could not but acknowledge the improvement in her painting tin, but she seemed, nevertheless, in no hurry to start. She re-arranged her paints, took off her hat and put it on again, and loitered about in so marked a manner that her brother could not fail to notice her hesitation.

"What's the matter now?" he enquired.

"You might come with me, Keith!"

"Oh, bother!"

"You know quite well I can't go alone."

"Why not?"

"Because Father said I mustn't sit sketching by myself."

"That's a horse of another colour. In that case, why did Aunt Bertha let you get ready?"

"She didn't. She's out, so I couldn't ask her."

"Taking French leave?" chuckled Keith.

"I thought it would be all right if you went too."

Keith groaned in reply.

"We need only walk for five minutes along the road, and then turn into the path through the wood," suggested Aldred. "There's a field of cut corn in front of the cottage; you could sit on the corn and read if you like."

"Not half so cool as here."

"Oh, Keith, you might be nice when it's holidays!" pleaded Aldred. "It's the only time I ever have anybody to go about with. I'm sure I do heaps of things for you; I was playing cricket with you all morning, wasn't I?"

"Yes, and a precious butterfingers you were, too. There, then, you needn't look so blue! I'll go, but on the one condition that you let me read in peace and quiet, and don't bother."

"I won't say a single word, if you don't want to talk. I'll be absolutely dumb and mum!"

"Well, I hardly believe you'll be able to hold your tongue to that extent. I'll allow you an occasional remark, but you mustn't keep up a continual flow of conversation. Where's my straw hat?—it's too hot for a cap. I think I'm an absolute saint to turn out on such a blazing afternoon!"

Having gained her point, Aldred ran readily enough to fetch her brother's hat, and set off with him down the drive in a state of beaming satisfaction.

Dingfield, the place where they lived, though only an hour's distance from London, was sufficiently in the country to afford a pleasant prospect of trees, meadows, and winding reaches of river. The hedgerows were thick with twining bryony and feathery traveller's joy; here and there the hips were reddening, and a ripe blackberry or two tempted them to linger upon the way. It was cooler than Keith had anticipated, for a fresh breeze was blowing from the Surrey Hills, sending white clouds in long streamers across the blue of the sky, and shaking down a few windfalls from the apple trees that overhung Farmer Walton's gate.

The two soon left the high road, and, after strolling leisurely through the welcome shade of the wood, climbed over a stile into a pasture, and after another five minutes' walking found themselves in a stubble field, within sight of the river. Here was the subject upon which Aldred had determined to try her brush. It was a picturesque old cottage, with red-tiled roof, lattice windows, a porch wreathed in purple clematis, and a garden gay with dahlias, looking attractive enough in the September sunshine to make even an amateur wish to commit its beauties to paper.

Aldred chose her point of view with great deliberation, and considerable taste for a girl of only fourteen. She fixed her easel where a couple of elders would make a background for the red roof, and where she could catch a pleasant angle of the gable window and a peep of the distance beyond. Having unpacked her portfolio, she settled herself on her camp stool and began to put in her sketch with rapid lines, working, indeed, more quickly than correctly, but nevertheless obtaining rather a good effect. Keith, finding a pile of corn stooks conveniently near, flung himself down in the shade, and, with a fern leaf to flip away flies, lay with half-closed eyes watching his sister's energetic pencil.

"How you go at it!" he remarked. "It makes me hot just to look at you!"

"Then don't look! I thought you wanted to read? You made me promise not to open my lips, and I haven't spoken a word since we came."

"Most heroic self-denial on your part, I'm sure! I believe I'm too lazy even to read. I like to lounge in the holidays, especially when it's getting so near the end."

"Only a week now to the fourteenth," said Aldred.

"Yes, worse luck! I wish it were a month!"

"And I am counting the days. I want the time to come so much!"

"It's a case of 'where ignorance is bliss', my dear girl. You've never been to school before; I have! You won't find yourself in such an anxious hurry to start off by next September, if I'm anything of a true prophet."

"I expect I shall. All the stories I've read about school sound delightful—the girls have such fun. I'm looking forward to going most immensely. It will be far nicer than having a governess at home. It's so fearfully slow while you're away at Stavebury. Aunt Bertha grows more prim and particular every day, and I never seem able to do a single thing right; it's scold and lecture, lecture and scold, from morning till night! As for Miss Perkins, I was sick of the very sight of her! You can't imagine how glad I was when she took her final departure. I said good-bye as nicely as I could, for decency's sake, and then rushed into the empty schoolroom and danced a jig and clapped my hands for joy, to think I need never do lessons with her there again."

Keith laughed. "I don't suppose she's crying her eyes out over you either," he observed.

"I'm sure she isn't. I've no doubt she's almost as delighted as I am. She's going to The Thorns, to teach Blanche and Minna Lawson. They're absolutely pattern girls, warranted never to do anything they shouldn't, so I hope she'll be happy at last. I find them insufferably dull."

"You may get a far worse mistress at school than Miss Perkins."

"I don't think so. You know, Mary Kennedy has been at The Grange, and she says Miss Drummond is a perfect dear. They have all kinds of games there too. It will be lovely to learn hockey and lacrosse; I've never played either before."

"School isn't all games, I can tell you," said Keith, pulling a straw from the stook and chewing it meditatively. "There's a jolly lot of grind to be gone through. You'll find you'll have to set that young head of yours to work in good earnest."

"I can easily do that," declared Aldred, tossing back her dark curls, "I've no fear at all of not managing my lessons. Why, when I cared to take the trouble, I could simply astonish Miss Perkins. I could work sums far quicker than she did, and I used to reel off French verbs so fast that sometimes she could hardly follow me, even with the book in her hand."

"All very well with a private governess, Madam Conceit! You've had no competition. Wait till you work with a class. At The Grange you'll probably find several other girls who can reel things off a little quicker."

"Then I shall go quicker still. I tell you, I mean to be top of my class, and head of the examinations too."

"Don't boast too much beforehand, or pride may bring a fall!" said Keith, speaking with the superior authority of his sixteen years. "You'll have to find your own level, Sis. The other girls may have ambitions as well as you, and will be ready to dispute for the head place."

"Then they won't get it! It's booked already for Aldred Laurence, and so is the tennis championship, and anything that's first and foremost in the way of hockey and lacrosse."

"Great Scott! What more?" exclaimed Keith, looking at his sister with quizzical amusement. "Are there no bounds to your ambition?"

"Well, I've often heard you say yourself that if one is to get on at school one must do well at games."

"No one tolerates slackers, certainly I'll allow that."

"I mean to be a general favourite," continued Aldred. "I want the girls to be tremendously fond of me, and ready to do anything for me."

"They won't jump into your arms all at once, I assure you."

"I'll make them like me! Just you wait and see! I can always make people care about me when I try hard enough."

"How about Miss Perkins?" suggested Keith dryly.

"Miss Perkins? Oh, well, I didn't even try! I disliked her so much, I wanted to get rid of her. But it will be a very different matter indeed when I go to The Grange. I don't mind undertaking that by the time I've been there a year I shall be the most popular girl, not only in my class, but in the whole school."

"Whew! That's a large order! Popularity isn't so easy to come by, Sis. It depends on a dozen things—sometimes, indeed, it seems almost an accident. If you work too hard for it, you may overstep the line, and find yourself sent to Coventry instead. I've known two or three fellows served that way."

"You always want to discourage me," declared Aldred, with a flush on her cheeks.

"No, I don't. But I think you've far too good an opinion of yourself. You need taking down considerably, and fortunately school will soon do that for you. You'll talk very differently from this at the end of your first term, or I'm much mistaken."

Aldred shrugged her shoulders. She was confident of her own success, and regarded Keith's warnings simply in the light of brotherly teasing. She said no more for the present, but gave her whole attention to her sketch, which had now arrived at the painting stage. She dabbed on the colours with the greatest assurance; there was no hesitation in the bold, rather clever strokes, and the picture, though somewhat "slap-dash" in style, was already beginning to bear a very fair resemblance to the scene before her.

"You're not the only one out working to-day," remarked Keith, after an interval of silence. "Here's Mr. Bowden himself sauntering down the field in search of a subject."

Aldred looked round and waved her hand to a tall, grey-haired gentleman, who, armed with a sketchbook, appeared to be jotting down the outlines of some of the corn stooks. On seeing her smiling face he came at once in her direction, and stopped critically behind her easel.

Mr. Bowden was an artist of considerable repute; he was a friend of their father's, and always had a pleasant word for Aldred when he visited at the house. Therefore she awaited his verdict with some anxiety.

"Very good, Aldred! I had heard you were fond of drawing, though I did not know you could do so well as this. But, my dear child, it's full of faults, all the same. The perspective of the front of the house is completely wrong."

"I'm afraid I don't know anything about perspective," pleaded Aldred. "I just drew it as I thought it looked. The cottage is so pretty, I felt I simply must paint it."

"That is the right spirit. Go on and try, even if you don't always succeed. I am glad to see you make an effort to sketch out-of-doors. There is no teacher like Mother Nature, and the attempt to reproduce a living tree, or a house, on paper will do you more good than a hundred copies. Why did you make the lines of your windows run up, when they so clearly ought to run down?"

"I don't quite understand," said Aldred, looking puzzled.

"Give me your pencil a moment, and I will show you."

"Oh, thank you!" cried Aldred, jumping up with alacrity. "Please take my camp stool, and then you will have exactly the same view as I have. It looks so different when one is sitting down."

Mr. Bowden good-naturedly installed himself in Aldred's place, and, taking her paint-box and brushes, began to give her a practical lesson in sketching from nature.

"The composition is not bad," he remarked, "but if you had brought in that far tree, which is considerably taller than the cottage, it would have raised the subject on the left-hand side of the picture, and given a pleasanter result. Shall I put in a touch to show you what I mean?"

"Oh, please!—as many as you like. It would be such a help to watch you!" replied Aldred.

"Very well, then. In the first place, I make the lines of your perspective slope down to their right vanishing point. Is not that better? Now, a dab of brighter blue in the sky, with a raw edge to give the effect of that white cloud. The trees need massing together, with a greater depth of shade to give roundness to them, and a branch just indicated here and there among the foliage. The stubble field needs a tone of richer and warmer yellow, while a few stooks here in the foreground would be the utmost improvement. Look how I am blocking them in, with strong light and shadow, and two or three ears marked definitely at the top, to show against the dark of the hedge beyond. There! Go on working yourself at the field and the distance. Paint moistly, and don't spare your cobalt blue."

"It's like magic!" said Aldred, reviewing the improvement in her sketch with immense satisfaction. "I hardly know how to thank you. I'm afraid I've been wasting your time dreadfully."

"No matter, if it has helped you," said Mr. Bowden, picking up his sketch-book. "I must go now, though, for I want to catch the effect of the late afternoon light on those marshy pools beyond the cottage. Don't forget the hints I have given you," and with a friendly nod to Keith he walked rapidly away, and was soon out of sight.

For some little time after Mr. Bowden had left, Aldred painted away industriously at her foreground. Keith, in the shelter of the stooks close by, was deep in his book; and there was no sound except the chirping of birds, or the lowing of cattle, to disturb her. How pleasant it was! She keenly enjoyed each touch of her brush, and tried hard to follow the directions which her kind old friend had given.

Fully half an hour had passed away, and her stubble field had made considerable progress, when voices in the pathway behind her caused her to look round.

It was Mr. and Mrs. Silvester, the vicar and his wife, who, bearing a basket, were walking in the direction of the cottage, no doubt with the intention of paying a visit to old Mrs. Barker.

Recognizing the little figure at the easel, they came at once to see what she was working at so briskly.

"Aldred, my dear! have you turned artist? This is an extremely good sketch. How long has it taken you?" asked Mrs. Silvester.

"I only began it this afternoon," answered Aldred. "We came here about three o'clock—didn't we, Keith?"

"It is really excellent!" exclaimed the Vicar. "I myself have had a little experience in painting, so I am able to judge. The composition of the picture is most artistic; I admire the way the tree has been arranged to just overtop the chimney, and the large corn stook to bring the eye down to the foreground. The perspective is correct, the light and shade have been handled in quite a masterly fashion, and the sky with the patch of cloud is particularly happy. I hope you are going to have drawing lessons at school. I am sure you have unusual talent, which ought certainly to be cultivated."

Keith, who had risen from his seat among the corn to greet the visitors, gave a peculiar, rather suggestive cough, but did not volunteer any remark. Aldred's eyes were very bright, and her cheeks pink, as she replied:

"I'm certainly fond of painting. I don't think I can do any more to the distance. I was just finishing the foreground when you came."

"Don't put another touch to it," said the vicar. "It is excellent just as it is. I beg that you will shut your paint-box, and leave it; it would be a mistake to work at it any more."

"I am most interested to have seen it," declared Mrs. Silvester; "it is delightful to find anyone with such a decided gift for art. You must make it your special study, and we shall look for great things from you when you have finished school."

She passed on with her husband, and as they walked towards the cottage the words "marvellous talent" and "astonishing cleverness" were wafted back by the summer breeze.

Aldred closed her paint-box as the Vicar had suggested. Somehow she did not feel inclined to continue her work; all the pleasure had suddenly faded away from it.

Keith had subsided once more into his former lazy attitude, and sat idly picking ears of corn, preserving an ominous silence. He waited until Mr. and Mrs. Silvester were safely inside old Mrs. Barker's garden, then burst forth.

"Well, of all the sneaks you're the biggest! Call that your work? Why, it's Mr. Bowden's!—all the best parts, at any rate, that they were praising so much. And you calmly took the credit for the whole! I wasn't going to speak and give you away, but I'll let you know what I think of you now."

"Oh, Keith! What could I do?" stammered Aldred, the tears welling up in her eyes and splashing down upon the paint-box. "Don't scold me so! I can't bear you to be cross with me."

"But you deserve it! Why didn't you say it wasn't really your own painting?"

"They never asked me if I had been helped," answered Aldred; "and, after all, it's my sketch, not Mr. Bowden's."

"Yes, your sketch, but improved absolutely beyond recognition. Look here! if you play these tricks at school you'll pretty soon find yourself the reverse of popular. Boys wouldn't stand it, and I don't suppose girls will either."

"It didn't strike me to say anything," sobbed Aldred. "Oh, Keith, don't look at me like that! Shall I run after them and tell them? I will, if you want. I'll go at once, if you'll only be friends with me again."

"No, they're inside the cottage, condoling with Mrs. Barker over her rheumatism. You'd only make yourself ridiculous if you followed them, and came out with a dramatic confession in the middle of the kitchen. I hate scenes. Do turn off the water-works, there's a good girl! Be a little straighter in future if you want to keep chums with me, though. Here, I'll help you to pack up your traps, and we'll go home to tea. Your sketch is still wet; if you carry that I'll bring on the rest."

Very crestfallen and miserable, Aldred took up her unfortunate painting, and began to walk away down the path towards the wood, leaving her brother to follow. In her brown holland dress and red poppy hat she made such a sweet picture against the yellow of the corn stooks that, in spite of his disapproval, Keith could not help looking after her with a certain amount of admiration. No one who met Aldred Laurence could have failed to be struck by her personality. She was very neatly and trimly made, and had a way of holding herself erect and looking alert that gave her a distinguished appearance, and seemed to raise her above the level of the average girl. Her lovely dark eyes, long, curling brown hair, and warm, rich colouring had a gipsy effect that was particularly picturesque. Her eyes were so bright and soft and expressive, her cheeks had two such bewitching dimples, and she smiled so readily and winningly in response to the smallest advance, that she generally made friends easily, and had won notice from strangers since the days of her babyhood.

To sober, downright, matter-of-fact Keith his sister was often a sore puzzle. Her eager, impetuous, excitable disposition, and many impulsive acts, were as foreign to him as an unknown language.

"Why need you work yourself up so tremendously over every trifle? What's the use of taking life so stormily?" he once remonstrated.

"I don't know," replied Aldred. "I seem to care so much more about everything than you do. I can't help it; I suppose it was born in me."

"Then it's high time you got it out of you!" remarked Keith, whose ideal was a state of unruffled calm on all occasions.

In spite of the difference in their temperaments the two were really attached to each other, and though Keith might not be demonstrative, he tolerated Aldred's devotion when they were strictly alone, though he would not allow her, as he expressed it, to "make an exhibition of him before other fellows".

Poor Aldred! She had a very warm and loving heart, and a perpetual hunger for affection that, so far, had failed to be entirely satisfied. Since the day, seven years before, when her mother had started on that long journey from which none return, nobody had seemed to understand her quite, or to know how to manage her aright. Her father, a clever barrister who went daily from Dingfield into London, was too absorbed in his profession to give much time or sympathy to his children. Having sent his son to school, and provided a daily governess for his daughter, he felt that he had done all that was required of him. The masters at Stavebury were responsible for Keith, and as for Aldred, if anything more was needful for her upbringing than Miss Perkins could give, surely his sister, who managed his house so admirably, could look after his motherless girl?

Unfortunately, though Aunt Bertha had great experience and excellent skill in the making of jams and the care of linen, she had no aptitude for the handling of human souls. She was a stout, bustling, unimaginative, prosaic person, without an atom of romance or sentiment in her composition. A nature such as Aldred's was beyond her comprehension. She tried to do her best for the child, but it was such an unsympathetic best that it had the unhappy effect of setting a barrier between herself and her niece which neither seemed able to pass. Long and lucidly would Aunt Bertha reason and expound, and enjoin habits of neatness, order, and punctuality. All to no purpose! Arguments never appealed to Aldred. She would listen with an air of don't-care indifference, and do just the same next time. Yet if her aunt could have given her one warm kiss, the battle would have been won. It was a sad pity, for the girl had in reality a very sweet disposition, though at present it was like a neglected garden, where a few choice blossoms might be found, struggling with ugly weeds that threatened sometimes almost to strangle the flowers.

The precise governess carefully chosen by Aunt Bertha had not helped matters. She found her pupil bright indeed, but only ready to work by fits and starts, and quite unmoved by fear of punishment, or promise of reward. So strong at last had the friction grown that Miss Perkins had herself resigned her post, and recommended that Aldred should be packed off to school.

"I have done my utmost," she said to Miss Laurence, "but I feel that I am a complete failure. I have no influence over Aldred, and she is not making the slightest progress. In the circumstances I cannot honestly continue to teach her. In my opinion a little strict discipline is what she requires, and the sooner she experiences it the better."

The decision to send her away (long held over her head as a threat), instead of daunting Aldred, had delighted her. Aunt Bertha was much relieved. She had dreaded a storm when the question was raised, and though she considered it a bad characteristic in a girl to be glad to leave home, she felt it removed a difficulty when her niece accepted the situation so readily.

To Aldred the idea of forming herself on the prim pattern of her aunt was intolerable. She was ready to copy anybody whom she loved and admired, but to be obliged to repress her enthusiasms, and reduce her ideals to the level of the commonplace, seemed like being forced into a box too small to contain her.

"Aunt Bertha never understands," she thought. "She says I must try to grow up now, and be sensible. If growing up means getting cold and calm and stupid, and taking everything as a matter of course, I'd rather not. I'll just stop a child always, however hard they may try to make me different!"

Such was Aldred at the time our story begins,—a mass of contradictions, so wayward and yet so winning, a mixture of good impulses and weak points, equally ready to join a crusade or to follow the multitude to do evil; waiting, like a gaily painted but rudderless vessel, to be launched on to the stormy ocean of school life.

CHAPTER II. MABEL FARRINGTON

BIRKWOOD GRANGE was a rambling, roomy stone house, built at the edge of a breezy common, within sight and sound of the sea. It was a pleasant spot for a school; beyond stretched the broad downs, covered with short, fine grass, through which the dazzling white road wound like a ribbon to the distant horizon. There was a sense of air and space as one looked over the green upland, where for miles the view was interrupted only by the sails of a windmill, or an occasional storm-swept tree, the slanting branches of which showed the direction of the prevailing gale. In front, the chalky cliffs descended sharply to the beach; and beyond them, now blue as turquoise, now gleaming silver, now inky black, as calm as a lake, or lashing into foaming spray, always changing, yet ever beautiful, lay the wide waters of the English Channel. On one side of the house was a walled kitchen-garden, and on the other a field for hockey; while in front a large lawn provided ample space for several tennis courts.

On the afternoon of September 14th The Grange presented an extremely lively and animated scene. Girls were everywhere—tall girls, short girls, fat girls, slim girls; some fair, some dark, some pretty and some plain; and all in a state of excitement, and chattering as fast as their tongues would wag. No anthill, or hive of bees about to swarm, could have seemed in a greater ferment; there was a constant hum of conversation, a continual patter of feet, and a succession of young people, always moving in and out, searching for friends, claiming old acquaintances, exchanging greetings, and passing on items of news. It was the first day of the autumn term; a fresh school year had begun, and the party of thirty-nine girls who constituted Miss Drummond's little community were once more assembled for a season of work and play. Several changes had taken place; most of the rooms had been re-papered and painted, and there were alterations in the time-table, a revised practising list, and an entirely modified arrangement of some of the classes.

Small wonder, therefore, that a babel of talk prevailed in every corner of the house, and that various groups of hair ribbons kept collecting and dispersing with the bewildering effect of a kaleidoscope, while such a general atmosphere of bustle and commotion pervaded the establishment as to turn the head of any onlooker in a complete whirl. Aldred, ensconced in an angle of a bow window, surveyed the whole spectacle, as yet, from the standpoint of an outsider. It is true, she had received a cordial welcome from Miss Drummond; she had been duly entered as a member of the Fourth Form; she had been allotted a desk in a classroom, a locker in the recreation-room, and a cubicle in a big, airy bedroom; and was already possessed of a pile of new books, a chest expander, and a hockey stick: yet, in spite of this initiation she was feeling decidedly like a fish out of water. She was not usually afflicted with shyness, but to find herself in the midst of a medley of strangers, all too occupied with their own affairs even to realize her existence, was a little disconcerting to even her easy self-confidence. She was beginning to wonder how long she would remain unnoticed, and was trying to screw up her courage to venture a remark to one of her nearest neighbours, when a plain girl in spectacles broke the ice.

"What's your name, and where do you come from?"

Aldred started at the abruptness of the question and turned to face the speaker, who continued with a smile: "We always put new-comers through a catechism. I want to know your age, and what class and dormitory you're in, and which teacher you're to learn music from, and whether you're going to take dancing and wood-carving. Oh! so you're in the Fourth—that's my form, as it happens. My name's Ursula Bramley, and I'm fourteen and a half. We have a very decent time at Birkwood. There's any amount of fun going on, as you'll soon find out. Wait till we start the Debating Society and the Cooking Class! Have you been measured yet for a gymnasium costume? Of course, there has not been an opportunity, but Miss Drummond is sure to see about it to-morrow—and a cooking apron too, if you haven't already got one."

Aldred replied as briefly as possible to these various interrogations, but Ursula seemed quite satisfied with "Yes" and "No" for an answer, and rattled on: "I'm rather sorry for you, being put in No. 2 dormitory, because you'll be with Fifth Form girls, and you can't expect them to be particularly chummy with you. If there had only been room, now, in No. 5! But we're full up, all six beds; there isn't even a corner for a shakedown. We have such jokes in the mornings, when we're getting up! It's a pity you'll be out of it. I'd like you to see Dora Maxwell acting a peacock; you'd simply scream! Of course, we daren't make too much noise, or we should have a monitress pouncing down upon us; but it's ever such fun, all the same. They're a very prim set in No. 2. They never lost a single order mark last term! Well, if you can't be in our dormitory you'll be with us in class, at any rate, and it isn't dull there by any means, I can tell you."

"How many girls are there in the Fourth Form?" asked Aldred.

"There were seven before, but you'll make eight. Why, most of them are in the room now, or on the lawn just outside, so I can point them out to you. That's Phœbe Stanhope standing by the fireplace,—the one with the long light pigtail and the blue blouse; she's talking to Lorna Hallam, and Agnes Maxwell is showing her camera to them both. Now, if you'll look through the window you'll see two girls walking arm in arm round the sundial; the fair one is Dora Maxwell, and the dark one is Myfanwy James. Dora is tremendously jolly; she and Myfanwy think of the most outlandish things to do. Why, one night they went to bed right underneath their bottom sheets, and put their pillows over their faces, and when Freda Martin (that's our prefect) came to turn out the lights she thought they weren't there at all, and was just going to make a tremendous fuss, when Myfanwy couldn't stand it any longer, and exploded! We six are in the same dormitory, and we're the greatest chums. We call ourselves 'The Clan', and each is pledged to back the others up through thick and thin, whatever happens."

"Who's the seventh girl in the class?"

"Mabel Farrington."

"And doesn't she belong to 'The Clan'?"

"Oh, no! Mabel wouldn't dream of such a thing."

"Why not?"

"Oh! because—well, she's rather particular. She's not very great friends with anybody."

"Don't you like her?"

"Like her? Yes; everybody likes Mabel. That's not the reason at all. Somehow she's a little different from other people. You see, her grandfather is Bishop of Holcombe, and her uncle is Lord Ribchester."

"You mean, she gives herself airs?"

"Not in the least; she's not at all conceited. But she never cares about playing tricks, and having all kinds of jokes, like the rest of us."

"Then she's a prig!"

"No, she isn't. Wait till you've seen her; she's extremely nice. As I said before, she always seems different—just a trifle above everyone else, perhaps."

"Which dormitory is she in?"

"She's allowed a bedroom to herself, and she's the only girl in the school who has one—even the monitresses have to sleep in cubicles."

"Why is she so specially privileged?"

"Her mother, Lady Muriel Farrington, is a friend of Miss Drummond's. I believe Mabel was sent here rather as a favour, because Miss Drummond was so anxious to have her at The Grange."

"Then you all make a fuss over her?"

"No, not particularly; but we certainly like her."

"I'm sure I shan't."

"You can't help it, when you know her. By the way, here she is now, coming in at the door. I must tell her who you are."

Aldred turned, and saw a girl of her own age, so remarkably pretty and attractive that, in spite of her preconceived prejudice against the aristocrat of the school, she could not repress a certain amount of admiration.

Mabel had a very fair complexion, with cheeks pink as apple blossom, a pair of frank, thoughtful blue eyes, straight features, and a quantity of beautiful red-gold hair that hung almost to her waist. Her expression was particularly pleasant and winning, and as she crossed the room in response to Ursula's call, and smiled a welcome to the new-comer, Aldred began already to reverse her unfavourable opinion.

"I'm glad we shall be eight in class now," said Mabel. "It's a much nicer number than seven. Don't you remember, last term Miss Drummond said she hoped we should get a new girl? Of course, we were Third Form then, but it has not made any difference to be moved up to the Fourth, except that we are going to have Miss Bardsley for a teacher, instead of Miss Chambers—we're just the same set altogether."

"I like our new classroom far better than the old one," remarked Ursula. "The desks are more comfortable, and there's a nicer view out of the window. From my place I can catch a little glimpse of the sea, if I screw my neck."

"Miss Bardsley won't let you crane your neck in school, I'm sure," said Phœbe Stanhope, who had joined the group. "She has the reputation of being much stricter than Miss Chambers."

"Ugh! Then I wish I could go back to the Third," declared Ursula.

"We'd a fairly easy time with Miss Chambers," said Lorna Hallam. "One could always give a headache as an excuse, if one didn't know one's lessons."

"I don't care for a slack teacher like poor Miss Chambers," put in Agnes Maxwell. "She has no more idea of keeping order than a jellyfish; I could teach as well myself."

"Go and tell Miss Drummond so, and propose that you should take the Third," laughed Ursula. "I should like to see her face when you suggest it!"

"There's the dressing-bell! Aldred, you must go and get tidy for tea, which will be ready in exactly ten minutes."

There was no doubt that Mabel Farrington was a particularly nice girl; the more Aldred saw of her, the more she liked her. Her popularity at The Grange was thoroughly well deserved, for it rested more on her character than on her social standing. She was extremely high-principled and conscientious, a plodding worker, and always anxious to uphold the general tone and credit of the school. If she had a fault, it was her exclusiveness. So far, though she was pleased with everyone, she had made no bosom friend, and, as Ursula had said, kept slightly aloof from the other girls in the form.

Aldred also found herself rather left out; "the clan" of six were so thoroughly absorbed in their own interests, so taken up with various amusements, secrets, and private jokes that could not be shared by anyone who did not sleep in their dormitory, that it was impossible for them to include her in their fun.

They were not unkind to her, but they simply took no notice of her; and as the Fifth Form girls in No. 2 dormitory were equally stand-off, Aldred's first week at The Grange was a very lonely one.

It was an unpleasant and unwelcome experience for her; she had come to school full of confidence that she would win immediate favour, and it was humiliating to find herself not appreciated as she had expected.

After her first catechism by Ursula no one had exhibited further curiosity about her home or her family; and any information which she volunteered was received without enthusiasm. It was plain that "The Clan" thought her of small consequence, and did not trouble to cultivate her acquaintance.

Aldred was not used to being overlooked; she felt both indignant and offended at this neglect. She almost wished she had never left home, or, at any rate, that she had been sent to some other school than The Grange.

"If I can't make them like me, I shall never be happy here," she said to herself. "They're a stupid set! Well, if I don't get along any better than this, I shall ask Father to take me away, and send me to Oakdene with the Ropers. They always admire me; Doris writes two letters to my one, and Sibyl fights with Daisy to sit next to me at tea!"

It is generally the unexpected that happens. Aldred had nearly made up her mind that she would never be popular with the Fourth Form, and would be obliged to remain a permanent outsider, when quite suddenly the whole aspect of affairs was altered.

The change arose from a most unanticipated quarter. One day Mabel Farrington came up to Aldred with an unusual warmth of manner, and an evidently newly awakened interest.

"By the by, Aldred, do you happen to live at Watersham?" she began.

"At Dingfield. It's really a part of Watersham, only the river runs between," replied Aldred, rather astonished at the question, for no one had seemed to care to hear about her home before.

"And were you staying at Seaforth in June?"

"Yes; we had rooms on the Promenade."

"I thought you must be the same girl! I've just had a letter from a cousin. I don't expect you've met her, but at any rate she has heard all about you, and she wrote to tell me. I'm so glad you have come to The Grange! I hope we shall be great friends. Will you sit next to me in class?"

Aldred's amazement was extreme. That Mabel Farrington, so exclusive and particular, should have singled her out, and actually wished to sit near her, was an honour which had been bestowed upon no one else in the school. It was evidently no empty compliment, but a genuine offer of friendship, for Mabel went promptly to Miss Bardsley and arranged for an exchange of desks, with the result that she and Aldred were placed side by side. At lunch-time she took Aldred's arm as they walked down the passage, she chose her for a partner at tennis during the afternoon, and sat talking to her during evening recreation.

She even made a more astonishing proposal.

"It's horrid for you to be obliged to sleep in No. 2, with Fifth Form girls," she said. "There's plenty of room in my bedroom for another bed. Would you care to join me? I should be delighted to have you, if you will."

The sudden fancy which Mabel had taken for Aldred could not fail to attract the notice of the other members of the Fourth Form. It was so unlike her to seek to be on such intimate terms with a classmate that at first they could scarcely believe the evidence of their own eyes. When they saw, however, that she appeared to have formed, not only an affection, but also an intense admiration for Aldred, they began to yield the latter a higher place in their estimation. As an ordinary new-comer, she had seemed of little importance; but as the chosen friend and elect companion of Mabel Farrington, she was at once raised to a very superior and important position. Girls who had hardly noticed her before, now made much of her; and her opinions were consulted, her remarks listened to, and her suggestions well received. It was an understood thing that to offend her would be to offend Mabel also, and to please the one was the best way of pleasing the other.

Aldred found this new state of things extremely gratifying. It was exactly what she had hoped for; success had come with a bound, and granted her the popularity for which she had craved. Added to this, she liked Mabel immensely, and keenly enjoyed her society. Once Mabel had unbent and thrown off her usual cloak of reserve, she proved a most delightful and winning comrade, and it gave a special zest to her confidences to feel they were shared by no one else. Aldred knew well that she was regarded as supremely lucky by the rest of the class, each one of whom would have jumped at the chance of being Mabel's room-mate, and envied her good fortune. She held her head a little high in consequence, and was ready almost to patronize those who, while they had had a much longer acquaintance with the school favourite, had not been considered worthy of her particular esteem.

It was about a fortnight after the establishment of this friendship, when the two girls had already grown very fond of each other, that Aldred happened one day to be standing inside the book cupboard in the classroom. It was quite a large cupboard, almost like a separate little room; and it had shelves all round, where spare exercise-books, bottles of ink, and boxes of chalk for the blackboard were kept. No one but the monitress was supposed to enter, and that only by the mistress's orders; so Aldred had no business there, and had gone in out of curiosity to see what it contained. She was examining the new pens, paper fasteners, bundles of pencils, and other articles which she found, when she heard voices in the classroom. Mabel Farrington and one or two other girls had evidently come in, and, to judge from their conversation, were discussing no less a person than herself. Aldred pricked up her ears. What were they saying about her? Strict honour urged her to step out of the cupboard at once, before she heard any more; but prudence advised her to stay where she was, and not to let her companions know that she had been prying in a place where she was not allowed to go: and it was the latter counsel that prevailed.

"Yes, I think she's pretty," said Phœbe Stanhope, "and she's very clever, and can make herself pleasant; but (if you'll excuse my saying so, Mabel) I can't quite see why you admire her so blindly as you do."

"Because she deserves it!" exclaimed Mabel, with enthusiasm. "She did such an absolutely splendid thing that I feel proud to know her."

"What do you mean?"

"I'll tell you. I didn't say a word about it before because I wanted to see if Aldred would mention it herself; but she's never hinted at the matter, and that's raised her higher still in my opinion. There are few girls who would not have made some reference to it."

"But what did she do?" asked Dora Maxwell.

"She was staying at Seaforth last June, and while she was there a terrible fire broke out in the middle of the night at the house where she was lodging. The people got safely on to the Promenade, and had sent for the fire engines, when suddenly it was discovered that the landlady's youngest little boy had been left asleep in the attic. The flames were blazing out at the windows, and the hall was filled with horrible, dense smoke. Nobody dared to go inside, and everybody said: 'Wait for the Brigade, and the proper fire-escape. One of the men will fetch him.' But

Aldred knew that every moment wasted might mean the loss of the child's life. She ran and dipped her pocket-handkerchief in the sea, and tied it over her mouth; then, without consulting anyone, she dashed into the house, and crept on her hands and knees up the stairs. She could just manage to breathe, but she reached the bedroom, and groped her way to the crib where the little boy lay whimpering with fright. He was only two years old, and luckily not very heavy, so she took him in her arms and crawled down the stairs in the same way as she had gone up, so as to get the purer air close to the floor. The people nearly went wild with excitement as they saw her stumble out at the door carrying the baby; and its mother was ready to worship her. The Brigade was such a long time in arriving that the flames had gained a complete hold before it came, and the attics were flaring like a bonfire. If Aldred had not seized the opportunity, and gone the very moment she did, the child would have been burnt to death! I believe it made a stir in Seaforth at the time. The newspapers wanted to print her portrait, but her father wouldn't allow it. He said 'his daughter had no wish for notoriety, and did not desire any public recognition of an act she had only been too happy to perform. She would be grateful if people would kindly take no further notice of it.' Now, you see why I think so well of Aldred! She's as brave as anyone in the *Book of Golden Deeds*, and yet so modest about what she has done that she's content to let it be quite forgotten."

"How did you hear, then?"

"I happened to mention in a letter to a cousin that we had a new girl at The Grange, called Aldred Laurence; and Cousin Marion wrote back, sending me a newspaper cutting that she had kept describing the fire, and saying she was sure that was the name of the 'little heroine' whom everybody at Seaforth had been talking about when she stayed there in June. She knew her home was at Watersham, and could tell me that she was dark and pretty, for she had sat next to her at a concert, one afternoon, on the pier. To make quite sure, I asked Aldred if she lived at Watersham, and if she had been at Seaforth in June; so when she answered 'Yes' to both questions, I was certain that Cousin Marion must be right."

"Aldred was brave!"

"Yes, and she showed such particularly nice, delicate feeling afterwards. It's a privilege to have such a girl at the school! Although she mayn't want us to say anything about it, she can't help our honouring her for it. I shall always feel quite different towards her for the sake of this."

In the shelter of the book cupboard Aldred had overheard every word. Mabel's account almost took her breath away. It was all a mistake. She had certainly never been in a fire, or risen to any such pitch of heroism. She remembered the circumstances, which had occurred just before her visit to Seaforth, and she had been struck at the time with the fact that the author of the deed bore the same surname as herself. The latter's name was, however, spelt with a W instead of a U, and the two families were not related, nor even acquainted. Aldred had not, indeed, been aware that the Lawrences lived at Watersham.

So this was the explanation of Mabel's violent attachment! She had been attracted, not by Aldred's real personality, but by qualities which she believed her to possess. What would she think, when she learnt that Aldred was not the girl she imagined? Suppose she were to drop the friendship as suddenly as she had taken it up? She might possibly prefer to have her bedroom to herself once more, and would feel no further interest in one who had not done anything particularly worthy of admiration. Aldred turned quite cold at the idea. If such a catastrophe occurred, all her popularity in the school would be lost. She was shrewd enough to realize that it depended entirely upon Mabel's goodwill, and that her position really resembled that of a Court favourite. It would be worse, far worse, to have to fall again into comparative obscurity than if she had never been thus made much of. Her pride could not tolerate the thought of being once more a nonentity in her class. To be held in high repute by her companions was the salt of life to her.

She knew perfectly well that she ought to walk out of the cupboard, confess to Mabel and the others that she had been listening to their talk, and explain the exact state of the case. It was the only straightforward course to take, and would prevent any further misconceptions. And yet, she hesitated. A swift and strong temptation had assailed her. After all, why need she tell? No one was aware that she had overheard this conversation, and nobody had so far made the slightest reference to her fictitious deed. She would act as if she were quite unconscious that they credited her with it, and it would be time enough to disclaim it when it was alluded to in unmistakable terms. The longer she could keep Mabel's friendship the stronger it would be likely to prove; and if the rest of the class had grown accustomed to treating her opinions with deference, they would probably continue to accord her a certain amount of consideration, from sheer force of habit.

She could not deliberately give up all that she had gained; it was too great a sacrifice to be expected from anybody! On some future occasion, when she had had sufficient opportunity to win their approbation on her own merits, she could casually enlighten the girls, and set the mistake right. She was confident that when they knew her better they could not fail to value her for herself alone, and this exploit would sink into insignificance. Besides, it was surely Mabel's fault, for jumping at once to a conclusion without making adequate enquiries. She could not help all the absurd things people might set down to her account, and it was not her business to go about the world correcting them.

The girls had left the classroom and run downstairs. She could now emerge from the cupboard quite unobserved, and no one but herself would be any the wiser for what had happened. For the present, at any rate, she would temporize; she would let matters remain as they were, and be guided by future contingencies. There was really no deception about it, because she fully intended to tell some time, when it was more convenient.

Thus Aldred drugged her conscience, and allowed herself deliberately to take the first step in a course which she knew in her heart was dishonourable and unworthy, and which she was afterwards most bitterly to regret.

CHAPTER III. THE MODEL COTTAGE

IN her supposed character of a modest and retiring heroine, Aldred rapidly secured the favour she wanted in the school. Since the afternoon when Mabel had confided to Phœbe and Dora the story of the rescue, the whole class had waxed enthusiastic. Though nobody openly mentioned the subject, she could feel a marked difference in the general attitude towards her; she was no longer only Mabel's friend, but somebody on her own account. That this new esteem was not truly her due caused her an occasional pang, but she would put the thought hurriedly away, consoling herself by reflecting that the girls were beginning to discover her good qualities, and to appreciate her as she deserved.

Her intimacy with Mabel increased daily. The latter seemed hardly able to make enough of her. The two were always together, and Mabel, who possessed many luxuries that do not usually fall to the lot of the average schoolgirl, was ready to share everything with her room-mate. Aldred found it decidedly pleasant to be, not only encouraged, but actually begged to help herself to an unlimited quantity of the most delicious scent, to use dainty notepaper, or a delicate pair of scissors; to be lent a most superior tennis racket, and allowed to borrow any of the delightful volumes that filled the bookcase in the bedroom. To do her justice, she was really grateful for all this kindness, and absolutely adored Mabel. Had she loved her less, she might, perhaps, have been more willing to hazard the loss of her affection; but the thought of the blank which such a calamity would entail made her keep silence, in spite of the reproachful accusations of her better self.

"It's such a delight to me to have found a real friend!" said Mabel one day. "I've told Mother about you, and she wrote that she was so glad. I think I must read you a little scrap of her letter. She says: 'Your description of Aldred Laurence pleased me very much—she seems just the kind of high-minded girl with whom I should wish you to be associated; and though I stipulated for you to have a bedroom to yourself, I do not object to your sharing it with her, if you like. Our friends naturally exercise a great influence over our characters, so I am glad you have made such a good choice. I am sure that, knowing our home standards, I can rely upon your judgment, and that you would not allow yourself to be intimate with anyone who is not thoroughly worthy of your confidence.' You needn't turn so red!" continued Mabel, who misunderstood the cause of Aldred's blushes. "Of course, Mother is extremely particular, but she seems quite satisfied. I hope she'll see you some day, and then she'll love you on her own account."

"Suppose she didn't?" hazarded Aldred.

"She couldn't help it. Mother and I have just the same tastes; we admire courage and spirit, and people who do things in the world. Nearly all Mother's friends are interesting in some way. Mr. Joyce is an explorer, and Mr. Hall has done grand temperance work; Miss Abercombie is an artist, and Miss Verney is helping to run a settlement in the slums. Mother says it does her good to know them, and spurs her on to try to do more herself."

"What does she do?"

"Oh, heaps! No one could live a busier life than Mother. She's president of ever so many societies and guilds! She looks after poor girls, and finds employment for them, and sends them to the country when they need holidays. Then, in our own village there are the Orphanage and the Cottage Hospital to visit, and the district nurse and the deaconess to help, and clothing clubs and local charities to manage. She opens bazaars, and gives the prizes at schools, and acts as judge at flower shows. When Father was in Parliament it was really dreadful; Mother could hardly get through her enormously long list. But he lost his seat at the last election, and she has had a little easier time since then."

"But need she do it, if she doesn't like it?" objected Aldred.

There was a puzzled look on Mabel's face as she answered: "You, of all people, to ask such a question! Of course, she feels bound to give what help she can. She says her social influence is her one talent, and she must use it wherever a good cause needs a champion. She would be terribly missed, if she stopped supporting those various societies. It's what I'm to take up myself when I leave school. You, I expect, will go in for some splendid work, like Florence Nightingale, or Sister Dora. I have a presentiment that your name will be handed down to fame."

The idea of devoting her life to such self-sacrifice absolutely staggered Aldred. She did not attempt, however, to shatter Mabel's dreams for her future, but only gave an ambiguous reply. When her friend was in this exalted mood, she evidently did not like to be checked, and the least hint that her high ideals were not shared would make a little rift within the lute, and destroy her confidence.

Now that she had secured what she considered her rightful place at Birkwood, Aldred was thoroughly happy in her new life. The Grange was a very up-to-date school, and Miss Drummond was an exceedingly enterprising and go-ahead principal, who kept in touch with all the latest educational methods, and was ever ready to give some fresh system a trial. This term she was devoting herself to an experiment which found great favour among her pupils. It was one of her pet theories that every woman, whether rich or poor, ought to have a thoroughly practical acquaintance with all the details of housekeeping, and she was determined to put this into operation. She had had a small cottage built in one corner of the grounds, and classes were held there regularly for cookery and still-room lore. The girls were taught to mix puddings, bake bread, make light pastry, and concoct many old-world salves and cordials. Miss Drummond would wax both enthusiastic and didactic when she aired her views on the subject.

"We can very well emulate our great grandmothers in this respect," she would say, "and thus make a happy combination of ancient and modern. Because you are studying French and algebra is no reason at all why you should not also know how to fry an omelette or boil a potato. A cultivated brain ought surely to be able to grasp domestic economy better than an untrained one, and an educated woman who is really helpful is worth more than an ignorant one. Even if you are never called upon to do things yourselves at home, you ought at least to know how they should be done, so that you need not set your maids unreasonable tasks, and expect impossibilities in the way of service. I think, also, that a great future for many of our English girls lies in the Colonies, where domestic help is often at a premium, and the most delicately nurtured lady must sometimes set to work, and be her own cook and laundress. If you profit by the classes you attend at the cottage, you will have an invaluable accomplishment, and one which may in some emergency prove more useful than anything else you have learnt."

Miss Drummond believed in putting all knowledge to the test of practice, so she instituted the plan of sending the girls in relays of three to the cottage every Saturday, and letting them undertake the entire work of the little establishment. Everything must be done by their own hands: the stove lighted—after the flues had first been intelligently cleaned—the rooms swept, dusted, and tidied; the midday dinner prepared, dished up, and cleared away; the crockery washed, and the kitchen left in apple-pie order. Miss Drummond herself and one of the other teachers were permanent guests at dinner; and the three housekeepers were each allowed to ask one friend to afternoon tea, so that there should be visitors to appreciate the various viands prepared.

The girls welcomed the experiment with the utmost enthusiasm. The cottage was to them a veritable doll's house, and they were supremely delighted at the prospect of directing the internal arrangements. As three were told off weekly for "domestic duty" there was just time during the term for each of the thirty-nine to have one trial, and "Cottage Saturday" became an event to which they looked forward with the greatest eagerness.

Instead of giving the upper forms the entire precedence, Miss Drummond sandwiched elder and younger girls in alternate weeks, so that several members of the Fourth Form secured an early chance. Aldred's turn happened to come the first week in October. To her great satisfaction, Mabel was bracketed with her for the same day, and Dora Maxwell completed the trio.

"It will be such fun!" declared Mabel. "We shall have to get our own breakfast. I hope we shan't make any idiotic mistakes."

"Grind the bacon, and fry the coffee?" laughed Aldred.

"Well, hardly so bad as that. But we shan't have anybody to ask. Miss Drummond says we're to be absolutely and entirely by ourselves."

"I wish we could do something rather out of the common," said Aldred; "something that nobody else has thought of yet! It would be such fun to surprise Miss Drummond!"

"Suppose we were to make some jam?" suggested Dora. "There are heaps of blackberries growing round the playing-field and the paddock. We could pick them this afternoon, and hide the basket."

"How about the sugar? There wouldn't be enough in the stores that are given out."

"We shall have to let Miss Reade into the secret, and ask her to buy it for us. We can pay for it out of our pocket-money."

"All right. I know there's a preserving-pan and plenty of jam pots at the cottage. It would be such a triumph, when Miss Drummond came to look round in the evening, if we could show her a row of jars neatly labelled 'Blackberry'."

"We'll do it, then. Let us get the basket and go to the paddock now."

There was no lack of fruit on the brambles, and the hedgerows yielded such a prolific harvest that in an hour the girls had picked all they required. They concealed their spoils carefully in a cupboard under the stairs, where hockey sticks, tennis rackets, and other possessions were generally kept. Miss Reade was sympathetic when they took her into their confidence, and promised readily to get them the sugar.

"Cook will bring it across and smuggle it into the scullery," she said. "I think Miss Drummond will be quite pleased to find you have tried something on your own initiative. By the by, I suppose you know how to make jam?"

"I do," replied Aldred. "I've often watched my aunt make it at home, and helped her, too. I remember exactly."

"Would you like a recipe?"

"I really don't think we need it, thanks."

"Well, I wish you all success," said Miss Reade "It is not my turn to have a meal at the cottage to-morrow, but perhaps the blackberry jam will appear at The Grange afterwards, and we shall taste it sometime at tea."

By half-past seven next morning the three housewives were ready, and attired in the regulation costume for the day's work. Each wore a holland overall with sleeves, and had her hair tightly plaited, to keep it out of the way.

Miss Drummond presented them solemnly with the key of the cottage.

"You will find most of the stores ready, either in the cupboard or in the larder," she said; "but the meat will be delivered at ten o'clock. It is a loin of mutton, and you may cook it in any one of the ways that Miss Reade has taught you. You can get what vegetables you want from the garden, and I leave both the pudding and the cakes for afternoon tea to your choice. Mademoiselle and I will come to dinner punctually at one o'clock, and I have no doubt you will have everything ready and hot and very nice."

"We'll do our best," replied the trio.

They rushed across to the cottage in great excitement, eager to commence operations. The place was a tiny bungalow, containing a sitting-room, a kitchen, a scullery, a larder, and a coal-shed. Most of its adornments were of amateur origin. Miss Drummond had wished it to be the special toy of the school; so while it was in progress of construction, she had encouraged the girls to prepare everything for it that they could possibly make themselves, even allowing them to help with the decorations. Handicrafts were much in vogue at Birkwood, and it was really astonishing what a number of charming articles had been contrived, all at a very small cost. The walls of the sitting-room were colour-washed a pale, duck-egg green, and the Sixth Form had painted round them a frieze, consisting of long, trailing sprays of wild roses, quite simply and broadly done, but giving a most artistic effect. The curtains of cream-coloured casement cloth were embroidered in pale-green *appliqué* by the Fifth Form; the Fourth had undertaken the cushions; and the Third had worked an elaborate and dainty table-cover. The pictures were mostly chalk and pastel drawings done by the best students of the art class; while the wood-carving class had contributed the frames. Carpentry lessons had produced the bookcase, the cosy corner, the two arm-chairs, and also many neat little contrivances, in the way of shelves and handy brackets. Every item spent on the furnishing had been carefully entered and added up by the girls, so that each should have an adequate idea of the cost of the wee establishment, and what it was possible to do at trifling expense.

Though the sitting-room was more æsthetic than the kitchen, the latter was regarded as the most important feature of the house. The walls were a pale terra-cotta, and were hung with a few brown bromide photographs; but there art ended and utility began. All the rest was strictly business-like. There was a small "settler's stove", with oven and boiler; and a complete stock of requisites for simple cookery—pots, pans, dishes, pastry-board and roller, lemon squeezer, egg whisk, and even a coffee grinder, a knife cleaner, and a mincing machine.

The three girls felt quite important as they took possession of their little kingdom for the day. It was almost like "playing at house", but there was a "grown-up" sensation of responsibility which differed from mere amusement. With two guests for dinner and three for tea, they certainly could not afford to waste their time, if they wished to make a worthy effort at hospitality.

"We'll get the stove going first," said Mabel, "and have our breakfast; then, as soon as we've cleared away and washed up, we can begin at once to think about dinner."

She set the example by seizing the flue brush and beginning to clear the soot from under the oven, while Aldred fetched sticks, and Dora ran with a bucket to the shed to break coals, hammering away at the largest lumps she could find with keen satisfaction. The fire was soon blazing and the kettle filled, and with so many hands to help breakfast was not long in preparation. The energetic Dora turned the handle of the coffee grinder, Mabel cut dainty slices of bacon and presided over the frying-pan, and Aldred laid the table and made the toast. They all agreed that their first meal was delicious, although Mabel had forgotten to warm the plates for the bacon, and the coffee was just a trifle muddy.

"It oughtn't to be," said poor Dora anxiously. "I'm sure I made it exactly the same way as Miss Reade showed us. I must manage better if we intend to serve any after dinner to Miss Drummond and Mademoiselle."

"And I must remember hot plates!" said Mabel. "I should be ashamed to face Miss Drummond if we left out such an important item as that. By the by, Aldred, did you fill the kettle again, so that we can have plenty of hot water for washing up? It takes a long time to heat the boiler."

Aldred jumped up rather guiltily. As a matter of fact, she had drained the kettle, and thoughtlessly placed it empty upon the stove. By good luck it had not been there long enough to crack, but the vision of what might have happened made her pensive.

"There seem so many little things to think about!" she declared. "While you're doing one, you just forget another. I can quite believe the story of King Alfred burning the cakes, though Miss Bardsley always says it's 'not based on sound historical evidence'."

"It's most natural, and has the ring of truth," agreed Mabel, "especially the woman saying he would be ready enough to eat them afterwards. I should have told him so myself, I'm sure."

"What are we going to give Miss Drummond for dinner?" enquired Dora. "Let us arrange that before we begin to clear away. The kettle can't boil for quite five minutes, so we may as well hold our council of war now."

After considerable discussion they decided to cut the loin of mutton into chops, and stew it with carrots and turnips; to have kidney beans for the second vegetable, and a plum tart and a corn-flour blancmange for the pudding.

"Couldn't we have some soup?" suggested Aldred.

"There's nothing to make it with. We've no stock or bones."

"You don't need any. It can be *bouillon maigre*, instead of *bouillon gras*—just water and vegetables, without any meat. A lady who lives in France was staying with us this summer, and she said they always have it like that on Fridays. They put all kinds of things from the garden into it—things we never think of using. It will be a compliment to Mademoiselle to give her a French dish."

"Hadn't we better stick to what Miss Reade has taught us?" returned Dora doubtfully.

"We're to have 'soups and broths' at the next lesson," said Mabel.

"We can't wait for the next lesson!" urged Aldred. "I'll undertake the soup, and you can do the stew. I might make some bread sauce as well."

"But no one ever takes bread sauce with stewed mutton!"

"Why shouldn't they? It will be a novelty. I believe they have it in Germany. It will make an extra dish on the table, at any rate. We want to give Miss Drummond a good spread."

Mabel and Dora demurred, but Aldred was so insistent that in the end they agreed to let her include both the soup and the bread sauce.

"But you'll have to be answerable for them," maintained Dora, "because we haven't learnt to make either, and we wanted to practise what we really know to-day, not to try too many fresh experiments."

"Oh, I'll take the responsibility!" declared Aldred lightly. "We shall have a splendid dinner now. We'll pick a few apples, and those big yellow plums, for dessert."

"We'd better write a menu, if we've so many courses," said Mabel.

"A good idea! We'll put it in French; it will just delight Mademoiselle. What a pity we didn't think of it sooner, and we'd have painted a lovely card on purpose! I suppose there wouldn't be time now, if I ran and fetched my paint-box?"

"Aldred! With all this cooking still to be done! We haven't even put away the breakfast things yet!"

"Well, the kettle's just singing; we'll wait till it boils. Have you a pencil, Dora, and a scrap of paper?"

The list of dishes looked quite imposing and elegant, when written in a foreign language. Aldred regarded it with pride, and copied it in her best handwriting:

MENU.

Potage aux Herbes.
Côtelettes de Mouton aux Légumes.
Sauce Anglaise.
Pommes de Terre au Naturel.
Haricots Verts.
Blancmange.
Pâté de Prunes.
Fromage.
Dessert.
Café.

"But why have you called the bread sauce *Sauce Anglaise*?" asked Mabel.

"I didn't know what to put. *Sauce de pain* doesn't sound quite right, somehow; and don't you remember some old Frenchman—was it Voltaire?—said the English were a nation of forty religions, and only one sauce? It's always supposed to be bread sauce, so I think *Sauce Anglaise* is a very good name for it."

The kettle by this time had boiled over, which necessitated a careful wiping of the fender and fire-irons. After the washing-up had been successfully accomplished, and the stove stoked, and the damper turned to heat the oven, the girls sallied forth with baskets to the kitchen-garden, to pick fruit and vegetables. Aldred, who was determined to concoct what she imagined to be a really French soup, made a selection of almost every herb she could find—sage, sweet marjoram, thyme, fennel, chervil, sorrel, and parsley, as well as lettuces, leeks, and a few artichokes.

"It shall be exactly like what Madame Pontier described to Aunt Bertha," she thought; "and I won't forget the *soupçon* of vinegar and olive oil, which she said was so indispensable. Miss Drummond will be quite amazed when she hears I've evolved it myself. I suppose some people have a natural talent for cooking, the same as they have for painting. Who first thought of all the recipes in the cookery books, I wonder? It's far more interesting to try something original than to make the same stew as we had last week with Miss Reade."

Mabel and Dora had hurried back with their baskets, and when Aldred, having secured her miscellaneous collection, followed them leisurely to the cottage, she found them already hard at work, disjointing chops, cutting up carrots and turnips, slicing beans, and peeling potatoes.

"We want to get the meat on in good time, and let it cook gently," announced Mabel; "then we can turn our attention to the sweets. Would you rather make the blancmange or the pastry?"

"I don't care much about either, if you and Dora want to make them," said Aldred. "I shall have quite enough with the soup and the bread sauce. I might look after the vegetables, if you like."

As the others agreed to this division of labour, Aldred retired to the scullery, and started operations. There was a small oil cooker here, which she thought she had better use, as there would not be room for everything on the kitchen stove. She chopped up all her various herbs, put them into a pan with some water, and then began to consider the question of seasonings.

"Even Aunt Bertha admitted that French people are cleverer than English at flavourings," she thought. "Madame Pontier said there ought to be a dash of so many things. I'll try a combination of all sorts of spices, not just plain pepper and salt." So in went a stick of cinnamon, a blade of mace, a few cloves, a teaspoonful of ginger, some grated nutmeg, and some caraway seeds. Aldred had not the least notion of how much or how little constituted a "dash", so she put a liberal interpretation on the term and added a teacupful of vinegar, and half a bottle of salad oil.

"There! That ought to be worthy of a *cordon bleu*," she said to herself. "Now I must let it simmer away, and it will be delicious."

She set her pan on the oil cooker, and ran out to the garden, to pick some flowers for the table. This was a part of the day's work that appealed to her more than the cookery, so she lingered for some time making an artistic combination of poppies, grasses, and sweet scabious. When she arrived back at the cottage, she was greeted by both Mabel and Dora with rueful faces.

"Your lamp has been flaring up in the scullery, and has made such a mess!" began Dora. "It's sent black smuts over everything! They came right through into the kitchen, and fell into the blancmange. I had hard work to fish them out."

"And the scullery looks as if it wants spring cleaning," added Mabel. "I'm afraid we shall have to put clean paper on the shelves."

Aldred rushed to ascertain the fate of her pan. Mabel had taken it off and turned the lamp out, but there was still a very nasty, oily smell in the air. Dora, who was the most practical of the three, examined the cooker and re-trimmed the wick.

"You won't have to turn it too high," she said. "These lamps always smoke very easily. We used to use a paraffin heater in our greenhouse at home, and it wasn't at all satisfactory. I should leave it only half on, like this, if I were you."

"It won't cook very fast!" objected Aldred.

"Well, you don't want soup to boil, only to simmer. We must have the back door open, to get rid of this smell. It's perfectly sickening! I'll help you to clean up, while Mabel finishes the pastry."

The catastrophe with the lamp was most annoying. The smuts had settled so persistently that nearly everything had to be taken down and wiped, or dusted.

"Miss Drummond may very likely peep into the scullery," said Dora. "It would never do for her to find it covered with blacks; she'd think we were dreadfully bad housekeepers. All the things in the cottage are so beautifully new and clean, it's a shame to have a speck anywhere. Isn't it time to put on the beans and the potatoes?"

The morning had certainly crept along very fast, and if the dinner was to be punctual to the moment, it was not any too soon to think of the vegetables. As Aldred had undertaken these for her province, she rushed into the kitchen and began to see about them at once, in such a flurry that she quite forgot the instructions she had received at the cookery class. Fortunately, the other girls were looking on, and brought her to book.

"You mustn't put the beans into cold water," shrieked Dora; "I've the kettle boiling on purpose. And where's the pinch of carbonate of soda, to keep the colour?"

"And the potatoes need salt," interposed Mabel. "They're old now, and quite floury. You shouldn't do them with a sprig of mint; that was for new ones."

"Finish the vegetables yourselves, then!" retorted Aldred, a little out of temper. "I haven't made the bread sauce yet."

"Don't mind about it!"

"Yes, I shall; it's down on the menu."

"That doesn't matter."

"It matters very much. I shall have quite time, if you two will lay the table. Only, don't disturb my arrangement of the flowers, because I've put them just right; and be sure you tilt the menu card exactly opposite Miss Drummond's place."

CHAPTER IV. DOMESTIC ECONOMY

AT exactly two minutes to one o'clock Miss Drummond and Mademoiselle arrived at the cottage, and were ushered by three rather nervous and anxious housewives into the sitting-room, where the table, at any rate, looked inviting, with its nice clean cloth and elaborately-folded serviettes. The girls had arranged among themselves that Aldred was to bring in and remove the soup and the cheese, Mabel the meat course and the dessert, and Dora the sweets and the coffee. While the others, therefore, were taking their seats, Aldred, with a good many misgivings, poured her *potage* into the little tureen which formed part of the dinner service. She had never tasted French vegetable soup, and doubted whether her compound bore the slightest resemblance to the wonderful *bouillon maigre* of which Madame Pontier had boasted; it seemed of such a particularly weak and washy consistency, the herbs were not half-cooked, and the salad oil was floating on the top, and refused to mix up properly, though she stirred it vigorously with a spoon.

"I'm afraid it hasn't boiled enough on this wretched paraffin cooker," she thought. "Well, it will have to do now; I can't keep them waiting. I'm glad Dora remembered the toast."

"A six-course dinner!" exclaimed Miss Drummond, picking up the menu with great approval. "This is more than Mademoiselle and I had dreamed of! We certainly never expected to find soup—it is quite a surprise! Where did you get the stock?"

"There wasn't any stock; it's made from vegetables," replied Aldred. "I heard a French lady tell my aunt how to do it, so I thought I'd try."

"*Potage aux herbes!*" ejaculated Mademoiselle, looking at the tureen with an interest half-gastronomical, half-sentimental; "ah, but that bring to me other days! I have not tasted *bouillon maigre* since I live with my *grand'mère* at Avignon."

"You must imagine you are back in Provence, then, Mademoiselle," said Miss Drummond, as she helped to hand the plates.

"It was a sweet thought to make it—*une idée tout à fait gentille*! The scenes of one's youth, ah, what it is to recall them to the memory! *Ma foi!* but I am again in the old white *château*: the green shutters are closed to keep out the warm sun; Jules, the *concierge*, carries in the dishes, treading softly on the polished floor; outside is the cooing of doves, and the tinkling of goat bells. *Grand'mère*, so stately, so erect, so gay in spite of her years, she sit at the table's head, and serve to all the portion. It is to me as if I were there!"

Steeped in these reminiscences of her childhood, Mademoiselle, with pleased anticipation, raised her spoon to her lips. Then, alas! alas! she spluttered, made a horrible grimace, and buried her face in her serviette.

"*Ah! mais c'est dégoûtant!*" she murmured faintly.

Aldred hurriedly tasted her own plateful. Mademoiselle had not exaggerated matters; a more unpleasant brew could not be imagined. The various vegetables and herbs were still half-raw, and had not imparted their flavour, so the soup seemed mainly a mixture of spices and salad oil, and had, besides, a suggestion of paraffin, owing no doubt to the flaring-up of the lamp.

Poor Aldred blushed hotly. She was covered with confusion at such a dead failure. The others had all politely sampled the soup, and then laid down their spoons; it was quite impossible for anybody to take it.

"Never mind, my dear!" said Miss Drummond kindly. "You tried to give us a surprise, and we are as sorry as you that it should have turned out so unfortunately. Even the best cook has to profit by experience, and the value of this little cottage is that it gives you the opportunity of learning from practice. You will be wiser another time. Perhaps your aunt's French friend will send you a written recipe, with exact quantities and instructions. It needs a very old housekeeper to make a dish from hearsay. Suppose you take out the tureen, and we will go on with the next course."

Mabel's and Dora's stew, made exactly as Miss Reade had shown them in the cookery class, was quite satisfactory. They had put in the right seasonings, and had remembered to brown and thicken the gravy. The potatoes and beans were also up to standard, which cheered Aldred a little. She was partly responsible for them, and had helped to prepare them, though it was Dora who had shaken the potato pan, and put the dab of butter among the beans. Miss Drummond looked mildly surprised at the addition of bread sauce, but she helped herself without comment, feeling pledged to taste all her pupils' efforts. Aldred had been obliged to draw upon her inventive powers for this also, as she had no recipe, and the result, though not so disagreeable as the soup, was far from palatable. She had made it exactly like bread and milk, without onion, butter, or cloves; and had even added a little sugar to it. She wished sincerely that she had not included it in the menu, or, at any rate, that she had not allowed it to be brought to table. She looked so conscious and distressed that Miss Drummond readily divined who was the author of the attempt, and charitably forbore to remark upon it, though she left her portion unfinished on her plate.

The rest of the dinner was really very creditable. Dora's blancmange was smooth, and Mabel's pastry light. Aldred had arranged the cheese and biscuits daintily on paper d'oyleys; and the coffee, a combined effort of the trio, was a great improvement upon that of the morning.

The three girls heaved a vast sigh of relief when Miss Drummond, after a tour of inspection into the kitchen and scullery, departed, expressing satisfaction both with the dinner and with the general neatness and order of the establishment. Mademoiselle had excused herself the moment coffee was finished. She had been very silent after the episode of the soup, perhaps her thoughts were in Provence, or perhaps she considered it a hardship that her duties should include being obliged to endure such amateur cookery.

"Hurrah! The worst part of the day is over," said Mabel. "I felt I couldn't breathe freely until dinner was done with, and Miss Drummond out of the house!"

"I'm quite exhausted with all our efforts," declared Dora, sinking into a basket-chair and tucking a cushion behind her head.

"Your efforts were successful," said Aldred ruefully. "I don't think Mademoiselle will ever forget my wretched *bouillon maigre*. I'm afraid she won't accept an invitation to dine at the cottage again."

"Well, she won't have us for cooks in any case, for we shan't get another day here now until next term. I wish our turns could come oftener!"

"Yes, we could do with a whole row of cottages."

"I'm afraid Miss Drummond won't build them."

"No, I suppose they cost too much."

The girls felt they had earned a rest after their labours, so they sat chatting for a while in the sitting-room before they began to clear away the remains of the feast.

"The others are looking forward tremendously to coming to tea," said Mabel. "It was nice of Miss Drummond to let us ask the whole Form."

"Well, we were allowed three visitors, and it would have been so hard to choose which. The two who were left out would have been so offended; and it really would have been hard on them, when they thought of the fun the rest were having."

"Look here!" cried Dora, starting up, "do you know it's a quarter-past two? If we're expecting five girls to tea at half-past four, we shall have to bestir ourselves and make some cakes."

"And there's the jam! We mustn't forget our precious blackberries," added Aldred.

An unpleasant surprise awaited them in the kitchen. They had forgotten the very existence of the stove while they were talking, and the fire was out. Until it was rekindled there did not seem much prospect of either cakes or jam. Dora and Aldred hastened to the rescue, while Mabel cleared the table, swept up crumbs, and generally tidied the sitting-room.

"We must manage to make it burn up quickly, or we shan't have the oven hot in time," said Aldred; and going into the scullery, she fetched the paraffin can, and poured a liberal amount over the pyramid of sticks and coal in the grate.

"Miss Reade said we were never to use paraffin!" objected Dora.

"Well, I suppose it's wrong in theory," answered Aldred, "but it's good in practice. I've seen the housemaid use it at home, when Aunt Bertha was out of the way. There's nothing like it for making a blaze. There! I've put on the lid, so if you will set a light to it, you'll see it will catch at once."

Dora knelt down in front of the stove, struck a match, and applied it to the paper. Then, instantly, a horrible thing happened. The paraffin flared up, and the strong down-draught from the stove pipe sent the flame suddenly straight out through the bars of the grate into her face. With a shriek she drew swiftly back; for the moment she thought she was blinded. Mabel came running in much consternation from the sitting-room, to see what had happened, and found Dora crouching on the floor with her hands over her eyes, and Aldred standing by, as white as a ghost.

"What's the matter? Are you hurt?" cried Mabel.

"Oh, I can see, after all!" shuddered Dora, cautiously peeping through her hands. "I never expected the stove to play me such a horrid trick! Is my face burnt?"

"No; but oh dear, your eyebrows and eyelashes are singed! They look so queer!"

Dora got up, and ran to view herself in the small mirror that hung over the dresser.

"I've certainly spoilt my beauty—what there was of it! And I've had a most dreadful fright, too!" she remarked.

"It was my fault!" quavered Aldred, who was horror-stricken at the accident. "I'd no idea the flame would rush out in front. You might have lost your sight!"

"Well, it can't be helped now," said Dora, with good-tempered philosophy. "We'd better keep this little episode as quiet as we can. I only hope Miss Drummond won't notice my eyebrows, and ask what I've been doing to them. We'll never try such a silly thing again, though it was very efficacious—the fire's blazing away hard. What about the jam? Can you look after it, Aldred? You said you knew how. Mabel and I will make some potato cakes, and some scones."

After the failure of the soup and the bread sauce, Aldred's supreme confidence in her powers was rather shaken; but she would not confess as much to her companions, and readily undertook to superintend the preserving. The blackberries were waiting in the basket, and the pounds of sugar had been smuggled in that morning by the cook, and were concealed under towels in a drawer.

Aldred wished now that she had not refused Miss Reade's recipe. There was no printed cookery book at the cottage, as the girls were not supposed to try experiments, but to carry out what they had learned in class, the instructions being written down in their notebooks.

"Still, jam really isn't difficult," she reflected. "There are no horrid seasonings and flavourings, only the fruit and the sugar. I don't see how I can go wrong over this; I've seen Aunt Bertha make it dozens of times!"

She set to work very providently and systematically. First she found the jam pots, wiped them, and placed them in readiness, then got the big brass pan and rubbed it carefully with butter, to make sure that not the slightest particle of verdigris could be left in it. She felt quite proud of herself for thus remembering her aunt's methodical ways. Next she measured the blackberries with a pint mug, and found that there were nearly five quarts, therefore four pounds of sugar would be just enough.

"I'll put the sugar in first," she thought, "and then, when it's boiling, drop in the fruit, like Aunt Bertha does. It keeps the blackberries whole, instead of letting them go squashy."

So on went the pan, and Aldred, armed with a big wooden spoon, stirred vigorously, wondering why the sugar did not begin to turn into a soft syrup, such as she had seen at home.

"There's a queer smell from somewhere!" exclaimed Mabel, who was at the table concocting potato cakes. "Is anything burning?"

"It's surely not my precious scones!" shrieked Dora, flying to the oven in hot haste, to ascertain the fate of the delicacies in question.

"Why, you only put them in a moment ago!"

"No, it's not the scones; they've hardly begun to cook yet," said Dora, much relieved. "Aldred, I believe it's your sugar. Why don't you stir it?"

"I am stirring," returned Aldred, who, indeed, was wielding the spoon with frantic zeal.

"What's wrong then? Let me try."

Aldred resigned her weapon, and Dora took her place at the stove; but she was already too late, for the sugar was rapidly turning into a black, solid mass.

"Lift off the pan!" cried Mabel. "Can't you see it's burning horribly? Oh, what a nasty, disgusting, sticky mess!"

"I don't know why it should have burnt," complained Aldred; "I was watching it the whole time."

"Did you put enough water into it?"

"Water! I didn't put in any at all," faltered Aldred.

"You unmitigated goose!" exclaimed Dora. "Why, even I know that sugar will burn by itself, though I don't pretend to make jam. You really are a bungler to-day! How many more silly things are you going to do?"

"Everyone's liable to make mistakes," said Mabel, coming to her friend's defence. "It was you who suggested the jam, Dora, and neither you nor I knew exactly the proper way."

"Evidently Aldred didn't either. Why couldn't she get a recipe from Miss Reade?"

"I thought I could remember," apologized Aldred, who was feeling decidedly crestfallen.

"Well, you've spoilt all the sugar, at any rate! And the blackberries are no use now, either. It's really too bad!"

"Oh, Dora, don't be cross, there's a dear!" entreated Mabel. "Aldred's fearfully sorry! I suppose we shouldn't have been so ambitious. I expect your scones will be lovely, and that will quite make up for the jam. Hadn't you better look at them again?"

Dora allowed herself to be pacified, though she felt she had more than one grievance against Aldred that day. She had refrained from any reproaches when her eyebrows were singed, but she was annoyed at her disfigurement, and thought that the various misadventures might have been avoided. She was considerably consoled, however, when she opened the oven door and caught sight of her scones. They had risen beautifully, and were done to a turn, just brown enough on the top, and nicely baked through.

"I believe they'll taste all right, when they're split in halves and buttered," she murmured, as she took them out of the tin.

"Help me with the potato cakes, Aldred," suggested Mabel, who was anxious to make up for Dora's snubbing. "You can stamp them out, and I'll do the rolling. And somebody fill the kettle! It is a quarter to four, and the girls are sure to be so punctual!"

"She'd better clean out the preserving pan!" grunted Dora. "It can't be left in this state. Miss Drummond will be round again at six, to inspect before we go. Those who make a mess must tidy up."

Aldred saw the force of the argument. She did not want to shirk the disagreeable task, nor put it off on to anybody else. Though she held rather too good an opinion of herself, it was not one of her failings to try to avoid her fair share of any work on hand. She began at once to clean the pan, and toiled away without asking any help from the others, though it was a lengthy and troublesome performance. She was obliged to scrape the burnt sugar off with a knife, and then scrub away with sand and brick dust and soap. It took her fully half an hour, and made her hands quite sore.

She had just finished, and put the humiliating row of jam pots back on to the scullery shelf, when a loud rap-tap sounded on the door.

"They're here—ten minutes too soon!" cried Mabel. "Go and let them in, Aldred. I'm taking out the potato cakes, and Dora's laying the table."

The five visitors arrived in the very highest of spirits, and with the best of appetites. They overstepped the bounds of politeness by sniffing the air appreciatively as they entered, and announcing themselves ready to eat anything and everything.

"I feel like a ragged-school child going to a treat!" announced Ursula. "As for Lorna, she's been banting in preparation; she hardly took any dinner."

"It's a libel!" protested Lorna. "I had quite as much as Ursie. What have you made? We're dying to know!"

"Where are your manners? Please to remember you're visitors. You're not to ask; you must wait until we bring the things on to the table."

Three hostesses and five guests seemed to completely fill the tiny sitting-room.

"It's so delightfully minute!" declared Phœbe Stanhope. "When I was a little girl, I always longed to make myself small, like Alice in Wonderland, and have tea in my own dolls' house. Now I feel as if I were really doing it at last!"

"There isn't room for us all at the table," said Mabel. "Dora, you had better let down that side leaf."

"It's an afternoon calling tea, not a sit-down schoolroom tea," explained Aldred.

"Three of you must sit in the cosy corner," commanded Dora, "and the other two may have the arm-chairs."

"But mayn't we help to bring in the things?"

"No, you mayn't! Agnes, I wish you'd sit down! If you were paying a real call, you wouldn't bounce up and try to peep into the kitchen."

"You came too early," said Mabel reproachfully. "We were going to have everything exactly ready for half-past four."

"Well, you might at least tell us how you've been getting on. Has it been fun spending the day here?"

"Simply scrumptious!" replied the trio.

"I'd like to do it again next week!" added Dora.

"It's the Fifth Form next Saturday, and after that it's my turn, with Phœbe and Myfanwy. When's this wonderful tea coming in? We're all waiting!"

"We'll make it now," said Mabel. "Aldred, will you put out the spoons?"

Dora had laid the best embroidered linen cloth on the table, set cups and saucers, and brought in the milk and a plateful of bread and butter. It only needed the teapot and the scones and cakes, therefore, to complete the feast.

"I hope you've made enough to go round twice!" said Ursula.

"Beautiful cakes, so rich and brown,Oh, how quickly you'll go down!Who for such dainties does not ache?Cake of the evening, beautiful, beautiful cake!"

sang Phœbe, trying to out-Alice *Alice*.

"How disgustingly greedy you are! I call it quite indecent. You don't deserve anything, except plain bread and scrape."

Mabel crossed the passage laughing; but as she opened the kitchen door her mirth was changed to mourning. There, with his fore-paws upon the table, stood Raggles, the shaggy yard dog, devouring scones as fast as he could gulp them down his capacious throat. Mabel uttered a cry of dismay, and, catching up the rolling pin, which was the nearest thing at hand, flung it at the intruder, who snatched a last mouthful, and bolted hastily through the back door.

"Oh, Dora! Aldred! Come and see what's happened!" cried poor Mabel, bursting into the sitting-room, oblivious of the fact that a model hostess ought not to air such domestic catastrophes in public. The visitors did not stand on ceremony, however, but seized the opportunity to make a dash for the kitchen, into which they had been longing to peep.

"I never dreamt of Raggles coming in! I thought he was tied up!" wailed Dora.

"We oughtn't to have left the back door open," said Aldred.

"It was so hot; one can't have the place all stuffy! Oh, the wretch! I wish they'd choked him!"

"Has he taken every one?" asked the disconsolate guests.

"All except three, and as he seemed to be licking the whole plateful, I don't suppose anybody would care to try what he's left!" replied Mabel.

"My lovely scones! And I had split them and buttered them!" moaned Dora, almost in tears.

"Well, we have the potato cakes, at any rate. Luckily, I put them on the top of the stove, to keep hot, and Raggles didn't find them out."

"We'd better eat them quick, before any more accidents happen," advised Aldred, hastily pouring the water on the tea, and heading the procession back into the sitting-room.

The potato cakes were a huge success. That was the universal verdict. They were light, and hot, and buttery, and the only fault to be found was that there were not nearly sufficient of them. Mabel handed the plate round with impartial justice, and there were only two apiece.

"Just enough to make one want more!" sighed Ursula, consuming the last delicious crumb.

"There's plenty of bread and butter, if you're hungry."

"But I'm not bread-and-butter hungry!"

"I'm sorry we've no jam!" apologized Dora.

"Oh, don't!" begged Aldred, who still felt humiliated at the fate of the blackberries.

"She didn't mean it!" interposed Mabel the peacemaker. "I vote we have some buttered toast, and anybody can hold it who likes to volunteer."

When Miss Drummond arrived at six o'clock she found the visitors gone, the tea-things washed, and the whole of the wee establishment in apple-pie order; while three flushed, rather tired little maids-of-all-work stood at attention, ready for her tour of inspection.

"Housekeeping isn't quite so easy and simple as it appears on the surface, is it?" she remarked. "In its own way, it has as many difficulties as Latin or mathematics, and needs as much learning. It's a very useful art, however, and worthy of cultivation. You'll have gained a little experience even in this one brief experiment, and your mistakes will teach you what to avoid next time. You have done very nicely, though, and I shall give you each a good report. Have you enjoyed your day at the cottage?"

And all three girls answered: "Immensely!"

CHAPTER V. OUT OF BOUNDS

ALDRED had never been to school before, but she was so happy at the Grange that she was sure no other place in the United Kingdom could be half so nice. Miss Drummond was certainly a delightful head mistress, and the model cottage was only one of her many original ideas. Following her theory of training her pupils in useful home arts, she allowed them to do many little things in the house that do not always come within the province of schoolgirls. Each classroom was provided with vases, and it was the monitresses' duty to keep these replenished, using leaves and berries when the garden supply failed. The prefects always arranged the flowers for the dinner-table, and the top girl in each Form had the privilege of attending to those in the drawing-room and in Miss Drummond's study. Those girls who gained ninety per cent in the monthly examinations were invited to the Principal's Wednesday afternoon "At Home", and helped to pass cups and entertain visitors, the one with the highest score being asked to pour out tea.

Miss Drummond encouraged the girls to talk to her, and tried to make the whole atmosphere as homelike as possible, allowing a tolerable amount of liberty, so long as it did not degenerate into licence. She would discuss topics of the day, books, music, art, or any other subject with her pupils, trying to make them talk easily and naturally, and take an intelligent interest in what was going on in the world.

"Conversation is like a game of ball," she would sometimes say; "it must be thrown backwards and forwards from both sides. There is nothing so aggravating as to be obliged to talk to a person who will persist in only answering with a negative or an affirmative. I have racked my brains sometimes to think of fresh topics, when all my leading remarks have been received with a 'Yes' or a 'No'. That is what I call dropping the ball. When you see people are making an effort to entertain you, it is only fair to play your part as well. I know you plead shyness, but shyness can be conquered if we try to forget ourselves, and think only how we can give pleasure to others. It is really a form of self-consciousness, and ought to be fought against as well as any other fault."

Games were not compulsory at The Grange, though Miss Drummond liked all to take part in the weekly matches. But she considered it was inadvisable to train girls to care for nothing but cricket and hockey, and wished them to take up a number of small interests, such as they could carry on afterwards at home. During recreation time she allowed specially chosen recruits to help her in superintending the garden and greenhouse, the poultry yard, and the bee-hives that were her particular hobby. These country occupations proved very popular, and to be one of Miss Drummond's "outdoor helpers" was an honour much sought after and keenly appreciated.

There was a large shed in the yard, where a joiner's bench had been fitted up, and on wet days this was devoted to carpentry or chip-carving, some of the best efforts being reserved for a small annual bazaar, generally held in aid of the Missionary Societies.

Sewing and embroidery were much encouraged. Miss Gray, the art mistress, taught the girls to design their own patterns, and had obtained some pretty results in appliqué and Oriental work. She was an enthusiast in handicrafts, and allowed many pleasant variations from the usual drawing course, thinking clay modelling, gesso, stencilling, wood-staining, and pyrography as important parts of an art training as line or brush work. The weekly afternoon spent in the studio was a revelation to Aldred, whose really artistic nature revelled in all these hitherto unknown delights. She took to them like a duck to water, and was absolutely happy moulding clay, or stamping backgrounds with the poker-work apparatus. She would have spent her whole leisure in the studio if that had been allowed, and would often beg a piece of clay, with which to practise modelling by herself.

Music, also, was not neglected at Birkwood. There were lessons in theory and harmony, as well as in piano playing and class singing. Sometimes the girls were taken to afternoon concerts, but these dissipations were generally reserved for winter, as there were so many other things in summer to fill up the days.

One Wednesday half-holiday, when she had been at The Grange for about a month, Aldred was sitting on the steps of the sundial, in company with Dora Maxwell, Myfanwy James, and Phœbe Stanhope The sundial was a place of general rendezvous in the garden. Here, as a rule, the tennis sets were arranged, sides chosen for croquet or basket ball, leaders elected, and disputes settled. It was as popular a spot as the market cross in a country town, and during play-hours was the universal centre for the whole school. The four girls had brought out books, and were enjoying reading, with intervals of chatting. Mabel was having a music lesson, so for once Aldred was apart from her almost inseparable companion.

"It will be so jolly when we begin hockey on half-holidays!" said Dora. "It's really been too hot for it so far; I quite agree with Miss Drummond in that."

"I'm always glad when the cold weather sets in, and we can settle down to all our ordinary winter arrangements," said Myfanwy. "I like the long evenings, when it's dark by tea-time, and we can sit round the fire and talk; it's really far more fun than the summer term."

"I love the summer best," said Aldred. "I like the flowers, and the leaves on the trees, and the birds singing. Winter seems lonely without them. I think it's so melancholy to have days and days without any sunshine!"

"I don't mind the evenings being dark, but I hate getting up before it's light," said Phœbe. "It's miserable to have to turn out of bed at seven o'clock on chilly November and December mornings. I'm never like the good boy in the story-books who gets up readily; it's always a wrench for me."

"We've hard enough work to rouse you, certainly," admitted Dora. "If it weren't for us, you'd be sweetly slumbering when the breakfast bell rings. I can't imagine how you'd manage if you had a room to yourself, instead of being in No. 5. Who wakes first, Aldred, you or Mabel?"

"Both together, generally," replied Aldred. "I don't see how anybody could sleep through such a fearful clatter as the bell makes. It gives me a horrible start every morning. It's worse than an alarm clock?"

"Oh, you'll get used to it in time!" declared Phœbe. "And then perhaps you won't notice it any more than I do."

The conversation was interrupted at this point by Freda Martin and Blanche Nicholls, two of the prefects, who came past arm in arm.

"What are you four doing here?" asked Freda briskly. "Why aren't you playing tennis with the others?"

"There isn't room," replied Phœbe. "The Fifth Form girls have got up a tournament, and they'll keep the courts all the afternoon."

"Can't you have a round at croquet, instead?"

"We don't feel inclined."

"Basket ball, then?" suggested Blanche.

Dora leaned back against the stone shaft of the sundial, and yawned luxuriously.

"No, we're simply enjoying doing nothing," she confessed.

"You lazy little wretches, you ought to be ashamed of yourselves! Get up and take some exercise! Look here! if you care to run in and ask for your exeats, you can come with us for a stroll to Chetbourne. There are two of you apiece for us, so it will be just right to make 'threesomes'; only, quick's the word, and don't forget to bring your gloves!"

The members of the Lower School were not allowed outside the grounds of the Grange without a teacher, except in very special circumstances; but the Sixth Form girls had the right of taking walks within certain bounds, if they went three together, and might occasionally extend the privilege to some of the younger ones, on the understanding that they were considered responsible for the latter. Each was only authorized, however, to give two such invitations in the course of a term, so that the lucky chance could fall to the lot of but a favoured few. In any case, no girl might pass through the gate without an exeat or special order from the head mistress, who always entered in a book the names of those who thus had leave of absence.

Phœbe, Aldred, Dora and Myfanwy sprang up with an absolute howl of joy. They had never anticipated such a piece of good fortune. The prospect of an outing was delightful, and they rushed at once into the house to secure the necessary permits from Miss Drummond, getting ready and returning with such record speed that the two prefects could not complain of being kept waiting. It was a beautiful afternoon in the middle of October, so warm and fine that it seemed more like the height of summer than autumn. Dahlias and hollyhocks were still in full bloom in the garden, the trees had scarcely begun to change colour, and, though the swallows had left, an industrious sparrow, mistaking the season, was flying with a piece of hay in her bill, as if actually contemplating another nest. The sun shone with an almost August glare as the girls left the Grange and started for their walk over the downs; but there was a pleasant breeze to temper the heat, and, as Freda declared, the dash of the waves always had a cool sound, at any rate. The road ran parallel with the cliffs, so that for the whole of the two miles they had an uninterrupted view of the sea, which lay calm and sparkling, with a gleaming sail here and there, or the smoke of a Channel steamer on the horizon.

"I've never been to Chetbourne," announced Aldred. "I suppose it's very jolly, with a promenade, and all that sort of thing?"

"It's the ordinary kind of seaside place," said Blanche Nicholls. "It's generally very full in the summer."

"Are there any entertainments on the pier?"

"Oh, yes!—pierrots, and a band."

"Shall we have time to go and hear them?"

"We're not allowed. Our bounds stop just at the beginning of Chetbourne. We mayn't go into the town, nor along the promenade."

"Why, what a swindle!" exclaimed Aldred. "I thought we were going to have some fun!"

"Isn't the walk enough for you?" asked Freda.

"It's very nice; but it would have been amusing to see a few niggers, or some performing dogs."

"The post office is our limit," said Blanche. "We always call a halt there. They have a splendid set of picture postcards, and some nice Goss china. A good many of us are collecting Goss."

"Then mayn't we go the least little scrap farther?" pleaded Aldred.

"Not a step!" replied Freda decisively.

Aldred said no more, and the six walked on, chatting of other matters, until they reached the outskirts of the town. The post office was a large shop, of a kind common at seaside resorts. A variety of miscellaneous articles were on sale—shell boxes, photograph frames, wicker baskets, cheap ornaments, and materials for fancy-work—and the younger girls found their allowances burning holes in their pockets, and stayed so long choosing souvenirs that their elders waxed impatient.

"Haven't you finished yet?" said Freda. "You must have turned over every postcard in the box. Blanche and I want to go to the bookseller's. I think we might leave you here for ten minutes. You'll be all right till we come back," and she departed with her fellow-prefect to a shop opposite.

The others finished their purchases and paid for them, then stood waiting until their escorts should return. The post office was a long building, and had two glass doors, one of which opened on to the main street, while the other led into a side road. To the latter door Aldred strolled leisurely, and stood gazing out at the general prospect.

"Is that the beach down there?" she asked Phœbe. "I almost think I can see bathing vans."

"Yes; this road leads directly to the parade. It's only about half a minute's walk."

"I should like immensely to take a look at the sea front."

"It's a beautiful promenade," said Dora. "It seems a shame you can't see it."

295

"Couldn't we just run down to the end of the road, and have one peep?"

"What about Blanche and Freda? They'd never let us."

"They wouldn't see us go out at this door, and we should be back before they were."

"All right! I'm ready, if you are."

"There can't be any harm in walking a hundred yards," added Phœbe. "Come along, Myfanwy!"

With one accord the four girls rushed out of the post office and tore down to the sea front. The promenade looked most inviting. The spell of warm weather had brought a number of autumn visitors to Chetbourne, so that there was quite a revival of the season. Children were digging on the sands, the seats and the shelters were full of people reading or chatting, and the constant stream of parasols, white flannels, and light dresses passing up and down opposite the Marine Hotel again suggested the month of August, rather than October.

"I believe the niggers are still here!" exclaimed Myfanwy excitedly. "Or perhaps they went away, and have come back again. Don't you see them at that corner by the tea-rooms?"

"There's certainly somebody with a banjo," said Phœbe. "I can't see for the crowd. Oh! I caught a glimpse then of a tall white hat and a red-striped jacket."

"I wonder whether it's the niggers or the pierrots?" said Dora.

"Do let us go and see!" begged Aldred. "It's such a very little way, we shan't be two minutes."

She seized Dora by the arm, and began to urge her in the direction of the music. Dora did not need much persuasion, and, as Phœbe and Myfanwy offered no remonstrance, they all marched briskly along the promenade. There was a spice of adventure in that, for they knew that they had no business to be there, and that if they were seen and recognized they might be reported to Miss Drummond, and get a severe punishment for breaking bounds. In any case, there were the prefects to be reckoned with. Blanche and Freda would be returning to the post office, and would be extremely angry to find that they had not waited.

"We'll manage to square them somehow," said Phœbe. "I don't think they'll tell Miss Drummond, although they'll probably scold."

"Of course, we shan't really stay a moment," maintained Dora. "We'll just rush straight there and back. They surely can't be very cross at that."

Yet, when they actually arrived at the rather congested corner where the light-hearted negro minstrels, with carefully blacked faces and striped collars, were making merry, they found it impossible not to stop and listen to the songs and jokes. The leader of the troupe was a humorist, and above the average of such performers; he kept his audience well amused, and it was not until he had sent round the inevitable hat, and bidden a polite adieu to the company, that the girls thought of stirring. Even then, their attention was at once claimed, first by a man with performing birds, and then by a Punch and Judy show. The poor little canaries were really clever, while the tragedy of wicked Mr. Punch is an ever-thrilling drama, and his squeaky voice has a peculiar fascination of its own. Time passed rapidly, and the four runaways began suddenly to realize that not only had they been gone much longer than a few minutes, but that they had wandered almost the whole length of the promenade.

"Why, we're nearly at the pier!" exclaimed Dora.

"We must turn back at once," said Phœbe.

"Let us buy a few chocolates before we go," suggested Aldred. "Isn't there a shop here, or an automatic machine?"

"There's a kiosk on the pier-head," replied Dora. "They sell the most delicious American popcorn there, in little boxes tied up with striped ribbons."

"Then we'll get some."

"It's a fairly long way to the end of the pier."

"Well, when we've been away so long already, I can't see that a few extra minutes matter."

"'As well be hung for a sheep as a lamb'!" quoted Phœbe.

"Yes; Blanche and Freda will wait, and they'll scold in any case."

"You'll have to pay for me, then," said Myfanwy, "for I haven't any money left."

"All right; I have plenty," responded Aldred, putting down her pennies on the counter of the toll gate, and pushing hastily through the turnstile. "Now we can run, if you like. How jolly it is on these boards! You can just see the water through the chinks."

The pier was even more interesting than the promenade. There were so many different kinds of automatic machines, which, by the magic of a penny in the slot, would set a team of miniature cricketers to work, and cause mimic soldiers to drill, or ships to sail across imitation oceans.

There was a little chalet where cheap jewellery and the polished stones of the neighbourhood were displayed; a fruit shop, and an emporium for sticks and fishing-rods. All these seemed to attract Aldred, and delayed her so much that the others were obliged to take her by the arms and tug her along towards the confectionary kiosk. She had just made an investment in chocolates and popcorn, and the girls were turning to hasten back along the pier, when Dora had an idea.

"Look!" she said; "the steamer's just starting. It always stops at the jetty, and it will take us to the other end of the promenade far faster than we can walk. It's only a penny fare."

"Yes, it would save time," agreed Phœbe. "Come along!"

The bell was ringing, so without waiting to ask questions the four ran down the steps and across the gangway on to the vessel. They were not a second too soon, for she started directly they were on board. The deck was rather crowded with passengers, but the four made their way to a fairly quiet corner, and managed to find seats. Several little coasting steamers ran between the pier, the jetty, the North End, and the lighthouse, and were much patronized by visitors in summer. It would only take a few minutes, so the girls calculated, to reach the first landing-place, which was close to the post office. Blanche and Freda would no doubt be waiting for them in a very irate frame of mind, but perhaps might be cajoled into not reporting the matter at head-quarters.

"Freda is particularly fond of popcorn, I know," said Myfanwy.

"We'll all cry *peccavi*, and say we're sorry," added Phœbe. "We certainly never intended to be away so long as this. It must have taken us half an hour."

"Perhaps they'll think we've started home," suggested Dora, "and imagine we're waiting for them on the downs."

"Well, we shall very soon see; we're nearly at the jetty."

"I wonder why so many people are taking portmanteaux with them for this tiny, little voyage?" commented Aldred, looking round at the passengers, most of whom seemed to be encumbered with some impedimenta in the way of luggage.

"How funny! I never saw them on one of these steamers before," replied Myfanwy. "Perhaps the people are visitors going to stay at the North End."

"There's the jetty," announced Dora; "we shall be off directly. Hallo! Why aren't we stopping? Oh, Phœbe! Myfanwy! Aldred! Look: we're actually going past it!"

CHAPTER VI. AN AWKWARD PREDICAMENT

THE girls sprang to their feet. It was unfortunately only too true; the vessel had steamed past the quay, and was heading out into the bay, away from the land.

The four looked at each other in consternation too great for words. What were they to do? Could anybody have imagined a more horrible situation? They must indeed have made some great mistake.

"Tickets, please!" cried the purser, coming round at this critical moment to collect the fares, and holding out his hand in anticipation.

"We—we haven't any!" faltered Dora. "We thought you stopped at the jetty."

"Why, no, miss. This is the Everston boat; we don't stop until Sandsend. You've got on the wrong steamer, that's what you've done. Didn't you see the notice up on the gangway? The North End boats have red funnels and a blue flag. A shilling each, please, to Sandsend, or half a crown to Everston."

"Oh, can't you turn back, and put us off at the jetty?" implored Dora, almost crying. "We don't want to go to Sandsend, and certainly not to Everston."

"And we're in a great hurry," added Aldred.

"Sorry, miss, but it can't be done! The captain won't stop the steamer for anybody," said the man, smiling.

"Not if we went and asked him ourselves?" begged Phœbe eagerly.

"Not for the Queen of England!" returned the purser, as he waited, shuffling the tickets and some loose change suggestively in his hand.

The girls felt in their pockets in vain. Most of their substance had gone on postcards and popcorn, and all they could muster among them was sevenpence-halfpenny.

"I'm afraid we haven't enough money. We only expected to pay penny fares to the jetty."

Dora's voice trembled a little. She felt so upset, she scarcely knew what she was saying, and the others looked equally solemn and concerned. The purser rubbed his chin, as if in doubt.

"It's an awkward case, certainly," he said. "I can't think what they were doing at the pier-head to let you come on without tickets. This boat goes to Everston, you see, and stays the night there, so we can't take you back to Chetbourne. You'd best get off at Sandsend, and walk home along the shore. I'll make it all right with the captain about the fares."

Were ever four wretched girls in such a predicament? It was a judgment with a vengeance on their naughtiness. To be carried away by the steamer and set down at such a remote place as Sandsend seemed an appalling prospect, and they were quite aghast at the idea.

"Well, we have got ourselves into a scrape!" exclaimed Phœbe, as soon as the purser was out of earshot.

"I was so sure it was the ferry-boat!" sighed poor Dora. "I feel as if I were to blame for proposing it."

"It wasn't your fault more than anybody else's," said Myfanwy. "I suppose we ought to have stopped to ask."

"We were in such a hurry!"

"How far is Sandsend from Birkwood?" asked Aldred.

"Six miles. It will take us a most fearfully long while to walk, and it's four o'clock now."

"Oh, dear! We shan't get in till supper. What will Miss Drummond say?"

"There'll be a regular hue and cry after us."

"What will Blanche and Freda do?"

"I suppose they'll go back, when they can't find us, and report us as missing. They wouldn't dare to stay in Chetbourne too long, and be late for tea."

"We're having a free excursion on the steamer, at any rate," said Aldred.

Dora appeared to think that a decidedly doubtful advantage. She was not a good sailor, and the sea was rough now that they were outside the bay. Phœbe, too, began to show signs of distress; and Myfanwy, usually so rosy and talkative, had suddenly grown unwontedly pale and pensive. Aldred was the only one who enjoyed the voyage; to the others it was the reverse of pleasant, and they were much relieved when the vessel at last arrived at Sandsend. They scurried across the gangway on to the quay with almost undignified haste.

"Oh, it is nice to feel oneself on terra firma again!" ejaculated Dora.

"Or 'terra-cotta', as the old lady remarked!" laughed Aldred. "I'm afraid you wouldn't appreciate a yachting cruise, Dora."

"I certainly shouldn't. Nothing would induce me to go. I should be lying in my berth the whole time, in a state of utter collapse and misery. No yachting for me, thank you!"

"We'd better ask somebody which is the right way," said Myfanwy. "We don't want to make any more mistakes."

They found, on enquiry, that the high road ran inland over the downs, and that, instead of it being only six miles to Birkwood, as Dora had supposed, it was in reality nearer nine.

"The road twists, and goes round by Greenstaple," said the old sailor who directed them. "It's only a matter of five miles if you went as the crow flies, but you'd maybe get lost on the downs. It's about the same distance along the coast, if you care to go by the shore. The tide won't be up yet awhile, and you'd have ample time to get round the headland, if you stepped out fairly well."

The beach sounded so much the most attractive route that the girls at once decided in its favour. It was a consideration to save four miles, and they all preferred the seashore to the hills. If they walked fast, they calculated that it would not take more than a couple of hours, and they would get back to school just before dark.

"We must 'step out', as the old man advised," said Phœbe. "No one must slack off, or lag behind."

It was all very well to make good resolutions, but quite another matter to keep them. The beach near Sandsend was an especially fascinating part of the coast. It abounded with little, shallow pools among the rocks, where such a variety of beautiful anemones, madrepores, sea-cucumbers, and other marine objects might be seen that it almost resembled an aquarium. None of these treasures were to be found at Birkwood, where the cliffs were of a different geological formation; indeed, these particular few miles of shore were a noted spot for zoologists, and could show more choice species than anywhere else within a radius of fifty miles. It was not astonishing, therefore, that the girls stopped to marvel at some of these flowers of the sea, to watch the anemones stretching out their delicate, brilliantly coloured tentacles, to admire the corallines or the many strange forms of zoophytes, to chase spider crabs, and to pick up rare shells, and gather some of the lovely seaweeds that fringed the pools. They quite forgot the time, and went dawdling on from one interesting rocky basin to another, wishing they had a glass jar, or a bucket, in which they could carry some specimens back to the Grange.

"Don't you think we might put a few anemones in our handkerchiefs?" suggested Aldred.

"Not an atom of use! They die directly they're out of water. We tried it once before, and it wasn't a success," replied Phœbe.

"We'll tell Miss Drummond about the place, and ask her to bring us for an expedition some day," said Dora. "The school aquarium needs replenishing badly."

They had been walking, or, rather, strolling for about an hour when they reached a small bay, which lay between two promontories. The water here was so low that they decided they might as well cross the sands, instead of keeping close under the cliffs; they made a bee-line, therefore, for the opposite headland, jumping over the narrow channels that intercepted their path. On the flat sandbank they found at least a dozen large jellyfish, left stranded by the tide. Aldred insisted upon picking up some of these and restoring them to their native element; and she kept poking about in so many heaps of seaweed, and investigating such a number of species, that the other girls began to despair of ever getting her back to Birkwood.

"We shall be all in the dark if we don't mind!" remonstrated Phœbe. "We've been sauntering along as if we had the whole day before us."

"And as if there were no tide! Just look behind you!" exclaimed Myfanwy.

Phœbe turned round uneasily. What she saw was enough to make her shout wildly to the others, and set off running as fast as she could towards the cliff in front. All the time they had been amusing themselves with the jellyfish, the water had been creeping stealthily and silently up, and had flowed in an ever-widening channel between them and the land. Except for a narrow space, which led to the rocks at the end of the promontory opposite, they were entirely cut off; and unless they cared to swim it was utterly impossible for them to reach the beach.

Most of them were good runners, and could do well enough at the school sports; but it seemed quite a different matter to race with the tide, and much too risky a performance to be appreciated. They just reached the rocks before the sands were entirely covered, and were obliged to splash anyhow through pools, getting their feet horribly wet, for there was no time to stop and take off their shoes and stockings.

Once on the promontory they were safe enough, and they began to make their way back towards the mainland, scrambling over the rocks, which were slippery and slimy with seaweed, and becoming extremely draggled in the process. There were several claps of distant thunder, and rain, which had been threatening for some time, suddenly descended in a drenching stream. The tide came thundering in, dashing great waves against the rocks, and sending showers of spray to join the rain.

The girls plodded steadily on, hoping that they would soon regain the beach; but it was hard walking, and they were getting wetter every minute. All at once they came to a full stop. In front stretched a channel of water so broad that through the blinding rain they could barely make out the opposite side, against which some very ugly waves appeared to be beating. They gazed at each other in blank dismay.

"Perhaps it's nothing but a creek, and we can get round it," said Myfanwy. "I'm used to this kind of coast in Wales. Let us try to our left; it looks fairly promising."

She led the way, and the others followed as best they could. It was a forlorn hope, however. The end of the promontory was completely surrounded at high water, and was temporarily turned into an island; and for the time being they were as completely stranded as a crew of shipwrecked mariners.

"I'm afraid it's no use," confessed Myfanwy, at last. "We've got ourselves into a tight place, and we shall just have to stay here until the tide goes down."

"Unless we could manage to swim," suggested Dora, looking dubiously over the channel to where some heavy breakers were booming against what seemed through the spray to be a steep and jagged precipice.

"Impossible!" exclaimed Phœbe, without any doubt in her voice. "We should be dashed to bits in that rough sea. There isn't a spot where we could land, even if we could struggle across. It would simply be madness."

"I don't want to try!" declared Aldred, with a shudder. "I can't swim, to begin with; and even if I could, I shouldn't venture through those waves. But what are we going to do?"

"Stop here till we can get off, I suppose," said Phœbe, shrugging her shoulders. "There's nothing else for it. We're in no particular danger, that's one comfort!"

"Let us climb higher up on to the rocks, and perhaps we may find some place a little out of the rain," proposed Myfanwy.

After considerable hunting about, they did at last come upon a ledge that shelved over so as to form a kind of cave; and creeping underneath, they squatted as close together as they could.

They were feeling the very reverse of jolly. It seemed anything but delightful to be sitting in a cramped position, wet through, without the chance of a meal, and with the prospect of spending perhaps the whole night in such unenviable surroundings.

"I'd give a great deal to be back in the classroom, learning my German prep.!" groaned Dora.

"I suppose an adventure never feels nice at the time," said Myfanwy.

"No. I can't help suspecting that Stanley, and Shackleton, and all the explorers didn't enjoy the fun of the thing until they got home and wrote books about it," agreed Aldred.

"It sounds so thrilling when you read it," continued Myfanwy; "but when you're cold and wet and hungry, it takes the romance away."

"I wish we hadn't eaten all our sweets," lamented Phœbe; "I'm simply starving!"

It had grown rapidly dusk; there was not even light enough to see their watches, but they calculated that the time must be about half-past six. They were not sure when the tide would be at the full, nor how soon it would go down again sufficiently to enable them to cross on to the mainland.

"We certainly can't stumble over these rocks in the dark," said Aldred. "Unless there's a moon, we're fixed here until morning."

"I can't remember whether there's a moon or not," sighed Dora. "The sun doesn't rise particularly early either—not until about six, I believe."

"What will they be thinking at the Grange?" said Myfanwy, whose tears were beginning to wander slowly down her cheeks at the misery of the prospect in store.

As to that, no one liked to hazard a guess. In all the annals of the school it had never been recorded that any girls had been lost before; and they knew that Miss Drummond must be in a fever of anxiety on their account. The rain kept on steadily, and the time passed by slowly—very slowly; the long hours seemed interminable. It was most forlorn and wretched to sit crouched under the rock, with the dripping rain beating in upon their wet clothes, listening to the sound of the water dashing below them.

"It's like a horrible nightmare," said Phœbe. "I wish I could wake up, and find myself in my own bed in No. 5!"

"It's so much worse now it's dark," groaned Aldred.

She was in a very dejected frame of mind, and would have burst out sobbing like a baby if she had not been too proud. Her friends were also in low spirits, and did not keep up their usual flow of jokes and chatter. All four snuggled as close together as they could, to keep one another warm, and sat silent, listening to the waves and the rain, till kind Mother Nature sent merciful sleep, and for a while at least they were able to forget their troubles.

Aldred had a long and confusing dream. She thought that she saw Mabel in danger of drowning, and that she plunged boldly into the sea, swam easily to her aid, and brought her back to shore amid the cheers of the school; and that Mabel was saying: "I knew you would come to the rescue. It's not the first time you have done a heroic deed!"

She woke with a start. The words seemed so clear, she could almost believe Mabel had really spoken them. Certainly she had done nothing particularly heroic that day; indeed, her conscience told her that she was mainly responsible for that unpleasant adventure. It was she who had begged the others to leave the post office, and urged them to go down the promenade and along the pier. But for her it would not have occurred to them to break bounds; they would have waited until Blanche and Freda returned, walked straight back to school, and considered that they had had an enjoyable afternoon, without transgressing rules. None of them, however, had accused her of this. They appeared perfectly ready to take the full blame—indeed, they had hinted that, as a new girl, she would probably escape the consequences of the escapade more easily than they.

"After all, it's mostly their fault, for they'd no need to come, even if I asked them," she decided hastily. "I'm not bound to explain everything and get into extra trouble. No one is likely to ask who suggested it."

She tried to stretch her cramped limbs, and felt so stiff that it was pain to move. But it was worse to remain in the same position; so, making an effort, she dragged herself up, and crept out from under the rock. The rain had stopped, and a full moon was shining outside, so clearly that she was able to consult her watch and ascertain that it was a little after ten o'clock. She roused the others immediately.

"Look—look!" she cried, shaking them eagerly. "It's bright moonlight! The tide will have gone down. We must try to get on to the sands at once."

Yawning and stretching, the girls emerged from the cave. It was sufficiently light for them to see their way over the rocks, so they set off without further delay in the direction of the shore. They were now able to cross easily at the place where the channel had stretched a few hours earlier, and found themselves, after a considerable amount of scrambling, on the beach at the farther side of the promontory.

It was the queerest walk home that they had ever experienced. Sands are generally associated with blue sky and bright sunshine, and those seemed very eerie and weird and strange in the moonlight, with the deep, dark shadows under the cliffs, and the sea gleaming silver in the distance. With one consent they took each others' arms. Aldred certainly did not feel sufficiently courageous to walk alone; moreover, she was tired, and could contrive to lean upon both Phœbe and Myfanwy, who were kind enough to pull her along without remonstrance.

The sands on this part of the shore were not very firm, and the girls' feet sank with every step, while they stumbled now and then over stones or clumps of seaweed. It took a long time to cover the three miles to Birkwood; the distance seemed twice as far as it would have done by day, and they were thankful when at last they found the path which they knew led up the cliffs to the Grange.

There was a light in the house; they could see it gleaming when they were still quite far off, and it seemed to hold out a promise of food and rest. As they opened the gate, the gardener's wife came running out of the lodge. She gave a shriek at the sight of them, and rushed straight up the drive to tell the news: and the four had barely arrived at the door before Miss Drummond herself came hurrying to meet them.

"Girls! Girls! Where have you been?" she cried, with such a look on her pale face that they realized for the first time what she must have suffered during all the hours of that anxious night.

Freda and Blanche (as the girls had supposed), not finding them at the post office, had imagined that they must have started home, and had returned without them. They had been greatly dismayed, when they arrived at the Grange, to discover that the four had not come back. They reported their absence at once, and a teacher started for Chetbourne, to try to find them. When darkness fell, and they were still missing, Miss Drummond, in the greatest alarm, applied to the police, and bands of searchers were looking for them in various quarters. It had never struck anybody that they could have gone on the steamer to Sandsend, which lay in the opposite direction to Chetbourne.

The four truants were very glad indeed of the hot baths and basins of bread and milk that were waiting for them. They did not equally appreciate doses of camphor, but did not dare to remonstrate, being only too thankful that Miss Drummond had forborne as yet to scold. The Principal's chief object was to get them to bed, and to ward off any risk of colds or rheumatism that might follow their many hours of exposure in wet clothes. Fortunately, her prompt measures had the desired effect, and no evil consequences ensued. The girls were allowed to sleep late the next morning, and when they arrived downstairs seemed quite free from all aches, pains, coughs, sneezes, and other suspicious symptoms. They were in dire disgrace, however, for now that Miss Drummond was reassured as to their health, she turned her attention to their conduct.

"I'm most dreadfully sorry about it," said Mabel to Aldred that evening. "You see, Miss Drummond has always trusted us so entirely at the Grange, and this is the first time anybody has ever gone out of bounds. She says it shakes her confidence in us. I'm afraid she'll stop all exeats for the Lower School. Of course, I know it wasn't your fault. You're a new girl, and how could you tell we weren't allowed on the promenade? You only went where the others took you. You'd no idea you were breaking the rules, had you?"

Aldred was brushing her teeth at the moment, therefore a grunt was her only means of reply. Mabel took it as the required denial.

"I was sure you hadn't," she declared triumphantly. "A girl who can do such splendid things always lives up to them. It was a mean trick to play on Blanche and Freda, when they had invited you all for a walk, but I was certain you weren't capable of it. Naturally, you're ready to take your share of the scolding (I shouldn't have tried to get out of that myself); but I'm so glad that I, at any rate, know you don't really deserve it!"

CHAPTER VII. FALSE COLOURS

THE thunderstorm that had added to the unpleasantness of the girls' adventure at Sandsend seemed to herald a complete change in the weather. The beautiful Indian summer, so warm and genial, so full of kindly sunshine, vanished suddenly, and autumn, cold and bleak, appeared in its place. A sharp frost in a single night worked havoc in the garden, blackening the dahlias, withering the nasturtiums, and reducing all the remaining annuals to a state of blighted ruin, so that what had one day been a flowery paradise was the next a scene of desolation. A strong easterly gale, following the frost, cleared the leaves from the trees before they had any chance of turning to crimson or gold, and stripped the last vestige of beauty from the hedgerows.

After this came days of pouring rain. The lawns and the playing-fields were sodden, the roads were deep in sticky mud, the row of bare elms dripped dismally on to the garden seats below, and the neglected sundial no longer told the hour of day, nor formed a centre for the throng of girls who generally haunted its steps.

"Baldur the Sun God is dead!" said Aldred, looking out of the window one damp afternoon at the cheerless prospect, and recalling Miss Drummond's lesson on Northern Mythology. "Loki has killed him with the piece of mistletoe, and he will never return to Asgard. All the Æsir are weeping for him, and the earth will be given up now to the frost giants and the spirits of the winds."

"Won't he ever come back?" said Mabel, falling in with her friend's humour.

"Just for a little while; but he always has to go in the winter, like Proserpine, who was bound to spend half the year with Pluto in Hades. I suppose there's no country, except the lost Atlantis, where it keeps summer all the year round."

"Why, you sound quite melancholy!"

"So I am."

"But why?"

"I don't know, except that it is so sad to see the summer gone."

Aldred could scarcely explain her attitude of mind, though she was conscious that the change in the world without affected her strongly. She had an extreme love of nature, an intense appreciation of beautiful things. No ancient Greek ever joyed in the sunshine more than she, or took greater pleasure in the scent of the flowers, or the blue of the sea and sky, or the song of the birds in springtime. Her artistic, poetical temperament was highly sensitive to all outward impressions; she was so keenly alive to the great, dramatic human tragedy and comedy that is being enacted around us, so in touch with the wonder and mystery of life, that what would pass unnoticed by many was to her the very essence of being.

Few people had ever sympathized with this side of her disposition. Her father had not realized it, Keith could not understand it, and Aunt Bertha had repressed it sternly. Modern schoolgirls are certainly not sentimental; they are more prone to laugh at poetic fancies than to admire them: and Aldred knew that on this score she would probably meet with ridicule from her form-mates. In consequence, she confined herself in public to the practical and prosaic, and, with the exception of an occasional private confidence to Mabel, kept her reflections locked in her own bosom.

There was certainly nothing in the atmosphere of the Grange to foster any tendency towards morbidness. The days were so fully occupied as to leave no time for dreaming. Though Aldred was clever, it took her whole energies to secure the place that she wished in the school. She was determined to be head of her Form, and, holding that object in view, toiled with a vigour such as nothing else would have wrung from her, and which would have caused unfeigned amazement to her former governess. It was not all plain sailing, for Ursula Bramley and Agnes Maxwell were also good workers; and even Mabel, though not specially bright, was very plodding and conscientious. Aldred soon found that she had to revise entirely her old method—that a careless German exercise could completely cancel a brilliant score in history, and that she must give equal attention to every subject if she wished to chronicle a record. The little tricks she had practised on Miss Perkins were not equally successful at Birkwood: she had tried reeling off her lessons very fast, so as to gloss over mistakes, but Miss Bardsley would allow her to finish, and then say: "Yes; now you may repeat it again, slowly. I did not quite catch the second person plural;" and Aldred, to her disgust, would be compelled to reveal her ignorance in a more deliberate fashion, and take the bad mark that ensued. She was at first a venturesome guesser, till her many bad shots drew scathing comments from her teachers and smiles from the rest of the Form.

"Even Lorna Hallam knows that Sir Philip Sidney didn't write the *Faerie Queene*, and she's supposed to be our champion bungler!" observed Ursula Bramley sarcastically, on one occasion. "As for history, you muddle up Thomas Cromwell with Oliver Cromwell! You'd better get an elementary book, and learn a few simple facts."

The girls would not tolerate Aldred's conceit. She quickly discovered that if she wished to be popular, it was unwise to claim too much credit for her achievements. The week after she arrived she had taken her place among the others at a singing lesson. Miss Wright, the mistress, began to teach the class the old English ballad, "Should he upbraid"; it was one with which Aldred happened to be familiar, so she at once took the lead and sang away lustily, beating time in a rather marked manner, and accomplishing the many little runs and trills with an air as if she considered herself indispensable. At the close of the lesson, as they were filing out of the room, she could not resist remarking to Ursula Bramley:

"It was a good thing I knew that song so well, wasn't it?"

"Why?" asked Ursula pointedly, looking her straight in the eyes.

Thus cornered, Aldred could hardly say that she thought the class would have managed badly without her aid; her tact told her that the remark would be unpalatable and indiscreet, so she quickly changed her ground.

"Oh! only that I find it difficult to learn new things," she replied, in some confusion.

"Indeed! Well, I suppose you'll improve when you've been here a little while," returned Ursula, with a meaning smile that was partly a sneer, and made Aldred decidedly red and uncomfortable.

During the earlier part of the term, try as she might, Aldred was not able to see her name in the coveted position of heading the list for the Fourth Form. One week she failed in geometry, another in French; if her German was correct, her arithmetic proved inaccurate, and some unexpected slip would pull her down. At the end of the sixth week, however, she at last dared to hope. She was aware that she had done unusually well, both in the ordinary class subjects and in the Friday morning examination; while Ursula, her chief opponent, had had an exercise returned, and received a bad mark for botany. The lists were always posted up on the notice-board in the corridor just before tea-time on Saturday afternoon, and there was generally a rush to read them. On this particular Saturday, Aldred determined to be the first to cull the news. She was too proud to allow herself to seem anxious, so she hung about the corridor, pretending that she was searching for a lost piece of india-rubber, and that she was thrillingly interested in the view of the dripping garden through the side window. At last Miss Drummond appeared, pinned the papers neatly on to the notice-board, and re-entered the library. Aldred strolled up as casually as she could; but Mabel, who had also been on the look-out, was before her.

"You're top! You're top!" shrieked the latter. "There it is: 'No. 1, Aldred Laurence.' Oh, how lovely! You've beaten Ursula by twenty marks. It's splendid! Come and see for yourself!"

Though inwardly she felt she had satisfied her ambition, Aldred took the announcement with the greatest outward sang-froid.

"Oh! am I?" she replied nonchalantly. "No, I don't want to see, thanks; I can take your word for it."

"How calm you are! I should have been fearfully excited if it had been: 'No. 1, Mabel Farrington.'"

"What's the use of getting excited? Let us go into the dressing-room, and wash our hands for tea."

Mabel linked her arm affectionately in that of Aldred, and accompanied her down the passage, talking as she went.

"I knew you would come out top, dearest!" she said. "You were certain to, as soon as you had grown used to the work here. It's always difficult for a new girl, when she has been accustomed to a different teacher; but I think you have fallen into Birkwood ways marvellously quickly. Don't you feel proud?"

"Not particularly."

"Well, I do, for you! To think of being twenty marks ahead of Ursula! It's a tremendous score! How do you manage to be so clever?"

"I'm not clever. It's sheer good luck, I expect."

"No, it's not good luck," said Mabel, putting back Aldred's dark curls with a caressing hand. "It's something far more, only you're too modest to acknowledge it. You're behaving just as you did at Seaforth. Oh, I've heard about that episode! We all know of it, though you may think it was done by stealth."

"What episode?" gasped Aldred, suddenly red to the tips of her ears.

"Don't blush so, darling! I won't speak about it again, if you'd rather not; but I should like to tell you how much I admire you, not only for what you did, but for the way you've tried to make nothing of it afterwards. It's only one girl in a thousand who would have had the courage to rush into that blazing house, and crawl upstairs and down again; or the presence of mind to tie a wet handkerchief over the little boy's mouth. I should never have thought of that, I'm certain. Do you mind my mentioning it to you just this once?"

Now was Aldred's chance. The occasion when she might deny her identity with the heroine of the fire had come at last! How easily the mistake could be corrected, and the matter set right! She looked nervously at Mabel, and words struggled painfully to her lips.

"I—I'm afraid—you——" she began.

"Yes, dearest?" There was a little thrill in Mabel's voice.

"You're—you're thinking too—too well of me——" stammered Aldred, trying desperately to take the fatal plunge.

Mabel simply smiled. Her blue eyes were gazing into her friend's with adoring affection; her face showed how deeply her feelings were stirred, and how earnestly she meant all she had said.

"I was at Seaforth——" continued Aldred.

"I know that."

"But—but——"

Oh, how hard it was to utter her confession! In the act, Aldred's resolution failed her; she stopped again, and was silent. Her embarrassment was most apparent.

"Would you really rather not speak of it, dear?" said Mabel gently.

Why did Aldred hesitate? Opportunity, like an angel of light, still tarried, and held open the door of honour. If she could only screw up her courage to the sticking-point!

"All right! If you don't like me to mention it, I'll say nothing more. I'm satisfied now I've let you know that your deed isn't absolutely hidden under a bushel. You're famous, in spite of yourself. You darling! I only wish I were worthier to be your friend."

Aldred shrank back at the words, and, disengaging Mabel's clinging arms, made an excuse to hurry away. She had the grace to be thoroughly ashamed of herself, and to feel that she could not bear any more praise at present.

"Why didn't I tell?" she moaned, in an agony of remorse. "I know I'm mean, and dishonest, and horrid, and the exact opposite of what she supposes. What would Keith say, if he knew? He'd never forgive me. He scolded me for not explaining that Mr. Bowden had painted part of my picture, and this is twice as bad. Keith is so absolutely honourable! I suppose I ought to go to Mabel now, and put things right. No, I can't! I simply can't! It would be worse than ever. I couldn't force myself to say it—the words would choke me!"

A letter from Keith had arrived only that morning, a particularly nice, jolly letter, full of chatty news and of such affectionate enquiries about her own doings at school that it seemed to bring her into closer touch than usual with her brother. She wanted so much to stand well in Keith's opinion; and she recalled with a groan what he had said to her in the cornfield about her sketch: "Of all the sneaks, you're the biggest!" and, "Be a little straighter in future, if you want to keep chums with me." Yes, she was a sneak; it was not a pretty epithet, but it was a true one. In Keith's eyes this affair would be serious; he would never tolerate such conduct for one single moment. If she wished to act up to his principles, she must undeceive Mabel immediately, her own self-respect told her that. Yet she could not bring herself to do it, and for a whole week she wavered, her conscience reproaching her bitterly, and her pride pleading and ever pleading to put off the evil moment.

"It's impossible to tell her straight out," she decided at last. "I'll write a letter and give it to her; that will be much easier, because I needn't stay to watch her read it. I know Keith would have gone and owned up; but then, I'm not Keith—I always mind things so much more than he does."

Having resolved to make an explanation through the medium of pen, ink, and paper, she retired, when tea was over, to the empty classroom, and set herself to the unwelcome task. How difficult it was! She scribbled sheet after sheet, and tore up one after another. Her confession looked so bald and paltry when she saw it in black and white! It seemed so awkward to explain adequately how the mistake had arisen. After five fruitless attempts, she at last managed to arrive at a result which, if it did not satisfy her, at least contained the truth. She placed it in an envelope, and addressed it to Mabel Farrington, then stood turning it over and over in her hand. Was this letter to break their friendship?—so small a thing to have such a fateful result? Well, if it must be, she had better let it be done as quickly as possible; it was no use delaying any longer. Bracing up her nerves, therefore, she went down to look for Mabel.

It being Saturday evening, there was no preparation. Relays of girls were having their hair washed in the bathroom, and others were finishing stocking darning, or various pieces of mending; tidying their drawers, putting out their clean clothes, and performing the many small duties that seemed to accumulate at the end of the week.

The Lower School recreation room happened to be temporarily deserted by its usual rollicking crew, and Mabel was there alone, standing warming her hands at the fire. She looked up brightly as Aldred entered.

"Come along!" she said. "Isn't this a glorious blaze? We've got the room all to ourselves for once, and we'll have such a cosy chat! Why! what's this you're giving me? A letter? From whom?"

"From me. It's something I want you to know," replied Aldred shortly; and she would have turned to leave the room had not Mabel caught her by the arm and forced her back to the fire.

"Don't run away!" she exclaimed. "You're the most absurd girl! What are you writing to me about?"

"You'll find out when you've read it," gulped Aldred.

"But why couldn't you tell me? What's the matter? You're actually crying! Dearest, have I done anything to offend you?"

"No, no! Do let me go, and then open the letter!"

"I shan't. You must stay here till I know why you are crying. Has anybody been nasty to you?"

"No; it's I who have done something wrong—I wanted to let you know—I'm afraid you'll never care for me afterwards—I daren't tell you—so please read it, and don't keep me now!"

Mabel looked puzzled, then suddenly enlightened; but instead of loosening her hold on her friend, she pulled her down on to the hearth-rug, before the fire.

"I understand!" she said. "Oh, Aldred, dear, I know all about that, you know!"

Aldred's face was a study.

"Yes, Agnes Maxwell told me before tea."

"What has Agnes to do with it?"

"Why, she heard you! She said all the others who had spoken English had reported themselves to Miss Bardsley, but she was sure you hadn't."

Aldred drew a long breath. It was quite a different crime that Mabel imagined she was confessing, a little slip that she scarcely recollected, and certainly had not intended to rake up. She had been guilty of expressing herself in her own language during the time set apart for French conversation that morning, but, having no desire to lose a mark, she had discreetly allowed her memory to fail her when the mistress asked if any girl had "communicated in English".

"I must say I was very astonished," continued Mabel, "and very disappointed that you, of all people, should not have told; it seemed so entirely different from what you are. I couldn't believe that you would go a whole afternoon letting 'perfect' be down in the register, when you ought to have had a bad mark. Of course, I knew you would tell before Monday—luckily, Saturday's marks count for next week."

Aldred said nothing. She sat on the fender, poking the little, soft volcanoes that oozed out of the coal, squeezing them down, and watching the jets of gas that followed.

"It was a funny idea to write it in a letter!" said Mabel. "You always do quaint things; I suppose it's because you're such an original girl."

"Aren't you going to read it?" asked Aldred, in a strained voice.

"Why should I? I know what's in it. No, it shall go down into that hollow in the fire. Give me the poker. There! What a blaze it makes!"

Aldred watched her confession flare up and sink into ashes in the heart of the hot coals; there was a strange look on her face, a look that her friend could not fathom.

"Suppose I had said nothing at all about it next week, and had kept the 'perfect', would you still have cared for me?"

"Oh, but you couldn't!" cried Mabel. "It's impossible! Why, it wouldn't be you to do such a thing!"

"But if——"

"There are no 'ifs'. I could never believe any wrong of you, darling; and yet——"

"What are you two crouching over the fire in the dark for?" exclaimed Dora Maxwell, bursting suddenly into the room. "We are going to act dumb charades in the hall, and Miss Drummond and the teachers are all there to watch. Come along! We've thought of some most lovely words, which I'm sure they'll never think of guessing."

So another opportunity was lost, and Aldred's secret was still untold. She dared not run the risk of breaking the friendship. If she was blamed for such a small fault, could she ever be forgiven for so much greater a deception? It was so sweet to be the very centre of Mabel's adoration, to be placed on a pinnacle, and loved with such rapturous devotion. Could she bear to see all this fade utterly, or even partially, away? No! She was glad and thankful that the letter had been burnt; she felt as if she had escaped from a great danger. She told Miss Bardsley about her "English communication", and took her bad mark with resignation; it was a small evil, compared with what she had avoided. There seemed no retreat now from the course she had taken; she could not in future plead the excuse that she was ignorant of her identification with the heroine of the fire. The affair had been mentioned so plainly that it was impossible for the most dense and obtuse person not to have understood the allusion. Had Mabel on the first occasion questioned her point-blank, I think she would probably have owned up immediately; but every wrongdoing bears its own ill harvest, and the second slip from the straight path is always easier than the first. Aldred persuaded herself that she had not told any deliberate lies, though she was fully aware that her silence made her equally guilty of falsehood. Finally, she tried to dismiss the whole thing from her thoughts. Mabel had promised not to speak of it again; surely it was finished with, and there was no need to trouble further? Yet it was a trouble. Deep down in her heart lay always the consciousness that she was sailing under false colours; every now and then Mabel would impute to her some better motive than really actuated her, or some virtue that she did not possess, and Aldred's inward monitor would give her an uneasy twinge, and remind her how very far she was below that high standard. There was also constantly present the dread that Mabel might learn the truth from some outside source; perhaps the cousin who had written to her before might hear more details, and write again, or some other friend might have been staying at Seaforth, and might know full particulars. The horror of the thought would make Aldred shudder with apprehension; she was living, she knew, on a bubble reputation, and at one word it might collapse, and change her pleasant Eden of appreciation and adulation into a blank desert of disillusion and contempt.

CHAPTER VIII. AMATEUR THEATRICALS

THE half-term had seen Aldred at the head of her form, and by dint of hard application she managed to keep her position there fairly steadily; with such a clever rival as Ursula to contend against, it was impossible to win the coveted prize every week, but she scored a success so often that her average record was higher than that of anyone else. Miss Drummond was manifestly pleased with her progress; it was not often that a new girl came so quickly to the fore. Aldred had been sent to her with a reputation for both shirking lessons and defying authority, so she flattered herself that the atmosphere of Birkwood had worked a change, and remedied both these defects.

Aunt Bertha, who was kept well informed of her niece's progress, wrote to express satisfaction.

"I am glad to hear you are settling down and becoming more reasonable," ran her letter to Aldred. "It is high time you learnt sense, and if you can turn into an ordinary, rational being at the Grange, it will be well worth having sent you there. I hope the improvement will show itself during the holidays."

"How hateful she is!" thought Aldred, tearing the letter angrily into little bits. "She always rubs me the wrong way, and makes me feel I'd like to do the exact opposite to what she wants. I don't get top to please her, at any rate! If she would improve during the holidays, perhaps I might too! I don't care what she thinks of me!"

Keith's approval was a different matter, and it was a keen pleasure to Aldred to be able to tell him of her triumph, and to receive his hearty congratulations.

"I know what it is to swat hard," wrote Keith, "so I think you've turned up trumps, and I'm proud of you. I'll take you into town as often as you like this Christmas, even to the National Gallery, though I detest the Old Masters."

With so much to fill up the time, the autumn term seemed to pass very quickly away. The weeks flew by, and dull November fogs were succeeded by early December frosts. It was no longer possible to go into the garden after tea; the days had closed in rapidly, and the lamps were lighted now by five o'clock. Every afternoon, when the weather allowed, the girls played hockey to keep themselves warm, and Aldred began to grow interested in the game, though she had not yet secured the proficiency that her ambition would have wished.

The situation of Birkwood, between the downs and the sea, so delightfully breezy and fresh in spring and summer, was decidedly cold in winter; Aldred was amazed at the number of blankets she required on her bed, and fully appreciated the hot brick that was allowed. Miss Drummond was indulgent in that respect. The bricks were placed every evening on a special stone intended for the purpose connected with the heating apparatus; by nine o'clock they were delightfully warm, and each girl carried her own upstairs, returning it next morning to its place.

"They're the greatest comfort; I should shiver all night without mine!" said Mabel. "I'm glad Miss Drummond lets us have them. One of my cousins goes to an absolutely Spartan school; they're obliged to wash in cold water always, and to take ice-cold baths, even in the depth of winter. Lilian put an india-rubber hot-water bag in her box, but she was not allowed to use it; the head mistress says she likes girls to be hardy. I think it must be wretched; we are better treated at the Grange."

Miss Drummond's arrangements were certainly calculated to make everyone at Birkwood as cosy as possible when the winds blew chill outside. There was always a cheerful blaze in the recreation room, and the girls were also permitted to keep up the fires in the classrooms, if they wished to do anything special there during the evening—a privilege of which they were glad to avail themselves towards the end of the term.

They were all very fond of acting, and each form intended to prepare a play for the last week. The strictest secrecy was observed about rehearsals.

"We don't want the others to have a hint of what we mean to do," said Phœbe Stanhope; "they mustn't even know the name of our act."

"And we must make all our dresses here too," said Myfanwy, "and any wigs, or moustaches, or anything we need."

"Shall we have time?" enquired Aldred.

"Yes; Miss Drummond excuses sewing when we're getting up theatricals. We may have the room to ourselves the minute we've finished prep. It gives us a good hour every night, and that ought to be enough, if we work hard."

"What are we going to act?"

"That's just the question."

"It's so difficult to decide!" said Mabel.

"I have a kind of notion that both the Sixth and the Fifth have chosen scenes from Shakespeare," observed Agnes Maxwell. "They keep talking in such grand language, and making quotations that aren't particularly appropriate! When Lilian Marshall wanted to call me back for something yesterday, she said: 'Tarry, Jew: the law hath yet another hold on you!' and the others sniggered."

"Then they'll be taking the Trial Scene from the *Merchant of Venice*. Yes, I'm certain they must be, because Eleanor Avery has a lovely red dressing-gown that they'll use for Portia's robe."

"And what about the Fifth?"

"Something from *As You Like It*, I fancy. Their classroom door was open as I passed last night, and I caught a glimpse of them painting scenery on great pieces of brown paper. It was evidently for a wood."

"It might be for *A Midsummer-Night's Dream*."

"Well, yes, of course it might."

"One thing is certain," said Lorna Hallam; "we mustn't decide upon Shakespeare."

"No; it would be too stale if we happened to choose the very same scene."

"Can't we have something comic?" suggested Myfanwy James.

"Yes, a short farce," agreed Ursula Bramley. "There are several very jolly ones in the book Miss Bardsley lent me. It would be quite a change."

"Where's the book? Let us look at it."

The little plays were mostly old friends with new faces. Well-known tales had been dramatized, and given a humorous element that made them very suitable for Christmas performances.

"They're screamingly funny!" said Phœbe. "I expect we shall die of laughing when we're acting. Shall we have 'Beauty and the Beast', or 'Bluebeard'?"

"Which has the easier dresses?" asked Mabel.

"They're pretty much the same, and there are the same number of characters, eight in each. We can't take 'Cinderella', because there are too many parts; and 'Goody Two Shoes' has too few."

"'Bluebeard' seems the more dramatic," said Aldred, hastily dipping into the book.

"Who votes for 'Bluebeard'?" queried Mabel.

Six hands went up immediately; so the matter was considered settled, Myfanwy and Agnes, who preferred 'Beauty and the Beast', being in the minority.

"And now we shall have to decide the caste," said Ursula. "I think the tallest ought to be Bluebeard."

"Oh, I dare say, when you're an inch above everyone else in the Form!" Agnes sounded indignant.

"No, we must draw lots for the parts, as we always have done," said Mabel. "It's the fairest way, because then nobody can complain. We're all pretty equal at acting, so it doesn't much matter who gets Bluebeard or Fatima. There are eight characters, so get eight slips of paper, Dora, and we'll write one on each."

"We must fold them exactly evenly," said Dora, "so that they all feel the same. What shall we shuffle them in? Can you make a place on your lap? Now, each girl must draw one in turn."

"Who's to begin?" said Aldred.

"The eldest. We always take it in order of birthdays. Nobody must unfold her slip until everyone else has drawn. Agnes, it's your turn first."

Aldred opened her paper with much anxiety, and read its contents with a frown. "An Attendant"—that was all! She was very disgusted to be obliged to take such a humble part, having hoped to get either Bluebeard or Fatima, or, at least, Sister Anne. She knew she could act well, and thought she certainly ought to be one of the more important characters in the play. It was particularly aggravating, because Fatima had been drawn by Lorna Hallam, the girl with the worst memory and the least dramatic talent in the class; and Bluebeard had fallen to the lot of little Dora Maxwell, whose chirpy voice would not be nearly so appropriate to the occasion as the deeper tones of Ursula Bramley. If anybody except Mabel had suggested the plan of deciding the caste by lot, Aldred would have disputed the matter hotly; but she did not like to argue with her chum, so she was obliged to suppress her feelings and agree with the best grace she could. Mabel herself was to be Sister Anne, Phœbe Stanhope and Myfanwy James were the two brothers, Ursula Bramley was the Beneficent Fairy, and Agnes Maxwell another attendant.

"We ought to alter some of the parts," Aldred could not help suggesting. "It's ridiculous for Ursula to be a fairy! She's too tall, and her hair is brown. Why can't she change with Dora?"

"No, thank you!" protested Dora. "I'm sick of being a fairy; because I'm small, and my hair is light, I'm always given a gauze dress and a wand. I'm tired of coming in disguised as a beggar woman, and then flinging off my cloak—it always catches on my wreath and pulls it crooked; and I've said I don't know how many ending-up speeches. I've drawn Bluebeard this time, and I mean to stick to him, whatever sort of a fairy Ursula makes."

"I shan't be such a bad one, I'm sure!" declared Ursula, rather offended. "You wouldn't make a better, Aldred; your hair's darker than mine."

"Well, I don't know how Lorna is going to learn all Fatima's long part," Aldred ventured to object; "she never gets through her recitations in class without a mistake."

"I'll manage, thank you!" retorted Lorna. "Besides, there's always the prompter behind the piano."

"The prompter! You ought never to rely on that!"

"I didn't say I was going to."

"Yes, you did! If people undertake a part, they ought at least to know the words, or let somebody else have it."

"I shan't give up my part at your bidding!"

"You're misunderstanding each other," interposed Mabel. "Aldred never meant she wanted you to give up your part, Lorna; I'm sure she was only sympathizing because she knows you find it hard to learn things."

"It's a queer form of sympathy, then!" grumbled Lorna. "I thought she wanted to be Fatima herself."

"Oh, no! That's most unlike Aldred. I wonder you could imagine for an instant that she would have such a motive! I think, when we decided to abide by the lot, it would be a mistake to have any changing; and we'd better set to work and learn some of our speeches, so that we can rehearse the first scene, at any rate, to-morrow. We must each borrow the book in turn, and keep looking at it in any odd moments we can spare."

"Yes; there won't be too much time, with all the costumes to think about as well," agreed the others.

Aldred mastered the dozen lines that fell to the Attendant in a few minutes, and handed the book on to Sister Anne. Feeling sure of her portion in the play, she could afford to criticize the others, and set to work to coach them vigorously at the evening rehearsal. Though some of them were not willing to fall in with her suggestions, she managed to make herself so prominent that, in spite of themselves, the girls allowed her to assume the leadership, and to constitute herself a kind of stage manager.

"Aldred is quite right," said Mabel, backing her up; "we certainly were not saying our speeches with half enough dramatic emphasis, and we weren't putting any spirit into them. I feel I was too tame."

"We haven't got as far as 'dramatic emphasis'," said Phœbe. "That would come afterwards."

"It's better to practise it as we go along, and as Aldred has had so much experience of private theatricals, we had better take her advice, and let her show us how it ought to be done."

Aldred's boasted experience was really confined to a few charades with the Rectory children at home; but she had considerable natural talent for acting, and could throw herself heart and soul into a part. It tried her very much to hear Fatima and Bluebeard give a dialogue as if they were repeating a lesson, to see the Brothers come strolling up to the rescue, instead of rushing in with hot haste; and to watch the very un-sylph-like movements of the Fairy.

"This is the way it should be done!" she would cry, and would go through the speeches herself, giving word and action as if she were really the character she was impersonating, her eyes flashing with enthusiasm and her cheeks aglow. Not one of her stage pupils could approach her fire, or the various delicate modulations of her voice; even Mabel, who tried her best, was very far behind.

"I can't put so much expression into what I'm saying!" declared Dora. "I have to think all the time whether I'm getting the words right."

"But you ought to know the words so well that you don't need to think about them—only to feel what Bluebeard would be feeling!" returned Aldred, who by this time could remember every separate speech in the play much better than the actresses themselves. "Can't you imagine yourself haughty and pompous, when you give Fatima the keys?"

"Why, no! I want to laugh!" giggled Dora.

Aldred stamped her foot; it was too irritating to see the part of Bluebeard usurped by one who had so little conception of his character. Dora's undignified rendering of the part was a constant annoyance. Fatima, too, was a great trial; she repeated her sentences in a monotonous, sing-song voice, without a vestige of passion.

"You take the keys from Bluebeard as if Miss Bardsley were handing you an exercise-book!" remonstrated Aldred. "And as for the cupboard scene, you look inside and say, 'Oh!' as casually as if there were nothing there!"

"Well, there is nothing there!" retorted Lorna, rather resentful of so much interference.

"Oh, Lorna! There are the horrid, bleeding heads of all the former wives. Can't you pretend you see them, and give a proper shriek? Do let us have the piece again! You ought to look half-curious half-frightened, as you open the door, and then, when you've taken one peep, you should scream, and fall back nearly fainting with horror!"

It seemed no use, however. In spite of all Aldred's coaching and practical illustrations, Lorna could not rise to the required pitch, and continued to give the thrilling scene with the utmost tameness. Aldred was desperate. She felt that the success of the play depended upon this particular situation being adequately depicted, and was determined that Lorna should be forced to give a genuine start; and with that end in view she hatched a little plot. The rehearsals took place in the classroom, and Fatima was accustomed to use the ordinary door, to represent that of the fatal cupboard. Aldred persuaded one of the servants to dress up in a sheet and wait about in the passage, so that when Lorna looked out she should see something calculated to surprise her. Nellie, an under-housemaid, willingly entered into the scheme, and even improved upon it, according to her own ideas, by whitening her face with flour, so as to make herself as ghost-like as possible.

Aldred felt quite excited when Scene III was begun. She managed, without attracting anybody's attention, to take a stealthy peep through the doorway. Yes, there was Nellie, standing quite ready, and horrible enough to make even Aldred jump, though she was expecting to see her. All was in good training, and Lorna was rapidly coming to the fatal lines. She delivered them with her usual lack of fire:

"The key fits well—now, wherefore should I fear?I will at last discover what's in here!Bluebeard's a hundred miles away in Spain;In ignorance no longer I'll remain.Turn, little key! Ope, door, for good or ill!Reveal your secret—know I must and will!"

She flung open the door, as she had done at every rehearsal, in an absolutely wooden manner, and with neither interest nor curiosity in her tone; but her expression changed when she saw the vision in the passage, and for once in her life she accomplished a very excellent representation of the part. She shrieked with a horror that was only too natural, and drew back with a face as white as that of the sham ghost outside.

The girls applauded furiously.

"Well done!"

"Good!"

"Splendid!"

"Why, what's the matter?"

"Lorna, are you acting?"

"Oh, I say! Catch her, quick; she's really fainting!"

CHAPTER IX. CHINESE LANTERNS

ALDRED'S plot had been only too successful. Lorna's nerves were not of the strongest, and the apparition in the passage had been utterly unexpected; so, although she did not actually lose consciousness, she lay for a few moments with her eyes shut, and considerably terrified the other girls.

"Bring some water, somebody!" said Mabel, who was kneeling on the floor, holding the luckless Fatima in her arms.

"I'll get it!" cried Aldred, springing up before anyone else could volunteer, and darting hurriedly out of the room. It had just occurred to her that she might probably be blamed for this incident, and she wanted to avoid that if it were still possible.

"You must go, Nellie!" she whispered to the housemaid. "The girls will tell Miss Drummond if they catch you, and you'll get into trouble!"

"But I thought it was to be a bit of a joke, miss!" remonstrated Nellie, who could not see where the fun had come in.

"They don't see the joke. You'd better run! Do you want Miss Drummond to find you playing ghost, when you ought to be turning down the beds?"

Aldred had been forcing Nellie along the passage as she spoke, and now she tore the sheet from the latter's shoulders, and flung it down the back stairs.

"Go and wash your face!" she commanded. "I didn't ask you to whiten it. You've made far more of this than I intended."

Nellie departed to the kitchen regions, highly offended. She considered she had been badly treated, but, as she certainly did not wish Miss Drummond to learn anything of the affair, she took Aldred's advice, washed her face, put the sheet away, and only aired her grievance to her fellow-servants.

Aldred, congratulating herself upon the success of her promptitude, fetched a glass of water to the classroom. Lorna had in a great measure recovered herself, but she was still pale and shaky, and anxious to claim sympathy.

"I saw something all in white in the passage!" she was assuring the other girls.

"Nonsense!" said Aldred brusquely. "How could you? Drink this, and you'll feel better."

"She must have seen something!" declared Phœbe and Ursula.

"Well, there's nothing there now, at any rate. Go and look for yourselves, if you don't believe me!"

"Perhaps the Third Form were playing us a trick," suggested Dora.

"It's extremely probable," returned Aldred. "Phyllis Carson loves practical jokes."

"It must have been Phyllis," said Lorna. "It looked very like her, and it is just the kind of thing she'd enjoy doing."

"It was a great shame of whoever it was, to give you such a scare!" said Mabel. "It's never safe to frighten people, and I hate sham ghosts myself.

Do you feel well enough to go on with the scene, or shall we stop for tonight?"

This incident (of which Alfred never divulged the authorship) had at least the desired effect of considerably improving Fatima's acting. Perhaps a nervous remembrance of what she had really seen returned to her in future when she opened the door, and supplied the lack of imagination; at any rate, she would give a very passable start and scream, and her whole manner was more interested and full of life. Even Bluebeard, owing to Aldred's exertions, learnt to suppress his ill-timed mirth, and to thunder as a domestic tyrant should; and the fairy, if not exactly graceful, to wave her wand elegantly, instead of brandishing it like a hockey stick or golf club. Having thus far perfected the business of the play, the girls turned their attention to costumes and scenery.

"We've only ten days left, so we must be very quick," said Mabel. "I've written home to Mother to send us anything suitable that she can spare. I think she'll let us have two gauzy veils and some glass bangles that she got in Jerusalem; they'd do nicely for Fatima and me. And perhaps she'll lend two daggers for the Brothers; but if she won't, we shall have to make cardboard ones, and cover them with silver paper."

"My sister has promised to send us some Chinese lanterns," said Phœbe. "They'll look lovely, and give quite an Eastern air to the thing."

"Yes, we want the first scene to look like a piece out of the Arabian Nights," agreed Agnes Maxwell. "I'm rather anxious about Dora's costume; how are we to manage the beard?"

"Would blue Berlin wool do?"

"Rather expensive—we should have to use so much of it."

"A piece of blue tissue paper, cut into shreds?"

"No, thanks! I should look like a fly-catcher!" laughed Dora.

"Then I don't know."

"I can manage a beard, if you'll leave it to me," said Aldred. "I have a splendid idea."

"What?"

"Get a piece of new rope, and untwist it and comb it out; the tow is exactly like stiff, white hair. Then we'll dip it in strong Reckitt's Blue, and let it dry."

"Splendid!" chorused the girls.

Aldred's fertile brain was full of plans and suggestions. She not only made a most successful beard, but contrived fierce moustaches for the Brothers, and (greatest triumph of all!) even twined the tow into long, flaxen ringlets for Ursula, which certainly suited her appearance as a fairy better than her own dark locks.

Each Form was to have its act on a separate evening during the last week of the term, and the Fourth was accorded the privilege of the opening performance.

"Miss Drummond calls it a 'privilege'," said Phœbe, "but I think it's a doubtful one! It's like singing the first song at a concert. I always hate starting anything!"

"We shan't be quite so much criticized as if we came last, though," said Myfanwy. "They can't compare our acting with the others'."

"No; and if the Sixth Form are getting up anything very grand and literary, 'Bluebeard' would sound pantomimey after it," agreed Mabel.

"And we shall have got ours over, and can enjoy the others' nights with free minds," added Agnes.

Nevertheless, it was a responsibility to feel that they must make a good beginning, and all worked hard to bring each little detail as near perfection as possible. The entertainments were always given in the dining-hall; it was a big room, with a door at each end, and had a brass rod fixed permanently to support a curtain, so that it was very convenient for performances. The actors could use the kitchen entrance, and have the large pantry beyond for a dressing-room, while the audience came in by the ordinary door.

The first scene was "An Apartment in Bluebeard's Palace", and the Form displayed all its ingenuity in trying to make a brave show of barbaric magnificence. Several gay shawls were hung over clothes-horses, and draped with scarves and sashes; the sofa, covered with a Turkish rug, represented an Eastern divan; Miss Drummond had lent a small Moorish table from the drawing-room and a hammered brass tray, with a quaint coffee-pot—contributions which greatly helped the Oriental effect. But the most precious "property" of all was the miscellaneous collection of Chinese lanterns that Phœbe's sister had sent. They were very fine ones, of various sizes, shapes, and colours; and added such a gala touch to the rest of the scenery as to make Bluebeard's Palace seem *en fête*.

"The difficulty is to know where to hang them," said Aldred, holding up a combination of red, blue, and green, and admiring the brilliance of the result.

"We must fix a string tight across the room," said Ursula. "We can fasten it to a picture clip on either side, and then the lanterns will hang all in a line, just above the divan."

"They'll look beautiful, because they'll shine exactly on Fatima's head," added Aldred.

"Oh, but we mustn't light them! Miss Drummond particularly said so; she's so terribly afraid of fire. We're only allowed to use them for ornaments."

"How stupid! What's the good of them, if they mayn't be lighted?" demanded Aldred impatiently. "They'd be perfectly safe!"

"I dare say they would; but Miss Drummond is nervous, and she won't let us, so that's an end of it!"

"Miss Drummond is most absurdly tiresome and fussy!" thought Aldred, when the string had been arranged, and the row of beautiful lanterns was swinging overhead. "There couldn't possibly be any danger when they're hanging so high; we wouldn't stick our heads into them!"

She was alone in the room, for the other girls had gone into the pantry to dress. She could hear from their suppressed giggles that they found the robing nearly the most amusing part of the performance. Her own costume would not take long to put on, so she was not at all in a hurry, and had lingered behind to add a few finishing touches to the scenery.

"Every one of them has a candle," she continued to herself. "I suppose Phœbe's sister made them quite ready; she evidently expected them to be lighted. It would be such a gorgeous illumination! I declare I'll try it, to see how it looks."

With the aid of a chair, she managed to set all the candles burning, and stood back against the curtain to admire the effect.

"It's perfectly lovely," she exclaimed; "like a real fairy tale palace! I never saw anything prettier—not even at the pantomime. Oh, I must leave them as they are! Perhaps Miss Drummond does not really mind, only she feels bound to give tiresome orders. What an astonishment it will be for the others, when they come back! Now I must fly!"

It was within twenty minutes of the opening of the entertainment, therefore high time for Aldred to dress. She scrambled into her long dressing-gown, and put on her turban without much enthusiasm; her part was so small that she knew she would attract little attention, and probably not receive even a clap. Mabel was already arrayed in the pretty, gauzy robes that her mother had sent, and made a charming Sister Anne, though her blue eyes, carnation cheeks, and red-gold hair were hardly of Eastern appearance.

"You might, of course, be a Circassian; they're often very fair," said Aldred. "You look far nicer than Fatima. If you're ready, let us go and take a last peep at the stage."

Aldred expected to give her friend a great surprise when she opened the door, but she was not prepared for the scene that greeted them as they entered the room. The lanterns, the beautiful Chinese lanterns, instead of hanging proudly on their string, and shedding a brilliant lustre over the scene, were lying here and there upon the floor and on the divan. By the greatest good fortune none had yet caught fire, but the danger was great, and at any moment the thin paper might be set in a blaze.

Aldred grasped the situation instantly. The flames, rising up from below, had burnt through the string, and brought the whole row crashing down. She rushed forward and began blowing out the candles as fast as she could; with Mabel's help it was only the work of a minute, and no damage was done, but it was a miracle that the flimsy scarves and the wreaths of paper flowers had escaped.

"Who can have lighted them?" exclaimed Mabel, her cheeks quite pale at the unexpected disaster. "We left all perfectly safe."

Aldred did not reply; she was busy adjusting her turban, which had tumbled off in her hurry.

"I wonder if it could be Dora?" continued Mabel. "She's such a scatter-brain, she always does silly things!"

"It does not matter so much who's done it, as how we're going to set these lanterns up again in time," replied Aldred. "Where's the ball of string? Here! you hold one end, and we'll thread it through; I'll soon climb up and fasten it. I'll pull the burnt piece off first. Raise it up a little higher, please. That's right! Now, just a thought tighter, and it will do."

"How splendid you are!" sighed Mabel admiringly. "You have such presence of mind, blowing out the candles so quickly, and getting everything right in less than five minutes; nobody could see that we've had an accident. It looks just the same. I should like to know who——"

"The audience is coming in!" interrupted Aldred. "We must scurry back and see if the others are ready. There isn't a second to be lost. Miss

Drummond can't bear to be kept waiting, and we promised to begin punctually at half-past."

The performance was an enormous success; of that there was not the slightest shadow of doubt. Thanks to Aldred's diligent drilling, the actresses "played up", and rendered their parts with a dramatic fervour that quite astonished the audience. Bluebeard threatened in a voice of growling thunder, and frowned fiercely in his character of tyrant. Fatima shrieked in such frantic agony when she opened the cupboard door that she made everybody start, and her swoon afterwards was particularly easy and natural; she scrubbed the incriminating stain on the key with desperate zeal, and pleaded for her life with heart-breaking sobs and an air of tragic appeal. Sister Anne looked out of the window with pitiful anxiety, and wrung her slim, white hands in melodramatic despair; while the Brothers dashed in with "neck-or-nothing" haste and slew the despot, who died with such groans and convulsive twitchings as to fully satisfy the cause of justice, and point an appropriate moral.

There was a storm of clapping at the end, as the principal "stars" formed in line to make their bows. Aldred, in her minor character, was standing at the back; but much to her amazement there was a sudden call for "Stage Manager", and Mabel dragged her forward to present her to the audience.

"Hurrah! Bravo! Well done!" cried both girls and teachers, who, knowing the previous achievements of the Fourth Form, recognized the amount of cleverness needed to have so enormously raised the standard of acting, and appreciated Aldred's exertions.

"You must have a better part yourself, next time, my dear," said Miss Drummond, as she offered her congratulations. "You can teach others so well that we should like to see you taking a leading character. Everything was beautifully managed; there were no delays, and no hesitations. The grouping and attitudes were most artistically arranged, and the dresses and scenery lovely. You have made an excellent start, and the other Forms will have to look to their laurels if they wish to beat the Fourth."

It was very gratifying to Aldred to feel that her trouble had really been rewarded with success. The other girls, who had grumbled at her coaching and criticism during the rehearsals, were pleased now that they found themselves able to perform in such a superior manner, and generous enough to acknowledge how much they owed her. For once she felt she had risen to the height of popularity, and her ambition was satisfied. It was a pleasant ending to her first term, and a favourable omen for those to follow.

There was only one little jarring note in all her happiness, and that was the accident to the lanterns. In the excitement of the play she had completely forgotten all about it, but Mabel mentioned the matter when they had gone to bed that night.

"It's so very strange who could have lighted them!" she said. "We all knew Miss Drummond had forbidden it."

"Whoever did will get into trouble, then, if any fuss is made," replied Aldred.

"Yes, if it were mentioned at head-quarters, of course; but I didn't think of telling Miss Drummond."

"What were you going to do?"

"Only ask the other girls. It surely must have been Dora!"

"If we begin to talk about it, perhaps someone may mention it outside the Form, and it would get to Miss Drummond's ears. She would be very angry."

"She certainly would, because it really was dangerous. If the string had broken through while any of us were underneath, we might have been burnt to death in our light, flimsy clothes."

"It's all ended safely now, though. Isn't it rather mean to try to ferret it out? You don't want to get someone into a scrape."

"I don't indeed!" agreed Mabel. "Perhaps, as you say, it's as well to let things be. Ursula and Dora are always quarrelling, and if Ursula turned spiteful and gave a hint to Miss Bardsley, she'd feel bound to make enquiries."

"And we should probably never be allowed to use Chinese lanterns again."

"Oh! That would be dreadful! Phœbe says her sister told her we could keep these at school, and I thought we might act 'Catskin' at Easter, and carry them in procession."

"Then, mum's the word!"

"Yes, you're right. You always do give good advice! Besides, it never struck me I might get anyone into trouble. You're such a thoroughly considerate darling, you make me quite ashamed of myself. What a glorious time we've had! I've enjoyed myself so much. Good night!"

Mabel turned over on her pillows, snuggled a little more cosily under the eider-down, and promptly went to sleep; but Aldred lay awake for a long time, thinking, and in spite of her brilliant triumph of the evening the tenor of her thoughts was far from satisfactory and agreeable.

CHAPTER X. A FROSTY JANUARY

SCHOOL broke up on December 18th, and the little community at Birkwood was soon scattered far and wide. Aldred thought that this Christmas was the most enjoyable one she had ever spent; she felt as if she had returned to Dingfield on an entirely different footing, and that now she had quite a new position at home. Her father, who had taken slight notice of her before, had missed her while she was away, and began suddenly to appreciate how much his daughter was to him, and to give her a larger share of his attention than had hitherto fallen to her lot. Aunt Bertha, whose former attitude had been one of continual criticism, stopped nagging and fault-finding, and treated her niece almost like a visitor, allowing many small indulgences which she had never been accustomed to sanction, and relaxing some of her stricter rules. It was plain that she thought Aldred much improved, and, as some of the chief causes of friction had now vanished, she was ready to forget old grievances, declare a truce, and try to make the holidays pass as smoothly as possible. She no longer ordered Aldred about as if she were a child in the nursery, and would even consult her wishes, or allow her to express an opinion of her own, realizing that the girl was rapidly growing up, and could not be expected to remain for ever in the background. This altered state of affairs was very much to Aldred's mind. She had always felt that her aunt had not treated her fairly, and it was partly the continual sense of injustice that had caused her rebellious attitude.

"I'll do anything for Aunt Bertha now she asks me nicely," she thought to herself. "It was when she used to speak so absolutely autocratically that she made me feel so angry. I'll fetch her what she likes, if she'll say 'Please', and 'Thank you'; but I can't bear to be sent trotting as if I were a baby of three."

If only Aunt Bertha had known this, and had taken poor Aldred by the "right handle" sooner, a very great deal of trouble could have been saved; but she was one of those complacently tactless people who try to impress the stamp of their own dominant personalities upon everyone alike, and who rule with an utter absence of sympathy. She had not understood Aldred's character, and had concluded, therefore, that there was nothing to understand. She was agreeably surprised now to discover the various pleasant qualities that had begun to develop under Miss Drummond's genial influence, and admitted, almost in spite of herself, that her troublesome niece was turning into quite a nice companion, and that her society could actually be an enjoyment as well as a care.

Keith also appeared to consider his sister a far more reasonable and sensible person since her return from the Grange. He was never very expansive, but he gave her more of his confidence than before, talked to her of his own school life, and seemed ready to spend the greater part of his time with her. It had always been Aldred's ambition to have Keith as her special property, but he had not been altogether willing to devote himself to her, and had often hurt her by his coolness. Now that they were both in a sense visitors at home, Aunt Bertha arranged plans that would include the pair, sending them together to visit picture galleries and museums, and other interesting places, for Keith was old enough to escort his sister, and could be trusted to take good care of her. In this way, with the addition of various parties and festivities, the four weeks passed very quickly, and the fifteenth of January brought Aldred's school trunk once more out of the box-room, and saw her started on her journey to Birkwood.

Though the holidays had been so pleasant, she was glad to return to school; she liked the life at the Grange, and the thought of seeing Mabel again was absolute rapture. The two had corresponded freely, but writing was not so good as talking, and she was longing for a delightful private chat, to hear all her friend's news and tell all her own. Mabel seemed equally delighted at their re-union.

"You darling! How I've missed you!" she exclaimed. "There are simply a hundred things I want to tell you. If there were not that tiresome silence rule, I should stop awake till twelve to-night. Leave your unpacking, and come and sit down on my bed for a minute or two; I'll help you to get straight afterwards."

"And Miss Bardsley won't be up just yet," said Aldred, accepting the invitation, regardless of the fact that the greater part of her wardrobe was still in her box.

"I told Mother all about you," continued Mabel. "You can't think how much she wants to see you. She's coming to town at the end of the month, and says she'll run down to Birkwood for an afternoon. I know she'll like you, and you can't help liking her—everybody adores Mother! I wish we were sisters, and that you lived at Grassingford, and that she was your mother too—how lovely that would be! But then, your own people at home would not spare you. It must be so dreadfully hard for them to part with you, even to go to school. When I know how I miss you for four weeks, I can sympathize with them losing you for thirteen. I don't know how they manage without you!"

Aldred did not say that she considered her family would not be quite so utterly inconsolable at her absence. She only kissed the sweet, pink cheek that was pressed against hers, and thought how blissful it was to occupy so large a place in Mabel's heart, and to find such a warm welcome awaiting her at Birkwood.

"There's nobody like you!" went on her adorer. "I stayed for a few days at Archdeacon Vernon's, at the New Year. His daughter is just my age, and Mother wanted me so much to meet her, for she said she was such an extremely nice girl. But she was absolutely nothing to you, dearest! I didn't feel I could ever be very fond of her; she's not so original, nor so jolly. No! I told Mother at once you were the only girl I had ever really cared for, and I couldn't do with another bosom friend."

Though Mabel was the chief attraction for her at Birkwood, Aldred was nevertheless glad to meet the rest of the Form, and to be in the midst of the lively school life again.

When the unpacking had been successfully accomplished, and supper was over, all the girls collected in a close group round the classroom fire, to compare notes about the holidays.

"I've been to Switzerland," said Ursula. "We went to Les Avants for the winter sports. It was simply glorious! I learnt to skate and to ski. I felt most fearfully wobbly at first, but it was lovely when one got into it; so was the tobogganing—one went skimming down slopes at a tremendous pace. The ice was all illuminated at night, and we had fancy dress carnivals; it was such fun!"

"Lucky you," said Phœbe, "to be in a place where there was real frost and snow! We've been grumbling at the wet weather continually. I wonder how long it is since we had an old-fashioned Christmas—the kind of thing one reads about in Dickens, I mean, when Mr. Pickwick went skating."

"People say 'a green Christmas makes a fat churchyard'."

"Well, I'm sure one gets more bad colds with pottering about in the rain than one would with skating."

"I believe it's freezing now. I shouldn't be at all astonished if we had quite a spell of hard weather."

"'As the days lengthen, the cold strengthens'," quoted Myfanwy, who was fond of proverbs.

"I wish it would! We've never had any deep snow, or really severe frost, since I came to the Grange."

Phœbe's prophecy concerning hard weather was literally fulfilled that very night. The thermometer descended with a run, and by next morning great, feathery flakes were falling silently, and turning the landscape into a white world. The girls were very excited, and watched anxiously, hoping that the snow would continue; and they rejoiced as each bush and shrub in the garden became more and more smothered.

"The outlines of the walks are quite lost," said Mabel exultingly, "and the tennis lawn looks like a huge iced plum cake."

"It's not much use for Brown to try to sweep a path, because it gets covered up directly."

"Yes, but he has to go and feed the hens, you see. I wonder if Miss Drummond will venture out to look at her Partridge Wyandottes? She's never missed going to them at four o'clock yet."

"I wish she'd let us go with her; I should love to tramp over the snow!"

"So should I; but she says we must none of us go farther than the shed. Brown has swept the courtyard at the back. If it's fine to-morrow, we'll have some fun."

After falling steadily for twenty-four hours, the snow stopped, and gave place to bright sunshine. Miss Drummond ordered dinner to be earlier than usual, and by half-past one the whole school was out upon the downs.

It was an ideal winter's day. The sky was clear, with the cold, pale blue of January, so different from the deep, warm azure of July. The sun, low down on the horizon, though it was still near its meridian, sent long, slanting rays over the white waste, catching the tops of the hills and making them shine and sparkle like diamonds. Each bush and tree was coated with rime, and edged with a tracery of delicate lacework. The snow, crisp and hard, crunched under the girls' feet as they walked, and here and there they could mark the track of a rabbit or a bird that had hurried through the cold, to shelter under the protection of some gorse-bush.

"It's just like fairyland! It might be part of the Frost King's Palace!" said Aldred. "I'm sure the Snow Queen has been here. I feel as if we ought to find Gerda hunting for little Kay—I expect she's just behind that bush, riding the Robber Maiden's reindeer, with her hands in the big muff. The Lapland woman and the Finland woman can't be far off."

"What do you mean?" asked Lorna Hallam.

"You benighted girl! have you never read Hans Andersen?"

"I believe I did, ages ago, but I've forgotten it all."

"So much the worse for you, then!"

"Why, one can't bother to remember silly fairy tales!"

"Hans Andersen is not silly; he's a classic."

"Quite right!" said Miss Drummond, who happened to overhear. "I consider the dear old Dane was one of the truest poets that ever lived. His writing has a purity of style that sets it on a very high pinnacle in literature, and his thoughts are most exquisite. No one who has really appreciated his lovely, tender stories can ever be quite vulgar and commonplace. He seems to take all the simple, everyday things, and wave his magic wand over them and turn them into enchantment."

"But the tales aren't true, Miss Drummond!" objected Lorna. "One can't see fairies."

"There is a meaning under it all, and the gist of the whole is, that if we persistently look at the beautiful side of everything, we are making our own fairyland, and seeing what is denied to those who dwell only on the prosaic and ordinary. It's a great quality to have, and one that brings a supreme enjoyment in life. If you're wise you'll cultivate it while you are young, and then you need never really grow old, because, although your hair may turn grey, you'll still keep the very principle of youth in your heart. Very few people can realize their ideals, so it is something to be able to idealize our real."

The place that Miss Drummond had chosen as the destination of their walk was a steep slope about a mile from the school. Here it was quite possible to make a good toboggan track, for there was a flat space in front and an easy way to climb up at the back. Half a dozen tea-trays had been requisitioned from the kitchen, to act as sleds.

"I wish we had a bob-sleigh!" said Ursula Bramley, who, after her experience in Switzerland, felt herself an authority on winter sports. "It's the hugest fun you can imagine, only you need two very good people to steer and act brake. Ours at Les Avants held a crew of six. My eldest brother used to take us down, and he only upset us once."

"I think little sleighs are better; they're not nearly so dangerous," said Agnes Maxwell. "A cousin of mine was fearfully hurt last winter at Samaden, in a bob-sleigh race; he fell on his head, and had concussion of the brain."

"Well, of course, you have to chance that. It needs pluck and skill if you're going in for racing; you mustn't be afraid for yourself—you could fall off a tea-tray, as far as that goes," said Phœbe.

"You couldn't do yourself much damage if you did," laughed Ursula; "the snow's not hard enough. Now, we shall have to go down the slope a good many times before we make a decent track of it."

"I wish we had more tea-trays! We shan't get very many turns each, I'm afraid," said Myfanwy.

Six girls from the Sixth Form had been chosen to start, and made a trial trip amid much cheering and excitement.

"It's perfectly lovely—just like flying!" they declared, as the improvised sleds drew up on the level ground at the bottom.

"Miss Drummond, won't you try?"

"Perhaps I may, when the thing is well started, but for the present I would rather stand and watch. It certainly looks very tempting, and worth an effort. Mademoiselle, shall you venture?"

"Nevaire!" shuddered poor Mademoiselle, who considered a walk in the snow quite a sufficient adventure. "I should have fear to place myself on a thing so insccure, and to let myself glide thus! Oh, no, it would be an act of folly! We have no snows in Provence, and I have been brought up to love other pleasures."

"You shall have the next turn if you like, Mademoiselle," said Esther Vaudrey, one of the pioneers. "It's really not difficult at all, if you know how to tuck up your feet."

"It makes one warm, at any rate," said Freda. "Who's going next? We'd better take it in Forms."

The sport proved extremely popular, and for the next hour relays of girls were constantly going down the slope; the track was soon as smooth as a slide, and really made a very good course, quite enough to satisfy everyone except Ursula.

"It's nothing to Les Avants! You should have seen that!" she kept assuring the others.

"Then I wish you would go back to Les Avants!" exclaimed Phœbe. "What's the good of belittling this all the time, and trying to make out it's so tame? I call it bad taste! If you can't enjoy it, we can, at any rate."

"I'd enjoy it if I had my own little sled, instead of a tea-tray."

"Nobody wants you to go on a tea-tray," said Agnes. "You can miss your turn if you like—I'll take it instead."

That, however, Ursula was not ready to allow. She appreciated the tobogganing as much as anyone, though she liked the triumph of referring to her Swiss achievements.

The fun waxed fast and furious. The girls were keen on racing, and would start six together from the top, at a given signal; then there would be a lightning descent down the slippery slide, generally ending in a roll in the snow at the bottom, from which they would spring up, powdered from head to foot, but laughing and quite unhurt.

Miss Drummond and most of the teachers took an occasional turn, but Mademoiselle remained firm in her refusal to venture into what she considered such imminent danger to life and limb.

"It is the sport of men!" she declared. "In my country, such things are not for *les jeunes filles*. They do not go out to slide in the snow."

"But don't you think our girls look much brighter and healthier, with this brisk exercise, than if we had kept them cooped up in the schoolrooms all this beautiful afternoon?" asked Miss Drummond.

"Perhaps—yes, that I will allow. But custom is strong upon us, and to me, I find it still strange to see what is permitted to your English *Mees*."

"I'm glad we are English," whispered Aldred to Mabel. "French girls must have a stupid time, if they're never allowed to toboggan, or to go in the snow. If I were sent to a French school I'd run away, and come back to Birkwood!"

"There's no place like the Grange," agreed Mabel, brushing the snow vigorously from her dress. "If there's any jolly thing that it's possible to do Miss Drummond thinks of it."

Miss Drummond certainly justified the character that Mabel gave her, for when the girls, very warm and rosy after their exertions, returned to the school at four o'clock, they found a surprise waiting for them. Brown, the gardener, with the aid of two or three labourers who had been called in to help him, had shovelled away the whole of the snow on the asphalt tennis court, and piled it as a wall all round. He had then brought the hose, and was now busy flooding the court to a depth of three or four inches.

"It ought to freeze hard to-night," said Miss Drummond, "and by to-morrow morning there should be a splendid surface. Those girls who have brought skates to school will be in luck, and I shall be able to arrange for those who have not. I have written to Wilson's, the ironmonger at Chetbourne, to send us out a parcel of several dozen to choose from."

The prospect of a skating rink in the garden was hailed with joy, and the anxiety of the school was great lest the frost should give way, and frustrate their verydelightful plans. The amusements of the cold spell so outweighed the discomforts that nobody (except poor Mademoiselle) grumbled at nipped fingers or chilly toes. Even Agnes Maxwell, who was a martyr to chilblains, suffered heroically, and did not wish for a thaw.

"It's quite the most severe winter I can remember," said Mabel, breaking the ice in her bedroom jug next morning. "I believe even my bottle of hair wash is frozen, and the glycerine cream is perfectly stiff; I shall have to melt it on the radiator before I can put any on my hands. Look at the window! It's covered with beautiful frost patterns."

"All the better for skating," said Aldred, who was trying to thaw her toothbrush. "I'm glad there has been no more snow to spoil our ice. I wish Miss Drummond would let us go out at once, after breakfast, instead of doing lessons."

Miss Drummond's good nature, however, did not extend to such a pitch of leniency as that, and the morning classes went on just as usual. About dinner-time, a young man arrived from Chetbourne with a large parcel of skates, and Aldred, who did not possess any of her own, was able to expend some of her pocket-money on a neat little pair.

"You've made a lovely choice!" said Mabel. "Mine are an old pair of my brother's that just fit me now; they're rather shabby, but they happen to be particularly good steel, and always 'bite' very well. There's the greatest difference in skates, in that respect."

"You'll have to help me," said Aldred, "for I've never even tried before, and I'm sure I shall be extremely stupid and clumsy."

"It will be the lame supporting the halt, then," laughed Mabel, "for I'm certainly not a crack skater myself."

By two o'clock the whole school was disporting itself on the ice. Some girls (Ursula Bramley, in especial) seemed quite at home there, and cut figures of eight with aggravating ease while their less fortunate comrades strove to balance themselves with outstretched arms, or sat down suddenly on the slippery surface.

"I'd no idea one could feel so absolutely weak in the knees!" declared Aldred, subsiding on to the snowy bank after a first struggle round the rink. "I'm like a baby learning to walk. I wonder if I shall ever manage to strike out properly? Look at Ursula—she's doing the 'Dutch roll'. I'm green with envy!"

"There's nothing like practice," said Mabel, getting up and making a gallant effort to accomplish the "outside edge", but speedily coming to grief over it. "Give me a winter in Norway, and I'd undertake to waltz on the ice; but what can one expect on the first day?"

CHAPTER XI. VENUS IN THE SNOW

THERE was generally sound sense in Mabel's arguments, though Aldred's impatience wanted at once to achieve great things. Skating, like everything else, has no royal road, and neither of the girls advanced much beyond the point of going alone. Aldred, rather to her chagrin, found she certainly could not compete with Ursula, and an aspiring dream of seeing herself queen of the rink vanished away. She was never without resources, however and as she was determined always to keep to the fore, she hit upon another means of making herself prominent. She remembered hearing that in Brussels, when snow falls, the most eminent sculptors of the city go to the Park and model snow statues, which are carefully guarded afterwards by the park keepers, and shown to the streams of visitors who flock to look at them. This was an idea worthy of being copied, and one of which she was sure nobody else would be likely to think. Abandoning her skates, therefore, one afternoon, she retired to the now deserted lawn, and set to work. The snow was not such an easy medium as clay, but it was in prime condition for her purpose, being soft enough to model, yet stiff enough to hold together. Aldred's scheme was decidedly ambitious, for she had decided to make a representation in snow of the Venus of Milo. She had chosen that for her subject because of its lack of arms and its flowing draperies, as she knew it would be quite impossible to reproduce a Flying Mercury or the Dying Gladiator. She had really a strong talent for sculpture, and contrived, with the aid of a framework of broomsticks, to give her statue a wonderfully good pose. She had brought out a photograph of the original, which she constantly consulted; and she worked away with great enjoyment, shaping the snow with deft hands, and using some flat pieces of wood and a palette knife from the studio as her modelling tools. She felt it was almost one of the most exciting things she had ever done in her life. The keen joy of creation, that true heritage of all who possess artistic ability thrilled her fingers, as she put dainty touches here and there, and watched the resemblance to the Venus evolve itself by slow degrees from her great mass of snow. She thought of Michelangelo, who saw the angel in a rough block of marble, only waiting to be released by his chisel, and felt as if she, too, were trying to free the goddess, and give her human form. For the time all thought of what the girls would say was forgotten, and she worked for the love of art alone, sighing with satisfaction as she successfully put in a delicate fold of dress, or a ripple of classic hair.

It was finished at last, even to the pedestal, and Aldred stepped back and looked at it with mixed feelings. She had done her very best; she dared not add another impress, from fear of spoiling it, yet she knew how far it fell short of her ideal.

"I wonder if Phidias used to be contented with what he'd done?" she thought. "I suppose he was the greatest sculptor that ever lived. I remember reading that Millais once went to an exhibition of his own pictures, and came away very dejected. Shall I ask them all to come and see it now? I want so much to show it, but somehow I hardly dare. I almost think I'll leave it for somebody to find out, and just go back to the rink and say nothing."

She had not counted, however, on Mabel, who, missing her friend for an unusual length of time, took off her skates and went to hunt for her, tracking her in the end by her footsteps in the snow. Mabel's amazement when she reached the lawn was only equalled by her admiration. She rushed off instantly to fetch all the girls to look, even venturing to knock at the study door and report her news at head-quarters.

Aldred's snow statue made quite a sensation at the Grange. Miss Drummond thought so highly of it that she had it photographed, and invited many of her friends from Chetbourne to come and see it. It was such a daring and original project for a girl of only fifteen to have carried out entirely alone that she felt it reflected credit on the school to possess so clever a pupil. Aldred was praised to her heart's content, and received so much attention from teachers and visitors that she could certainly consider herself, for the time being, the most important person at Birkwood. She was petted by the prefects, invited to skate by members of the Sixth Form who had ignored her existence before, and asked so often for her autograph that she grew almost tired of signing her name.

"There's to be a picture of your statue in the School Magazine," said Mabel rapturously. "That's a tremendous compliment, because Miss

Drummond generally says it's too expensive to have illustrations. I'm going to ask her to have your photograph put in as well—just a tiny head, from that splendid snapshot which Dora took when you came last September. It would fit into a corner of the same page, and show the 'portrait of the artist'. I'll make up the extra money myself, if it will cost more to print. I shall bespeak six copies: I want to send one to Cousin Marion—she's gone to live in Germany for a year; she'll be so interested, because, you know, it was she who was staying at Seaforth last year, and who first told me anything about you."

Aldred's face fell. In a moment all the zest seemed to have faded out of her pleasure. This was indeed a grave danger. "Cousin Marion" had seen her namesake at Seaforth, and would probably recognize that the two faces were not the same; even a badly printed portrait might not conceal the lack of likeness. Would Mabel ever forget that wretched episode? Why must it always be raked up in this tiresome way? Whenever she thought it was safely consigned to oblivion, it appeared to rise again like a ghost, and threaten the destruction of her position. True, she had done much since she came to Birkwood to strengthen her hold on Mabel's affection, but she knew that her one deed of supposed heroism was the basis of their friendship, and the groundwork of her general popularity; and she trembled to think what the effect might be if this foundation stone were removed.

"I don't want my photograph blazoned abroad," she said, almost crying. "I'd rather Miss Drummond didn't put either me or the statue in the Magazine. Promise me, Mabel, that you won't send a copy to anybody, if she does."

"But why shouldn't I?" said Mabel, much surprised.

"Because I don't wish it. The statue was a stupid thing, after all; far too much fuss has been made of it. I'm sorry I didn't knock it down as soon as it was finished!"

"Aldred! how can you say so?"

"Well, I'm tired of hearing about it, anyway," returned Aldred, "and I hope you won't mention it to your cousin; it makes me feel silly to have such a tremendous 'cock-a-doodling' over all my stupid little performances, which really aren't worth it."

"Well, I won't, if you so particularly ask me not to," said Mabel, in a disappointed voice. "But you can't always hide everything; it's not fair to the world if all the brave and clever things that are done must be suppressed—they're such a help and encouragement to other people. I, for instance, am ever so much better for having known you; you've been quite an inspiration in my life. My mother had a friend like that (it was Lady Betty Blakeney, who is now so famous) who had a tremendous influence over her, and first made her want to help poor people, and take up the work she does now; and she always hoped I should meet somebody who would be as much to me as her friend was to her. But I never did until you came to Birkwood."

It seemed useless to protest; the more Aldred tried to shuffle out of her rôle of heroine the more Mabel admired her modesty and her other imagined excellencies. Mabel was a girl who loved to idolize celebrities; it was partly a necessity of her nature, and partly a habit that had been cultivated at home by her mother, who had a kindred weakness. Before the two girls knew each other, Mabel had been obliged to confine her worship to book favourites; then, having met, as she thought, the realization of her ideal, she could not resist the temptation to endow her with the combined virtues of Portia, Rebecca, Ellen Douglas, Grace Darling, Flora Macdonald, and the "Nut-brown Maid", without stopping to put the various qualities to the test, and make sure that they actually existed. It is always better to err on the right side, and think too highly than too ill of people, but Mabel's mistake was to take Aldred so utterly on trust, and to blind herself wilfully to the many small indications of character that might easily have shown her that her idol was very far from perfection.

Aldred could not feel easy until she had made sure that the snapshot portrait was not to be included in the next number of the Magazine. She was afraid Mabel might break her promise, and send a copy surreptitiously to her cousin, and then the mischief would be done. She did not dare to mention the matter at head-quarters; it would appear conceited on her part to suggest that the idea had been broached, and she would feel very humiliated if Miss Drummond were to say: "Oh, no, my dear! I never dreamt of putting it in!"

A plan occurred to her, however, by which she could defeat her friend's too enthusiastic project. She borrowed the negative from Dora on the pretence of wanting to look at it, and in handing it back managed to drop it and step on it, breaking it beyond all chance of repair. She apologized profusely for the accident.

"It was most clumsy of me!" she declared. "Could we possibly patch it up again, do you think?"

"No, we couldn't!" said the aggrieved Dora. "It would show a mark right across the face, however carefully we joined it. I've tried piecing negatives together before, and they're not worth the trouble of printing."

"Well, it was only a picture of me, not the lovely one you took of Miss Drummond and Mademoiselle."

"No; I'm glad it was not that. But I promised this to Mabel; she asked me last night if I could find it, and I've had such a hunt through all my negatives! She'll be quite cross that it's broken."

"You must put the blame on me, then, for it was my fault."

Secretly Aldred was exultant.

"I know Dora only took one print from it," she said to herself, "and that was spoilt in the fixing bath. It's impossible to take snapshots in midwinter, so I believe I'm safe for the present. I shall discourage Mabel strongly from buying a camera. I hope she won't get one given to her on her birthday! I'm glad her Cousin Marion has gone to Germany, so that she won't meet Mabel for a year, at any rate. So far as I can tell, she is the only person who has seen that Lawrence girl and knows what she is like."

The ice lasted for a whole fortnight, a totally unprecedented record in the annals of Birkwood, which, on account of its position near the sea, did not often come in for so severe an experience of frost. The rink proved the greatest success; the ice was apt to get cut up and rough by the afternoon, but when everyone had left, the gardener would turn the hose over it, so that by next morning there was once more a splendid, smooth surface.

January 29th happened to be Miss Drummond's birthday. The girls were accustomed to prepare some little surprise for her on such occasions, and generally acted a play in honour of the event; and the evening was always considered a holiday. This time, however, Miss Drummond announced that, instead of being entertained by her pupils, she wished to provide a treat for the whole school.

"It is full moon," she said, "and we shall have a carnival on the ice. The rink will be illuminated, and I expect we shall all find it quite a novel experience to skate by torchlight. Mind you don't catch colds beforehand! Anyone who is heard sneezing will have to stay indoors."

"It is a lovely idea!" said Phœbe, as the Fourth Form discussed the project afterwards. "We shall have the most glorious fun! I'll ask Miss Drummond if we may hang up the Chinese lanterns round the rink; it would be quite safe to light them out-of-doors, and they'd look so nice!"

"I hope I shan't have toothache again," said Dora. "Do you think Miss Drummond would let me go out if I muffled my head in a big shawl?"

"No, I'm sure she won't, nor Lorna either, if she persists in that noisy coughing. If you can't smother it, Lorna, you and Dora will have to keep each other company in the classroom, and miss all the fun."

"Oh, that would be too bad! I'll manage somehow to get well enough, if I swallow every nostrum under the sun. Will you lend me your carbolic smoke ball? and I'll try it to-night."

In spite of many remedies suggested by sympathetic friends, Lorna was, however, obliged to forego the festivities. Miss Drummond was inexorable where health was concerned, and would not allow colds to be trifled with.

"Perhaps if I'd tried all the different recipes I might have cured it," said Lorna dolefully. "I've been recommended hot buttermilk and treacle, and honey with lemon, and black-currant tea, and elder syrup, and spirits of nitre, and ammoniated quinine, and to tie a wet handkerchief and a stocking round my throat, and sit with my feet in mustard and water!"

"I think the cures sound worse than the cold," said Dora, who was nursing a swollen face. "I've resigned myself to staying indoors. We shan't be the only ones, for there are at least eight others on the sick list. I don't much care; I'd rather sit near the fire and keep warm than skate with a raging toothache. No, I'm afraid I can't eat any chocolates, though it's kind of Miss Drummond to have sent us a box full."

"If you look out at the landing window, you can just catch a peep of what is going on," said Mabel. "We'll tell you all about it afterwards. And if you're wise you'll let Miss Bardsley take you to the dentist to-morrow, and have that tooth out."

At half-past seven those members of the school who could show a clean bill of health wrapped themselves up warmly, and sallied forth to the carnival. The garden was really a beautiful sight. The full moon shone down upon the snow, glinting on the frosty branches of the trees, and showing cold and pale in contrast to the line of flaming torches that encircled the rink. All Phœbe's Chinese lanterns had been put up, and a number of others, which belonged to the Fifth and Sixth Forms; so that the scene resembled Aladdin's palace, with its rows of red, blue, yellow, and green lamps. It seemed very romantic to skate amid such surroundings, and the girls felt as if they were stepping into a picture or a scene from a play, as they took their first strokes, over the ice. Two friends of Miss Drummond had brought a mandoline and a guitar, and played lively selections, sometimes giving a song with a chorus, in which all could join, when the whole school swung round to the tune of "Oh! dem golden slippers" or "The old folks at home". The oil stove from the cottage had been requisitioned, and stood in a snug corner, keeping warm a large can of beef-tea, from which steaming cupfuls could be ladled from time to time by anyone who wanted refreshment; and a tray full of hot turnovers, which one of the maids carried from the house, was highly appreciated.

As a wind-up to the festivities, everyone made an attempt to dance Sir Roger de Coverley—a very funny proceeding indeed on the ice, where strokes had to be substituted for *chassés*, and the ranks were apt to be abruptly broken by someone sitting down suddenly, with more swiftness than grace. Miss Reade and Miss Bardsley were heading the line, and passing under the upraised hands of Maude Farnham and Rose Turner, two of the prefects, when unluckily Rose tipped a little too far forward and lost her balance. Down she came with a crash, and in her fall she clutched wildly at Miss Bardsley, and not only brought both the teachers to their knees, but upset six couples who were following close behind and could not stop. There was quite a tangle of prostrate figures upon the ice, and much laughter as the girls picked themselves up, and tried to re-form the lines. Amidst the general scramble, nobody noticed for a moment that Miss Bardsley was really hurt; when she attempted to rise, however, her foot was so painful that she sank back with a groan.

"I'm afraid I must have sprained my ankle!" she exclaimed.

It was a case for "first aid", and the members of the ambulance class had very soon shown the advantage of their training by taking off the teacher's skates and boots, improvising a stretcher, and carrying her into the house, where Miss Drummond set to work at once with hot fomentations and bandages. Unfortunately, the mischief was greater than anyone supposed, for when the doctor from Chetbourne arrived next morning he declared that a bone was broken, and that the ankle must be put into splints.

Naturally, this was a very awkward occurrence just at the beginning of the term. Miss Bardsley would be disabled for some weeks, and in the meantime, who would take her Form? For a few days one of the prefects did duty, while Miss Drummond wrote post-haste to a scholastic agency, to secure a teacher as locum tenens.

It was difficult to find anyone who was disengaged and could come at so short a notice, and Miss Webb, the mistress who finally arrived, was hardly to the taste of the Fourth Form. She had been a private governess in a family, and was not accustomed to class teaching; and the girls discovered in the first half-hour that she had not the slightest notion of how to enforce discipline.

"She told me to stop talking, and when I didn't, she simply took no notice!" chuckled Dora Maxwell.

"And she said: 'Ursula, dear, please do not fidget with your pencil,' in such a mild, apologetic little voice!" laughed Ursula. "Miss Bardsley would have glared, and said: 'Ursula, take a forfeit!'"

"She doesn't know anything, really, about the lessons," said Aldred scornfully. "She kept looking at the book all the time, to follow what we were saying."

"And you remember that sum that came out so funnily? I'm sure the answer was wrong in the book, and I wanted her to work it on the blackboard, but she wouldn't," put in Dora.

"Because she couldn't!" sneered Aldred. "She's evidently no good at arithmetic. We know more ourselves than she does!"

"And when we were having physical geography, and I asked her why the moon really had phases, she said it depended on the tide!"

"Well, she had got rather flustered, and put it the wrong way," interposed Mabel. "Of course, she meant that the tide depended on the moon."

"Then why didn't she say so?"

"You muddle her by asking so many questions."

"Miss Bardsley never gets muddled; she always explains things so that one can understand exactly. As for Miss Webb, at the end of her physical geography, I feel as if I weren't sure whether the sun goes round the earth, or the earth round the sun."

"Well, it must be difficult for her, poor thing! to come here at a few hours' notice and have to take up another mistress's work," said Mabel. "I expect she's taught from quite different books, and doesn't know how far we are on in anything."

"It's not exactly that," said Phœbe. "I'm sure Miss Bardsley could set to work on someone else's Form, and manage their lessons in five minutes. The real trouble is that Miss Webb hasn't been used to teach in the way we learn things at Birkwood. She's old-fashioned, and expects you just to repeat what's in the book, and never minds whether you really understand it or not."

"That's fearfully out-of-date!" said Ursula. "She must have been educated a very long time ago. I wonder how old she is?"

"Quite fifty, I should think. Her hair is very grey," said Aldred. "She's older than Miss Drummond, I'm certain, and oh! what a vast difference there is between them! Miss Drummond is the cleverest person I know, and Miss Webb is a perfect noodle!"

"I don't see what's the use of troubling to learn her stupid lessons; they can't do us any good."

"Well, we must be able to reel off something, or she'd give us bad marks, and Miss Drummond would scold."

"Yes, that's the worst of it."

"Freda Martin made a far better teacher; I wish she could have gone on taking us!"

"So do I; but, you see, she has her own work. She is going in for the Matric. next summer."

"Well, I vote we give ourselves an easy time with Miss Webb. We'll learn just enough to satisfy her and no more; and if we feel inclined to talk in school we'll talk!"

CHAPTER XII. THE NEW TEACHER

It was very naughty of the girls thus to take advantage of poor Miss Webb, who was doing her utmost, according to her lights, to fill the gap occasioned by Miss Bardsley's enforced absence. She had no natural gift either for imparting knowledge or for keeping control over unruly wills, and had, indeed, quite mistaken her vocation. Teaching was to her, not a pleasure, but a weary grind to which she must continually brace her nerves; she could not help showing how distasteful it was, and her lack of enthusiasm was reflected in her pupils. Her classes were chaotic. The girls whispered, laughed, and played tricks upon one another with impunity; her faint remonstrances had not the slightest effect, and the more nervous she grew, the more out of hand they became.

Ursula Bramley, who prided herself on her wit, would delight in asking questions calculated to expose the mistress's ignorance, or to trip her up in some obscure branch of knowledge. She would come into school well primed with educational posers, and keenly enjoyed Miss Webb's discomfiture. She would meet all the unfortunate governess's attempts at evasion with firm determination, nailing her to the point until poor Miss

Webb seemed more in the position of a candidate undergoing examination than a teacher conducting her own class.

"Baiting the cobweb," as Ursula called it, was the grand amusement of the Form, and it was very seldom that the victim emerged triumphant from the ordeal. Schoolgirls are thoughtless creatures, often very heartless, and it never struck the Form what pain they were inflicting upon a proud and sensitive lady, whose misfortunes obliged her to gain her living at an uncongenial occupation. To them she was simply a tiresome old bore, an object of mirth or contempt; and the agony that she endured in private did not enter into their calculations.

Mabel alone took no part in this unseemly state of disorder. Soon after the advent of Miss Webb she had developed a slight attack of influenza, and was laid up in the "hospital", a large room at the top of the house reserved for purposes of isolation. She was not seriously ill, but Miss Drummond was so afraid of infection being spread through the school that she kept Mabel away from the others for a longer period than was really necessary.

The latter certainly would not have countenanced any rudeness or discourtesy in class, but, her good influence being removed, Aldred was only too ready to follow the example of the others, and, as a cheap and ready means to win popularity, became one of the ring-leaders in the daily mutiny, vying with Ursula as to which could be the more clever at their teacher's expense. All kinds of petty annoyances were resorted to. If Miss Webb wished to write on the blackboard, the chalk would be missing, or the duster mislaid. The desk lids were banged, books dropped feet scraped noisily, or the door was slammed on purpose. The girls would wilfully misunderstand the plainest directions, make ridiculous mistakes in their essays or exercises, and altogether try how far they could put the patience and good temper of the long-suffering mistress to the test.

One morning Miss Webb, in a feeble effort towards reform, announced that she intended next day to give the Form a viva voce examination upon the work taken since her arrival, and that she would submit the results to Miss Drummond.

This was a blow, for the girls had learnt their lessons so badly lately that not one of them was prepared, and they knew that the low standard of their marks would mean trouble with the head mistress.

"It's absurd to give us an exam, when it's not even the middle of the term!" exclaimed Dora, in much indignation.

"And a viva voce, too! We always have written ones at Birkwood," said Agnes, "with properly typed questions."

"Suppose none of us pass? Miss Drummond will be absolutely savage!" said Phœbe uneasily.

"Yes; she was not at all pleased with our reports last week," agreed Lorna.

"She asked how it was I had so many mistakes in my German exercises, and why my problems were all wrong."

"And she looked at the writing in my book, and said it was a scribble," added Myfanwy.

"What are we going to take for the viva voce?" asked Aldred.

"Everything. It's to be from nine to eleven—a regular catechism in Roman history, and physical geography, and English literature, with grammar and parsing thrown in."

"Miss Webb said she would even ask us French verbs, and weights and measures," wailed Dora. "I know I shall fail! I'm no good at viva voces. I can remember the past preterite of *s'en aller*, or how many square yards there are in a square pole, when I'm writing an exercise, or doing a sum; but I never can think quickly enough when I'm asked point-blank. It all goes straight out of my head, and it's just coming back to me by the time the next girl is answering."

"Viva voces really are not fair," grumbled Myfanwy. "The nervous ones always do badly, however much they know."

"And when you don't know, it's still worse!" continued Lorna. "Miss Bardsley never gives them, at any rate, and that's quite sufficient reason why Miss Webb shouldn't."

"I call it quite impertinent for a temporary teacher to make such an innovation!" said Ursula loftily.

"Especially when Miss Bardsley is a B.A., and Miss Webb hasn't been to college."

"Yes. She has no business to alter any of our Form arrangements. We told her what we were accustomed to do, and she ought to stick to that, instead of introducing her own ways."

However much the girls might murmur in private, they could not openly rebel, or refuse to submit to the examination. It never struck any of them to take their books and set to work during recreation time, to try to make up arrears. They much preferred to grumble, and bewail their hard luck.

"I hope she'll begin with literature and physical geography," said Phœbe. "I can manage fairly well with those, because it's easy enough to give examples of a dactyl and hexameters, or to describe a volcano; but when it comes to Roman chronology, I shall be done for! I can't remember the dates in the least, or the right order of the battles, or the names of the generals."

"We must try to spin out the first part," suggested Aldred. "We'll answer as slowly as we possibly can, and then there won't be so much time left for the Roman history. We can't go on again after eleven, because of the singing class and science."

"That's a good idea! Will everyone please remember not to hurry? I wonder if I could manage to drawl like Lorna?" chuckled Phœbe. "She always takes twice as long as anyone else to bring out her remarks!"

"I don't!" protested Lorna.

"Yes, you do. You needn't be so indignant; it's an accomplishment that we're all envying just at present, and longing to acquire!"

Preparation that evening, which ought to have been devoted to a steady recapitulation of forgotten dates and events, was conducted with the half-heartedness into which, under Miss Webb's slack rule, the attention of the class had unfortunately degenerated. The girls learnt with one eye on their books and the other on their neighbours; they made signs, talked on their fingers, and passed notes under the desks. Occasionally, when matters were really too bad to be ignored, Miss Webb would pluck up courage to venture a remonstrance, when there would be a brief interval of work; but within five minutes Aldred would be drawing caricatures on the fly-leaf of her grammar, Ursula uttering a vamped-up sneeze, and Dora signalling to Myfanwy behind Agnes's back. It was a farce of study, and at the end of two hours nobody had really made any headway or gained any fresh items of knowledge to use in the forthcoming ordeal.

Miss Webb gave a sigh of relief when the clock struck and her unpleasant task was over, and the girls popped their books untidily into their desks, and bolted from the room with a noise and hustling at the door such as they would not have dared to indulge in if Miss Bardsley had been there.

Next morning at nine o'clock the examination began. All took their seats, not at their own desks, but on a couple of forms placed in front of the blackboard, an arrangement insisted upon by Miss Webb, and carried out rather sulkily by the girls, who objected to be so directly under the teacher's eye. For once, Miss Webb really managed to enforce her authority. She separated Dora and Phœbe, the worst whisperers, peremptorily ordered Aldred not to loll, and told Ursula, who made an attempt at "baiting", to confine herself to answering questions, instead of asking them.

"Anyone who does not behave properly will take a forfeit, and this morning I shall subtract the forfeits from the general totals of the examination," she announced, looking quite stern and determined.

Rather impressed by this unexpected burst of spirit on her part, the girls sat up straight, and gave their minds to the subject in hand. It was certainly very necessary for them to concentrate their attention, for both facts and figures proved coy, and apt to refuse to come at the call of memory. Miss Webb was methodical: she held the register in her hand, and recorded every girl's answer immediately it was given, entering it as right or wrong. The roll that resulted was hardly one of honour. Nobody covered herself with credit, or made even a tolerable show of information. Often a question would pass round the whole Form, and the number of misses to each name began greatly to outbalance the marks. The girls looked solemn. It was one thing to neglect Miss Webb's lessons, but quite another affair to have their deficiencies thus relentlessly written down and submitted to Miss Drummond, who would be sure to institute a close enquiry into the reason for such a universal failure. Everything seemed to go wrong, even English literature, upon which Phœbe had counted. Instead of taking examples of metre, Miss Webb asked for the chronological lives of authors, and lists of their works; or for the plots and principal characters of Shakespeare's plays. Physical geography fared no better, for she demanded an exact definition of terms, and very precise explanations of various phenomena, and would take no half-replies. She had evidently prepared carefully for the examination, and (when she was not continually interrupted by irrelevant questions) had a far better grasp of her subjects than her pupils had supposed.

The time dragged on slowly. No morning had ever seemed so long, in the opinion of the girls. The weary rounds of literature and physical geography were succeeded by English grammar, with a discomfiting interval of French verbs. Aldred, surreptitiously consulting her watch, found it was just after half-past ten. Nearly half an hour, therefore, must elapse before lunch, and Miss Webb was already opening the Roman history primer. A look of horror passed along the Form. If their other subjects had been weak, this was decidedly weaker. Not one could remember a quarter of what she had learned. They had hoped that, as this subject was the last on the list, it would have been left so late that only a few pages could be covered; they certainly had not calculated on spending twenty-five minutes at it.

"I shall miss every turn!" thought Aldred. "It's dreadful! I've done so fearfully badly already. I believe I've only got about thirty per cent., and this will put me lower still. Miss Drummond never passes anyone on less than half marks. What can we do?"

She caught her breath, for an idea had suddenly flashed into her mind—an idea so daring, although so feasible, that its boldness almost frightened her. The small clock on the chimney-piece was not going, and Miss Webb generally kept time by the striking of the great clock that stood on the landing outside. If this clock could be put forward, the Form might be dismissed almost at once, instead of enduring the purgatory of any more horrible questions. Of course, there would be the danger of discovery, and consequently of getting into a serious scrape, but Aldred decided that something must be risked. A cold from which she was suffering gave her the necessary excuse.

"Please, Miss Webb, may I go for a clean pocket-handkerchief?" she asked.

Miss Bardsley would not have allowed any girl to leave the room during an examination, but her substitute was more lenient.

"You must be very quick, then, Aldred," she replied. "If you lose your turn I shall count it as a miss."

Aldred was up and out of the door in a minute. Once on the landing she glanced cautiously round, to make certain that nobody was in sight; then, boldly opening the glass front of the clock, she moved the hands till they pointed to three minutes to eleven. She returned to her place, ostentatiously displaying the clean handkerchief, just as the Form were wrestling with the Punic Wars, and by a lucky chance got the date of the battle of Cannæ, which was the only one she knew.

"What was the policy of Rome after this defeat?" asked Miss Webb.

Lorna could not remember, and the question passed on to Phœbe, who made a bad shot and answered wrong. Dora, Agnes and Myfanwy missed entirely, and Miss Webb was in the act of turning to Aldred, when the clock outside began to chime.

The teacher looked surprised, and glanced at her watch.

"I must surely be late!" she remarked. "I make it only twenty minutes to eleven."

"The landing clock is always right," volunteered Ursula, who, being doubtful herself as to the policy of Rome in that particular emergency, was as relieved as Aldred.

Miss Webb did not dispute the matter, but closed her book. Perhaps she also was not sorry to find it was lunch-time sooner than she had expected. The girls did not need telling to go; they rose in a body, and fled downstairs in hot haste.

"It isn't really eleven yet!" panted Aldred, when they had reached the comparative safety of the hall. "Oh, don't make such a noise! Miss Drummond will hear us, and come out and send us back. Let us rush outside, into the carving-shed!"

"We knew it wasn't!" exclaimed Dora. "We all had our watches. How clever of you to put on the clock! I guessed in a second what you'd done."

"I wonder how soon Miss Webb will find out the mistake?" said Myfanwy. "The bell hasn't rung yet; she didn't think of that!"

"Well, I never was so glad to finish any exam in my life," avowed Phœbe. "Wasn't it detestable?"

"As bad as the Inquisition. It was a regular torture chamber. My unfortunate brains have been on the rack for two hours."

"Not quite two hours!" chuckled Aldred.

"No, thanks to you! but for an hour and forty minutes, at any rate."

"We must all have failed hopelessly; not a single one of us can possibly have scraped through."

"Yes; but it would have been worse still if we had gone on missing for other twenty minutes."

"Rather! Miss Drummond will be quite cross enough as it is, when she looks at the register."

The girls judged it discreet not to go indoors too soon for lunch, waiting until the pantry was likely to be full, lest their early appearance might excite comment.

Singing was from ten minutes past eleven to twelve, and after that came science, with Miss Drummond, until one, both classes being held in the lecture-hall, so that there was no further lesson with Miss Webb that morning. A hockey match was played in the afternoon, which caused such excitement that the affair of the clock was forgotten for the time being; but it returned only too forcibly to the girls' minds, as they walked in to evening preparation. Would Miss Webb have found out the trick played upon her? And what steps would she take? They could not suppose that she would submit tamely, and ignore the whole circumstance. The most poor-spirited governess expects to keep her pupils in their classroom during school hours, even though she may not be able to exercise control over them while they are there. Would she show herself to be angry? or, worse still, would she report the matter to Miss Drummond? If so, trouble was in store for them.

Miss Webb, to their surprise, did neither. Her line of conduct was totally unexpected. She announced, quite calmly and briefly:

"I find that a mistake was made this morning in the time, and that you lost twenty minutes of your examination. By noting your marks during the ten minutes we spent on Roman history, I have been able to calculate the general average that you would have received during the entire half-hour, and, as a result, I have added one right answer and eight misses to each of your names on the register, and ten extra misses to Aldred Laurence, in lieu of forfeits."

The girls groaned inwardly, but they knew they were checkmated. If they dared to remonstrate, Miss Webb would probably expose the entire episode to Miss Drummond, so they wisely said nothing.

They certainly well deserved all they had received, particularly Aldred, who for once had been a little too clever. Her additional bad marks placed her at the bottom of the list, a position she had never occupied since she entered the school. She was very irate in consequence.

"I detest Miss Webb!" she declared. "It was a disgustingly mean way of her to take revenge on us. How could she tell I had altered the clock?"

"Any idiot could have guessed that!" returned Dora. "It was perfectly simple to put two and two together; we all knew."

"Well, I think it was nasty of her, all the same, and I mean to pay her out."

"If you can."

"Oh, I'll manage it somehow!"

"Better not boast too soon."

"All right! Just wait and see!"

It was perfectly unreasonable of Aldred to feel aggrieved because Miss Webb had asserted her authority; but she chose to consider that she had been unfairly treated, and that she was justified in nursing her wrath. She cast about for some means of turning the tables and annoying the mistress, but it was rather difficult to hit upon anything safe; she had no wish to get herself into serious trouble, and knew that any open defiance would be reported at head-quarters.

"It must be something she can't fix specially upon me," reflected Aldred; "something that any of us might have done. The whole class dislikes her, so I shall really be acting champion for the rest; only, I think I won't tell them anything about it beforehand; it shall come as a surprise."

After serious cogitation, she decided to chalk Miss Webb's chair, so that her black dress should show a white impression of the cane seat and back.

"She won't know," thought the girl, "and of course we shall none of us tell her, and she'll be going about the school looking such a guy! She'll wonder why everybody is smiling."

By nine o'clock next morning Aldred had her unpleasant surprise already prepared. She had managed to slip into the classroom before breakfast, and to chalk the chair thoroughly; and she now sat in her place, laughing in anticipation. Miss Webb was punctual. She entered in her usual rather flurried, undignified manner, and was about to close the door after her, when she suddenly opened it wide again to admit—Miss Drummond and Mabel! This was a totally unlooked-for event. Aldred had not known that Mabel was returning to class that day, as it had been reported that she was to remain in hospital for the rest of the week; and she certainly did not expect the head mistress. Mabel walked quietly to her own desk, and Miss Drummond (alas for Aldred!) sank straight down on the chair that Miss Webb at once politely offered her.

"I have come this morning, girls, to say a few words to you," began the Principal. "I have examined your marks for the last three weeks, and also the list of the viva voce examination that you had yesterday. I wish to tell you that I am extremely dissatisfied. I have never seen such a low average from the Fourth Form, and I am sure that you are none of you doing your best. I cannot possibly allow such a state of affairs to continue; it is a disgrace to the school! I am greatly disappointed, as I had hoped for better things from you. It has been a very hard task for Miss Webb, who kindly came to help us in an emergency, to take up another teacher's work at so short a notice, and I believed that you would have realized her difficulties, and have made an effort to help her in every way in your power. Instead of this, you appear to have taken advantage of Miss Bardsley's absence to neglect your work. As I cannot trust you to do your preparation adequately and thoroughly in your own classroom, I am going to make a new arrangement, and you will bring your books each evening into the lecture-hall, and sit with the Sixth Form, when I can myself see that you are not wasting your time. I have also asked Miss Webb to bring me the register at the end of each morning. I shall check your marks, and any girl who, as I consider, has fallen below her usual standard, will stay indoors during the afternoon, to learn the lessons in which she has failed."

If Miss Drummond looked grave, the Form looked utterly crestfallen and ashamed. The girls sat perfectly still, gazing at their desks, for nobody dared to meet the Principal's eyes. As for Aldred, she was filled with blank dismay. It was bad enough to be scolded for ill-prepared work, but what was going to happen when Miss Drummond got up from her chair? That she hardly dared to guess, and she would have given everything she possessed if she could have recalled her silly act. She was kept for some time in suspense, as the head mistress called for their exercise-books, and insisted upon examining them all minutely, and asking various searching and awkward questions as to the reason for so many mistakes and misspelt words, and such bad writing. The Fourth Form had never endured such an unpleasant quarter of an hour, and Aldred, between her present discomfiture and her apprehension of what was to come, felt as if she were passing out of the frying-pan into the fire.

The dreadful moment arrived at last. Miss Drummond handed the exercise-books back to the monitress, and rose up. Aldred's trick had answered only too well: the pattern of the cane seat was imprinted most plainly upon the head mistress's handsome dress. As she turned for an instant to consult the time-table, everybody noticed it, and a universal gasp of horror passed round the room. Miss Webb blushed hotly, and hesitated as if in doubt what to do; then, apparently plucking up her courage, she nervously informed the unconscious Principal of the state of affairs. Miss Drummond looked keenly first at the chair and then at the girls.

"Who is responsible for this?" she asked, in a constrained voice.

There was no reply.

"I will give whoever has done it one more chance to confess."

Still Aldred held her peace.

"Very well! I am exceedingly sorry for the girl who is wilfully concealing this; her own conscience will tell her how mean and despicable is her conduct. I consider this an act of such silly childishness and utter folly that in itself it is hardly worthy of my notice; the worst fault by far is the moral cowardice of the girl who has not the courage to own up, and offer an apology. It adds, I am sorry to say, to the bad opinion of the class that I have already been obliged to form. No, thank you, Miss Webb, there is no need to fetch a clothes-brush; I will ask one of the servants to attend to my dress, and to bring a wet cloth to wipe the chair before you use it yourself."

Aldred managed to avoid the other girls both at lunch-time and at afternoon recreation, making Mabel's return an excuse for devoting herself exclusively to her friend. She was most anxious not to be questioned on the subject of the chair. She was afraid she might be suspected of having played the trick, and did not see how she was to shield herself without a point-blank denial. Greatly to her relief, a bad cold from which she was suffering was pronounced influenza by Miss Drummond, who promptly packed her off to the hospital. She was not very ill, so it was a luxury to be an invalid for a few days, to miss classes, preparation, and practising, and to sit by the fire with an interesting book, and be fed up with beef-tea and jelly.

Mabel, who had completely recovered, was the only visitor allowed, a matter for which Aldred was devoutly thankful.

"It's perfectly horrid in school just at present," said Mabel, who ran up every afternoon to bring her news. "We have to do prep, with the Sixth Form, and Miss Drummond sits there herself, as well as Miss Forster, and keeps looking at us, to make sure that we're working. We hardly dare to lift our eyes from our books even for a second, and the room is so still that if anyone drops a pencil it makes quite a sensation. Before we go, each girl has to tell what marks she has gained or lost during the day. It's a regular confession! I can tell you, we have to be fearfully careful, and not make any more mistakes than we can help. It won't last long, though, because I hear Miss Bardsley is quite able to walk now with a stick, and she's to come back to class in a week from to-day."

"How blissful!" sighed Aldred. "Will Miss Webb be going, then?"

"Yes, on Saturday. I'm very sorry for her. Of course, she's not interesting, but she really did her best, poor thing, and I think the girls have behaved abominably. I wonder who chalked her chair?"

"Haven't they found out?"

Aldred's voice was very quiet, and she did not look at Mabel as she spoke.

"No. Everybody denies it flatly. I believe it lies between Phœbe and Dora. Ursula actually had the cheek to suggest that you must have done it! I was so angry with her!"

"You always stand up for me."

"I should think so!—I know you so well, dear. But Ursula is always jealous of you, and is inclined to be rather spiteful. I was obliged to take a very high hand with her. I said I should refuse to speak to anyone who connected your name again with the affair, and whoever spoke a word against you in future would quarrel also with me. That soon put them down. They're rather anxious to keep friends with me just now, because my aunt is staying at Chetbourne, and has sent me a box for Wednesday's *matinée* of *Julius Cæsar*. She asked Miss Drummond to allow me to go with one of the teachers and any friends I liked. I only wish you were wellenough! I invited Miss Webb promptly. She and Miss Forster are to take us."

"Oh, I'm so glad Miss Webb is going!"

"Yes, I think she's pleased; but I'm sure the girls don't deserve a treat, and I believe I'll ask the prefects instead of them. It would really serve the Form right to be left out. The way they treated poor Miss Webb was most unchivalrous."

"Unchivalrous? Is that the right word?" queried Aldred, rather puzzled. "I thought chivalry was only for men, and that it meant fighting in tournaments, with your lady's favour fastened to your helmet, like they did in the Middle Ages."

"That was part of it, but Mother says real chivalry is for everybody, for girls as well as boys, and we can practise it nowadays, because it simply means refusing to profit by anyone else's weakness. The knights in olden times were bound by their vows of knighthood to defend all who couldn't protect themselves, and—oh, dear! I can't explain myself properly, but don't you see that, when poor Miss Webb was so stupid and helpless, we were bound to behave well and learn our lessons, simply because she wasn't strong enough to make us on her own account, and it was so cowardly to take advantage of her? That would have been chivalry."

"I think I understand," said Aldred, staring hard at the fire.

"Yes, I knew you would, though the others don't in the least, I'm afraid. I'm glad to say they're a little ashamed of themselves, though, and they're quite nice to Miss Webb now. By the by, we've started a subscription in the Form, to make her a present before she goes. You'd like to give something, wouldn't you?"

"Very much indeed. Please put my name down for ten shillings."

"A whole half-sovereign! How generous you are! Most of us have only given half-crowns. We shall have twenty-five shillings now, and that ought to buy something really nice. Miss Drummond has promised to get it for us in Chetbourne. We don't know whether to choose a russia leather writing-case or a silver-topped, cut-glass scent bottle. I think you ought to have the casting vote, as you're giving so much more than anyone else."

"No; you settle it with the rest of the Form. I don't mind which, but it must be what the others like best."

"Well, I'll tell the girls what you say. I must go now, because Miss Drummond said I mustn't stay more than half an hour."

"Here are my keys," said Aldred. "If you'll unlock the workbox on my dressing-table, you'll find the half-sovereign in the lid. I can't go downstairs myself to fetch it."

"All right. I shall put your name first on the list."

"Oh, please don't! I'd rather have it last of all, if you don't mind."

The half-sovereign was conscience money, Aldred reflected sadly, as she returned to the fireside after bidding her friend good-bye. There was neither real pleasure nor merit in her gift, only a wish to make expiation for a fault that she dared not openly confess. She was like the Norman barons of old who gave large sums to the Church, to try to atone for the sins they still went on committing. She had no intention of explaining or setting the matter of the chair right, and her most earnest hope was that Mabel had succeeded in turning away the suspicions of the other girls from her, or, at least, in closing their mouths.

"They won't like to mention it any more, from fear of offending Mabel," she thought. "There's not one of them who would risk a quarrel. I expect I'm safe enough, and needn't worry about it: but oh, dear! Mabel thinks I'm so generous, and everything that's noble and splendid and good; I wonder what she would say, if she knew me as I really am!"

CHAPTER XIII. ALDRED PAYS A VISIT

Miss Bardsley, after nearly six weeks' absence from school, returned to her work with renewed zeal, and under her judicious rule the Fourth Form was once more the abode of order and attention, Miss Webb's brief interlude was soon an old story, and Aldred, except for the inward monitor that insisted on recalling unpleasant things, was troubled with no awkward reminiscences, or demands for an explanation which she was not prepared to give. The days were so full and so busy at the Grange that the girls were generally occupied with the affairs of the moment, and they had neither time nor inclination for recollections of an episode that had reflected so little credit upon the Form.

The spring term was often called "Indoor Science Term", because on Wednesday evenings Miss Drummond gave lectures that were intended as a preparation for the botanical and zoological rambles held during the summer. In May, June, and July the girls would be taken to search for wild flowers upon the downs, and for marine specimens of all kinds on the beach; and it was Miss Drummond's object to enable them to understand beforehand what they were likely to find. Sometimes she had a magic lantern and sometimes a microscope, and always she had something interesting to tell and to show, whether it was the marvels of plant life or the wonders of the seashore; and she could make her nature stories sound as thrilling as human ones.

There were attendances also at concerts and University Extension lectures at Chetbourne, to which the school went in relays; Miss Drummond liked to keep her girls in touch with the outside world, and did not wish them to remain continually shut up in the Grange, as if it were a nunnery. At mealtimes, though she banned politics, she generally discussed the news of the day and any great events that were happening, so that nobody could plead ignorance of current topics. At the Debating Society all kinds of questions were aired and argued, the opposing papers being entrusted to members of the Fifth and Sixth Forms, though the Lower School was allowed to express its opinion. The meetings were conducted in a strictly business-like and orderly manner worthy of a college society, having been organized by Miss Forster and Miss Bardsley, who were both well versed in Girton traditions. Aldred enjoyed them immensely, and, finding several opportunities of putting in a few words, did not hesitate to avail herself of her chances. She was not shy, and had perhaps inherited a propensity for discussion from her barrister father, so she was able to do herself ample justice, and to reflect credit upon the Fourth Form.

"You simply squashed Freda on the subject of Socialism," said Mabel, after one particularly successful little speech. "Her thesis went all to pieces when you nailed her to the point, and she couldn't prove anything. I wish I had such clear brains! You see the weak spots in people's arguments immediately, and then you can bowl them over like ninepins."

Mabel herself had no gift of eloquence, so she appreciated Aldred's powers all the more, and was immensely proud of her success.

"I can't imagine how I lived before you came to school," she sometimes remarked. "I was a wheel without an axle. Now everything I do centres round you, and the best of it is that Mother likes you too!"

To both of the girls the great event of the term had been the night spent by Mabel's mother at the Grange. Lady Muriel Farrington not only had a warm friendship for Miss Drummond, but held both her personality and her methods of teaching in admiration and respect, and for this reason had entrusted her with her daughter. When up in town, she sometimes paid flying visits to Birkwood, as she knew that Miss Drummond would allow her to do so without disturbing the general routine of the school. She had been exceedingly anxious to come on this occasion, partly because Mabel had had influenza, and she wanted to assure herself that she was quite strong again; and partly because she wished to meet Aldred, and ascertain what kind of girl had gained such an intense, dominating influence over her daughter. She was extremely particular as to the friendships Mabel should form, considering her choice of companions one of the most important features in her upbringing; and she had been most careful to allow no intimacy with anyone whom she had not herself seen and approved.

Mabel's letters had been so entirely filled with accounts of Aldred, to the exclusion of all other topics, that her mother felt it was high time to investigate this new and absorbing interest, and either give her sanction or take some steps to put an immediate stop to it. She had come to the Grange prepared to be very critical, and even censorious; but once introduced to Aldred, she had immediately fallen under the spell of her striking appearance and winning manners. No one knew better than Lady Muriel, however, that a picturesque exterior is not always an index to the mind; so she had a long talk with Miss Drummond about Aldred's character, and received such a favourable report that her fears were quite set at rest.

"I find your friend utterly charming," she said in private to Mabel, who was waiting in some anxiety to hear the verdict. "She is a most fascinating girl, evidently very clever and intelligent, yet so sweet, sympathetic, and winsome. I hear good accounts of her from Miss Drummond, who says she is entirely truthful, honourable, and straightforward (that was a question I particularly asked), and that she has a splendid reputation in the school. I am going to invite her to stay with us during the Easter holidays, and I hope very much that her father will allow her to come."

Mabel's rapture knew no bounds. She felt that she now had an official seal on her friendship, and she was longing to take Aldred home with her, and show her all the places that she had so often described.

"You'll see the house, and the park, and the lake, and our Alpine garden, and the tanks where we grow water-lilies, and our village club and library, and all Mother's pet schemes and hobbies," she announced gleefully. "We'll have a perfectly delightful time! Grassingford always looks particularly pretty in spring, when the trees are just coming out, and we'll get Father to take us about in the motor, so that you can see the country. Do you ride?"

"A little," said Aldred. Her achievements in that line were limited to a donkey at the seaside, but she was not going to confess her lack of experience.

"Then we'll have some glorious scampers on Belle and Beauty. Belle really belongs to Geoffrey—that's my stepbrother, who is married, and lives a mile away—but he lends her to me sometimes, and I am sure he will this Easter if I ask him. I must take you to see Geoffrey and Rosamond, and my wee niece Margot. She's only five months old, and I haven't seen her since she was in long clothes. Then there are my cousins at the Rectory; I know they'll simply fall in love with you. Oh, I'm absolutely longing to introduce you to everybody and everything!"

Aldred's father readily gave his consent to the proposed visit, so April fifteenth saw the two girls starting off together for the holidays. Miss Bardsley took them up to town, and placed them safely in the train at King's Cross; and they would have no further change until they reached Helmsworth, the junction for Grassingford.

They were in a very exultant and hilarious frame of mind, literally bubbling over with excitement. They managed to restrain themselves while they were under Miss Bardsley's eye, but directly the train started, and she had waved a final farewell from the platform, they allowed their wild spirits to have free play, and laughed to their hearts' content, waltzed between the seats, gave three cheers for the breaking-up, and chattered like a pair of magpies. Fortunately, they had the compartment to themselves, or they could not have indulged in such enjoyable frivolities except at the risk of being taken for lunatics.

"I managed to buy a box of chocolates and a bag of pears," announced Aldred, triumphantly producing a parcel. "Miss Bardsley said there wasn't time, but I got the newspaper boy to run to the refreshment room while she bought our tickets."

"She's given us about ten thousand last directions! Can you remember any of them?" said Mabel.

"Never a one!" laughed Aldred. "The engine was snorting so loudly, I couldn't hear a single word."

"And I could only catch a word here and there. I have a general impression that we aren't to hang out of the window, or speak to strangers, and that we must call the guard if anyone disagreeable gets into the carriage."

"Well, we had all that before, from Miss Drummond!"

"And not to lose our tickets!"

"As if we should! I always keep mine in this inner pocket; it was made in my coat on purpose. I'm much more likely to lose my temper with so many instructions—we might be babies, five years old! I wonder Miss Bardsley did not tie a luggage label to each of us, marked, 'Perishable Goods, at Owner's Risk'!"

"Yes, or 'Live Stock; Immediate,'" suggested Mabel. "Then we could have gone in the guard's van, and she would have been perfectly easy about us."

"There's only one outrageous thing that always tempts me," declared Aldred. "I do so want to pull down the cord, and stop the train!"

"A five pounds penalty if you indulge yourself, my dear."

"If I had five pounds I would, just for the sheer fun of it. All the people would rush out of the carriages, to see what was the matter. It would make such a sensation! By the by, how can the guard know who has pulled the cord? Suppose we simply looked innocent and astonished when he came to our compartment, he couldn't tell it was either of us; I don't think he could possibly know."

"As a rule, people only signal to stop in some great emergency, and then they would be anxious to call for help."

Aldred reached up, and put her hand tentatively on the cord.

"Shall I?"

There was real intention both in her eyes and in her voice.

"No, no! Aldred, stop! How can you think of doing such a dreadful thing!"

"I was only in fun, you dear goose!" said Aldred, with a rather forced laugh.

Mabel heaved a sigh of relief.

"Of course you were; what a silly I was to imagine you could be in earnest! You gave me quite a shock, all the same. I never saw anyone pretend so cleverly as you."

"Suppose I had pulled it? What would you have said to the guard when he arrived?"

"Why, naturally I should have told him at once."

"Would you, truly? Are you sure?"

"What else could I have done?" Mabel looked rather puzzled, and distressed.

"You wouldn't really—and have me fined five pounds?"

Mabel's face suddenly cleared.

"Oh, I understand what you mean!" she cried triumphantly. "No, I shouldn't have the chance, because you would already have told him yourself! You naughty girl, how you love to tease me! I'm extremely stupid at seeing jokes."

"Well, I haven't five pounds to waste, at any rate," replied Aldred, leaning back in her corner. "If I were a millionaire, I might be tempted. What's the time? I feel very much inclined to investigate that basket of lunch."

It was a six hours' run by express to Grassingford, and before they arrived at Helmsworth Junction the girls grew thoroughly tired of the journey. They made the lunch spin out as long as possible, ate pears and chocolates, looked at the illustrated papers, and varied the monotony by taking little walks up and down the corridor.

"I get so stiff if I sit still all the time," declared Aldred, in reply to Mabel's objection that Miss Bardsley would have preferred them to remain in their seats. "Besides, the better view is on this side of the carriage, and we can't see it properly from our compartment."

Mr. Farrington met them at Helmsworth Junction, where they changed from the express to a local train; and at Grassingford a motor was waiting to take them to the Hall.

Aldred thought she had never seen such a beautiful house, when a turn of the drive gave her a first glimpse of Mabel's home. It was built of grey stone, with towers and turrets, like a castle. The main entrance was under a carved archway that led into a courtyard, around which lay some of the principal rooms. A splendid wistaria covered one wall, and an equally fine magnolia another, while the greater part of the courtyard was devoted to an Italian garden, gay flower-beds in quaint shapes radiating from a fountain that stood in the middle.

Within, the house was as handsome as without. Mabel's father and mother had travelled much in foreign countries, and had picked up many treasures during their wanderings. There were lovely statues of Carrara marble, priceless Venetian glass, exquisite inlaid Italian cabinets, and carved oak cupboards from Germany; Chinese ivories and Indian lacquer work, Moorish lamps, rich Oriental draperies, Persian rugs, and Turkey carpets—to say nothing of pictures by old masters and modern artists, and a multitude of curios—embossed daggers, antique coins, Etruscan ornaments, old Nankin porcelain, Delft and Majolica, Roman vases, Greek urns, Sicilian jars and statuettes, and a medley of other articles, either ancient or modern, gathered from almost every corner of the world.

"It's like a museum!" said Aldred, when Mabel showed her some of the more interesting among the contents of the many cabinets.

"Yes. Dad and Mother have a perfect mania for bringing things home from abroad. They like to have specimens from every country they have been to, and each year the collection seems to grow bigger."

"Have they ever taken you abroad?"

"Not yet. Mother says I shall enjoy it so much more if I wait until I know enough really to appreciate it properly. I'm to go when I leave school, and spend a whole winter travelling in France and Italy and Greece; but Father says that before I start he will give me an examination in the old Italian masters and in Greek architecture, and if I don't pass he'll leave me behind."

Mr Farrington was a connoisseur in all matters of art and archæology; he took keen pleasure in adding continually to his already large collection, and considered the finding of a genuine Van Eyck in a second-hand dealer's shop at Rheims the greatest triumph of his life. His special hobby, however, did not absorb the whole of his time. He had represented his county in Parliament, and though he had lost his seat at the last election, he found much to occupy him in local affairs. He was a magistrate, a Poor Law Guardian, and Chairman of most of the charitable institutions in the neighbourhood, taking an active interest in the Hospital, the Blind Asylum, and the Orphanage. In all his philanthropic work, Lady Muriel was his right hand. She was slightly socialistic in her tendencies, and had preferred to marry plain Mr. Farrington, a commoner and a widower, though she could have made a brilliant match in her own circle. She was thoroughly happy, however, in the sphere that she had chosen, and, troubling little about society, gave herself to a career of usefulness. She personally superintended the Workhouse Orphanage, knowing every child there by name; and spent one afternoon weekly at the Blind Asylum, reading or singing to the inmates, and inspecting their knitting and straw plaiting. She had instituted a library and reading-room at Grassingford village, and was collecting funds to add a men's club and a lecture-hall; while the building of a mission church in an out-of-the-way corner of the parish was mainly owed to her energy and enterprise. A secretary was obliged to deal with her large correspondence, for she was practically interested in the temperance cause, in Women's Guilds of Help, the Fresh Air Fund, and the Boy Scout movements, all of which involved much trouble and considerable business ability, if they were to be a success.

In spite of her many duties, Lady Muriel always made time in the holidays to devote herself specially to her daughter. Mabel adored her mother, and was absolutely happy if she might accompany her on some errand of mercy, or take part in any of her various schemes. She liked to be asked to address envelopes, to write lists of names, or to discuss the programme for a village concert or the prizes to be offered at a flower show; and was already beginning to grow quite clever at organizing small local affairs. This Easter, Aldred was included in the conclaves, and made her first acquaintance with public and parish work. She had seen nothing of the kind at her own home, and it was a revelation to her to find how interesting it was to help other people. She and Mabel between them marked all the articles for Lady Muriel's stall at a bazaar, and were allowed to take special charge of the sweet department, selling dainty boxes of home-made bon-bons, and enjoying themselves immensely over it. They also arranged the sports for a party given to the Orphanage at the Hall, and worked very hard, distributing cups of tea and plates of cake; starting races and games of "Aunt Sally"; and generally amusing the children, and trying to give them a happy time.

"Aldred is simply splendid at this kind of thing!" said Mabel enthusiastically to her mother. "She keeps everybody going, and sees that all the little ones are playing too; they're so apt just to stand about and stare, you know. She thought of the loveliest games for them, and told them long fairy tales afterwards. They were absolutely delighted."

"I'm so glad to find she is a kindred spirit, and sympathizes with our work," replied Lady Muriel. "You have been most fortunate in your choice of a friend."

Though Aldred was thus initiated into the busy round of life at Grassingford Hall, the Farringtons did not neglect to entertain their guest, and provided plenty of amusement for her. She was taken in the motor to see all the sights of the neighbourhood—the beautiful mediaeval castle at Bonbridge, which still possessed moat, drawbridge, and portcullis in excellent preservation; the quaint old town of Bingdale, with its encircling walls and turreted gates; the valley of Malden, where the woods were in their spring glory, and the primroses were an absolute dream of delight; the ruined abbey at Dinvaux, which could boast of early Saxon carvings; and, last but not least, the view from the summit of Charlton Hill, whence five counties might be seen at once.

Though Mabel was Lady Muriel's only child, she had stepbrothers and stepsisters, who were married, and lived within reasonable distance. Several enjoyable visits were paid to their homes, for Mabel was very proud indeed of her various little nephews and nieces, and anxious to show them all to Aldred.

"I can't expect you to admire them as I do," she declared, "but they really are dears! I never know which is my favourite—Vera, with the thick, yellow curls; or Betty, with her big brown eyes. Miles is the cleverest, but Barbara says such funny things, and the baby is the most fascinating little rogue. They all came to spend Christmas Day with us, and it was so delightful!"

The cousins from the Rectory were frequently at the Hall, and were always ready to make up a set of tennis, or contribute to a musical evening. There were two girls, who had turned up their hair, and three boys, who, to Aldred's great astonishment, went to the same school as Keith, the eldest being actually in both his Form and dormitory. Aldred was quite excited at the discovery, and only wished her brother could have been there, to share the pleasure in her new acquaintances.

This holiday at Grassingford was the first visit that Aldred had paid alone, and she found it delightful to be free from Aunt Bertha's chaperonage, and a guest on her own account. It marked an epoch in her life to be thus transplanted into somebody else's home, and to see other people's ways. One thing that particularly struck her was that, in spite of their wealth and position, the Farringtons were extremely natural and unaffected. Mabel seemed quite accustomed to wait upon herself, and very ready to perform little services for others; and the family life was so simple, it might have served as a model for any cottage in the village. Aldred began to understand why Lady Muriel had selected Miss Drummond's school for Mabel, and to see in many of the arrangements at Birkwood the strong influence emanating from Grassingford.

She was very quick at picking up new ideas, and learnt many things at the Hall that she had not known before, whether points of social etiquette or fresh channels of thought.

"We shall make you into quite an antiquarian yet," said Mr. Farrington, who enjoyed explaining his curios to an interested listener. "You're already beginning to note the difference between Etruscan and Roman ornamentation, and to recognize a Greek coin when you see it. Tell your father to take you abroad when Miss Drummond has finished with you. It's the best coping-stone to put on any girl's education, and enlarges her mind in a wonderful way. In my opinion, six months on the Continent, studying the museums and art galleries, is worth three years at college. If he hasn't time to take you himself, he'd better let you go with us, and be a companion for Mabel."

"Oh, that would be too absolutely glorious!" exclaimed Aldred, with sparkling eyes.

CHAPTER XIV. AN ALARM

THE Easter holidays were for three weeks, and to Aldred each day seemed more enjoyable than the one before. She was thoroughly at home at Grassingford, and felt as if she could have wished to remain there for ever. She had become a great favourite with both Mr. Farrington and Lady Muriel: her bright ways entertained them, and they were glad also for Mabel to have a companion of her own age.

"You seem more like a sister to me than Nora or Adelaide," said Mabel one day. "They were both married when I was quite tiny, so I haven't seen a very great deal of them—not having them living in the house, I mean. And Sibyl and Ida at the Rectory are older than I am, too. Francis is the nearest to me—he's seven months younger—but then he's a boy, and that isn't in the least the same as having a girl friend, is it? I couldn't talk secrets to him! Mother says she will invite you as often as your father will spare you, so we can look forward to plenty more delightful times together. We shall call the little blue bedroom your room now, and it will always be ready and waiting for you to come back to it."

This was a very desirable state of affairs to Aldred. She was quite content to be half-adopted by the Farringtons, and to know she was such an acceptable and welcome addition to their household. She had never felt herself of any great importance at her own home, but here she was constantly considered, her opinion being asked and her wishes consulted; and she was well aware that with Mabel, at any rate, her will was almost law. She knew how greatly the rest of the girls at school had envied her this visit, and how it would raise her yet higher in their estimation when she returned to Birkwood. She would certainly have a good excuse in future for taking the lead in her Form, and letting the others plainly realize that they had not had her advantages.

It is at moments like this, when we are complacent with fortune, and think our happiness will never be moved, that Fate sometimes steps in, and with stern hand topples over all our schemes of self-advancement, and threatens us with utter desolation.

In the very last week of Aldred's visit, when she was at the height of enjoyment and gratification, and was beginning to consider herself almost a permanent fixture at the Hall, something happened—something that she might have anticipated, indeed, yet a contingency that had never occurred to her, and therefore as unexpected as unwelcome.

One morning, after the arrival of the post-bag, Mabel came running up to her friend with a look of bright animation on her face.

"From Cousin Marion!" she exclaimed, waving a letter enthusiastically in her hand. "She writes that she's staying at Evington, and wants us to go over and see her. I'm so glad, for I always wanted to introduce you to her."

It was a very innocent remark of Mabel's, but it came upon Aldred like a bolt from the blue. Cousin Marion—the very person of all others in the world whom she most dreaded to meet! The shock was so great that she was obliged to clutch with trembling fingers at the back of a chair, to support herself. On no account must she allow her emotion to be noticed, so she waited for a few seconds until her voice was steady enough to reply.

"Your Cousin Marion! Why, I thought she was in Germany!"

"So she was, and had intended to stay for a year; but the baths did her so much good that the doctor said she was practically cured, and might return to England for the summer, at any rate. I'll read you a piece out of her letter. She says: 'It is ages since I saw you, so ask your mother to bring you on Thursday, and include your heroic little friend in the invitation. I well remember seeing her on the pier at Seaforth, but had not the pleasure of making her acquaintance'—Why, what's the matter, Aldred? Are you ill?"

"I'm afraid I must be bilious this morning, I feel so shaky, and headachy, and queer!"

"Oh, I'm so sorry!" Mabel was at once all sympathy and concern. "You must come and lie down on the sofa, and I'll fetch you my bottle of eau-de-Cologne. There! Now you'll feel more comfortable. Would you like some soda water, or lemon juice? I believe it's a very good thing. I never remember your having a bilious attack before."

"I don't often," said Aldred, who, indeed, was seldom troubled with illness of any kind.

"I'll ask Mother if she can give you some medicine. You must get well by to-morrow! We couldn't possibly go to Evington without you. Think how disappointed Cousin Marion would be—and so should I, for I'm looking forward so much to taking you!"

In spite of herself, Aldred could not stifle a groan of despair.

"Do you really feel so poorly? Are you in pain? Perhaps we ought to send for the doctor. I'll go and fetch Mother immediately; she's a splendid nurse."

"No, no! Please don't!" cried Aldred. "I dare say I shall be better soon. I don't want to make a fuss, and upset everybody."

"You never do that, you're too unselfish and considerate. I know how ill you must feel, to mention it at all. I hope it's nothing serious!" and Mabel rushed off in quite a fever of excitement and alarm, to fetch her mother.

Lady Muriel was kindness itself.

"I expect you are a little overdone, dear child," she said. "We have been working you rather hard at sight-seeing, and perhaps letting you stay up too late. After the regular hours at school, the holidays are sometimes apt to upset young people. If your head aches, wouldn't you like to go to your bedroom, and rest quite quietly?"

"Yes, please," said Aldred.

She was devoutly thankful for the suggestion. Her one longing was to be alone, so that she might realize the blow that threatened her, and plan some means of averting it. Mabel's well-meant sympathy was almost agony in the circumstances; all she wanted was time to collect her thoughts. It was with a sense of intense relief, therefore, that she allowed herself to be put to lie down in her room. Lady Muriel drew the dark curtains across the window, rang for a siphon of soda water, and, having done everything in her power for the comfort of her young guest, took her departure, bearing with her the reluctant Mabel.

"Couldn't I just stay in the room, in case Aldred wants anything?" the latter pleaded. "I wouldn't speak a word."

"No, no! Aldred must be left quiet. If she can go to sleep, she may possibly feel better in the afternoon."

For once Aldred was quite glad to be rid of her friend. She hoped no one would disturb her for a long while, for she wished thoroughly to review the situation. This was indeed a catastrophe! A visit to Cousin Marion!—Cousin Marion, who would be sure to remember the appearance of the girl she had seen on the pier at Seaforth, and would realize in a moment that the two were not the same. She would no doubt express surprise at the difference, then questions would be asked, and the whole of the wretched affair would have to come out. It meant a complete exposure, and what the sequel would be Aldred dreaded even to imagine.

"They would call me a hypocrite and a deceiver, and so I am!" she thought bitterly. "I couldn't stay any longer in the house. I should be obliged to go home immediately; and what excuse could I give to Aunt Bertha for cutting short my visit? She would insist upon worrying the truth from me, and I should get into equal trouble at home. Keith would hear, and he would never forgive me. I don't believe I could even return to Birkwood, if all the girls at school were to know about it too."

She felt as if she were standing on the edge of a precipice, and that at any moment the frail ground might give way under her feet, and plunge her into the depths of the abyss. "Cousin Marion" seemed her evil genius; from the very first Aldred had been haunted by the fear of this meeting. It was wrong to wish people ill, but she regretted with all her heart that the German spa had effected so speedy a cure, and that the doctor had given permission for the invalid to return to England.

"I've been practising a fraud for the last eight months," she groaned, burying her face in the pillow. "I'll allow that much to myself, though I'll try to hide it from everyone else."

The agony she was enduring made her really feverish, for distress of mind is often far harder to bear than pain of body. She had gained all she wanted—popularity at school, a complete hold upon Mabel's affection, and a permanent invitation to a house where it was an honour to be received as a guest. And now, must all this be lost? The friendship had grown so necessary to her that she felt she could not live without it, and the prospect of estrangement and cold looks was appalling. At any cost she must manage to avoid this fatal expedition to Evington. She would sham illness, and ask to remain in her bedroom, so that they could not possibly include her in the party. To be sure, she would miss everything that was going on; but that was nothing, in comparison with the horror of an introduction to "Cousin Marion".

"If she comes over here, and asks to see me, I must have something infectious!" thought Aldred. "I wonder if I could rub anything on me to bring out a rash? Nettles might do it, only I can't go out to pick them. Was any wretched girl ever in such a desperate strait?"

She had had so little experience of ill health that it was rather difficult for her to feign symptoms. She had mentioned biliousness to Mabel on the spur of the moment, as it was the first idea that came into her head; but she had rarely suffered from an attack. She remembered, however, that it included a bad headache, and a disinclination to consume anything except soda water and biscuits.

"I shan't dare to touch proper meals, no matter how hungry I am," she reflected. "I expect I shall be nearly starving before to-morrow is over. I wish now I had said I had a sore throat, and then perhaps they would have been afraid of influenza, and have isolated me at once. Oh, dear! Mabel's tennis party is to be this afternoon, and I shall have to stop here and lose all the fun. Francis Farrington asked me to be his partner, and he plays so well that I'm sure we should have beaten all the others!"

She was shedding hot, bitter tears, not so much of regret for the long months of deception as of chagrin for the pleasure she must needs forgo. She was sorry, indeed, for the course she had taken, but it was not real repentance, only a wish to escape disagreeable consequences. Aldred had much to learn yet before she could set the desire for right above the love of approbation, or practise truth for its own sake.

When Lady Muriel and Mabel came to see her, about one o'clock, they found her with red eyes, a flushed face, and a genuine headache.

"You must lie still," said Lady Muriel, after feeling her hot hands. "You seem quite feverish, and mustn't on any account try to get up and race about at tennis; it would be the worst thing possible for you. I'm so grieved about it, dear!"

"It's most disappointing!" echoed Mabel. "I should like to stay and spend the afternoon with you, only it would be so rude to the other visitors. Perhaps I can keep running in between the sets."

"No, don't!" protested Aldred. "You're indispensable, and will be needed out-of-doors all the time. You mustn't bother about me."

At present she much preferred her friend's absence. She was afraid she might not be able to play her part adequately, and that the loving, watchful eyes might discover how little she really ailed. Mabel also would be sure to talk of nothing but her Cousin Marion, in the circumstances the most unpalatable topic possible.

There was no lunch for Aldred that day; she ate three biscuits, the utmost limit she felt she dared allow herself, and drank some soda water. She longed for roast beef and potatoes, but knew that an invalid who could demand such solid fare would scarcely receive credence.

"I suppose I can hold out until to-morrow evening," she thought, "but after that I shall be obliged to confess to an appetite."

She spent an extremely dull afternoon, listening wistfully to the sound of voices wafted from the tennis lawn. There were no books in her room, and she had not liked to ask for one, lest the request should be taken as a sign of her recovery. She was virtually a prisoner, and though her solitary confinement was self-constituted, it was no less wearisome on that account. She was able to indulge in a cup of weak tea and a slice of thin, dry toast at four o'clock, but her supper was as unsatisfying as her lunch, and she felt nearly famished when her solicitous hostess, after performing every possible kind service, finally left her arranged for the night.

Oh, how she yearned to get up next morning, and present herself at the breakfast table! It seemed intolerable to be obliged to spend another day in bed on starvation diet, but she was forced to restrain herself, and to look subdued and suffering when her attentive friends paid their early visit.

"I hoped you would feel better to-day," said Lady Muriel, with real concern in her voice. "I shall telephone for Dr. Rawlins, and ask him to call and see you first thing, before he begins his rounds. I feel responsible to your father for you, and it is well to be wise in time."

In spite of Aldred's protestations, Lady Muriel insisted upon sending for the doctor, who came promptly in response to her message. He examined his patient carefully, took her temperature, felt her pulse, and made her put out her tongue. He looked at her so attentively, and with such keen eyes, that Aldred could not help turning rather red. Did he know, she wondered, that she was only shamming, and was he going to denounce her as a humbug? His expression, however, was inscrutable, and after asking her several questions, to which she gave reluctant replies, he turned to Lady Muriel.

"I think you have no cause for uneasiness," he said. "It is merely a slight, temporary indisposition, which will soon pass. I will make up a bottle of medicine that ought to do her good."

"Mr. Farrington feared it might be motor sickness," observed Lady Muriel. "We have taken her about so much in the car, and the motion certainly affects some people."

Aldred caught at the suggestion as a drowning man clutches at a straw.

"Yes, it must be that. I'm sure it would make me sick to go in the motor again," she volunteered eagerly, raising herself on her elbow in her excitement, but sinking back languidly on to the pillow as she caught the doctor's contemplative eye.

"We wished very much to take her to Evington to-day, but I'm afraid she's not fit for it, poor dear child!" continued Lady Muriel.

"Let her stop at home, then," replied Dr. Rawlins, whose tone was hardly so sympathetic. "There is not the slightest need, however, for anyone else to stay on her account. She is much better left alone, and I forbid Mabel to come into her room until this evening."

"I should scarcely like to leave her," objected Lady Muriel anxiously. "It is such a responsibility to have the charge of someone else's daughter!"

"Install one of the housemaids as nurse, to see that she takes her medicine. No, Lady Muriel! As your physician, I insist that you go out for some fresh air. I have your health to consider as well as that of your young guest. She'll be in no danger while you are away."

The medicine arrived shortly after the doctor's departure—much too soon, in Aldred's opinion. It was a huge bottle, and was labelled: "Two tablespoonfuls to be taken every two hours". Anything more absolutely disgusting Aldred had never tasted; it seemed a combined mixture of every disagreeable drug in the pharmacopœia. Burke, an elderly servant, had been placed on duty in the sick-room, and informed her patient that she had received express orders from Dr. Rawlins himself not to omit a single dose.

"He told me most particularly, miss, that you were to have it," she announced, in reply to Aldred's violent objections. "He said it was most important, and if I couldn't get you to take it I was to telephone for him, and he'd come himself and make you!"

Aldred swallowed her nauseous draught at a gulp. She was not anxious to receive another professional visit. She had gathered from the doctor's manner that he diagnosed the nature of the case, though he did not care to offend Lady Muriel by expounding his opinion. It was ill-natured of him, the girl thought, to give her so severe a punishment; he could not understand her motives, and he might have treated her with more consideration. The one redeeming point of the medicine was that it utterly spoilt her appetite, and took away all desire for food; and she was enabled to show a genuine lack of interest in the beef-tea and jelly that were sent up for her.

Another long, long day dragged itself out. Aldred was in the very lowest of low spirits. She had ventured to beg for a book, but Burke promptly replied that the doctor had forbidden either reading or conversation, and had recommended her to keep perfectly quiet. So there was nothing for it but to lie with half-closed eyes, listening to the everlasting click of Burke's knitting needles, an irritating sound in itself, and made worse by its monotony. Aldred counted the spots on the muslin blindsand the roses on the chintz bed curtains, and tried to imagine faces in the pattern of the wall paper; she recited in her mind every piece of poetry that she knew, and as much as she could remember of the play the girls had acted at Christmas. She was even reduced to repeating French verbs, to relieve her utter boredom; and hardly knew whether to be glad or apprehensive when Mabel paid her a visit at seven o'clock.

"We've had a glorious afternoon," said the latter. "The road was free, so we spun along, and got to Evington in an hour and a half. Cousin Marion was so delighted to see us! She'd have been very disappointed if we hadn't gone."

"I'm so glad you did!" put in Aldred.

"But she was fearfully disappointed not to see you, darling, and so sorry when we told her you were ill. We talked about you for quite a long time. Didn't your ears burn this afternoon?"

"I didn't notice."

"Well, I'm sure they ought to have done so. I won't tell you all we said, because you don't like to be praised, but you'd have been very flattered if you'd heard. Cousin Marion remembers you quite distinctly."

"I shouldn't know her."

"I dare say not; you wouldn't notice her particularly at Seaforth. By the by—isn't it absurd?—Cousin Marion actually thought you had sisters!"

"Why should she suppose so?" Aldred's voice was uneasy.

"She said they were with you, and so like you—one a little older, and the other younger."

"How ridiculous!"

"Yes, I told her you are the only girl. Perhaps you had some friends with you at the concert?"

"I expect I had. I really can't remember now."

"And another funny thing: she said she was sure your name was Mary."

"So it is, Aldred Mary, after my mother," replied Aldred, thankful to be able to say what was really the case, though she knew her truth was only further aiding her deception.

"That explains it, of course. I suppose the newspaper forgot the 'Aldred', and simply put 'Miss Mary Laurence'. Newspaper reporters often make mistakes."

"So do other people," thought Aldred, though she did not say it aloud.

"We were so anxious for Cousin Marion to come over to Grassingford," continued Mabel. "Mother wanted to bring her home with us this afternoon, to stay for a few days, but she wouldn't be persuaded. She says her doctor has forbidden her to motor."

"Then won't she be coming at all?" Aldred tried to speak unconcernedly, but she could not quite banish the anxiety from her tone.

"Ah, I knew you wanted to see her! No, dear, I'm sorry to say it's impossible. She's still too great an invalid to take more than a gentle little drive in a landau. She might have come by train, but she decided that it would be too much for her. I'm afraid you won't meet her now, as we go back to school on Wednesday."

So the danger was over! The relief was so intense that Aldred had to bury her face in the pillow to hide her feelings. Her ruse had been successful, and for the present, at any rate, she might consider herself safe.

"I've tired you out!" exclaimed Mabel self-reproachfully. "I might have remembered your poor head. How stupid and thoughtless I am! Good night, darling! I've missed you terribly all to-day. It will be absolute bliss when you're yourself again."

When Dr. Rawlins arrived next morning, he found that his bottle of medicine had been like the quack nostrums advertised in the newspapers, and had worked a lightning cure.

"I knew it would have a beneficial effect," he remarked, with a twinkle in his eye that only Aldred understood.

"Then you think she may really come downstairs, Doctor?" asked Lady Muriel, who was still a little worried.

"Most decidedly! There's nothing to prevent it. The sooner she's out in the fresh air the better. A game of tennis would be the best tonic I can prescribe. Her medicine? Oh, well, she's so wonderfully improved that I'll excuse her from finishing the bottle! She might keep it, in case she's ever troubled with the same symptoms again."

"Isn't he nice?" said Mabel enthusiastically afterwards. "I always like Dr. Rawlins so much. I think he's the kindest man I know. I often say it's almost worth while being ill, to have him come to see one. And he's simply enormously clever!"

"He certainly seems to cure his patients quickly," replied Aldred, with doubtful gratitude.

CHAPTER XV. ON THE RIVER

ALDRED had found the family at the Rectory a decided addition to the attractions of Grassingford. The girls, although they were "out" and "finished", were very companionable, and made much of both Mabel and her friend; as for the boys, when first their stiffness and shyness had worn off, they proved exceedingly jolly. Mabel was on excellent terms with her cousins, who were frequent visitors at the Hall, and might always be counted upon to take part in any fresh plans or projects.

On the Monday following Aldred's sudden illness and recovery, she and Mabel were invited to spend the afternoon at the Rectory. It was their last opportunity, as they were to start for the Grange first thing on Wednesday morning, and Tuesday must be reserved for packing and saying good-byes.

"We're all off this week," said Francis Farrington, as the visitors were welcomed and borne away into the garden. "We are due back on

Thursday, worse luck! I could have done with another fortnight. I hate school!"

"You lazy boy!" said Mabel.

"All right! I'm lazy if you like. I wonder, though, how you'd care to change places with me, and be in old Barlow's Form. He's the most fearful Turk, and gets as savage as a bear if one doesn't construe properly—very different from your Miss Drummonds and Miss Bardsleys."

Mabel laughed.

"Shall I go to Stavebury with Piers and Godfrey, and you can take Aldred back to Birkwood?"

"Done! It would be jolly good fun—for me, at any rate. I should be living in clover."

"Except for the work—you mustn't forget that."

"Work! I don't call your lessons work! They seem mostly cookery and wood-carving, varied by hockey and tennis."

"Don't be nasty! We have to use our brains during school hours and prep., though we do have jolly times in between. You needn't laugh at cookery, for you were ready enough to eat the queen's cakes that Aldred and I made last week."

"I'm not laughing. They were delicious; I only wish you'd make some more! All the same, don't you suppose that the amount of grind you go through is anything like equal to ours; if you had old Barlow to set your exercises, you'd soon find out."

"Well, you don't want girls to swat as hard as boys," said Piers, who was rather fond of airing his opinions on various topics. "Spoils their complexions! They're put in the world to do the ornamental."

"Are we, indeed, sir? Thank you!" replied Mabel, with a mock curtsy. "I wonder what you know about complexions, by the by? As for exerting ourselves, we can do quite as much as you, in our own way."

"Granted, so long as you keep to your own way, and don't poach on ours!"

"Here, you two, stop bickering!" said Godfrey. "When Piers begins an argument he'll hold forth for hours together. We don't want to discuss 'Women's Sphere', or the 'Education Question'! Leave these to the Debating Society, and let's enjoy ourselves! How would Mabel and Aldred like to come with us to Holt's farm? The pater wants us to take a message there. It's only three miles away, and Aldred, at any rate, hasn't seen the river."

"I've never been to Holt's farm either," said Mabel "I haven't even crossed the ferry."

"It would be better fun than tennis," agreed Piers. "Our court seems a very poor affair after the one at the Hall; it's hardly worth playing on."

Both Mabel and Aldred felt disposed for a walk. It was a fresh and bright afternoon, and the prospect of seeing a new part of the neighbourhood was attractive. Mabel often went out riding on horseback, or in the motor with her parents, and thus knew the high roads for many miles around; but unless she accompanied her cousins, she seldom explored the lanes and by-paths.

"In one way it's much jollier to go on foot," she declared. "You can stop to pick flowers, or climb on to banks; and I do so enjoy getting over stiles!"

"You'll have enough of them this afternoon," laughed Francis. "There are at least twelve to cross, if we go through the fields by the river."

"Are Sibyl and Ida coming with us?" asked Mabel.

"No, they think the Grants may be calling, so they don't dare to be out. Would you each like a stick? We've an assortment here, in the umbrella stand; this is a nice little one with a crooked handle for Aldred, and I can recommend this cherrywood for you, Mabel."

The country at Grassingford was exceedingly pretty. It was not grand, nor mountainous, but was well wooded and dotted with picturesque farmsteads. There were deep lanes, with high hedges, which at the present season of the year were a mass of flowering hawthorn; and every little copse and spinney showed blue with hyacinths. There was a delightful spring-like feeling in the air, that combination of sun and breeze, bursting buds, and opening leaves which promises returning summer, renews all the vitality of human beings, and sets us singing like the birds for the mere joy of being alive. Such days seem echoes of the Golden Age slipped out of Paradise, days when we want to forget houses and cities and civilization, and go into the fields to learn the lessons Mother Nature has to teach us—lessons as old as the hills, but fresh every year, when they are fraught with the mystery of new creation.

The path to the river lay across fields, and it would have been difficult to find it without a guide who knew the way. It zigzagged between patches of growing corn and hay, turned sharply round corners, and for a short distance even led down the half-dry bed of a stream.

"The fact is, it isn't a proper path at all," said Francis. "It's only a short cut that we found out for ourselves; it saves a mile."

"It's lovely! I should want to come by it, even if it were a mile longer instead of shorter," said Aldred, who always preferred the romantic to the practical. "How do you manage when the stream is full?"

"Oh! we can't get along unless we wade. We came once last winter and had to turn back; the water was up to this stone, a regular rushing torrent, very different from what it is now. Can you scramble over this wall? Take my hand. Now, you see, we are in the lane, and we shall get to the ferry in a minute."

The old-fashioned ferry was a most picturesque feature of the tidal river, a large, flat-bottomed boat being worked on chains, which stretched from one bank to the other. Sometimes a horse and cart, or a flock of sheep, would be taken over, as well as ordinary passengers, the whole cargo being slowly wound across the water by the ferryman, who turned a creaking windlass on board. The whole arrangement seemed a delightful survival of days when no one was ever in a hurry, and life revolved on leisurely wheels, as different from our modern rush and excitement as a bullock cart is from a motor car. Aldred was fascinated with the quaint contrivance, and anxious to cross on it; but Francis had other projects.

"I say! Wouldn't it be jolly if we could get Pritchard to lend us his small boat, and row ourselves up the river to Holt's farm?" he suggested.

"Ripping!" said Godfrey. "Why not?"

"It's not a bad idea," said Piers; "but have you fellows brought any money with you? for I haven't."

"I've left my worldly wealth in my other trousers' pocket," admitted Godfrey. "Francis, you'll have to pay the piper."

"All serene!"

"I wonder what he'd charge?"

"I don't know, but we can ask him. Here he is now. You'd like a row, girls, wouldn't you?"

"Immensely!" said Mabel.

"Oh, I do hope he'll let us! It would be such fun!" added Aldred.

"We want to know if you'll hire out your small boat," said Francis to the ferryman. "What would you charge to let us have it for an hour, or perhaps a little longer?"

Pritchard stroked the short, grey stubble on his chin reflectively.

"Are you sure you can manage a boat amongst you?" he queried.

"Of course!" answered Francis, rather loftily. "We all know how to row; we're as accustomed to the river as you are yourself."

"I don't know about that," said Pritchard, smiling. "You haven't got fifty years at the back of you yet. It'll take a fairly strong arm to pull the lot of you, especially against the tide. The boat's bespoke for half-past four too."

Francis complacently felt his muscles, as if to suggest that he was quite equal to the occasion.

"Say what you want for it," he replied.

"We'll undertake to bring it back in heaps of time," interposed Godfrey.

"How would half a crown be for the hour?"

"I'm afraid I've only got a two-shilling piece with me," said Francis, coming down a little from his high horse.

"And two shillings is the usual price without a boatman," added Piers.

"I'd a deal rather you had a boatman with you, only I can't spare the time. Well, I don't want to be hard on you; we won't quarrel over the sixpence. One of the oars is spliced, and you'll have to be careful of it. Thomas, help to run down the boat, will you?"

With the help of two strong pairs of arms, the *Maid of Llangollen* went grating along the shingle towards the river. She was short and broad, and evidently not intended for racing. The boys inspected her with a critical eye.

"She's a dreadfully heavy old tub," said Piers, "but she's seaworthy, and I dare say we shall have some fun out of her."

"Who's to row stroke?" said Francis.

"I am, of course," answered Piers, in a tone that admitted of no dispute. "Godfrey may have the other oar, and you can steer."

"And what may we do?" asked Mabel.

"The ornamental, of course! You and Aldred can just sit and enjoy yourselves."

"We'd much rather take our share of the work."

"Well, perhaps we'll let you have a turn by and by, if you're so particularly anxious."

Pritchard by this time had run the boat down the bank and rowed her round to a small jetty, from which it was easy to board her.

"There's a nice place for you misses here, in the stern," he said. "Be careful! It's wet in the bottom. There's a tin can under the seat, if you want to bale her out."

It was most delightful on the river. In spite of her clumsy build, the *Maid of Llangollen* seemed to glide along in the easiest manner. Mabel and Aldred leaned back luxuriously in the stern of the boat, trailing their hands in the water, and watching the regular dip of the oars. The party were all in the best of spirits, and began to exchange jokes and sing songs.

"Yo di diddle diddle dee,Five jolly sea-dogs are we.We've to heave the anchor, and our friends all hankerTo join our companee!"

chanted Francis.

"Is that original?" asked Mabel.

"Of course it is! Don't you know my remarkable style by this time? I'm the coming poet!"

"A modest one, at any rate!" laughed Aldred.

"Oh, it doesn't do to hide one's light under a bushel! Nobody believes in you nowadays unless you advertise yourself."

"I thought self-praise was no recommendation."

"Quite a mistaken idea! To alter Shakespeare a little, one can say: Sweet are the uses of advertisement!"

"You must give us a better specimen of your poetry before we'll believe in you," said Mabel. "I shall call you a doggerel rhymster at present."

"All right! How do you like this?—

'Tis unkind, most naughty Mabel,Your poor cousin's lines to labelAs but trashy, worthless rhymesOnly fit for strolling mimes.Don't you see the genius burningIn each verse that I am turning?Some fine day—I'll give a hint—You may see my name in print!"

"It will be among the advertisements, then," said Aldred. "I suppose you really made up that one?"

"Certainly; a poor thing, but mine own," said Francis, with an attempt at a bow. "You needn't clap, because, after all, I'm rather modest, and it might raise a blush on my cheek."

"We weren't going to—though we'd like to see the blush, I assure you!"

"Would you like another verse? I'm waxing poetical: I suppose it's a matter of practice."

"No, thanks, we've had enough!" exclaimed Piers. "You'd better drop poetry, and stick to steering; you've nearly bumped us into the bank more than once."

"Can't I have a turn at rowing now?" asked Mabel. "You promised I should."

"All serene!" said Piers. "You may take my oar. Steady! Don't go upsetting us!"

"Then let me have yours, Godfrey," said Aldred. "I do so want to try too!"

"It's the spliced one," said Godfrey, "but I don't suppose you're likely to smash it."

It was the first time Aldred had ever tried to row, and it was much harder work than she had supposed.

"Look here! you're not feathering your oar properly," commented Piers. "You oughtn't to put it in so deep, nor bring it out with a jerk. Watch how Mabel is doing it."

"Oh, I know!" replied Aldred rather impatiently. She did not like to receive any criticisms, and, setting her feet firmly, gave a mighty pull. The next instant over she went on her back, and away went the oar into the water. Luckily, Piers had plenty of presence of mind. He put out his hand and caught the oar just as it was floating past the stern.

"We very nearly lost it!" he remarked. "It was luckily near enough to reach."

Aldred retired into the stern again, feeling decidedly crestfallen, all the more so as Mabel was getting on nicely. Her friend's efforts did not last long, however; she soon declared that her hands would be blistered, and relinquished her seat to Piers, who was longing to be in command again.

"It's far better for you to look on," he said. "Girls aren't much good at rowing."

"How about Grace Darling?"

"Oh, well, she was the exception that proves the rule!"

"Here we are, close to the farm!" exclaimed Godfrey. "We must try to find a good landing-place."

They decided that it was not worth while for all to leave the boat, so Francis volunteered to get out. He ran across a field to the farm, delivered

383

his father's message, and was back almost before the others had time to grow impatient.

"We must turn her about now," said Piers. "Oh, thunder! It's later than I thought; we shall have to hurry up, if somebody wants the boat at half-past four. Francis, you had better take Godfrey's oar."

Once on the river again they found that their return was a very different matter from their former journey. The tide was running out in a fast and strong current against them, and though Piers and Francis tried their utmost, they could scarcely make any headway. It was a heavy boat for two boys to manage, and the possibility of their being back in time seemed doubtful.

They had gone perhaps two-thirds of a mile, when suddenly there was a harsh, grating sound under them.

"Hallo! We've run aground!" cried Francis.

This was bad news indeed, but it was only too true. They had not known that a sandbank was there; on their way up they had passed over it easily, but the tide was going out so rapidly now that already it was almost uncovered. The boat seemed stuck fast, and although the boys made every effort, they were not able to free her with their oars. They pulled off their boots and stockings, and, jumping overboard, tried to push or drag her from the shoal, but all to no purpose; she was sunk so deeply in the soft sand and gravel that they could not move her an inch.

"What are we to do?" asked Godfrey.

"Stay where we are, I suppose, till the tide floats her off again," replied Piers.

"It's a pleasant look-out, anyhow!" said Francis.

"And Aunt Winifred will be wondering where we are, too, if we don't turn up for tea," added Mabel.

"It's a pity we didn't bring some tea with us, and we could have had a picnic," said Aldred. "I'm so thirsty!"

"There's nothing to offer you but the river, I'm afraid."

"No, thanks, it's too muddy for my taste."

"'Water, water, everywhere, nor any drop to drink!'" quoted Piers.

"And what our thirst will be ere long,One doesn't like to think!"

rapped out the irrepressible Francis, whose muse was not quenched even by this disaster.

"We're in a fix, and that's the solemn truth," said Godfrey.

They were, indeed, in a most awkward predicament. By the time the tide was high again it would be midnight, and they certainly could not see to row in the dark. There was every prospect that they would have to spend the night on the shoal, without tea or supper, or extra wraps.

They waited for perhaps an hour and a half, while the sandbank grew to quite a respectable island. There were woods on either hand, so it was most unlikely that their plight would be noticed from the shore; their only chance of relief was from a passing boat—a faint hope, for as a rule there were very few craft on the river.

"I begin to understand how a shipwrecked mariner feels when he's waiting for a sail!" said Aldred.

"I believe I'd trade my watch for a plateful of bread and butter," said Francis.

Godfrey suddenly stood up in the stern and waved his hat.

"A boat! A boat!" he cried eagerly. "Hallo, there! Hi!"

Francis and Piers immediately joined him in making such a noise that nobody but a deaf person could have ignored it. The fisherman who was rowing in their direction evidently realized the situation; he signed to his mate to stay in the channel, then, clambering overboard, came wading in his tall boots on to the island.

"Why, it's Sam Ball, who sings in the choir!" exclaimed Godfrey.

Their rescuer regarded them with a rueful grin.

"You've got yourselves into a precious mess here!" he said briefly.

"Can you help us to pull her off?" returned Piers anxiously.

"Pull her off! Couldn't do it with a team of horses! She'll have to stop where she is until the tide floats her. I'll take you off, and that's the best I can do for you. Hoist one of them young misses on my back; I'll carry them first."

He waded with Aldred to his own boat, returning to fetch Mabel, and the boys scrambled after him as best they could.

"It's Pritchard's boat, isn't it?" he said. "I'm passing the ferry, so if you like I'll tell him what's happened. If you cross through the wood there, and turn to the right of the iron gate, you'll find your way straight to the village."

The boys went home in rather subdued spirits.

"We shall have to go down to the ferry this evening and explain things to Pritchard," said Piers. "I hope he won't cut up rough about the boat."

"I'm afraid he'll want compensation," said Francis, "I split that spliced oar with trying to shove her off."

"What an abominable swindle! It'll take half our next term's cash. I don't believe the pater will stand it for us."

"I'm sure he won't, after that little affair of the rifle and old Carter's dog!" put in Godfrey.

"Well, never mind if we have to pay up. We shall survive it, I suppose," said Francis. "We're making Mabel and Aldred look quite uncomfortable. It seems a stingy trick to take them out rowing, land them on a sandbank, and then spend all the rest of the time growling over the damage. But I know one thing: if ever we have that boat again, I'm going to make a chart of the river first, and mark down all the shoals!"

CHAPTER XVI. AN OPPORTUNITY

MABEL and Aldred returned to Birkwood on terms of even closer intimacy than before. There is always a difference between a companion who is only an acquaintance at school and one who shares the many little home associations and interests that make a bond of union apart from the other girls, and give innumerable subjects for those confidential talks which are the chief joy of friendship. The bedroom that had once seemed entirely Mabel's was now taken up with joint possessions. Aldred had helped to buy the new gipsy table that stood in the window, and had embroidered half of the table-cloth that covered it. The cushion for the wicker chair was a present from Lady Muriel to both the girls; and the knick-knacks that they had brought back with them were so entirely mixed that it was difficult to tell which belonged to either. "All things in common" was Mabel's motto, and Aldred, who certainly got the better of the bargain, was only too ready to agree.

It was high summer now at the Grange—glorious, golden days, when the sea breeze, or the wind from the downs, tempered the warm sunshine, and established Birkwood's reputation for a bracing climate. As many lessons as possible were held in the garden. Each form had its own special open-air classroom, and the girls easily accommodated themselves to working out-of-doors.

"When you're accustomed to it, it's no harder than working in the house," said Ursula. "Of course, just the first day we can't help staring about a little, to look at birds and things, but we soon get over that. We're none of us babies, to need four walls round us to keep our attention, and it is so very much nicer."

The Fourth Form "room" was at the corner of the big lawn, under the shade of a large oak, almost exactly in the place where Aldred had made her statue of Venus in the snow. How different the garden looked now in its summer dress! It was difficult to believe that the asphalt court had ever been frozen and turned into a skating rink.

"I shall never forget our ice carnival," said Miss Bardsley. "My ankle is hardly strong yet, and I'm afraid it will always be thicker than the other."

"You had a long holiday, though," urged Phœbe: "six whole weeks!"

"An enforced holiday is no pleasure; I would far rather have been at my work. I don't feel that you've made up yet for all you lost while I was absent."

"Is that why we have a double allowance of Roman history now?" queried Ursula.

"Certainly it is. You must finish the book this term, if we have to take extra lessons on it. You naughty girls, don't pull such faces! You ought to be interested in the Emperors."

"Father says some day he'll take me to Rome, and I shall see all their marble statues," observed Mabel.

"Lucky girl!" said Miss Bardsley. "I was fortunate enough to spend one Easter holiday in Rome, and saw the busts of the Emperors at the Capitoline Museum. They're the most beautiful likenesses in the world. You'll appreciate Roman history when you've been to the Forum, and the Colosseum, and all the other famous places."

"Why can't we study history that way?" suggested Ursula. "Suppose you were to take us all to Rome for a month, and we learnt about Romulus and Remus when we were sitting on the Capitoline Hill, and about Trajan in Trajan's Forum, and Diocletian in Diocletian's Bath, and Nero at the Colosseum: it would be so interesting, and we should really remember it!"

"No doubt that is the ideal method; but think of the expense! I am afraid most parents would grumble at the school bills, if teaching history involved a visit to the scene of each occurrence. No! You're supposed to study all this beforehand, and then, when you have a clear idea of ancient and mediaeval times, you can go abroad with an understanding of what you'll see."

"But why shouldn't there be a mutual exchange of schools?" continued Ursula, who liked to discuss questions with Miss Bardsley. "Suppose a class from an Italian school were to come to the Grange for a month, and we were to go and take their place: they'd learn English games, and we should see the old temples and amphitheatres, so we should each have something we couldn't get in our own country."

"It would certainly be a splendid means of learning languages, especially if such an exchange could be effected with a French or a German school. But I fear we are not ripe for that yet; there are too many difficulties in the way of such international visiting. In years to come perhaps the State will organize it, and we shall see little bands of children starting with their teachers to study foreign life and get rid of insular prejudices. It would have to be a special department of the Board of Education."

"If Father gets into Parliament again I'll ask him to bring in a Bill for it," said Mabel. "He's very keen on Secondary Education."

There was so much to be done at Birkwood during the summer term that the days did not seem nearly long enough, though the school rose half an hour earlier than in winter. The girls played cricket as well as tennis, worked in their gardens, and were taken for walks on the downs or on the shore. These expeditions generally had a scientific object in view, wild flowers being brought home to be pressed and added to the school collection, or the pools left by the tide investigated for specimens to enlarge the already flourishing aquarium. There is an old saying: "If you are good, you are happy"; but Miss Drummond believed in the reversing of that moral process, on the theory that "if you are happy, you are good", considering that young girls, at any rate, would be more likely to grow up with nice minds and true instincts if all their environment was beautiful, and their days were filled with pleasures calculated to elevate and refine. There were few of her pupils on whom her system had not the desired effect, and the one or two failures had been gently eliminated, so as not to contaminate the rest.

With Aldred especially Miss Drummond's method had worked well. She was very different from the ill-disciplined girl who had arrived at the Grange last September. The pleasant but carefully ordered regime seemed quite to have counteracted her aunt's injudicious management, and she would have been utterly ashamed now of behaviour in which a year ago she had gloried. This improvement was largely due to Mabel's influence. The latter's implicit faith in her began to rouse a desire to become actually what her friend believed her to be. She conquered many little weaknesses, lest Mabel should notice them. She had soon found that a cross word or an unkind speech, the evasion of a rule, or the shirking of some small duty, would bring a look of puzzled surprise to the latter's face; and rather than that Mabel should be disappointed in her, she kept a tight hand on herself, and would repress anything of which her friend did not approve. It was not the loftiest of motives, but it was the first time in her life that Aldred had ever really tried to join the ranks of those who are striving upwards, and even a faint-hearted effort is better than none at all.

There are occasionally people in this world who seem to have the faculty of drawing the very best out of those with whom they come in contact. They create their own atmosphere, and by the strength of their winning personalities rouse all the sleeping good in others. Such a friend was Mabel, and Aldred, despite her false position, could not fail to be influenced by daily living with a character so much sweeter and more self-controlled than her own. Though she was still content to take credit that was not her due, she was gradually altering her standard, and beginning slowly but surely to realize that life consists of far more than the gratification of the moment, and that righteousness is a higher goal than pleasure.

One morning, when the girls were sitting chatting round the sundial at eleven o'clock recreation, they noticed the telegraph boy from Chetbourne ride up on his bicycle and deliver a message at the door.

"No alarm for any of us, I hope!" said Phœbe. "It's rather silly, but I always feel a little scared when I see one of those yellow envelopes, and wonder if anything has happened at home."

"And yet people send telegrams about everything," said Myfanwy. "Probably this is only to offer Miss Drummond seats at a concert, or to tell her somebody's coming to visit the school."

"Oh, I dare say! But I get nervous, all the same; telegrams so often mean bad news."

Phœbe's apprehensions were justified in this case, though not on her own account. When morning school was over, the prefects reported that Miss Drummond had been suddenly called away.

"She has a mother living somewhere in the North, who is most seriously ill, and is scarcely expected to recover," explained Freda Martin. "She sent for a carriage at once, and started off to catch the 1.13 train at Chetbourne. I hope she'll arrive in time. She was most fearfully upset and distressed, and couldn't make any arrangements; she only said Miss Forster was to take her classes, and she would come back as soon as she could."

This unexpected event naturally caused great commotion at the Grange. Miss Drummond had never before been absent during term time, and, though the other mistresses did their best in the circumstances, all seemed rather helpless without her. The principal taught the Sixth Form herself, and also took science classes throughout the school, so it was difficult to arrange to supply her place, it being impossible to engage another teacher, as had been done during Miss Bardsley's absence. By combining some of the classes, and omitting the science, Miss Forster managed to arrange fairly well; but as she had not been definitely placed in command over the entire establishment, she did not like to usurp too much authority on her own account. No one, therefore, seemed actually at the head of affairs, or really responsible; and there was a general feeling of disorganization and slackness.

"It's horrid without Miss Drummond!" said Mabel. "Nobody seems to know anything, or to be able to do anything while she's away. Even the medicine cupboard is locked up."

"That's no loss, I'm sure!" returned Aldred.

"Well, as it happens, it is. I've such a splitting headache, I was going to beg for sal volatile."

"Perhaps Miss Forster may have some."

"I asked her, but she hadn't; and then Mademoiselle came fussing along, wanting to know what was the matter. When I told her I had a headache, she declared it might be the beginning of something infectious, and said that I must sleep in the hospital to-night, and she would examine me to-morrow morning, to see whether a rash had come out. 'Ve cannot be too careful vile Mees Drummond is avay!' she said."

"But you're not really going?"

"I shall have to. I'd have asked Miss Forster to interfere, but she'd hurried away by that time. I've come to collect my night things now."

"What a ridiculous swindle! Can't I go too?"

"No; remember, it's a case of isolation!" said Mabel, smiling.

"But you'll be afraid to sleep there all alone."

"Oh, no, I shan't! Mademoiselle offered to send Hunter—she's generally told off for hospital duty—but I said I'd rather not have her. I'm not a scrap ill; it's only my head."

"And Mademoiselle's idiotic nonsense! I never heard of such a silly notion as to pack you off there! She's absolutely mad!"

"Well, it can't be helped. There's no one to appeal to. Mademoiselle is as much in authority, I suppose, as Miss Forster, or Miss Bardsley, or anybody else."

"The school seems lost without Miss Drummond."

Feeling decidedly a martyr, Mabel, taking the various possessions she needed for the night, marched upstairs to the hospital.

"If it's anything catchable I'll catch it too!" Aldred called after her. "You're not to be ill up there without me! You may choose measles, or scarlatina, or anything you like; I'm quite agreeable, so long as I can have a share in it!"

"It's for Mademoiselle to decide the complaint to-morrow!" laughed Mabel, already half-way down the passage. "I don't mind what it is, so long as she doesn't declare it's suppressed smallpox, and have me re-vaccinated as a precaution. Good night!"

Aldred felt injured and aggrieved at her room-mate's banishment. It was really very tiresome and unnecessary of Mademoiselle to have insisted upon it.

"She's a Jack-in-office!" thought Aldred. "If she were head of the school, I should ask to be taken away. How particularly slow and stupid it is without Mabel! She's forgotten her bedroom slippers, by the by. I wonder if I dare take them up to her? On the whole, I think I'd better not; I suppose she'll manage without them."

It was a warm evening, and light until very late. Aldred undressed leisurely, and took a last delicious sniff at the roses that framed her window before she jumped into bed. She was tired, and dropped asleep almost immediately, falling into a confused dream, in which Mabel and Mademoiselle and measles were hopelessly mixed. The doctor had come to see Mabel, and had prescribed a huge bottle of nasty medicine, labelled "Two quarts to be taken every two hours". He was coming again, and was ring-ring-ringing at the front-door bell. Why did not one of the servants go to the door? And why was Mademoiselle sounding the gong? It was not dinner-time yet. Would nobody stop her? It would make Mabel's headache worse. In her dream, Aldred rushed downstairs, and tried to hold Mademoiselle's arm; but the clanging grew louder and louder, and with a start she awoke and sat up in her bed, half-awake.

The noise was actual fact. Somebody downstairs was hammering the gong, with frantic, jarring strokes; while the big bell that rang for classes was clanging lustily. There was a curious smell in the air, very different from the scent of the roses outside; and there was also a ruddy light, surely neither that of the moon nor of the rising sun. Before Aldred had time to do more than rub her eyes, hurried footsteps resounded along the passage, her door was flung open, and a voice cried: "Fire! Come at once!"

The girls at Birkwood had been trained in fire drill, and Aldred knew immediately what she must do. Her heart was beating quickly, and her hands were trembling, but she flung on her dressing-gown, slipped her feet into her slippers, seized a pocket-handkerchief and dipped it in the bedroom jug (all the work of three seconds), and dashed without further delay down the stairs.

The landing and hall were filled with dense clouds of choking smoke. To get to the front door was like passing through the mouth of a cannon, and Aldred felt almost suffocated before she reached the fresh air. In the garden several agitated teachers were trying to review an even more panic-stricken crowd of girls and servants. Mademoiselle was sobbing hysterically, and though all the teachers were striving each to number her own flock, they kept getting in one another's way, and missing count and having to begin again. Nobody seemed responsible, or in command. The gardener rushed about distractedly with buckets of water, assuring everyone that he had sent for the fire brigade from Chetbourne. The servants shrieked and wailed, and neighbours who came running from various farms and cottages on the downs only added to the general noise and confusion.

From one of the windows of the upper story flames were bursting, throwing a red glare over the garden. By this livid light Aldred pushed her way among the excited, jostling girls, scanning each face, and asking one constantly reiterated question: "Where's Mabel?"

Nobody knew. Nobody seemed to have noticed, in the general confusion, that she was not with them.

"Where's Mabel?" Aldred's voice was frantic with alarm.

"Isn't she with you?" asked Miss Bardsley wildly. "I opened your door and called you both. Oh, girls, if you would only keep together, I could tell if you were all here!"

"She was sleeping in the hospital!" cried Aldred, disregarding the teacher's request, and tearing away to interrogate Mademoiselle—a vain errand, for the unfortunate French governess had fallen in a dead faint upon the grass.

Aldred grasped the fact only too speedily that there was but one terrible answer to her question. *Mabel was in the burning house, for nobody had gone to warn her!* Without a moment's hesitation, she rushed back to the front door. There was no alternative; the emergency was all-compelling. Mabel was in imminent and pressing danger; no one realized it, or had even missed her, and there was no time to appeal to Miss Forster or Miss Bardsley. She, Aldred, alone and on her own responsibility, must save her friend. There was not a second to be lost; already it might be too late, for the blaze was fast making headway. From the open door clouds of smoke belched forth as if from a furnace, and Aldred was driven back with blinded eyes choking and gasping for breath. It was her own fault. How stupid she was to forget, in her excitement, what she had learnt at the fire-drill practice! Her dripping pocket-handkerchief was still clasped, almost unconsciously, in her hand; she tied it rapidly over her nose and mouth, then, dropping on to her hands and knees, she began to crawl along the hall in the direction of the staircase. The difference was marvellous. Down on the ground the air was comparatively fresh and clear—she could see the bottom of the umbrella stand and a pair of Miss Drummond's goloshes quite plainly; while only a foot higher the atmosphere was dense and impenetrable. The wet handkerchief also made breathing easier, and though her eyes were smarting and the heat was very great, she found it quite possible to get along. With half-closed eyelids, and her mouth well to the floor, she crept up the stairs; each one seemed a victory gained, and a step nearer to the accomplishment of her purpose. Oh, how many there were, and how interminable was the passage at the top! The heat grew more intense, and a roaring, crackling sound warned her that she was reaching the west wing, where the flames were raging worst and had burst through the windows.

The hospital was on the top story, so there was another staircase to be mounted. Dared she do it? Every fresh step cut off her retreat, and put another bar between herself and safety. Yet Mabel was there, solitary, unaided, in the midst of awful peril. No, she could not abandon her, come what might! She would face death with her friend, rather than leave her to perish alone.

She never remembered quite how she dragged herself along; her nerves were strung to the highest pitch, her brain felt bursting. The room she was in search of was over the kitchen, where the fire had originally broken out. Fortunately, it was a little clearer there, and Aldred was able to stand up; and by groping her way along the walls, she found the handle and flung open the door of the hospital.

"Mabel! Mabel!" she cried vehemently.

There was no reply. The room was filled with smoke, but the glare outside made just enough light to distinguish objects.

"Mabel! Are you there? Mabel!"

Aldred was in an agony of apprehension. There were several beds in the hospital, and she ran from one to the other, feeling in them with eager hands. They were empty. Had she, after all, come on a vain quest? Mabel must have heard the alarm bell, and have escaped and joined the others in the garden! Aldred's heart almost stopped beating, as for a moment the horror of the situation overcame her. Her search was quixotic, fruitless—she had risked her life for nothing! She moved instinctively to clutch a bedpost to steady herself, and as she did so her foot touched something soft. With a cry she dropped upon her knees. Mabel was lying on the floor just by the bedside, where she must have fallen, overpowered by the smoke, in an effort to make her way to the door.

With frantic hands Aldred dragged her friend across the room, and by sheer effort of will hoisted her up, so that her head might reach the open window. It was a task far beyond her ordinary powers, but in such moments a strength not our own is often given to us. The fresh air soon restored consciousness, and Mabel, to Aldred's intense relief, opened her eyes.

"What is it? Where am I?" she asked confusedly.

"The house is on fire, dear, and I don't know how we are to save ourselves. Stay where you are, and go on getting the air; I'm going to see if we can manage to get back down the passage."

Directly Aldred opened the door she realized that escape in that quarter was impossible. A roaring sound and a glare at the end of the landing told her only too plainly that the staircase had broken into flames. She shut the door again hurriedly, and, returning to the window, shouted with all her might. Would anybody hear, and if so, could they help? The Fire Brigade had not yet arrived from Chetbourne, and it was unlikely that there would be any ladder about the place long enough to reach to the top story of the house.

"Help! Help! Hallo!" Her voice sounded so thin and weak, compared with the crackling of the flames, she feared it would not carry far enough. Mabel, still in a half-dazed state, clung to her wildly, trembling and shivering with terror.

Would no one ever come? They were all watching the front of the house, and had completely forgotten the back.

At last! There was a shout from below, and a sudden rushing and noise, as the ever-increasing crowd poured round the corner.

"Fetch a ladder!"

"It's too short!"

"Tie two together!"

"There aren't two!"

"Tell them to jump!"

"No! No! They'd break their necks!"

"Someone go in and fetch 'em!"

"Impossible! The stairs are ablaze!"

"Does anyone hear the engine coming?"

"Not a sign of it yet."

"Then God help them, for we can't!"

The room was getting hotter and hotter. Aldred could hear the roar of the flames in the passage now. How long would the door keep them out? It was plain that, unless both girls were to perish, something must be done, and that instantly. Disengaging Mabel's clinging arms, Aldred propped her against the window-sill, then groped her way through the dense smoke across the room. The six beds in the hospital were always kept made up, perfectly ready for use. Aldred pulled off the twelve sheets one after the other, and carried them in a bundle back to the window, where, with trembling hands, she knotted them firmly together, just as Miss Drummond had shown in the fire-drill practice. She dragged forward the nearest bedstead till its foot almost touched the sill, and, fastening her improvised rope round a post, pulled it hard, to make sure that the knot was safe.

"Mabel," she said loudly, "we must try the sheet dodge. I'm going to lower you down. Let me tie this end round your waist, quick!"

"No! No!" cried Mabel, who had somewhat recovered her scattered senses. "I'll lower you! I'm the bigger, and stronger than you. Here, give me the end!"

"I shan't. You must go! Mabel, I insist! This is no time for arguing. My mind's made up, and I shall make you!"

Aldred was fastening the knot as she spoke, with quick fingers. She would take no denial. Had she not come to rescue her friend, and was she to be so easily gainsaid?

"But, Aldred! Aldred! If I go first, who will lower you afterwards?"

"I'll slip down somehow."

"You know you can't! It's saving me at your own cost!"

The heat was terrific, and the roar on the landing had increased sevenfold. With a crash the door fell in, and a sheet of flame burst like a furious living thing into the room.

Aldred turned almost fiercely upon Mabel.

"For your father's and mother's sake! Think of them!"

Her nature was the stronger and the more masterful of the two. She had always been the dominating influence, and now, in this great and awful crisis, her will prevailed. Without further ado she pushed Mabel over the window-sill, and, clinging with all her might to the sheet rope, let her down as carefully and gently as she could. It was a great effort to regulate the descent of such a heavy dangling weight, but she feared to let her burden go with a run, lest Mabel's head should be dashed against the wall of the house. Oh, what a fearful, dizzy depth it seemed from the upper story to the ground! The crowd below stood stock-still, pressing tightly together shoulder to shoulder, and gazing upward, voiceless and almost breathless with suspense. Would Aldred's frail strength accomplish the task? The fire within had gained a grip of the room, and shone behind her head like a halo. Still she did not flinch or falter; she kept her nerve, and paid out her rope piece by piece, manœuvring the knots over the window-sill, and remembering every necessary precaution.

The flames rolled nearer. Strangely enough, now that death was almost at arm's length, she felt perfectly cool and collected, and far calmer than she had done when first she had entered the room. Every thought and effort of her being was concentrated on Mabel's escape; after that, she cared nothing. Only a few yards now! She set her teeth, and hung on grimly. She was nearly spent, but she just managed to control the last quick rush as the rope's burden fell at length into the dozen eager hands upraised to help. The crowd had waited in silence, but now a roar rose up from below of deafening cheers and loud shouts of encouragement.

"Come down yourself!"

"Try hand over hand down the sheets!"

"Don't waste a minute!"

"Pluck will win yet!"

"We're all waiting to catch you, if you fall!"

But Aldred, standing exhausted and panting by the window, had no strength left for further effort. The heat of the flames and the smoke were overpowering. She had kept up by sheer effort of will until her friend was in safety; now the world seemed suddenly to be turning round her. There was a rushing in her ears, and her eyes grew dim. Through a thick haze she saw the crowd beckoning to her, and one man, more daring than the rest, begin to scale the rope, in the hope of rescuing her. He could never reach her in time, she thought vaguely; and she was too faint and giddy to let herself down hand over hand, as they were calling to her to do. She almost wished they would leave her alone; her work was done, Mabel was safe, and that was all she cared.

Why was the crowd suddenly turning round and hurrahing? The people were breaking up in wild confusion, and parting so as to leave a wide path in their midst. There were sounds of galloping horses and grinding wheels. What did it all mean? Aldred's fading senses just grasped a vision of men in bright helmets, of a great ladder that seemed to advance faster than the wind, and of a tongue of flame that shot out from the room behind and enveloped her, and the fact that a strong arm at the same instant clutched her and snatched her away; then she went down—down—down, and everything sank into blank nothingness.

But the crowd below cried: "Thank God! The Fire Brigade came in the nick of time!"

CHAPTER XVII. LOSS AND GAIN

Owing to the strenuous efforts of the Brigade, the fire at the Grange was at last got under control; and though the main staircase was gone, and the west wing a wreck, all the eastern portion of the building was saved.

The new day showed a scene of great desolation—blackened walls, and staring, empty windows; garden and lawn trodden into a waste by trampling feet, and littered with broken glass, pieces of timber, and the remains of charred furniture; the greenhouse smashed to atoms; the sundial knocked over; and both pergola and rosery in ruins. The lecture-hall, one classroom, and the bedrooms that lay over them were untouched—a most fortunate circumstance, as they provided a shelter for the girls, who were all clad in dressing-gowns and bedroom slippers. As soon as they were assured of the safety of that part of the house, the teachers marshalled the school there, access being easily gained through a French window. This wing, a later addition to the Grange, possessed a separate staircase, and had only communicated with the main building by means of a long passage and a door. At present, therefore, it proved a general asylum of refuge. The firemen collected and carried round any articles they could find which would be of use, and, since both larder and pantry had escaped, provisions, cups and saucers, and kettles soon made their appearance.

The classroom was turned into a temporary kitchen, and the servants, with the aid of the gardener, set to work to prepare breakfast. The girls who occupied the bedrooms over the lecture-hall lent various garments to the rest, so that by eight o'clock everybody was at least clothed and fed, though very much upset and agitated by the terrible occurrence.

A telegram was dispatched at the earliest opportunity to Miss Drummond, but it would not be possible for her to arrive until the evening. In the meantime, what was to become of her pupils? They could manage for the day, but it would be impossible to put the whole thirty-nine into three bedrooms. The Rector of the parish came to the rescue by at once assuming the direction of affairs, and making arrangements to send all home by the morning trains, himself advancing the money for their railway tickets. Most of the girls were travelling as far as London, where Miss Forster and the prefects undertook to see each safely started for her destination. In the circumstances, it seemed much the wisest thing to be done; the girls could not recommence lessons that term, and the sooner they were out of the way the better.

And where was Aldred? Speeding by express like the others, to tell her astonishing tale at home? No: in the midst of all the general excitement and confusion, she lay utterly unconscious of her surroundings. She had been carried into the bedroom over the classroom, and the Rector had sent for the nearest medical man, and for a nurse from the infirmary at Chetbourne.

"Can we save her, Doctor?" asked Miss Bardsley, who had applied first aid, and done everything in her power, considering the limited means at her command.

"She is badly scorched, and is suffering from a severe shock to the system," replied the doctor gravely. "Still, with careful nursing I think we may pull her through. You have telegraphed for her people? That is well.

Absolute quiet is essential. I am thankful the other girls are leaving this morning."

"It is a blessing her good looks are spared," said the nurse, bending down to admire the pretty, pale face, mercifully unscathed by the fire. "I have not needed even to cut her beautiful hair."

"By some strange chance, or rather Providence, the tongue of flame that shot out so suddenly only caught her below the waist," explained Miss Bardsley. "The fireman had just seized her in his arms, and her head was thrown forward over his shoulder. One second later, she might have been burnt to death."

"How did the fire originate?" asked the doctor.

"Through carelessness in the kitchen, I am afraid; but it is difficult to tell until we can make proper enquiries. We are leaving everything for Miss Drummond to investigate herself."

"And this child? How was it she was left in the burning house?"

"She went to warn Mabel Farrington, a companion, who, without my knowledge, had been sleeping in the hospital, a room on the top story. In the darkness and confusion it was almost impossible to count all the girls. I had not specially missed Mabel. I had already been to her bedroom to rouse her with the others, and had not realized that she was not there. The teacher who had ordered her removal to the hospital fainted when the fire broke out, so of course could offer no information. Only Aldred knew of Mabel's whereabouts, and she, without consulting anybody, must have made her way up the tottering staircase to save her friend. The first knowledge I had of the matter was when I heard the crowd shout, and saw the two girls screaming at the window. We were frantic, but powerless to help. There was no long ladder on the premises, and all we could do was to wait for the arrival of the Brigade. Aldred made a rope of sheets and let Mabel down in safety; but the flames had taken such a hold of the room that there was no time for her to follow."

"Then she has saved a life!" said the doctor. "She'll be a little heroine among you, when she gets well."

"Ah, yes—when she gets well!" replied Miss Bardsley anxiously.

Poor Miss Drummond, called from her mother's sick-room, arrived that evening to find the Grange half-wrecked. Fortunately, she was well insured, and would suffer no pecuniary loss, but apart from that it was quite a sufficient catastrophe. Her school could not reassemble until the house was repaired and redecorated; and many treasures had been destroyed which it would be impossible to replace.

"You must try to look on the bright side of things," said the Rector, who was present to receive her. "The damage might have been much worse. Mr. Southey, your architect, came this morning to make an inspection, and told me he would be able to have all in order for you to re-open in September. And the garden will soon recover itself; you will be astonished how quickly everything will grow up again. As for the little patient, she is much better this evening, and the nurse considers her out of serious danger. When we think of the tragedy that might have occurred, we must feel only too grateful that all your flock escaped with their lives."

"It is indeed a cause for thankfulness," said Miss Drummond. "I cannot tell you what anxiety I have suffered during to-day's journey. The telegram only gave the briefest message, and did not assure me of everyone's safety. I was left to imagine the worst, and the long hours in the train were agony. Fortunately, I left my mother on the high road to recovery, so that is another subject for gratitude. I shall be able to remain here now without feeling that my presence is absolutely necessary in the North. How very good it was of you to pack off the whole school so promptly this morning!"

"It was really an easier task than I anticipated. They all seemed accustomed to travelling. One of the girls, however, utterly declined to depart with the others, and I was obliged to permit her to remain. I thought you could reason with her better than I."

It was Mabel who had refused point-blank to leave the Grange, and who, now that Miss Drummond had returned, begged most earnestly not to be sent away.

"Let me stay near Aldred!" she implored. "I won't be the least trouble. I'll sleep anywhere—on a sofa, or a camp bed, or anything. No, I know I shouldn't be allowed in her room, but I should hear the doctor's report every morning and evening, and know how she was. And perhaps I might be of some help. I could carry trays upstairs, and wait on the nurse. I'd do anything in the world for Aldred! I like to feel I'm in the same house with her, and if I have to go it will simply break my heart. I'll write to Mother to-night, and if she agrees will you say 'Yes'?"

Neither Lady Muriel nor Miss Drummond could resist Mabel's piteous appeal. She was always rather a privileged pupil at the Grange, so for this once she was accorded her own way. The doctor grew accustomed to find her wistful face waiting in the passage at the conclusion of his visits, and liked to see the look of relief spread over it as he gave her a hopeful bulletin in passing. He would not consent to any visits, for he feared Mabel's presence would recall Aldred's memory of the fire, and he particularly wished to keep her from all excitement.

"Her friend is the last person whom it would be advisable to allow in the room," he declared. "She must not even peep round the door without my express permission."

It was hard for Mabel to be thus excluded, but she was sensible enough to understand the reason for her banishment, and did not attempt to transgress the doctor's orders.

So far Aldred, though she had quite regained consciousness, had never made the least reference to that terrible night. She recognized those around her bed—Miss Drummond, Aunt Bertha, who had come over immediately, and remained in close attendance on her; her father, who paid flying visits to see her; the nurse, and the doctor—but she made no enquiries for others, and did not even ask if Mabel were safe. Her burns were after all not very severe, and she seemed to be suffering more from general collapse. As day after day passed, and she still continued in the same state, her case began to puzzle the doctor.

"She ought to be making more improvement," he said. "She is no better now than she was a week ago. Her mental attitude does not satisfy me at all. Please watch her closely, and see if you can ascertain the reason for this set-back."

"I will do so," answered the nurse, who had had great experience with convalescent patients, and knew how often an apparently trifling cause can hinder recovery.

The result of her observation she communicated to Miss Drummond.

"I am certain the poor child has something on her mind," she declared. "It is this that makes her so restless and uneasy. I've several times found her crying, though she evidently didn't want me to notice it. She lies awake for hours during the night, and I'm sure it is not merely the pain of her burns that troubles her. Her eyes follow you round the room with the most pathetic gaze. I believe she's longing to confide in you, if she could only get you to herself, and that it would be the greatest comfort to her."

"Then I will stay alone with her this evening, when her aunt has gone to bed," replied Miss Drummond. "If it is really as you say, that will give her the opportunity she wants."

The nurse always went on duty at nine o'clock, at which hour Miss Laurence retired to her own room. Miss Drummond had so far acted as an extra assistant to both, so she was able, without making her motive too apparent, to say that she was taking the nurse's place for the night. She did not wish to excite Aldred unnecessarily, only to afford her a chance of a private talk if she wished for it. She thought there was a look of gratitude in the dark eyes at this arrangement, but she could not be quite sure; so, having made her patient as comfortable as possible, she shaded the lamp, and left her to go to sleep.

For a long while Aldred lay fairly still, though by occasional restless movements the head mistress knew that she was wideawake. A pitiful little sigh at last brought Miss Drummond to her side.

"Can I do anything for you, dear? Are you in pain?"

"No, thank you—it isn't that."

"Something is worrying you, all the same?"

There was no reply.

"Is it anything you would like to tell me?"

"How did you guess?"

"Never mind how I guessed. Just remember that I'm your friend, and that I'm anxious to give you all the help I can. Don't be afraid! Let me know the trouble, and perhaps between us we can manage to set it straight."

Miss Drummond had the rare quality of absolute tact and sympathy. She said no more, only took her pupil's hot hand, and waited patiently for her to begin.

It was a great effort for Aldred to utter her confession, but when once she had made a start she poured out the whole story of her false career at school from its very commencement, keeping nothing back, and mentioning even the affairs of the Chinese lanterns, Miss Webb's chalked chair, and the feigned illness at Grassingford.

"I couldn't bear to meet Mabel again, after what happened at the fire, and allow her to go on thinking me so much better than I am," she concluded. "I'd like her to know all—yes, every single horrid thing that I've done! She can never love me the same, but I'd rather make a clean breast of it, and lose her friendship, than feel so unutterably mean. Will you tell her, please? I haven't the courage to do it myself."

"To be sorry for our faults is the first step on the right road," said Miss Drummond. "It is a sad story, Aldred, and I don't condone anything, though it is a little comfort that you have at least done the very deed for which you took false credit at the beginning. Whether Mabel's friendship will stand the test or not, I cannot say; your plain and only course is to acknowledge the deception, and leave it for her to decide, and to set to work yourself to redeem the past. Now, I can allow no more talking. Remember, I am deputy nurse, and it is my business to see that you shut your eyes and go to sleep."

Aldred seemed so much calmer and easier next morning that the doctor was surprised at the change.

"If she only continues to improve at this rate, we shall soon have her well," he reported. "Keep her as cheerful as you can, and—yes—if she is asking so particularly for her friend, it will be advisable not to thwart her."

Aldred's one feverish anxiety was to see Mabel, though she did not know whether she more longed for or dreaded the visit. The nurse, to whom Miss Drummond briefly confided an outline of the circumstances, decided, though she feared the effect of so much excitement, that it was better to get the meeting over than to allow her patient to remain in a state of such great suspense.

"I want Mabel with me alone," said Aldred, and she pleaded so hard that even Aunt Bertha was judicious enough to consent.

Propped up on pillows, Aldred gazed with nervous eyes as her friend entered the room. Mabel had evidently been crying bitterly, and had not entirely regained her self-control as she came and stood beside the bed.

"Miss Drummond has told you?" queried Aldred eagerly.

"Yes, she has told me everything. I can't deny that it has been a most terrible shock. I had believed in you and trusted you so utterly. I thought you hadn't a single fault. But oh, Aldred! Miss Drummond has been talking to me; she says we were both wrong, and that I was partly to blame for expecting too much. She told me I had set up an idol, and it was right that it should be broken down; that no human being is faultless, and that we must look for our example to the one perfect Pattern, Who can never disappoint us. Shall we start quite afresh now, with Him for our ideal, and try to help each other?"

Aldred's face was buried in the pillow; she was sobbing too much to reply.

"I haven't thanked you yet for saving me," continued Mabel. "It was a braver thing by far even than what I supposed you had done, because you risked so much more."

"I'd have given my life for you gladly!" gulped Aldred.

"I know, and I feel almost unworthy of such love."

"Will you kiss me, to show you can forget what's past?"

Mabel bent her head. It was a kiss of complete reconciliation and forgiveness, and Aldred, with a glad leap of her heart, felt that the friendship that she had striven to build upon the shifting sand of a false reputation was founded at last upon the rock of self-sacrifice and mutual endeavour.

THE END

BOOK EIGHT.
THE NEW GIRL AT ST. CHAD'S

A Story of School Life

CHAPTER I. HONOR INTRODUCES HERSELF

"Any new girls?"

It was Madge Summers who asked the question, seated on the right-hand corner of Maisie Talbot's bed, munching caramels. It was a very small bed, but at that moment it managed to accommodate no less than seven of Maisie's most particular friends, who were closely watching the progress of her unpacking, and discussing the latest school news, interspersed with remarks on her belongings.

Maisie extricated herself from the depths of her box, and handed a pile of stockings to Lettice, her younger sister.

"What's the use of asking me?" she replied. "Our cab only drove up half an hour ago. I feel almost new myself yet."

"So do I, and horribly in the blues too," said Pauline Reynolds. "It's always a wrench to leave home. I'm perfectly miserable for at least three days at the beginning of each term. I feel as if——"

"Oh, don't all begin to expatiate about your feelings!" broke in Chatty Burns. "We know Pauline's symptoms only too well: the first day she shows aggressively red eyes and a damp pocket-handkerchief; the second day she writes lengthy letters home, begging to be allowed to return immediately and have lessons with a private governess; the third day she wanders about, trying to get sympathy from anyone who is weak-minded enough to listen to her, till in desperation somebody drags her into the playground, and makes her have a round at hockey. That cheers her up, and she begins to think life isn't quite such a desert. By the fourth morning she has recovered her spirits, and come to the conclusion that Chessington College is a very decent kind of place; and she begins to be alarmed lest her mother, on the strength of the pathetic letter, should have decided to let her leave at once, and should have already engaged a private governess."

"You're most unsympathetic, Chatty!" said Pauline, smiling in spite of herself. "You don't know what it is to be home-sick."

"I wouldn't parade such a woebegone face, whatever might be the depths of my misery," returned Chatty briskly.

"I'm always glad to come back," declared Dorothy Arkwright. "I like school. It's fun to meet everybody again, and arrange about cricket, and the Debating Society, and the Natural History Club. There's so much going on at St. Chad's."

"No one has answered my question yet," remarked Madge Summers. "Are there any new girls?"

Chatty wriggled herself into a more comfortable position between Adeline Vaughan and Ruth Latimer.

"I think there are about a dozen altogether. Vivian Holmes says there are four at St. Bride's, three at St. Aldwyth's, two at the School House, and two at St. Hilary's. I saw one of them arriving at the same time as I did, and Miss Cavendish was gushing over another in the library; and Marian Spencer has brought a sister—she introduced her to me just now."

"But what about St. Chad's?"

"We've only one, I believe, though Flossie Taylor, the Hammond-Smiths' cousin, has moved here from St. Bride's. She was always destined for a Chaddite, you know, only there wasn't room for her till the Richardsons left."

"She's no great acquisition," said Dorothy Arkwright. "I hate girls to change their quarters. When once they start at a house, they ought to stick to it."

"Well, she wants to be with her cousins, I suppose," put in Madge Summers. "Who's our new girl?"

"I don't know. I haven't heard anything about her."

"Perhaps she hasn't arrived yet."

"Sh! Sh!" said Pauline Reynolds, squeezing Madge's arm by way of remonstrance, and pointing to the closely-drawn curtains of the cubicle at the farther end of the room. "She's here now."

"Where?"

"There, you goose!"

"What has she shut herself up like that for?"

"How should I know?"

406

"Perhaps she's unpacking," suggested Dorothy Arkwright.

"If she is, she'll finish it quicker than Lettice and I can," returned Maisie Talbot. "Why can't you be hanging up some of those skirts, instead of sitting staring at me? Yes, this is a whole box of Edinburgh rock, but you shan't have a single piece, any of you, unless you get off my bed at once."

"Poor old Maisie, don't grow excited!" murmured Ruth Latimer, appropriating the box and handing it round, though no one attempted to move.

"But look here! what about this new girl?" persisted Madge. "Hasn't anybody seen her?"

"No. She's been in there ever since she arrived."

"Don't talk so loud; she'll hear you."

"I don't care if she does."

"I want to know what she's doing."

"I can tell you, then," said Chatty Burns, in a whisper that was more audible by far than her ordinary voice.

"What?"

"Crying! New girls always cry, and some old ones too, if you take Pauline as a specimen."

"I'm not crying now!" protested Pauline indignantly. "And how can you tell that the new girl is?"

"I'm as certain as if I'd proved a proposition in Euclid. Why should she have drawn her curtains so closely? If she's not lying on her bed, with a clean pocket-handkerchief to her eyes, I'll give you six caramels in exchange for three peppermint creams!"

"Then you're just mistaken!" cried a voice from the end cubicle. The chintz curtain was pulled aside, and out marched a figure with so jaunty an air as to banish utterly the idea of possible homesickness or tears.

It was a girl of about fifteen, a remarkably pretty girl (so her schoolmates decided, without an instant's hesitation), and rather out of the common. She had a clear, olive complexion, a lovely colour in her cheeks, a bewitching pair of dimples, and a perfect colt's mane of thick, curly, brown hair. Perhaps her nose was a little too tip-tilted, and her mouth a trifle too wide for absolute beauty; but she showed such a nice row of even, white teeth when she laughed that one could overlook the latter deficiency. Her eyes were beyond praise, large and grey, with a dark line round the iris, and shaded by long lashes; and they were so soft, and wistful, and winning, and yet so twinkling and full of fun, that they seemed as if they could compel admiration, and make friends with their first glance. The girl walked across the room in an easy, confident fashion, and stood, with a broad smile on her face, beaming at the seven others seated on Maisie's bed.

"Why shouldn't I pull my curtains?" she asked. "If I'd been pulling faces, now, you might have had some cause for complaint. You look rather a nice set; I think I'm going to like you."

The girls were so surprised that they could only stare. It seemed reversing the usual order of things for a new-comer, who ought to be shy and confused, to be so absolutely and entirely self-possessed, and to pass judgment with such calm assurance upon these old members of St. Chad's, some of whom were already in their third year at Chessington College.

"Perhaps I'd better introduce myself," continued the stranger. "My name is Honor Fitzgerald, and I come from Kilmore, near Ballycroghan, in County Kerry."

"Then you're Irish!" gasped Chatty Burns.

"Quite right. First class for geography! County Kerry is exactly in the bottom left-hand corner of the map of Ireland. It's a more hospitable place than this is. I've been here nearly two hours, and nobody has offered me any refreshments yet. I'm simply starving!"

She looked so humorously and suggestively at the Edinburgh rock that Madge Summers promptly offered it to her, regardless of the fact that the box belonged to Maisie Talbot.

"Come along here," said Ruth Latimer, trying to make a place for the new girl on the bed by pushing the others vigorously nearer the end.

"No room unless I sit on your knee, while you get up and walk about," declared Honor. "There! I knew you would!" as Madge Summers fell with a crash on to the floor.

"Seven little schoolgirls, eating sugar sticks;

One tumbled overboard, and then there were six!"

"Thank you. I think I prefer to 'take the chair', as the dentist says. There only seems to be one in each cubicle, but as I'm the visitor——"

"Take care!" screamed Maisie. "My clean blouses!"

"What am I doing? I declare, I never saw them. There, I'll nurse them for you while I eat this delicious-looking piece of pink rock."

The new girl was so utterly different from anybody else who had ever come to St. Chad's that the others waited with curiosity to hear what she would say next.

"Well?" she enquired coolly at last. "I suppose you're thinking me over. I should like to know your opinion of me. They tell me at home that my nose turns up, and my tongue is too long. But I didn't turn up my nose at the Edinburgh rock, did I?—and as for my tongue, it fits my mouth, as a general rule, though it runs away sometimes."

"When did you come?"

"What class are you in?"

"Have you seen Miss Cavendish yet?"

"How old are you?"

"Have you been to school before?"

"Do you know anyone here?"

"Why did you come to St. Chad's?"

The questions were fired off all together from seven pairs of lips.

"One at a time, please!" returned Honor. "I'm older than I look, and younger than I seem. You mayn't believe me, yet I assure you I've only had three birthdays."

"Rubbish!" said Chatty Burns.

"It's a fact, all the same."

"But how could that be?" demanded Pauline Reynolds incredulously.

"Because I was born on the twenty-ninth of February, and I can't have a birthday except in a leap year. That accounts for anything odd there is about me; so if you find me queer, you must just say: 'She's a twenty-ninth of February girl', and make excuses for me. As for the other questions, I've never been to school before; I've seen Miss Cavendish, but I haven't heard yet what class I'm to be in; five minutes ago I didn't know anybody here, but now I know—how many are there of you?—one, two, three, four, five, six, seven, eight, nine!"

"Have you unpacked yet?" asked Maisie, returning to her box, which Lettice had been steadily emptying.

"Only about half."

"I think we had better come and help you, then."

"Better finish our own first!" grunted Lettice, for which remark she was promptly snubbed by her elder sister.

"Miss Maitland will be up at eight o'clock to look at our drawers," said Chatty Burns. "She'll expect you to have everything put away, and your coats and dresses hung in the wardrobe."

"We have to be so fearfully tidy here!" sighed Adeline Vaughan. "A warden comes round each morning, and woe betide you if you leave hairs in your brush, or have forgotten to fold your nightdress!"

"It's just as bad at St. Hilary's," said Madge.

"And worse at St. Bride's," added Ruth Latimer.

"My father wanted me to be at the School House," said Honor, "but Miss Cavendish wrote that it was full, so I was entered at St. Chad's instead."

"Yes, you generally need to have your name down for two years before you can get a vacancy at the School House," said Dorothy Arkwright. "It's the popular favourite with parents, because Miss Cavendish herself is the Head; but really, St. Chad's is far nicer. We all stand up for our own house, and I know you'll like it."

"There's the tea-bell! Come along! we must go at once," interrupted Chatty Burns.

"Won't they wait for us?" enquired Honor, beginning to wash her hands with much deliberation.

"Wait! She asks if they'll wait!" exclaimed Adeline Vaughan.

"One can see you've never been to school before!" commented Maisie Talbot. "No, you certainly haven't time to comb your hair now. You had better follow the rest of us as fast as you can."

St. Chad's could accommodate forty pupils, and Honor found a place assigned to her in the dining-hall near the end of a long table, which looked very attractive with its clean white cloth, its pretty china, and its vases of flowers in the middle. She had a good view of her schoolfellows, more than half of whom seemed of about the same age as herself, though there were tall girls, with their hair already put up, and a few younger ones who had apparently only just entered their teens. Grace was sung, and then the urns began to fill an almost ceaseless stream of cups, while plates of bread and butter circulated with much rapidity.

"We're late to-day," explained Honor's neighbour, "because the train from the North does not get in until five. Our usual tea-time is four o'clock, after games; then we have supper at half-past seven, when we've finished evening preparation. Did you bring any jam? Your hamper will be unpacked to-morrow, and the pots labelled with your name. I expect you'll find one opposite your plate at breakfast. Jam and marmalade are the only things we're allowed, except plain cakes."

Tea on the first afternoon was generally an exciting occasion at St. Chad's. There were so many greetings between old friends, so much news and such various topics to be discussed, that conversation, in a sufficiently subdued undertone, went on very briskly. The girls had enjoyed their Easter holidays, but most of them seemed pleased to return to school, for the summer term was always the favourite at Chessington College.

"Have you heard who's in the Eleven?" began Madge Summers. "They've actually put in Grace Shaw, and she bowls abominably. I think it's rank favouritism on Miss Young's part. She always gives St. Hilary's a turn when she can."

"She was a Hilaryite herself," returned Adeline Vaughan. "That's the worst of having a games mistress who's been educated at the school; she's sure to show partiality for her old house."

"And yet in one way it's better, because she understands all our customs and private rules. It would be almost impossible to explain everything to a new-comer."

"What about the house team?" asked Ruth Latimer. "Is anything fixed?"

"Not yet. There's to be a practice to-morrow, and it will go by our scores."

"I shall stick to tennis," declared Pauline Reynolds. "One gets a fair chance there, at any rate, and we must keep up the credit of St. Chad's in the courts. I don't know whether we've any chance of winning the shield. I wish we could get a real champion!"

"You should see Flossie Taylor play!" burst out Edith and Claudia Hammond-Smith, who were anxious to bring their cousin forward, and to ensure her popularity among the other girls.

"I've not heard that she made any record at St. Bride's," remarked Dorothy Arkwright, who resented Flossie's removal to St. Chad's.

"She hasn't had an opportunity. She only came to school last Christmas, and it wasn't the tennis season. Wait till you see her serve!"

"Miss Young will have to be judge, not I," replied Dorothy coldly.

"Flossie is in your bedroom, Dorothy," announced Claudia. "She has the cubicle near the fireplace."

"If you're sleeping in the bed next to mine," said Flossie, eyeing Dorothy across the table with a rather patronizing air, "I sincerely hope you don't snore."

"Of course not!" responded Dorothy, in some indignation.

"At St. Bride's," continued Flossie, "one of my room-mates snored atrociously. I used to have to get up and shake her, and pull the pillow from under her head, before I could go to sleep."

"You'd better not try that on with me!"

"I would, in a minute, if you kept me awake."

"It is a shame she's not in our room," interposed Edith. "We've asked Miss Maitland to let her change with Geraldine Saunders, and I think perhaps she may. We want Flossie all to ourselves; I do hope she'll let us!"

"So do I!" retorted Dorothy feelingly. "The Hammond-Smiths are welcome to their cousin, so far as I'm concerned," she whispered to Chatty Burns; "I don't like her. She's trying to show off. Edith and Claudia are making far too much fuss over her."

"They always gush," commented Chatty. "Still, I dare say Flossie will need taking down a little."

"It would do her all the good in the world," replied Dorothy. Then, turning to the Hammond-Smiths, she remarked aloud: "There's a new girl here who may be just as good as your cousin, for anything we know. Honor Fitzgerald, do you play tennis?"

"I can play, but how you'll like it is another story," answered Honor. "We two," nodding at Flossie, "had better try a set by ourselves, and then you can choose the winner."

"I'm sure I don't care about it, thank you." Flossie's tone was supercilious.

"All right! We don't force ourselves where we're not wanted in my part of the world."

"Is that Ireland? Then I suppose your name is Biddy?"

"Certainly not!"

"I thought all Irish girls were called Biddy; are you sure you're not?"

"My name is Honor Fitzgerald."

"Really! I'm astonished it isn't Mulligan, or O'Grady."

The Hammond-Smiths giggled, and poked Effie and Blanche Lawson.

"Isn't Flossie funny?" they whispered delightedly.

"I think she's very rude," observed Dorothy Arkwright. "I call that an extremely cheap form of wit."

"Irish names are often rather peculiar," drawled Claudia Hammond-Smith.

"They're quite as good as English ones, and sometimes a great deal more ancient and aristocratic," returned Honor.

"One for Claudia, and for Flossie Taylor too!" said Dorothy to Chatty Burns.

"Paddy, for instance," interposed Flossie, who saw that the Lawsons were listening, as well as her cousins. "St. Patrick and pigs always go together, in my mind. I suppose you keep a pig in Ireland?"

"Don't answer her!" whispered Honor's neighbour. "They're only teasing you because you're new. They want to see how much you'll stand."

But poor Honor was unaccustomed as yet to schoolgirl banter, and could not abstain from replying:

"Does it matter whether we do or not?"

She spoke quietly, but there was a gleam in her eye, as if her temper were rising.

"Not in the least! I only thought all Irish people cultivated pigs."

"It's no worse than keeping a cat, or a dog."

"My dear Paddy, of course not! Still, I shouldn't care to have the creatures in the drawing-room. Take a little more bread and butter. I'm sorry we've no potatoes to offer you."

The Hammond-Smiths and the Lawsons tittered, and Dorothy Arkwright was about to state her frank opinion of their behaviour when Honor's pent-up wrath exploded.

"We don't keep pigs in the drawing-room," she exclaimed. "There's a saying that it takes nine tailors to make a man, so if your name is Taylor you can only be the ninth part of a lady!" Then, realizing that her upraised voice had drawn upon her the attention, not only of all the girls, but also of Miss Maitland, she flushed crimson, scraped back her chair, and fled precipitately from the room.

Miss Maitland looked surprised. It was an unheard-of thing for any girl to leave the tea-table without permission. Such a breach of school decorum had surely never been committed before at St. Chad's! There was a very complete code of etiquette observed at the house, and to break one of the laws of politeness was considered an unpardonable offence.

"She's made a bad beginning," whispered Ruth Latimer to Maisie Talbot. "It's most unfortunate. It was really the fault of Flossie Taylor and the Hammond-Smiths. They needn't have teased her so."

"Still, it was silly of her to lose her temper," replied Maisie. "She stalked out of the room like a queen of tragedy. Miss Maitland can't bear girls who give way to their impulses; she despises what she calls 'early Victorian hysterics', and I quite agree with her."

"Yes, we must learn to be stoics here," said Ruth; "and as for teasing, the wisest thing is to take no notice of it."

A monitress had been dispatched to fetch Honor back, but in a short time she returned alone, and reported that she could not find her. Miss Maitland made no comment, and as the meal was now over she gave the signal of dismissal. Most of the girls went to the recreation room, but Maisie Talbot, who had not yet quite concluded her unpacking, ran straight upstairs. Noticing something move behind a curtain in the corner of the bedroom, she pulled it aside. There was Honor, sitting in a queer little heap on the floor, and rubbing her eyes in a very suggestive manner. She jumped up in a moment, however, and pretended that she was only arranging her boots.

"I'd finished tea," she remarked airily, "so I thought I might as well empty my box, and put my dresses away in my wardrobe."

"You'll have to ask Miss Maitland's leave next time, before you march out of the room, or you'll get into trouble," said Maisie. "If it weren't your first evening, you'd be expected to make a public apology. Of course, Flossie Taylor and the Hammond-Smiths were aggravating, but you should just have laughed at them, and then they'd have stopped. We don't behave like kindergarten children here."

Maisie spoke scathingly. She was a girl who had scant sympathy with what she called "babyishness", and disliked any exhibition of feeling. And, after all, she only voiced the general opinion of the school, which, by an unwritten law, had established a calm imperturbation as the height of good breeding.

"I don't care in the least what any of you think!" retorted Honor, and she hung up her skirt with such a jerk that she broke the loop.

Yet, although she spoke lightly, she evidently did care. She was very quiet indeed all the rest of the evening, and hardly spoke at recreation.

Chatty Burns sat down next to her and tried to begin a conversation, but Honor answered so briefly that she very soon gave up the effort in despair, and moved away; while the other girls were so interested in their own affairs that they did not trouble to remember their new schoolfellow. At nine o'clock prayers were read, and everybody went upstairs to bed.

When the lights were out, and the room was in perfect silence, a strange, suppressed noise issued from Honor's corner. It might, of course, have been snoring; and Honor explained elaborately next morning that Irish people often have a peculiar way of breathing in their sleep—an affection from which she sometimes suffered herself.

"All the same, I don't quite believe her," confided Pauline Reynolds, who occupied the next cubicle, to Lettice Talbot, a more sympathetic character than her sister Maisie. "I know what it is to feel home-sick, and to smother one's nose in the pillow! If that wasn't sobbing, it was as like it as anything I've ever heard in my life."

CHAPTER II. HONOR'S HOME

For a full understanding of Honor Fitzgerald we must go back a few weeks, and see her in that Irish home which was so far away and so utterly different from Chessington College. Kilmore Castle was a great, rambling, old-fashioned country house, built beside an inland creek of the sea, and sheltered by a range of hills from the wild winds of Kerry. To Honor that was the dearest and most beautiful spot in the world. She loved every inch of it—the silvery strips of water that led between bold, rocky headlands out to the broad Atlantic; the tall mountain peaks that showed so rugged an outline against the sky; the brown, peat-stained river that came brawling down from the uplands, and poured itself noisily into the creek; the wide, lonely moors, with their stretches of brilliant green grass and dark, treacherous bog pools; and the craggy cliffs that made a barrier against the ever-dashing waves, and round which thousands of sea birds flew, with harsh cries and whir of white wings.

Its situation at the end of a long peninsula made Kilmore Castle an isolated little kingdom of its own. On the shore stood a row of low, fishermen's white-washed cabins, dignified by the name of "the village"; but otherwise there was no human habitation in sight, and Ballycroghan, the market town and nearest postal, railway, and telegraph station, was ten miles off.

Trees were rarities at Kilmore; a few stunted specimens, all blown one way by the prevailing gale, grew as if huddled together for protection at the foot of the glen, but they were the exception that proved the rule; nevertheless, under the sheltering walls of the Castle Mrs. Fitzgerald had managed to acclimatize some exotic shrubs, and to cultivate quite a beautiful garden of flowers, for the temperature was uniformly mild, though the winds were boisterous. Brilliant St. Brigid's anemones, the poet's narcissus, tulips, jonquils, and hyacinths bloomed here almost as early as in the Scilly Isles, and made patches of fragrant brightness under the sitting-room windows; while in the crannies of the walls might be seen delicate maidenhair and other ferns, too tender generally to stand a winter in the open.

Born and bred in this far-away corner of the world, Honor had grown up almost a child of nature. Her whole life had been spent as much as possible out-of-doors, boating, fishing, or swimming in the creek; driving in a low-backed car over the rough Kerry roads; galloping her shaggy little pony on the moors; following the otter hounds up the river, and sharing in any sport that her father considered suitable for her age and sex. She was the only girl among five brothers, and in her mother's opinion was by far the most difficult to manage of the whole flock. All the wild Irish blood of the family seemed to have settled in her; the high spirits, the fire, the pride, the quick temper, the impatience of control, the happy-go-lucky, idle, irresponsible ways of a long line of hot-headed ancestors had skipped a generation or two, and, as if they had been bottling themselves up during the interval, had reappeared with renewed force in this particular specimen of the Fitzgerald race.

"She's more trouble than the five boys put together," her mother often declared, and her friends cordially agreed with her. Mrs. Fitzgerald herself was a mild, quiet, nervous, delicate lady, as much astonished at her lively, tempestuous daughter as a meek little hedge-sparrow would be, that had hatched a young cuckoo. Frankly, she did not understand Honor, whose strong, uncontrolled character differed so entirely from her own gentle, clinging, dependent disposition; and whose storms of grief or anger, wild fits of waywardness and equally passionate repentance, and self-willed disobedience, alternating with sudden bursts of reformation, were a constant source of worry and anxiety, and the direct opposite of her ideal of girlhood. Poor Mrs. Fitzgerald would have liked a docile, tractable daughter, who would have been content to sit beside her sofa doing fancy work, instead of riding to hounds; and who would have had more consideration for her weak state of health. She appreciated Honor's warm-hearted affection to the full, but at the same time wished she could make her realize that rough hugs, boisterous kisses, and loud tones were hardly suitable to an invalid. Suffering as she was from a painful and incurable complaint, it was sometimes impossible for her to admit Honor to her sick-room, and for weeks together the girl would hardly see her mother. It was through no lack of love that Honor had failed to give that service and tenderness which, in the circumstances, an only daughter might so fitly have rendered; it was from sheer want of thought, and general heedlessness. Some girls early acquire a sense of responsibility and care for others, but in Honor these qualities were as undeveloped as in a child of six.

Many were the governesses who had attempted to tame the young rebel, and bring her into a state of law and order, but all had been equal failures. She had learnt lessons when she felt inclined, and left them undone when she was idle; and she had managed to make life in the schoolroom such a purgatory that it had been difficult to persuade any teacher to stay long at the Castle, and cope with so thankless a task as her education.

It had been of little use to complain to her father, the only person in the world whose authority she recognized; he was proud of his handsome daughter, and, except when her temper crossed his own, was apt to indulge her in most of her whims. Matters had at last, however, come to a crisis. An act of more than usual assumption on Honor's part had aroused Major Fitzgerald's utmost indignation, and had caused him suddenly to decide that she was spoiling at home, and that the only possible solution of the difficulty was to dispatch her to school as soon as the necessary arrangements could be made for her departure.

The incident that led to this resolution was very characteristic of Honor's headstrong, impulsive nature. She was passionately fond of horses, and for some time had been anxious to possess a new pony. It was not that she loved Pixie, her former favourite, any the less; but he was growing old, and was now scarcely able to take a fence, or carry her in mad career over the moors, being only fit for a sober trot on the high road, or to draw her mother's Bath chair round the garden. To obtain a strong, well-bred, fiery substitute for Pixie was the summit of Honor's ambition. One day, when she was with her father at Ballycroghan, she saw exactly the realization of her ideal. It was a small black cob, which showed a trace of Arab blood in its arching neck, slender limbs, and easy, springy motion. Though its bright eyes proved its high spirit, it was nevertheless as gentle as a lamb, and well accustomed to carrying a lady. Its owner, a local horse-dealer, was anxious to sell it, and pressed Major Fitzgerald to take it as a bargain. Honor simply fell in love with it on the spot. She ascertained that its name was Firefly, and begged and besought her father to buy it for her. But on this occasion he would not yield, even to her utmost coaxing. He did not wish to keep another pony in the stable, and he considered the price asked was excessive, and entirely beyond the present limits of his purse.

"No, Honor, it can't be done," he said. "You must be content with poor old Pixie. I have quite enough expenses just now, without running into such an extravagance."

"But couldn't I have it instead of something else?" pleaded Honor.

"There's nothing we could knock off, dear child," replied her father.

"I could do without a governess," suggested Honor hopefully. "I'd set myself my own lessons, and learn them too. Oh, Daddy, darling, if we gave up Miss Bury, wouldn't you have money enough to buy Firefly?"

Major Fitzgerald laughed in spite of himself.

"I consider Miss Bury a necessity, and not a luxury," he replied. "A governess is the very last person we could dispense with. I should like to see you setting your own lessons! Remarkably short and easy ones they would be! No, little woman, I'm afraid Firefly is an impossibility, and you must just try to forget his existence."

Unfortunately, that was exactly what Honor could not do. She thought continually about the beautiful black cob, and the more she dwelt on her disappointment the more keenly she felt it. She considered, most unreasonably, that her governess was the alternative of the pony, and that if she were without the one she might possibly acquire the other. Her behaviour had never been exemplary, but on the strength of this grievance she grew so unruly, so disrespectful, and so absolutely unmanageable that Miss Bury at length refused to teach her any longer, and, after an interview with Major Fitzgerald in the library, packed her boxes and returned home to England.

Honor viewed her exodus with keen delight. It seemed the removal of an obstacle to her plan. She went in to luncheon determined to broach once more the subject of Firefly, hoping this time to meet with better success. She saw at once, however, from her father's face, that he was not in a suitable mood to grant her any favour. He was much annoyed at the governess's departure, for which he had the justice to blame Honor alone; and he was worried with business matters.

"That tiresome agent has not sent the telegram I expected," he announced. "I shall be obliged to go over to Cork, to consult my solicitor. Tell Murphy to have the trap ready by two o'clock, and let Holmes pack my bag. I shall probably be away until Friday evening."

As soon as her father had started for the station, Honor sauntered out in the direction of the stables. It was one of her mother's bad days. Mrs. Fitzgerald was confined to her room, therefore Honor, released from Miss Bury's authority, felt herself her own mistress. Finding Fergus, the groom, she ordered him to saddle Pixie, and make ready to accompany her on a ride. Fergus was devoted to "Miss Honor", and would never have dreamt of disputing any command she might give him; before three o'clock, therefore, her pony was at the door, and, dressed in her neat blue habit, she was ambling away in the direction of Ballycroghan. It was a leisurely progress, for poor Pixie's gait was slow, in spite of his best endeavours, and Honor loved him too well to urge him hard.

She was determined to call at the horse-dealer's, and to ascertain if Firefly were still for sale. Perhaps, when her father returned home, she might catch him at a favourable moment, and be able to cajole him into changing his mind and buying the cob. Mr. O'Connor, the horse-dealer, lived at a large farm on the way to the town, and, to Honor's intense delight, the first object that met her eyes on approaching the house was Firefly, feeding demurely in a paddock to the left of the road. By an equally lucky chance Mr. O'Connor happened to be at home, and came hurrying out at once when he saw "one of the quality", as he expressed it, drawing bridle at his door.

"Good afternoon! I see you still have the black cob," began Honor eagerly.

"Yes, missy," replied the horse-dealer, "and I was thinking of sending a message to your father about him this very day. It's the good fortune to see you here! I've had a man over from Limerick who's anxious to take him—a tradesman who'd run him in a light cart—but I didn't close the bargain at once. I said to my wife: 'Firefly is too good a breed to carry out groceries. I'd rather be for selling him to the Castle. Miss Fitzgerald took the fancy for him, and I'll not be parting with him till I've had word again from the Major.' Maybe his honour will be wanting him, after all? But sure I must know at once, for the Limerick man will be here at noon to-morrow, and I've promised to tell him one way or another."

"Could you possibly wait until Saturday?" asked Honor.

The dealer shook his head.

"I can't afford to miss a sale," he replied. "I've had the cob on my hands for some time; it's just eating its head off, and it's anxious I am to get rid of it."

Honor was in a fever of excitement. Firefly, so spirited and so aristocratic, whose delicately shaped limbs looked only fit for leaping brooks, or cantering over the short grass on the uplands, to be sold to a tradesman, and to run between the shafts of a cart that delivered groceries! It seemed a degradation and an outrage. She could not dream of allowing it; she must save him at any cost from such a fate.

"Must you absolutely have an answer to-day?" she asked.

"Yes, missy. I fear I couldn't put off Sullivan any longer than noon to-morrow. He's a touchy man, and ready to carry his business elsewhere."

"Very well, then, that settles the matter. We will take the cob. You may send him over to the Castle this evening."

Honor spoke in such a high-handed manner that the dealer never guessed she was acting on her own authority. As she had made a special visit to the farm, accompanied by her groom, he imagined she must have been entrusted by Major Fitzgerald with full powers to buy the pony if she wished.

"Many thanks to you, missy! It's the fine mistress you'll make for Firefly. My respects to his honour, and the price shall be the same as I was asking him before."

The price! Honor had quite forgotten that. Weighed against Firefly's possible future, it had seemed an unimportant detail. She remembered now, however, that her father had considered it extravagant, and declared he could not afford it. The thought was sufficient to check her joy suddenly, and to send her home in a sober frame of mind that was well justified by the sequel.

Major Fitzgerald's wrath, when he arrived on the Friday and found the black cob installed in the stable, was more serious than his daughter had ever experienced before.

"It was a piece of unwarranted presumption!" he declared. "I shall not allow you to keep the pony. It must be sent back to O'Connor's, and resold at the first opportunity. As for you, the sooner you are packed off to school the better. We have indulged you too much at home, and it is time indeed that you learnt to submit to some kind of discipline."

The proposal to send her away to school was a terrible blow to Honor. At first she appealed to her mother, begging her to plead with her father and try to persuade him to alter his resolution. But Mrs. Fitzgerald, while regretting to part with her troublesome daughter, was so convinced of the wisdom of the proceeding that, instead of interceding, she applauded her husband's decision.

"I can't ever like England!" sobbed Honor. "I'd rather have our mountains and lakes and bogs than all the grand streets and houses. I'm Irish to the core, and I don't believe any school over the water can change me. There's no place in the world like Kilmore. I love even the cabins, and the peat fires, and the pigs, and the potatoes! I shan't forget a single stick or stone of it, and I shall never know a moment's happiness till I'm home again."

After considerable hesitation, and the examination of a large number of prospectuses, Major and Mrs. Fitzgerald had determined to send Honor to Chessington College. It had a wide and well-deserved reputation, and Miss Cavendish, the principal, was understood to give much individual attention to the characters and dispositions of her pupils. Added to this, it was situated within a few miles of the Naval Preparatory School where Dermot, Honor's younger brother, had been for the last two years; so that they knew from experience that the neighbourhood was bracing and healthy.

"It's a comfort, at any rate, that I shall be near Dermot," said Honor, as she sat watching while her mother superintended the maid who was packing her boxes.

"I'm afraid you won't see much of him, dear, during term-time," replied Mrs. Fitzgerald. "He will not be able to visit you, I'm sure; neither will Miss Cavendish allow you to go out with him."

"Why not?" demanded Honor.

"Because it would be against the rules."

"Then the rules are absurd, and I shan't keep them."

"Honor! Honor! Don't speak like that! You have run wild here, but at Chessington College you will be obliged to fall in with the ordinary regulations."

"They'll have hard work to tame me, Mother!" laughed Honor, jumping up and dancing a little impromptu jig between the boxes. "I don't want to go, but since I must, I mean to get any enjoyment I can out of it.

After all, perhaps it may be rather fun. It's deadly dull here sometimes, when the boys are at school, and Father is busy or away."

Mrs. Fitzgerald sighed. In her delicate health she could scarcely expect to be a companion for Honor, yet when she thought of how few years might be left them together, the parting seemed bitter, and she was hurt that her only daughter would evidently miss her so little. Young folks often say cruel things from mere thoughtlessness, and unintentionally grieve those who love them. In after years Honor would keenly regret her tactless speech, and blame herself that she had not spent more hours in trying to be a comfort, instead of a care; but for the present, though she noticed the look of disappointment that passed over the sensitive face, she did not fully realize its cause, and the words that might have healed the wound went unspoken.

At length the preparations were concluded, and the time had almost arrived to bid farewell to Kilmore Castle and the surrounding demesne. Honor's friends in the village mourned her approaching departure with characteristic Irish grief.

"Miss Honor, darlint, it's meself that will be hungerin' for a sight of yez!" cried old Mary O'Grady, standing at the doorway of her thatched cabin, from which the blue peat smoke issued like a thin mist.

"And it's grand news entoirely they'll be afther tellin' me too, that ye're lavin' the Castle, and goin' over the seas!" put in Biddy Macarthy, a next-door neighbour of Mary's. "It's fine to think of all the iligant things ye'll be seein' now!"

"Bless your bright eyes, it's many a sad heart ye'll lave behind yez!" added Pat Conolly, the oldest tenant on the estate.

"England can never compare with dear Ireland, in my opinion," replied Honor, with a choke in her voice. "There's no spot so sweet as Kilmore, and all the while I'm away I shall be wishing myself back in the 'ould counthree'!"

"Will ye be despisin' this bit of a present, Miss Honor?" said old Mary, producing a cardboard box, from which, out of many folds of tissue paper, she proudly displayed a large bunch of imitation four-leaved shamrock. "My grandson Micky brought it for me all the way from Dublin city, and I've kept it fine and new in its papers. Sure, I know it's not worthy of offerin' to a young lady like yourself, but I'll take it kindly if ye'll deign to accept it."

"Of course I'll accept it!" returned Honor heartily. "It's very kind of you to give it to me. It shall go to school with me, as a remembrance of Ireland, and of you all."

"The four-leaved shamrock brings good luck to its wearer, mavourneen; may it bring it to you! And whenever ye look at the little green leaves, give a thought to the true hearts that will be ay wishin' ye a speedy return."

The last day came all too soon, and Mrs. Fitzgerald, with tears in her eyes, stood at her window, watching the disappearing carriage in which Honor sat by her father's side, waving an energetic good-bye.

"Surely," she said to herself, "school will have the influence that we expect! The general atmosphere of law and order, the well-arranged rules, the esprit de corps and strict discipline of the games, all cannot fail to have their effect; and among so large a number of companions, and in the midst of so many new and absorbing interests, my wild bird will find her wings clipped, and will settle down sensibly and peaceably among the others."

CHAPTER III. THE WEARING OF THE GREEN

Chessington College stood on a breezy slope midway between the hills and the sea, and about a mile from the rising watering-place of Dunscar. It was a famous spot for a school, as the fresh winds coming either from the uplands or from the wide expanse of channel were sufficient to blow away all chance of germs, and to ensure a thoroughly wholesome and bracing atmosphere. The College prided itself upon its record of health; Miss Cavendish considered no other girls were so straight and well-grown as hers, with such bright eyes, such clear skins, and such blooming cheeks. Ventilation, sea baths, and suitable diet were her three watchwords, and thanks to them the sanatorium at the farther side of the shrubbery scarcely ever opened its doors to receive a patient, while the hospital nurse who was retained in case of emergencies found her position a sinecure.

The buildings were modern and up-to-date, with all the latest appliances and improvements. They were provided with steam heat and electric light; and the gymnasium, chemical laboratory, and practical demonstration kitchen were on the very newest of educational lines. The school covered a large space, and was built in the form of a square. In the middle was a great, gravelled quadrangle, where hockey could be practised on days when the fields were too wet for playing. At one end stood the big lecture-hall, the chapel, the library, and the various classrooms, the whole surmounted by a handsome clock tower; while opposite was the School House, where Miss Cavendish herself presided over a chosen fifty of her two hundred pupils. The two sides of the square were occupied by four houses, named respectively St. Aldwyth's, St. Hilary's, St. Chad's, and St. Bride's, each being in charge of a mistress, and capable of accommodating from thirty to forty girls. Though the whole school met together every day for lessons, the members of each different house resembled a separate family, and were keenly anxious to maintain the honour of their particular establishment. Miss Cavendish did not wish to excite rivalry, yet she thought a spirit of friendly emulation was on the whole salutary, and encouraged matches between the various house teams, or competitions among the choral and debating societies. The rules for all were exactly similar. Every morning, at a quarter to seven, a clanging bell rang in the passages for a sufficient length of time to disturb even the soundest of slumbers; breakfast was at half-past seven, and at half-past eight everybody was due in chapel for a short service; lectures and classes occupied the morning from nine till one, and the afternoon was devoted to games; tea was at four, and supper at half-past seven, with preparation in between; and after that hour came sewing and recreation, until bedtime. It was a well-arranged and reasonable division of time, calculated to include right proportions of work and play. *Mens sana in corpore sano* was Miss Cavendish's favourite motto, and the clean bill of health, the successes in examinations, and the high moral tone that prevailed throughout pointed to the fulfilment of her ideal. Most of the girls were thoroughly happy at Chessington College, and, though it is in girl nature to grumble at rules and lessons, there was scarcely one who would have cared to leave it if she had been given the opportunity.

It was to this new, interesting, and exciting world of school that Honor unclosed her eyes on the morning after her arrival. She opened them sleepily, and, I regret to say, promptly shut them again, and turned over comfortably in bed, regardless of the vigorous bell that was delivering its warning in the passage. Punctuality had not been counted a cardinal virtue at Kilmore Castle, and she saw no special necessity for rising until she felt inclined. She had just dropped off again into a delicious doze when once more her peace was rudely disturbed. The curtain of her cubicle was drawn back, and three lively faces made their appearance.

"Look here! Don't you know it's time to get up?" said Maisie Talbot, administering a vigorous poke that would have roused the Seven Sleepers of legendary lore, and caused even Honor to yawn.

"You'll be fined a penny if you're late for breakfast," added Lettice, "and that's a very unsatisfactory way of disposing of one's pocket-money."

"And makes Miss Maitland particularly irate," said Pauline Reynolds.

"Honor Fitzgerald! do you intend to get up, or do you not? Because if you don't, we shall have to try 'cold pig'!" Then, as there were no signs of movement, Lettice carried out her threat by dabbing a wet sponge full in Honor's face, while at the same moment Maisie wrenched back the bed-clothes with a relentless hand.

"We're doing you a real kindness, so you needn't be cross, Miss Paddy Pepper-box!" said Lettice. "Just wait till you've seen Miss Maitland scowl at a late-comer, and you'll give us a vote of thanks."

"I'm not cross," said Honor, laughing in spite of the violation of her slumbers. Lettice spoke so merrily, it was impossible to take offence, even at the nickname. "But I think you use rather summary measures. The sponge was horribly cold and nasty."

"It's the only way to get people to bestir themselves," said Lettice complacently. "I've had experience with sleepy room-mates before."

"We always try the water cure at St. Chad's," added Maisie. "We've given you quite mild treatment, as it was a first case; we might have used your bedroom jug, instead of a sponge."

Owing to her companions' efforts, Honor was in time for breakfast—a fortunate circumstance for her, as, after the episode at the tea-table on the preceding evening, her house-mistress would not have been ready to overlook any deficiency in punctuality.

There was always a short recess between breakfast and chapel, which the girls called a "breathing space", and during which they could revise exercises, sharpen lead pencils, and take a last peep at lessons. This morning everybody seemed to be assembling in the dressing-room for this brief interval, and there Honor repaired with the others.

"I hear you've been put in the Lower Third, Paddy," said Lettice Talbot. "Vivian Holmes told me so just now. It's my form. Maisie and Pauline are in it too."

"Isn't Maisie above you?" asked Honor, looking at the sisters, the elder of whom overtopped the younger by nearly a head. "She is in inches, at any rate."

"I'm only a year older than Lettice, though I am so much taller," explained Maisie. "I suppose I ought to be in a higher form, but she always manages to catch me up. I make up my mind every term I'm going to win a double remove and leave her behind, yet somehow it never happens to come off. I'm much better at cricket and hockey than at French and algebra. But after all, it's rather convenient to have her in the same form: she's sure to remember what the lesson is when I forget, and I can borrow her books if I lose my own."

"Yes, I have to work for both," complained Lettice. "Maisie won't even copy her exercise questions; she always relies on me."

Maisie certainly made her younger sister useful. She expected her to fetch and carry, tidy both their cubicles, and generally maintain a very subservient and inferior position. On the other hand, though she tyrannized over Lettice herself, she would not allow anybody else to do so, and was ready to take her part and fight her battles against the whole school.

"I'm glad we're in the same class," remarked Honor, with an approving glance at Lettice's round, smiling face. "Perhaps I shall ask you to copy the exercise questions too. My memory is not particularly good where lessons are concerned. Who else is in the Lower Third?"

"Ruth Latimer, my greatest chum."

"We allow ourselves chums," put in Maisie, "but we're not at all romantic at Chessington. We don't swear eternal friendships, and exchange locks of hair, and walk about the College with our arms clasped round each other's necks, and write each other sentimental notes, with 'sweetest' and 'darling' and 'fondest love' in them. That's what Miss Maitland calls 'early Victorian'. We're very matter of fact here. Still, when we choose a chum we generally stick to her, and don't go in for all that nonsense of 'getting out of friends', or not speaking, as they do at some schools."

Honor was about to ask more questions, but at that moment Vivian Holmes, the monitress and head girl of the house, came bustling into the room.

"You haven't got your sailor and jersey yet, Honor Fitzgerald," she said. "Miss Maitland asked me to give them to you. Here they are, both marked with your name, so that they needn't be mixed up with anybody else's. You're to take this hook, and this compartment for your shoes, and this locker to keep your books in. I've put labels on them all."

Honor looked without enthusiasm at the knitted woollen coat, and with marked disfavour at the white sailor hat, with its band of orange ribbon.

"I can't wear that!" she ejaculated.

"Why not?" enquired Vivian, in surprise.

"There's an orange band round it."

"Orange is the St. Chad's colour," explained Vivian. "We all have exactly the same hats at Chessington, but each house has its own special ribbon—blue for the School House, pink for St. Aldwyth's, scarlet for St. Hilary's, and violet for St. Bride's. I thought you knew that already."

"If I had, I'd have insisted upon going to another house," declared Honor tragically. "You ask me to wear orange? Why, the very name of 'Orangeman' sets my teeth on edge. I'm a Nationalist to the last drop of my blood; we all are, down in Kerry."

Vivian smiled.

"Don't be absurd!" she said, in rather an off-hand manner. "Our hats have nothing whatever to do with politics. Here are two long pins, but if you prefer an elastic you can stitch one on," and without deigning to argue further she walked away.

Honor stood turning the hat round and round, with a very queer expression on her face. She was a devoted daughter of Erin. Her country's former glories and the possible brilliance of its future as a separate kingdom could always provoke her wildest enthusiasm; to be asked, therefore, to don the colour which in her native land stood as the symbol of the union with England, and for direct opposition to national independence, seemed to her little short of an insult to her dear Emerald Isle. There were still five minutes left before she need start for chapel, so, making up her mind suddenly, she rushed upstairs to her bedroom. She would show these Saxons that she was a true Celt! They might compel her to wear their emblem of bondage, but it should be with an addition that would proclaim her patriotic sentiments to the world.

Hurriedly hunting in her top drawer, she produced a yard of vivid green ribbon and the bunch of imitation shamrock that old Mary O'Grady had given her as a parting present. Then she set to work on a piece of amateur millinery. There was little time to use needle and thread, but with the aid of pins she managed to twist the ribbon into several loops, and to fasten the shamrock conspicuously in front. She looked at the result of her labours with great approval.

"One could almost imagine it was St. Patrick's Day," she said to herself. "Nobody could possibly mistake me now for a Unionist. I'm labelled 'Home Rule' as plainly as can be." Then, hastily pinning on her hat before the mirror, she ran downstairs, humming under her breath:

"So we'll bide our time; our banner yet

And motto shall be seen,

And voices shout the chorus out,

'The Wearin' o' the Green'!"

The girls at Chessington College were all dressed exactly alike, in a uniform costume of blue serge skirts, with blue or white cotton blouses for summer, and flannel ones for winter. On Sundays they wore white serge coats and skirts, and for evenings white muslin or nuns' veiling. They were allowed a little latitude in the way of embroideries with respect to best frocks, but their everyday, ordinary clothes were required to be of the school pattern, with the addition of sailor hats and knitted coats, for use in running across the quadrangle on wet or cold days. Miss Cavendish considered that this rule encouraged simplicity, and provided against any undue extravagance in the matter of dress. She did not allow rings or bracelets to be worn, and the sole vanity permitted to the girls was in the choice of their hair ribbons.

Punctually at twenty-five minutes past eight each morning the bell in the little chapel began to give warning, and by half-past every member of the school was expected to have taken her seat, and to be ready for the short service held there daily by the senior curate of the parish church at Dunscar. In twos and threes and small groups the girls came hurrying in answer to the call of the tinkling bell. Though they laughed and talked as they ran across the quadrangle, they sobered down as they neared the door, and, each taking a Prayer Book from a pile laid ready in the porch, passed silently and reverently into the chapel. Every house had its own special rows of seats, and the sailor hats that mingled like a kaleidoscope in the grounds were here divided into their several sets of colours, though sometimes varied by a gleam of ruby or amber falling from the stained-glass windows above. The singing was musical and the responses hearty, while into his five minutes' explanation of the lesson for the day the clergyman generally managed to compress much helpful thought, sending away some, at least, of his hearers braced up for the duties that awaited them.

On this particular morning anyone accustomed to the ordinary atmosphere of the place might have been aware that something of an unusual character was in the air.

There was an undercurrent of unrest, a turning of heads, a subdued rustling, even an occasional whisper; and the head mistress, realizing at last that some outside cause must be distracting the minds of her pupils, glanced up, and, following the direction of all eyes, saw a sight that filled her with unfeigned astonishment. Among the neat rows of orange-banded sailor hats in the benches marked "St. Chad's" was one trimmed with large and obtrusive knots of emerald-green ribbon, which drooped over the brim, while a bunch of imitation shamrock finished the front. It seemed to stand out so conspicuously from its fellows that it resembled a succulent palm tree growing in the midst of a sandy desert, and could not fail to attract the attention of the whole school. How such an irregularity had crept in amongst the uniforms of the college Miss Cavendish could not comprehend; it must form the subject of an after enquiry, and in the meantime, stilling with a reproachful glance a faint whisper in her vicinity, she joined in the singing of a psalm with her usual clear intonation. When the service was over, however, and the girls began to file away in orderly line, she spoke a few, rapid words to a monitress, who at once passed quickly out by a side door.

As the extraordinary green hat made its appearance in the quadrangle it was greeted with quite a buzz of excitement by the girls assembled outside. Only a few of them, comparatively, knew Honor by sight, and the rest were asking who she was, and to which house she belonged. The common feeling was distinctly unfavourable. Apart from the unseemliness of such an exhibition in a sacred place, new girls were not expected to make themselves conspicuous, or to introduce innovations; either was considered an impertinence on their part: so the general verdict was that Honor had done a dreadful thing, and public opinion was dead against her. She, however, held up her head as proudly as though her absurd hat had been the latest creation from Bond Street.

"It's a tribute to my native land!" she said airily, in response to a chorus of questions. "Sorry you don't like it, but it's my first attempt at hat-trimming, and I flattered myself it wasn't bad for a beginner. St. Patrick for ever! I made up my mind before I started that I'd keep up the credit of the shamrock on this side of the water, and I've done my best. Hurrah for old Ireland!" Then, as if her feelings were absolutely too much for her, she took her skirt in her hands, and began to dance an old-fashioned Kerry hornpipe, humming a lively Irish tune to supply the music.

The girls stared in amazement at the mad performance. "She's showing off!" declared some, but others laughed, and watched with a kind of fascination, for the dance was striking and original, and the movements were unusually graceful.

Honor's triumph, however, was short-lived. Vivian Holmes forced her way through the crowd, and, laying her hand on the shoulder of the obstreperous new-comer, told her to report herself at once in Miss Cavendish's study. The lookers-on scuttled away to their classes without being told; they were half-ashamed of having taken so much notice of a new girl. Lettice Talbot, turning round, caught a glimpse of Honor walking blithely away, with a jaunty smile on her face.

"As if a visit to the head mistress meant nothing at all!" she gasped.

"She'll soon find out her mistake," replied Ruth Latimer grimly. "Miss Cavendish can reduce one to a quaking jelly when she feels inclined."

Honor was in one of her wildest, most reckless moods, and the prospect of a passage of arms with the principal of the College was as the call of battle to a knight of old. In her conflicts with her governesses at home she had invariably come off best, and it pleased her to think she had now the opportunity of trying her will in opposition to that of the ruler of this little kingdom.

Miss Cavendish's study was a beautiful and unusual room. It was built in accordance with an old-world design, and in shape resembled an ancient chapter-house. The richly carved chimney-piece, the dark panelling of the walls, and the straight-backed oak chairs helped to carry out the prevailing note of mediaevalism, which was further enhanced by a large, stained-glass window, filled with figures of saints, that faced the doorway. To enter was like going into the peace and serenity of some old cathedral, and, notwithstanding her defiant frame of mind, a feeling of something akin to reverence crept over Honor as she crossed the threshold. Her impressionable Celtic temperament could not fail to be influenced by outward surroundings: she had a great love of the beautiful, and this room satisfied her æsthetic tastes.

The head mistress was standing beside the hearth, which, though devoid of fire at this season of the year, was piled up with newly cut logs. In her long, clinging black dress, the light from the halo of St. Aldwyth in the window falling on her regular Greek features, and touching with a ruddier gleam the pale gold of her rippling hair, Miss Cavendish looked an imposing and commanding figure. Born of a good family, the daughter of a high dignitary of the Church, she was by nature a student, and after a brilliant career at Girton she had for a time devoted herself to scientific research, arousing much interest by her clever articles in various periodicals; but feeling that her true vocation was teaching, she had turned her attention to education, and, gaining a reputation in the scholastic world, had in course of time been elected as the principal of Chessington College, a post which she filled with dignity, and greatly to the satisfaction of both governors and parents. Not a remarkably tender woman, she was perhaps more respected than loved by her pupils; but she had great powers of administration, and managed to impress upon her girls a strict sense of duty and responsibility, a love of work, a fine perception of honour, and a desire to keep up the high tone and prestige of the school.

She turned her clear, cold blue eyes on Honor, as the latter entered the room, with a scrutinizing gaze, so comprehensive and so full of authority that, despite her intention of showing a bold front, the girl involuntarily quailed.

"Come here, Honor Fitzgerald," began Miss Cavendish, in a calm, measured tone. "I wish you to explain to me why you have taken it upon yourself to alter the costume which, you are well aware, is obligatory for all attending the College."

"I can't wear orange," replied Honor, plucking up her courage for the battle; "it's against my principles."

"There are right principles and wrong principles; we will decide presently to which class yours belong. On what grounds do you raise your objection?"

"I'm Irish," said Honor briefly, "so I prefer green."

"That is no reason. We have many nationalities here, and do you imagine that every girl can be permitted to carry out her individual taste? Tell me why you suppose such a rule was framed."

"I don't know," returned Honor rebelliously.

"Then you must think, for I require an answer."

Honor stared at the fireplace, at the bookcase, with its richly bound volumes; at the window, where the red robe of St. Hilary made such a glorious spot of colour; at the table, covered with books and papers; and finally her glance went back to the head mistress, whose eyes were still fixed on her with that steady, embarrassing gaze.

"Was it to make everybody look alike?" she replied at last, almost as if the words were dragged from her lips.

"Exactly! Then, to return to my original question, why, knowing this fact, did you presume to break the rule?"

Honor was again silent. Somehow her intended bravery seemed to desert her.

"I met your father, Major Fitzgerald, yesterday," continued Miss Cavendish. "I understand that he held a command in the Royal Munster Fusiliers, and did splendid service in the Boer War. Kindly tell me what explanation he would have given to his general if he had appeared at church parade minus his uniform."

"Oh, but he wouldn't have done that!" exclaimed Honor in horror.

"Why not?"

"Why! because he is a soldier. How could he? The uniform is part of the service."

"And what is the first duty of a soldier?"

"To obey orders," answered Honor, with a spark of apprehension in her eyes.

"You are right. Now, what would happen to a regiment if each individual, instead of obeying his superior officer, were to follow his own inclinations?"

"It would go to pieces."

"And what occurs when a soldier commits any breach of regulations?"

"He is court-martialled and punished."

"Is that just?"

"Yes."

"But why?"

"Oh, because—because—it's the Army, and they must! There couldn't be any discipline without."

"Exactly! You are an officer's daughter, and you evidently appreciate the vast importance of good discipline. Now, we are a little army here. Every girl, as a member of this community, is bound to preserve its rules, which have been wisely framed, and deserve to be faithfully kept. You have been guilty of a very grave breach of our regulations, and by your own showing you merit punishment. Do you consider this to be just?"

"Yes," returned Honor, meeting the head mistress's look firmly.

"We have an esprit de corps at the College," continued Miss Cavendish, "which makes each girl anxious to keep up the credit and prestige of the school. When you have been here a short time, and have learnt the tone of the place, I believe and trust that you will be truly ashamed of the remembrance of your appearance in chapel this morning. It is for this reason I shall not punish you, though you have yourself acknowledged that punishment would be only an act of justice. As for the matter of principle to which you referred, so far from advancing the good fame of your country, you were bringing it into disrepute. If you imagine it was a particularly patriotic deed to flaunt the shamrock in a wrong place you are much mistaken. We have had Irish girls here before, and I have always been able to rely upon them for the maintenance of our high standard. You may go now, Honor, and remove that foolish trimming from your hat; and remember that, as you have been christened 'Honor', I shall expect you to live up to your name."

Honor left the room more subdued than she would have cared to acknowledge. The calm, well-balanced arguments had completely disarmed her. She had entered in a reckless mood, almost anxious to be scolded, that she might have the chance of showing how little she cared; and now, for perhaps the first time in her life, she had been compelled to think seriously and sensibly upon a subject.

Very few teachers would have taken the trouble to reason thus with a pupil, but Miss Cavendish had her special method of education, and believed in paying particular attention to each girl's individuality. "Different plants require different cultivation, if you are to obtain good results," was one of her axioms. "You cannot successfully grow roses and carnations with the same treatment." She had seen at once, partly from her own observation and partly as the result of a talk with Major Fitzgerald, that Honor was an unusual and difficult character; and she wished to obtain a hold over the girl's mind from the very outset. It was part of her system to train her pupils to keep rules rather from a recognition of their justice and value than from a fear of punishment; therefore she regarded the ten minutes spent in the study as, not wasted time, but an opportunity of sowing good seed on hitherto neglected ground.

Vivian Holmes was waiting for Honor outside the door of the study. After conducting her to the school dressing-room, she produced a pair of scissors and ripped the offending green trimming from the hat in stony silence.

"May I keep them?" Honor ventured to ask, for it went to her heart to see her bunch of cherished shamrock torn ruthlessly from its place and flung aside.

"As you like," replied Vivian, "so long as they are not seen here again." Then, with a look of utterly crushing scorn, she burst out: "You needn't think that what you have done is at all clever. It's not the place of a new girl to show off in this way, and you'll gain nothing by it. I am responsible for St. Chad's, and I don't mean to have this kind of nonsense going on there; so please understand, Honor Fitzgerald, that if you give any more trouble, you may expect to find yourself thoroughly well sat upon!"

CHAPTER IV. JANIE'S CHARGE

The four-leaved shamrock having so far belied its reputation, and brought bad luck instead of good upon its wearer, Honor put it away in her drawer, with the resolve not to test its powers again until she was back in her own Emerald Isle, where, perhaps, it could exercise its magic more freely than in the land of the stranger.

Her first day at school was satisfactory, in spite of its bad beginning. She took her place in her new class, and made the acquaintance of Miss Farrar, her Form mistress, and all the seventeen girls who composed the Lower Third Form.

After the quiet and solitude of Kilmore Castle, to be at Chessington College seemed like plunging into the world. It was almost bewildering to meet so many companions, all of whom were busily occupied with employments into which she had not yet been initiated. It was an especially fresh experience for Honor to belong to a class, instead of learning from a private governess, and she much appreciated the change. It interested her to watch the faces of her schoolfellows, and to listen to their recitations, or their replies to Miss Farrar's questions. The strict discipline of the place astonished her: the ready answers, the total lack of whispering, the way in which each girl sat straight at her desk, giving her whole attention to the subject in hand; the prompt obedience, even the orderly manner of filing out of the room for lunch, all were as unusual as they were amazing to one who had hitherto behaved as she liked during lessons. She felt for the first time that she was a unit in a large community, and began to have some dim perception of that esprit de corps to which Miss Cavendish had referred during their interview in the study.

In spite of her previous laziness and neglect of work, Honor was a very bright girl, and she contrived even in that first morning to satisfy Miss Farrar that she was capable of doing well if she wished. Perhaps, after all, the four-leaved shamrock had sent her a little luck, for she happened to remember a date which the rest of the Form had forgotten, and won corresponding credit in consequence. When one o'clock arrived she arranged her new textbooks and notebooks in the desk that had been allotted to her next to Lettice Talbot.

"Did you get into a fearful scrape with Miss Cavendish, Paddy?" whispered the latter eagerly. "Do tell me about it!"

But Honor pursed up her mouth and looked inscrutable. She was unwilling to divulge what had passed in the study, and Lettice's curiosity had perforce to go unsatisfied.

On her arrival at St. Chad's Honor had been given a spare cubicle in the bedroom occupied by the Talbots and Pauline Reynolds. On the following afternoon, however, Miss Maitland sent for Janie Henderson, a girl of nearly sixteen, and informed her that a fresh arrangement had been made.

"I am going to put you and Honor Fitzgerald together in the room over the porch," she said. "I hope that you will get on nicely, and become friends. I want you, Janie, to have a good influence over Honor, and help her to keep school rules. She does not yet know our St. Chad's standards, and has very much to learn. I give her into your charge because I am sure you are conscientious, and will try your best to make her wish to improve and turn out a worthy Chaddite. You may carry your things into your new quarters during recreation-time."

"Yes, Miss Maitland," answered Janie, with due respect. She dared not dispute the mistress's orders, but inwardly she was anything but pleased. She did not wish to leave her present cubicle, and looked with dismay at the prospect of having to share a bedroom with this wild Irish girl, towards whom as yet she certainly felt no attraction.

Janie Henderson had a painfully shy and reserved disposition. Hitherto she had made no friends, invited no confidences, and "kept herself to herself" at St. Chad's. She was seldom seen walking with a companion, and during recreation generally buried herself in a book. Slight, pale, and narrow-chested, her constitution was not robust; and though a year and a half at Chessington College had already worked a wonderful improvement, she was still far below the ordinary average of good health. She was a quiet, mouse-like girl, who seldom obtruded herself, or took any prominent part in the life of St. Chad's—a girl who was continually in the background, and passed almost unnoticed among her schoolfellows. She had little self-confidence and a sensitive dread of being laughed at, so for this reason she rarely offered a suggestion, or an opinion, unless invited. She often felt lonely at school, but her shyness prevented her from making advances, and so far nobody had offered her even the elements of friendship. It sometimes hurt her to be thus entirely ignored and left out, but she had grown accustomed to it, and, shutting herself up in her shell, she followed the motto of the Miller of Dee:

"I care for nobody, no, not I,

Since nobody cares for me."

She was obliged to share in the daily games, which were compulsory for all; but she never joined in the voluntary ones unless she were specially asked to do so, to make up a side, and then she played with an utter lack of enthusiasm. "Moonie", as the girls called her, was a bookworm pure and simple. She had read almost every volume in the school library; it did not matter whether it were biography, travels, poetry, essays, or fiction, she would devour any literature that came her way. She lived in an imaginary world, peopled by heroes and heroines of romance, who often seemed more real to her than her schoolmates, and certainly twice as interesting. Half the time she went about in a dream, and even during lesson hours she would let her thoughts drift far away to some exciting incident in a story, or some mental picture of her own. It appeared as if Miss Maitland could not have picked out two more opposite and unsuitable girls to share a bedroom than Honor Fitzgerald and Janie Henderson; but she had good reasons for her choice. Not only did she hope that Janie's sober ways would steady Honor, but she also thought that Honor's high spirits would have a leavening effect upon Janie, who was sadly in need of stirring up.

"I wish I could shake the pair in a bag!" she confided to a fellow-teacher. "It would be of the greatest advantage to both."

There was at least one compensation to Janie for being obliged to change her quarters. No. 8, the room over the porch, was a special sanctum, much coveted by all the other Chaddites. It was arranged to accommodate only two, instead of four, and was the beau-ideal of every pair of chums. It had a French window opening out on to a tiny balcony, and, having been originally intended for one of the mistresses, was furnished rather more luxuriously than the rest of the bedrooms. There was a handsome wall-paper, a full-length mirror in the wardrobe, a comfortable basket-chair, and also what appealed particularly to Janie—a large and inviting bookcase, with glass doors. She conducted her removal, therefore, with less dissatisfaction than she had at first anticipated.

"I call you lucky," declared Lettice Talbot. "I only wish I could go instead. Everyone on our landing is envying you. I shall be rather sorry to lose Paddy—I think she's a joke."

"Especially as we're to have Flossie Taylor instead," said Pauline Reynolds. "It's a poor exchange. I can't stand Flossie; she gives herself airs."

"She needn't put them on with us," observed Maisie. "I've had a quarrel with her already. She was actually trying to make Lettice pick up her balls for her at tennis!"

"Lettice always picks up yours," suggested Pauline.

"That's a totally different matter," declared Maisie.

"I wish Miss Maitland would have let Flossie join the Hammond-Smiths," said Lettice. "I can't imagine why she is making such changes. Oh, here's Honor! Do you know, Paddy, you have got notice to quit?—in fact, you're going to be evicted from No. 13."

Honor had already been informed of the fact by the house-mistress herself. She appeared to take the news with the utmost sangfroid.

"I don't care in the least which room I have," she replied. "All I bargain for is a room-mate who doesn't use 'cold pig' in the mornings. I haven't forgotten your wet sponge."

"You ungrateful Paddy! It was for your good."

"If you call me Paddy I shall call you Salad!"

"You can if you like. It's rather a pretty name, and has a juicy, succulent sound about it."

"Make haste, Honor, and clear your drawers," grunted Maisie. "Here's Flossie Taylor coming down the passage with her arms full of under-linen."

No. 8, like all other bedrooms at St. Chad's, was divided by a curtain that could be drawn at pleasure. At present, however, this was pulled aside for the mutual convenience of the occupants of both cubicles. To Janie the burning question to be decided was the possession of the bookcase. She tried to imagine that it was nearer her bed than Honor's, but justice forced her to come to the conclusion that it stood exactly in the middle, between the two. With heroic self-denial she offered her companion the first choice of its shelves before she put away her own little library.

"But I haven't brought any books with me," declared Honor. "You're welcome to the bookcase, so far as I'm concerned. We can take turns at this luxury," sinking into the basket-chair.

"Don't you ever read?"

"Very seldom."

Janie went on arranging her volumes in silence, the poets on the top shelf, by the side of her edition of Scott's novels, and the miscellaneous authors below. She touched each book tenderly, as though it were an old and dear friend, opening one occasionally to glance at a favourite passage; and she became so absorbed in her occupation that she utterly forgot Honor's presence.

"There! I've stowed away all my possessions," remarked the latter at last. "I don't know whether Miss Maitland judges a room by a tidy bookcase. She said she was coming up presently, to see if we had put our things straight."

Janie started guiltily. She, who was expected to be the mentor and to keep her companion up to the mark, was certainly the defaulter in this instance. Her bed and the chairs were strewn with various articles, and nothing seemed as yet in its right place.

"I couldn't help dipping into that book," she confessed. "It's a collection of old Irish fairy tales and legends. It was given me yesterday, before I left home, and I've scarcely had time even to look at it."

"Are they nice?"

"Lovely, to judge by the one I've just sampled!"

"Then do tell it to me! I hate reading, but I'm an absolute baby for loving to be told old tales."

"I? Oh, I couldn't!" exclaimed Janie.

"Yes, you can—while I'm helping you to put all these things into your drawers. Do, mavourneen! I want to hear the Irish story."

When Honor's grey eyes looked pleadingly from under their long, dark lashes, and a soft blarney crept into her voice, there were few people who could resist her. Janie flushed pink; she was so seldom asked to do anything for anybody! She had no natural gift for narrative, but she made an effort.

"There was once an Irishman called Murtagh O'Neil," she began, "and he was walking over London Bridge, with a hazel staff in his hand, when an Englishman met him and told him that the stick he carried grew on a spot under which were hidden great treasures. The Englishman was a wizard, and he promised that if Murtagh would go with him to Ireland, and show him the place, he would gain as much gold as he could carry. Murtagh consented, so they went over to Bronbhearg, in Kerry, where there was a big green mound; and there they dug up the hazel tree on which the staff had grown. Under it they found a broad, flat stone, and this covered the entrance to a cavern where thousands of warriors lay in a circle, sleeping beside their shields, with their swords clasped in their hands. Their arms were so brightly polished that they illuminated the whole cave; and one of them had a shield that outshone the rest, and a crown of gold on his head. In the centre of the cave hung a bell, which the wizard told Murtagh to beware of touching; but, if at any time he did so, and one of the warriors were to ask: 'Is it day?' he was to answer without hesitation: 'No, sleep thou on!' The two men took as much as they could carry from a heap of gold pieces that lay amidst the warriors, and Murtagh managed accidentally to touch the bell. It rang, and one of the warriors immediately asked: 'Is it day?' when Murtagh answered promptly: 'No, sleep thou on!' The wizard told him that the company he had seen were King Brien Borombe and his knights, who lay asleep ready for the dawn of a new day. When the right time should come the bell would ring loudly, and the warriors would start up and destroy the enemies of Erin, and once more the descendants of the Tuatha di Danan should rule the isle in peace. When Murtagh's treasure was all finished, he went back to the cave and helped himself to more. On his way out he touched the bell, and again it rang; but this time he was not so ready with his answer, and some of the warriors rose up, took the gold from him, beat him, and flung him out of the cave. He never recovered from the beating, but was a cripple to the end of his days."

"And serve him right, too!" declared Honor. "Brien Borombe was a great hero of Ireland."

"Yes, there's one of Moore's *Irish Melodies* that begins: 'Remember the glories of Brien the brave'," said Janie.

"Are there any more stories about him in that book?"

"I'm not sure, but there are tales about fairy raths and changelings and leprechauns and pookas and banshees, and all kinds of extraordinary creatures."

"Then we'll have one every day, please! I think you're a first-rate story-teller. You're almost as good as old Mary O'Grady. I've often sat by her peat fire and heard about the banshee and the leprechaun; only, she believes in them. I'm so glad I've moved into this bedroom! I like you far better than those girls in No. 13."

When Miss Maitland came upstairs to inspect No. 8, she found Honor and Janie already on a more favourable footing than she had dared to hope, the latter chatting with a vivacity that no one at St. Chad's had hitherto imagined she possessed. Once she had broken the ice of her shyness, and had broached her beloved topic of books, Janie had plenty to say; and, as Honor was also in a communicative mood, the pair seemed well started on the high road to friendship.

It was fortunate for Honor that she had found a congenial room-mate, as her first days at Chessington proved rather a time of trial. She was woefully and terribly home-sick. It seemed an absolute uprooting to have been torn away from Kerry, and she considered that nothing in her new surroundings could make amends for the change. Her pride upheld her sufficiently to prevent her from showing any outward signs of misery before the inquisitive eyes of her schoolfellows, but every now and then the yearning for Kilmore would rise with an almost unbearable pain, and she would have to fight hard to keep her self-control. Maisie Talbot, she was sure, would regard home-sickness as "early Victorian", and consequently worthy of contempt; and she was determined not to give either Maisie or any of the others an opportunity of laughing at her.

She felt very keenly the confinement and restraint of school life. To be obliged to study lessons and play games at specified hours, all within a certain limited area, seemed an utter contrast to the freedom in which she had hitherto revelled; and she would long for a scamper with Bute and Barney, her two terriers, or a sail with her father down the creek and out into the Atlantic. She would pour enthusiastic descriptions of her home into Janie's ears, until the latter felt she knew Kilmore Castle and its demesne, and the little fishing village, with its peat smoke and its warm-hearted peasants; and the rocks and the moors and the stream, and the green, treacherous bogs, almost as well as Honor herself.

Notwithstanding her former reputation for unsociability, Janie, at the end of three days, had completely lost her heart to this wayward, impulsive daughter of Erin. It was true, Honor was apt to be trying at times. Her gusts of hot temper, petulance, or utter unreasonableness were rather disconcerting to anyone unaccustomed to the Celtic disposition;

but they never lasted long, and Janie soon found out that her friend rarely meant what she then said, and was generally particularly lovable after an outburst, with a winsome look on her face and a beguiling, endearing tone in her voice that would have gained forgiveness from a stone.

With the rest of the members of St. Chad's Honor was also on good terms. She could be very amusing and full of racy Irish humour when she liked, and would send the girls into fits of laughter with her quaint sayings and funny stories. Her nickname of "Paddy Pepper-box" stuck to her, and she certainly justified it occasionally.

"She's like a volcano," declared Lettice Talbot. "Sometimes if you tease her she starts with a bang, and lets off steam for five minutes. Then it's all over, and she's quite pleasant again, until next time."

"I'd rather have that than sulking, at any rate," said Dorothy Arkwright. "A storm often clears the air."

"It's not much use chaffing her, either," said Madge Summers, "for she always seems to get the best of it."

"Yes; if she's down one minute she'll bob up again the next, like a cork."

Honor's humours were apt to overflow into the region of practical jokes. These were generally played on such genial recipients as Lettice Talbot and Madge Summers, but occasionally she would venture on more dangerous ground. One afternoon, at the end of her first week at Chessington, she was in the dressing-room, changing her shoes in preparation for cricket, when Ruth Latimer interposed.

"I forgot to tell you, Paddy! Games are off to-day."

"Why?" asked Honor in astonishment, for the hour and a half in the playing-fields was as strict a part of the college curriculum as the morning lessons.

"Because it's the Health Testing."

"What's that?"

"A kind of medical examination," explained Dorothy Arkwright. "We always have it at the beginning of each term, to make sure that, as Miss Cavendish expresses it, we are 'physically fit for the duties of school life'."

"Oh!" said Honor, looking rather aghast at the prospect.

"You needn't pull such a long face, Paddy," said Lettice. "We none of us mind; indeed, we think it's a joke."

"We have a lady doctor, you see," said Ruth, "and she's so jolly, she keeps one laughing all the time."

"What does she do?"

"Oh! weighs us, and sounds our lungs, and tests our eyes, and measures our chests."

"You'll have to draw a deep breath, and to put out your tongue, and to let her look at your teeth," added Lettice.

"And if any girl is really very much below standard," said Dorothy, "she is 'turned out to grass'. That means that she only does half-lessons."

"Of course, she has to be rather bad for that," remarked Ruth.

"It's never been my luck yet!" lamented Lettice.

"I should think not, with those fat, red cheeks! You couldn't look delicate, however hard you tried."

"It happened to Janie Henderson, though, in her first term. How little did you weigh, Moonie?"

"I'm sure I forget," returned Janie, who had joined the group.

"But you had to be fed up on cream and beaten eggs and all kinds of things. I remember how we envied you."

"Are you weighed in stones or pounds here?" asked Honor.

"In stones. It's very puzzling to some of the Colonials, because they're accustomed to American machines that register in pounds. They have to do a sum before they can calculate the result."

"When does this exam. come off?"

"Some time this afternoon. We go up in relays. It's St. Chad's turn to-day. On Wednesday it was the School House, and on Thursday, St. Aldwyth's. Then on Saturday it will be St. Hilary's and St. Bride's. It takes nearly a week to get through the whole school."

The medical examination was to be conducted at the sanatorium, and Dr. Mary Forbes was already installed there, and busily employed, when Honor and her classmates arrived.

"She begins with monitresses, and then works downwards," explained Dorothy. "I don't expect it will be our turn for half an hour yet, but we're obliged to stay here, to be ready in case we're called."

"It's not nearly so alarming as the dentist's," said Ruth.

The waiting-room was full of girls, who were beguiling the time with jokes and banter and lively chatter. Lettice, Ruth, and Dorothy soon mingled in the crowd, and forgot all about their Irish companion until the voice of Vivian Holmes was heard announcing:

"Next—Ruth Latimer, Chatty Burns, Madge Summers, and Honor Fitzgerald."

"Where's Honor?" asked Lettice. "She was here just now."

"Why, she's there!—actually outside in the garden," replied Dorothy.

"What's she doing, dodging about the rockery?"

"Someone call her—quick!"

Honor came running in, looking rather flushed and hot, and with a curious, bulgy appearance about her blouse.

"Where have you been?" demanded Ruth, but her question went unanswered, for Vivian whisked the four girls with scant ceremony into Dr. Mary Forbes's consulting-room. Time was too precious to be wasted, and the monitress was something of a disciplinarian. Honor sat watching with deep interest while first Ruth, then Chatty, and finally Madge were duly examined and passed as "sound". She was called then, and after her name and age had been entered on her chart, and her height taken, she was told to step on to the weighing machine. Round swung the pointer, and stopped at 8 stone 4 lb. Dr. Mary looked at the dial almost incredulously. She thought there must be something wrong with the machine.

"Stand off for a minute," she said, "while I examine the weights. I must have made a mistake."

Honor obeyed, with a very solemn face. She appeared to be taking the matter with unusual seriousness. Dr. Mary readjusted the lever, and even oiled the machine; but when Honor stepped on to it again it registered exactly the same.

"It's most extraordinary!" exclaimed the lady doctor. "For a girl of your height and slight build I have never known such a record," and she gazed at Honor's rather slender proportions in amazement.

"I expect it's bones," volunteered Honor. "The Fitzgeralds are a big-boned family."

"Your bones would have to be of cast iron, to bring you up to eight stone odd," cried Dr. Mary. "The machine must be at fault. It's absurd, on the face of it—a small, slim girl like you!"

"Perhaps it's the change of air since I arrived," said Honor innocently, but at the same time she looked at Madge Summers with a very mischievous expression on her face.

"She's up to something!" thought Madge, and nudged Ruth, though she dared not venture to whisper.

"Of course, we eat a great deal over in Ireland," continued Honor. "There is nothing like potatoes for making one grow. I saw in the *British Almanac* that they were twice as nourishing as anything, except herrings and oatmeal; and we have those too in Kerry."

"I think, in that case, we must try Banting," said Dr. Mary, who must have caught Honor's glance, for she suddenly took hold of her, and began feeling her carefully.

"Ah!" she exclaimed; "so these are the extra bones, are they?" and diving into her patient's pocket, she drew out stone after stone, and as many more again that had been tucked down in the front of the white flannel blouse.

The doctor was a good-tempered woman, with a strong sense of humour, and, instead of scolding, she laughed heartily at having been taken in by such a trick.

"I've had patients who shammed ill before," she declared, "but never such a scandalous case of imposition as this."

"Well, the girls told me the weight was to be reckoned by stones," said Honor, with a twinkle in her eye, "so I thought I'd better come well provided. I'm not at all sorry to be rid of them, if they're not wanted."

"Get on to that machine again immediately!" commanded Dr. Mary, with an effort to be severe. "Ah! 6 stone 5 lb. is rather a difference. It's lucky for you I didn't put you on starvation diet to reduce you. Don't try to be so clever again, or I shall have to perform an operation to get rid of your cheek!"

Madge, Ruth, and Chatty had sat chuckling with subdued delight during the interview, and the moment they were out of the room they published the story abroad, for the edification of the others.

"She thinks of such funny things!" laughed Madge, "things that nobody else would ever dream of doing."

"I was afraid she'd get into a fearful scrape," confessed Chatty.

"Oh, Dr. Mary Forbes is too jolly to mind!" said Ruth. "She was far more amused than cross. If it had been Miss Maitland, or Miss Cavendish, now! But I should imagine that even Honor Fitzgerald would scarcely dare to play a practical joke upon either of them!"

CHAPTER V. A RIDING LESSON

The College had reopened on a Tuesday, so that by her first Sunday Honor had been at school five days. In her own estimation it seemed more like five months, but as she had left home on 24th April, and the Shakespeare calendar in the recreation room (a leaf of which was torn off punctually each morning by the monitress) only recorded 29th April, she was obliged reluctantly to acknowledge the evidence of the almanac, and realized that twelve whole weeks must intervene before the joyful termination of what she considered her banishment from Erin.

Sundays were made very pleasant at Chessington. In the morning the girls attended the parish church at Dunscar. In the afternoon they might read, or stroll about the grounds where they pleased, an indulgence not permitted on weekdays. During the summer term they were allowed to carry their four-o'clock tea into the garden. All was laid ready by the servants in the dining-hall, and each girl might pour out her own cup, and, taking what bread and butter she wished, retire with a few select companions to some nook under the trees, or a seat in an ivy-covered arbour.

From half-past four to half-past five was "silence hour", which everyone was required to devote to reading from a special library of books carefully chosen for the purpose by Miss Cavendish.

"I won't call them Sunday books," she sometimes said, "because I consider our religion would be a very poor thing if it were only kept for one day in the week. What we learn in this quiet time we must apply in our busy hours, and let the helpful words we read influence our ordinary life and go towards the building of character, which is the most invaluable of all possessions."

At half-past six there was a short service in chapel; and the rest of the evening, after supper, was given up to the writing of home letters.

All the routine of the school was still new to Honor, and she felt very strange and unusual as, precisely at ten o'clock, she took her place among the lines of Chessingtonians marshalled in the quadrangle preparatory to setting off for church. Miss Cavendish gave the signal to start, and the two hundred girls filed along two and two, all dressed alike in white serge coats and skirts and best sailor hats, with their house colours, the blue ribbons of the School House leading the way, followed by the pink of St. Aldwyth's, and the orange, violet, and scarlet of St. Chad's, St. Bride's, and St. Hilary's, respectively.

"I believe it's considered one of the sights of the neighbourhood to see us parade through the lich-gate," said Lettice Talbot, who happened to be walking with Honor. "Visitors stand in the churchyard and try to count us. They make the most absurd remarks sometimes; I suppose they think we shan't overhear what they say. Really, they seem to look upon us as a kind of show, and I quite expect we shall be put down in the next edition of the guide-book as one of the attractions of Dunscar. Of course, we take no notice. We walk along with our noses in the air, as if we weren't aware that anyone was even thinking of us; but all the same we feel giggles inside when we catch a whisper: 'They look like angels dressed in white!' or, 'What a pile of washing they must make!'"

Honor had been looking forward immensely to this Sunday morning, for she hoped she might have an opportunity of seeing her brother Dermot, who was at Dr. Winterton's school. Dermot was her favourite among her five brothers, and the thought that Orley Grange and Chessington stood only a mile and a half apart had so far been her one thread of comfort. To catch even a distant glimpse of Dermot would be like a peep at home, and she felt that a moment's talk with him would be sufficient to send her back to St. Chad's rejoicing.

The students of the College occupied the whole of the left aisle of the church, and the right aisle was reserved for Dr. Winterton's pupils. As a rule, the girls arrived early and took their seats first; and they always passed out by a side door, so that they seldom met the boys in the churchyard. Should they happen to do so, however, it was etiquette to take no notice of them, even though some might be relations, or intimate friends. Honor was unaware of this rule, which her classmates, not knowing she had a brother at the Grange, had not thought of mentioning to her.

On this particular Sunday either Miss Cavendish or Dr. Winterton had slightly miscalculated the time, for the two schools arrived at exactly the same minute. As there was not room for all to march in together through the lich-gate, the boys were drawn up like a regiment, and waited for the College to go by. The girls sailed past with well-bred unconsciousness, their eyes fixed discreetly upon the Prayer Books and hymn-books that they carried—all except poor impulsive, unconventional Honor, who made a sudden dart out of the line, and snatched rapturously at a brown-faced, curly-headed boy, by his coat sleeve.

"Dermot! Dermot! I *am* glad to see you!" she exclaimed, in a voice that could be heard from end to end of the ranks.

"Oh, I say, Honor! Stow it!" murmured the boy in an agonized tone, turning as red as fire, and trying to back away from her.

Naturally Honor's unexpected and unprecedented act caused a great sensation. Lettice Talbot stopped when deserted by her partner, and the girls behind her were obliged to halt too. All wondered what had happened, and, in spite of their excellent training and good discipline, their curiosity got the better of them, and they craned their necks to look. Miss Farrar saved the situation by hurrying to Honor, seizing her by the shoulder, and forcing her back into her place; then the long line once more moved forward, and the Chessingtonians, slightly ruffled, but trying to carry off the affair in a dignified fashion, marched with admirable coolness into the church. If Honor had a little, surreptitious cry behind her Prayer Book, she managed to conceal the fact from the neighbours on either side of her in the pew; and if her eyes looked suspiciously red, and there was a slight tendency to chokiness in her voice as she walked home after service, Lettice Talbot, at any rate, was tactful enough to take no notice, though she seized the opportunity of explaining the school code of decorum, and was severe in her censure.

"You ought to have told me before," said Honor. "How could I know that I mustn't speak to my own brother?"

"I didn't even know you had a brother," returned Lettice; "and I never dreamt you'd do such an idiotic thing as rush at him like that. He evidently didn't appreciate it."

"No! I thought he'd be more glad to see me," gulped Honor, not the least part of whose trouble had been Dermot's cold reception of her enthusiastic greeting.

"How silly you are! Does any boy care to parade his sister before his whole school? I expect he'll get tremendously chaffed about this, poor fellow! Really, Paddy, you ought to know better!"

Considerably chastened by Lettice's crushing remarks, Honor subsided into silence, and only reopened the subject when, in company with Janie Henderson, she had retired after dinner to a spot overlooking the playing-fields. It was a warm, beautiful afternoon, a day when you could almost hear the buds bursting and the flowers opening. The two girls spread their jerseys on the grass, and sat basking in the sunshine, watching a lark soar up into the blue overhead, or the seagulls flapping leisurely round the cliffs; or listening to the caw of the jackdaws that, in company with a flock of starlings, were feeding in a neighbouring ploughed field. The sea lay a sparkling sheet of pearly grey, and Honor looked wistfully at its broad expanse when she remembered that its farther waves washed the rocky shores of Ireland.

Janie was the only girl at St. Chad's to whom she cared to mention her home. With the others she could exchange jokes, but not confidences; and though she returned their banter with interest, she did not look to them for sympathy. Janie seemed altogether different from the rest; she never laughed at Honor, and even if she remonstrated, it was in such a gentle, apologetic way that the most touchy of Celtic natures could not have taken offence.

Miss Maitland had not overlooked the episode of the morning. She had had a few words to say after their return from church, and Honor, in consequence, was feeling rather sore, and ready to pour out her grievances into her friend's ears.

"It's too bad!" she declared. "If you can't speak to your own brother, to whom may you speak, I should like to know? It seems absurd that Dermot should be living at the Grange, not two miles off, and yet we're never to see one another. I thought I should at least meet him once a week, and now I mayn't even say, 'How do you do?' without being scolded as if I had committed a highway robbery."

"Is he your favourite brother?" asked Janie.

"Yes; he's the nearest in age to me, and we're great chums. We have the wildest fun during the holidays—we dare each other to do the maddest things we can think of!"

"What kind of things?"

"Well, one day, when old Biddy Macarthy was ill with quinsy, we got up early and took her cart to Ballycroghan market, and Dermot sold all her chickens for her. He talked away like a Cheap Jack, and made such fun, people nearly died with laughing. You see, most of them knew who he was, and it seemed so absurd to hear him proclaiming the virtues of Biddy's fowls. Then we filled the cart with seed potatoes, as a present for her; and tore home so fast that the traces broke, and the donkey ran straight out of the shafts. We fell on the road, nearly buried in potatoes, but luckily we weren't hurt. We managed to catch the donkey, and to mend the traces with a piece of string; then we had to put all the potatoes back. Biddy laughed so much when we told her about the adventure that it cured her quinsy; and she said she never had such a splendid crop of potatoes as from those we brought her that day from Ballycroghan. That was Dermot's joke; but I think mine was quite as much fun."

"What was yours?"

"I saved up my pocket-money to get a little pig, to give to old Micky, the cobbler. Dermot and I walked over to Ennisfellen fair to buy it, and drove it home with a string tied to its leg. As fast as we pulled one way it ran another, and just as we got to Micky's cabin the string snapped, and off the pig bolted down the village, and ran straight into the open door of the school. The children chased it round and round beneath the forms, and caught it at last under the master's desk. Oh, we have lively times at Kilmore! Then once Dermot and I ran away, and went to see Cousin Theresa at Slieve Donnell. Nobody knew where we were for two days, and people were hunting all over the country for us. They thought we must have been drowned, or have fallen into the bog."

"But weren't your father and mother fearfully anxious?" asked Janie, who had listened almost aghast to the recital of those wild escapades.

"Well, Father was rather cross about that, certainly. He was never really very angry, though, until the last time, when I——"

But here Honor stopped. On the whole, she decided she would not relate the story of Firefly. She could not quite understand the expression on Janie's face, and she began to doubt whether her friend would altogether sympathize with her. Instead, she plunged into a detailed description of her elder brothers, telling how two were preparing for the Army at Sandhurst, how another was at Oxford, and the fourth was studying law.

"I suppose you are nearly always with your mother, as you are the only girl," said Janie.

"Well, no," admitted Honor. "She's so delicate, and so often ill. I'm afraid I give her a headache."

"My mother is delicate too," confided Janie. "She has most dreadful neuralgia sometimes. I bathe her head with eau-de-cologne, mixed with very hot water, and it always does her good. She calls me her little nurse. Have you ever tried hot water with eau-de-cologne for your mother's headaches?"

Honor had never dreamt of offering any help or assistance to anyone in sickness. The idea was quite new to her, and that Janie evidently expected her to be her mother's companion and right hand surprised her. She had already met with many astonishments at St. Chad's, where most of the views of life seemed different from her old standards. She scarcely liked to confess that she was of so little use at home, and hastily turned the conversation back to her brother Dermot.

"Do you think if I were to ask Miss Cavendish, she would let him call to see me?" she suggested.

Janie shook her head.

"I'm quite sure she wouldn't," she replied. "The rules are so strict about visitors. Nobody but our parents is allowed, except an occasional uncle or aunt—never a brother. You'd better not suggest it."

"Then I shall have to go and see him."

"How could you, Honor? Don't be so unreasonable!"

"I thought I might find an opportunity some day," said Honor reflectively. "One never knows what may turn up. Dear old Dermot! It would be hard luck to be within two miles of him for a whole term, without exchanging a single word."

"Well, if you do, you'll get into a far bigger scrape than you'll like. You'd much better wait until the holidays, when you'll probably both travel home together," advised Janie.

There certainly were no opportunities at Chessington College for paying calls. Except on half-holidays, the girls seldom went beyond the school grounds, the large playing-fields providing a wide enough area for exercise. The members of the Fifth and Sixth Forms were allowed to go out occasionally, within specified bounds, if they went three together; but the younger ones had not attained to such a privilege.

"We mayn't even put our noses through the gate of the quad," said Lettice Talbot, in reply to a question from Honor, who chafed sorely against the rule; "not unless we can get a special exeat from Miss Cavendish, and that's only given once in a blue moon. It's no use looking volcanic, Paddy! You'll have to grin and bear it."

"It's as bad as being in prison," grumbled Honor.

"Nonsense!" snapped Maisie Talbot. "You have cricket or tennis for nearly two hours every afternoon. What more can you want? I'd rather play games myself than do anything else."

"You can't expect to do just as you like at school," remarked Dorothy Arkwright, who sometimes joined with Maisie in "squashing" Honor.

"The riding lessons begin next Thursday," said Lettice, with an attempt at consolation. "They are very jolly. Mr. Townsend always takes the class a trot over the Tor. You said you were to learn riding?"

"It's the one lesson I begged for," replied Honor. "I could have dispensed with Latin, or German, or mathematics."

"Maisie and I are to begin this term; we're looking forward to it tremendously!"

"You are lucky," said Pauline Reynolds enviously. "I'd give all I possess to be going with you. I've never ridden anything more interesting than a rocking-horse, or a donkey on the sands; and one doesn't get much of a canter for six-pence!"

"I believe I'm horribly nervous, and I don't mind confessing it," declared Lettice. "The idea of being perched on a great, tall horse makes me shake in my shoes. When it begins to trot I shall drop off—I know I shall!"

"Don't be so silly!" protested Maisie. "You can stick on to Teddie at home all right. Honor Fitzgerald, can you ride?"

"Bareback, if you like," said Honor. "Dermot and I used to take our old pony and practise what we called 'circus performances'. Pixie quite entered into the spirit of the thing, and would walk along gently while we stood on his back."

"I hear Mr. Townsend brings very fresh horses," said Lettice, with a shiver of apprehension. "I do hope he'll choose me a quiet one!"

"The fresher the better for me," said Honor. "I'm just longing for a good gallop."

"But suppose it runs away?"

"Then it will have to take me with it. If it's any kind of a beast with four legs, I'll undertake to make it fly."

"I heard that Mr. Townsend's horses aren't worth the fag of riding," observed Flossie Taylor, who had joined the group.

"There speaks the voice of envy! You wouldn't say so if you were taking the lessons," retorted Maisie.

"People who are accustomed to hunt at home don't care about hired hacks," drawled Flossie, in her most supercilious manner.

"It all depends on the sort of hunting," returned Honor, who was never at a loss. "If it's only 'hunt the slipper', I'll admit it's not much of a training, and you might be afraid of your seat."

The riding course was a special feature of the summer term at Chessington. It was an "extra", not part of the ordinary school curriculum, as were the games. A master came from Dunscar, and would escort select little parties of girls for a trot upon the Tor, a stretch of moorland not far from the College. Mr. Townsend did not care to take out many pupils at once, so on the following Thursday afternoon only seven horses were waiting in the quadrangle. The Talbots, Ruth Latimer, and Honor represented St. Chad's, while two girls from St. Hilary's and one from St. Bride's completed the party. Lettice confessed to a very superior and elated feeling as the reins were laid in her hand and the cavalcade began to move, particularly as Flossie Taylor and the Hammond-Smiths were just setting off for tennis, and could not help witnessing the start, though they resolutely looked the opposite way.

"Flossie always tries to be extremely grand herself, and make other people seem small," whispered Lettice.

"Fortunately, one needn't take people at their own estimate," replied Maisie, whose downright nature much disliked Flossie's habit of bragging.

To all the seven girls it was a delight to find themselves passing under the archway of the big gate, and away along the road towards the Tor. A chestnut called Victor had fallen to Honor's share, and though he was very tall in comparison with her old favourite Pixie, she nevertheless sat him well.

"She looks just like the picture of Diana Vernon in our *Rob Roy*," remarked Lettice to Maisie, gazing with admiration at the upright, graceful figure of her schoolmate, who seemed perfectly at home in the saddle.

Lettice was getting on much better than her modest protestations beforehand would have led her friends to expect. Violet Wright, the girl from St. Bride's, was quite a beginner, and Mr. Townsend held her horse by a leading rein; while Gwen Roby, from St. Hilary's, looked rather solemn, as if she were not altogether sure that she was enjoying the experience.

"I've ridden before," she explained, "but only on a small pony, and this feels so very different."

At first the party went at a walking pace, but on coming to a good, level stretch of road the master gave the order to trot, and his pupils were able to test the capacities of their steeds. Honor, at least, was most unwilling to pull up when Mr. Townsend called out "Halt!" I am afraid she did not want a lesson, only a scamper through the fresh air; and she listened impatiently while the master explained the right position of the whip, the hold on the snaffle, and the principle of rising elegantly in the saddle.

"It's all very well to talk of principles," said poor Violet, who happened to find herself next to Lettice; "I expect a little practice will be of more use to me. At present I jog up and down like a sack of flour, and it's all I can manage to stick on anyhow. I know I shall be as stiff as a board to-morrow!"

"When we reach the Tor we may manage a short canter," said Mr. Townsend, "but for the present I wish you to keep together. Now then, young ladies, please, elbows in and heads up! Hold the reins rather short in the hand, and take care not to bear on the curb!"

"It's no fun, is it?" remarked Honor, as she passed Ruth Latimer. "Are we only going to walk in a stupid row, and then trot for about ten yards? I thought we should be flying along, like a hunt. I'd rather be on Pixie at home; I could always make him go when I tickled his ears. If we don't hurry up a little more I shall try it on this horse, and see if he won't break into something more interesting than a snail's pace."

"Oh, Honor, do take care!" remonstrated prudent Ruth.

But Honor did not stop to listen, and pushed on ahead of the others, swishing her whip about in a manner that drew instant reproof from the master. They had left the highway, and were now on a road leading across the open moor. On one side the cliffs descended steeply to the sea, and on the other rose bare, rolling hills, covered with short, fine grass, the sails of a windmill or an occasional storm-swept tree alone breaking the line of the horizon. It was a very suitable place for a canter, and after a few preliminary remarks Mr. Townsend started his flock on what seemed to most of them a rather mad career, following closely himself in their wake, to continue his instructions:

"Courage, Miss Roby! Miss Talbot, you are leaning over in your saddle! Miss Lettice, your elbows again! Miss Wright, you must learn not to grasp the pommel. Don't drag the rein! Miss Latimer, keep a light hand! What, tired already? Well, I won't work you too hard just at first."

A little shaken and agitated by the unwonted exercise, the girls checked their horses to a walk. They were none of them practised riders, and all were glad that no more was expected from them for the present. Honor, however, was some way on in front, and, instead of pulling up, as she was told, she gave her horse a switch across the flank and a tweak on the ear, such as she had been accustomed to bestow on her old pony at home. The effect was magical. Seaside hacks are not generally prone to run away, but this one had a little spirit left in him; he resented his rider's liberties, and, feeling the soft grass under his feet, fled as if he were on a racecourse.

"Miss Fitzgerald! Miss Fitzgerald!" shouted Mr. Townsend, but he might as well have spoken to the wind. Honor had found her opportunity, and was quick to seize it. Instead of attempting to pull up Victor, she let him have his head. She had no desire to check his pace, the motion was so exhilarating; and she could not resist the temptation to display her horsemanship before the rest of the class. The unfortunate master dared not desert his other nervous and inexperienced pupils to give chase, and in a few minutes she had left the remainder of the party a mile behind. They could see her tearing past the coastguard station, where an old man with a telescope yelled wildly to her to stop; past a windmill, where children and chickens scrambled in hot haste out of her path; and away over the moor, until she quite disappeared from sight.

The girls were in a panic of alarm. Mr. Townsend turned rather white, but preserved his presence of mind, and, leading his little company straight to the coastguard station, made all dismount, and tied up the horses. Then he set out himself in pursuit of the runaway.

Honor, meanwhile, continued her "John Gilpin" galop. On and on she flew, her hair, as the fairy tales say, "whistling in the wind". It occurred to her at last that she might be going too far, and she made an effort to pull up. But it was of no avail; Victor had got the bit firmly between his teeth, and nothing could hold him. Luckily, the girl did not lose her nerve, but waited until she could tire him out, and get him in hand again; and I verily believe she would have succeeded in mastering him, and turning him safely on his homeward course, had not the way been unexpectedly barred by a fence. The poor old horse must have been a hunter during some period of his life; he went at the fence like a greyhound, and cleared it nimbly: but there were a trench and a rough bank on the farther side, and as he alighted he stumbled, flinging Honor violently from the saddle. Mercifully, her foot came clear of the stirrup, and she rolled safely into a bed of nettles, while Victor, scrambling up again, made off without her over the crest of the hill.

Honor picked herself out of the nettles as quickly as she could. No bones were broken, and, except for some painful stings, she was none the worse for her adventure.

Nevertheless, the situation was awkward. There she was on the open moor, many miles away from Chessington, and obliged to make her way home to St. Chad's as best she could. She climbed over the fence, and, holding up her habit, set out to walk back in the direction in which she had come.

It seemed slow progress compared with riding, and she began to wonder how long it would take her to retrace her steps. She had not gone more than half a mile, however, when she met Mr. Townsend, who had at last succeeded in reaching her. His relief at finding her alive and unhurt was almost too great for words. He put her quietly on his own horse, and led it by the bridle back to the coastguard station, where the rest of the girls were waiting, very anxious to know what had become of Honor, and very rejoiced when they saw she was safe.

There was no further riding lesson that day. As Maisie Talbot explained afterwards to a select company of interested friends: "I'm sure Mr. Townsend was frightfully angry, but he scarcely said a word. He only took us straight home at once, in a kind of solemn procession. He had to walk himself, leading Honor's and Violet's horses, so of course we went horribly slowly; and he looked so savage that nobody dared to speak."

"What possessed you, Paddy?" asked Lettice.

"I had an idea of going to see Dermot," confessed Honor. "I thought if I rode straight up to the Grange, and asked leave from Dr. Winterton, perhaps he'd let us have half an hour together."

"Well, you are the silliest goose! Why, the Grange is in exactly the opposite direction! Will you never learn sense?" and Lettice collapsed with laughter.

"Mr. Townsend is having a long talk with Miss Maitland at this present moment," announced Ruth Latimer.

"Then I'm glad I'm not you, Paddy!" chuckled Lettice.

Nobody ever knew the details of Mr. Townsend's interview with the house-mistress, or what explanation he gave of the affair. Though he was perfectly persuaded that it was Honor's own fault, it was difficult for him to blame her for what might, after all, have been a mere accident; so, beyond a few words of warning about the danger of whipping her horse without proper orders, she did not on this occasion receive the scolding that she certainly merited.

Victor was found on the hills six miles away from Chessington, gently cropping the grass, and allowed himself to be caught by a passing farmer. He was not used at the riding lessons again. Honor was in future given the tamest and least-spirited of the mounts, and for the next two lessons was even kept strictly to the leading rein.

"She's fearfully disgusted about it," said Lettice, "and it certainly is a humiliation, when she can ride so well. It's quite the worst punishment Mr. Townsend could possibly have given her, and I expect he knows it!"

CHAPTER VI. THE LOWER THIRD

The Lower Third Form at Chessington College numbered seventeen pupils, eight of whom were members of St. Chad's. In addition to Honor, these included Maisie and Lettice Talbot, Ruth Latimer, Pauline Reynolds, Janie Henderson, Effie Lawson, and Flossie Taylor. The teacher, Miss Farrar, was rather a favourite with her class. Though she could well uphold her authority, and maintain the good discipline that was universal in the school, she was not so strict as some of the other mistresses. She had a very pleasant, genial manner; she was a capital tennis player, and no mean figure at hockey and cricket; she was a prominent supporter of the Debating Society and the Natural History Union; and was altogether so cheerful and brisk that "jolly" was the word generally applied to her. Honor liked Miss Farrar, and, according to her lights, really made a heroic effort in the direction of good behaviour. Her conduct was certainly immeasurably superior to what it had been with her governesses at home, and yet, judged by Chessington standards, it was frequently irregular and unorthodox. With her best endeavours, she could not grasp the fact that education is a very solemn affair, and a school-room about the last place in the world where one should try to be funny. She never seemed able to be absolutely serious, and at the least opportunity her Celtic humour would flash out, and not only upset the gravity of the class, but sometimes even cause Miss Farrar to have a difficulty in keeping her countenance.

She was a slightly disturbing element in the Form. When it was her turn to answer there would be an air of general expectancy in the room; the didactic language of the textbooks was often paraphrased by her lips into something of a more racy description, and even her mistakes were as delicious as her quaint methods of stating facts. Miss Farrar occasionally suspected her of intentionally giving wrong replies, for the sheer satisfaction of causing amusement; but it was difficult to prove the charge, since, however ludicrous her statements might be, she never under any circumstances laughed at them herself, and all the while her large, grey Irish eyes would be fixed upon her teacher with the innocence of a baby.

Thanks to Janie Henderson's assiduity, Honor conformed tolerably well to the ordinary rules. Mindful of Miss Maitland's charge, Janie considered herself responsible for Honor, and was continually ready to jog her memory about what exercises must be written, what lessons learnt, and what books brought to class, all of which were details that her friend would not have troubled about on her own account; but in spite of her exertions the poor girl often saw her protégée in trouble.

"The worst of it is," she admitted to herself, "that one never knows what to expect. Honor is a darling, but she does such peculiar and extraordinary things, she almost takes one's breath away. If I could be prepared for them beforehand, and warn her, it might be of some use; but I can't, so she's bound to get into scrapes."

Undoubtedly, very unprecedented happenings took place in the Lower Third—happenings such as had never occurred before Honor's advent. Who but she would have thought of tilting two books together and emptying the inkpot on the top of them, when asked to describe a watershed? Yet she looked genuinely astonished when the vials of Miss Farrar's wrath descended upon her, and said almost reproachfully that she was only trying to give a practical illustration.

One day she smuggled Pete, the kitten from St. Chad's, into class, and shut him inside her desk, where he settled down quite comfortably, and slept peacefully through the French lesson. But in the middle of algebra, Honor, who hated mathematics, managed to give him a surreptitious pinch, with the result that a long-drawn, impatient, objecting "miau" suddenly resounded through the room. Miss Farrar gave quite a jump, and looked round, but could see nothing. Honor sat bolt upright, with arms folded and eyes fixed attentively on the blackboard, as if she were sublimely unconscious of any noise in her vicinity.

"What can it be? It sounds like a cat," said Miss Farrar, peering about on the floor, and even peeping into the cupboard where the chalk and the new books were kept.

The girls jumped up, and pretended to look under their desks. Most of them had an inkling of the situation, but they were human enough to enjoy an interruption in the midst of difficult equations.

"Perhaps it's a mouse in the wainscot that's not feeling quite well this morning," suggested Honor, though it would have needed an absolute giant of a mouse to give vent to the unearthly yowl in which Pete had indulged. She said it, however, rather too innocently on this occasion. Miss Farrar was not dull, and had suspected from the beginning who was at the bottom of the mischief; indeed, it was easy enough by this time to trace the noise to the right spot, for the kitten had begun to scratch, and lifted up its voice in a series of emphatic wails, evidently protesting vigorously against solitary confinement.

Miss Farrar walked straight to Honor's desk and opened it, when out jumped Pete, purring with satisfaction, and arching his back as if in expectation of petting. The teacher seized him by the scruff of the neck and gave him to Janie Henderson, at the same time quelling the unseemly mirth of her class with a withering glance.

"Carry this kitten back at once to St. Chad's," she commanded. "Honor Fitzgerald, you will learn two pages of Greek chronology, and repeat them to me before school to-morrow morning. Lettice Talbot, take a forfeit! Girls, I am astonished at you! Open your books instantly, every one of you! Gwen Roby, read out your answer to Example 37."

Though Honor was popular with most of the members of her Form, she was never on very good terms with Flossie Taylor. Flossie had a sharp tongue, and liked to make sarcastic remarks; and though Honor would promptly return the compliment, and often "squash" the other completely, continual bickering did not promote harmony between the pair. Flossie was occasionally capable of certain dishonourable acts, which always drew upon her Honor's utmost indignation and scorn. The latter could not tolerate cheating or copying, and spoke her mind freely on the subject.

"Well, I'm sure I'm not nearly as bad as you!" Flossie retorted once. "You do the most outrageous things. I never mixed the French and history exercises, nor dipped the chalk into the red ink!"

"It's worse to crib someone else's work," protested Honor, "because that's sneaky and underhand. What would Miss Farrar say if she knew you wrote dates on a slip of paper and put it inside your dictionary, and then copied them when you pretended you were only looking how to spell a word?"

"Miss Farrar won't find out, and what the eye doesn't see the heart doesn't grieve for!"

"But it's so mean!"

"You turning Mentor!" sneered Flossie. "Really! I wonder what we may expect next? Come, girls, and hear our most righteous and well-conducted Paddy preach a homily on 'How to be the pattern pupil'!"

"Paddy is quite right," declared Maisie Talbot, taking up the cudgels for once on Honor's behalf. "There's a difference between her way of breaking rules and yours. She mayn't be exactly a shining example to the class, but, at any rate, she's always square and above-board, and that's more than I can say for you!"

"We're none of us saints," added Lettice, "but we've never gone in for cribbing at Chessington. No other girl in the Form ever does it."

It was not only as regards the question of fairness in her work that Flossie failed to reach the standard of honour current in the Lower Third. She had many little meannesses, so small in themselves as to be hardly worthy of notice, yet enough in the aggregate to exhibit her character unfavourably.

One morning, just as the girls were going to their desks, Maisie Talbot suddenly remembered that it was Miss Farrar's birthday.

"We ought to say something about it," she whispered to Lettice. "I wish we had thought of it before, and bought her some flowers. How stupid we were to forget!"

"Are you sure it's her birthday? How do you know?" asked Flossie, who was standing near, and overheard.

"I'm absolutely certain. I have her name in my birthday book," replied Maisie.

Flossie said no more just then, but the moment Miss Farrar came into the room she stood up and wished her "Many happy returns", in the name of the whole Form, before either Maisie or Lettice had the opportunity to say a word.

They were most annoyed to be thus forestalled.

"It was our idea," protested Lettice afterwards. "You didn't even know it was Miss Farrar's birthday before we mentioned it."

"And yet you calmly took all the credit, and made yourself the mouthpiece of the class!" exclaimed the equally indignant Maisie.

"I suppose I had as good a right as anybody else to offer congratulations," laughed Flossie. "You should have brought yours out a little quicker."

Flossie might be appreciated by her cousins, the Hammond-Smiths, and their particular friends, the Lawsons and the Palmers, but she was certainly not a favourite in her own Form. Nearly everybody had a squabble with her upon some pretext. Even Janie Henderson, whose retiring disposition involved her in few disputes with her schoolfellows, found a cause for complaint. It was one of the ordinary regulations that the girls should each take the office of warden for a week in turn, the duties being to give out any necessary books, clean the blackboard, distribute fresh pens and blotting-paper, and collect any articles that might be left in the room after lesson hours. By general custom all pencils, india-rubbers, or other stray possessions were put into what was known as the forfeit tray, whence their owners might reclaim them by paying the penalty of the loss of an order mark. Each girl had her pencil-box, in which she was expected to keep her own property; but many things were usually left lying about, and the warden always made a careful search at one o'clock.

The most cherished object in Janie's desk was a little, pearl-handled penknife, which she greatly valued. She guarded it zealously, lending it as seldom as she could, and taking good care that it was always returned to her immediately. One unfortunate day, however, she had been sharpening her pencil at the close of the arithmetic lesson, and in the preoccupation of correcting her answers she laid her treasure down, and forgot all about it. She remembered it after dinner, and ran back to the schoolroom to rescue it, but it was nowhere to be found.

"It must have been put in the forfeit tray," she said to herself. "I shall get it to-morrow, though it will cost me an order mark, worse luck!"

She looked eagerly next morning when Miss Farrar produced the tray, but her penknife was not among the lost property. She made a few enquiries in the class, but nobody professed to have seen it, and she was obliged to abandon it as hopelessly gone.

It must have been quite a week after this that one evening, when the St. Chad's girls were sitting in the recreation room, Flossie pulled her handkerchief from her pocket, and in so doing whisked out a pearl-handled penknife. She stooped in a hurry to recover it, but it had fallen under a little table, close to where Pauline Reynolds was sitting, and the latter picked it up instead.

"Hello! This is Janie Henderson's knife," exclaimed Pauline. "Look here, Janie! Isn't this the one you lost?"

"Of course it is," affirmed Janie. "I can tell it by the small blade. There's a tiny piece broken off at the end."

"Where did you get it, Flossie?" enquired

"I found it when I was warden," replied Flossie. "How should I know it was Janie's?"

"You might have asked whose it was," said Maisie. "You've no right to pocket things when you're warden!"

"I wrote a 'Found' notice about it," declared Flossie.

"I never saw any notice," put in Janie.

"Where did you pin this wonderful paper?" asked Pauline.

"On the dressing-room door."

"Where nobody would ever dream of looking!" returned Maisie. "Why couldn't you put the knife on the forfeit tray?"

"I really don't know! What's the use of making such an absurd fuss about trifles?" said Flossie, linking her arm in Norah Palmer's, and turning away.

"I call them principles, not trifles," murmured Maisie; "it's just on the same lines as the cribbing, not quite open and square. I wish Flossie had stayed at St. Bride's; I certainly don't consider her a credit to St. Chad's."

The quarrels between Honor and Flossie occasionally rose to the level of a miniature war. The latter never lost any opportunity of flinging ridicule and contempt on all things Irish, and Honor, who resented a slur on her native land more than a personal injury, could not keep her hot temper within bounds. It was, of course, very foolish to take any notice of Flossie's taunts, and so her friends reminded her.

"The more you blaze up, the more she'll tease, of course," said Maisie.

"Why can't you keep calm, and pretend you don't hear her?" said Pauline. "She doesn't try it on with us."

"You're such a set of stolid Anglo-Saxons!" declared Honor. "You never get roused about anything."

"It's bad form, my dear girl! Hysterics are out of fashion. We don't go in for them at Chessington."

"But you really are entertaining when you're aggressively Celtic, Paddy!" said Lettice. "I own I can't resist taking a rise out of you myself sometimes, just for the fun of seeing you explode."

"You ought to have been born Red Indians!" retorted Honor. "I like people with a little fire. What's the good of having feelings, if one's not to show them?"

"You show them so hard," laughed Lettice, "you make yourself quite ridiculous! I'm sure I shouldn't think one of Flossie's silly jokes was worth making any fuss about."

This was very excellent and practical schoolgirl wisdom, but unfortunately Lettice preached a philosophy of stoicism to which Honor had not yet attained. At the least provocation her fiery Irish blood always asserted itself, and she would flare up, albeit she was conscious that, by so doing, she was affording her enemy the keenest satisfaction, and was providing amusement for the other girls, who enjoyed "hearing Paddy break out".

One morning the feud came to a crisis. When Honor opened her desk she found inside a neat little collection of new potatoes, and on the top, pinned to the biggest, a paper in Flossie's handwriting, bearing these lines:

HONOR'S WISH

Oh, Erin, moist Erin, how damp are thy showers!

I would I were back 'mid thy pigs and thy rills!

The "tater" to me is more dear than thy flowers,

And I relish the rain on thy ever-wet hills.

Honor could not help laughing at this, in spite of the aspersion on the climate of her country. Such a quip, however, could not go unrequited, and she sought for means of retaliation. She decided that Flossie deserved a "booby trap", and fled back early to the classroom after lunch, to set it for her. It was a rather difficult and delicate operation, for she did not wish to catch anybody else by mistake. She balanced a big dictionary so that it rested on the top of the door and the lintel of the doorway; then, stationing herself inside the room, she held the handle firmly, lest someone should disturb her arrangement by flinging back the door, which was just sufficiently wide open to allow a single person to enter. She peeped every now and then into the passage, on the look-out for Flossie, and admitted each returning girl with caution and due warning.

"Here she is at last!" whispered Lettice, who was naughty enough to enjoy practical jokes, and, after admiring the preparations, had offered to act scout.

"Is she really coming in next?"

"Yes; she's walking in front of May Thurston and Dorothea Chambers."

"Are you certain?"

"Absolutely."

"Then tell me when!"

"Now!"

Honor pulled open the door, and down crashed the dictionary, tumbling full on the head, not of Flossie Taylor, but (oh! horrible miscarriage of justice!) of Miss Farrar herself. At exactly the wrong moment the teacher had popped out of the next classroom, and, as Flossie had stood politely aside to give her precedence, she had walked straight into the trap destined for her pupil.

The dictionary was heavy, and in its fall its sharp corner caught Miss Farrar on the cheek. She stopped, almost dazed by the sudden blow, and, pressing her handkerchief to her face, drew it back marked with a red stain. At the sight of the blood Honor uttered a shriek, and, rushing from the room, fled down the passage, as if to escape from the horror of what she had done. In almost a state of panic she ran across the quadrangle, and, turning into the garden, sought refuge inside the tool-shed. Here she was found some time afterwards by Janie, who had been sent to look for her, and had vainly searched St. Chad's and every other likely spot of which she could think.

Honor never did things by halves; if she wept, she wept, and at present she was a perfect Niobe, almost drowned in tears. When she saw Janie she gave her streaming eyes a hasty mop with a very wet pocket-handkerchief.

"Have I killed her?" she asked, in a tragic whisper.

"Of course not!" replied Janie. "It was only a small cut on the cheek. It's all right now it has been bathed with cold water."

"I was afraid they'd bring it in murder," groaned Honor. "Oh, the ill luck of it, that it should have been Miss Farrar! And the dictionary came down with such a frightful bang! I can never look her in the face again."

"You'll have to!" said Janie. "I was sent to fetch you back at once. You needn't be afraid, Miss Farrar has taken it so nicely."

Poor Honor's apologies and the depths of her genuine remorse would have melted the hardest of hearts, much more that of her teacher.

"We'll say no more about it," declared Miss Farrar. "All the same, remember that I cannot allow such things to happen in the classroom. You might have hurt Flossie very seriously. No, my scratch is nothing! It will be healed directly. But if you are really sorry, Honor, you must give me your most solemn promise that you will never play such a dangerous practical joke again."

CHAPTER VII. ST. CHAD'S CELEBRATES AN OCCASION

During her first few days at Chessington, Honor had considered the College as little better than a prison; but as time went on and she grew more accustomed to the routine, she began to reverse her opinion. After all, it was pleasant to have companionship. The various fresh interests, the many jokes, amusements, and constant small excitements inseparable from a large community of girls seemed to open out a new phase of existence for her.

"I'd no idea what school was like before I came," she confided to Janie. "Of course, the boys were always talking of the things they did, and of the fagging and bullying and ragging that went on, but I was sure they were piling on the horror for my benefit, and that it wasn't really as bad as they pretended."

"Why, no one bullies at girls' schools," said Janie.

"I know they don't; but Derrick and Dermot stuffed me with all kinds of ridiculous tales, just for the sake of teasing. They said that Chessington was exactly on the model of a boys' college, and that if girls learnt Latin and mathematics, and played cricket and hockey, and had a gymnasium and a debating society, it put such a masculine element into them that they couldn't refrain from using brute force, instead of any other means of persuasion. They declared it was a natural sequence, and I must make up my mind to it. Derrick even offered to teach me to box before I came, as a useful accomplishment!"

"Did you accept?"

"No, thank you!—not after the way I'd seen him knock Brian about. I suppose brothers are always teases."

"I've no experience, because I haven't any brothers. I've nobody except Mother; but she's as good as a whole family combined." When Janie mentioned her mother her eyes always shone, and her face would light up. It was evident the two were everything to one another, and that the separation during term-time was a hardship.

"I didn't want to go to school at all," continued Honor; "not, of course, because I believed Derrick's absurd stories, but simply because I was so fond of home that I hated to leave."

"That's just how I felt. Mother and I had such a delightful time together, I was sure Chessington couldn't be half so nice."

"What used you to do? You've scarcely told me anything about your home, though I often talk about Kilmore."

"We live in quite a quiet place," began Janie, "though it's not so out-of-the-world as Kerry. Our house is at Redcliffe, a village a few miles from Tewkesminster. It's a beautiful country. There are lovely farms, with red-tiled roofs and big orchards and picturesque barns; and there's a splendid old castle overlooking the river. And then the trees! You ought to see our trees! These about Chessington look the most wretched, stunted things, after our grand oaks and elms. It's a great fruit-growing neighbourhood; we have heaps and heaps of apples and pears and plums and apricots in our garden. They're simply delicious when they're ripe. Then Tewkesminster is so quaint! There are all kinds of funny little side streets, with cottages built at odd angles; and there's a market cross and several old churches, as well as the Minster. Mother is extremely fond of painting, and sometimes she takes me out sketching with her. I can't draw very well yet—most of my attempts are horrid daubs! but Mother is such a good teacher, she always makes one want to try."

"Hadn't you a governess?" asked Honor.

"Yes. Miss Hall used to come every day from Tewkesminster; but I had a few lessons from Mother as well, in drawing, and Greek history, and English literature. We used to read books aloud in the evenings—Shakespeare, or Dickens, or sometimes Tennyson or Wordsworth. We got through a tremendous amount of poetry in the winter, when it was dark early, and we had nothing else to do, except sit by the fire. We read all *Marmion* and the *Idylls of the King* and *Lalla Rookh*, as well as shorter pieces. Mother reads aloud most beautifully; it's delightful to listen to her. Then in summer-time we used to go country walks, and find wild flowers, and bring them back and hunt out their names in the botany book. I kept a Nature Calendar, and put down everything I noted—when the first violets were out, and when I heard the cuckoo, or saw a swallow for the first time in the year; and what birds' nests I found, or butterflies, or moths, or caterpillars. Sometimes I drew pictures of them as well. I had a whole row of specimen sheets pinned round the school-room at home. Then one day a wretched doctor told Mother that Tewkesminster was too relaxing a place for me, and recommended Chessington. I begged and implored not to be sent away, but Mother said the doctor was quite right, and that I was far too grown-up for my age, and an only child ought to have young companions, so I must certainly go to school at once. I was absolutely miserable my first term. I'm a little more used to it now, but I begin to count the days to the holidays directly I get back to St. Chad's. There are still eight weeks before we break up!"

Janie spoke of home with the intense longing of a girl who is not naturally fond of the social side of life. She was out of her element at Chessington, and the strenuous bustle and stimulating whirl of the place, which began to mean so much to Honor, were repugnant to her quiet, reserved disposition. In every big school there are Janies, isolated characters not quite able to run the pace required by the inexorable code of public opinion, interesting to the one or two who may happen to discover their good points, but to the mass of their companions merely names and faces in class. Some of them do fine work in the world afterwards, yet the very qualities that help them to future success are not those to bring present popularity. They are not for the many, but for the few, and only show their best to an occasional friend whose sympathy can overstep the wall of shyness that fences them round.

With Honor alone Janie was at her ease, and she would chat away in their bedroom with a sprightliness that would have amazed the other members of St. Chad's, if they could have heard her. The two girls got on well together. Their opposite dispositions seemed to dovetail into one another, and so to cause little friction; and Miss Maitland, whose observant eyes noticed more than her pupils imagined, was well satisfied with the result of her experiment. Janie kept Honor up to the mark in the way of work; she would generally go over dates or difficult points in the lessons while they were dressing each morning, and it was chiefly owing to her efforts that Honor held a tolerably high place in her class. The latter often wished that she could have performed a like service for her friend in respect of athletics, but Janie was hopeless at physical sports, and endured them only under compulsion.

Every afternoon, from two o'clock till a quarter to four, all the girls were required to take part in organized games, under the direction of Miss Young, the gymnastic mistress. They were allowed their choice between cricket and tennis, but during the specified hours they must not be absent from the playing-fields, as this systematic outdoor exercise formed part of the ordinary course of the school. Now and then it was varied by a walk, and occasionally by an archery or croquet tournament; but these were reserved for insufferably hot days, and the time, as a rule, was devoted to more active pursuits. The cricket pitch lay to the west of the College, a splendid, level tract of ground, commanding a glorious prospect of low, undulating hills, cliffs bordering a shingly beach, and the long, blue stretch of the Channel beyond. All the healthy moorland and sea breezes seemed to blow there, filling the lungs with pure, fresh air, and well justifying Miss Cavendish's boast that Chessington was the most bracing place in the kingdom for growing girls. Even Janie's pale cheeks would take a tinge of pink as she ran, unwillingly enough, in chase of a ball; and the majority of the school would come in at four o'clock flushed and rosy, and very ready indeed for the piles of thick bread and butter that awaited them in the various dining-halls.

Honor took to the games with enthusiasm. Having served an apprenticeship in the Beginners' Division at cricket, and having shown Miss Young her capacity in the way of batting and bowling, she was allowed a place in the St. Chad's team.

It happened that on the very day of her promotion her house played St. Hilary's, and there was great excitement about the match, because the latter was generally considered the crack team of the College. That afternoon, however, the Hilaryites did not quite justify their reputation. Perhaps the St. Chad's bowling had been extra good; at all events, the St. Hilary side was dismissed for sixty-seven.

Honor's heart was beating fast when at length her innings arrived, and, taking her bat, she walked to the wicket. Every eye, she knew, would be fixed upon her play. A new girl, she was standing her trial before the school, and on the result of this match would largely depend her position during the term. She had played cricket during the holidays with her brothers, and all Derrick's rules came crowding into her mind as she tried to imagine that she was on the dear, rough old field at home, with Brian to bowl, and Fergus for long-stop, and Dermot and Osmond to field, and criticize her strokes afterwards.

She held her bat well, keeping her left shoulder to the bowler and her eye on the ball. The bat was a light, new one, which the boys had given her as a parting present, and she felt she could wield it easily. During the first over she played steadily, but did not attempt to score. It was one of

Derrick's pet maxims that it was folly to try to do so until you had taken the measure of your opponent, and she wished to gain confidence.

In the next over her partner, Chatty Burns, made a single, which brought Honor to the opposite wicket. Gertrude Humphreys's bowling was more to her taste; it might be described as fast and loose, and Honor, unlike most girls, did not object to swift bowling, having been accustomed to it from Brian and Derrick. The first ball she received came down at a good pace, but well on the off side of the wicket. This was just the chance she had been waiting for, and a well-timed cut sent it flying to the boundary for three. The rest of the over was uneventful, Chatty having evidently made up her mind to be careful. Winnie Sutcliffe now took up the bowling at the other end, but her first ball, being a wide, served to increase the confidence that Honor had felt in breaking her duck. The next ball, though straight on middle stump, was a half-volley; Honor stepped out to it with a feeling of exultation, and a moment later it was soaring over the bowler's head for four.

"Good!" "Well hit, Honor!" "St. Chad's for ever!" "Hurrah!" ejaculated the Chaddites.

Success like this often turns the batter's head, but Honor remembered in time the many cautions she had received from her critical brothers, and the next ball, being of good length, she played quietly to long off for one. Chatty now received the bowling, and, encouraged by Honor's success, made what the girls afterwards described as the finest leg hit they had ever seen. Certainly it was a good stroke, taken quite clean and square, and as it cleared the boards it was marked down six amid rapturous applause. After that runs came more slowly for a time, and neither girl appeared inclined to take any risks. This careful play, however, began to wear down the bowling, especially Gertrude Humphreys's, which became decidedly loose. Honor, seeing her chance, suddenly began hitting about her with a spirit and vigour that almost sent the Chaddites delirious with delight, while even Miss Young was seen laughing and smiling with Miss Maitland in a manner that seemed to imply no small self-congratulation on her choice for the last vacancy in the team.

The Hilaryites were looking decidedly glum at this marked change in the fortunes of the game. Grace Ward, their captain, at the end of the over quietly rolled the ball to Ida Bellamy, famed for her slow "twisters". Her first essay pitched well to the leg side, and Honor, who rather despised "slows", made a mighty stroke at it, not allowing for the break, and missed it altogether. With her heart in her mouth she glanced rapidly round at the wicket, expecting to see her bails fly; but luck was on her side, for the break had been a little too great, and the ball just cleared the off stump.

"A good thing Derrick isn't here," said Honor to herself. "I should never have heard the end of that!"

It was very hard to resist the temptation to hit out, dangerous though she knew it to be, and it was with a sensation of relief that she saw the ball travelling off for a single to long field, thus leaving the rest of the over to Chatty, who, neither so ambitious nor so impatient, played it out without giving the much-longed-for chance of a catch. By this time sixty was up on the board, of which Honor had contributed twenty-eight, to the great satisfaction of all concerned.

But Grace had not played her last card. She had evidently decided on a double change of bowling; for, when the fielders had crossed, Irene Richmond was seen at the wicket. Irene's bowling was peculiar; it was left-handed, which is quite uncommon in a girl, and the more difficult on that account. The Chaddites looked at one another with smiles that were less spontaneous.

Certainly Irene might with advantage have been put on before. Her style, though by no means swift, was most awkward to play. Chatty received the first ball, which beat her completely, though luckily it did not touch the wicket. A minute later she made a single, and Honor felt rather blank, as it was now her turn to face the bowling. One of Derrick's pet rules, however, came into her mind: "When you're in doubt, watch each ball carefully, till you get your eye in"; and by dint of adherence to this, she played out the over with safety.

The slow bowling at the other end, though it looked so simple, was full of weird pitfalls, into one of which Chatty fell an easy victim. She played too soon at a short-pitched ball, and spooned a catch to mid-on, who took good care not to drop it. Chatty retired rather ruefully, but was consoled by the applause she received from the pavilion, her twenty-three runs being regarded as a handsome contribution.

Maisie Talbot came in next. Being tall and athletic for her age, she had a long reach, which she employed successfully in driving the first ball she received right along the ground into "the country" for three. This seemed to disconcert the bowler; the next one she sent down was an easy full pitch. Honor waited till just the right moment, and then, with a fine swing of her bat, sent the ball clean over the boundary for six, a performance that quite "brought down the house", even the Hilaryites joining in the cheering. For a moment no one seemed to have realized how the score was going, but when seventy went up on the board there was a wild rush for the pavilion, for the match was won.

Honor's friends were loud in their congratulations, and Janie, who had been an excited spectator, was almost as proud as if the success had been her own. Vivian Holmes herself actually expressed approval.

"Well played, Honor Fitzgerald!" she said. "I expect some day you'll be a credit to St. Chad's."

As Vivian was generally more ready to "squash" new-comers than to encourage them, this was indeed high praise, and Honor felt inspired to continue her exertions, having the white ribbon of the College team as the object of her ambition.

Great were the rejoicings of the Chaddites at their triumph over St. Hilary's. Something in the way of a celebration seemed necessary to immortalize the occasion, and that evening, after a hurried conference among the elder girls, it was given out that, with Miss Maitland's permission, an impromptu fancy-dress ball would take place in the recreation room at 8.30 precisely.

"We're just to come in any kind of costumes we can manage to contrive," said Lettice Talbot, who, wild with excitement, had carried the thrilling tidings to the younger contingent. "Miss Maitland is going to dress up, and so is Miss Parkinson. The cook is making some lemonade; I hope it will be cold in time, but even if it isn't it will be rather nice hot. Oh, would you advise me to go as a flower-girl, or do you think Queen Elizabeth would be better?"

"I should suggest a Merry-andrew at the present moment," said Ruth Latimer, as Lettice, unable to contain her glee, went hopping round the room. "You could easily put a different coloured stocking on each leg, cut sheets of tissue paper to make a short, frilled, sticking-out skirt, borrow the toasting-fork from the kitchen and hang it with ribbons for your bauble, and there you are!"

"Jolly!" exclaimed Lettice. "I'll do it. Will you lend me your scarlet sponge-bag? It would make the very cap I want."

It was fortunate that Vivian Holmes and her fellow-workers had reserved the announcement of the proposed fête until after preparation, otherwise very few lessons would have been learnt at St. Chad's. The girls finished supper with record speed, and filed out of the dining-hall at least ten minutes earlier than usual, all anxious to flee upstairs and begin the delightful but arduous task of robing themselves in character.

Miss Maitland was the owner of what she called a "theatrical property-box". It held a store of most invaluable possessions, which she had collected from time to time and put by to serve for charades or tableaux. There were old evening dresses and cloaks, feathers, shawls, a few hats, artificial flowers, bright-coloured scarves, beads, bangles, and cracker jewellery, even some false moustaches and beards, a horse pistol, and a pair of top-boots. These she placed entirely at the disposal of the girls, telling Vivian Holmes to distribute them so as to allow as many as possible to have a share. Vivian was strictly impartial, and doled out the treasures with the stern justice of a Roman tribune. They did not go very far, however, among forty Chaddites; so, of necessity, at least half of the costumes had to be composed hastily of anything that came to hand.

The apparelling was a lively process, to judge from the sounds of mirth that issued from the various cubicles; and so many different articles were borrowed, lent, and exchanged that it was a wonder their respective owners ever managed to claim them again. Strict secrecy was observed, the occupants of each bedroom denying even a peep to their next-door neighbours, who, though full of their own preparations, could not fail to exhibit curiosity when such exclamations as, "Oh, how lovely!" or, "It's simply screaming!" were wafted down the passage.

Nowhere was the excitement keener than in No. 8, though Honor and Janie had the fun all to themselves. The latter had decided to go as a friar. She had contrived a capital monk's habit out of her waterproof, tied round the waist with the cord that held back the window curtains. The hood formed the cowl, a dictionary made a very passable breviary, and a hockey stick served as a pilgrim's staff.

"You're just like a palmer returning from the Holy Land," declared Honor.

"Or the 'Friar of Orders Grey'," said Janie, "who—

"'Walked forth to tell his beads,

And he met with a lady fair

Clad in a pilgrim's weeds!'

"I ought to have a rosary, but there isn't anything that would do in the least for it."

"Never mind! One must imagine it is in your pocket. Even palmers couldn't tell their beads all day long. You look a most unsuitable figure to dance! I'm afraid they would turn you out of your monastery, if they caught you."

Honor was determined to enact the part of Dick Turpin. She had corked herself the most ferocious moustaches, and made a cocked hat out of brown paper; and was now only waiting for a certain cloak, the horse pistol, and the pair of top-boots, which Vivian had promised to bring her if Barbara Russell, one of the elder girls, did not want them.

"I heard Barbara say she meant to be a shepherdess," she said, "so she couldn't possibly wear top-boots. I don't believe anybody else has thought of a highwayman. I wish Vivian would be quick!"

She was in a ferment of excitement. A festivity such as this was an event in her life. She could hardly bear to wait, and would have been down the passage in search of the missing properties, only she did not wish to exhibit her beautiful moustaches before the right time.

"Vivian won't be long," Janie assured her. "She is the most dependable person I know; when she says she'll do a thing, she does it. Oh, here she is now!"

Honor sprang to the door, but her face fell as she saw the monitress arrive empty-handed.

"I'm dreadfully sorry!" announced Vivian. "Barbara decided, after all, to be Oliver Cromwell, so of course she wanted the cloak, boots, and pistol. I've brought you a few bangles and a wreath of flowers, if they'll be of any use to you; I've nothing else left. I must fly! I've to get into my own costume."

Poor Honor! It was a bitter disappointment. She had counted so much on representing Dick Turpin that to have to forgo the part seemed little short of a tragedy.

"I can't do a highwayman in nothing but a pair of corked moustaches!" she exclaimed dolefully.

"It is a pity," sympathized Janie, "but of course it can't be helped. If we're very quick we shall just have time to think of something else. Could you manage a fairy, with the bangles and the wreath and a white petticoat?"

"A fairy! No! Do I look like a fairy? I'm so cross, it would have to be a goblin. I know what I'll do; I shall go as an Arab."

"With the towels wound round you, I suppose?"

"They're not big enough; I must use my sheets," and Honor, suiting her action to her words, ruthlessly disarranged her bed.

If the towels were too small, the sheets proved too large. In spite of Janie's efforts (much hampered by her cassock and cowl) they refused to drape elegantly. Honor lost all patience at last, and, seizing her scissors, ripped the offending sheets in halves with uncompromising fingers.

"Oh, Honor, what have you done? How could you? Oh, what will Miss Maitland say?" shrieked Janie, almost in tears.

"I don't care!" declared Honor recklessly.

In her present excited state she would have torn up her best dress with equal readiness. She was elated with her success in the cricket field—what the Scotch call "fey"; and so long as she gratified her present whim, she had no thought at all for the future.

"I must have some costume," she continued, "and we ought to go downstairs at once. They're my own sheets, so what does it matter? It isn't as if they were school property; I brought them from home with the rest of my linen—they're marked 'H. Fitzgerald' in the corner."

"You'll get into a shocking scrape, all the same," said Janie, who was horror-stricken at her friend's lawlessness.

There was no time, however, to think about consequences. The gong was giving the signal for the parade to begin, and various gigglings and exclamations in the passage warned them that the other girls were already issuing from their rooms. Honor hastily finished her Arab toilet, and without further delay the pair joined the rest of the masqueraders in the hall.

Here a brilliant scene awaited them. Considering the scanty materials at command, quite marvellous results had been accomplished. The costumes were most gay and varied, and many of them showed extreme ingenuity on the part of their wearers. Lettice Talbot had carried out Ruth Latimer's idea for a Merry-andrew with great success, and was evidently endeavouring to sustain the character by firing off bad puns, or facetious remarks on the appearance of her friends. Dorothy Arkwright, in a blue evening dress and a black velvet hat with feathers, made a dignified Duchess of Devonshire; and Pauline Reynolds, whose long, golden hair hung below her waist, came arrayed as Fair Rosamond. There were several Italian peasants, a Cavalier, a Roundhead, and a matador. Agnes Bennett, one of the elder girls, impersonated the Pied Piper of Hamelin. By pinning two dressing-gowns (one of red and one of buff) together, she had well imitated the "queer long coat from heel to head, half of yellow and half of red", worn by the mysterious stranger; and, with her pipe, hung with ribbons, at her lips, seemed ready to charm either rats into the

Weser, or children into the hillside. Edith Hammond-Smith was a fairy, and Claudia a pierrot; while Flossie Taylor, in an Eastern shawl, and with bangles tied on for ear-rings, looked a gorgeous Cleopatra.

Chatty Burns, in a tartan plaid, made a typical "Highland lassie". Effie Lawson, with her hair plaited in a tight pigtail, and her eyebrows corked aslant, had, with the aid of a coloured bedspread and a Japanese umbrella, turned herself into a very creditable "Heathen Chinee"; and Maisie Talbot, who found materials waxing scarce after she had finished arraying Lettice, had flung a skin rug over her shoulders, painted her face in streaks of red and black, and come as a savage. Adeline Vaughan had an original and rather striking costume. She called herself "Scholastica", and had decorated herself with a double row of exercise books, suspended by ribbons round her waist. Pencils, india-rubbers, pens, and rulers were fastened to all parts of her dress; and a College cap, borrowed from Miss Maitland, completed the effect.

The funniest of all, however, was Madge Summers, who represented a sausage. She had been elaborately got up for the part by her room-mates. They borrowed a coloured table-cloth from the kitchen, the reverse side of which was a pinky-fawn shade; then they padded Madge carefully all over, so as to make her the right shape, swathed her in the table-cloth, and fastened it down the back with safety-pins, tying it tightly round her neck and ankles. She could scarcely manage to walk, much less dance; and she was so hot in her many wrappings that her face burnt—so she assured her friends—as if she were already on the frying-pan: but if she could not take an active part in the proceedings, she had the satisfaction of attracting an immense amount of attention.

The girls chose partners in the hall, and marched in procession into the recreation room, where Miss Maitland (a stately Marie Antoinette) acted hostess, and received her guests with the assistance of Miss Parkinson (a Spanish gipsy) and Vivian Holmes (hastily attired as a troubadour).

"It is indeed a carnival," said Miss Maitland. "The costumes are splendid, and all deserve hearty congratulations. We shall have to take votes as to which is the best. We haven't thought of the music yet; it seems almost presumptuous to ask Queen Cleopatra to play a waltz for us, but perhaps she will condescend thus far. We can't ask the sausage, for she hasn't any arms! The troubadour and the Pied Piper ought to do their share, and the Merry-andrew must give us a *pas seul*."

Everybody declared the evening to be the greatest success. The lemonade, fortunately cold, was delicious, and so were the biscuits that Miss Maitland, through lack of any other dainties, had provided as refreshments. Half-past nine came far too soon, and the dancers, hot, flushed, and excited, were forced reluctantly to abandon the festivities and betake themselves upstairs to tear off their grandeur.

Honor slept between the blankets that night, and her slumbers were haunted by a vision of Miss Maitland, as an avenging spectre, arrayed in the mutilated sheets. The dream was certainly prophetic, for the house-mistress was extremely angry on discovering the damage done, and gave Honor a lecture such as she richly deserved.

"You will stay in from cricket to-day, and mend the sheets," she decreed, at the conclusion of the scolding. "You will find them ready fixed by two o'clock. I shall expect the seams to be neatly run, and the edges turned over and hemmed."

Honor groaned. After the excitement of yesterday's match, she had been looking forward to the cricket practice; moreover, she hated sewing. But there was no appeal. Each house-mistress had authority to suspend games, if necessary, so she was compelled to pass a weary afternoon at a most uncongenial occupation.

"It's hard labour!" she exclaimed, when Janie ran in at four o'clock. "Finished! No! I've only run one seam, and hemmed about six inches. I feel like the 'Song of the shirt' (only it's the song of the sheet instead). 'Stitch, stitch, stitch', and 'work, work, work'! My fingers are getting quite 'weary and worn'. There's one comfort, at any rate: Miss Maitland won't be likely to keep me away from preparation, and as the clothes go to the wash to-morrow, perhaps she'll let one of the maids do the rest of this, and give me some other penance instead. I'd rather learn five chapters of history, or a scene from Shakespeare; and I'd welcome a whole page of equations—I would indeed!"

"I'm afraid it's a vain hope," said Janie. "Miss Maitland always sticks to her word."

She proved right; Miss Maitland was inexorable. The discipline at Chessington was strict, and any mistress who gave an order was accustomed to enforce it rigorously. Honor was obliged to forgo the triumphs of the playing-fields until the very last stitch had been put in her sheets—a punishment which was severe enough, if not entirely to work a reform, at any rate to sober her considerably for the present.

CHAPTER VIII. A MYSTERIOUS HAPPENING

"I wonder how it is," philosophized Ruth Latimer, "that one always seems to like some girls so much, and detest others? There are certain people who, no matter what they do, or even if their intentions are good, always rub one up the wrong way."

"Natural affinity, or the reverse, I suppose," answered Maisie Talbot. "I'm a great believer in first impressions. I can generally tell in five minutes whether I'm going to be friends with anyone or not; and I find I'm nearly certain to be right in the long run."

"I suppose I must have a natural antipathy, then, against Flossie Taylor," confessed Honor candidly. "It didn't take me as long as five minutes to discover my sentiments towards her."

"I don't wonder," said Lettice. "Flossie is a bounder!"

"What's that?"

"Oh, Paddy! You've lived at the back of beyond! A bounder means—well—just a bounder; putting on side, you know."

"How particularly lucid and enlightening!"

"It means someone who tries to make herself out of more consequence than she really is," explained Maisie. "Flossie is continually dragging into her conversation the grand things she has at home, and the grand people she stays with."

"She doesn't mention them naturally, as anyone might do without being offensive," said Ruth Latimer. "She parades them just to show off, in a particularly obtrusive and objectionable manner."

"And we think that very bad taste at Chessington, because, of course, almost all of us have quite as nice homes and friends, only we don't care to boast about them."

"It looks as if you hadn't been accustomed to decent things, if you're always wanting to let people know you possess them," added Lettice.

"The worst of it is," continued Maisie, "that she's having a bad influence at St. Chad's. The Hammond-Smiths and the Lawsons and the Palmers follow her lead implicitly, and she's completely spoiling Rhoda Cunliffe and Hope Robertson. They used to be quite different before Flossie came. I don't think Jessie Gray and Gladys Chesters have improved either lately. It seems such a pity, because we've always prided ourselves that St. Chad's was the best house in the College, and we don't want this kind of element to creep in."

"What can we do?" asked Ruth Latimer.

"Suppose we form a league against it! All the nicer girls would join, and if Flossie and her set see that we really vote them bad style, perhaps they'll have the sense to drop it."

"All right. Put me down as your first member. What's the name of the Society?"

"We might call it the 'Anti-Bounders'. It has a brisk, rolling sound that's rather jolly."

"The A.B.S. for short," suggested Honor.

"And the rules?" asked Ruth.

"Those could be short and sweet—something on these lines:

"1. No member is to make an unnecessary or ostentatious display of wealth or valuables.

"2. No member is to brag constantly of high connections or titled friends.

"3. Members are to consider, not money, but culture, as the standard of public estimation at St. Chad's; and to remember that the essence of good breeding is simplicity.

"4. Any member transgressing any of these rules will be blackballed."

"Excellent!" said Ruth. "It puts what we mean in a nutshell. Now, we must write that out, and try to get signatures. We might add a fifth rule, about not doing sneaking tricks; it's decidedly necessary."

"And our motto could be *Noblesse oblige*," proposed Honor.

The "Anti-Bounders" met with favour among a large proportion of the Chaddites, but with much derision from Flossie and her friends, who lost no opportunity of ridiculing the league, nicknamed its members "The Pharisees", and threw open scorn upon its rules. Nevertheless, in spite of their opposition, the society was strong enough to work a decided improvement, particularly among a certain section who were ready to trim their sails according to the prevailing wind, and to follow blindly the general consensus of public opinion. In future any girl guilty of inordinate bragging was christened "Chanticler", and a warning "Cock-a-doodle-doo!" would advise her of the fact without further explanation.

"It's quite enough!" said Maisie. "We don't want to rub it in too hard, but just to let them see that we notice. Jessie Gray is better already, and although Flossie and Claudia make so much fun of us they're really extremely nettled, because they thought themselves the absolute perfection of good style, and it has been a great blow to them to discover that three-quarters of the house consider them bad form."

It was a constant annoyance to Maisie, Lettice, and Pauline that Flossie should occupy the fourth cubicle in No. 13 bedroom, and they often wondered why Miss Maitland had placed so uncongenial a companion in their midst—"especially when Adeline Vaughan is with the Hammond-Smiths in No. 10," said Lettice. "If we might only make an exchange, everybody would be satisfied."

Miss Maitland, however, had reasons for her arrangements, which she did not care to explain. She knew far more of the inner life of the house than the girls suspected, and hoped that by a judicious sandwiching of different elements certain undesirable traits might be eliminated, and the general tone raised. Though she was often aware of things that were not entirely to her satisfaction, she was wise enough not to interfere directly, but by careful tactics to allow the reformation to work from within, experience having taught her that codes fixed by the girls themselves were twice as binding as those enforced by the authorities.

The bedrooms at St. Chad's were on two floors, Nos. 9 to 16 being on the upper story, and Nos. 1 to 7 on the lower. No. 8, occupied by Honor and Janie, was the higher of two small rooms built over the porch, and occupied a position midway between the two floors, being reached by a short flight of steps from the landing below. In No. 4 slept Evelyn Fletcher, the youngest girl in the house. She shared the room with an elder sister and two cousins, all three members of the Sixth Form. Though Evelyn was thirteen, she was very small and childish for her age, and was treated rather as a pet by the Chaddites. She was a pretty little thing, with appealing blue eyes, fluffy hair, and a helpless, dependent manner. It was the great trial of her life that she was obliged to go to bed more than an hour before the other occupants of No. 4. She had a morbid horror of being alone in the dark—a horror that, through a sensitive dread of being laughed at, she had so far confessed to no one, but which, all the same, was very real and overwhelming. Night after night she would lie with the curtain of her cubicle half-drawn, and the door ajar so as to catch a gleam of light from the landing, listening with every nerve on the alert for she knew not what, and enduring agonies until the welcome moment when her sister Meta came upstairs. It was, of course, very foolish, but her terror was probably due to a dangerous illness from which she had suffered some years before, and which had left a permanent delicacy.

One evening the younger girls had retired as usual, and everything was very quiet in the upper stories. Evelyn lay wideawake, sometimes straining her ears to catch a sound from the ground floor below, and sometimes burying her head in her pillow. Suddenly she sat up in bed, with wide-open, terror-stricken eyes. On the opposite wall there gleamed a strange, dancing light, which appeared and disappeared and reappeared again, flickering faintly from floor to ceiling. There seemed no explainable origin for it, and Evelyn's mind at once turned to the supernatural. A silly maidservant at home had been accustomed to ply her with ghost stories, all of which now recurred to her memory. What was it, that unnatural, luminous halo on the opposite wall? It was moving nearer to her, and had almost reached the curtain of her cubicle, when, with a choking little gasp, she sprang out of bed, and darting into the corridor ran shrieking upstairs, her one idea being to escape from the mysterious apparition.

Her screams not only roused all the girls on the higher rooms, but brought up Vivian Holmes, who had been crossing the hall at the moment, and felt it her duty as monitress to go and investigate.

"What's all this noise about?" she asked. "Evelyn, what's the matter? Has anything frightened you?"

"It's something on my wall," panted Evelyn; "something white, that moves."

"What was it like?"

"I don't know—I can't describe it."

"Perhaps it was a ghost," said Honor, in a hollow voice; "they come softly, this way," and, pulling a horrible face, she moved slowly forward with a gliding motion, her white night-dress completing the illusion.

Trembling from head to foot, Evelyn turned and clung to the monitress.

"Stop that, Honor!" exclaimed Vivian sharply. "It's a wicked thing to frighten anybody. Come along, Evie! I'll go with you to your room, and we'll try to find out what this mysterious 'something' is. Go back to bed at once, all the rest of you!"

After making a thorough inspection of No. 4, Vivian found that the uncanny light was, after all, very easy of explanation. It was nothing but the reflection from a lamp outside, and the swaying of the blind had been responsible for the movement. Having shown Evelyn the unromantic origin of her spectre, the monitress left her, apparently pacified, and went downstairs.

In the upper rooms all was soon in absolute stillness. The girls took Vivian's advice and retired to bed again, laughing at having been disturbed for so trivial a cause.

"Evelyn Fletcher is a goose!" said Flossie Taylor. "She'd run away from her own shadow."

"She is rather silly," agreed Maisie Talbot. "I've no patience with people who imagine ghosts!"

Maisie's own nerves were of the stoutest. She certainly could not sympathize with superstitious fears, and neither flickering lights nor possible spectres would have distressed her in the least.

"When people shriek at nothing and rouse the whole house, they deserve to have something to shriek at," remarked Flossie.

But Maisie was in the act of hopping into bed, and only grunted in reply, while Pauline and Lettice were already half-asleep. Flossie lay for a minute or two pondering over the affair, then got up again very softly. First, she felt on her washstand for her tooth powder, and dabbed her face plentifully with it till she was sure it must be white all over; then she took the towel, and arranged it over her head, to hide her hair. In every bedroom at St. Chad's there were a candle and a box of matches, in case the electric light should suddenly fail; Flossie groped for these and found them, and, taking them in her hand, left the room on tiptoe.

"Where are you going?" asked Maisie drowsily, but receiving no reply, she did not even trouble to open her eyes.

Once outside the door, Flossie lighted her candle. She was determined, in spite of Vivian's warning, to play a trick upon Evelyn.

"She needs teasing out of such rubbish," she said to herself. "Vivian Holmes always makes an absurd fuss of her—quite spoils her, in fact. I think the best way to cure people is to laugh at them."

Creeping softly downstairs, she switched off the electric light at the end of the lower landing, and, shading her candle with her hand, passed along in the darkness to No. 4. Without pausing a moment she entered, holding up one arm in a dramatic attitude, and making her eyes glare wildly from her whitened face. The effect was beyond all that she had anticipated. Such a scream of agonized fear came from the bed in the corner that, alarmed at what she had done, Flossie turned and fled. As she ran through the door she realized that somebody was hastening along the dark passage, and, afraid of being discovered, she turned suddenly and rushed up the short flight of steps that led to Honor's bedroom, blowing out her candle as she went. She crouched for a few moments outside the door of No. 8, then, hearing no footsteps pursuing her, she ventured to steal down again and make a dash for the stairs and the upper landing, where she whisked into No. 13 with all possible speed.

"It was a narrow shave!" she said to herself. "If that was Vivian, and she had caught me, I expect she'd have made herself uncommonly disagreeable."

In the meantime, Vivian had returned to the recreation room, and told the story of Evelyn's groundless fears to the elder girls assembled there.

"A shock of this kind is extremely bad for Evie," said Meta. "She had a nervous fever four years ago, and has been so fragile and highly-strung ever since. She was sent to Chessington because we hoped the bracing air might do her good. I remember she used to have night terrors when she was a wee child, but we thought she had quite got over them."

"She looks very white and delicate," said Vivian. "She's all eyes. If she were my sister, I should like to see her less 'nervy'."

"Perhaps I had better run upstairs to her," said Meta, rather anxiously. "Now I think of it, I remember she always seems most relieved when May and Trissie and I make our appearance at nine-thirty."

Meta found the landing in total darkness, a most unusual occurrence, as the electric light was always left on there. She felt her way along by the wall, and as she did so she was aware of somebody coming towards her from the opposite end of the long corridor. Whoever it was carried a light in her hand, so small as to make only a faint glimmer, but enough to allow Meta to perceive that she turned into No. 4. The next moment a cry of frantic fear issued from the room. Meta hurried forward, her heart throbbing wildly, while the figure, rushing from the room, and showing in its hasty flight a white-veiled head, darted up the steps to No. 8, and disappeared, light and all.

It did not take Meta more than three seconds to reach her sister's bedside. Strangled sounds issued from under the clothes, where Evelyn lay cowering in mortal terror; and again, as Meta placed her hand on the bed, came that convulsive, half-stifled cry.

"Evie! Evie dear! Don't you know me?" exclaimed Meta.

Realizing at last who stood near, Evelyn sat up and flung her arms round her sister. She was in a most agitated, hysterical condition, trembling and quivering with sobs. Meta soothed her as well as she could, and requested Vivian, who had followed to see that all was right, to switch on the bedroom light, and also the one in the passage.

"Someone must have intentionally turned it off," she said, "on purpose to play this trick."

"I know I'm silly!" choked Evelyn, more reassured now that the room was no longer in darkness, "but I can't help it. I really thought it was a ghost."

"Who is responsible for this?" asked Vivian indignantly.

"Honor Fitzgerald," replied Meta, without hesitation.

"Are you sure?"

"Whoever it was ran back into No. 8. Janie Henderson would never dream of doing such a thing, so it must have been Honor."

"She certainly was pretending to be a ghost upstairs," said Vivian. "I shall go and tell her my opinion of her," and she departed with a very grim expression on her face.

Janie and Honor were half-asleep when Vivian, like an avenging angel, entered No. 8.

"Look here, Honor Fitzgerald!" she began, "if you try any more of those senseless practical jokes, I shall report you to Miss Maitland. I'm monitress here, and I don't intend to have this kind of thing going on at St. Chad's."

"What's the matter?" asked Honor, rubbing her eyes.

"Matter, indeed! You know as well as I do. It was a cruel, mean trick to play upon a nervous, delicate girl like Evie Fletcher."

Honor was considerably astonished. She, of course, knew nothing of Flossie's escapade, and imagined that the monitress must be referring to the few words she had said on the upper landing.

"Why, Evie didn't seem to mind all that much!" she retorted.

"You've frightened her most seriously, and I consider it so dangerous that I'd rather you were expelled from the school than that it should happen again. I don't want to get you into trouble at head-quarters if I can help it, so I'll say nothing if you'll promise me faithfully that this is absolutely the last time you'll ever act ghost."

"Of course I'll promise. I didn't intend to upset Evie. I think both you and she are making a great fuss about nothing," replied Honor, lying down once more.

"I'm disgusted with you, Honor Fitzgerald! If you can't realize the mischief your thoughtlessness has done, you might at least have the grace to be sorry for it! To amuse yourself by playing on the fears of a timid girl, younger than you, is the work of a coward—yes, a coward! That's what I consider you!" and Vivian turned away, full of righteous wrath, and wondering whether she had adequately fulfilled her monitorial duty, or whether she ought to have said even more.

CHAPTER IX. DIAMOND CUT DIAMOND

Honor was both amazed and indignant at Vivian's stern rebuke. She appealed to Janie in self-justification.

"I don't understand it," she declared. "I only screwed up my face, and said ghosts glided. I stopped at once when Vivian asked me. How could Evelyn have been so fearfully frightened just at that?"

"I can't imagine," said Janie, "except that she's such an extremely nervous girl."

"It's too bad to blame me on that account."

"Vivian is generally very severe."

"She's always down on me! I'm continually in hot water, and half the time I don't know exactly why."

It was not until the next afternoon that Honor learnt of the practical joke that had been practised upon her schoolfellow. As she was washing her hands in the dressing-room she chanced to overhear a few remarks between two or three girls who were discussing the affair, and at once questioned them about it.

"Of course Meta knew it was you, Honor!" said Ruth Latimer, rather reproachfully.

"Why of course?" asked Honor.

"Because it couldn't be anyone else. You're always playing tricks upon someone."

"It's a case of 'give a dog a bad name', then. I'm innocent for once."

"But the ghost ran up the steps to No. 8!"

"That's only 'circumstantial evidence'. I certainly didn't do it. Janie can tell you that I never left the bedroom."

483

"Yes, I could take my oath in a law court, as a reliable witness," vouched Janie.

"Then who was it?"

Honor shook her head.

"Ask me a harder!" she said briefly.

Flossie, who was standing near, looked rather conscious, but volunteered no explanation.

"It's a most peculiar thing," said Ruth. "Somebody must have been the ghost, I suppose."

"Unless it were a real one!" suggested Flossie. "It might——"

"What nonsense! Nobody believes in ghosts, except, perhaps, Evelyn," interrupted Ruth scornfully. "Of course, it was a girl playing a trick. The only question is, who?"

"Could it be May or Trissie Turner?" suggested Flossie.

"Impossible! Evelyn's own cousins—and in the Sixth Form, too!"

"It's very extraordinary!"

"It ought to be properly cleared up," said Lettice Talbot.

"Suppose we ask every girl in the house if she knows anything," proposed Dorothy Arkwright.

"No; Meta begged us to let the matter drop," replied Ruth. "She says Evelyn is extremely sensitive about it, and can't bear the subject alluded to."

"Evelyn looked very ill this morning," observed Dorothy.

"Yes; Meta says she has had a severe shock, and the least reference to it might upset her again."

"So it will have to remain unexplained?"

"I suppose so," said Flossie. "It seems a complete mystery."

"Why, Flossie!" exclaimed Maisie Talbot suddenly, "didn't I hear you get up last night, after Vivian had gone downstairs and we had marched off to bed again? I remember I called out to you, but I was too sleepy to wake up properly. I verily believe it must have been you who frightened Evelyn. Honestly now, was it?"

Flossie turned very red. She would have continued to shield herself at Honor's expense if it had been any longer possible, but she was not prepared to tell a direct falsehood. There was no way out of it but to confess.

"What a storm in a teacup!" she replied, shrugging her shoulders. "It's absurd if one can't play the least joke without a monitress interfering and making a ridiculous fuss. It was only meant for fun; I should have laughed if anybody had done it to me."

"It's no laughing matter," said Maisie gravely. "In the first place, though Evelyn may be silly, you had no right to frighten her; and in the second place, you deliberately let the blame rest on Honor's shoulders."

"Vivian ought to be told of this," declared Dorothy.

"Yes, she must know at once," added Ruth.

"Oh, please don't go sneaking to the monitress on my account!" interposed Honor. "If Meta wants the affair to drop, it shall. Both she and Vivian took it for granted last night that I had acted the ghost in No. 4; they never asked me, or gave me a chance of denying it, so I shan't trouble to undeceive them. If Vivian has such a poor opinion of me already, she shan't think me a tell-tale in addition. As for Flossie, she's not worth noticing."

"But telling a monitress isn't like telling a teacher," objected Ruth.

"It savours of sneaking, and I prefer to leave it alone. What does it matter? I don't care about anybody's opinion!"

Honor was on her high horse. She had been much hurt by Vivian's injustice, and all the Fitzgerald pride was roused within her. Notwithstanding the girls' remonstrances, she would not allow herself to be cleared of the false charge.

"The whole thing is altogether beneath me," she remarked, as she stalked haughtily away.

"It's no good trying to persuade her," said Lettice. "When she puts that set look on her face, arguments are absolutely useless."

"On the whole, I think I rather admire her for saying nothing," commented Maisie. "It's more dignified than making a fuss. I can't tolerate tale-bearing myself. It would have got Flossie into a terrific scrape with Vivian, and probably with Miss Maitland as well."

"Flossie doesn't deserve to go scot-free," said Ruth, with a glance at the flaxen head that was discreetly disappearing through the door.

"She won't!" asserted Lettice. "Honor is the most contrary, queer, impossible, perverse girl I've ever met. She'll let Flossie off easily now, but she'll make her pay for it in some other way. I could see it in her eye. She was as cool as a cucumber outside, but I'm sure that was only the crust over the crater, and that there was the usual volcano inside. It's bound to find a safety-valve, so Flossie had better look out for squalls!"

Lettice was right. Honor was certainly in a most unenviable frame of mind. She considered that Vivian had treated her unfairly in assuming her to be guilty without making any proper investigation.

"It's the first time a Fitzgerald has ever been called a coward!" she said to Janie.

The word rankled in her memory even more than the monitress's high-handed manner.

"Then you must use every opportunity of showing that you're the reverse," replied Janie. "You'll have to live the thing down. I expect the truth will come round to Vivian's ears in course of time, and I'm sure that she'll think far better of you than if we had gone at once to her with a long accusation against Flossie. If Flossie herself had offered to tell, that would have been different; but she didn't rise to such a pitch of heroism."

"One wouldn't expect it from Flossie Taylor!" said Honor contemptuously, as she hurried off to her music lesson.

I am afraid Honor's scales that day were anything but a satisfaction to Fräulein Bernhardt, the piano teacher. Her mind was so abstracted that she kept continually playing wrong fingering, or even an occasional wrong note in the harmonic minors. Her study was little better, and her piece a dead failure. The mistress, with characteristic German patience, set her to work to try to conquer a couple of difficult phrases, through which Honor stumbled again and again, each time with the same old mistakes, until the end of the half-hour.

"I find you not yet fit to take share in ze evening pairformance!" sighed poor Fräulein, whose musical ear had been much distressed by this mangling of her favourite tarantella. "Zere must be more of improvement before ve render ze piece to Mees Maitland. You say you not vish to play in publique? Ach, so! Zat is vat zey all say; but it is good to begin young to get over ze fear—vat you call ze 'shyness'—is it not so?"

Fräulein Bernhardt was an excellent teacher—patient, conscientious, and enthusiastic. She tried to inspire all her pupils with her own love for music, and with some indeed she succeeded, though with others it proved a more difficult task.

"I'm almost impossible!" avowed Lettice Talbot. "I believe I'm nearly as bad as the old fellow who declared he only knew two tunes—one was 'God Save the King', and the other wasn't."

"You certainly have a particularly leaden touch," agreed Dorothy Arkwright. "The way you hammer out Mendelssohn is enough to try my nerves, so I'm sure it must be an offence to Fräulein."

"I think it's stupid to be obliged to learn the piano when you've absolutely no taste for it," yawned Lettice. "I'm going to ask Father to let me give it up next term."

"Don't!" interposed Vivian Holmes, who happened to overhear Lettice's remark. "I went through that same phase myself, when I was fourteen. I implored my mother to allow me to stop music, and she had nearly consented when I met a lady who advised me most strongly to go on. She said she couldn't play herself, and regretted it immensely now she was grown-up, and would be thankful if she could manage even a hymn tune. So I did go on, and now I'm very glad. I'm certain you'll like it better, Lettice, when you've got over more of the drudgery."

"Perhaps it will never be anything but drudgery for me!"

"Oh, yes, it will! We shall have you taking part in the 'Friday firsts' yet."

On the first Friday in every month Miss Maitland held a "Mutual Improvement Evening", at which all who were sufficiently advanced were expected to contribute by playing, singing, or reciting. These were quite informal gatherings, only Chaddites being present. Miss Cavendish considered it good for teachers and pupils to meet thus socially, and a similar arrangement obtained at each house. To many of the girls, however, it was more of an ordeal to be obliged to perform before their schoolfellows than it would have been to play to strangers.

"I'm always nervous, in any case," said Pauline Reynolds; "but strangers don't criticize one openly afterwards, whatever they may think in private. I feel it's perfectly dreadful to have Fräulein and Miss Maitland and Miss Parkinson sitting on one side, and all of you in a row on the other!"

"But we're very polite," urged Lettice. "We say, 'Thank you!'"

Honor had not yet been considered proficient enough to take an active part in the monthly entertainment, but Flossie's name was one of the first on the list. She played the violin remarkably well, better than almost anybody else at Chessington; and as she was seldom nervous, her pieces were generally very successful. The day following Evelyn Fletcher's fright happened to be "Mutual Improvement Friday". The girls only spent a short time at preparation, and then went upstairs to change their dresses.

The meetings were always held in the drawing-room, and were rather festive in character. Miss Maitland tried to make them as much as possible like ordinary parties; she received the girls as guests, encouraged them to converse with herself and the other teachers, and had coffee served to them during the evening.

On this particular occasion Flossie made a very careful toilet, and she certainly looked nice in her pretty, embroidered white muslin dress, her fair hair tied with big bows of palest blue ribbon. She took a last glance at herself in the looking-glass, then, seizing her violin, which she had brought to her cubicle, she prepared to go downstairs.

In passing Miss Maitland's bedroom on the lower landing, she noticed that the door stood open, and that no one was within. There was a large mirror in the wardrobe, and, catching a glimpse of her own reflection as she went by, she stopped suddenly, and could not resist the temptation to run in for a moment and take a full-length view of herself as she would appear when she was playing her piece. She raised her violin and struck a suitable attitude, and was immensely pleased with the result that faced her—the dainty dress, the blue bows, the coral cheeks, flaxen hair, and bright eyes all made a charming picture, and the position in which she held her instrument was particularly graceful. She drew her bow gently over the strings, to observe the curve of her slender wrist and well-shaped arm. It was gratifying to know that she would make such a good appearance before her schoolfellows. Once again she played a few notes, for the sheer satisfaction of watching her slim, white fingers in the glass.

Alas for Flossie! That single bar of Schubert's Serenade was her undoing. Honor chanced to be passing the door at the identical moment, and, hearing the strain of music, peeped inside. She grasped the situation at a glance.

"Oho, Miss Flossie! So I've caught you prinking!" she said to herself. "You're evidently practising your very best company smile for this evening. What a disappointment it would be to you, now, if you were not able to play that piece after all!"

Honor had a resourceful mind. Very gently she put her hand inside the door and abstracted the key, which, with equal caution, she fitted into the keyhole on the outside; then, quickly shutting the door, she locked it, and ran away before Flossie had even discovered that anybody Was there. The latter naturally noticed the slight noise and turned round, but she was too late; and though she rattled the handle, and knocked and called, it was of no avail. Honor, as it happened, had been the last girl to go downstairs, and there was nobody left on either landing to hear even the most frantic thumps. Flossie rushed to the electric bell, hoping to bring a servant to her assistance; but it was out of order, and would not ring. She was in a terrible dilemma: if she made too much noise one of the teachers, or even Miss Maitland herself, might come upstairs to see what was the matter; on the other hand, there she was locked up fast and secure, missing the "evening", and with an equal chance of being found out in the end, and asked to give some explanation of her presence in the mistress's room.

In the meantime, Honor went downstairs chuckling. She entered the drawing-room in the highest of spirits, paid her respects to Miss Maitland, and found a seat close to the door. The musical part of the performance, she ascertained, was to come first, and after coffee there were to be recitations, and a dialogue in French. A neat programme had been written out and was laid on the top of the piano, so that it could be referred to by Vivian Holmes, who was conductress of the ceremonies.

It was late already, and the proceedings began immediately. The room was crowded, and amongst the forty girls nobody seemed to have particularly remarked Flossie's absence, and no enquiry was made for her, until the close of the song that preceded her violin solo.

"Where is Flossie Taylor?" whispered Vivian then, with a look of marked annoyance on her face. "Her *Serenade* comes next. She ought to be standing by the piano. Has anybody seen her? Please pass the question on."

She paused a moment or two in great impatience; then, as no Flossie put in an appearance, she turned to Meta Fletcher and May Turner, who followed on the programme, and asked them to begin their duet.

"I can't wait for anybody," she remarked. "If Flossie isn't ready, I must simply miss her out. We've almost too many pieces to get through in the time."

The rest of the music went off successfully. Nobody broke down, or even made a bad stumble, a subject of much self-congratulation to several nervous performers and of great relief to Vivian, who, as monitress of the house, always arranged the little concerts as a surprise for Miss Maitland, the latter preferring that the girls should settle all details amongst themselves, instead of leaving matters to a teacher.

Coffee was brought in at eight o'clock, after which the recitations began immediately. At this state of the entertainment Honor felt magnanimous. She did not want to involve Flossie in serious trouble, so, slipping quietly away, she ran upstairs, unlocked the door of Miss Maitland's bedroom, and released her prisoner.

The disappointed violinist emerged looking decidedly glum.

"It's a nasty, mean trick you've played me, Honor Fitzgerald!" she burst out.

"No meaner than you played on Evelyn Fletcher—not half so bad, in my opinion. I'm sorry to say you're too late for your solo. The music's over long ago, and they're hard at work reciting Shakespeare at present."

"Just what I expected! And it's all your fault!"

"You're very ungrateful! You ought to be most relieved to be let out before Miss Maitland caught you," retorted Honor. "What an opportunity to point a moral on the fatal consequences of vanity!" Then, as Flossie flounced angrily away: "You've never thanked me for unlocking this door yet. I thought we were supposed to cultivate manners at St. Chad's. If Vivian asks where you've been, I suppose you'll tell her?"

"I certainly shan't! And you'll be a sneak if you do."

"All right, all right! Keep your little temper! You may make your mind easy; I don't intend to do anything of the sort," called Honor, watching Flossie's back as her victim hurried out of earshot down the passage. "It has been a delightful evening," she continued to herself; "really quite the jolliest since I came to Chessington. I'm afraid I've had the lion's share of the enjoyment, but that couldn't be helped. It certainly is a most immense satisfaction to feel that Flossie Taylor and I are now exactly quits!"

CHAPTER X. HONOR FINDS FAVOUR

Honor was undoubtedly finding Chessington College a totally different place from Kilmore Castle, and in the six weeks she had spent there she had already learnt many lessons quite apart from textbooks. The wildest bird cannot fly with its wings clipped, and at school Honor was so bound round with conventionalities and restrictions that she never dreamt of raising such turbulent scenes as had sometimes been her wont at home. The calm, firm administration of Miss Cavendish, Miss Maitland's wise control, and Miss Farrar's brisk authority, all seemed indisputable; and even the regulations of Vivian Holmes might not be defied with impunity. The Fitzgerald pride could not tolerate a low place in class, therefore Honor prepared her work carefully, so that she might be above Flossie Taylor and Effie Lawson, emulation urging her to efforts which love of learning alone would not have effected. She did not indulge so frequently as before in either "tantrums" or bursts of temper, for these provoked such ridicule from the other girls that she felt rather ashamed of them; and even her overflowing spirits began to be modified to the level of what was considered "good form" at Chessington.

There is a vast power in public opinion, and Honor, who at Kilmore had lived according to a model of her own choosing, now found herself insensibly falling in with the general tone of the College, and acquiring the mental shibboleths of her schoolfellows. Naturally all this was not accomplished at once, and "Paddy Pepper-box", as she was still nicknamed, had many outbreaks and relapses; but by the time the half-term arrived, Miss Maitland, in a long talk with Miss Cavendish, was able to report that "Honor Fitzgerald was marvellously improved".

"She has the elements of a very fine character," said the house-mistress, "though at present it is like a statue that is still in the rough block of marble: it will take much shaping and carving before the real beauty appears. There is sterling good in her, in spite of certain glaring faults. She is at a most critical, impressionable age, and will require careful management. Everything depends upon what standards she forms now."

Though the whole atmosphere of St. Chad's had its effect upon Honor, she owed more than even Miss Maitland guessed to the influence of Janie Henderson. Janie seemed to have the power of drawing out all that was best in her friend's disposition. In some subtle fashion she appeared to demand the good, and, by presupposing it was there, to bring it actually into existence. Many new ideas of duty, consideration for others, and self-restraint, that had never before occurred to Honor, now began to take root and grow—feebly at first, but the seed was there, and the fruit would come afterwards. It was Janie who put the first suggestion into her mind that life was more than a mere playground, and that other people have paramount claims on us, the fulfilling of which can bring a purer joy than that of pleasing ourselves; Janie who, by implying what a comfort an only daughter might be to father, mother, and brothers, made her realize how utterly she had so far failed to be anything but a care; and Janie whose high ideals and aspirations raised future possibilities of helpfulness of which she had not hitherto dreamt, for until she came to St. Chad's Honor had not heard of girls taking up careers, or fitting themselves for any special work.

"I don't mean earning one's own living," said Janie. "Neither you nor I will probably ever have to do that, and Mother says it is hardly right for women who have independent incomes to overcrowd professions, and drive out those who are obliged to keep themselves. What I want is to settle on some useful thing, and then to do it thoroughly. I've a large family of cousins in town, and they all are so busy, each in a different way. One has trained as a Princess Christian nurse, and now goes three days a week to give help at a crèche. She took me once to see the babies; they were the very poorest of the poor, but were beautifully clean, and so good. Beatrice simply loves them. Then Millicent, the second girl, has learnt wood-carving and metal-work, and takes a class at a Lads' Recreation Club. One of her boys has turned out so clever that he has been sent to the Technical Schools to study 'applied arts'. Milly is tremendously proud of him, particularly as he comes from such a wretched, lost, drunken home. Barbara is very musical—she teaches singing at a Factory Girls' Club; and Mabel helps with a Children's Happy Evening Society."

"But can you do those kinds of things in the country?" asked Honor.

"I'm going to try, when I leave school. I thought if I could learn ambulance work I could have a 'First Aid' class for the village girls. Most of them don't know how to dress a burn, or bind up a wound. I have another scheme too."

"What's that?"

"It's so ambitious, I'd better not talk about it. Perhaps the ambulance work will be enough for a beginning, and the other could follow. Well, if you insist upon my telling you, I should like to get up a lace-making industry among the girls in our village. I read an article in a magazine about someone who had revived the old Honiton patterns at a place in Devonshire."

"A few of the women make lace in our neighbourhood," said Honor.

"How splendid! Then you could start the same at Kilmore, and we could keep comparing notes, and get specimens sent to exhibitions—the 'Irish Industries', you know, or 'Peasants' Handicrafts'. It's such a pity that everything should be done by machinery nowadays! Why, you might have quite a thriving colony of lacemakers at Kilmore—the women could be working at their 'pillows' while the men are out fishing. If I begin at Redcliffe, will you promise to try the experiment too?"

Such a proposal as introducing a new occupation for the tenants on her father's demesne almost took Honor's breath away; yet to her active mind it was rather attractive, and she drew a rapid mental picture of the little barefooted colleens of Kilmore seated at their cabin doors, plying the bobbins with deft fingers. Janie's ardour was infectious, and if Honor were not yet ready to agree to all her plans, at least she caught enough enthusiasm to be interested in the subject, and to admit that it was a dream worthy some day of realization.

In the meantime, the ordinary school course gave ample scope for the energies of both girls. Janie, though a great reader, was backward in many subjects, and was obliged to study hard to keep up with the rest of the class; while Honor, naturally far more clever, had not been accustomed to apply her brains in any systematic fashion. The work of the Lower Third was stiff enough to need constant application, unless the girls wished to earn the reputation of "slackers", a distinction which neither coveted. Besides their mental exertions, Honor, at any rate, wished to maintain her credit in the playing-fields. Janie had long ago given up all hope of becoming a good cricketer, or even a moderate tennis player. She was not fond of exercise. To use her own phrase, she "hated to be made to run about". Her ideal of bliss was to be left to wander round the grounds with a book; but as this was permitted only on Sundays, she was forced on weekdays, much against her inclination, to take her due part in the games. She even went the length of envying Muriel Cunliffe, whose sprained ankle did not allow her to hobble farther than the garden for five weeks; and hailed with delight the occasions when the school filed out for a walk on the moors, instead of the usual routine of fielding, batting, or bowling, all of which she equally detested.

During the latter part of the summer term, when the weather was sufficiently warm, swimming was included among the outdoor sports. There was a large bath behind the gymnasium, and here every girl was obliged to learn her strokes, and to be reported as "proficient", before she was allowed to venture on a dip in the ocean. Those who reached the required stage of independence were taken in classes of about twelve to practise under the critical superintendence of Miss Young. The bathing-place was a sheltered cove among the cliffs, not far from the College, and reached by a footpath and a flight of steps cut in the rock. On the strip of shore stood a big wooden hut, partitioned off into small dressing-rooms; and a causeway of flat stones had been made down to the water, to avoid the sharp flints of the shingly beach.

Janie, though not an expert swimmer, had passed her novitiate, and thoroughly enjoyed a leisurely round of the bay, with as much floating included as Miss Young would allow. To Honor the sea was as a second element. She had been accustomed to it from her babyhood, and was as fearless as any of her brothers. She soon gave proof of her ability in the bath, and was straightway placed among those Chaddites who were privileged to visit the sea.

It was a glorious afternoon in the middle of June when she started for her first trial of the waves of the Channel.

"It can't be anything like so rough as the Atlantic," she declared. "I've swum out sometimes when there was a swell on, and it was quite difficult to get back."

"Of course, we're not allowed to go when it's rough," said Janie. "To-day I expect it will be as smooth as a millpond. I'm so glad you're not a beginner, and only learning to struggle round the bath!"

"So am I. To judge from Madge Summers's achievements yesterday, it doesn't look like a pleasant performance. She appeared to be trying to drown herself."

"Madge is horribly clumsy! I don't believe she'll ever manage to keep afloat properly. She always flounders unless she has one foot at the bottom. Pauline Reynolds wouldn't venture into the water at all at first; Miss Young had to push her in. I shall never forget how she shrieked; and she was so frightened, she actually swam three strokes!"

"Poor old Pauline! It was hard luck on her."

"Yes, it couldn't have been particularly nice. I didn't altogether appreciate learning myself, with a row of horrid Hilaryites sitting on the diving-board and jeering at my best efforts. However, 'those bright days are o'er', and now 'I hear the ocean roar', as the poem says."

Each Chaddite was required to carry her own bathing costume and towel, and to wait in the quadrangle for Vivian Holmes, who was to escort the party down to the cove. Miss Young was already on duty, superintending a batch of Aldwythites, who were to have the first half-hour in the water, and who must vacate the dressing-hut before the second contingent arrived.

"I wonder if there'll be any trippers to-day," said Lettice Talbot, winding her towel artistically round her hat, and letting the ends fall like a pugaree. "Sometimes excursionists from Dunscar walk along the beach, and insist upon stopping to look at us."

"Are they allowed?" asked Honor.

"We can't help it. The beach is common property, and though the College got permission to put up a wooden shanty, it has no power to prevent anybody who likes from coming past. Some people are the greatest nuisance. They bring cakes and bags of shrimps, and sit down on the rocks to eat them while they watch us."

"What cheek!"

"Yes; we glower at them in as withering a manner as we can, but they don't seem to mind in the least. I suppose they think we're part of the seaside amusements, like the niggers, or the pierrots."

"Fortunately, that doesn't happen often," said Ruth Latimer. "We've only been really annoyed once or twice; Lettice loves to exaggerate. The cove is about the quietest spot on the whole shore. Here's Vivian; it must be time to set off."

Honor was in her liveliest spirits as they walked along the cliffs. She was overflowing with Irish blarney and nonsense, asking absurd riddles and making bad puns, and sending the other girls into such fits of laughter that Vivian called them to order.

"Don't be so horribly noisy!" she said. "Honor Fitzgerald, I wish you were more sensible."

"I'm very contrite," replied Honor cheerfully. "You see, I've never been taught to be serious-minded. I'm quite ready to learn, though, if you'll set me someone to copy. Would this be better?" and she put on an expression of such lugubrious gloom that the rest could not suppress their mirth.

Vivian did not seem to appreciate equally the humour of the situation. She was rather jealous of her position as monitress, and not unwilling to show her authority. Moreover, she was responsible for the conduct of the girls, who were expected to comport themselves discreetly on a public footpath.

Honor was not a favourite of hers. Vivian considered her too forward, and thought she made a troublesome element at St. Chad's. In her opinion, a new-comer in her first term ought not to attempt to obtrude herself, but should follow the lead of those who had been some years at the school. She told her rather sharply, therefore, to come and walk with her, and made the others go two and two, in a due and orderly fashion.

"I see some people coming along the cliffs," she said, "and I should be most ashamed if it were reported that the Chessington girls don't know how to behave themselves."

"I wonder whether she's taking the opportunity to try to improve Paddy's mind on the way," laughed Lettice to Ruth Latimer.

"She'll have a difficult task, then," remarked Ruth. "I can't imagine Paddy engaged in very deep and serious discourse."

By the time the St. Chad's party had climbed down the rocky steps on to the beach, the Aldwythites were just emerging from the hut, a lively, bareheaded little company, spreading their hair to dry in the wind and sunshine.

"It's simply delicious in the sea to-day," they called out; "quite warm, and as calm as possible."

The Chaddites had soon donned their bathing costumes, and went scampering down the causeway to take the coveted plunge into the waves.

"I don't know anything more glorious than the first few strokes of one's swim," said Lettice, floating for a moment or two by Honor's side. "I'm sure a frog couldn't enjoy it more, and a duck simply isn't in it!"

Honor seemed as much at home in the water as the fishes, and Miss Young, after watching her progress near the shore, gave her permission to go with the more advanced members of the class for a tour of the bay.

"I shall not be far off myself," she remarked, "and of course you must come back the instant I call to you."

"Miss Young generally stays close to the girls who aren't so much used to it, in case they should get cramp, or turn giddy," explained Lettice. "Beatrice Marsden and Ivy Ridgeway are only beginning, so I expect she'll paddle about with them in four feet of water. Janie Henderson never ventures very far either."

Once out in the bay, Honor began to distinguish herself, greatly to the delight of her admiring friends. She swam on her side and on her back, dived to pick up stones, and even contrived to make a wheel.

"How plucky you are!" exclaimed Lettice. "I should never dare to attempt such feats; but then, I haven't the sea to practise in at home. Look at Chatty; she's trying to do a wheel too. I know she'll come to grief. Chatty! Do you want us to have to practise life-saving?"

"No, thank you," said Chatty; "I was only seeing what I could manage. Look here! suppose we swim right round the bay. We can take a rest every now and then by floating and towing each other along."

Though there were no excursionists on the shore that day, the girls noticed a small boat bobbing about near the point of the cliffs. It contained three people, who were evidently visitors from Dunscar. A young man in his shirt sleeves, with a pocket-handkerchief tied over his head, was rowing in a very awkward fashion, as if it were the first time he had handled a pair of oars; while his companions, girls of about sixteen and seventeen, kept jumping up and changing places, or leaning suddenly over the side to catch pieces of seaweed.

"Vivian might complain of their laughing," said Lettice. "Just listen to them! Aren't they fearfully vulgar?"

"Cheap trippers come over for the day, no doubt," said Chatty. "Look! One of the girls is pretending to throw the young man's hat overboard, and he's trying to clutch it."

"The silly things! They're making that boat heel over far more than I should appreciate, if I were inside her," remarked Honor. "I don't believe they know there's any danger."

"I wonder they were allowed to go out without taking a boatman. I'm sure it's not safe," said Lettice.

The three young excursionists were still struggling and fighting over the hat when round the corner of the headland came the steamer from Westhaven, steering much closer to the shore than was her custom. She had started late, and her captain was trying to make up for lost time; and, in consequence, she was going at top speed. Her screw made such a tremendous wash that in a moment the sea was as rough as if there had been a storm. The bathers felt themselves tossed about like corks, and struck out as hard as they could for the shore, trying to keep abreast of the waves that threatened to overpower them. The next moment there was a chorus of wild, agonized shrieks, and the little cockle-shell of a boat whirled rapidly past, upside down, the young man and one girl clinging desperately to it, with white, terror-stricken faces. The other girl was nowhere to be seen. She rose in a few seconds, however, struggling violently, and sank again; then, when she came up for the second time, she had drifted a good distance farther on, and was strangely quiet.

The Chaddites had been separated by the sudden shock of the unexpected occurrence. Lettice found it as much as she could manage to keep her head above water, and Chatty acknowledged afterwards that she had never before felt in such danger of her life. Honor, however, was swimming fast in the direction of the drowning pleasure-seeker, and seized her just as she was on the point of going down for the third time. Luckily the poor girl had lost consciousness, and so did not grip her rescuer, or it might have ended fatally for them both. As it was, Honor was able to put her arm under her and keep her afloat while she called loudly for help.

But no one could come immediately. The heavy sea had got Ivy Ridgeway into difficulties, and Miss Young dared not leave her while she was still out of her depth; and the others were only able to save themselves: so Honor was obliged to do her best alone. By this time the steamer had stopped and was lowering one of its boats, but it took several minutes before the latter could be launched.

"Hold on a bit!" the sailors shouted encouragingly to Honor; and once they were clear of the vessel, they rowed with a will.

They reached the pair at last, and lifted the unfortunate girl, insensible and helpless as a log, over the gunwale.

"Better let us take you in too, miss!" said the coxswain to Honor.

"No, thanks; I'm all right," she replied, and, turning round, she swam straight back to the shore.

The passengers on the steamer gave cheer after cheer as they watched the little figure making its way so pluckily; and more than one person heaved a sigh of relief when it arrived in shallow water, and walked out on to the beach.

Meanwhile, the boat had picked up the young man and the other girl, who had clung to their upturned craft till they were in the last stage of exhaustion.

Poor Miss Young actually shed tears when she saw all her class safe and sound on dry land once more—a weakness of which her pupils never knew her to be guilty before or after.

"I'm not sure if I don't feel a little bit weepy myself," said Maisie Talbot. "Lettice is not a remarkably strong swimmer, and when I saw her so far out in the bay I thought—But there! it's over now, and I won't imagine horrible tragedies."

"It was a near shave for several of us," said Chatty soberly.

Honor took the whole affair with the utmost coolness; indeed, she insisted upon treating it almost as a joke.

"One doesn't always have the luck of picking up a mermaid," she declared. "I may find Father Neptune, or the Sirens, if I go a little farther; or perhaps I might drag back the sea serpent, as a neat little specimen for the school museum. If the trippers are often going to provide us with such entertainment, we shall have very lively times at bathing."

"All the same, I'm sure she's more upset about it than she pretends," said Lettice. "Her hands were trembling so much when she was dressing, she could scarcely button her blouse. It's just like her, though; she'd rather say something funny any time, than look serious."

Miss Young praised Honor highly for her "splendid bravery and presence of mind", and Miss Maitland added warm words of commendation. As for the Chaddites, they could scarcely make enough of her. "No other house can show such a record," said Maisie enthusiastically. "We've beaten St. Hilary's hollow!"

"And even the School House," added Chatty, "though their monitress once stopped a runaway donkey on the shore."

"Paddy, we're proud of you!" said Lettice.

"Please don't say any more about it!" protested Honor. "I was only enjoying myself. I feel a great deal prouder when I've finished a sum in cube root, because I simply hate arithmetic. Swimming is as easy to me as walking, and I'm sure you'd each have done the same if you could."

Naturally, Honor was the heroine of the school, especially as the affair got into the newspapers, and the Royal Humane Society wrote to say that she would be presented with a medal in recognition of her courage. The father and mother of the girl whose life she had saved called with their daughter at the College, and begged to be allowed to express their gratitude, so Honor was sent for by the head mistress. She would have been glad to avoid what seemed to her an embarrassing interview, but there was no escape.

"These people have come on purpose to see you," said Miss Maitland; "it would be not only discourteous but unkind if you were to refuse to speak to them."

Honor had not been in Miss Cavendish's study since the memorable occasion when she had so injudiciously sported the shamrock, and as she entered the beautiful, old-world room again she could not help a feeling of wonder at how much had happened since she had first set foot there, and of relief that this second summons should be for approbation, instead of blame. She would give no account afterwards of what took place, or what the girl's parents said to her, though Lettice was full of curiosity and pressed her for particulars.

"Look here!" she exclaimed; "if anybody says another word to me about this business, I shall leave St. Chad's and go across to St. Hilary's. I should be sorry to desert you all, but I'm sick of the very sound of 'life-saving'! As for the medal, I'm thankful to say it will be sent to me by post during the holidays, so there'll be no dreadful ordeal of presentation. Now, I've told you as much as I intend, so please go away, and let me do my preparation in peace!"

CHAPTER XI. A RELAPSE

Towards the end of June there was a burst of very warm weather, so sultry and hot as to make games, or any form of violent exertion, almost an impossibility. Ruth Latimer fainted one day when she was fielding, after which Miss Cavendish absolutely prohibited cricket in the blazing sun, and set to work to devise other means of occupation. The girls themselves would have been ready enough to lounge about all the afternoon in the grounds, chatting and doing nothing, but of that the head mistress did not approve; she considered it might tend to encourage habits of gossip and idling, and much preferred that everyone should have some definite employment. She temporarily altered the hours of work, setting preparation from two until four, so that in the evening the school might be free to go out and enjoy the breeze that often rose towards sunset. In the circumstances, this really seemed a better division of time, for during the early afternoon it was actually cooler in the house, with sunblinds drawn to protect the windows, than out-of-doors; and though there were many groans at having to learn lessons and write exercises immediately after dinner, on the whole the change was regarded with favour. General public opinion would have decided on swimming as the most suitable occupation in the state of the thermometer, but since the events related in the last chapter Miss Cavendish would not allow more than eight girls to go into the sea at once.

"It is as many as Miss Young can undertake to be responsible for," she said. "Steamers are frequently passing between Westhaven and Dunscar, and they seem to take a course nearer the coast than formerly. The wash from them is so exceedingly strong that it is wiser to run no risks."

Bathing, therefore, was conducted in small detachments, and though fresh relays went each day to the cove, it took so long to work through the whole school that nobody seemed to have the chance of a second turn. Miss Cavendish, however, was never at a loss. Everyone with the slightest aptitude for drawing was provided with paper and pencil, and taken out to sketch from nature. Those who possessed paint-boxes were encouraged to work in colours, and the head mistress, who had herself no little skill, gave many useful hints on the putting-in of skies and the washing of middle distances. Janie Henderson, who was naturally artistic, and had been accustomed to try her 'prentice hand at home, found herself at a decided advantage, and won more credit in a single week than she had hitherto gained in a whole year at Chessington.

"You've scored tremendously, Janie," said Honor, who revelled in her friend's brief hour of triumph. "Vivian Holmes was most impressed by your sketch of the cliffs. I heard her telling one of the Aldwythites about it. She said you were quite an artist. There, don't blush! I'm particularly rejoiced, because Vivian is so superior, and always does everything so much better than everybody else, and yet her picture wasn't half as good as yours, and she knew it."

"Vivian paints rather well, though."

"Oh, yes, tolerably! But she hasn't your touch. She muddles her greens, and her trees get so treacly! She's not really clever, as you are."

Honor had not brought a paint-box to school, but Janie lent her a brush and a tube of sepia and a china palette that she had to spare, so that she was able to attempt studies in monochrome, if she could not try colour.

"They're horrid daubs," she declared. "I don't pretend to have the least atom of talent; I only drew these because Miss Cavendish said I must. It's art under compulsion."

"Like the man who painted the pictures for some Moorish sultan," said Janie. "I've forgotten the exact facts of the story, but I know he was taken prisoner, and was marched with a long line of other wretched captives to learn his fate. The sultan asked the first on the list: 'Can you paint?' and when he answered 'No', ordered his head to be chopped off. Seven more were asked the same question, and given the same doom. Then, when it came to an Englishman's turn, he said 'Yes', although he knew as much about drawing as the man in the moon. The sultan spared his life, and ordered him to begin at once to decorate the walls of the palace, so he was obliged to try. I believe the pictures are still there, and people go to look at them because they're so extraordinary. I wish I could remember where the place is!"

"I should certainly like to see it," said Honor. "My productions would have been unique. I think I should have represented battle scenes, and put smoke to hide everything, and then have said it was impressionistic! The sultan was as bad as the Queen in *Alice in Wonderland*, who cried, 'Off with her head!'"

"They're absolute autocrats," said Janie. "I read a story of another who had a pet donkey, and sent for a philosopher and commanded him to teach it to talk. The poor old sage expected his last hour had come, but luckily an idea occurred to him. He said he would do so, but it would take seven years. He thought that in the meantime either the sultan might die, or the donkey might die, or he himself might die."

"And what happened?"

"Oh, I don't know! Like all good stories, it ends there."

"How disappointing! I want to hear the sequel. I suppose the philosopher might have poisoned the donkey."

"Or, perhaps, somebody poisoned the sultan. It was an amiable little way in those days of getting rid of an unpopular monarch. By the by, to go back to the subject of drawing, Miss Cavendish says there's to be an exhibition of all the sketches at the end of the term. They're to be pinned up round the gymnasium, and she'll ask an artist friend to come and judge them, and mark them first, second, and third class. Perhaps she may even set a special competition for a prize."

"You'll win, then, if she does. I'm certain Marjorie Parkes's painting is no better, though the St. Bride's girls have been crowing tremendously over her."

"Don't pin your hopes to me! I'm a broken reed. If I want to do a thing particularly nicely, I never can. All my most successful hits have been made when I wasn't trying."

"Yes, that's often the way. I always say my highest scores at cricket are really flukes. Here's Lettice coming to criticize. Don't look at my sketch, Lettice, it's abominable! You may admire Janie's as much as you like."

"I think you've both been very quick," said Lettice. "I've only drawn in about half of mine yet. But I can generally manage to make a little work go a long way! I came to tell you that it's time to pack up. And I have a piece of good news as well; it has been so much cooler to-day that Miss Cavendish says we may be more enterprising to-morrow. I don't know what's arranged for the other houses, but St. Chad's is down for a botany ramble. Isn't it jolly? I shall like it much better than sketching. Miss Maitland is to take us, and we're to walk along the hills towards Latchfield. There's to be an archery tournament as well, and we may go to that instead, if we like, only we must put our names down to-night. The lists for both will be hung up in the hall. I know which I shall choose."

"So do I," said Janie. "I've never hit the target yet, so it's not much use my entering against Blanche Marsden and Trissie Turner and Sophy Williams. A ramble sounds lovely. Honor, do come! I'm sure you're not keen on bows and arrows!"

"I haven't tried, so I can't tell. A tournament doesn't seem exactly the place, though, to make one's first wild shots, and I've no time even for an hour's practice. If it's to be botany versus archery, I think I'll put my valuable autograph on the side of science."

No one could be more capable of leading a botanical ramble than Miss Maitland. She was a close student of nature, and not only loved plants and flowers herself, but could make them interesting to other people. The beautiful collection of pressed specimens in the school museum was mostly her work, and she was regarded as the best authority on the subject in the College.

"I'm often so glad we're at St. Chad's," said Janie. "Miss Maitland is a thousand times nicer than any of the other house-mistresses. The Hilaryites are very proud of Miss Hulton because she writes for the *Scientific World*, the Aldwythites plume themselves on Miss Paterson's double first, and the Bridites worship Miss Daubeny since she did that splendid climb in the Alps last summer; but Miss Maitland is so jolly all round, I like her by far the best. Of course, the School House girls say the very cream of Chessington is to be with Miss Cavendish, but I think a head mistress is pleasanter at a distance, one always feels so much in awe of her."

"Yes; I'm afraid I should never feel quite at ease with Miss Cavendish," avowed Honor. "At St. Chad's we seem almost like a big family."

The College stood in the midst of a pretty country, and there was no lack of walks in the neighbourhood. At exactly half-past four on the following afternoon a party of sixteen Chaddites set off under the wing of Miss Maitland, and turned at once in the direction of the woods that led to Latchfield, by a deliciously green and shady path. The warm sun, pouring between the thick leaves, made little radiant patches of golden light among the deep shadows under the trees; the whole air seemed alive with the hum of insects; and here and there rang out the sharp tap of a woodpecker, or the melancholy "coo-coo-coo" of a wild pigeon.

"The birds are generally very silent in such sultry weather," said Miss Maitland. "They sing at dawn and again at sunset, but you hear little of them in the heat of the day. Those doves probably have a nest at the top of that tall ash. I think I can see some sticks among the leaves on that big bough."

Some pieces of honeysuckle twined round the low undergrowth of bushes, and tall foxgloves reared their purple spikes in every small, open glade. The girls gathered these as their first specimens.

"I wonder why they're called foxgloves?" said Lettice. "They've nothing to do with foxes."

"It's simply a corruption of 'good folks' gloves', meaning 'fairies' gloves'," said Miss Maitland. "People gave the plants much more romantic names in olden days than modern scientists do. I confess I like 'Queen of the Meadows' better than *Spiræa Ulmaria*, and I think 'poor man's weather-glass' a far better description of the scarlet pimpernel than *Anagallis arvensis*. We shan't find many flowers here, among the trees; but I'm hoping we may come across some orchids when we get on to the moors."

They had been walking uphill all the time, and, as soon as they were clear of the woods, found they had reached a high table-land, covered with pastures, through the midst of which flowed a stream, whose rushy banks were gay with purple loosestrife, Ragged Robin, and yellow spearwort. It was a famous place in which to botanize, and the girls were allowed to disperse and hunt about for specimens, and came back every now and then to show their finds to their teacher.

"Adeline Vaughan is the only one who knows much about the natural orders, or the proper scientific terms," said Lettice. "It seems rather funny, because she's a Londoner, and doesn't belong to the country."

"Country people aren't always the best authorities on the subject," said Miss Maitland. "I know some who go through life with deaf ears and blind eyes, and never hear or see what is all around them. The main thing is to have enthusiasm, and then, it doesn't matter where your home is, you'll manage to enjoy nature, even if it is only at second-hand, from books."

"And there are always the holidays," said Adeline. "We went to Switzerland last August, and I found twenty-seven different specimens just in one walk."

"Before I came to St. Chad's," confessed Lettice, "I used to think daisies were the flowers of grass, and not separate plants—I did indeed!"

"You certainly know better now," laughed Miss Maitland. "We can get so much pleasure from things when we have learnt even a very little about them. Every leaf or blade of grass becomes a marvel, if we begin to examine its structure, and look at it through the microscope. There is nothing so wonderful as the book of nature, and it is always there, ready to entertain us when we wish to read it."

It was much cooler and breezier up on the hills, though even there the air had a sultry feeling, and a dull, heavy haze was creeping up from the sea.

"It looks like thunder," said Miss Maitland. "I should not be surprised if we were to have a storm to-night. We had better turn towards home now; but we'll go back by the cliffs above Sandihove, instead of through the woods."

It was rather a difficult matter to get the girls along, so many interesting discoveries were made on the way—first a patch of pink-fringed buck-bean, growing at the edge of the stream; then a clump of butterfly orchis; and last, but not least, a quantity of the beautiful "Grass of Parnassus", the delicate white blossoms of which were starring the boggy corner of a meadow. Miss Maitland was kept quite busy naming specimens, and everybody had a large bunch of treasures to carry home. Janie Henderson and Adeline Vaughan, being the two chief enthusiasts of the party, walked on either side of the teacher, discussing matters botanical; and the others straggled in little groups behind. Honor found herself walking with Lettice Talbot, who was in a more than usually sprightly frame of mind, bantering and teasing, and turning everything into fun.

"I've learnt the names of so many new flowers," she declared, "that I'm sure I shall get a bad mark for history to-morrow. My brain is small, and only capable of holding a certain amount. When fresh things are put in, out go the old ones, or else I mix them completely up. I shall probably say that Oliver Cromwell was born at Marsh Cinquefoil, and that Charles the First belonged to the family of Ranunculaceæ. Paddy, you look rather glum! What's the matter? Don't you like botany? Or are you longing for your native wilds in Kerry? Is that a surreptitious tear trickling down your cheek?"

"Surreptitious rubbish!" laughed Honor. "I wasn't thinking of anything so romantic. I was looking at that little white village below us, and wondering if it can boast of possessing a shop."

"Then I can satisfy you on that point. It does—a very small shop, where they sell tea, and red herrings, and tinned provisions."

"Do they sell peppermint humbugs, or raspberry drops?"

"I dare say. I believe I remember some big bottles in the window."

"Then let us go and buy some. I haven't had any sweets since I came to St. Chad's. I'm simply yearning for butter-scotch or chocolates!"

"Don't talk of them! So am I! There's only one slight drawback, and that is, that we're not allowed!"

"Why not?"

"How can I say why? It's one of the rules: 'No girl to enter any shop, or make purchases, without special permission from her housemistress'."

"Then run on and ask Miss Maitland if we may. She's in a particularly good temper tonight, so she'll probably say 'yes'. I have some pennies in my pocket."

"All right. One can but try!" replied Lettice, and hurrying after the teacher, who was a little distance in front, she made her request.

She came back to Honor shaking her head gloomily.

"As I thought!" she announced. "Miss Maitland says 'No'. We're not to pass the shop at all; we're to keep to the upper road that skirts above the village."

"How disgusting!" grumbled Honor. "It would only have taken a minute longer. I'm sure there's no need to be in such a tremendous hurry. Lettice! Suppose we were to dash down this lane, we could go to the village and catch the others up at the crossroads. I can see the path quite plainly from here. We couldn't possibly miss it, and we could run all the way."

"Whew! But how about breaking rules?"

"Bother rules! Miss Maitland shouldn't make so many, and then they'd be better kept. It is ridiculous if girls of our age mayn't walk five yards by themselves. We're not infants in arms!"

Lettice hesitated, glanced to see if anyone in front was looking, or whether anybody was close behind, then yielded to the voice of the temptress.

"It's horribly risky, but it would be a joke!" she said.

Honor was in one of her self-willed moods that evening, ready to dare or do anything. In her heart of hearts she was offended because Janie should have walked on with Adeline and Miss Maitland, and left her behind. She was of a jealous temperament, and had enjoyed keeping her friend as her own private and particular property. It seemed quite a new state of affairs for Janie to be conversing in so animated a manner with anybody but herself, and the change was the reverse of pleasant.

"They're so interested in their talk, they've completely forgotten me!" she thought. "Very well; so much the better! They won't notice what we're doing. I'm not going to keep all these silly regulations. One might be in the nursery, to have to ask leave for such an absurd little thing as buying a pennyworth of sweets."

The two girls ran as fast as they could along the lane, Honor looking reckless and rather stubborn, and Lettice decidedly guilty. It was certainly a most deliberate act of disobedience, and one that, if they were caught, would involve them in very disagreeable consequences. The discipline at Chessington was so perfect that it was seldom any pupil ever dreamt of even questioning a mistress's orders; and Lettice, in her two years at St. Chad's, had never done such a naughty thing before. She felt almost frightened at her own daring, but very excited, and ready to follow Honor to the end of the adventure. They hurried into the little shop and made their purchases as quickly as possible, though the old woman who served them did not understand the meaning of the word "haste", and weighed out butterdrops and caramels with exasperating deliberation. The pair stood by almost dancing with impatience, and when the packets were at last ready, snatched them up and rushed off with all speed.

"This way!" cried Honor, turning sharply to the left through an open gate. "I noticed the path particularly when we were on the hill above, and this is a short cut back to the road."

"It looks as if we were going into an orchard," objected Lettice.

"No; I'm sure I'm right. We shall get out through those apple trees at the top of the bank."

The pathway, however, merely seemed to lead to a field, and ended at a gate that was securely fastened by a piece of wire.

"I believe there's a stile across there," panted Honor, hot and out of breath with running. "Don't bother to undo that wire! We'll climb over. Here, take my hand!"

It was a vain hope. On closer examination the supposed stile proved to be only part of a fence. The meadow was surrounded by a quickset hedge, so thick as to be an insuperable barrier.

"I must have taken the wrong turning, after all," said Honor blankly. "What a fearful nuisance! We shall have to go back."

"It's all very well to say 'go back'!" exclaimed Lettice, turning and clutching at Honor's arm. "Look at what is in front of us!"

Honor stopped short as suddenly as her companion. Directly facing them was a large bull: it had been feeding in the ditch when they entered the field, and thus they had not perceived its presence; but now it had walked across, and was standing exactly opposite the gate, completely cutting off their return to the footpath.

"Perhaps it mayn't be really savage," said Honor, with a slight quiver in her voice. "Shall we walk a little nearer, and see if it takes any notice of us?"

"No! No! Don't!" implored Lettice. "I'm terrified even of cows, and this is a monster. I'm sure it's dangerous—it has a ring in its nose!"

Honor looked round the pasture in dismay. She felt as if they were caught in a trap. How were they to make their escape while that huge beast stood between them and safety?

"We'd better go to the hedge again," she said. "Perhaps there may be some little hole where we can scramble through into the next field."

They beat a cautious retreat, not daring to run from fear that they might attract the bull's attention. But the farmer had mended his fences only too well; they did not find the smallest opening, search as they would.

"What are we to do?" demanded Lettice distractedly. "We can't stay all night in the field, yet if we call for help that creature will come rushing at us. Oh, Honor, look! It's seen us now!"

The bull had certainly become aware of their proximity. It was gazing at them in an uneasy fashion, sniffing the air, and pawing the ground restlessly. It gave a roar like the growling of thunder, and began to walk slowly in their direction. With white faces, the girls backed nearer the fence. Perhaps the heat, or the flies, or the unusual appearance of two strangers in its meadow irritated the animal, for again it gave a loud, rumbling bellow, and, lowering its horns, made straight for the intruders. Shrieking with fright, Honor and Lettice plunged into the hedge, scrambling anyhow through quickset and brambles, scratching their hands and faces and rending their dresses in the struggle, their one object being to escape from the horror behind them. With torn blouses and fingers full of thorns they issued from the opposite side, and rolled down a bank before they were able to stop themselves.

Honor sprang up promptly, and looked anxiously back. Fortunately, the bushes were far too thick and high for the bull to leap over.

"We're quite safe now!" she exclaimed, with a gasp of intense relief.

Lettice, sitting on the bank, indulged in a private little cry. She was very agitated and upset, and was trembling violently.

"I thought we were going to be gored to death," she quavered. "Oh! has it gone away? It's dreadful to feel it's still so near us!"

"We'd better get on as fast as we can, and put another field between it and us," said Honor, pulling her companion to her feet. "There are some hurdles over in that corner that we can climb, and then we shall be absolutely out of danger."

Honor's short cut proved a very long one before the two girls once more found themselves on the high road. There was not a sign of the rest of the party to be seen, so they began to walk home as briskly as their shaken nerves would allow. They had not gone far, however, before they met Miss Maitland, who, with Janie Henderson and Maisie Talbot, had come back to look for them.

"You naughty girls! Where have you been?" the house-mistress exclaimed, in righteous wrath, as the dilapidated pair made a conscience-stricken approach.

There was nothing for it but a full confession, and a very disagreeable ten minutes followed for both. Miss Maitland knew how to maintain discipline, and would not overlook such a flagrant breach of orders.

"I had distinctly forbidden you to go," she said. "I am extremely disappointed, for I thought I could have depended on your sense of honour to behave as well behind my back as if you had been walking in front. You may be most thankful to have escaped from a danger into which your own disobedience led you. I am sorry that our pleasant ramble should have ended so unfortunately; it will be very difficult for me to rely on either of you again."

CHAPTER XII. ST. KOLGAN'S ABBEY

"After what happened on Latchfield Moors," remarked Vivian Holmes, one afternoon about a week later, "I think it is extremely good of Miss Maitland to allow Honor Fitzgerald and Lettice Talbot to go to the picnic to-morrow. I shouldn't have been in the least surprised if she had left them both out, and I should certainly have said it served them right."

Vivian was at an age when stern justice appears more attractive than mercy. She kept rules rigidly herself, and had scant patience with those who did not, serving out retribution in her capacity of monitress with an unsparing hand. She was perhaps too hard on prodigals, but her influence and authority undoubtedly did much to maintain the high standard of St. Chad's; and if she were not altogether popular, she was, at any rate, greatly respected.

Honor's last delinquency had placed her more than ever on Vivian's bad list. The monitress considered that it completely cancelled the bathing episode, and regarded "that wild Irish girl" as the black sheep of the house, ready to lead astray such innocent lambs as Lettice Talbot who were impressionable enough to be influenced by her example. Miss Maitland, though grieved at such a relapse from the marked improvement that Honor had shown, was fortunately a better judge of character. She knew that old habits are not overcome all at once, and that it takes many stumblings and fallings and risings again before any human soul can struggle uphill. She did not want Honor to be discouraged, and hoped that if the girl felt herself trusted she would make an effort to be more worthy of confidence.

"I put you on your parole," she said to her. "It would be impossible for me to take you to Baldurstone if I imagined you were capable of a repetition of what occurred last week. I think, however, that I need feel no anxiety on that score."

"I promise faithfully," said Honor, and she meant it.

Vivian's opinions largely led popular feeling, and as Honor did not hold a high place in her estimation, the other Chaddites also, in consequence of the affair on the moors, slightly ostracized "Paddy", letting her understand that they did not altogether approve of her. Lettice Talbot suffered a severe snubbing from her elder sister, in addition to Miss Maitland's censure.

"It was such shockingly bad form!" declared Maisie. "Why, you might have been two little Sunday-school children, running away from your teacher to buy common sweets at a small village shop! I'm utterly ashamed of you. We don't do such things at Chessington. No wonder Miss Maitland was amazed and disgusted. Yes, I know Honor Fitzgerald is listening; I'm very glad, because she'll hear what I think of your fine adventure."

Honor undoubtedly felt much crestfallen to find that what she had regarded as spirited independence was labelled "bad form" at the College. On reflection it struck her that, apart from all rules, it had perhaps been scarcely polite to rush away, in direct opposition to the expressed wishes of one who had been taking so much trouble to make their walk interesting. In common with all the Chaddites, she keenly appreciated both Miss Maitland's personality and her knowledge of nature lore, and had enjoyed the expedition on the hills immensely.

To be left out of the picnic would have been a bitter disappointment. It was the great event of the summer term. Each house took its excursion on a separate day, as Miss Cavendish considered that the whole school made too formidable an invasion for any place. St. Hilary's and St. Aldwyth's had already respectively visited Weyland Castle and Eccleston Woods, and it was now the turn of St. Chad's to choose a destination. Miss Maitland had made a list of several interesting spots, which were well worth seeing, and had put the matter to a general ballot, with the result that by a majority of eight the votes fell in favour of St. Kolgan's Abbey at Baldurstone.

"It's the nicest of all, and Miss Maitland's favourite," announced Lettice.

"I chose it for three reasons," said Honor: "first, because it's the farthest off, and I like to have a long journey; secondly, because we're to go most of the way by steamer, and I love being on the sea; and thirdly, because Flossie Taylor wanted Haselmere Hall."

"What a very intelligent and desirable motive!" sneered Vivian Holmes, who happened to overhear. "You evidently go on the principle of pig philosophy. As a matter of fact, Miss Maitland said she had no preference."

"I was speaking to Lettice," retorted Honor. "I suppose my motives are my own business?"

"Oh, certainly! They're not of the slightest interest to me."

"Vivian's rather snappy this evening," whispered Lettice, as the monitress stalked away. "I believe she voted for Haselmere herself."

"Then I'm doubly glad it's to be Baldurstone. Even if people are monitresses, they've no need to think it's their mission to squash everybody else perpetually. I can hardly make the least remark without Vivian sitting upon me."

"You always answer her back, you see, and she thinks that's cheek in a new girl."

"I'm not new now."

"Yes, you are—you're not through your first term yet. Vivian says it takes a whole year to become a full-blown Chaddite, and until you've thoroughly assimilated Chessington ideas you oughtn't to presume to air outside opinions."

"What bosh!"

"No, it's not bosh. You see, we all think that Chessington is the only girls' school in England, and that St. Chad's is the one house at Chessington. One must keep up the traditions of the place, and it wouldn't do to let every fresh comer take the lead. You'll have to knuckle under, Paddy, and eat humble pie. Vivian has been here for five years—she's simply a 'Chaddite of the Chaddites'. That's why she was chosen monitress. You'll have your chance when you get to the Sixth Form."

"Shall I ever climb so high up in the school? If I were head of the house, though, I'd be rather less hard on new arrivals."

"Oh, no, you wouldn't! By the time you've gone through the mill yourself you'll want to grind everybody else. There's an attraction about the St. Chad's code; you'll like it better when you're more used to it, and when you've forgotten any pettifogging notions you may have brought from anywhere else."

"You're outspoken, at any rate!"

"Certainly! I believe in plain, unvarnished truths."

Honor had already discovered that fact, and also the further one that whatever a girl's position might be at home, it made no difference to her standing at the College, where each was judged solely and entirely on her own merits. She had once unfortunately alluded with a touch of pride to her family pedigree, but she rued her mistake in a moment, for Vivian, with uplifted eyebrows, had enquired in a tone of cutting contempt: "Who are the Fitzgeralds?"

A large public school is indeed a vast democracy, and members are estimated only by the value they prove themselves to be to the commonweal: their private possessions and affairs matter little to the general community, but their examination successes, cricket scores, or tennis championships are of vital importance. All, to use an old phrase, must find their own level, and establish a record for themselves apart from home belongings. Honor was beginning to realize that among two hundred girls she was a mere unit, and that her opinions and prejudices counted as nothing against the enormous weight of universal custom. It was quite a new aspect of life, so new that she was not sure whether she liked or disliked it; although, if she had been given her choice of remaining at the College or returning to the old, slipshod, do-as-you-please régime of her schoolroom at Kilmore, she would have decided most emphatically, despite strict rules, scoldings, snubs, and unwelcome truths, in favour of Chessington.

Nobody wished to lie in bed on the morning of the picnic; even Honor, to whom early rising was still one of the greatest banes of existence, actually woke up before the bell rang, and had the triumph of rousing her sleeping companion, a reversal of the customary order of things that afforded her much satisfaction.

"It's delightful to think that St. Chad's is going off for a jaunt, while all the other houses will have lessons just as usual," she remarked. "I'm sure I shall enjoy it twice as much when I think of Christina Stanton and Mary Nicholls toiling through equations and physics."

"It will be their turn to chuckle next week, when St. Bride's has its holiday," said Janie. "You'll feel rather blue then."

"No, I shan't—not if we've had our fun first. I shall turn philosophical, and say: 'You can't eat your cake and have it', and 'Every dog has his day', or any other little platitude I can think of. In the meantime, it's our day, and I'm glad to see it's a particularly fine one."

At precisely nine o'clock, just when the rest of the Chessingtonians were filing into classes, the Chaddites were assembled in the quadrangle, and at a signal from Miss Maitland started off, two and two, to walk to Dunscar, where they were to catch the steamer to Avonmouth, the nearest point for Baldurstone. Everything seemed delightful—the brisk march in the fresh morning air, the bright sunshine, the glinting, sparkling sea, the foam churned up by the steamer's revolving screw, the cries of the seagulls, and the steady motion of the vessel as she headed out of the bay. The breeze in the Channel was exhilarating, and so cool as to make the girls appreciate Miss Maitland's wisdom in having insisted upon all bringing wraps.

"I thought it seemed as foolish as carrying one's winter fur and muff on a broiling day like this," commented Lettice, "but I really think I should have been cold without my coat. It's marvellous what an enormous difference there is when you get well away from land."

Lunch was taken on the steamer, and they did not arrive at Avonmouth until half-past one. They were landed in small boats, for there was no pier, and vessels of any considerable size could not cross the harbour bar. Miss Maitland counted up her forty pupils as they stood on the jetty—a precaution that seemed more of a formality than a necessity, as everyone had taken good care not to be left behind.

"We have exactly three and a half hours here," she said. "The steamer will be back at five o'clock. That gives us plenty of time to walk to the Abbey, and enjoy the ruins. I have ordered tea to be ready for us as soon as we return on board. We shall be very hungry by then, I'm afraid, but there is nowhere to buy refreshments in this tiny place."

Avonmouth was, indeed, only a little fishing village, composed of an irregular row of cottages, huddled together on the beach, and a small, not-too-clean inn, which looked as if it would be quite incapable of providing even seats for a party of forty-three, to say nothing of cups and saucers.

"We're such an army!" said Vivian. "If we were to have tea here we should clear the whole place of provisions. I don't suppose there'd be enough milk and bread and butter to go round."

"Couldn't they have been ordered beforehand?" asked Lettice, who had a leaning towards picnic meals. "We might have sat on the grass outside the inn."

"Yes, no doubt. But suppose the day had been wet and we hadn't come, then all the things would have been wasted. A steamer is generally prepared to cater for any number of people."

St. Kolgan's Abbey stood about two miles from the village, on a headland overlooking the sea. It was a steady toil uphill the whole way, but the glorious view at the top was ample reward for the hot climb between high walls. The beautiful old ruin faced the Channel, and commanded a wide prospect of blue waves, flecked here and there with little, foamy crests.

"I wonder if that's the coast of Ireland, on the other side?" remarked Honor, shading her eyes with her hand to gaze over the dancing water.

"I'm afraid the wish is father to the thought," said Ruth Latimer. "I don't honestly see anything that can possibly be construed into a distant coast line, and I've about as long sight as anybody in the school. Don't you want to come and listen to Miss Maitland? She's going to tell us a story about St. Kolgan, who founded this place."

Honor followed to the corner of the fallen transept, where Miss Maitland was installed on a fragment of broken column. The girls, in various attitudes of comfort, had flung themselves on the grass within earshot, prepared to listen lazily while revelling in the calm, tranquil beauty and the old-world atmosphere of the scene. It seemed so peaceful, so far removed from the bustle and noise of our hurrying, pushing age, that they could almost throw their minds back through the centuries, and imagine they heard the vesper bell tolling from the tower overhead, and the slow footfalls of the monks pacing round the cloister to those carved seats in the choir of which the very remains were so exquisite.

"Yes, Baldurstone is a wonderful spot," began Miss Maitland. "I don't believe any place in the neighbourhood has older traditions. St. Kolgan was a British saint, and his legend has come down to us from the very earliest times. You know that there was a thriving and orthodox Celtic Church in Britain long before St. Augustine's 'introduction' of Christianity—a Church that was so important and vigorous that it contributed three bishops to the Council of Arles in A.D. 314, and several to the Council of Nicæa in 325, thus showing that it formed a part of united Christendom. It sent missionaries both to Ireland, where St. Patrick preached the Faith, and to Scotland, where St. Ninian spread Christian teaching in the north. Then came the invasion of the heathen Norsemen, the Angles, Saxons, and Jutes of history, who burnt and plundered every sanctuary they could find, slaying the priests at the altars, destroying both prelates and people, and forcing the Britons to take refuge in the woods and mountains. Though driven westward, the Celtic Church did not perish, and every now and then some devoted monk would try to establish himself among the worshippers of Thor and Odin. Such a mission was extremely dangerous, for so intense was the hatred of the pagan conquerors for the religion of the New Testament that it was almost impossible for a Christian teacher to show himself among them and live.

"At about the beginning of the seventh century, when the Saxons had spread so far westward as Dunscar and Avonmouth, and were practically masters of all the country round, a monk called Kolgan came over from Ireland with a little band of brethren, and prevailed upon Osric, the chief, or 'under king', of the district, to allow him to settle at Baldurstone. Those Celtic pioneers built a small monastery, and worked very earnestly among the people, some of whom they persuaded to become adherents of the Cross. Osric, though a pagan himself, tolerated them for the sake of his British wife, Toura, and for a while they went unmolested. When Osric died, however, the chiefdom fell to Wulfbert, a fierce warrior, who was determined to annihilate by fire and bloodshed any faith that had taken root among his subjects. In daily peril of their lives, Kolgan and his monks stayed on, knowing that if they deserted their post the last light of Christianity in the district would flicker out. One day a cowherd, who had been cured of a dangerous wound at the little settlement, came running to warn the brethren that Wulfbert and a band of armed men were advancing against them; and he besought them at once to flee into the woods. Kolgan marshalled his trembling companions, and, giving them the altar vessels to carry into a place of safety, sent them straightway to seek refuge in the vast forest that stretched ever northward and westward beyond the dominion of the Saxons.

"He himself was determined to remain. He knew that many of those who were coming with Wulfbert had, in Osric's time, been converts, either openly or secretly, of the Church; and he hoped, even at the eleventh hour, that he might recall their lost allegiance. Alone, with a cross uplifted in his hand, he stood at the door of the monastery to meet the Norsemen. The fierce band paused in amazement at the sight of his temerity; it was something those savage men had not known before. The swift rush through the battlefield of the warrior who hoped by slaughter to gain Valhalla, they could understand; but this calm courage in the face of death was beyond their experience. Kolgan seized the opportunity of the moment's respite to appeal to them in the name of the Trinity, and thundered out a denunciation against those who forsook the Faith. A few trembled, but Wulfbert, rallying his ranks, cried: 'Cowards! Are ye afraid of the empty words of an unarmed priest?' and rushing forward, he struck the first blow with his battle-axe.

"Kolgan fell where he stood, the little settlement was plundered and ravaged, and for the time it seemed as though his work had been of no avail. But brighter days were in store for the Church; slowly and gradually Christianity had begun to spread, not only from Celtic, but from Saxon sources, and before many years were past Wulfbert himself had accepted baptism. The monastery was by his special desire rebuilt in honour of St. Kolgan, and became afterwards one of the greatest centres of learning in the west country. For nine hundred years it flourished, till at last it was suppressed in the reign of Henry VIII, and the buildings, untended and neglected, fell into the state that we see now."

"And is this actually the place built by Wulfbert?" asked Ruth Latimer.

"Oh, no! That must have been a very rude and primitive erection; probably it had wattled walls, and a thatched roof. The Abbey was reconstructed more than once, and the present ruins are the remains of fourteenth-century work."

"What a shame that it should have been destroyed!" said Dorothy Arkwright.

"Yes and no. One much regrets the ruin of so lovely a place, but the monks had grown idle and self-indulgent, and were as different from the founders of their order as could well be imagined. The old, self-sacrificing spirit had passed away; and the days were gone, too, when the monastery had stood as the sole centre of light in a dark age, at once the substitute for school, college, hospital, and alms-house, as well as the home of painting, literature, music, and all the refined arts. When any custom or institution, however beautiful, becomes effete, the ruthless hand of progress sweeps it away, and supplants it with something else, leaving us only ivy-covered ruins to show us what our forefathers loved and valued."

"How grand St. Kolgan was!" said Vivian. "I think it was simply splendid the way he stood at the door and braved the Saxons!"

"Yes; but to me the truest part of his heroism was not his death, but his life. It needed far greater self-denial and true courage to spend each day in trying to teach a wild and hostile people, making long and fatiguing journeys, and suffering the loss of every joy that earth could offer him, than it did to summon up the supreme spirit to meet martyrdom. It is just the same in most of our lives," continued Miss Maitland, with a glance in Honor's direction; "it takes more real and strenuous effort to do plain, ordinary things, obeying rules and keeping our tempers, than one occasional very brave thing; and, though I would not for a moment depreciate the latter, I think that in the aggregate the others are of greater importance. Anybody, however, who can do a courageous deed is capable of living up to it every day, and thus rising to a still higher level. We must consider ourselves as failures unless we are trying to develop the very best that is in us."

When Miss Maitland and the girls had dispersed to explore the ruins more thoroughly, Honor lay still on the grass, gazing hard at the wide, shining expanse of sea. Janie stayed too, and sat abstractedly plucking daisy-heads and pulling them to pieces, or crumbling little pieces of mortar from the wall. For a long time neither spoke.

"I believe Miss Maitland was having a shot at me," said Honor at last; "only, I don't understand exactly what she meant."

"I do," returned Janie. "She thinks that you're capable of very much more than ordinary people."

"I can't imagine why!"

"Because it's in you. You've brains, and pluck, and 'go', and all kinds of things that other folks haven't. You might do such a splendid amount in the world some day!"

"I, my dear girl!" cried Honor in amazement. "Why, I'm sure I'm not up to much!"

"You could be, if you tried."

"There are some things that aren't possible, however hard one tries. I can no more be really and truly good than you could win the Atalanta race at the sports!"

The colour flushed into Janie's thin cheeks. Her lack of physical prowess was sometimes rather a sore subject to her. Though she did not enjoy games, she would, nevertheless, have dearly liked the credit of excelling in them. For a moment or two she did not reply. She was considering hard, and making up her mind on a difficult point. When she spoke, it was with a touch of diffidence and hesitation in her voice.

"Suppose I could win the 'Atalanta', would you think it possible to be what Miss Maitland wants you?"

"Indeed, I'd think anything possible!" replied Honor, with more truth than politeness.

"Then shall we make it a bargain—if I win the race, you're going to try your very hardest?"

"Turn over a new leaf, in fact?"

"Yes."

"All right; I've no objection. I should like to see you flying round the quad!"

"And I should like to see you doing other things! Will you promise, then?"

"On my honour, if you want."

"Very well. Give me something as a pledge."

"You can have this small compass," said Honor, rummaging in her pocket. "It's rather a treasure. Brian brought it me from Switzerland, and it's made of agate."

"All the better, because you'll want to have it back. I'll give you my silver fruit-knife, which I'm equally loath to part with. We must each keep each other's token until after the sports."

"And then?"

"Ah! that remains to be seen," said Janie, as she rose and strolled leisurely away.

All the Chaddites agreed that the visit to Baldurstone was one of the most interesting excursions they had ever taken, and that the ruins were the most picturesque in the neighbourhood, far exceeding Weyland Castle, favoured by the Hilaryites; and Clayton House, the destination of St. Bride's. The memory of their delightful day was sufficient to carry them through the ordeal of recapitulation that always preceded the examinations, necessitating an extra half-hour of preparation in the evenings, and, as Lettice described it, "concentrating one's unfortunate brains to absolute splitting point".

Whether Lettice's mental exertions were sufficient to bring her to such an unhappy crisis was a question on which her class mistress might have expressed some doubt, though she herself thought she had proof conclusive one afternoon during the week following the picnic. She ran in from the grounds in quite a state of excitement, and hailed a group of friends assembled in the recreation room.

"Girls!" she exclaimed, "I've seen a vision, a most extraordinary and peculiar sight! You wouldn't believe what it was! I happened to be at the bottom of the garden, and in that quiet path behind the laundry I actually saw Janie Henderson tearing up and down, as if she were doing the last spurt of a Marathon."

"Janie Henderson! Impossible!" cried everybody.

"Just what I said. I rubbed my eyes, and came to the conclusion that I'd been overstudying, and must be suffering from a delusion. Do I look queer?"

"Not in the least; your cheeks are as red as peonies."

"Well, my eyesight must be defective, then, for I certainly thought I saw her."

"You've been dreaming!"

"It's about as likely as seeing Miss Cavendish performing with a skipping rope."

"Yes, it's absurd on the face of it. It must have been somebody else."

"A case of mistaken identity."

"There are heaps of girls the same height, and with long, light hair."

"No doubt. I was a fairly good distance off too. And yet," added Lettice to herself, as she went to change her cricket shoes, "I verily believe it was Janie Henderson, after all!"

CHAPTER XIII. MISS MAITLAND'S WINDOW

While the weather continued to be so hot and close, Miss Maitland allowed the girls to spend their evening recreation in the garden, so that they might have a blow of fresh, cool air before they went to bed. They enjoyed sitting under the trees with books or fancy work, though as a rule their tongues wagged so fast that there was little display of industry with their needles.

"I hate sewing," confessed Honor, "and it's no use pretending I like it."

"This piece of embroidery has lasted me three terms, and it isn't finished yet," said Maisie Talbot, leisurely snipping off a thread, and pausing before she chose another piece of silk.

"I don't have to look at my knitting," said Chatty Burns; "but then, I'm Scotch, and every Scotchwoman knits."

"You're getting on so fast, it will do for me as well," said Honor, lying comfortably on the grass with her hands clasped under her head, and watching Chatty's rapidly growing stocking. "It's a 'work of supererogation', and that always leaves a little virtue over, to count for somebody else."

"I didn't say I'd hand the extra merit on to you," retorted Chatty.

"You can't help it. If there's so much to spare it must go somewhere, and I'm the idlest person; it will naturally fly to make up my deficiencies."

"What a fallacious argument!" declared Maisie.

"Do you know," interrupted Ruth Latimer, "that it's exactly a fortnight on Friday to the end of the term?"

"Know! I should think we do know!" replied Lettice. "I expect each one of us is counting the days, and longing for the time to come, if I'm any sample of the rest of the school. I say, 'One more day gone', every night when I get into bed."

"It's glorious to think the breaking-up is so near," said Pauline Reynolds. "What are you all going to do in the holidays?"

"We're starting for the Tyrol at the beginning of August," said Ruth. "We want to have a walking tour. We shall leave our heavy luggage at Botzen, and then tramp off up the mountains with just a few things in knapsacks on our backs, and stop at chalets and little inns ('guest-houses', as they are called there) on the way. We shall feel most delightfully free, because we can go any distance we like, and shall not be bound to arrive at any special place by any special time. That's the beauty of a walking tour."

"How far can you go in a day?" asked Honor.

"It just depends. If one is in the hot valleys, quite a short distance knocks one up; but when one gets the real mountain air, one can march along without feeling the least scrap tired. I once did twenty miles in Switzerland, but that's my record."

"And a pretty good one," said Pauline, "particularly as one oughtn't to reckon miles in Switzerland; one counts mountain climbing in hours."

"Yes, I've sometimes been deer-stalking at home," said Chatty, "and it's a very different affair toiling uphill over the heather from walking on a flat road. We're not going away this summer. Father has taken some extra shooting, and we're to have a big house-party instead. It's great fun! I like helping to carry the lunch in the little pony trap on to the moors; and we have jolly times in the evening—games, and music, and dancing. Have your people settled any plans yet, Pauline?"

"They talk of Norway. It would be glorious to see the midnight sun, and the lovely pine forests. I've wanted to go ever since I read *Feats on the Fiord*."

"You won't find it so romantic as that," laughed Ruth Latimer. "Things have changed since the time Harriet Martineau wrote about it. There are no pirates nowadays, to try to kidnap bishops and burn farms. You might, perhaps, find Rolf's wonderful cave, but I'm sure there isn't a peasant left who believes in the water sprite, and the Mountain Demon, and Nipen, and all the rest of the spirits of which Erica was so afraid."

"Perhaps not; but the country's just as beautiful, and I shall see the fiords, if I haven't any adventures there. I didn't say I wanted to meet pirates among the islands; on the whole, I should prefer their room to their company."

"Well, I wish you just one adventure, to keep up the element of romance. Perhaps your boatman will row you into the middle of the fiord, and demand your purse before he consents to take you back to the vessel; or you may be shipwrecked on a sunken rock, and left stranded in the Arctic Circle, dependent on the hospitality of the Laplanders!"

"No, thanks! I believe their tents are disgustingly dirty. I hope I may see a Lapp settlement, all the same, and also a few seals. I'm afraid a whale, or an iceberg, is too much to expect."

"Where are you going, Lettice?" enquired Chatty.

"Nowhere in particular, unless Maisie and I are asked to our aunt's. But we shall have jolly fun at golf and tennis. When one has been at school the whole term, one likes to be at one's own home, and to meet all one's friends again. It feels such ages since one saw them."

"Yes; the middle part of the term always seems to drag dreadfully, and then the last comes with a rush, and the exams. are on before one knows what one is doing."

"Don't talk of exams!" cried Pauline. "I expect I shall fail in every single one. I'm completely mixed up in chemistry, and I never can remember dates and names properly. My history paper will be a series of dashes: 'War with France was renewed in ——, when the English gained the decisive battle of ——, in which the Prince —— was slain and the Duke of —— taken prisoner. By the Treaty of —— a truce was concluded', &c."

"Perhaps Miss Farrar will think it's a guessing competition," remarked Honor.

"I dare say she will. I wish we needn't have exams., or marks, or any horrid things, to show whether we've done well or badly."

"I can get on tolerably with facts," said Lettice, "but I'm always marked 'weak' for composition. Miss Farrar says I use tautology and repeat myself, and that my grammar is shaky and my general style poor. She told me to take Macaulay as a model, but I can no more copy other people's ways of writing than I could improve my features by staring at the Venus de Medici."

"Poor old Salad! You're not cut out for an authoress."

"I'm certainly not; I'd rather be a charwoman! I don't aspire to be editress of the school magazine, I assure you, nor even a contributor. By the way, Honor, why don't you send something? I'm sure you could."

"I did think of it," replied Honor. "I was going to make a nice little series of acrostics on all of your names. I did one about Chatty, and showed it to Janie; but she said that it was far too slangy, and Vivian would never pass it, so I tore it up, and felt too squashed to go on."

"Oh! what was it?" exclaimed the girls. "Can't you remember it?"

"I'll try. I believe it went this way:

"C hatty Burns is just a ripper!

H air's the colour of a kipper;

A nd her face so round and red is

T hat you'd think her cheeks were cherries.

T hough we often call her 'Fatty',

Y ou depend we're nuts on Chatty."

"What a shame!" cried the indignant original of the acrostic. "My hair's auburn, it's not the colour of a kipper!"

"We certainly call you 'Fatty', though," laughed Lettice. "I think the poem is lovely!"

"It's a good thing you tore it up, all the same," said Ruth. "Vivian would have been simply horrified. We have a crusade against slang at Chessington, and 'ripper' is one of the words absolutely vetoed. We only say 'jolly' by stealth."

"I'm sure 'jolly' ought to be allowable. I saw it in a book in the library: 'as jolly as a sandboy', was the expression."

"What is a sandboy?" asked Lettice. "The phrase is always quoted as the high-water mark of bliss."

"I've never been able to find out," said Ruth. "I suppose it's either one of those wretched little urchins who dive for pennies, or an ordinary donkey boy. But this is what Miss Farrar calls 'a digression from the subject'. I want to hear if Honor has written any more acrostics."

"I made one on Lillie Harper," replied Honor. "It had an illustration, too, done very badly, in just a few crooked strokes, like little children draw:

"L illie is a dab at cricket;

I depict her at the wicket.

L ook how tight her bat she's grasping,

L eaving all the fielders gasping!

I have done this sketch in woggles,

E specially to show her goggles.

"It ought to have the picture to really explain it," said Honor regretfully; "I'm sorry now that I tore it up. I began a piece on the exams. too; it was a parody of 'The boy stood on the burning deck', but I can't get beyond the first verse:

"The girl sat at the hard, bare desk,

Whence all but she had fled;

Her fingers they were stained with ink,

And aching was her head."

"Oh, go on! It would be so nice!"

"It's impossible to think of any more."

"The time rolled on, she could not go

Without her teacher's word,"

improvised Ruth.

"That teacher, taking tea below,

Her sighs no longer heard,"

finished Honor. "Only, Miss Farrar wouldn't be taking tea in the middle of an exam. No, it can't be done!"

"Then we must put 'To be continued'," said Ruth.

"Make another acrostic, Paddy!" urged Lettice.

"Acrostics are too hard, because one is hampered by keeping to the letters of the girls' names," objected Honor. "Limericks are much easier. How would this do for Vivian Holmes?—

"There was a head girl of St. Chad's,

Who was subject to fancies and fads;

When we tried to talk slang,

She declared it was wrong,

And said she considered us cads."

"Good!" laughed Ruth. "Only, of course, Vivian wouldn't dream of using such a word as 'cad'. Now, I've got one about you:

"There's a girl at our house we call 'Paddy':

She's not 'goody-goody', but 'baddy';

She loves practical jokes,

Or to play us a hoax,

Though we tell her such tricks are not 'Chaddy'."

"Very well, Miss Ruth Latimer! I'll return the compliment," said Honor. "How do you like this?—

"There's a girl at our house who's called Ruth:

She is fond of an unpleasant truth;

She says she is seeking

To practise plain speaking,

But we think she is merely uncouth."

"I don't mind in the least," declared Ruth; "in fact, I'm rather flattered than otherwise."

"Make one about Maisie or me," implored Lettice. "You can say as nasty things as you want."

"Nothing could possibly rhyme with Lettice," announced Honor after a moment's cogitation, "or with Salad either. I might do better with Maisie. Let me see—crazy, hazy, daisy, lazy—I think those are all. Will this suit you?—

"There's a girl in this garden called Maisie;

At lessons she's horribly lazy,

But she's splendid at sports,

And at games of all sorts,

While o'er cricket she waxes quite crazy."

"What are you all laughing at?" enquired Flossie Taylor, sauntering up to join the group, and taking a seat on the grass.

"Limericks. Honor is winding them off by the yard. Now, Paddy, let us have one about Flossie! Quick, while your genius is burning!"

"It's only flickering," laughed Honor, "but I'll try:

"There's a girl at St. Chad's who's named Flossie;

She tries to be terribly 'bossy',

She sets us all straight

(Which is just what we hate),

And makes us exceedingly cross(y)."

"Oh, what a fearfully lame rhyme!" said Lettice.

"I know it is, but I couldn't think of any other word. If you're offended, Flossie, you can go away."

"I'm not silly enough to care about such trifles," replied Flossie loftily.

"You've quite left out Janie," said Lettice, "and there she is sewing all the time, and as usual never offering a single remark. Janie Henderson, why don't you talk?"

"You don't give me a chance to put in a word," protested Janie. "Perhaps I'm like the proverbial parrot, which couldn't talk, but thought all the more."

"You mean that I do the talking, and not the thinking?"

"I didn't say so."

"But you implied it. You deserve a horrid Limerick, and I shall make one myself. Wait a moment, while I rack my brains. Oh, now I've got it!—

"Miss Henderson, otherwise Jane,

May think very hard with her brain,

But it never comes out,

So she leaves us in doubt

If there are any thoughts to explain.

"There! You can't retaliate, because, as Honor says, there isn't a rhyme for Lettice."

"It's a good thing, for we might get too personal," interposed Chatty. "I think we've been over the margin of politeness as it is. Suppose we change the subject. Do you know, the honey dew is dropping from this lime tree overhead and making my knitting needles quite sticky!"

"It would be a lovely tree to climb, the boughs are so regular," said Honor, gazing into the green heights above.

"I don't believe I could go up a tree if a mad bull were after me," asserted Pauline. "I should just collapse at the bottom, and be gored to death, I know I should!"

"It isn't difficult," declared Honor. "You've only to catch hold of the branches, and keep swinging yourself a little higher. I've climbed ever so many trees in our garden at home."

"I should like to see you do it here, then."

"Very well! I'll show you, if you don't believe me."

The lime tree in question stood close to the house—so near, in fact, that some of its boughs brushed the windows. Miss Cavendish had several times decided to have it cut down, thinking it interfered with the light; but Miss Maitland had always begged that it might be spared a little longer, saying she loved its cool shade.

Honor swung herself quite easily from branch to branch, while the group of girls below watched her with admiration.

"You look like a middy going up the main-mast," said Ruth.

"Or a monkey at the Zoo," added Lettice.

"That's the voice of jealousy," remarked Chatty. "Lettice is green with envy because she can't do it herself."

"A squirrel would be a happier simile," suggested Ruth.

"She's getting along very quickly," said Pauline.

Half-way up the tree Honor paused and looked down.

"Hallo!" she cried, "I'm just by Miss Maitland's study. I shall go in, and pay her a call. Ta-ta!" and she disappeared suddenly through the open window.

"What will Miss Maitland say if she's there?" exclaimed Lettice.

"I don't believe she'd be cross," said Maisie. "She'd be amused to see anybody come in so funnily."

Honor was absent only about a minute, then her beaming face peeped from the window once more.

"Miss Maitland's not at home," she announced. "I've left my card with the footman, and said I'd call again another day, in my aeroplane. Keep out of the way down there—I'm coming!" and down she came, with a rush and a scramble, arriving quite safely, however, with only her hair ribbon untied and her hands a little grazed.

"You see, it's really a very easy matter," she explained; "we do far harder things in the gym."

"Can you find a good foothold?" asked Flossie.

"Oh, yes! There are heaps of places that seem made on purpose to put your toe in. It's almost like a ladder."

"Here's Vivian!" said Chatty. "I'm afraid she's come to call us in."

"What a nuisance! I don't want to go to bed."

Chatty had accurately guessed the monitress's errand.

"It's nearly nine o'clock," proclaimed Vivian. "Didn't you hear the bell? I rang it at the side door."

"We didn't hear a sound," replied Lettice. "But then, we were all laughing so much. Honor Fitzgerald has just been climbing the lime tree, and she went right through the window into the study."

"Honor Fitzgerald is a hoyden, then," said Vivian. "And what business had she to go inside Miss Maitland's room? It was a piece of great impertinence."

"I'm sorry I told you," said Lettice ruefully.

"I wish Vivian could have heard the verse you made about her!" whispered Pauline to Honor. "Is hoyden a dictionary word, or not? I'm afraid I should have said 'cheek' instead of impertinence, but I'm not a monitress."

The girls had entered the dressing-room, and were putting away books and sewing materials in their lockers, when Maisie exclaimed:

"Oh, what a bother! I've left my work-basket on the grass. It was open, too, and if there's a heavy dew my scissors and crewel needles will be covered with rust. Lettice, do go and fetch it for me!—there's just time."

Lettice was so accustomed to wait upon her elder sister that she did not even remonstrate, but turned straightway and ran into the garden to fetch the lost property. It had grown suddenly very dusk, almost dark. The lime tree stood out tall and black by the side of the house, and the bushes were dense masses of shadow. Lettice had to grope for the basket, but found it at last, and began to retrace her steps along the hardly-discernible path. She was about twenty yards away from the lime tree when a slight noise made her look back, and she noticed the figure of a girl swinging herself down by the branches in the same way as Honor had done. Whoever it was alighted on the ground gently, and rushed off into the bushes before Lettice could see her face, though it would have been too dark, in any case, to distinguish her features. It was all done very quickly, and so silently that, except for the first sound, there was scarcely a rustle.

Lettice was in a great hurry, and did not stop to make any investigation; indeed, she did not trouble to give the matter a thought. It seemed a trifling little incident, not even worth mentioning to the others; yet it was one that she was to remember afterwards, in view of certain events that followed, for it was destined to make a link in the strangest chain of circumstances that ever occurred at St. Chad's.

CHAPTER XIV. A STOLEN MEETING

Honor had hurried with the other girls from the garden, laughing and joking as she went, and was almost in the act of running into the house when quite unexpectedly something happened, something utterly amazing and out of the common, and which was to be fraught with entirely unlooked-for consequences. As she put her foot on the first of the steps that led to the side door a figure moved silently from under the shade of a lilac bush close by, and, tapping her upon the arm, drew her aside with a whispered "Sh-sh!"

Honor suppressed an exclamation of astonishment, and, peering through the dusk to see who thus accosted her, recognized Annie, an under-housemaid who had only lately come to St. Chad's.

"I've been waiting to catch you alone, miss," whispered the girl, "and a difficult matter it's been too. I didn't dare speak to you before the other young ladies. I'm to give you this letter, safe into your own hand. I'd never have done it if I hadn't promised so faithful—it's almost as much as my place is worth!"

"What is it? Who sent it?" asked Honor, taking the note.

"It's from one of the young gentlemen at Orley Grange, and I was to be sure you got it secretly. Put it in your pocket, miss, and run indoors! I must be off to the kitchen," and without another word Annie turned and fled, as if relieved to have accomplished her errand. Full of curiosity, Honor entered the house. The clock had not yet struck nine, so, seeing that the light was on in the dressing-room, she peeped inside. Fortunately, nobody was there, and she was able to go in and read her letter free from all observation. Its contents appeared to occasion her no little perplexity and dismay, for she knitted her brows and shook her head as she replaced the envelope in her pocket. She went, however, to the recreation room, where the rest of the girls were assembled waiting for the bell that always rang to proclaim bedtime; but she was in such an absent and abstracted frame of mind that several of her friends noticed and remarked upon it.

"What's wrong with Paddy?" asked Lettice. "She's shut up suddenly, like an oyster. I can't get a word out of her."

"I can't imagine," said Pauline. "I spoke to her just now, and she didn't seem to hear me."

"It's most unlike her," commented Ruth. "She generally goes to bed with so many jokes and parting shots."

To-night Honor walked upstairs with unwonted staidness and gravity. She went quietly into her cubicle and drew the curtain, and answered so briefly when her room-mate spoke to her that the latter was almost offended.

"Perhaps she's only tired though," thought Janie charitably. "This hot weather is enough to wear anybody out. I don't always care to talk myself."

Janie was certainly not a girl to push conversation where it was evidently not wanted, so the pair undressed in absolute silence. From Honor's cubicle came sounds that suggested that its occupant was fumbling with a key and unlocking a box, but as she did not volunteer any explanation, her room-mate made no comments. When Vivian arrived at half-past nine to switch out the light, both girls were in bed.

Next morning Janie woke suddenly just as the grey dawn was growing strong enough to show faintly the various objects that were in the room. Some unusual noise had disturbed her, and she lay listening intently. She could hear stealthy movements in the next cubicle, and wondering what her friend was doing, she popped out of bed and peeped round the curtain. There was Honor, fully dressed, and in the act of putting on her hat.

"What's the matter?" asked Janie anxiously. "Honor! where are you going?"

"I hoped I shouldn't waken you," replied Honor in a whisper. "Hush! Don't talk loud, because with all the windows so wide open the girls in No. 6 can hear quite plainly when we speak in this room."

"All right. But do tell me why you're getting up at this extraordinary hour?" said Janie, in a subdued tone.

"I'm in a dreadful fix! I must meet Dermot down on the beach soon after five o'clock."

"Meet Dermot! Your brother? But why?"

"He's in such a scrape, and I have to get him out of it."

"How do you know?"

"One of the servants slipped this note into my hand last night, as we came in from the garden. You can read it if you like."

Janie took the letter, which was written in a scrawling, boyish hand on a piece of paper apparently torn out of an exercise-book. It ran thus:—

"Dear Honor,

"I am in the most awful row, and if I can't get a sovereign by to-morrow morning I shall be done for. I owe it to Blake. I haven't time to tell you the whole affair, but I have been an absolute idiot. Blake wants the money, and he's a mean sneak. He says if I don't pay up he'll let on about something that I'm trying to keep dark. He really means it, too, and if it gets to the Head's ears I shall be expelled. Can you possibly lend me anything? I'd have written to the Mater, but I hear she has one of her bad attacks, so it wouldn't do to upset her. As for the governor, he'd be furious if he knew. He told me last term that if I ran into debt I needn't trust to him to get me out of it, for he wouldn't stir a finger to help me, and would give me a thrashing for my pains. He must not know on any account. It is of no use writing to Brian or the others, because it is so near the end of the term they're sure to have no money left. Have you spent all yours? I am going to get up before five o'clock to-morrow and climb out through the dormitory window, and go along the shore to the beach below Chessington, just by your bathing-place. Can you manage to do the same, and bring me any cash you can gather? Perhaps Blake might take something on account, if you haven't the whole. The janitor has promised to go with this letter to St. Chad's; he says he thinks he can get it smuggled in through his niece, who is a servant there. But he won't have time to wait for an answer, so the only way to give me the money is to meet me on the shore. I am awfully sorry to have to ask you to do this, but it is the one chance I have left, and if you knew what a hole I am in I think you would be sorry for me. I must stop now. The bell is ringing.

"Your loving brother,

"Oh, Honor! Are you going?"

"Of course I am. I wouldn't fail Dermot at such a pinch. Luckily I have the money too. I shall let myself out by the dressing-room window, and climb over the fence at the end of the cricket field. It won't take very long. I shall be back before any of the servants are stirring."

"But it's such a frightfully risky thing! Suppose you were caught, you'd certainly get into a scrape."

"I shall have to take the risk. Dermot will get into a far worse scrape if I don't go. I couldn't bear to think of him waiting for me on the shore, and finding I never came. Hush, Janie! Please don't ask me any more. I've made up my mind."

Honor had put on her tennis shoes, and now stole very softly out of the room and down the passage. Janie went to bed again, though certainly not to sleep. She heard the stairs creak, and wondered if anyone else were awake in the house, and would notice the compromising sound.

"Oh, dear! What is to be done?" she thought anxiously. "It's fearfully naughty of Honor, yet I sympathize with her wanting to help Dermot. I believe I should have gone myself, if I'd had a brother of my own in trouble. Major Fitzgerald must be a very stern man; they both seem too frightened of him to tell anything, and their poor mother is so ill she mustn't be disturbed. I'm sorry for Honor. I hope she won't be long away; I shall be wretched till she comes back. Somebody might see her from a window, even if no one hears her in the passage, and then—I don't like to think of the consequences!"

Honor was indeed determined to do her utmost for Dermot. Of all her five brothers, he was the dearest. Rather younger than herself, he had been her inseparable companion in nursery days, when the pair had shared everything, from sweets to scoldings, with strictest impartiality. Honor had never forgotten the terrible parting when her father had decreed that Dermot was old enough to go to school—how she had cried herself sick, and how absolutely lonely and deserted the Castle had seemed when she was obliged to wander about and amuse herself alone. She had grown accustomed in time to solitary rambles, but she had always looked forward to her brother's return with keenest anticipation, and regretted bitterly that holidays were so short.

That Dermot was in trouble and wanted her was now the one thought uppermost in her mind, and rules were entirely ignored in her desire to see him and speak with him. Though she was determined to carry out her project she knew, however, that it was a most unorthodox and unwarrantable proceeding to leave St. Chad's at such an hour, and on such an errand, and she had no desire to be caught and prevented from going.

She stole along the landing, therefore, as softly as possible, pausing every now and then to listen if all were quiet. The whole house seemed to be sound asleep, and not a door opened as she passed. Once down the stairs and in the hall she felt safer, and hurrying quickly into the dressing-room, she easily unbolted a French window that led into the garden.

Was that a step on the stairs? Honor was not sure. She dared not go back to ascertain, but, rushing outside, fled as fast as she could round the corner in the direction of the cricket pitch.

"Whoever it was will find the bird flown," she said to herself. "Perhaps I was mistaken, though, and only imagined I heard somebody."

A glance at the little watch pinned to her blouse told her that she had not much time to lose. She did not wish to keep Dermot waiting, for she knew he would be in a fever of anxiety until she made her appearance.

"I hope he has managed to get off safely," she thought. "It must be more difficult to leave a large dormitory than a small bedroom; still, I don't suppose any of the other boys would try to stop him, or would tell afterwards."

She had now reached the playing-fields, and she climbed over the fence that separated them from a neighbouring pasture. A few hundred yards, and a stile brought her to a path along the cliffs that led to the bathing-place.

Dermot was first at the tryst. Even before Honor began to descend the flight of steps she caught sight of his familiar figure on the beach below. He was pacing impatiently up and down, glancing first one way and then another, until at length he happened to look upwards in the right direction, and saw her. He waved his hat, and came eagerly along the shingle to meet her.

"All right, Dermot! I've brought you the sovereign!" she cried, anxious to relieve his mind at once.

"Really? Oh, I say, Sis, it is good of you!"

There was no long line of grinning schoolboys to jeer, nor sedate Chaddites to disapprove, so Honor hugged her brother this time to her heart's content. It seemed so delightful to see him again that she almost forgot for the moment upon what errand she had come, only realizing that he was there, and that she had him all to herself. The remembrance of his trouble, however, quickly returned to her.

"Come and tell me everything," she said, drawing him towards the bathing-hut. "We can sit on these steps and talk."

"I was rather doubtful whether my letter had reached you," began Dermot; "I'd to settle with the janitor, and at first he said that the College was so strictly kept, it would be quite impossible. Afterwards he gave way and said he'd try, but I couldn't see him again to ask if he'd really managed the affair; I had just to come to the cove on chance. I can tell you I was glad when I saw you coming down the rocks. Oh, Honor, I've got myself into the most awful mess!"

"How is it? I don't understand. Who is this Blake?"

"He has a place in Dunscar, a kind of second-rate veterinary surgeon's business; and he sells dogs, and rats, and rabbits, and even does a little mole-catching, I believe—rather a low-class sporting chap, in fact. Roper took me to the kennels one day, to see a spaniel. Some of our fellows keep dogs there, and Blake looks after them. Well, I liked the spaniel; it was a perfect beauty! Roper said Blake only wanted ten shillings for it, and it was an absolute bargain. He advised me to buy it and keep it at the kennels. I'd run through all my cash by then, but Blake said I could go on tick if I cared; and I thought it was a pity to miss the chance, because if I didn't have the dog, Jarrow was going to take him."

"I suppose you mayn't keep dogs at school?" said Honor.

"Rather not! You'd have liked this one, Honor! His name was Terry, and he was as jolly as poor old Doss used to be. He got to know me directly, and he'd come jumping and trying to lick my face. He was clever, too; he could do all kinds of tricks—trust for a biscuit, and lie down and die, and give three barks for the King. I grew so fond of him, and I meant to take him home with me in the holidays. Well, I hadn't been able to go to the kennels for several days, and when at last I managed to run down there Blake told me that Terry was dead and buried. He looked so shifty when he said it that I had my suspicions at once. I don't believe Terry died at all; I'm sure Blake sold him to somebody else, who has taken him away."

"Oh, what a shame!" exclaimed Honor.

"It's just like the fellow, though—he's an atrocious cad! Of course, I couldn't prove anything. I could only say that Terry had looked all right when last I saw him, and it seemed a queer thing for him to pop off so suddenly; but then Blake rounded on me with all sorts of medical terms, and said he'd made a post-mortem examination, and could give me a written certificate. As if that would have been of any use! Well, the long and short of it was, we had a quarrel, and Blake turned nasty. He said he wanted the money I owed him for the dog, and he gave me an immense bill for its keep. It was quite ridiculous; he made out it had eaten pounds and pounds of Spratt's biscuits every week, and that he'd bought fresh meat for it too. I'm sure he hadn't! I disputed every item; but he said if I wasn't satisfied I could refer the matter to the Head. The whole affair came to exactly a sovereign. I couldn't possibly pay it—I hadn't more than a few shillings left in the world. I tried to get him to give me tick for a little longer, but he was as surly as a bear, and threatened that if I didn't turn up with the money by Wednesday, he'd send in the bill to the Head."

"I suppose that would mean a big row?"

"Simply terrific! You see, the kennels are out of bounds; besides which, we've all been warned we're to have nothing to do with Blake. The Head said he was a rascal, and any fellow who went to his place would do so at the risk of expulsion. I was an idiot to let myself get mixed up in such a business, but Roper, and Graveson, and several others had dogs, and I was so taken with that black spaniel! I thought and schemed how I could find a way out of it. I didn't dare to write home to the Mater: if she's well enough to read her own letters, she'd be in quite a nervous state of mind about it; and if she's ill, then the governor will open them all for her, and you know what he'd say!"

"It would be as bad as when I bought Firefly," replied Honor. "He was most fearfully angry that time."

"And he'd be harder on me than on you, because you're a girl. He couldn't thrash you, however much he might scold you. I've had a little experience of his hunting-crop before, and it's not exactly pleasant."

"Yes, I remember—when you took the cartridges out of his gun cupboard."

"Well, I say, Honor, I mustn't stay here too long; I've got to be back before anyone's about the place, you know."

"Did you get off all right?"

"Oh, yes! I dropped out of the dormitory window on to a piece of roof near, and let myself down by the spout. It was quite simple."

"How about climbing up again?"

"Easy as A B C."

"Well, here's the pound, at any rate."

"Thanks immensely! How is it you're so flush of cash?"

"I'm not. I've hardly any of my pocket-money left. This is my Jubilee sovereign."

"Not the one Uncle Murtagh gave you?"

"Yes."

"Oh, Honor, I am sorry! I scarcely like to take it."

"Don't be absurd! You must!"

"But you had the thing as a locket, and vowed you'd never part with it."

"It can't be helped. Vows are sometimes better broken. Uncle Murtagh told me to keep it until I happened to want it very badly, and I'm sure we need it to-day."

"Well, I do, at any rate, though it seems rather a swindle to commandeer your particular, pet treasure. I'll have to borrow it now, I'm afraid; but I'll get you another some time, I promise you faithfully."

"I don't care in the least, so long as you get out of this scrape," protested Honor.

The sun was already so high that its bright rays, reflected in a little pool near their feet, warned the pair that it was no longer safe to delay their parting.

"It's a quarter to six!" exclaimed Dermot, looking at his watch. "I must absolutely fly. I'll run all the way to Dunscar. I hope you'll get back quite safely into the College. You were a perfect trump to come. Good-bye; I'm off!"

Honor stood watching him until he had disappeared round the rocks at the end of the cove, then half-regretfully she climbed up the steps again on to the headland. She returned to St. Chad's the same way as she had come, walking across the pasture and climbing the fence of the cricket ground. She found the French window in the dressing-room still ajar, and bolted it on the inside before she went upstairs. All was still quite quiet in the hall and on the landing, and she was able to regain her room without any alarms.

Janie looked up nervously as the door opened. She had been lying awake, suffering far more anxiety on her friend's behalf than Honor had experienced for herself, and she gave a sigh of intense relief on hearing that the interview was successfully accomplished.

"I've been thinking it over," she said, "and I really believe it would have been much the best to go straight to Miss Maitland and tell her about it. She's very kind and sympathetic; perhaps she would have let you meet Dermot, and then you could have gone openly, and without all this dreadful stealing up and down stairs."

"I daren't risk it," replied Honor. "Suppose she had said 'No'? I should have been far worse off than if I hadn't asked. Besides which, she might have insisted upon telling Dr. Winterton. That's quite within the bounds of possibility; and then I should have given poor old Dermot away."

"On the whole, wouldn't it be more satisfactory for Dr. Winterton to know?"

"Janie! How can you suggest such a thing?"

"Well, if, as you say, this man Blake is a scamp, and has really sold the dog, it ought to be enquired into. If it were all exposed, perhaps he would be obliged to leave Dunscar and go to some other place, and that would be much better for the boys at the Grange."

"But in the meantime Dermot would be the scapegoat."

"I don't believe Dr. Winterton would expel him, if he went and owned up himself. He'd be rather angry, I dare say, but then the thing would be over, and there'd be no more fear of being found out. If Blake is such a dishonest man, he may send in the same bill again."

"Dermot said he should make him give a receipt for the money. No, Janie! You don't quite grasp the case. You've no brothers of your own, so how can you understand boys?"

"Then couldn't you have asked your father?" pleaded Janie desperately. "It seems—please don't be offended!—not quite straight to be suppressing the whole affair like this."

"You don't know my father, or you wouldn't suggest it. He can be very stern, particularly with the boys. They always say he's more of a martinet at home than ever he was in the Army. Yes, I know you tell your mother everything, but mothers are much more lenient than fathers. I'd tell mine, if she weren't ill. It's no use arguing, Janie! I'm sorry if it isn't all on the square, but Dermot was in a very tight place, and I felt bound to help him, even if I had to do something rather wrong."

CHAPTER XV. SENT TO COVENTRY

Though Honor had seen nobody, either in leaving or re-entering St. Chad's, her morning adventure had not been so entirely unobserved as she imagined. Vivian Holmes, who was a light sleeper, had awakened by the unfortunate creak that had been made by the stairs. Always mindful of her duties as monitress, she had jumped up and cautiously opened her door, and was just in time to peep over the banisters and catch a glimpse of Honor's back disappearing down the hall. She hurriedly returned to put on her dressing-gown and bedroom slippers, then followed as rapidly as she could. When she arrived downstairs, she found the French window leading into the garden open; but Honor was well round the corner, and running fast towards the cricket field. Vivian was very much disturbed and distressed. She scarcely knew what she ought to do. She ventured a little way into the grounds, but not a trace of any truant was to be seen, so she thought it useless to search far. One of the girls must have gone out; on that point she was absolutely certain.

"I'm almost positive it was Honor Fitzgerald," she said to herself. "It looked exactly like her, although I only saw her back for a moment."

Vivian was extremely conscientious, and felt personally responsible for all under her charge at St. Chad's. She was apt to err on the side of severity, but she honestly strove to do her duty, and to see that the rules were duly kept. In this case, however, she was in a difficulty. There was no rule to prevent a girl getting up early and going into the garden, because it had never occurred to Miss Maitland that anyone would wish to rise before the usual dressing-bell. Vivian knew that Honor had been accustomed to much liberty in her Irish home, and that she greatly chafed against the constraints of school life. What was more probable than that, waking at dawn, she had longed for a breath of the cool morning air, and was taking a stroll round the grounds?

"She may have a headache, or have slept badly," thought the monitress, with an endeavour to be charitable. "These hot nights are very trying, even with both one's bedroom windows wide open."

After all, it was not a very desperate offence, and there seemed no need to report it to Miss Maitland. Vivian determined to listen for Honor's footsteps and catch her on the stairs as she came back, or, at any rate, to tax her with the affair later during the day, and point out that in future such early rambles could not be allowed. In the meantime, she went back to bed, and, in spite of her resolution to intercept the returning wanderer, fell asleep again, and heard nothing until the bell rang at a quarter to seven. In the busy whirl of occupations that followed, there was no opportunity for any private conversation with Honor, either before or after morning school; and immediately dinner was over, all the Chaddites rushed off to watch a croquet tournament between mistresses and monitresses, in which Vivian herself was taking part. The day, therefore, passed exactly as usual, and it was not until after tea, when the girls were just going to preparation, that anything particular occurred.

At precisely half-past four o'clock Janie Henderson chanced to be walking down the passage when she saw the door of Miss Maitland's study suddenly open, and Vivian Holmes come out, looking so greatly agitated and upset that Janie stopped in amazement.

"Why, what's the matter?" she exclaimed, for she was on sufficiently friendly terms with the monitress to venture the enquiry.

"A great deal's the matter!" replied Vivian. "The worst thing that has ever happened at St. Chad's, or in the whole College. I'd give all I possess in the world to have nothing to do with it! I wish I weren't monitress! Where's Honor Fitzgerald? I have to find her."

"She's practising," said Janie. "Shall I fetch her?"

"Look here!" returned Vivian. "Honor sleeps in your room; did you hear her get up very early this morning and go out?"

Janie's tell-tale face betrayed her at once, though she would not have attempted to deny the fact, in any case.

"Then I'm sorry, but you'll have to come to Miss Maitland too," said Vivian. "It's a hateful business altogether, and after our splendid record at St. Chad's, and the way we have all tried so hard to keep up the standard, it hurts me more than I can tell you. I can't bear to get Honor Fitzgerald into trouble! I simply couldn't have believed it of her, though I'm afraid it's only too plain. She's been very naughty sometimes, but she always seemed extremely straightforward, and I never dreamt she could be capable of an affair like this. We shall have to tell the exact truth, Janie; there's nothing else for it, and she must clear herself as best she can. I'm afraid she's bound to be expelled. It's a terrible disgrace to the house. Yes, go and fetch her now; the sooner we get it over the better."

Janie walked down the passage in the utmost perplexity. She could not account for Vivian's excited diatribe. What had Honor done to bring disgrace upon St. Chad's? It was, of course, a very irregular thing to run away at daybreak to meet her brother, but it was no worse than many of her other scrapes, and did not seem an offence of sufficient gravity to warrant such an extreme measure as expulsion from the school.

"Vivian is always hard on Honor," thought Janie. "Perhaps, after all, she's making an unnecessary fuss, and it won't turn out to be so dreadful as she says. Tell the truth! Of course I shall do so; Vivian needn't remind me of that!"

Janie called her friend as quietly as possible from the piano. There were several other girls in the room, and she did not wish them to know anything about the affair. She only whispered therefore that Honor was wanted in Miss Maitland's study at once, and did not add any explanation, thinking it better not to mention Vivian's remarks, as she had not understood them herself. Honor put her music away calmly enough, and closed the piano. She knew that the summons must have reference to her morning adventure, and anticipated a scolding; but it was not the first she had received at St. Chad's, and she thought the punishment would probably not exceed two hundred lines, or, perhaps, a few pages of poetry to be learnt by heart.

The two girls hurried to the study, and, after knocking at the door, entered in response to Miss Maitland's "Come in". The house-mistress was seated at her writing-table, talking to Vivian, and turned round at their approach. She looked worried, and had a sterner expression on her face than they had ever seen there before.

"Honor Fitzgerald," she began, "I have sent for you because a very unpleasant thing has occurred, which I hope you may be able to explain to me. Last evening I was sitting writing at this table, and laid a sovereign down just at this corner. I was called away, and left the room for about ten minutes, or a quarter of an hour. When I returned, I found to my astonishment that the money was gone. I searched everywhere, and it had certainly not fallen on to the floor, nor was it amongst my papers; so I can only conclude that someone must have come in and taken it. I have made careful enquiries as to who was seen near my study last night, and I hear that you climbed up the lime tree and entered the room by the window shortly before nine o'clock. Is that so?"

"Yes, Miss Maitland," replied Honor, without any hesitation. "I did come in, but I only stayed a minute. I didn't go near the table, and I didn't see the sovereign. If I had, I certainly shouldn't have touched it."

Miss Maitland sighed.

"I was afraid you would say that, Honor! My dear child, it would be better to tell me the truth, and confess at once. We have the clearest proof that you, and only you, must have taken it, so it is no use denying it any more."

"I should like to know what proof you mean, Miss Maitland?" said Honor, in a strained voice.

"This letter," replied the mistress, producing Dermot's note. "It was found on your bedroom floor this morning by the upper housemaid, who brought it at once to me. It was given you, I find, by one of the under servants, who much regrets now that she was persuaded to deliver it secretly. It shows me, of course, your motive for taking the money."

"But I did not take it!" said Honor. "I said before that I didn't see it, and I mean it."

For answer Miss Maitland turned to Janie.

"Janie Henderson, did Honor Fitzgerald leave her bedroom before five o'clock this morning?"

Poor Janie whispered, "Yes", though the word almost choked her. That she, of all people, must be a witness against her friend seemed too cruel to be endured.

"Did Honor mention to you where she was going?"

"To the bathing cove."

"And her errand?"

"To meet her brother."

"Did she say that she meant to take him the money he needed?"

"I believe—yes—I remember she did," stammered Janie, almost bewildered by this cross-questioning.

"Did she seem to you in any way conscious that she was doing wrong?"

Janie paused. She recalled only too plainly Honor's words: "I'm sorry if it isn't all on the square, but Dermot was in a very tight place, and I felt bound to help him, even if I had to do something rather wrong".

"I am waiting for your answer, Janie."

"I—I—think she seemed—sorry!"

"Did she mention to you where the money came from that she was taking to her brother?"

"No, she said nothing about it."

"That will do for the present, Janie. Now, Vivian, I wish you to tell me if you saw Honor Fitzgerald go along the hall early this morning?"

"It looked like Honor; I could be nearly certain," faltered Vivian, rather hesitatingly.

"It was, so you needn't mind saying so!" interrupted Honor, who had been listening attentively to this evidence. "I admit that I went out, and ran down to the beach, and met Dermot. I never wanted to deny that. But I certainly didn't even see the sovereign, much less take it."

"Let us have the truth, Honor," urged Miss Maitland. "I believe that you yielded to a sudden temptation, and I am very sorry for you, since I think you did it entirely for your brother's sake. If you will confess now, I will promise to deal leniently with you."

"I can't confess what I haven't done," said Honor. She had turned very white, but she did not flinch in the least.

"Nevertheless, you handed money to your brother on the shore?"

"Yes. I gave him a sovereign, but it was my own, and not yours."

"Honor! Honor! It is no use holding to such a palpably false story. Where could you get a sovereign? You banked your pocket-money with me at the beginning of the term, like the rest of the girls; it was only a small amount, and you have spent it weekly."

"I had a sovereign, all the same," answered Honor. "It was a Queen Victoria's Jubilee one, with a hole in it, which my uncle had given me. I wore it as a locket, and kept it inside my green work-box. Last night I took it off the chain. That was the piece of money I gave to Dermot."

"Did Honor ever show you this locket?" asked Miss Maitland, turning to Janie.

The latter shook her head sadly. How she wished that she could have replied in the affirmative!

"Then the only way in which your words can be proved, Honor, is to trace your sovereign. Possibly your brother has not parted with it; or we could find the man to whom he paid it. A Jubilee gold coin with a hole in it is so uncommon that it could easily be identified. I am personally acquainted with Dr. Winterton, so there will be no difficulty in calling and asking his co-operation in the matter."

"Oh, don't ask Dr. Winterton—please don't!" implored Honor in much agitation. "I'd rather leave things as they are than that!"

Terrible as was the indictment against her, she felt she would not clear herself at her brother's expense. To allow Miss Maitland to call at Orley Grange would expose Dermot's peccadillo to his headmaster, and involve him in as serious a trouble as her own. If one or other must be expelled, she would rather it were herself. She, of the two, had less to fear from her father's anger; and, besides, there was a further reason. Dermot was destined for the Navy, and was very shortly to take the entrance examination for a cadetship; were he expelled from his training school, he would be prohibited from competing, and by another year he would be above the required age, and therefore no longer eligible as a candidate. To put any hindrance in the way of his success might ruin his whole future career. At all costs she must shield him, come what might.

"Then you wish me not to pursue the enquiry, Honor?" continued Miss Maitland. "Remember, it is the only way of clearing up this most unfortunate affair."

"I can't help it! The sovereign mustn't be traced. It was my own, all the same. Indeed I am telling the truth!" blurted out Honor, in great distress.

"I am sorry I cannot believe you," returned Miss Maitland coldly. "I thought better of you than this. You have given much trouble during your term here, but I considered you at least to be strictly honourable. I am most bitterly disappointed, and even now I will offer you a last chance. I perhaps took you by surprise, and you were not prepared to acknowledge what you had done. I will let you think the matter over until to-morrow morning. If you come to me then, before chapel, and confess the truth, I will forgive you; but if you still persist in denying it, I shall be forced, though sorely against my will, to take sterner measures. For the credit of our house and of our school, we cannot allow such things to happen at St. Chad's."

"I have told you the truth now, Miss Maitland," answered Honor, with a certain dignity in her manner. "I can only say the same to-morrow and every day. I don't know who has taken your money. I may do naughty things sometimes (indeed, I often do), but if you knew us Fitzgeralds at home I think you would scarcely have accused me of this."

Honor walked into preparation outwardly calm, but inwardly she nursed a burning volcano. She had great pride of race, and had often gloried in the honourable name which she bore. That a Fitzgerald should be suspected of so despicable a crime as stealing a sovereign seemed little short of an affront to her whole family. It was a blot on their good repute such as had never been placed there before. In days gone by her ancestors had fought duels for far less insults; now, however, she was obliged to submit to that horrible charge without making any attempt to defend herself. The one means of proving her innocence was closed to her. For

Dermot's sake she must endure to be thought a thief! Yes, a thief! She repeated the word under her breath, and the very sound of it seemed to sting her. A Fitzgerald a thief! Oh, it was impossible to bear the reproach! Surely even Dermot's future could not compel her to such a sacrifice? Yes, it must and should. She knew it was the dream of his life to become a Naval cadet, and that her father and mother also cherished hopes for their youngest son's success. She seemed, like the Argonauts of yore, "'twixt Scylla and Charybdis". Which was the worse she could hardly decide, for Dermot to miss his examination, or for herself to be sent home under the slur of such a false accusation. Both seemed equally bad, but she reasoned that the former would involve more disastrous consequences, and, therefore, was the greater evil of the two.

She sat with her French grammar before her, mechanically looking at the pages; but her thoughts were so busy that she did not take in a single word of what she was reading, and would scarcely have known, if asked, whether she was studying French or geometry. What must she do? Some answer must be given to Miss Maitland to-morrow morning, and only one was possible. At all costs she would persist in her determination not to allow the affair to be mentioned to Dr. Winterton.

Janie, meanwhile, was in a hardly less disturbed state of mind. Never for a moment was her faith in her friend shaken. The mass of evidence was certainly strong, but it did not convince her. She knew Honor too well for that, and would have taken her word against all the world. Though she could not understand the particular reason for screening Dermot at such an enormous cost, she appreciated the fact that Honor was prepared to brave anything sooner than allow enquiries to be made at Orley Grange.

"It's that that looks so bad," thought Janie. "Of course, Miss Maitland thinks she made up the tale about her own sovereign, as she seems so afraid of having to produce the proof. Oh, dear, what a terrible tangle it all is! I wish that Honor had trusted me more at the very beginning, when she first received the letter. She didn't even want to let me know she was stealing out to meet her brother, only I happened to wake. I was so taken by surprise I didn't say half what I should have liked! If I could have persuaded her last night to go and tell Miss Maitland, she couldn't have been suspected. It's too late now, unfortunately, and I can't imagine how the affair will end."

Vain regrets were futile, so Janie with an effort concentrated her mind upon her lessons, and the two hours of study dragged slowly to a close. The evening was wet, and it was impossible to go into the garden, therefore all filed into the recreation room, with the sole exception of Honor, who lingered behind, putting away her books. Ill tidings fly apace, and within two minutes of the close of preparation every girl in the house had heard that Honor Fitzgerald had taken a sovereign from Miss Maitland's room, and refused to "own up". The news made the greatest sensation. Such a thing had not occurred before in the annals of the College. It seemed a stain on St. Chad's that could never be wiped out, and for which no amount of tennis shields, champion cups, or other triumphs would ever compensate. How could the Chaddites hold up their heads again? They, who had ranked in reputation next to the School House, would now sink to a lower level than St. Bride's! A hush fell over the whole community, as if some dreadful calamity had taken place. The girls stood in little groups, whispering excitedly; consternation and dismay were on all faces, for the honour of the house appeared a personal question to each. Maisie Talbot suddenly voiced the universal verdict.

"Anyone who's capable of bringing this disgrace upon us deserves to be sent to Coventry, and cut dead!" she announced, loudly enough to be heard by everybody.

There was a common murmur of assent, which stopped instantly, however, for the object of their opprobrium walked into the room. As she entered the door, Honor became aware of the hostile feeling against her. All eyes were turned in her direction, but there was recognition or welcome in none. It was a terrible thing to meet the cool stare of nearly forty companions, and feel herself thus pilloried for general contempt, yet not for a moment did she flinch. White to the lips, but with her head held up in silent self-justification, she moved slowly down the room, running the gauntlet of public disdain. Did I say all had abandoned her? No, there was one who remained faithful, one who was, not merely a fair-weather friend, but ready to believe in her and stand by her through the severest ordeal. Janie, the shyest girl at St. Chad's, who never as a rule raised her voice to venture an opinion or a criticism on any subject, came boldly to the rescue now. Stepping across to Honor, she took her firmly by the arm; then, almost as white and haggard as her friend, she turned and faced the rest.

"I think you will be very sorry for this afterwards," she began, in a voice that astonished even herself by its assurance. "It is not right to convict anybody without a trial, and Honor has not yet been proved guilty. I'm absolutely certain she is innocent, and that in time she'll be able to establish her good name. We've known her for a whole term now at St.

Chad's, and she has gained a reputation for being perfectly truthful and 'square'. The charge against her is so entirely opposite to her character that I wonder anyone can credit it."

"Let her clear herself, then!" replied Maisie Talbot. "It ought to be easy enough, if she is really innocent. In the meantime, the honour of St. Chad's is being trailed through the dust!"

Excited comments and indignant accord greeted these words. All evidently were in agreement with Maisie, and determined to blackball Honor as a vindication of their zeal for the credit of their house. The supper-bell fortunately put an end to the unpleasant scene, and nobody was surprised when Honor, instead of walking into the dining-hall with the others, marched straight upstairs to her cubicle. Miss Maitland noticed her empty place at table, but made no remark. Perhaps, like the girls, she felt her absence to be a relief.

When Janie went to No. 8 at nine o'clock she found her friend already in bed, and feigning sleep with such persistence that she evidently did not wish to be disturbed. Always tactful and thoughtful, Janie drew the curtain again without attempting any conversation. She knew that Honor's heart must be too full for speech, and that the truest kindness was to leave her alone.

CHAPTER XVI. A RASH STEP

Honor's sleep was undoubtedly of a very pretended description. She lay still in bed, pressing her hand to her burning head, to try to calm the throbbing in her temples and allow herself to think collectedly. She must decide upon what course she meant to take, for matters could not go on thus any longer. Before nine o'clock to-morrow morning she must again face Miss Maitland, and take her choice between betraying Dermot and her expulsion from St. Chad's. In either case, the danger to her brother seemed great. If Miss Cavendish wrote to Major Fitzgerald, asking him to remove his daughter from the College, he would naturally come over to Chessington and make full enquiries as to the reason. She would not be able to face her father's questions, and Dermot's secret would come out, after all. How might this most fatal consummation be avoided?

"If I were only at home, instead of here, then Father wouldn't be able to go and call at Orley Grange," she said to herself.

It was a new idea. She wondered she had not thought of it before. She would solve the problem by running away! She would thus meet her father at Kilmore Castle, instead of in Miss Maitland's presence at St. Chad's; and could avoid many awkward questions, simply saying she had been accused of taking a sovereign, and leaving out Dermot's part in the story altogether.

The prospect was immensely attractive. She felt scarcely capable of once more confronting the cold scorn of her companions. Home seemed a haven of refuge, an ark in the midst of a deluge of trouble, the one place in the wide world where she could fly for help. Perhaps her mother might be better, and well enough to see her, and she could then pour out her perplexities into sympathetic ears. But how to get to Ireland? It was impossible to travel without money, and she had less than a shilling left in her purse. She knew, however, that a line of steamboats ran from Westhaven to Cork; if she could walk to the former place she thought she could persuade the captain of one of the vessels to take her to Cork by promising that her father's solicitor, who lived there, would pay for her when she arrived. Mr. Donovan had often been on business at Kilmore Castle; she knew the address of his office, and was sure that he would advance her sufficient to pay for both the steamer journey and her railway ticket to Ballycroghan.

The first thing, therefore, to be done was to leave the College as early and as secretly as she could. She did not dare to go to sleep, but lay tossing uneasily until the first hint of dawn. Sunrise was at about four o'clock, so soon after half-past three it was just light enough to enable her to get up and dress. Miss Maitland had sent a glass of milk and a plate of sandwiches and biscuits for her supper the night before, but she had left them untouched on her dressing-table. Now, however, she had the forethought to drink the milk and put the biscuits and sandwiches in her pocket. The face which confronted her when she looked in the glass hardly seemed her own, it was so unwontedly pale, and had such dark rings round the eyes. She moved very quietly, for she was anxious not to waken her room-mate.

"Janie mustn't know what I intend, or she'll get into trouble for not stopping me," she thought. "It's a comfort that she, at any rate, doesn't believe I've done this horrible thing, and that she'll stand up for me when I'm gone."

She listened for a minute, till the sound of her friend's even and regular breathing reassured her; then, drawing aside the curtain, she crept into the next cubicle. Janie was lying fast asleep, her head cradled on her arm. With her fair hair falling round her cheeks, she looked almost pretty. Honor bent down and kissed the end of one of the flaxen locks, but too gently to disturb its owner; then, with a scarcely breathed good-bye, she left the room. She had laid her plans carefully, and did not mean to be discovered and brought back to school; so, instead of going downstairs, and thus passing both Vivian Holmes's and Miss Maitland's doors, she went to the other end of the passage, where the landing window stood wide open, and, managing to climb down by the thick ivy, reached the ground without mishap. She crept through the garden under the laurel bushes, and, avoiding the cricket field, scaled the wall close to the potting shed, helped very much by a large heap of logs that had been left there ready to be chopped. Once successfully over, she set off running in the direction of the moors, and never stopped until she was quite out of sight of even the chimneys of St. Chad's. Then, hot and utterly breathless, she sat down on the grass to rest.

It was still very early, for the sun had only just risen. The air was fresh and pleasant. Behind her lay green, round-topped hills, and in front stretched the sea, smooth as glass, with a few small, white sails gleaming in the distance. Innumerable rabbits kept scuttling past. One small one came so near that she almost caught it with her hands, but it dived away into its burrow in a moment. She brought out her sandwiches and biscuits, and began to eat them. She was hungry already, and thought wistfully of breakfast. The bread had gone rather dry and the biscuits a little stale, but she enjoyed them, sitting on the hillside, especially when she remembered all she had escaped from at St. Chad's. She felt that, once back in dear old Ireland, her difficulties would be nearly at an end, and she registered a solemn vow never to cross the Channel again, except under the strictest compulsion. The last fragment of biscuit having vanished, she got up and shook down the crumbs for the birds; then, turning towards the hills, she struck a footpath which she thought must surely lead in the right direction. Westhaven, though twenty-five miles away by the winding coast road, or the railway, was only twelve miles distant if she went, as the crow flies, over the moors. The authorities at the College, she imagined, would never dream of looking for her there. When they discovered her absence they would probably suppose she had gone to Dunscar, and would enquire at the station, and search the main road; but, of course, nobody would have seen her, and there would be no clue to her whereabouts.

She was so pleased to have such a good start that she felt almost in high spirits, and strode along at a fair pace, keenly enjoying the unwonted sense of freedom. It was very lonely on the moors, and not even a cottage was to be seen. The path was hardly more than a sheep track, sometimes nearly effaced with grass, and she had to trace it as best she could. After some hours she began to grow tired and desperately hungry again. She wondered how she was to manage anything in the way of lunch; then, hailing with delight the sight of a small farm nestling in a hollow between two hills, she turned her steps at once in that direction. She had a sixpence and two pennies in her pocket, and thought that she might perhaps be able to buy some food.

The farm, on nearer acquaintance, proved a rather dirty and dilapidated-looking place. Honor picked her way carefully through the litter in the yard, and was about to knock at the door, when a collie dog flew from the barn behind, barking furiously, showing his teeth, and threatening to catch hold of her skirt. Much to her relief, he was called off by a slatternly, hard-featured woman, who, hearing the noise, came out of the house with a pail in her hand, and stood looking at her visitor in much amazement.

"I want to know," said Honor, "if you can let me have a glass of milk and some bread and butter, and how much you would charge for it."

"We don't sell milk here," replied the woman, shaking her head. "I've just put it all down in the butter-pot, so I'm afraid I can't oblige you."

"Oh!" said Honor blankly. Then, "I should be so glad of a little bread and butter, if you can let me have it."

"Are you out on a picnic?" asked the woman. "Where are the rest of you?"

"No, I'm by myself," answered Honor. "I'm walking across the moors to Westhaven."

"To Westhaven? You're on the wrong road, then. That path will lead you out at Windover, if you follow it."

Poor Honor was almost dumbfounded at such unexpected bad news.

"Have I gone very far wrong?" she faltered. "I must get on to Westhaven as fast as I can. Perhaps you can tell me the right way?"

"Aye, I can put you on the path, if you want," replied the woman; "but you'll have a good long bit to go."

"Is there any village where I could buy something to eat? I've had nothing since breakfast," said Honor, returning again to her first and most pressing need.

"No, there ain't," said the woman; then, apparently softening a little, "Look here, I don't mind making you a cup of tea, if you care to pay for it. The kettle's boiling. You can step in if you like."

Glad to get a meal in any circumstances, Honor entered the squalid kitchen, and tried not to notice the general untidiness of her surroundings, while the woman hastily cleared the table and set out a teacup and saucer, a huge loaf, butter, and a pot of tea. The dog had made friends, and crept up to Honor, snuggling his nose into her hand; and a tabby cat, interested in the preparations, came purring eagerly to join the feast. Honor did not know whether to call it late breakfast, dinner, or tea, but she told Janie afterwards she thought she must have eaten enough to combine the three, though she only paid sixpence for it all. She finished at last, and got up to go; then, remembering the long walk still in store for her, she gave the farmer's wife her remaining twopence for some extra slices of bread and butter to take with her.

"It's a tidy step for a young lady like you, and a-going quite alone too," said the woman, eyeing Honor keenly as she led her round the side of the cottage, to point out the right path. "You've come from over by Dunscar, I take it?"

"Oh, I'm a good walker!" replied Honor, who did not wish to encourage enquiries. "I shall soon get along. Thank you for coming so far with me."

"You're welcome," said the woman. "I hope you'll keep the path, and reach there safe; but if you'll take my advice, you'll turn round the other way and go straight back to school. You'd just get there by tea-time."

Honor started at this parting remark, and hurried on as fast as she could. How did the woman guess she had run away from the College? Of course!—she had forgotten her hat. Everyone in the neighbourhood of Chessington knew the unmistakable "sailors", with their coloured ribbons and badges. She might have remembered they would easily be recognized, and blamed her own stupidity and lack of forethought. She hoped no message would be sent to Miss Cavendish, and looked round carefully to see if she were being followed. Yes, she could certainly see the woman now, calling a boy from a field, and pointing eagerly in her direction. They would perhaps try to take her back against her will, and she would be marched ignominiously, like a prisoner, to St. Chad's.

"That they shall never do!" she thought, and choosing a moment when the pair were passing round the front of the house, she turned from the path and scrambled up the bed of a small stream on to the hills again. She decided that so long as she knew the right points of the compass, it would be quite easy to find her way, as she could walk in a line with the path, only higher up on the moor, where she would be neither seen nor followed. She flung her hat away, determined that it should not betray her again; and, on the whole, she liked to have her head bare, the wind felt so fresh and pleasant blowing through her hair. For a while she went on briskly, then, coming across a spring, which rose clear and bubbling through the grass and sedges, she took off her shoes and stockings, and sat dabbling her feet in the water, watching a pair of dragon flies, and plaiting rings from the rushes that grew around.

She stayed there so long that when she happened to look at her watch she was startled to find it was nearly half-past four.

"I must push on," she said to herself. "I've a long way to be going yet. I wonder what time the steamer starts for Cork, and if I shall find it waiting in the harbour?"

She was quite sure that she had come in exactly the same direction as the path, but somehow she did not seem to be getting any nearer to civilization. On and on she wandered, hour after hour, seeing nothing before her but the same bare, grass-covered hills, till she began to grow alarmed, and to suspect that after all she had completely missed her way. The sun was setting, and as the great, red ball of fire sank behind the horizon, her spirits fell in proportion. What was she to do, alone and lost on the hills? Even if she could reach Westhaven in daylight, she would not like to be obliged to go to the quay in the dark; and suppose there were no night boat, like the mail steamer in which she had crossed from Dublin to Holyhead, where could she go until morning? She had not foreseen any of these difficulties when she set out, it had all appeared so easy and simple; but she saw now what a risky adventure she had undertaken. She was almost in despair, when luckily she came across a track sufficiently trodden to indicate that it probably led to some human habitation. It was growing very dusk indeed now, but she could just see to trace the path, and she hurried hopefully on, till at length the lights of a farm-house window shone out through the gathering gloom.

At first Honor thought of knocking boldly at the door and asking for food and shelter; but then, she reflected that the people of the house would think it most strange for a nicely dressed girl to present herself so late in the evening with such a request, and would be sure to ask awkward questions, and might possibly send a messenger to the College to tell of her arrival, detaining her there in the morning until Miss Cavendish or Miss Maitland arrived to fetch her. Even supper and a bed, welcome though they might prove, would be too dearly bought at such a price; and she determined, instead, to spend the night in a barn, the door of which stood conveniently open. It was half-filled with newly made, sweet-smelling hay, on to which she crept in the darkness; and flinging herself down, she drew some of it under her head for a pillow. A strange bed indeed, and very different from the one in her cubicle at St. Chad's! But at least she was free to go when she pleased; she meant to be up at daybreak, before anyone on the farm was astir, and to-morrow she would surely reach Westhaven and the steamer, and be able to start for that goal of all her wanderings—home.

It is easy enough before you go to sleep to resolve that you will rouse yourself at a certain time, but not quite so simple to carry it out, especially when you happen to be dead tired; and Honor's case was no exception to the rule. Instead of waking at dawn, she slept peacefully till nearly eight o'clock, and might even have slept on longer still if the farmer and his son had not chanced to stroll into the barn on their way to the stable. The boy was walking to the far end to hang a rope on a nail, when he suddenly ran back, with his eyes nearly dropping from his head with surprise.

"Dad!" he cried. "Dad! Come and look here! There's a girl sleeping on the hay!"

Honor, newly aroused, was just raising herself up on her elbow; she had not quite collected her senses, nor realized where she was. Startled by the voices, she jumped up, with the instinctive impulse to run away; then, seeing that two strangers stood between her and the open door, she sat down again on the hay and burst out crying.

"There! There!" said the farmer. "Don't you take on so, missy; we ain't a-goin' to hurt you. Tom, you'd best run in and fetch Mother hither!"

"Mother", a stout, elderly woman, arrived panting on the scene in a few moments. No lady in the land could possibly have proved kinder in such an emergency. She kissed and soothed poor Honor, took her indoors and gave her hot water to bathe her face and wash her hands, and finally settled her down in a corner of the delightfully clean farm-kitchen, with a dainty little breakfast before her.

Honor felt sorely tempted to unburden herself of her story to this true friend in need, but the dread that she would be sent back to St. Chad's kept her silent, and she only said that she had been lost on the moor, and was anxious to get to Westhaven, and to go home as speedily as possible, all of which was, of course, absolutely true. Mrs. Ledbury, no doubt, had her suspicions; but, seeing that questions disturbed her guest, with true delicacy she refrained from pressing her, and suggested instead that, as her husband was driving into Westhaven market that morning, he could give her a lift, and save her a walk of nearly seven miles.

Honor jumped at the opportunity; she felt stiff and worn out after her yesterday's experiences, and much disinclined for further rambles; so it was with a sigh of genuine relief that she found herself seated in the high gig by the side of the old farmer.

"Good-bye, dearie!" said Mrs. Ledbury, tucking a shawl over Honor's knees, and pressing a slice of bread and honey into her hand, from fear that she might grow hungry on the road. "You run straight home when you get to Westhaven! They'll be in a fair way about you, they will that! It gives me a turn yet to think of you sleeping in the barn all night long, with rats and mice scrambling round you, and me not to know you was there!"

Mr. Ledbury was evidently not of a communicative disposition; he drove along without vouchsafing any remarks, and Honor was so lost in her thoughts that she did not feel disposed to talk to him. Her great anxiety now was to catch the steamer to Cork; she wished she had some idea of the time of its starting, and only hoped that it did not set off early in the morning, for to miss it would seem almost more than she could bear. The gig jolted slowly on over the uneven road, till at length the moor gave way to suburban villas and gardens, quickly followed by streets and shops; and they finally drew up in the busy market-place of Westhaven.

Mr. Ledbury helped Honor to dismount, and having thanked him and said good-bye, she turned round the nearest corner; then, once safely out of his sight, she set off as fast as she could for the harbour. Partly, perhaps, because she enquired chiefly from children, whose directions were not very clear, and partly because it is generally difficult to find one's way in a fresh place, it was a long time before she saw the welcome gleam of the water and the masts of the shipping; and then, after all, she found she had come to the wrong quay, and it was only by dint of continual asking that at last she arrived at the particular landing-stage of the Irish steamers.

"Want the boat to Cork, miss?" said the weather-beaten seaman to whom she addressed her question. "Why, she's bin gone out an hour and a half ago. She was off at eleven prompt. When will there be another, did ye say? Not till eight to-night, and she's only a cargo."

Honor's hopes, which had managed to sustain her spirits so far, dropped to zero at this bad news. There she was, penniless, in a strange town; and how could she get through all the long, weary hours until the evening? Gulping down a lump in her throat, she asked the sailor if the cargo vessel were already in the harbour, and if it were possible that she might go on board now, and wait there till it should be time to set sail.

"We're expecting of her in every minute," said the man, looking at Honor curiously. "You can speak to the captain when she comes. Maybe he'd let you, maybe he wouldn't; I shouldn't like to give an opinion"—which, to say the least, was not consoling.

Honor walked on a little farther down the landing-stage, trying to wink back her tears. She was in a desperate strait, and almost began to wish she had never left St. Chad's. Suppose the captain would not take her without the money for her passage? Possibly he might not know Mr. Donovan's name, and would think she was an impostor; what would she do then? She turned quite cold at the idea, and had to sit down on a bulkhead to recover herself, for she felt as though her legs were shaking under her.

She did not remember how long she sat there. A noise and bustle behind presently attracted her attention, and turning round, she saw that a steamer was arriving, and that the sailors were busy catching the thick cables and fastening the vessel to the wharf. The gangway was thrown across, and a few passengers stepped on shore. They had evidently travelled steerage—two or three women, with babies and bundles, and a party of Irish labourers come over for the harvest, with their belongings tied in red pocket-handkerchiefs; but after them strode a tall figure, with a grey moustache, at the sight of whom Honor sprang up from her seat with a perfect scream of delight, and raced along the quay like a whirlwind, to fling herself joyfully into the gentleman's arms.

"Father! Father!" she sobbed. "Oh, is it really and truly you?"

CHAPTER XVII. JANIE TURNS DETECTIVE

Honor being safely in her father's charge, we must leave her there for the present, and return to Chessington, to see what was happening in the meantime at St. Chad's.

Janie's slumbers had been quiet and undisturbed until half-past six, when she woke with a start, feeling almost ashamed of herself for being able to sleep when her friend was in trouble. She got up at once, and peeped round the curtain into the other cubicle, only to discover, too late, that the bird had flown. She looked on the dressing-table to see whether a note might have been left, but to her disappointment there was nothing. Honor had vanished mysteriously, leaving not the least sign or clue behind her. Where had she gone? Janie could scarcely venture a guess. Such a daring scheme as a return to Ireland did not even suggest itself to her less enterprising mind. Perhaps, she thought, Honor might have set out to try to find the man Blake, and ask him to come and show the Jubilee sovereign to Miss Maitland; but this seemed so at variance with her determination of last night that Janie could hardly consider it probable. She wondered if it were her duty to go and tell Miss Maitland immediately, but came to the conclusion that, as the bell would ring in a few minutes, she might put off giving the information until she had dressed.

Her news naturally caused the greatest consternation at headquarters. Steps were taken at once to institute a search for the runaway. Miss Cavendish communicated with the police, who, exactly as Honor had anticipated, enquired at the railway station and the pier at Dunscar, in case she had taken the train or the steamer; and caused the high roads to be watched. It did not occur to anybody that she would have ventured on such an undertaking as to cross the moors, and she had the advantage of several hours' start, so that, from her point of view, her plan was a success.

"You should have come to me instantly, Janie, when you made the discovery that she was gone," said Miss Maitland reproachfully. "We have lost at least three-quarters of an hour through your delay."

Poor Janie burst into tears. It had been very hard to be obliged to reveal the fact of her room-mate's flight at all. She felt that, utterly against her will, she had the whole time been the principal witness in Honor's disfavour, and that every word she had spoken had helped to confirm unjust suspicion. She would have made an attempt to plead her friend's cause if Miss Maitland had looked at all encouraging, but the mistress was anxious to waste no further time, and dismissed her summarily from the room.

Janie had taken the affair as much to heart as if the disgrace were her own. It seemed so particularly unfortunate that it should have happened, because, since their talk at St. Kolgan's Abbey, she had thought that Honor was making increased efforts, and that Miss Maitland had noticed and approved the change. Now all this advance appeared to be swept away, and in the opinion of both teachers and girls her friend was not fit to remain any longer on the roll of Chessington.

Although the Chaddites tried to keep their shame hushed up, the news leaked out somehow, and very soon spread through the entire College, where it instantly became the one absorbing topic of conversation. Owing to her prowess at cricket, and her friendly, amusing ways, Honor had won more notice than most new girls among her two hundred schoolfellows; but, in spite of her undoubted popularity, she was universally judged to be guilty. The general argument was that the money was missing, that somebody must have taken it, that Honor was known to have needed it desperately, and that her action in running away showed above everything that she dared not stay to have the matter investigated.

Janie thought that no day had ever been so long. The hours seemed absolutely interminable. Her lessons had been badly prepared the night before, and won for her a reproof from Miss Farrar; and her thoughts were so constantly occupied with wondering where Honor had fled that she could scarcely attend to the work in class, and often answered at random. Her head was aching badly, and her eyes were sore with crying, neither of which was conducive to good memory, or lucid explanations; so she was not surprised to find at the end of the morning that her record was the worst she had had during the whole term.

The afternoon was cool after the rain of the previous evening, and games were once more in full swing. Dearly as she would have liked to shirk her part in them, Janie was not allowed to absent herself; but she played so badly that she drew Miss Young's scorn on her head, to say nothing of the wrath of the Chaddites.

"You missed two catches—simply dropped them straight out of your hands! You're an absolute butter-fingers!" exclaimed Chatty Burns indignantly.

Janie was too crushed by utter misery to mind this extra straw. She retired thankfully to the pavilion as soon as she was allowed, feeling that missed catches or schoolmates' scoldings were of small importance in the present state of general misfortune.

"If I could only find out who took the sovereign!" she thought. "Honor certainly did not, so somebody else must have. Who? That's the question. I wish I were an amateur detective, like the clever people one reads about in magazines. They just get a clue, and find it all out so easily, while the police are on quite a wrong tack. The chief thing seems to be to make a beginning, and I don't know in the least where to start."

Neither tea nor preparation brought her any nearer to solving the difficulty. After supper she went into the garden, taking her work-basket and crochet with her. She was in the lowest of spirits, and blinked away some surreptitious tears. Weeping was not fashionable at St. Chad's, being classed as "Early Victorian", and she wished to hide her red eyes from the other girls; for this reason she hurried down the long gravel path behind the rows of peas and beans, and found a snug place by the tomato house, where there was a convenient wheelbarrow to sit upon. She had not been there more than five minutes when, to her surprise, she was joined by Lettice Talbot.

"I've been hunting for you everywhere, Janie!" announced Lettice. "I shouldn't have found you now, only I caught a glimpse of your pink hair ribbon through a vista of pea-sticks. Is there room for two on this barrow? Thanks; I'll sit down then. Look here! I want to tell you how glad I am that you stuck up for Honor last night. I know Maisie and all the rest think she took that wretched sovereign, but I declare I don't. Poor old Paddy! I'm certain she never could; I would as soon have done it myself."

"I'm so thankful to hear you say this," exclaimed Janie. "I was afraid I was the only one who believed in her."

"A few of our set are beginning to come round; Ruth Latimer is certainly wavering, and so is Pauline Reynolds. But naturally they all say: 'If Honor didn't take it, who did?'"

"That's exactly what I should like to find out," sighed Janie.

"Miss Maitland is absolutely certain that she left it on her table, and that it was gone when she came back within a quarter of an hour; also, that it hadn't fallen down anywhere in the room," said Lettice, with the air of a judge weighing evidence. "Where is it, then?"

"I've thought and thought," replied Janie, puckering up her forehead, "but I can't get any nearer. If we could prove, now, that someone else had been in Miss Maitland's room, it might quite alter the case."

"Why, what an idiot I am!" exclaimed Lettice, suddenly bouncing up from the wheelbarrow.

"What's the matter?"

"It's only just occurred to me! I suppose a really clever person would have thought of it at once. I'm afraid my brains don't work very fast. Oh, what a jubilee!"

"Lettice Talbot! Have you gone mad?"

"Not quite, but a little in that direction."

"Do explain yourself!"

"Well, you recollect when Honor climbed up to the window? We all went into the house afterwards, and then I ran back to fetch Maisie's work-basket. I saw a girl climb down the lime tree, and run away into the bushes."

"Are you sure?"

"I could not be mistaken."

"Then this is most extremely important."

"I know it is. I can't imagine how I never remembered it before. They may well call me 'Scatterbrains' at home! I certainly shouldn't have done for a barrister, if I'd been a boy."

"Could you tell who it was?"

"No, I wasn't near enough. I only saw her for a moment. If I had caught a glimpse of her face, it might have been of some use; but everybody wears the same kind of blue skirt and white blouse at Chessington, so it's quite impossible to recognize any particular girl when you see nothing but her back."

"Unless you could find somebody else who happened to have seen her too."

"No one else was there at the time."

"We must make enquiries," said Janie excitedly. "It really seems a clue. We won't leave a stone unturned, if we can help it."

"I should be very glad to get poor Paddy out of trouble," replied Lettice. "The slur on our house will be just the same, though, whichever Chaddite may be the culprit. It's only moving the disgrace from one person to another."

"We must see that the blame is put on to the right pair of shoulders, though; it's not fair for Honor to bear it unjustly."

"Indeed it isn't. What would be the best way to begin?"

"We need a witness. I wonder if Johnson was about at the time, and noticed anything?"

"A good idea! We'll go and find him. I believe I saw him just now, shutting up the greenhouse."

After a rather lengthy search, the girls at last discovered the old gardener putting away his tools in the potting shed.

"Johnson, please, we want to ask you a question," began Janie. "Were you near St. Chad's at nine o'clock on the night before last; and did you happen to see anyone climbing the lime tree that stands close to the house?"

Johnson stroked his chin reflectively.

"It couldn't have been last night," he replied, after a few moments' consideration. "I was in Dunscar then. It must 'a been the night afore that. Aye; I did see one of you young ladies go up that lime tree. I remember it, because she climbed that smart you'd have thought she was a boy. In at the window she gets, and I watches her and thinks it's well to have young limbs. It's not much climbing you'll do when you're nigh sixty, and stiff in the joints with rheumatism besides!"

"What was she like?" enquired Janie eagerly.

"Had she long, dark hair?" added Lettice.

"Nay, it was fair hair. There was a light in the room, so as she comes back through the window I sees her as plain as I sees you now. I knows her in a minute. It was the young lady as every Sunday morning pesters my life out of me to cut her a rose for her buttonhole: Miss Taylor, I think she's called."

"Flossie!" exclaimed Janie. "I know she always begs for roses."

"Then it was Flossie!" said Lettice. "I had an uneasy feeling in the back of my mind all the time that it was she—it looked like her figure. It seemed too bad to suspect her, though, when I had absolutely no proof."

"There can be little doubt about it now."

"Shall we go straight to Miss Maitland, at once?"

"I don't know. I'm not sure if it wouldn't be better to ask Flossie herself about it. She may be able to explain it; and, at any rate, I think we ought to warn her before we say anything, and then we shan't seem to have told tales behind her back."

"She doesn't deserve any consideration," grumbled Lettice.

Janie's conscience, however, required her to be scrupulously fair. She could not bear to take an advantage, even of one who must be shielding herself at the expense of another.

"We'll give her a chance," she decided emphatically.

The next step evidently was to search for Flossie. She was not in the garden, but after a diligent quest through the house they eventually found her in her own cubicle, engaged in the meritorious occupation of tidying her drawers. It was an unpleasant task for the two girls to voice their suspicions, but one that nevertheless had to be done.

Somewhat to their surprise, Flossie sat down on the edge of her bed, and burst out crying.

"Oh, I knew it would come! I knew it would!" she sobbed. "What am I to do? Oh, I've been so wretched all day! I believe I'm quite glad it has come out at last."

"Flossie, did you take that sovereign?" asked Janie.

"Yes—no—at least—yes! Only, I didn't know I was taking it!" groaned Flossie, trying in vain to find her handkerchief, and mopping her eyes in desperation with a corner of the sheet instead.

"What do you mean?"

"I'll tell you. Oh, it's such a relief to tell somebody! Of course, I was there when Honor climbed up the lime tree, and after you had all run indoors I thought it would be fun to see if I could go up too. It was quite easy, and I jumped through the window without any difficulty. There was nobody in the study, but the electric light was turned on. I walked over to the writing-table, and I remember noticing the sovereign lying at the corner, on the top of a pile of letters. There were ever so many papers strewn about, and some of them were our house conduct reports for the term, which Miss Maitland was evidently just beginning to fill in. I was so anxious to see if mine was there that I stretched over and took some of them in my hand, to look at them. Then I thought I heard a step in the passage, and I didn't want to be caught, so I popped them quickly back, and went down the tree a good deal faster than I had gone up. I took off my blouse as usual that night, and put it away in my middle drawer, and next day I wore a clean one. Then this morning, when I was dressing, I looked at the first blouse, to see if it were really soiled and ready for the laundry. To my horror, out tumbled a sovereign on to the floor! I can only suppose it must have slipped inside my turnover cuff, when I reached across the table; I certainly hadn't the least idea it was there. I couldn't think what to do! I hoped I might be able to smuggle it back on to the table, and I've been watching all day, but there has never been the slightest opportunity to go into the study. I didn't dare to tell Miss Maitland, from fear she would think I'd taken it on purpose. She wouldn't believe Honor, so I thought she wouldn't believe me either. Oh! isn't it all dreadful?"

"It is indeed," said Janie; "especially as Honor has had to bear the blame. It isn't the first time she has acted scapegoat for you!"

"I know what you mean," sobbed Flossie. "Vivian thought it was she who shammed ghost that night when I played a trick upon Evelyn Fletcher. I didn't intend to get Honor into trouble. I was very sorry about it; still, what could I do?"

"Do! Why, you ought to have told Vivian at once. Any girl with a spark of honour would have known that."

"You'd better make a clean breast of everything now," suggested Lettice.

"I daren't! I daren't!" cried Flossie, in an agony of alarm.

"I don't believe you need be afraid of Miss Maitland," said Janie. "You've only taken the sovereign by accident. She would be far more angry with you for not owning up."

"If you don't tell her, I shall go to her myself," threatened Lettice.

It was dreadfully difficult to screw Flossie's courage up to the required point. She declared she could not and would not make the necessary confession.

"I'll write to my mother to send for me to go home, and it can come out after I'm gone," she declared.

Lettice lost her temper and indulged in hard words, which, so far from altering Flossie's decision, only made her more obstinately determined. Fortunately, Janie had greater patience.

"I'm sure you'll be brave enough to do it for Honor's sake," she said. "You'll feel far happier and more comfortable when it's over. I know it's hard, but it's right, and we shall all think so much better of you afterwards than if you shirked telling, and went home. You could hardly come back again here if you did that. Be a true Chaddite, and remember our house motto: 'Strive for the highest'. I'll go with you to Miss Maitland, if you like."

In the end, Janie's counsel prevailed, and Flossie, very tearful and apprehensive, allowed herself to be led to the study, to return the sovereign and explain how it came into her possession. Miss Maitland proved kindness itself. She was immensely relieved to find that the whole affair was due to a mischance, and that none of her girls had been capable of committing a dishonest act. It wiped a blot from St. Chad's, and restored the house to its former high standing.

"If we could only find Honor Fitzgerald," she declared, "my mind would be at rest."

CHAPTER XVIII. THE END OF THE TERM

Major Fitzgerald's astonishment at meeting his runaway daughter on Westhaven Quay was great, but he was extremely thankful to find her safe and sound. He had received a telegram from Chessington informing him of her flight, and had started immediately for the College, coming from Cork to Westhaven by a night cargo vessel, as he thought that a quicker route than by the ordinary mail steamer from Dublin to Holyhead.

He at once took Honor to a hotel, where he engaged a private sitting-room and ordered luncheon; then he set to work to demand an explanation of what was still to him an absolute puzzle and mystery. In spite of her determination to suppress all mention of Dermot's embarrassments, Honor speedily found herself pouring out the whole of her troubles into her father's ears. She was no dissembler, never having been accustomed to concealment, and possessing naturally a very open character; so, with a few skilful questions, the Major easily drew from her the entire story.

She had prepared herself to expect a stern rebuke, but to her surprise her father seemed far more pained than angry.

"I thought my children could have trusted me!" he said. "You will find, Honor, as you go through life, that no one has your interest at heart so truly as your own father. Perhaps I have erred on the side of severity, but it is no light responsibility to keep five high-spirited lads under control, to say nothing of a madcap daughter. My father brought me up on the rule of 'spare the rod, spoil the child', and I thought modern methods produced a less worthy race, so I would stick to his old-fashioned principle. I have taken far harder thrashings in my boyhood than I have ever bestowed on Master Dermot. All the same, I believed you knew that, though I might sometimes appear harsh, I meant it for your good, and that I was the best friend you had in the world."

"You are, Daddy, you are!" cried Honor, clinging round his neck.

"Well, little woman, you must have more confidence in me another time, and come boldly and tell me your scrapes. I would rather forgive you a great deal than feel that you kept anything back from me. You've been a very foolish girl, and have got yourself into sad trouble. Your mother is wild with anxiety about you."

"How is Mother? Is she still so ill?" quavered Honor.

"She was much better until yesterday, when we received Miss Cavendish's telegram. Naturally, that upset her very much. I have wired to her already, to say that you are safely here with me."

"Oh, Daddy, let us go home to Mother at once!"

"No, my dear!" said Major Fitzgerald decidedly. "I couldn't let you return to Kilmore with such an accusation resting against your name. We must face that, and get it cleared up. I shall have a talk with both Miss Maitland and Miss Cavendish. Don't you see that by running away you are practically admitting yourself to be guilty? It was the silliest thing to do! Come, don't cry! We'll get to the bottom of the matter somehow."

"But you won't tell Dr. Winterton?" implored Honor, whose tears were more for her brother than for herself.

"I won't promise. It may be necessary to do so. You needn't fear Dermot will miss his exam.; I should of course stipulate that he must take it. I don't believe, however, that he would be expelled. It is so near to the end of the term, and if he secures a pass he will be leaving the Grange in any case, to join his training ship. The young rascal! He certainly deserves his thrashing. He's always up to some mischief! There, dry your eyes, child, I won't be too hard on him! In the meantime, we must think of getting back to Dunscar. We can just catch the 2.40 train. The sooner we arrive at the College and ease Miss Cavendish's mind, the better. I must buy you a hat as we walk to the station, and then perhaps you'll look more respectable."

It seemed to Honor as if an immense weight had been lifted from her mind. She began for the first time to understand her father, and to realize how much he thought of and cared for his children's welfare. The knowledge drew her nearer to him than she had ever been before. Her troubles seemed over now that he had taken the responsibility of them;

she wished she had trusted him sooner, and felt that he was indeed, as he had said, her best and truest friend.

Miss Maitland was greatly relieved that afternoon when her missing pupil was restored to her, and congratulated herself that the mystery had been solved, and that she was able to give a full explanation to Major Fitzgerald of what had occurred.

The latter listened with close attention to her account.

"Pray don't apologize for having accused Honor falsely," he said. "As house-mistress, it was your plain duty to act as you did, and the evidence seemed overwhelming. I don't exonerate my little girl altogether; she had no right to take the law into her own hands and meet her brother in defiance of rules, and, still worse, to run away from school; neither had she any business to climb through the window into your study. She deserves a thorough scolding, but I think she is truly sorry, and that the consequences of her foolishness have been punishment enough."

"We will say no more about it," replied Miss Maitland; "it is an unpleasant episode, which we shall be only too glad to consign to oblivion. Honor has shown us already that she is capable of better things, and I shall expect much from her in the future."

The runaway received a warm welcome from the Chaddites, who much regretted their hasty action in condemning her without sufficient proof.

"I'm afraid I misjudged you before, Honor," said Vivian Holmes. "Flossie has told me that it was she who shammed ghost. It's a pity there have been so many misunderstandings, but I'm glad you weren't responsible for Evelyn's fright."

Vivian spoke kindly, but without enthusiasm. She was ready enough to acknowledge Honor's innocence, but she still did not altogether approve of her, and considered that there was much room for improvement before she became a worthy member of St. Chad's. The monitress had no sympathy with lawlessness, and preferred girls who upheld the school rules, instead of breaking them. Undue exuberance of spirits during a first term was in her eyes presumption, and not to be countenanced by a monitress who did her duty.

She need not have been afraid, however, that the black sheep of her flock was going to indulge in any more lapses from the strict path of convention. Honor had returned in a very subdued frame of mind, and gave no further occasion for reproof.

She took the girls' apologies for sending her to Coventry in excellent part.

"If you really believed I'd stolen the sovereign, you were quite right," she remarked briefly. "Anyone who'd done such a thing would have richly deserved that, and worse. I care quite as much as you all for the honour of the house."

To Janie alone, the one friend who had taken her part and stood up for her when the whole school was against her, could Honor turn with a sense of absolute confidence; the bond between them seemed closer than ever, and she felt she owed a debt of gratitude that it would be difficult to repay. Janie's joy at this happy ending to what had appeared a scholastic earthquake was extreme; and, though she gave Lettice the credit that was due, she could not help experiencing a little satisfaction at her own share in elucidating the mystery. She had worked hard to clear her friend's name, so it was delightful to reap her reward.

The sensation caused by the events of the last few days was soon forgotten by the majority of the girls in the excitement of the examinations. For the next week the whole College lived in a whirl of perpetual effort to marshal scattered facts, or recall forgotten vocabularies. The classrooms, given over to pens, ink, and sheets of foolscap paper, were the abodes of a silence only disturbed by the occasional scratching of a pen, or the sigh of a candidate in the throes of attacking a stiff problem. To Honor the experience was all new. She tried her best, but found it difficult to curtail her statements sufficiently to allow of her answering every question, in spite of Miss Farrar's oft-repeated warning against devoting too much time to one part of the paper. She was, of course, at a great disadvantage, as she had spent only one term at Chessington, and the examinations were on the work of a whole year; but she nevertheless acquitted herself creditably, and actually gained higher marks than several girls who had come to school the preceding September.

"I feel as if I'd been in a battle!" she announced, when at length the ordeal was over and the last set of papers handed in. "My fingers are soaked with ink, for my fountain pen leaked atrociously; but it wrote so much quicker than an ordinary one that I didn't dare to abandon it."

"You'll soon get the ink off," said Lettice. "Miss Maitland always puts plenty of pieces of pumice stone and slices of lemon in the dressing-room at examination time. I'm sure I've failed in geometry, and I shall be very much surprised if I find I've scraped through in physics."

"I feel just as doubtful over English language," said Chatty Burns. "But it's no use worrying ourselves any more; we can't correct mistakes now, whatever stupid ones we may have made."

"And we can just have a few peaceful days until the sports," added Lettice.

The end of the term was always celebrated by a gathering of parents and friends, at which the girls gave exhibitions of their skill in running, jumping, or some of the physical exercises that they had learnt with Miss Young. This year the programme was to include military drill and flag signalling. The latter was a new departure in the school, but one that everybody had taken up with enthusiasm. Little bands of the most expert performers had been selected, and these practised diligently in the playing-fields, waving their messages with great accuracy and dispatch.

"It might come in useful if there were a war," said Lettice; "and, at any rate, it will be very convenient at home. I mean to teach some friends who live at a house close by, and we shall be able to stand at our bedroom windows and talk with our flags."

"It will be fun out yachting," said Madge Summers. "We can signal any vessel we pass, and ask her name, and where she is going, and all kinds of questions."

"I wish Miss Young would teach us heliography next term," said Honor. "I should like flashing messages with looking-glasses."

"We'll ask her; but we shall have to wait nearly a year. We only have hockey in the winter term, with gymnasium work when it's wet. Are any of your people coming over on Thursday?"

"I'm afraid not—it's such a long way from Kerry! My mother is still ill, and my father is busy."

"That's a pity!" said Lettice. "We all like our parents to turn up for the sports. There's generally an absolute crowd."

As Lettice had indicated, a large number of visitors made their appearance on breaking-up day. The quadrangle and playing-fields were gay with summer dresses and parasols, and everywhere girls might be seen conducting little parties of friends over the College buildings.

"The whole place seems topsy-turvy," remarked Honor. "You can go where you like, and actually speak in the laboratory without forfeits! Even the library is turned into a tea-room!"

"Yes, there are no rules this afternoon," replied Janie.

The sports were held in the cricket ground, and began punctually at half-past four. Forms had been brought from the school, to make seats for the spectators and for those of the girls who were not taking part in the proceedings.

"I like a large audience," said Chatty Burns; "it's rather inspiring. Of course, it makes one nervous, but, at the same time, it puts one on one's mettle. I always do better when there are plenty of people to watch."

"Especially when one feels that one is working for the credit of one's own house," said Ruth Latimer. "We all want to see the orange ribbon to the fore to-day."

"I'm afraid we've very little chance of winning anything," groaned Madge Summers. "The Hilaryites are almost sure of the long jump. Mona Richards beats the record. They call her 'The Kangaroo'!"

"And the School House will get the high jump," said Lettice. "We haven't anybody so good as Lois Atkinson."

"How about the Atalanta race?"

"Doubtful. I expect it will go to Aldwyth's, or Bride's. They've been training their champion runners the whole term, while we were concentrating our energies on cricket. No Chaddites have even entered, I believe! Chatty, you ought to be in it."

"It seemed no use putting down my name. I was practising last week—you remember, we had a general trial of all the houses?—and I soon found I hadn't a ghost of a chance."

"Well, St. Chad's must content itself with its cricket laurels. We've got the cup for this year, at any rate."

The first portion of the programme consisted of military drill and physical exercises, in which the whole school took part, showing a readiness and promptitude of action worthy of a regiment. Miss Young had prepared a little surprise for the visitors. At the end of the display, the girls suddenly ranked themselves so that their sailor hats, viewed from a distance, formed the College motto: "United in effort"; then, at a sign, they moved again, and the greeting, "Welcome to Chessington" appeared instead. Naturally, this caused much applause, and many congratulations were offered to Miss Cavendish on the excellent discipline prevailing throughout.

The flag signalling was confined to a picked band, so the greater portion of the girls now joined the spectators, only those who had entered for the various competitions remaining in a separate corner of the field.

"I'm glad we have five Chaddites at flag work," said Chatty Burns; "it's a larger proportion than any other house. But there our triumphs are likely to end."

"We won't give up too soon," said Lettice. "There's an old proverb: 'You're never killed till you're dead'. We might manage to score, after all."

In spite of Lettice's sanguine anticipations, St. Chad's did not appear likely to win any triumphs on this occasion. The long jump, as everyone had expected, fell easily to Mona Richards, who thoroughly justified her nickname of "Kangaroo", and caused the Hilaryites to hold up their heads with the proud consciousness of victory. The high jump seemed at first of more doubtful issue; both Dorothy Saunders, of St. Bride's, and Rachel Foard, of St. Aldwyth's, ran Lois Atkinson very close, and the School House had almost made up its mind to a beating when the luck suddenly turned, leaving Lois mistress of the event.

The next item was the "Atalanta Race", so called because each competitor was obliged to pick up three apples during its course, and present them duly at the winning post—not an easy feat to accomplish, as it was possible to drop the first and second in the hurry of snatching at the third.

"There are eleven in for it," announced Lettice, as the candidates began to take their places at the starting-point. "Five scarlet ribbons, two pinks, three violets, and one blue. Not a single Chaddite, alas! Yes, I believe there actually is! Look, there's an orange hat walking up, to make a twelfth!"

"Who can it be?" asked several of the girls, straining their eyes to catch a glimpse of the last comer, who was rather hidden behind the others.

"She's about Pauline's height," said Lettice. "No; Pauline is over there, with Madge and Dorothy. It's not tall enough for Effie Lawson, nor fat enough for Claudia Hammond-Smith. Can it possibly be Adeline? Why, girls, by all that's wonderful and marvellous, it's Janie Henderson!"

Janie's appearance among the trained runners in the Atalanta race was indeed sufficient to cause the most unbounded astonishment. Her general dislike of active exercise was proverbial. It was well known that she only played games under the strictest compulsion, and throughout her school course she had earned the not unmerited reputation of a "slacker". That she, the most unathletic and altogether unlikely girl in the College, should have calmly taken her place as the sole champion of St. Chad's in so difficult a race seemed nearly incredible.

"I wonder Miss Young let her!" gasped Ruth Latimer in horror. "She's bound to fall out immediately."

"And it will bring more discredit on the house than if no one had tried," added Chatty Burns. "I'd have gone in for it myself, only Vivian begged me not to."

"I call it a regular swindle!" said Maisie Talbot. "Honor, did she tell you of this mad scheme?"

"Not a word!"

There was a curious expression on Honor's face as she answered, a look of mingled surprise and enlightenment. She had not forgotten the talk at St. Kolgan's Abbey, and she alone of the whole school knew the motive that had prompted Janie to such an amazing action, and could account for this apparent inconsistency of conduct.

"I never dreamt of her really doing it!" she murmured, under her breath.

"Someone ought to stop her in time!" exclaimed Lettice indignantly.

So far, however, from placing any hindrance in the way of Janie's attempt, Miss Young, on the contrary, appeared to be giving her a few words of encouragement and final advice.

The course was to be three times round the cricket ground, an apple to be picked up in each circle. Heaps of early green codlins from the orchard had been disposed at regular intervals, and competitors might select from which pile they wished, so long as they took neither more nor less than the one required specimen in every round, the object being to prevent a general scramble. There were to be no handicaps, so the twelve girls were drawn up in even rank, each girl with one foot on the white line, and her eyes fixed on Miss Young, in readiness for the signal to start. It was an anxious moment.

"One! Two! Three—off!"

They were gone, a row of young athletes, each bounding forward in the ardent hope of outstripping the rest, and gaining the coveted silver cup of victory. The race was always a great feature of the Chessington sports, but to-day, to the members of one house at any rate, it afforded a spectacle of more than ordinary interest. The eyes of all the Chaddites seemed riveted upon Janie, and they watched with frantic excitement to see how she would conduct herself in the struggle.

"She's keeping well up with the rest," whispered Lettice.

"And has a very light, swinging pace," replied Ruth.

"She's actually ahead of Connie Peters already!" said Chatty.

"And gaining on Christina Willoughby!"

"There! She's picked up her first apple!"

"And passed Blanche Hedley!"

"If she only goes on at this rate, St. Chad's may begin to hope."

"Too good to last, I'm afraid."

"She's begun the second round!"

"She's flagging a little!"

"No, she isn't! She's saving herself for a spurt. There! I told you so! She's passed Christina now!"

"I can hardly believe it's Janie Henderson who's running. It doesn't seem possible!"

"Well, of course, she's extremely light; that gives her a great pull over most of the others."

"But I didn't know she could run at all!"

"Perhaps she didn't either, until she tried."

"She's picked up her second apple!"

"And Alice Marsh has nearly knocked her over, through rushing to the same heap."

"Never mind! it hasn't really hindered her."

"She and Nettie Saville are almost equal now!"

"How well she keeps up!"

"There she goes, past the post again!"

"This is actually the last round!"

"And that's her third apple!"

"She'll let it fall!"

"No, she won't; she's got them quite tight!"

"She's up to Nettie!"

"No—Nettie is spurting, and gaining fast!"

"Janie must push on!"

"Hurrah! Nettie has dropped an apple, and she'll have to stop, and pick it up."

"Janie is ahead of everyone!"

"If she wins, it will be a triumph for the orange ribbon!"

Thus the girls, with continuous anxiety, followed the events of the race, all unknowing that Janie was playing for a far higher stake than they realized, and that on the result of that race hung, not only the honour of St. Chad's, but the future of a human soul, capable of infinitely so much more than it had yet achieved.

"They're all putting on steam! Oh, look! Alice Marsh is almost even!"

"And so is Christina!"

"And Connie Peters has gained what she lost at first!"

"Janie mustn't fail now!"

"Nettie has passed her!"

"Then she'll lose, for a certainty!"

"Oh, dear! I hardly dare look!"

"She won't! She won't! She's making a last dash! She's in front of Nettie! She's gaining—three feet—four feet! Well done, Janie! Go on! Go on! You're safe! Don't flag now!"

"Oh! Hurrah for St. Chad's! She's actually won!"

The wild delight of the Chaddites at this most marvellous and unexpected achievement was beyond all bounds. They cheered themselves nearly hoarse, and waved their handkerchiefs in the exuberance of their joy. To have gained the Atalanta race was a score for their house which, added to their previous cricket successes, would place it on the highest pinnacle of the athletic records of the year.

"And to think that my delicate Janie should be capable of such a feat!" exclaimed Mrs. Henderson, who had watched the contest with hardly less excitement than the Chaddites themselves. "Chessington has been the making of her, and I cannot thank you enough, Miss Cavendish, for your care of her general health. She is another girl from what she was two years ago. The doctor always told me that plenty of exercise would be her salvation, but I could never persuade her to run about at home."

"I am as delighted as you at the change," declared Miss Cavendish. "Janie has shown us quite a new phase to-day, and we shall take care that she keeps up to this standard."

Janie herself, panting and flushed with victory, heard the applause almost as in a dream. It was sweet to her ears, yet it was not the reward for which she had striven. Her eager gaze searched down the long line of clapping girls till she found Honor's face. For a moment their eyes met, but in that one swift glance she read all she wished to learn, and could interpret without the medium of language her friend's unspoken thoughts: "It was a bargain. You have kept your part of it, and I will keep mine."

The Honor who returned to Ireland next day was indeed changed from the one who had left home in disgrace only thirteen weeks before—so much more thoughtful, sympathetic, and considerate, with such higher ideals and nobler aspirations, that she scarcely seemed the same: an Honor who could tread softly in her mother's room, and give the required tenderness to that dear one who was to be spared so short a time to her; an Honor who, while keeping all her old love of fun, could forget self, and turn her merriment into sunshine for others. Character is a plant of slow growth, and she was not yet all she might be; but she had set her foot on the upward ladder, and whether at school, or at home, or in after years, life to her would always mean a conscious effort towards better things.

It seemed to her as if she had been away years, instead of only three months, when she and Dermot (who had passed his examination for a Naval cadetship) drove from Ballycroghan along the well-known road to Kilmore. The villagers stood at their cabin doors waving a greeting; her father, and actually her mother too, were waiting for her on the Castle steps when she arrived; and her four elder brothers had collected all the dogs of the establishment to join in a warm, if somewhat uproarious reception.

"I believe everything looks glad to see me," said Honor, "the very house, and the trees, and the birds, and the flowers in the garden! I'm going to have the most glorious holidays, and enjoy every hour of them. It feels almost worth while to have been thirteen weeks at Chessington, for the joy of such a coming home again!"

THE END

Manufactured by Amazon.ca
Acheson, AB